FEDERATION CHRONICLES

THE COMPLETE SERIES

KEN LOZITO

Published by Acoustical Books, LLC

KenLozito.com

Cover design by Jeff Brown

IF YOU WOULD LIKE TO BE NOTIFIED WHEN MY NEXT BOOK IS RELEASED VISIT

WWW.KENLOZITO.COM

ISBN: 978-1-945223-56-3

ACHERON INHERITANCE

1

He didn't wake up. To wake would suggest that he'd been sleeping, when he'd actually just sort of become aware. It was as if someone had flipped a switch and he started processing information. First came a vague awareness that startled his mind into a heightened state of activity. Then, a feeling of increased urgency expanded from the diminutive depths, as if he'd suddenly forgotten something important. He tried to open his eyes. Nothing happened.

System diagnostic running.

These words appeared amid the black void of his thoughts. A few moments later, various diagnostic windows flashed, and a status report appeared.

Warning.

Low-power mode.

Less than 30 percent of power remaining.

Recommendation: Deteriorating power cell should be replaced for optimal performance.

Configuration update required.

Please wait . . .

He frowned, or at least tried to, but nothing happened, which instantly made him want to even more. He couldn't feel anything. He couldn't even open his eyes, but he'd seen the status windows, so he wasn't blind. His racing thoughts went into overdrive. He tried to move—first his arms and then his hands. Nothing. He felt the urge to inhale, but it was only an urge—just a longing to take a deep lungful of sweet, precious breath—and it wasn't happening.

He couldn't breathe and wondered why he wasn't gasping. He should be struggling to breathe, but he wasn't, and his thoughts flatlined. He wouldn't panic. He was awake but couldn't move or feel . . . anything. There was no kinesthetic awareness to indicate whether he was lying down, strapped to a chair, or dangling in the air.

Not a good sign.

Maybe someone had drugged him, and he hadn't fully awakened yet. There were drugs that could induce paralysis, and maybe they were wearing off. He tried to remember the last thing he'd been doing. Had he been hurt? Medication to block pain receptors could explain a lot, including the paralysis. Where was he? He felt another urge to frown, remembering what it felt like as his eyebrows knitted together, his gaze narrowed, and his jaw tightened with the gritting of his teeth, but as he commanded his muscles to do those things, they just sort of . . . stalled, as if there was something blocking his muscles from actually moving.

Veris initiation complete.

System startup complete.

Autonomous mode has been activated.

Limited storage available.

A small image appeared in the void that surrounded him. He focused on it, and the image rushed toward him until the void disappeared. He was in a dreary room with smudgy, broken windows and long, thick cobwebs, and he had the impression that he was sitting. He looked down to a crusty, dirt-laden floor. Howling winds gusted from outside, sending layers of dust swirling into a lazy cyclone. Scummy residue trailed a path from the broken windows to the ground. Across from him were charging stations that housed different-sized humanoid robots. They were covered with a swarthy, crumbling shell that must have taken years of exposure to accumulate. These remnants of abandoned robots were all offline, without any indication of power.

He glanced down at his legs, and his thoughts screeched to a halt. His legs were gone! In their place were thick, metallic legs with an intricate set of connectors and actuators running to his feet. But they weren't *his* feet; they were something else. Each foot had three large, elongated toes and a broad, thick heel. They shifted, seemingly of their own accord, as if their range of motion was being tested.

He jerked backward at the movement and heard the mechanical whine of actuators fighting against their restraints in a cradle unit. Looking down, he saw that his chest was broad and comprised of overlapping plates that flexed when he moved. A whitish-blue power source glowed from between the plates. There was a series of symbols on his left side, and after a few seconds, a translation appeared on his internal heads-up display.

Agricultural Unit – 92.

Repairs have been completed, and the unit is cleared for duty.

Something disconnected from his back with a snap-hiss, and he slumped forward. The table he'd been sitting on dropped down and became part of the wall. As he landed on his feet, he saw the metallic toes spread and adjust to keep him standing. He flailed his arms for a few moments, trying to keep his balance. Everything felt uncoordinated and slow. He tried to move his head, and the movements were jerky, as there were actuators in his neck that hadn't been moved in a long time.

The one thing he knew for sure was that he hadn't been drugged. He felt as if he was remotely operating a mechanized unit for the first time, except that there was no system lag. Was this someone's idea of a joke?

Self-diagnostic?

The words appeared on his heads-up display—HUD—and he initiated the command.

Cannot run self-diagnostic now. Still restoring backup from remote storage. Please wait . . .

Thanks for nothing. That wasn't very helpful. He was apparently stuck in an agricultural unit, and he didn't know what he was supposed to do. This wasn't funny anymore. Why had he thought this could've been a practical joke? His mind was functioning much like his current body, like neither had been used in a really long time, but his mind suddenly began to race with an all-compelling need to remember.

He needed . . .

He *needed.*

He . . .

Partial data restored.

Veris restore procedure for the consciousness transference protocol has enacted emergency protocol number 736 in accordance with the Veris mandate of preserving core Personality Matrix Construct into the system.

He read the message again. "Consciousness transference protocol" stood out amid the amber lettering on the translucent window. Consciousness transference . . . His consciousness had been transferred, and something was trying to restore it from backup. Someone was restoring *him* into this machine.

He tried to bring up a command menu on the HUD.

Identify.

The system response puzzled him. It had just restored him, so shouldn't it already know who he was? He froze there, his thoughts racing as he tried to make sense of all the information coming at him.

I'm a robot? No, not a damn robot! I know who I am.

He repeated that thought over and over again.

I know who I am.

I know who I am.

I. Know. Who. I. Am.

He glared at the system prompt that showed its last query in dispassionate amber lettering.

Identify?

A surge of hope coursed through him as his name pierced the veil of confusion surrounding his thoughts.

"Quinton Aldren," he said, his voice sounding slightly modulated. He tried to clear his throat—which he didn't have—and repeated his name.

"Quinton Aldren," he said, much more clearly this time.

Identification confirmed. Partial restoration of Personality Matrix Construct has confirmed the viability of the individual in this unit.

Quinton reread the message with an increasing awareness that he knew about Personality Matrix Constructs. PMCs were human-consciousness-to-machine interfaces. He tried to remember more, but the information just wasn't available. He was *sure* he knew more about it, but something . . . He looked down at his body and understood.

A quiet hum came from a maintenance drone as it sank slowly to the floor. Its spherical chassis had multiple appendages, some of which looked to have been torn off, but one of them reached in his direction. Its power indicators went dark, and the drone was dead.

Quinton felt a second presence snap to existence in his mind. It was as if someone had just appeared next to him, but nobody was there.

VI interface initiated. Designation—Radek.

A virtual intelligence should be able to help him out.

"Radek, are you online?" Quinton asked.

"Diagnostics are still running," Radek said a few moments later. "Diagnostics complete. Virtual Intelligence Designate Radek responding."

"Excellent. Now, maybe you can answer a few questions for me. Why have I been restored into this agricultural unit?" Quinton asked.

"Emergency reactivation protocols were initiated," Radek replied.

Quinton felt as if his thoughts were wading through a muddy barrier.

"Radek, putting my consciousness into this agricultural unit violates PMC protocols. It shouldn't have worked, even under emergency conditions."

"Personality Matrix Construct's standard operating procedures were overridden."

"By whom?" Quinton asked.

"Information is unavailable."

"Unavailable . . . how's that?" Quinton paused for a moment, trying to strangle his growing irritation with the useless VI. He glanced down at the maintenance drone. "Were you in control of this drone?"

"Affirmative. It was required to transfer the Energy Storage System to Agricultural Unit 92."

"You're telling me that I've been stored in an ESS, which you then stuck in the chest of this agricultural unit—a damn *garden* robot," Quinton said.

More of his knowledge became available. It shouldn't have worked. PMCs required a high level of haptic capabilities in order to avoid malfunction. The PMC was a way of preserving his consciousness, requiring that he feel human, or else—

"Your summation of the events is an oversimplification," Radek replied, and Quinton could've sworn the VI sounded a little agitated.

"Not from where I'm standing."

"Per emergency procedures, I found the best solution given the constraints I was called to deal with," Radek said.

Quinton looked out at dark gray skies through the shattered remnants of what had been windows. He was in a garden storage shed for service bots. He didn't have any idea where he was, and he certainly didn't know why he was there. He needed Radek's help if he was going to figure out what had happened. He needed the VI's cooperation, but VIs could be finicky. They weren't sentient, but they could be singularly uncooperative if given the right motivation.

"It sounds like you did the best you could," Quinton said. "How long did you have to search before you found this body?"

"One hundred eighty-seven days, fifteen hours, and thirty-three minutes."

Oh crap, Quinton thought. Radek seemed to sense this, but Quinton reminded himself that VIs couldn't read minds.

"The ESS was in a critical state and in danger of imminent failure. Use of this agricultural unit was the only option."

Quinton didn't doubt what Radek said. If Radek had searched for a hundred eighty-seven days to find a suitable host for his PMC, then he was in danger.

"Where are we?"

"Unknown."

That's great, Quinton thought. Radek was just as much in the dark as he was.

"Is there a governing body we can contact?"

"Negative. There are no settlements with active inhabitants that I've observed."

Six months searching and no one to contact. Quinton glanced out the window at the ash-covered landscape and then looked around the room. This planet had suffered some kind of disaster. A readout on his HUD showed that the atmosphere was still breathable, meeting minimum requirements to survive—not that breathing air was an obstacle for him in his current form.

Quinton tried to recall why he'd been uploaded into a PMC and stored in the first place but found that he couldn't remember.

"Radek," Quinton said, "my memory access is restricted. Is the ESS intact? Was it damaged?"

"The ESS is undamaged and fully intact. However, because of the limitations of the agricultural unit, you have limited access to the ESS. This is required so you can fully utilize the unit the PMC is currently housed in."

Quinton took a few steps across the shed, then turned and paced back to the other side. Each step he took demonstrated more confidence as he learned the capabilities of the agricultural unit. There was significant risk involved with a PMC being loaded into a less capable machine. PMC degradation would occur if the consciousness inside lost its connection to being human. Quinton tried to feel whether he was losing himself and then shook his head. How was that *supposed* to feel?

There were several loud pops as something slammed into a nearby building. Quinton spun around at the noise and glanced toward the maintenance drone on the ground. There were gashes cut into its sides, and several of its limbs were missing.

"I must advise you that there are hunter mechs currently searching for you," Radek said.

A new pathway engaged in Quinton's mind, and he had access to new data stored in the ESS. "Hunter mechs! What do they want with me?"

"The hunter mechs are specifically tasked with destroying PMCs."

That couldn't be right. Nothing about this situation was right.

Quinton heard something crash from within a nearby building. "They must have control units. Can't we override them?" Quinton asked, stepping toward the door as he tried to engage the communications systems of the agricultural unit.

"I advise against that," Radek said quickly. "They can detect open comms signals. These units have been pursuing me for many days. I already tried an override command, which didn't work. Those systems are locked out from any comms unless they're coming from whatever command central gave them their instructions in the first place."

That made the hunter mechs no better than mindless drones. Why would they hunt PMCs?

"Radek, I need access to your analysis of those units if I'm going to decide how to deal with them. If they're just basic mechs, I should be able to disable them."

"Data is available, as you requested."

A report appeared on his HUD, and Quinton accessed the log data. There wasn't anything like a detailed analysis, and Radek had been severely limited in his capabilities while operating the maintenance drone. His top priority had been to preserve the Energy Storage System that Quinton's Personality Matrix Construct was stored in, which was all fine and good, but it meant he didn't know what he was facing, and they were getting closer to his position.

2

QUINTON STEPPED OUTSIDE but stayed close to the side of the building so he could watch for the mechs.

"How do you know they're hunting PMCs?" he asked.

"When they scanned the maintenance drone and detected the ESS, they became hostile."

The Energy Storage System—ESS— was a miniature reactor the size of a fist. The low energy output of the leuridium core made it durable and long-lasting, ideal for the data storage requirements of a PMC. The ESS had a unique identifier that made it easy to detect. Quinton glanced down at the agricultural bot body that contained his consciousness. He didn't think the robot's chest could shield it from the mechs.

He looked up at thick, dreary clouds pressing on top of him and felt as if he were staring at a tidal wave about to sweep him away in a violent upheaval of destruction and doom. A bellowing rumble came from overhead. Weather-worn buildings that were sagging under the weight of wet volcanic ash lined the streets, fading into the misty fog.

Quinton moved to the other side of the street. Loud banging sounds came from inside the nearby buildings, followed by screeches that came in rapid succession as the mechs forced their way through a heavy door. The agricultural unit was capable of highly acute sound sensitivity and depth perception, probably meant for the delicate work of maintaining the exotic gardens that had once been here.

He heard three distinct sound sources from various areas of the building. The mechs weren't trying to hide what they were doing.

He glanced around at the crusty brown ash that covered the buildings and saw more fall from the sky in a sleety mix of snow. Peering closely at the clusters of ash as they fell, he realized that the agricultural unit's optics were able to perceive each unique crystalline structure marred by the particulates filling the air. Where was the ash coming from? The agricultural unit must have had smell receptors, but he was glad they weren't working. Atmospheric readings on his internal heads-up display showed high levels of sulfur. Skipping the smell of rotting decay was perfectly fine with Quinton.

"I need to know what you plan to do," Radek said.

The VI's question startled him out of his thoughts because Radek was just a voice. Although there was a highlighted section of his HUD that flashed when Radek spoke, it was still off-putting. Quinton checked the agricultural unit's systems to see what was available.

"Radek, update preferences for our normal interactions to require the use of a holographic representation."

A small sphere that was a semi-transparent silver hovered in the air a few feet away from Quinton's head. "System preferences have been updated."

That was better.

"I wonder if we have a case of mistaken identity," Quinton said. "Maybe the security mechs just detected a power signature that's not in their data repositories. Given how things look around here, they're probably still following some kind of latent security protocol. You said they hunted you for days, but did you see any people here? Is there anyone we can go to for help?" Quinton asked.

"There were very few online systems, and no life signs were detected. I was lucky to find this agricultural unit."

Quinton's gaze flicked upward in irritation. He was about as far away from what he considered "fortunate" as he could get. He was sure the VI assistants that were part of his PMC were working overtime, managing the interface between him and the machine he was stuck in, but why belabor the point that his current form was the best the VI could find? Radek was just the manifestation of multiple VIs that were part of the PMC.

Quinton had limited access to his memories, but now that everything was online, he remembered going through extensive training before his consciousness was uploaded into an ESS, even if it wasn't *the* ESS that was in this specific bot. He couldn't recall the actual memories of his training, but the skills were there, and the link that the VIs were associating with hinged on the fact that Quinton had been trained. It was supposed to set him at ease so he could focus, but it just brought attention to the fact that he wasn't anywhere he'd expected to be, which meant that something had gone utterly wrong. Without complete access to his memories, how was he supposed to come up with a solution? He was stumbling in the dark, but he had his training. The possibility of a partial upload had always existed, as well as a chance that the unit the ESS was installed in would have limited capacity, which was what Quinton was dealing with thanks to Radek inserting him into this garden-variety robot.

"It was the only unit available, and it doesn't quite meet the minimum requirements for a PMC," Radek said, making Quinton wonder if the VI *could* read his thoughts.

Quinton accessed the scan data from Radek's encounter with the mechs. They were accurately identified as Veris Hunter Model Mechs, but that was just the base unit. They could represent any number of mech types, but they all had strict protocols for preserving human life, and an ESS housing a PMC qualified as a living being. These mechs shouldn't harm him, unless they were military mechs, in which case the restrictions on human life could be rescinded. If Quinton was identified as the enemy, they would attack. Radek's attempted communication with them had likely been interpreted as just another drone delivery system, which was different from someone who was actually alive.

He had to find out if the mechs would hunt him. If he tried to sneak away and was detected, there was very little chance of him being able to reason with them. He walked out to the middle of the street and shouted, "Hello!"

The glowing holographic sphere bobbed up and down to get his attention. "I must advise against this. Hostiles in the area," Radek warned.

"Noted. Now stop distracting me," Quinton replied.

The orb disappeared. VIs helped the PMC interact and cope with being in another form other than a human host. To help facilitate this connection, they were required to act human, but they were machines. Radek was a virtual intelligence, and sometimes they just got things wrong.

Three mechs emerged onto the street a short distance from where Quinton stood. They had extremely long arms that protruded from their stocky wedge-shaped main bodies. Long legs connected to a black-armored pelvis. They'd probably been designed to run at high speeds, using all of their limbs. Serial numbers for each mech appeared on Quinton's HUD, which were transferred as some kind of default broadcast. This was encouraging because they might listen to him. But what struck him as odd was just how old the mechs looked. The orange stripes along their torsos and down their arms were faded and looked to have been scraped off in several areas. They must've been bright when the mechs were in service. He had no idea how long these mechs had been running around. How could they still have power? The fact that they did indicated that there must be a charging station in service nearby.

The three mechs regarded Quinton for a few moments, and he raised his arms to the side in a non-threatening gesture of compliance. The mechs squatted lower in an aggressive posture.

"Wait a minute," he blurted, his voice going high. "I'm not a danger to you. My name is Quinton Aldren, and I'm a Personality Matrix Construct temporarily stored in this agricultural unit. I need help. Transferring my identification now."

A beam of light came from one of the mechs and highlighted an area on Quinton's chest for a few seconds before going out. The three mechs remained motionless, and Quinton was beginning to agree with Radek that this was a bad idea. He tried opening a comlink to the three mechs, thinking that perhaps they had suffered some kind of damage and were attempting to communicate with him.

They weren't.

The mechs shared a data communication session, which Quinton was able to decipher because they weren't using any security protocols.

. . . Target hostile: negative.

ESS power signature confirmed.

Must retrieve.

The three Veris mechs began striding toward him. Each step they took seemed to impact the ash-laden ground, and Quinton stepped back.

"Wait a second. I'll go with you," Quinton said.

. . . *Agricultural unit loss is acceptable.*

Retrieve ESS for disposal.

Quinton felt a wave of panic surge through him. They wanted the ESS. What did they want with the ESS? They were going to . . .

They were charging toward him now.

3

QUINTON STAGGERED BACKWARD, nearly losing his balance, and ran. The robot's feet adjusted to the rough terrain, giving him better traction, and his enhanced hearing noted the quick, powerful cadence of the hunter mechs hastening to catch up with him.

There were dozens of abandoned greenhouses nearby, covered in a thick, crusty layer of dirt, and ash coated their windows in a grimy grayish brown. Quinton bolted toward a narrow path between them and pivoted, hoping to throw the mechs off his tail.

He raced away from them as he heard at least one of the mechs crash into the building. Quinton emerged from between the greenhouses and turned right, rushing toward an impressive main building that, despite the current climate, had retained hints of its former glory. Atop a broad staircase were mounds that must have been statues, which Quinton recognized by the elevated pedestals. An enormous dome sat on top of the main building, flanked by two long side wings. Large sections of the roof had been peeled off the upper levels, but the main entrance above the grand marble staircase looked intact. He'd try to lose the mechs inside while he searched for a vehicle.

Quinton heard the stomping of heavy metallic footfalls coming from the rooftop of the building beside him. A hunter mech kept pace with him, gingerly running along the rooftops. Amber-colored eyes locked onto him, piercing the gloom from within narrow sockets in its dark helmet.

The sky brightened as pale moonlight shone through a break in the billowing storm clouds. The mech must've veered away from the others, circling around to cut him off. Quinton swerved away from the greenhouses and darted toward the main building. The mech leaped off the roof and chased him, rapidly closing the distance.

He ran up the grand staircase past thick stone columns to the shadowy interior. His vision cleared as his night vision engaged. Just beyond the doors was a wide reception desk with kiosks. Quinton ran past the reception area, the hunter mech right on his heels. A loud blast of sound came from behind him, and his foot was bumped to the side, shoving him off balance. He stumbled, and the mech knocked him off his feet. Quinton went down and skidded to a stop on the smooth floor as dust billowed into the air.

He scrambled to regain his feet, searching for anything he could use for a weapon. The agricultural unit was equipped with a focused sonic blaster, but it wouldn't respond. It was dead, just like he'd be in a few seconds if he couldn't stop the mech. He hastened back as the mech stalked forward, but it leaped toward him, grabbing hold of Quinton's outstretched hands. He struggled to push the powerful mech off of him, but he couldn't.

Dammit, Radek, why did you have to put me into such a pathetic machine?

Quinton pushed with his feet, and they slid farther into the building. The mech atop of him tried to block Quinton's feet with its own. He knew that if he could just keep moving, there was at least a chance he could break free.

The mech began angling them toward a nearby wall.

No, this is not good.

The mech was going to use the wall as leverage to overpower him. Quinton tried to change direction, but the mech had momentum on its side. As they drew near the wall, the mech pivoted on its lower body, anchoring itself to the wall, which jolted them both to a stop. The mech leaned toward Quinton's chest, where the ESS was housed. Two smaller arms sprang from a hidden compartment in its chest and pulled hard on Quinton's chest plate. He twisted away, trying to prevent those damn small arms from getting his ESS. The mech climbed higher on the wall, lifting Quinton off the ground.

Oh, crap.

He was completely at the mech's mercy. He had to do something, or else his brief existence as a PMC was going to end. What separated humans from machines was an unwavering drive to preserve life. When push came to shove, both humans and animals alike would fight for their lives until their very last breath. A PMC wasn't required to breathe, but the indomitable will to live was just as strong.

Quinton wouldn't give up without a fight. He accessed the agricultural unit's systems menu and felt a rush of hope surge through him as he finally found something he could use.

Weapons!

Hidden within the forearms were hardened alloyed blades meant for chopping and cutting thick branches.

The mech grabbed his chest plate and pulled hard. Quinton brought his feet up to its body and angled his palms upward as the blades sprang from his wrists, punching through the mech's hands. Quinton pressed his feet into the mech and pushed away from its grasp. He landed on his feet, and the mech's head turned toward him in surprise. Quinton sprang up, stabbing the blade through its narrow eye socket. He hung there for a moment, using his whole weight to sever the mechanical innards of the hunter mech. Sparks burst from the wound, and Quinton dropped back down to the ground.

The mech flailed its arms and struck Quinton's shoulder, almost knocking him down. Damage alerts flooded his internal heads-up display as a klaxon alarm blared from the mech. He glanced back toward the entrance of the building and heard the other two mechs running up the stairs. He'd gotten lucky, but he didn't want to take on two hunter mechs at the same time. They'd probably already called for reinforcements, so more were on the way. Quinton turned and ran, eager to put as much distance between him and the hunter mechs as possible.

"There is a power source in this building. There might be a working terminal available for use," Radek said.

"Where?"

"Sub-basement level five."

A route for him to take was highlighted in front of him. Quinton followed the path to a wide, long staircase amid an open atrium with exhibits and walkways on both sides. Thunder roared outside, and rain began to fall through a massive hole in the roof overhead.

"What's down there?" he asked.

"My guess is some kind of control room."

"You guess!" Quinton said, reaching the bottom of the stairs.

He'd tried to keep his voice down, but the mechs must've heard him. He noted the echoes of the security mechs from the top floor, but they hadn't followed him yet. What were they waiting for?

"I have access to the same information as you. This unit has a sensor range for detecting power lines, which is understandable given the occupation for which the unit was designed."

Radek was correct. This unit was once a highly sophisticated garden robot whose lifespan would have been severely limited if it hadn't been able to detect hidden power cables and conduits. Quinton had never thought about it before, and even if he'd been an expert in these kinds of machines, he wouldn't have remembered because of his limited access to the ESS.

Gah! He really wanted to grit his teeth, but he couldn't. The robot didn't have a mouth, but its head had somewhat anthropomorphic features.

He dashed toward a hallway that led to elevator doors, going to the one farthest away and prying open the door. There was no power to the elevators, so he'd have to climb down the shaft. He spotted a metallic ladder to his left and began his descent. The elevator doors squeezed shut, and he was in near darkness. The only light came from the slight glow of his ESS that has been partially exposed when the mech tried to rip it out of his chest. The mech had been trying to tear his heart out, but the ESS was more than just his heart. It contained everything that made Quinton who he was. PMCs were sophisticated uploads of the human consciousness, wrapped in a framework of assistant virtual intelligences.

Quinton didn't know the circumstances that surrounded his apparent reactivation. He didn't even know what planet he was on, and because of the limited capacity of the machine he was housed in, he couldn't access any of his memories.

Every time he climbed down a rung on the ladder, there was an audible click, like several gears grinding into place. When the mech had struck his shoulder, it must've damaged the socket. The sound would surely be detected by the hunter mechs when they came for him.

Instead of climbing down one rung at a time, Quinton decided to let himself drop. Before he could gain too much velocity, he grabbed hold of a rung to slow his descent, and his body jerked to a halt. The agricultural unit was designed for climbing. Trimming tall trees was probably one of its duties. He didn't know what he would do if his arms were torn out of their sockets, but he needed to reach the lower level—fast.

He soon came to the fifth level and made his way over to the door, forcing it open and climbing through. As he walked down the dark, quiet maintenance corridor, he noticed that the outside elements hadn't penetrated there, and the corridor was untouched. The sensor data on his HUD showed that the power source was just up ahead in one of the side rooms.

Quinton hastened toward it and opened the door. A phalanx of workstations illuminated the area in an azure glow, and he walked to the nearest one. A holoscreen flickered on. The data displayed was slightly blurry from the aged projector hidden inside the workstation, but the status window showed the batch of commands that had been submitted by the last person who'd used the station. They'd initiated a shutdown protocol because of some kind of emergency. Given how things looked aboveground, Quinton was certain it was something catastrophic. As the system refreshed, a barrage of offline messages began spewing on the holoscreen. There was no info-net for him to connect to. He could only find the coordinates to an evacuation center. It must've been a broadcast emergency message that instructed the workers to go to a specific evacuation place. He brought up a map, and it highlighted a path for him to follow. There was a lot of open ground to cover, and with the hunter mechs coming for him, he wasn't sure if he'd make it.

He still had access to local systems, and he tried to find a maintenance work area. He was hoping to find some kind of vehicle he could use. An alert appeared on his HUD. The power core in the agricultural unit was depleting, showing that he had less than 25 percent power remaining. Quinton had no idea what the longevity of the power core inside him was, but the unit must've been stored for quite some time, and it was probably well beyond its expected lifespan. He was running out of time.

"You should go to the evacuation center," Radek said.

Quinton stepped away from the workstation. "Thanks for the tip," he said bitterly.

He left the control center and shook his head. Radek was just trying to help keep him on task, and he had to focus. He had to do one thing at a time in order to escape. He couldn't afford to dwell on what he didn't know, but he couldn't help but blame Radek for his current predicament. Rationally, he knew it wasn't the VI's fault. It, too, had been activated after the upload to the ESS, but given what was happening, he felt he was entitled to a bit of irrationality. It wasn't as if Radek had feelings anyway.

There was no way for Quinton to call for help, and now he was thinking that there would be nobody to answer his call even if he was able to make one. He began making his way to the maintenance work area. Hopefully, there would be some kind of vehicle the groundskeepers used. Otherwise, he'd have to continue running from the hunter mechs. If there *was* a vehicle, and it was still connected to a charging station, perhaps it would be enough to get him to the evacuation center.

4

The maintenance area was located at the ground level. Rather than risk another encounter with the hunter mechs, who no doubt wanted to exact revenge for what Quinton had done to their sneaky comrade, he decided to find another way to reach the ground level. Making his way through the dark hallways of the building, he found a staircase and began climbing to the upper level. He kept expecting to feel the exertion of climbing the steps. It was natural to think that since he was exerting himself, he'd feel the results of those efforts regardless of how physically fit he'd been. At least, he *thought* he'd been in good physical condition before he'd been uploaded into an ESS, but he couldn't know for sure. He just had a feeling that he had been. Something in the way he moved suggested a familiarity of movement, a familiarity that could only come from the habits formed in his brain, but what if he was wrong? There was no heavy breathing or burning thighs as he mounted the stairs. Instead, there was nothing but an efficiency of motion as he climbed as fast as he could. With his mechanical limbs, he was taking the steps two at a time. The hunter mech had damaged his shoulder, and whenever he lifted his left arm, he once again noted a clicking sound from the actuators. Raising his arm higher than shoulder level resulted in it dropping, as if it couldn't support its own weight. The blade in his left forearm was only partially retracted because it was bent from his fight with the mech.

Quinton reached the ground floor and slowly opened the door. He stepped into the dark corridor and peered toward a wide doorway that led to a maintenance garage. Pale light from the outside cast shadows beyond the doorway, and he froze. The hunter mechs would be searching for him. The shadows stirred in the pallid light, and a gust of wind moaned in the distance.

Quinton raised the sensitivity of the bot's auditory sensors. Rain splattering the roof high above him registered in stunning clarity of sound, as if time had slowed to a crawl. A soft groan came from the upper floors that were exposed to the elements. He remained still and logged the sounds, carefully cataloging them and minimizing their impact so he could listen for the mechs. He waited there, alone in the darkened corridor, hoping the mechs weren't nearby. Several minutes passed with nothing but the quiet cadence of a stream of rainwater splashing the ground inside the maintenance garage. He crept toward the door.

Satisfied that there were no mechs waiting to ambush him, Quinton reduced the auditory system sensitivity to normal levels. Inside the garage were vehicles and other bots in charging stations along the walls. He detected faint power signatures from some of the bots and vehicles, but he'd need to inspect them to determine whether they had enough power to be of use.

Rainwater streamed through a jagged opening in the roof of the garage toward the outer wall. It looked as if the roof had been peeled away in order to see inside. Something must have crashed and bounced off the structure with sufficient velocity to cause that kind of damage. If the hunter mechs had a giant older brother, something from a military arsenal, then he was as good as dead.

A steady stream of water made its way toward the main doors. Lightning flickered brightly, pushing the shadows back into sudden retreat, and Quinton headed toward the outer doors. There were several large vehicles off to his right that looked as if they were meant for hauling heavy things. Their thick wheels were nearly as tall as he was. The lack of counter-grav vehicles meant that this estate or museum was a throwback to a historical time before the advent of the current tech, or he might be on a fringe planet that had limited resources. It could be both, but Quinton wouldn't find that out by staying in this garage.

He headed to the door control panel and saw that it still had power. The maintenance area must have been on its own backup power after it had been cut off from the main building. The bots and vehicles in the garage weren't what he considered cutting edge, but they were built to be relatively self-sustaining—at least under normal circumstances. Given the state of things outside, he wondered how long things had been so bad here. Power cores being what they were, they would take tens of years to deplete and maybe more, even without proper maintenance.

Next to the main doors was a smaller door where workers entered. Quinton walked over to it and pulled it open. Outside, he could see what had once been a sprawling garden, with paths he could just barely see under the slushy ash. Map markers, pulled from the agricultural bot's memory core, appeared on his HUD. There were several paths across the vast estate that he could take to the evacuation center. The ash-covered fields had the appearance of dingy gray snow, and Quinton's sensors detected high levels of sulfur. Such high concentrations indicated that not only did the air smell like rotten eggs and decay, but he'd have a strong aftertaste in his mouth if he were in his body.

He doubted anything was left alive in the region. In addition to looking like a hellish landscape of a dying world, the atmosphere was slowly poisoning anything left alive. He couldn't wait to get out of there.

Streaks of gray and black stretched across the way, and even though the remnants of tree-covered paths were only a short distance away, he'd be way too exposed if he tried to make a run for it.

"Quinton, you must hurry. You need to cross the field to reach the evacuation center," Radek advised.

"I don't think so," Quinton replied.

"I don't understand. Staying here doesn't bring us any closer to our objective."

"You're supposed to help me, Radek. I can't just go running blindly out there. Can you tell me if any hunter mechs are waiting to ambush us? That's where I'd be if I were them. I'd be keeping watch, and as soon as my target left the building, I'd pounce," he said and shook his head. "For a virtual intelligence that's supposed to help me, you're not being very helpful. Now, just give me a few seconds to think."

He watched the open field. There was *some* cover from the trees that hadn't toppled over, but they were leaning to their sides under the heavy weight of the ash, ensuring their eventual demise. He tried to calculate how long it would take him to reach that area, and he didn't like his chances. Radek was right about one thing. He couldn't stay here, but that didn't mean he should make a mad dash across an open field, begging for the hunter mechs to run him down. He had to be smarter than that. He needed cover . . . or a distraction. Quinton glanced behind him at all the vehicles and the maintenance bots. Some of them still had power. They wouldn't last long, but they might last long enough for what he was planning.

He glanced at the main doors where ice glistened on the gray metallic surface in frozen rivulets. It wasn't enough to prevent the doors from opening, but he doubted they'd open quietly, which meant they'd draw the mechs' attention.

He crossed to the other side of the garage and brought up a control terminal. The main screen showed the status of the machines in the charging stations. Almost half of them were without power, but there were multiple outdoor maintenance bots for which he was able to bring up the startup sequence. These bots were less sophisticated than the unit he was in. No doubt, they were meant for working away from the view of the patrons who visited this place. The medium-sized maintenance bots had four mechanical arms, as well as a continuous tread system at the base. As they went through their startup sequences, they did a system check. Their mechanical arms went through a range of motion to test their mobility and the continuous tread systems clustered together, raising the bots up several feet. All twelve of them bobbed up and down as they went through their checks.

Only four large autonomous vehicles still had power. Quinton accessed their control systems next and began activating them. One of them quickly came online but failed during its startup sequence and became unresponsive. He accessed another one, and it lasted a whole thirty seconds longer than the first one had before it failed. Quinton swore in frustration. Thankfully, the remaining two passed their systems startup test and waited for orders. He passed the control protocol from the control terminal over to his own systems so he wouldn't need to stay at the physical terminal, then stepped back and turned to survey his squad of decoy bots. Dim amber light gleamed through the crust-covered, multi-sensored heads of the maintenance bots. A soft hum came from each one as they waited for him to command them.

Quinton walked over to the main doors and used the controls to open them. The door mechanism struggled for a few moments before the actuators were able to pull the two massive doors to the side, and rain and wind gusted in a soft howl through the opening. The door tracks screeched in a protest loud enough to be heard over the storm.

There's no going back now.

He scanned the area outside for a few moments and then accessed the medium-sized bot control interface. He tasked half the bots to perform a general maintenance patrol mode, and they quickly sped outside, heading away from the maintenance garage. Quinton waited a few moments and then ordered one of the large haulers to head to the western side of the vast estate. The large metallic wheels adjusted the treads to give it traction, and the hauler drove away at a leisurely speed at first, gradually increasing its velocity.

The rest of the medium-sized bots came to the doorway and waited, followed by the remaining large hauler. Quinton climbed up the side of the hauler and glanced inside the open storage bed. Pieces of scrap metal were piled inside.

He scrambled over the side and onto the bed. The scrap metal was partially covered, and he squatted down toward the front. He ordered his small squad of robot henchmen out into the storm, and he followed.

Radek had updated Quinton's HUD to show where the other bots had gone. The coordinates he'd given this group were to take them directly across the field as fast as they could. He hoped it would confuse the hunter mechs.

The large hauler jostled back and forth as it crossed onto the rugged path. Quinton turned around and glanced behind them, seeing two shapes appear on the roof of the museum. The hunter mechs quickly surveyed the scene of the fleeing robots and then leaped to the ground. They split off, each mech heading toward different groups of maintenance bots, but neither was heading toward him. His distraction had worked.

The hauler was running with minimal power, and its systems were throwing up warnings about the depleting charge. Quinton increased the vehicle's speed, knowing it would cut the life of the hauler's power cell to little more than a handful of minutes, but he needed more speed than endurance. The hunter mechs were able to quickly traverse the rough terrain, galloping on all of their limbs.

Quinton was about to turn around when he saw a third mech appear on the rooftop. Its dome-shaped head had a jagged puncture where one of its eyes had been. A few fleeting sparks burst from the opening. It scanned the area and seemed to focus on him. He sank down, trying to hide behind the pile of scrap metal. Just then, one of the hauler's wheels slipped, and the vehicle began to slide for a few moments before regaining traction. The storage bed jerked to the side, and Quinton was jostled out from cover. He looked back at the roof in alarm, hoping the mech hadn't seen him.

He was wrong.

The mech leaped off the roof and hit the ground at a run.

Quinton commanded two medium-size bots to circle back and intercept the mech. There was a bright flash off to the side, and then a squeal sounded from a maintenance bot as one of the hunter mechs tore it apart. Sparks burst from its power core, and the mech darted toward its next victim.

Quinton took control of the large hauler, overriding the autonomous drive systems. He jerked the steering controls toward the tree-lined path, and the entire vehicle tilted to the side as it swerved. The hauler bounced wildly for a few moments, and he clutched onto the handrail inside the storage bed. The adaptive wheels quickly engaged deformation protocols, and the ride smoothed out as the vehicle continued over rough terrain.

He looked to the left and saw a mech chasing the maintenance bots. They didn't look anything like Quinton's agricultural unit, which made him wonder just how sophisticated the targeting systems of the hunter mechs actually were. They seemed to be chasing almost anything that moved, and his only option was to get away from them as fast as possible.

He ordered the four remaining bots in front of them to form a phalanx behind the large hauler. The mech he'd fought inside the museum had made quick work of the medium bots he'd sent over to it. Their remains littered the ground in pieces. The mech's one good eye gleamed hatefully in stark contrast to the greenish fluid that had splattered over its chassis.

Quinton made it to the forest path, and the hauler bludgeoned through the lower tree branches that splintered apart on impact. He saw small dark shapes scampering among trees, keeping pace with him. Something big slammed into the side of the hauler. It lurched, jostling his hold on the handrail, and he slipped back onto the pile of scrap. An armored, metallic claw reached over the side. The mech had finally caught up to him.

He extended the blade from his forearm and slammed down on the mech's hand with all his might. The hand severed at the wrist, and the mech dropped and rolled away, but Quinton's blade was wedged into the side of the storage bed. He yanked his hand back, trying to free the blade, and it snapped at the base of the tang.

The vehicle leveled off, and he peered around. Eight sets of amber-colored eyes gleamed menacingly in the darkness. Reinforcements had arrived, and their heads bobbed slightly as they raced toward him. Quinton recalled all the maintenance bots, but their numbers had diminished rapidly. He overrode their crash-avoidance systems, and they threw themselves at the mechs. Several mechs went down in a tangle, and Quinton lost sight of them.

"Obstruction ahead. Secure your position," Radek warned.

Quinton spun and saw that the corpse of a thick tree was blocking part of the path. He grabbed onto the handrail and increased the speed. Several dark, furry shapes leaped from the nearby trees and landed inside the hauler's storage bed. The creatures' fur was matted and dirty, but their wide eyes gleamed in the dim light.

The hauler slammed into the obstructing tree, causing it to jerk violently, and it bounced off another fallen tree on the other side of the path. The furry little critters screeched as they scrambled to grab hold of something. One of them flew through the air and disappeared from view. Quinton watched as one of the larger animals helped the others climb the scrap pile near the rear of the vehicle. They hadn't paid any attention to him at all.

Quinton heard two mechs close in behind the hauler. They sprang up and yanked the rear hatch, hard. The hinges bent and the hatch flung open, causing the pile of scrap to start spilling out of the bed. Several of the furry creatures tumbled down despite the efforts of the larger male trying to help them. One of the mechs snatched at the scrap, pulling it, along with the creature, toward him. Quinton lurched forward and flung a metallic shaft at the mech. The shaft slammed into its chest, knocking it off balance.

A third mech raced behind the hauler, desperate to find a way into the vehicle. With a firm grip on the handrail, Quinton tried to grab another piece of scrap metal, but the mech was faster. The clawed hand gouged at the end and heaved itself into a lunge toward him. The furry creature scrambled back, squealing in terror as the large mech was about to flatten him. Quinton dove and plucked the creature out of harm's way. He rolled, so his back slammed into the side of the storage bed while cradling the animal. Then he shoved at the last scrap pile with his feet, sending fragments of metal flying toward the mech's head.

The mech flailed blindly before falling off the back and tumbling out of sight.

"Obstruction ahead. We must slow down," Radek said.

Quinton pulled himself up. The frightened creature tried to escape from his grasp, but he held onto him and looked toward the front of the vehicle. The hauler was speeding toward a tall barricade that stretched across the path. It looked reinforced and solid. There was no way around it, and there was no way he was going to break through it like he'd done with the tree. He glanced back and saw the remaining mechs about to make another attack run. Quinton increased the vehicle's velocity to the maximum and climbed out of the storage bed toward the front of the vehicle. After the initial burst of speed, the hauler began slowing down. Its power core was depleting rapidly. A system alert appeared, showing that there was a containment breach in the power core.

The mechs closed in on them. Quinton held the furry creature in one hand and then leaped into the air just before the vehicle slammed into the barricade. He cleared the barrier, hurtling through the air like a slow-moving missile. The ground raced up to meet him, and he spun to the side, clutching the furry rodent to his chest protectively. As he crashed to the ground, a large explosion blazed into the night. He rolled for a few feet and then skidded to a stop but quickly regained his feet. The creature glared at him as if Quinton had somehow mishandled it. He squealed loudly, and Quinton dumped it to the ground.

"You can take your chances with them if you want," he said and started running.

He didn't need to look behind him to know that there were more mechs making their way to his position. He was out of range of the maintenance bots, but he doubted there were any left online.

The evacuation center wasn't far. Something scrambled up his leg, and he glanced to the side, seeing the creature riding on his shoulder. It was his good shoulder, and he couldn't lift the other arm high enough, even if he wanted to shoo him away. He left him alone and ran toward the evacuation center.

5

QUINTON DARTED DOWN THE STREET, passing empty shops along the way. Their darkened interiors flashed by as lightning gleamed brightly overhead. He came to a large marketplace and peered through the broken windows to the dark recesses inside. Abandoned nests and dead animal skeletons were piled outside various alcoves, occurring too regularly to be random. A community of predators had lived there but must have moved on when they depleted the food source.

Quinton kept wondering about what had happened here. Had the calamity affected the entire planet? Volcanic ash was indicative of a major catastrophe, but with enough warning, there were ways to prevent even a caldera from blowing. If they'd evacuated the region, that probably meant the disaster had been extensive. Hopefully, he'd find some kind of transportation that could get him out of the area and leave the mechs behind. The evacuation center was his best hope for either finding transportation or contacting someone who could help.

Holographic signs pointed the way to the center. Quinton hurried down abandoned permacrete streets, passing buildings that had entire floors exposed where the walls had crumbled, exposing the superstructure that kept the buildings standing. The gusting winds shrieked through the openings in a furious buildup and then relented.

Rubble crowded the sides of the streets, and an analysis of it appeared on Quinton's HUD. Outlines of human skeletons were detected within the rubble. The bodies had long since decomposed, but the analysis capability of the agricultural bot was designed for fine-tuning. His sensors were able to decipher the intricacies of delicate plant life, and the detail of the analysis surprised him. It was something he hadn't been expecting. The owners of this machine had configured it with features he'd underestimated. Unfortunately for him, none of those things would help him when the mechs finally caught up with him. Even though the mechs that had been on the hauler must have been destroyed, he knew more had been nearby.

He reached the end of the street and ran around a corner, seeing that the evacuation center was several hundred meters away. Barricades blocked the entrance, and long lines of abandoned vehicles were crammed together, filling the space leading up to it. Quinton ran between them. A watchtower still stood to the side of the barricade, and he peered at the dark shape inside.

ACN Plasma Assault System.

The words appeared on his HUD.

"Radek, what's with the ident of the tower defenses?"

"The identity of the tower defenses was pulled from your ESS," Radek replied.

The other tower had toppled over the barricade, and Quinton began climbing it.

"Are you saying that I have detailed schematics of weapons systems available?" Quinton asked, hoping he'd found some useful skill he hadn't known he had.

He couldn't recall that ability from the little he could remember of his PMC training, but there might have been improvements since he'd first been uploaded and stored into his original ESS. PMC modification, which included the enhancements, required the consent of the person, and under the circumstances, Radek should be able to inform him if any such enhancements had occurred.

"Negative, there are no additional technical libraries stored in the ESS. The identification was from your own knowledge."

Quinton reached the top of the barricade and began sliding down the other side.

"My own knowledge," he said. "But why can't I remember having the knowledge in the first place?"

He stopped his descent. A maze of designated queues meant to manage the people leaving this place extended another hundred meters from where he was. How many people had come through here? The lines must have been immense.

He leaped to the ground and began making his way across the maze, going in as straight a line as possible, but he saw that there were more personnel barricades on the other side that funneled people to a specific pathway beyond. Quinton didn't know which would take him directly inside, so he angled for the nearest one and hoped for the best.

"Radek, you never answered my question."

"Apologies. I've been interacting with the VI interface that manages all the VIs. To answer your question, it has to do with the limitations of this unit. VIs operate to assist you without you having to consciously ask for it. They're monitoring all sensory inputs. Due to the limitations of the unit, they cannot allow direct access to your extensive memory libraries, but they can allow the factual knowledge, giving you information to help you with things like identification of a variety of systems."

Quinton considered this for a few moments. The VIs managed the Personality Matrix Construct's connection to the ESS. His consciousness was mainly stored in the ESS, but the parts that allowed him to inhabit the agricultural bot functioned separately, as if they were two distinct units. But there *was* a connection, which meant that the VIs had access to the majority of knowledge—his knowledge and experiences— stored in the ESS. Quinton didn't like that one bit. This meant he'd be living with VI gatekeepers that were called upon to decide which knowledge he needed and then make it available. He should have access to everything. Instead, he was walking—or, in this case, running—around with a form of selective amnesia that was under the dominion of a VI. What made it even worse was the fact that Radek hadn't realized this was happening, which led Quinton to believe that even Radek was functioning in a diminished capacity. Compounded with the current situation of running for his life, this meant he was one step away from some kind of failure. Either this unit would cease to function, or the bottleneck between his PMC and the ESS would cause the entire system to freeze up.

He stopped his racing thoughts from distracting him when he could least afford it. He just needed to keep moving forward. His furry little freeloader let out a low squeal, and Quinton stopped. He glanced behind him toward the large barricades and increased the sensitivity of his auditory systems. Filtering out the rapid breathing of the creature on his shoulder, he was able to hear the brisk thump-thump of its heartbeat as it increased. He raised the sensitivity further and could just make out the artificial cadence of hunter mechs in the distance. They must have found his trail. He returned the configuration of the auditory system back to normal and ran inside the evacuation center.

A warning flashed on his HUD. The power meter for the agricultural bot—him— was decreasing rapidly and would soon reach critical levels.

The unit's power meter minimized to the upper-right corner of his HUD and, trying to ignore it, he sprinted inside the evacuation center through another security check-in, wondering how many of these things the people of this world had had to go through before they could leave. He glanced at a veritable mountain of discarded personal belongings and sped down a long hallway. Lightning flashes illuminated a wide-open waiting area ahead of him, and he ran toward it. Once through the doorway, numerous lightning flashes revealed ash-laden sleet free-falling outside in glistening waves. It collected on the ground in drifts that nearly reached the tops of high landing platforms.

He peered at the rows of landing platforms.

They were empty.

Quinton ran toward the window, searching for a ship. Personnel tubes extended from the waiting area to empty landing platforms. The sky lit up again, showing the graveyard of a massive transport station without any ships. There was nothing here.

He kept walking in a half-shuffle, stopping periodically to look outside, hoping to spot something he might have missed. He slowly scanned the area, praying that one of his internal VIs would spot something and highlight it on his HUD.

"Radek, I don't see anything out there that we can use."

"Confirmed. It appears that all ships have left this center."

Big help that was, he thought and quickly dismissed it. He leaned toward the window, searching. He was at ground level, which didn't give him a good view of the area, so he glanced over to the side at a small building that looked as if it was some kind of control center. He saw the curvature of the landing field area, and judging the central location of the dark building, he could climb to the top and get a better vantage point.

Quinton scuttled toward the nearest tunnel leading out of the evacuation center and entered. He kept going until he found an emergency exit and emerged outside. His furry companion let out a soft cry and burrowed his face into Quinton's neck, shielding himself from the acid rain. There was nothing he could do for the creature, no shelter he could give him. The best he could do was to get out of the toxic atmosphere as quickly as possible.

He raced toward the control center and bolted up the staircase that led to the entrance. Once inside, the creature shook itself, and flecks of water and slimy ash flicked into the air. To his left was a wide window that stretched the length of the control center, giving him a perfect—though disheartening—view of the empty landing area for the transport station.

"Come on," Quinton said. "Give me something I can use."

He peered outside and then noticed a dim light glowing from one of the workstations to his right. He hastened over to it and engaged the holo-interface. The console flickered to life, and the screen showed the most recent status. As he quickly scanned through the data, he noted that there was a date for the last entry, but without knowing the current date, he didn't know how much time had passed since the system had last been updated.

All the loading platforms had a status of "open," meaning that they were waiting for a shuttle or other transport vehicle to arrive. Quinton scrolled through the screen, reading page after page of the same thing. He was stranded here. There was another flash on his HUD, warning him that his power core had reached critical emergency levels. He needed to get to the nearest charging station.

Quinton shook his head in frustration and glared at the holoscreen, which was full of information that wouldn't help him, but he kept scrolling until he reached the end. There were no other ships. Then he noticed something different about the last entry.

Emergency launcher track system offline.

This wasn't the important part. If he'd had his human eyes, they would have widened in exultation. One of the tracks showed that there was a small escape craft with a status of needing repairs. Quinton verified the location and looked out the window. Across the landing field was a series of tracks that led off into the distance and curved out of sight.

He saw a door to the outside on the far side of the room and darted over to it. He rushed through and leaped over the railing, forgoing the staircase altogether. He didn't have time. He needed to get to that ship and figure out what was wrong with it so he could escape.

A few minutes later, Quinton finally reached the emergency launcher track system to find a long tent covering the temporary hangar. Its frayed edges flapped in the wind, and long tears along the top provided no shelter underneath.

The track systems curved away before raising in a steep incline, and he looked for anything that could be blocking the track. His enhanced vision outlined an obstruction about halfway down the track before it curved upward. He'd have to clear it. Quinton peered down the row of empty loaders until he saw an elongated shape with a booster engine on the back.

He raced toward it, and his excitement spiked. The loader's terminal was still active. It was a simple standalone access terminal for the planetary escape pod, which had limited flight capabilities and was designed to dock with a space station. He brought up the terminal, and it attempted to establish a connection to the space station that this evacuation center fed into.

Attempting to establish a link.

Connecting . . .

Connecting . . .

"Connect, dammit."

Connection established. Downloading updated coordinates to station alpha.

"Yes!"

While the navigation data was downloading, Quinton brought up the pod's status to determine why it was offline. The creature jumped off his shoulder and scurried back under the tent cover while he accessed the pod's computer.

Escape Pod 4110.

Status – Life-support system failure.

Abort launch sequence . . .

He quickly checked the remaining systems for the escape pod. They were still operational. The only thing was that the pod's life-support system had malfunctioned. Whoever was here must not have had time to repair it, or perhaps they hadn't needed to. But Quinton didn't need life support. He didn't need oxygen or an atmosphere to survive. What he didn't know was how long the metallic alloy of the agricultural bot could withstand the frigidness of outer space, but he could deal with that. The pod would still protect him. He began the launcher's startup sequence, which would take a few minutes to initialize.

Quinton ran next to the track, quickly closing in on the obstruction across it. A tangle of twisted metal from another track lay across the one he needed. He pulled at it, clearing away pieces until he got to a heavy section that just wouldn't budge no matter how hard he pulled. He climbed over to the other side and saw where it was wedged in tight. Quinton extended the remaining blade from his right forearm and selected the option on his HUD for shearing. The blade split into two, and he began cutting near the wedged section. In a stroke of good fortune, the alloy of the blades was stronger than the material used for the track, and he was able to cut through it. He made quick work of it and then tore loose the last of the debris.

He spun around and ran back toward the pod. The control panel inside cast a bluish glow on the vehicle's interior. Quinton glanced at the launcher platform, looking for the creature, but it was gone. It had probably run off. He checked the pod's status on the terminal and approached the open hatch. He was taking one last glance around when lightning flashed, and his gaze sank to the ground, seeing flashes of amber reflected upon the watery surface.

Hunters!

The mechs had found him. Six of them galloped toward him, closing the distance in a rush of speed.

Quinton scrambled through the hatch and closed it. He sat down and had to buckle himself in before the controls would allow him to initiate the launch.

Something scurried on the floor, and Quinton saw that the furry creature had already climbed aboard. A mech slammed its fists on the outer hatch, and the escape pod rocked to the side before settling back into place. He thought it was going to break through. If it did, the automatic safety systems would abort the launch.

As the hunter mech drew back for another strike, Quinton engaged the launch system. There was a sudden burst from the booster, and the planetary escape pod raced down the track, quickly reaching maximum speed. He was thrown back into the seat, and his furry companion screeched as he was pinned against the wall. The pod angled upward and then it was in the air. The secondary boosters engaged in a blast of energy as the pod reached escape velocity.

A warning flashed across the holoscreen.

Life support offline.

Interior atmosphere minimal.

Quinton glanced at the creature and then opened the panel beneath the console. There was an emergency life-support face mask inside. He snatched it out and grabbed the little furball, which scrambled his stubby legs.

"Easy there, Stumpy. I'm trying to help you."

He fit the mask over the creature's face. It formed around his head, the material configuring in a tight seal, and oxygen flowed inside. The panicking creature calmed down after a few moments of breathing the fresh air.

"Power levels critical. I must shut down systems to conserve power," Radek said.

Before Quinton could voice any kind of protest, everything around him began fading. His thoughts came to a halt, and all sensory input crawled to a stop as if his mind were frozen. Then, nothing.

6

System diagnostic running.

Quinton snapped back to awareness and stared at the words on his HUD. A few quick diagnostics completed, and his motor functions returned to normal.

Again . . .

Where am I now?

He didn't open his eyes because, as far as he knew, the agricultural bot he was housed in didn't have any eyelids. It was more that he gradually became aware of his condition and the sensory input the optics provided.

He was still inside the planetary escape pod, but the hatch was open. Somehow, he was lying on his side on the floor. He glanced at the upper-right corner of his internal HUD, which showed that his power meter was charging, and he jerked his head back in surprise. His power core had been charged to almost 50 percent. He started to push himself up and the actuators in his left shoulder gave out, but he caught himself with his other hand. He still had that damn damaged shoulder to deal with, but at least he was awake.

Outside the hatch, emergency lighting was engaged in the corridor. He glanced at the floor and saw that a thick power cable came in from the outside and was attached to a port on his back. Someone had connected him to an emergency charging station.

"Radek, are you there?" Quinton asked.

"System startup is nearly complete."

"Do you know where we are?"

"Station identification is Gateway Station in the Zeda-Six Star System. You went into emergency standby mode to preserve functionality. Once the pod was within range of the station, their automated systems guided it into this docking bay. I did a search and discovered that I would be able to request an emergency power supply authorization if I declared you caretaker of a living creature."

"You made me Stumpy's caretaker?"

"It was a calculated risk, but I didn't want to give the station's computer systems a reason to deny the request."

Quinton realized the little creature wasn't completely useless after all. "Good call. I guess if you'd told the system I was a PMC, it might have ejected the pod so some station jockey could use it for target practice."

"I kept you in standby until the unit had charged more than 50 percent," Radek explained.

They'd escaped the hunter mechs and made it to a space station, and he had Radek to thank for it. "I guess I owe you one."

Radek paused for a moment as its silvery holographic orb hovered in the air. "I'm afraid I don't understand." The orb pulsed when the VI spoke.

"You helped me, Radek. You got me hooked up to a power supply to recharge this machine."

"PMCs are a distinct entity apart from the physical form they are housed in. I made an effort to keep the unit performing. It's one of my primary objectives."

Quinton shook his head. "It's called appreciation, Radek. I was expressing my gratitude. I know VIs understand this concept."

"I understand the concept. I'm merely pointing out that it is unnecessary."

"Well, I disagree, but let's just drop it. Have any station personnel arrived?"

"Other than the automated system response, we have not been contacted."

Quinton didn't like the sound of that. He stood up and attempted to access the space station's computer systems, but there were no active connections available. Glancing around the escape pod for a moment, he realized that the emergency faceplate he'd stuffed Stumpy inside was now empty. The agricultural bot was equipped with sensors to detect a whole library of residues, so tracking Stumpy would be easy, but he couldn't spend a lot of time doing it. He wondered if he should have left the critter but quickly recognized that anything left on the planet, at least in the region they'd been in, was likely dead or dying. Leaving Stumpy would have been a death sentence, but Quinton wasn't sure if bringing the creature up here was any better.

He walked out of the escape pod and into the narrow corridor. To his right, the corridor led to the station's interior. The station's automated systems had docked his small vehicle on a long arm that was designed for escape pods, and the corridor was lined with empty pods whose occupants had long since exited them. There must have been a mass exodus from the planet, and he once again wondered what had happened to make the planet so uninhabitable. Severe volcanic activity explained some of it, but not the mechs.

His sensors detected that there was an atmosphere being maintained on the space station, but it was minimal. Apparently, it had been some time since anyone had come here. Life-support systems had automatically initialized the artificial atmosphere with the detection of Stumpy.

The power line that was tethered to the access port in his back retracted into the wall as he walked down the corridor. The main port was at the end, and when Quinton reached it, the cord detached from his access port and disappeared behind a panel on the wall.

He thought it was more important that he find the people who operated the space station rather than staying to continue charging. They might have a better housing unit for his ESS. Hopefully, he'd be able to get some information about where he was and whether other PMCs had been sent out across the galaxy. He tried to remember what the standard protocol was for PMC reactivation, but he couldn't. However, he was pretty sure he wasn't supposed to be dumped in an agricultural bot, no matter how sophisticated it was. This thing was barely able to accommodate the ESS where the bulk of Quinton's PMC was contained.

He called out, hoping that somebody would hear him, but there was no reply. The station should have been monitoring for verbal communications at the very least, so why hadn't it responded? There was really no way for him to get lost because there was only one way to go. He came to a larger corridor, and there was a sign that pointed the way to central processing and main transport.

Quinton followed the signs and eventually made his way to an information terminal. Somebody had designed this part of the station for minimal human interaction, which he supposed made sense. If people were evacuating the planet, they wouldn't be on the station for very long.

The information terminal came online, and Quinton accessed it. This entire section of the space station must have been offline because the information terminal didn't have the current status readily available. But then, Quinton had no idea how large the space station was because he'd been unconscious when the pod arrived.

He heard the pitter-patter of tiny clawed feet and saw Stumpy coming toward him. The creature stopped and regarded him for a few moments, twitching his head to the side and fully extending his large floppy ears. Deciding that the danger was minimal, Stumpy came closer, but the status screen suddenly flashed, and data began populating the screen. Quinton ignored Stumpy.

Searching for the next available transport ship.

None available. Please head to central processing.

Quinton glared at the holoscreen. He made a swiping motion, and the status screen minimized. He searched through the options, trying to find a map of the station so he could see the layout of the place and locate a hangar. He finally found a map and saw that this station was one of more than twenty positioned around the planet. It *was* a mass exodus.

He studied the map. The station looked like it had been cobbled together from spare orbital platforms. Usually, inhabited systems had a singular space station that was the transport hub for the planet. If there were mining facilities throughout the star system, then there might be smaller stations. But Quinton had the feeling he wasn't on either of those kinds of space stations. Someone had deployed this setup quickly, which meant that it lacked some of the essential systems he would have expected to find. Also, there were no people. He was alone.

His thoughts began to race, focusing on nothing that would help him. He found himself wanting to take a deep breath, but he couldn't, and there was no physical release of tension that might have brought a moment's peace. Instead, his fear just gathered into an overwhelming intensity. He looked around at the metallic walls of the space station and staggered back a few paces, letting out a half-formed snarl.

Who had done this to him?

A small voice in his mind urged him to calm down, and he wanted to comply, to think rationally. He should be able to do that, but he couldn't. He was stuck inside this lifeless machine, trying to keep a firm hold of his sanity, and it was slipping away.

I just need to focus. I just need to see.

Quinton spotted a viewport off to the side, but it was closed. They all were. He stomped over to the information terminal and opened all the viewports. All around the circular room, the metallic shields sank toward the floor, revealing a planetary view directly in front of him. A massive storm covered any landscape that would have been in sight, and only faint flashes of lightning emerged through the tempest. He glanced toward the horizon, looking for signs of life, but all he saw was an expanse of grays and whites that had extended far from the poles.

He walked around the central hub and saw the other arms of the station where escape pods had docked. Above him were massive docking platforms where transport ships had docked to fly people away from there.

He peered out of the viewports, looking for the other stations, but couldn't find any. Something shimmered in the sunlight, but Quinton couldn't tell what it was. It looked like some kind of metallic mass that was reflecting the light from the star. He returned to the terminal and bypassed the generic options on the main screen, establishing a link to the station's communication systems. Then, he sent out a general comms signal and waited. There were several automated replies —not from other stations but ship systems. He didn't care. He activated the station's auto-dock procedures, sent the commands to the ships, and waited for the ships to acknowledge the broadcast. Three of them replied immediately, and Quinton watched for them to fly to the station.

He shook his head. The ships weren't far, but it was going to take them some time to reach the station. He walked back toward the viewport of the planet and watched the massive storm clouds that covered the entire continent. There was something almost hypnotic about the way the swirling masses moved together. Out of the corner of his eye, he noticed something that pierced the clouds. A large grouping of objects began to glow as they reached escape velocity and headed toward the station. Were they escape pods? He returned to the info-terminal, but the automated docking systems weren't detecting any incoming pods from the planet.

Quinton looked back toward the viewport. A flash of panic erupted inside him just as the first of the objects slammed into the nearby docking arm. Klaxon alarms sounded and bulkhead doors slammed shut, cutting them off from the damaged part of the station. He backed away and heard Stumpy screech as he scurried away from the sound of the alarms.

Quinton glanced out of the viewport and saw more objects speeding toward the station. Two realizations slammed themselves into the forefront of his mind

—there was a planetary defense cannon on the surface of the planet, and somehow the hunter mechs were using it to destroy the space station he was on.

Quinton backed away from the viewports.

He had to run.

7

QUINTON OPENED a comlink to the space station's computer systems using his connection to the information terminal as an access point. He ordered the door on the other side of the control center to open and ran toward it. Stumpy scampered ahead of him down the corridor that curved out of sight.

He needed to get to the smaller docking bays on the far side of the station that faced away from the planet. As he ran, he scanned for new comlink access points because his current connection to the onboard systems was tenuous at best. If the planetary defense cannons hit the processing center, he would be cut off until he found another information terminal to patch into. It shouldn't take him this long to find a remote access point.

As the seconds went by, Quinton felt a gnawing doubt nibble away at his thoughts.

"Radek, are you able to help me with access to the station's systems?"

He checked the station's tracking systems, and one of the ships he'd called for was minutes away from docking with a maintenance port.

"Try scanning for open comlink interfaces," Radek replied. "They should be standard on a station of this design."

"What do you think I've been trying to do?" Quinton said.

The bulkhead door ahead of him wouldn't open, and Stumpy scurried back and forth in front of it—a furry ball of frightful intensity. Quinton checked the command status of the bulkhead door, and it wasn't responding. Then his access to the space station's systems severed. He was cut off.

A loud clang came from behind him, followed by a series of pops. The floor trembled under his feet, and everything lurched to the side as his view of the planet spun out of view. The station was spinning! The defense cannons must have hit a vital system for maintaining its orbit.

Quinton searched the control systems of the agricultural bot for magnetic boots to help stabilize him, but there weren't any. He cursed inwardly, simultaneously acknowledging that there was no reason for the bot to be equipped with magnetic boots. There was still some artificial gravity, but the centrifugal forces of the spinning space station exerted more force than the standard point-seven-five g-force maintained by the field.

He was pushed against the outer wall, and he crawled toward the bulkhead door. Light flashed by the open window. The station wouldn't be able to maintain its location in lower orbit. Quinton didn't know how long he had before the station broke apart in the planet's atmosphere. Unless his luck changed, it wouldn't be long.

He reached the bulkhead door and squatted down to pull open the manual override. He yanked hard on the lever, and the door opened a little. He grabbed onto one side of the door and pushed. Both sides of the door retracted. Stumpy hastened through, and he followed.

Quinton ran, his feet pounding on the outer wall of the station.

"Radek, did you detect anything?" he asked.

The wall curved upward, and Quinton climbed toward the opening of the adjacent hall. The little furball had already reached it and let out a screech before disappearing from view. Quinton had the impression that the little creature was telling him to hurry in furball language.

It took him a few moments to realize that Radek hadn't responded to him. Quinton accessed the agricultural bot's comms systems, and they were stuck in a comms loop, unable to connect to anything. He killed the process, temporarily shutting down his data communications capabilities, then brought them back up. He engaged the signal-acquisition protocol, which was a limited broadcast from the transmitter located on his head.

Signal acquired.

Authorized access granted.

Welcome to emergency gateway station.

The words appeared on his HUD, along with a gold emblem of the triangular bow of a warship on a black background. Quinton felt a few moments of satisfaction, immediately followed by suspicion. Why hadn't Radek told him about the faulty comms subroutine? It should have been easy for the VI to detect, unless the VI interface was functioning at a limited capacity just like Quinton was.

He glanced at the emblem, thinking it looked familiar. He tried to force the memory from his ESS, but it didn't work. Some low-level VI interface had decided that this information was nonessential.

Quinton slammed his fist against the wall and used the hardened alloy of his fingers to gouge a fingerhold. He thought he might have heard a growl from the bot's vocalizer. He pulled himself up and climbed to the top. Stumpy was already way down the corridor, and the furball stopped and glanced back at him for a moment before continuing.

With entry to Gateway Station's systems, Quinton had more access to the data he needed.

"Apologies, Quinton," Radek said, his silver orb shimmering nearby. "My capabilities were temporarily impaired due to a faulty module inside the agricultural bot's central processing unit. I was freed from the impairment when you stopped the associated tasks, and I have managed a workaround. I see that you now have systems access."

"Are you serious? You should've—" Quinton stopped himself from making a snarky reply. Everything was falling apart, including the bot his PMC was housed in, and he had no idea how long it would function. How many internal systems would need to fail before his PMC ceased to function? If that happened, his life would be in Radek's limited virtual hands, and who knew if Quinton would ever regain consciousness in those circumstances. He had to get to the ship and get away from the space station as quickly as possible. Then he could decide what to do next.

An alert popped up on his HUD. The automatic docking systems were attempting to abort the docking procedure.

"No, dammit, stop aborting the dock," Quinton growled.

He initiated an override and engaged the station's mobility thrusters. Enough of them came online to slow the spinning space station, and the approaching ship was able to get on a safe approach vector. At least now he had a ship docking closer to his location than before.

With the station stabilizing, it was easier for him to move toward his destination, although he knew it wouldn't last—not with the planetary defense cannons tearing the station apart. He accessed a video feed and saw that the projectiles from the defense cannon had decreased. Maybe they were running out of ammunition.

Quinton hastened down a narrow corridor between sections of the station, glancing at the section heading to make sure he was in the right place.

Successful dock of the ZS-Novo.

The status of the ship appeared on Quinton's HUD. The other ships he'd initiated a broadcast to weren't responding now. They'd aborted the docking procedure, so this was his only chance to get off the station. The ship was at the far end of a long corridor where escape pods normally docked.

Quinton ran down the corridor, and the station lurched to the side again, causing him to stumble. He banged into the wall and nearly fell into one of the open doorways of an empty escape pod. Stumpy screeched from somewhere ahead of him, and he could tell by the sound that he was going to have to climb to reach his ship. The axis at which the remains of the space station was spinning was trying to push him off the wall, and he had to hold on. If he let go, there'd be no way for him to stop himself and he'd just crash into the far wall at the end of the corridor, likely destroying the agricultural bot altogether.

He crawled along the wall like a spider. The station began to spin faster, and Quinton didn't know how much time he had. He began taking short leaps, ignoring the fact that if he failed to grab hold of the bulkhead walls at the precise time, he was going to die.

The escape pod doorways blurred by as he sped past them. He reached out with his hands and attempted to slow himself down, but the actuator in his left shoulder gave out and he misjudged his approach. Instead of grabbing hold of the bulkhead wall, he began to tumble. He heard the little furball screeching but didn't know where it was.

Quinton grunted with effort as he tried to anticipate where his body was going to be in relation to the out-of-control space station. He banged against the bulkhead wall and a series of impact alerts appeared on his HUD.

Panic swelled up inside him. This was it. He was going to die. He tried to grab the bulkhead wall again but couldn't get a firm grip.

Then time slowed down—literally.

"What the . . ." Quinton began to say, and then a new sub-window appeared on his HUD.

Frame rate increase.

Warning: Power consumption increase.

He finally understood. One of the advantages of a PMC was the ability to speed up the perception of time beyond what he would've been capable of in his own body. The agricultural bot was still tumbling out of control, but his perception of it had slowed down. He could pick the precise moment to slow himself down.

Quinton looked around and found a handhold that was part of the bulkhead wall. He was going to bounce off the adjacent wall, and by his estimation, it would send him right to the handhold.

He slowed the frame rate to 20 percent that of real time, then angled his body to try to control how he bounced off the wall.

It worked.

He was heading right toward the handhold. Quinton reached out with both hands, his body slowly spinning. He brought his legs and feet together as if he were a missile. Then, he grabbed the handhold. His feet jerked past him, but he was able to hold on and stop.

He blew out a breath that came out as an audible hissing sound from the agricultural bot's vocalizer. He didn't need to breathe, but there were some things that were embedded as habits in his consciousness that he couldn't let go. A proper housing unit for his PMC would have been able to compensate for the nuances that came with being human.

He adjusted the frame rate to normal time and heard Stumpy from farther down the corridor near where the ship was docked. Quinton began climbing toward it. On the other side of the corridor, inside a vacant escape pod door, he saw Stumpy, wide-eyed with terror as he clung onto the central console.

"You're not showing off now, are you?" he said.

Stumpy turned toward him, and his saucer-shaped eyes narrowed. His clawed feet gripped the console and his tail went rigid as he tried to keep his balance.

"This is what happens when you run off ahead." He looked around, trying to think of a way to cross over.

"The ship is just ahead. You must escape as quickly as possible," Radek said.

Quinton glanced up the corridor to the open docking bay door where his ship waited for him. "Are you suggesting I just leave him here? No moral compass, Radek?"

"A VI is incapable of determining moral choices. That is left up to the PMC."

He found Radek's reply peculiar, but he wasn't sure why. He'd brought Stumpy with him on a whim. The furry creature would have died if he hadn't, just as he would surely die if Quinton left him where he was now. If he tried to save him, there was a chance they'd both die. But if he could save the creature, Stumpy would most likely die at a later date, and Quinton would feel better about it now at least.

Stumpy held onto the central console, and now his feet and tail dangled in the air as he scrambled to hold on.

"Hang on, I'm coming," he said.

He tried not to think of how stupid he'd feel if he botched this and ended up dead. At least he'd only feel that way for a few seconds, and then he wouldn't be thinking of anything at all. The edges of Radek's holographic orb glistened, but the VI didn't say anything.

Quinton brought his feet under him and changed the configuration of the bot's feet so he could grab onto the handhold. The agricultural unit was designed with climbing in mind.

He increased his frame rate so time slowed down, and he waited for the space station's spin to approach its apex. When it did, he launched himself across the corridor directly toward the open hatch of the escape pod. Then, he grabbed the outer hatch and stopped himself from landing inside and crushing the little fella.

He set his frame rate back to normal time. His body dangled inside the escape pod, and he reached with his foot toward Stumpy. The escape pod was bigger than the one he'd flown to the station on, and he couldn't quite reach where Stumpy was, but he was as close as he was going to get.

"You're going to have to jump," he said.

Stumpy bobbed his head a couple times, as if judging the distance to Quinton's foot, and looked as if he was going to make the jump a few times, but Quinton's patience was growing thin. He didn't have time for this.

"I'm going to leave you here." He shook his foot, dangling it in front of the little furball. "Come on," he said and beckoned with his arm.

Stumpy's gaze locked onto Quinton's foot, and his body went rigid. There was a quick shuffle and a leap. The furry little creature grabbed on, scampered up to his shoulder, and held on tight.

Quinton climbed out of the escape pod and headed toward the ship. He had to time his movements with the momentum of the space station as it spun. A few frame rate adjustments later, he was climbing into the ship.

The ZS-*Novo* was a light transport star jumper-class ship. He closed the outer hatch, went through the airlock, and walked out onto a decent-size storage area compared to the size of the ship. From there, he headed for the bridge. Crusty flecks of pale green paint from the walls and ceilings littered the floor. He glanced at a CO_2 scrubber that was in a recess on the wall. A buildup of black mold surrounded the scrubber, and Quinton was able to detect mold spores in the atmosphere. Not the healthiest air to breathe, but he'd worry about that after they escaped.

The *Novo*'s bridge was rather small. There were two chairs in a small circular room that was above the level he'd entered. He sat down in one of the chairs, and

Stumpy scampered off his shoulder, but he didn't pay attention to where the little furball went next. He needed to check the ship's systems and get away from the space station. Since this was a civilian ship, there was very little security between him and the *Novo*'s systems. It also helped that the last captain hadn't done a proper shutdown of the systems. They'd probably been in a rush to get on one of the large evacuation ships.

The *Novo* was equipped with a second-generation Paxton jump drive, which had limited range, but it should do the job of getting him to another star system. Anything would be better than where he was. Three holoscreens appeared in front of him, and he was able to see outside the ship for the first time. The bridge was located near the front of the ship, seeming to ride on top of the storage area.

Quinton opened a comlink to the *Novo*'s systems so he could interact with the computer directly. The *Novo* ship computer recognized that a new captain was on the bridge and had status reports ready for him. A proximity alarm flashed on the centermost holoscreen.

A video image showed that the planetary defense cannon had resumed its bombardment on the station. Those damn mechs must have reloaded them. The space station was essentially a large shaft with spindly docking arms that had escape pods attached. Many had broken off as the space station was blown apart.

Quinton got the engines ready and waited, intending to use the space station's rotation to help him escape. It wouldn't do him any good to release the docking clamps and be flung toward the planet. In that case, he'd have to expend precious energy flying away from the planet, and he didn't know how well the ship could maneuver through a field of projectiles from a mag cannon.

He noticed that the rate of fire seemed to be focused on another part of the space station, so the mechs probably believed he was still there. He released the docking clamps and engaged the engines. As the ship cleared the station and flew away, Quinton felt an urge to sit back in his chair and sigh, but neither was necessary. For the first time since he'd awakened, he felt like he had a few moments to catch his breath.

He set a course to take them away from the planet. Not only did he need to reach the minimum safe distance to execute an FTL jump, he also needed to allow the navigation computer time to refresh the star charts to align with a destination he had yet to pick.

"Okay, Radek. Time for us to talk."

Quinton looked at the power meter on his HUD. The power levels for the agricultural bot had fallen below 50 percent. Increasing his frame rate had drained the power core. He needed to keep that in mind. He queried the ship's systems, looking for a way to continue charging the bot's power supply, but couldn't find anything. That was problem number one that he'd have to work on.

"Radek, are you there?"

A silver orb appeared on one of the holoscreens. "I'm here, Quinton. I thought it better to show myself using the ship's power systems rather than the limited capacity of the bot."

"Can I leverage the ship's computer systems to gain additional access to my ESS?" Quinton asked.

"Offloading like that poses an extreme risk to PMC stability and the ESS."

"How extreme of a risk?"

"Instability in the ESS, which could lead to severe degradation of the PMC."

"Okay, Radek, next time just tell me it'll kill me and we can keep this simpler."

"Understood."

"Why am I here?"

"I don't understand the question," Radek replied.

Quinton took a few moments to gather his thoughts. "You said there was an activation signal from somewhere, and there was an ESS located on Zeda-Six. Somehow my PMC was stored there."

"I believe this is accurate. Transference of a PMC to an ESS poses a great risk to PMC stability. There is a strong probability that you were stored in the ESS prior to it being located on this planet."

That was something, at least. PMCs were highly complex, and Quinton didn't want to think that someone or something had transferred all that data from somewhere while looking for an open ESS. "Where was I first activated?"

"In a data archive facility on Zeda-Six."

"Whose data archive facility?"

"Unknown. The facility reacted to the activation signal."

"Where did the activation signal come from?" Quinton asked and then shook his head. There was no way Radek would know this because he would have been activated at the same time. "Never mind. Is there anything you can tell me about the activation signal itself? Do you have a record of it?"

"No, when the ESS was activated and there was no acceptable storage unit for it, I was tasked with finding an acceptable one. Any record of the initial activation signal must still be at the facility on the planet," Radek replied.

Returning to the planet wasn't an option. He recalled that Radek had encountered the hunter mechs shortly after his activation. Going back there would help only if he had no other option. Quinton opened a comlink to the space station and found that part of the communication system was still online. Most star systems had a communication hub with built-in redundancies. He requested a data dump of the communication log from the space station. He didn't know how long it would remain online and didn't want to risk being cut off. When that was done, he could review it on the ship.

"Radek, analyze the communication logs and see if you can pinpoint the activation signal. I need to know where it came from."

The silver orb on the holoscreen went still, and a few moments later the data on the screen changed. "I've identified the signal, but I'm unable to determine its origin."

Quinton studied the raw data of the communication signal. It looked like gibberish, and incomprehensible data could mean only one thing: Whoever had sent the signal didn't want to be found. This made tracking it more complicated. He'd have to give it some more thought. He saved a copy of the data, then opened the *Novo*'s navigation systems and began looking at the star charts. They hadn't been updated in over fifty standard years. A lot could change in that time, but staying there wasn't an option.

The holoscreen to his right flickered and showed a plot of the Zeda-Six Star System. He was moving away from the planet but noticed that another ship had entered the system and was heading toward the planet. It wasn't on an intercept course with the *Novo*, but he was reluctant to open a comlink to the ship. The plot updated with other ships that were in orbit around the planet, and he noted that they were small vessels like the one he was on. Given his original reception, Quinton had to assume that everything in the star system could be hostile.

He brought up the Paxton jump drive, and while it was charging, he picked a nearby star system called Lantus as a destination. He'd never heard of it before, but he needed to get away from this place, and he didn't want to break the jump drive by having it fold space to a destination much farther away.

A communications holoscreen came to prominence. The ship that had just entered the system was trying to initiate contact, but something was wrong. The hailing package was just a ship-to-ship identity request.

SN-Seeker-901.

He'd never heard of the designation "SN," and "Seeker" was a class of ship, not a ship name. Ship designations utilized federation names as part of their identification.

The SN-Seeker-901 hailed them again and then changed course.

"Definitely not friendly," Quinton said and checked the status of the jump drive.

The SN-Seeker-901 increased its speed and was now on an intercept course.

The Paxton jump drive finished charging, and its status changed to green. He was far enough away from the planet's gravity well that he could initiate the jump.

The ZS-*Novo* light transport ship jumped out of the star system.

8

THE LANTUS STAR system was home to a massive red giant star. An initial subspace scan of the system revealed a couple of Jovian planets with a few hundred moons orbiting them in clusters, but nothing else was detected—no automated mining platforms, no research stations. Nothing. Not even an interstellar communications relay.

Quinton looked at the scan data on the holoscreen in disappointment. The star charts had shown that both a communications relay and mining platforms were present in this star system. Again, he felt an urge to sigh or frown or maybe even press his lips together, all of which the agricultural bot couldn't do. Instead, the bot's vocalizer made a soft buzzing sound that he supposed could have been considered a growl. He made a mental note to change whatever setting was associated with it.

He glanced at the controls for the ship's monitoring systems on the bridge, wanting to get a better look at the agricultural bot. He didn't have a clear image of what he even looked like. But it wasn't him, he reminded himself. He wasn't the bot. This was just a platform that his PMC was housed in for the moment. It was temporary. He repeated the thought in his mind a few times before shifting his focus to something else. Maybe now wasn't the best time to find out what he looked like.

He hadn't altered his course since entering the star system. While he waited for the jump drive to recharge, he searched the navigation system. He needed to pick a system that would likely have a communication hub so he could track the activation signal that had found its way to Zeda-Six.

The *Novo* wasn't designed for extensive travel beyond a local cluster of stars, which was why the star charts in the navigation systems had limited information. He didn't know if he was located along the galactic fringes or was in one of the core systems. His thoughts suddenly became blank, as if they'd been blocked by an invisible barrier.

"Radek," Quinton said, "I'm stumbling around here in the dark without full access to the ESS. I don't even know which federation or star empire I'm located in."

"Understandable," Radek replied, "but I don't think you fully appreciate just how precarious a position you're in. Ship diagnostics indicate that even though this ship can still operate, it's been derelict for at least fifty years. Jump drive systems for this ship haven't been calibrated since the star charts were updated. The computer systems are inadequate to transfer even a small percentage of the sophisticated data in the ESS. It wasn't designed for—"

"All right, I get it," Quinton said irritably. He remained motionless on the bridge for a few moments. "This ship and this bot are all I have to work with."

An alert appeared on his internal heads-up display. The bot's power meter plummeted by more than 10 percent before stopping at 38 percent. Then another alert appeared, informing him that part of his power core had ceased to operate. The error log gave a manufacturer code for Veris, who had built the bot.

He didn't know how much time he had. If he lost power here, no one would ever find him. He'd be lost forever. Someone had sent that activation signal just like someone had stored his PMC onto an ESS and left it on Zeda-Six. He needed to figure out who that was, but more importantly, he needed to find another body— something that could handle the ESS so he could have full access to his memories. Then maybe he could find whoever thought it had been a good idea to store an ESS with Quinton's PMC on what he suspected was a fringe-colony world. Someone had hidden him away to be activated at a later date, and he needed to understand why.

Quinton returned to scouring the star charts for a destination. Radek was right—the ship had severe limits. He had to assume that the next FTL jump might be his last, so he had to make the most of the destination he chose. He moved the star chart to the main holoscreen and then calculated the limits of the jump drive. A sphere surrounded a smaller portion of the star charts. There wasn't much here in such a remote location, but he did see a reference to Shangris Spaceport. The spaceport would be his best chance to get some help or, at the very least, find some information. Maybe they'd even be able to swap out his power core, or better yet, maybe he could find a better bot to use since this one wouldn't last much longer. He needed something that was designed for a PMC with full haptic interface capabilities.

He was getting ahead of himself. He looked back at the holoscreen, uploaded the coordinates to the navigation system, and left the bridge. As soon as the jump drive recharged, he could be underway.

"Your power core is failing," Radek said.

"I know."

"I would advise you to stay on the bridge."

Quinton walked down the short corridor, glancing at the failing atmosphere scrubber as he passed it, and then entered the storage area. There were several rows of storage containers. He brought up the shipping manifest, hoping there would be something he could use.

"I can't do anything on the bridge. I need to recharge my power core," Quinton said.

"This ship doesn't have droid support capabilities," Radek said.

"You're right; it doesn't, but some of these storage containers have their own individual power cores that connect to the ship's reactor. I'm going to have a look at them."

Radek was quiet for a few moments. Quinton imagined him as an old man with gray hair, a harsh gaze, and a quizzical furrowed brow, ripe with disapproval. Quinton chuckled.

"I don't see the humor in this," Radek said.

The VI's comment confirmed that he was incapable of reading Quinton's thoughts. From what little he could remember of his training to become a PMC candidate, VIs weren't supposed to be able to do that. But there had been so many things that were unorthodox in what Radek had been called to perform that he wouldn't put it past the original designers to keep certain capabilities secret.

"I need a new body," Quinton said. "Actually, I need *my* body."

"It is doubtful that your original body has been preserved, but I don't have any knowledge regarding it."

He walked down a row of storage containers, some of which were nearly as tall as he was. "What *do* you know then?" he asked as he squatted down to look at the container's identification.

"All PMCs have their DNA backed up and recorded in case the PMC decides to abandon its artificial existence and return to a biological form," Radek said.

Quinton stood up. He'd asked the question without really expecting an answer. "Wait a second. Are you saying that somewhere out there is a record of my DNA, and it can be used to grow me a new body?"

"Precisely," Radek replied. "This safeguard was put in place for all PMCs and was part of the standard PMC creation protocol."

If he could track the activation signal, this would lead him to where his DNA was recorded. He just had to survive long enough to find it.

He checked all the storage containers that were patched into the ship's reactor. There was a small charging station for the salvage gear stored in a work area in a side room. Inside the kit was a power bypass module, and Quinton studied it for a few moments. One of the connections looked like it could be attached to the side port of the agricultural bot. He tried to attach it and was able to force the connectors to make contact. It wasn't seamless, but he thought it would work.

He grabbed one of the other connectors and plugged it into an open port on the workbench.

Nothing happened.

Quinton stared at it expectantly, then initiated a remote access session to the ship's systems. He found the controls for the power regulator on the workbench, throttled the power output down to the lowest setting, and then turned it on.

Quinton snapped back to consciousness.

System diagnostic running.

Power surge detected.

Emergency disconnect.

32 percent power remaining.

He cursed inwardly. He'd nearly overloaded the bot's power systems. He was about to call out to Radek when he heard Stumpy's guttural screech.

"What the hell is that thing?" a man asked.

"I don't know. Shoot it if it comes back," another man said in a deep voice.

There were two men aboard the ship? How long had Quinton been out of it? He accessed the ship's systems. It had successfully jumped to the star system where the Shangris Spaceport was located.

"See, Becker, I told you coming back to this old spaceport was a good idea. There's some good salvage on this little ship," one of the men said and laughed.

"It'll be a good haul. Lennix will be pleased. Hey, Simon, where you going?"

Quinton heard someone walking toward him.

"Relax, Becker," Simon said. "I'm just having a look around. There's a small workshop over here. I also think I saw that creature run this way."

Quinton accessed the video feed and saw two men in the storage area. One of them was tall and broad shouldered, and a scar that went from his chin to his neck made him look as if he had a permanent scowl. The second man was much smaller but stocky, with russet, reddish-brown skin. Quinton didn't get a good look at his face before the man headed for the bridge.

"I need you on the bridge, Simon," Becker said.

"I'll be there in a second."

"You're not going to believe this," a disembodied third man said. "Becker, you need to get up here."

"Hang on, Guttman," Becker said. "Simon. Bridge. Now," he bellowed.

Quinton heard Simon come to a halt outside the workshop and sigh. "Fine," he said and walked back the way he'd come.

"This ship came from Zeda-Six," Guttman shouted.

"Not likely," Simon muttered under his breath.

Quinton activated another video feed on the bridge and saw that the three men were looking at the nav system's data on the main holoscreen.

"That's crap," Becker said, leaning over Guttman at the controls.

"It says it right there," Guttman said, trying to shove Becker away.

Becker backhanded the salvager, knocking him out of the seat. Then, he grabbed Guttman by the metallic collar of his spacesuit and hauled him into the air with a growl. "Who do you think you're shoving?"

Guttman grunted in pain, the collar pressing into his neck. "Sah . . . sah . . ." he rasped. "Sorry!"

Becker glared at the man, who coughed in an attempt to breathe in some air. Then Becker dropped him to the ground.

Quinton watched as Simon stood in the doorway.

"Listen up," Becker said. "Out here, it's my way or the airlock. It's your choice, and I don't care which you choose. Get it? You worthless meat-bags mean nothing. All of you are replaceable. Understand?"

"Yeah, I get it," Guttman said and spat on the floor. The biometric sensors showed that there were droplets of blood mixed in with the expelled substance.

"I'm not your friend," Becker said and turned toward Simon. "That includes you, rookie."

Simon hastily brought his hands up in a placating gesture. "I'm here. What do you need me to do?"

"What took you so long?"

Simon jutted a thumb behind him. "I was looking around in the storage area. There's a workshop back there."

Becker shook his head and stepped toward Simon. The smaller man's back bumped against the wall, and he gasped nervously.

"I'm here now. Just tell me what you want me to do," Simon said.

Becker leaned toward him like menacing doom incarnate. "Do you think Crowe cares about who you work for? There's no special treatment."

Simon looked away. "I know. *I know*," he sputtered.

Quinton saw an energy signature detection on the video feed, and the source was the palm of Simon's hand that he kept at his side. He might have been terrified, but it didn't appear as if he intended to go down without a fight, and Quinton guessed that Simon's dark-haired, boyish looks made people underestimate him.

Becker straightened. "Get on that system and tell me if it's been compromised."

The energy signature vanished, and Simon scrambled over to the pilot's seat.

Guttman had finally caught his breath. "Who would lay a trap way out here?"

The sides of Becker's lips lifted into a smirk. "I would," he drawled. "A juicy piece of salvage out here in the middle of nowhere and a group of salvagers," he said, his beefy hand making a circular gesture with his index finger, "come to claim it and bring it back to base?"

"Yeah, but you just put a suppressor on the comms systems."

Becker shook his head. "Suppressors don't stop rogue transmitters designed to come online after certain conditions have been met. Things like engaging a jump drive. Forcible access to the ship. Latent check-in intervals for subsystems."

Guttman considered this for a few moments and nodded, turning his attention back toward the holoscreen.

Becker raised his hand to his ear. "Go ahead, Oscar."

"Captain, we finished scanning the hull and didn't find anything out of place. The ship looks clean," Oscar said.

Becker nodded. "Good work. Simon, patch us into the *Ravager*'s systems."

"Done, and the ship hasn't been compromised," Simon said.

"Well then, how the heck did it get out here?" Guttman asked.

"The ship's computer has logs for two recent FTL jumps. Given the state of the jump drive, we're lucky the ship is in as good a shape as it is," Simon said.

"Why is that?" Becker asked, peering at the data on the main holoscreen. Then he turned toward Simon.

"It's been in standby for almost fifty years and then received a recall request for a place called Gateway Station in the Zeda-Six Star System."

"See," Guttman said. "I told you it was from Zeda-Six."

Becker's gaze narrowed. "A recall," he said, then unholstered the weapon on his hip.

Quinton peered at it. A tactical overlay appeared on the video feed, and an enhanced view of the weapon appeared.

Particle sidearm.

Model: FCC-Tilion.

Status: Charged.

"What's wrong," Guttman asked and pulled out a similar weapon.

"We have a stowaway," Becker said.

"There aren't any life signs on the ship other than that small thing we saw before," Simon said.

"Then they're shielded," Becker said and stepped toward the door, using part of the frame for cover as if he expected to be attacked. "All right, I want every part of this ship checked. Simon, you check the storage area. Guttman, you're with me. We'll look in engineering and work our way to the storage area."

Quinton thought about increasing his frame rate to give him time to think about what he could do but decided not to. The salvagers didn't look like reasonable people to him. Becker certainly looked like the shoot-first-and-ask-later type of person. He could stand up and try to reason with them but doubted they'd help him.

"Wasn't Zeda-Six an Empire colony?" Guttman asked.

"Maybe," Becker replied. "This region was controlled by the Tilions."

"Actually, the last federation to control this sector was the Acheron Confederacy," Simon said.

Quinton watched as the slight man worked his way through the storage area, a small sleek sidearm in hand.

"Acheron, phaw," Guttman said brusquely. "The galaxy is much better off without 'em."

"It's ancient history," Becker said. "Now, be quiet."

Quinton filed the information under his to-be-reviewed pile, along with everything else. He'd fought the hunter mechs on Zeda-Six, but three armed men in an enclosed space without room to maneuver might be too much for him, especially now that his power core had suffered damage. If he started a fight, he wasn't sure that he'd be able to finish it. Even if he could somehow incapacitate the three men, there was still an unknown number of people on the other ship. No, his odds were much better if he just pretended to be the broken-down agricultural bot that he appeared to be. If anything, it would buy him some time.

Quinton heard Simon approach the workshop. The young man stood in the doorway for a moment, then holstered his weapon and came over to him.

"What do we have here?" Simon said and proceeded to have a closer look at him.

Quinton felt all kinds of conflict while Simon poked and prodded his systems. His sense of personal space was being violated, and it took every shred of his control to ignore it.

Simon pulled out a palm scanner and began running a scan of the bot's systems. "Heh, still online," he said quietly. "How did you get here?"

Quinton watched as Simon leaned over to examine his damaged arm. He nodded to himself in response to the conversation that was taking place inside the young man's mind.

"That's weird," Simon said. "Why would there be . . ."

Dammit, he's going to detect the ESS.

The ESS was shielded and hidden inside the agricultural bot's chassis, but still. If that scanner could detect it, then all bets were off.

Heavy footfalls came toward the workshop, and Simon quickly stopped scanning.

"What you got here?" Becker asked.

Simon stood up. "No one's here. Just this bot."

Becker stepped inside the workshop and gave Quinton a quick once-over. "What kind of bot is that?"

"It's an agricultural unit. No idea how it got on the ship. Someone must have been trying to repair it before abandoning it here. I'd like to claim it as my cut from the salvage, if that's all right with you," Simon said.

Becker's gaze narrowed and he peered closer at Quinton, as if trying to guess whether he was missing something valuable.

"It's not worth much. I mainly want it for parts. This model has a pretty good haptic system," Simon said.

Becker frowned. "Haptic system?"

"Yeah, it must have been designed for delicate work, which requires a pretty good haptic system for sensory input. It's not worth much. Who has gardens to tend to these days anyway?" Simon said.

Careful. You're overselling it, Quinton thought.

"Gotcha!" Guttman cried out from the other room.

Becker frowned and looked back out the doorway. Stumpy's screeching could be heard throughout the storage area.

Becker and Simon left the workshop.

"This thing is ugly," Guttman said. Stumpy twisted and squirmed, trying to break free. His tail lashed back and forth. "What's with the little spines on its back?"

"Careful," Simon warned, and Guttman froze while trying to hold the struggling animal away from his body. "They contain a neurotoxin. If you come into contact with it, it will cause paralysis and then permanent blindness."

Guttman's eyes widened. He hastily dropped the creature and vigorously wiped his hands on his legs, then paused for a moment to search for imagined residue on his fingers.

Simon snickered, and Becker glanced at him. Then the large man laughed uproariously.

Guttman's eyebrows pulled together, and he sneered. "Why you little son of a—"

"All right, enough," Becker said, and Guttman halted.

"I don't know what it is," Simon said. "Doesn't look that dangerous."

Guttman glared at the younger man. "I'm not gonna forget this, noob. You're just a tech. You just wait. When we—"

"Save it," Becker said. "Let's get this ship ready to transport. Guttman, head back to the *Ravager* and tell Oscar we're ready to move on."

Guttman gave Simon a venomous look and then walked toward the airlock. Becker regarded Simon for a few seconds. "You got some spine, kid. If that bot means so much to you, then I'll let you claim it."

"Thank you, Captain," Simon said.

"Go secure it for transport. It looked like someone had it wired up for something. I don't want it interfering with the jump drive when we leave," Becker said.

Simon headed back into the workshop and disconnected the wires to Quinton's chest. A warning appeared on Quinton's HUD, but at least he hadn't lost a charge in the bot's power systems. Now all he had to worry about was whether Simon was going to strip out the parts that were connecting him to his humanity. PMCs required a certain level of physical interaction with their environment, or the experience would become too artificial. The garden bot was equipped with specialized haptic systems necessary for working with delicate plant life, which was absolutely essential for Quinton to feel as human as he could. The alternative was psychosis. This was why PMCs were uploaded into special automatons designed to mimic key features of the human body and experience—senses beyond sight but no less important, including smell and touch. He supposed that with limited access to his memories and a bot that wasn't designed to house a PMC, he should count himself lucky to be functioning at all.

Simon stopped what he was doing and regarded Quinton for more than a few seconds. He seemed to be waiting for something, his face a mask of concentration. Quinton remembered that Guttman had called Simon a tech expert. Had Simon figured out what Quinton was? Had he detected the ESS? Quinton had no idea. He felt like Simon was staring him down, as if they were determining who was going to blink first.

Quinton smiled inwardly. He definitely had the advantage there. He could easily wait out the young man.

Becker bellowed for Simon to report to the bridge, and Quinton heard Simon sigh.

"I'll deal with you later," Simon said and left the work area.

Quinton thought he might have been talking about Becker but then suspected that Simon was referring to him. There was nothing he could do. He'd wait to see where they were going and then decide what to do next.

9

THE SALVAGERS more or less ignored him. Quinton overheard Becker talking about other things they'd salvaged from the spaceport. He monitored the *Novo*'s systems as Simon put nonessential systems into standby. After determining that it was unsafe to use the *Novo*'s jump drive, they flew the ship onto a secure docking platform attached to the salvager's ship.

Quinton accessed the external video feeds and got his first view of the *Ravager*. He'd expected the ship to be some type of cargo carrier, but it looked more like a smaller munitions supply-class ship that would have been used by any of the galactic federations. He peered at the heavily damaged hull, looking for the ship's identifier. Without it, he didn't know which federation or star empire the ship had come from. He wondered how the salvagers kept it space worthy. The supply ship was designed for a small crew and only had one light mag cannon located midship. The cannon looked like it had been maintained in serviceable condition and was probably enough of a deterrent for other opportunistic salvagers but not enough for earnest ship-to-ship combat. He spotted a few armored panels that looked to house point-defense turrets, but he couldn't be sure. The rear artillery section still had the mounting structure for another mag cannon, but it had been stripped away and the salvagers had built up the platform to store large cargo that couldn't be brought inside.

The *Novo*'s docking clamps engaged the platform, taking up a large section of it. The small ship was only one piece amid a crowd of space salvage they'd managed to extract from the station.

Quinton listened to the open comms chatter. Becker was monitoring the area for other ships, almost like he expected to be attacked. The small number of crew that had come aboard the *Novo* must have been Becker's way of testing new recruits.

He kept an eye on Simon until he was ordered off the ship. After that, he sat in the workshop, pretending to be a lifeless robot. Simon had captured Stumpy by disabling the artificial gravity. The loss of gravity had stunned the creature, and Simon had stuck him in a bio-storage container. Quinton hadn't heard so much as a peep from him, which was probably for the best.

A short time after the salvagers had secured Quinton's ship, they'd flown away from the small space station. He tried to think of some way to escape, but the salvagers were on high alert. They'd notice if Quinton used the *Novo*'s escape pods. Even if he were able to leave undetected and somehow make it to the derelict space station, there was no guarantee that anything there would help him. Staying put was his best choice and kept his options open. Now all he needed to worry about was where they were taking him.

There was a bright azure flash as the *Ravager*'s jump drive engaged and the open comms chatter went quiet. Quinton hated being kept in the dark. The *Novo*'s systems were on standby, and if he started switching things on, someone would notice. He'd simply have to ride this out.

He glanced at the power meter in the upper-right corner of his HUD. It was holding at 38 percent. Power consumption while he waited in the workshop was minimal. At least he had that going for him.

FTL jumps were almost instantaneous, but they did cause a temporary gap in sensor coverage. A field of stars appeared on the video feed. He couldn't listen in on the *Ravager*'s comms systems, but he assumed they were checking in with their destination. The outside imagery began to change as the salvage ship flew toward its destination. The journey didn't take long, and none of the salvagers returned to the *Novo*. Maybe Simon *hadn't* guessed that the agricultural bot was something more than what it seemed.

The *Ravager* entered an approach vector to a large asteroid base. Asteroid movers helped maintain the orbit of the mineral-rich rock. Although it wasn't quite the size of a dwarf planet, it was close enough that it could support a space colony. Quinton spotted several large hangar bays that were built into the craggy side of the asteroid. There was a significant amount of ship traffic going to and from the base. Legions of delivery drones hauled shipping containers to some of the bigger ships, maintaining their position at a space docking platform.

The *Ravager* headed toward one of the remote hangar bays with the least traffic. As they came closer, Quinton spotted numerous station defenses, which made him think that this had once been a military station converted into what looked like an extensive salvage operation. All he had to do was find an alternate power source or an alternate body to use, both of which would buy him the time he needed to figure out where the activation signal for his PMC had come from. Gaining full access to the ESS would be a tremendous bonus, but he needed to focus on one thing at a time.

The ship passed through the hangar bay shields and flew toward an offloading landing pad. As soon as they were through the shield, multiple network connections became available from the station, and Quinton pulled up the list. They were mainly for personal comms traffic rather than data feeds, which made sense. The salvager's security protocols had to assume that all ship systems in the bay were unsecured and therefore required further screening before data access was allowed. He remembered Simon giving Becker the green light that the *Novo*'s ship systems were clean. He needed to wait until he was offloaded before trying to gain system access to the space station or else risk being detected.

Quinton didn't have to wait very long. Counter-grav lifts attached themselves to the *Novo*'s hull, and the small ship was lifted off the *Ravager*. All the salvaged items were offloaded onto the platform, and dock workers began to categorize them. He watched them from the *Novo*'s external video feeds. A group of dock workers gathered outside the ship. He saw Becker's towering form jab a beefy finger toward them, and the workers stopped. Becker turned back to speak to someone else. Simon came into view, and Becker gestured toward the *Novo*. Simon nodded, and he and Guttman hastened over.

He watched Guttman's stocky, dark-skinned form stride ahead and begin speaking with the dock workers. Without the EVA suit, Quinton saw Guttman's belly push against his shirt, and the additional weight lent extra skin to his already protruding eyes.

After Guttman finished speaking with the workers, he and Simon came aboard the *Novo* and began unloading the ship. Quinton saw Guttman glare at Simon as the young man walked up the loading ramp. He was probably still angry about Simon's little joke. While the dock workers offloaded the cargo containers, attaching them to portable power generators, Simon entered the work area where Quinton was.

Simon gave Quinton a brief once-over and then turned to the array of tools in the workshop. He did a quick job of cataloging the items and then began gathering them into a container in the middle of the floor. Simon accessed his wrist computer, and Quinton saw a new data connection appear on the agricultural unit's systems.

Simon looked at him and sighed. "Someone really didn't like you," he said while reading the data on the holoscreen. He pulled up a damage report and pressed his lips together. "It looks like you can still move, though, so let's give this a try. All right, stand up."

Quinton saw that Simon had enabled vocal command mode. He'd need to be compliant and maintain the guise of cooperation. He'd thought Simon had guessed what he was, but he must have been wrong.

He stood up.

"Good." Simon nodded and gestured toward the container. "Grab that container and follow me."

Quinton walked toward the container, which was almost overflowing with spare parts and tools from the workshop. He squatted down and lifted it, but it wobbled because of the damaged actuator in his left shoulder. Some of the tools slipped off the top and dropped to the floor.

Simon picked them up and put them back on top. "Damaged shoulder joint. I can fix that. That power core will need replacing too."

You have no idea, Quinton thought.

Simon left the workshop, and Quinton followed him. As they walked down the loading ramp, Guttman glanced in their direction, scowling.

"What do you think you're doing?" Guttman asked as he stormed over to them.

"Claiming what's mine. You can take it up with Becker if you want."

Guttman narrowed his gaze. "Yours," he sneered.

"I loved that little scene on the bridge—you know, when you tried to shove Becker. You probably thought it was me," Simon said and frowned in mock consideration. "I'm sah, sah, sorry," he said, mimicking Guttman. "It must have been hard to speak while you were being choked."

Guttman inhaled explosively. "You little bastard, I'll—" He reached toward Simon.

Quinton tilted the container to one side and a small avalanche of tools spilled onto Guttman's feet, tripping the man. He set the container down, hastening toward the mess while bumping into Guttman, sending him sprawling onto the floor. Simon glanced at Quinton, a curious frown on his face. Then, the dock workers laughed uproariously. It had all happened so quickly that Guttman found himself on the ground, looking completely baffled as to how he'd gotten there. He glowered toward Simon.

"Hey, I'm sorry about that," Simon said. "That bot has a bad shoulder and it gives out." He quickly reloaded the container.

Becker walked over. He looked at Guttman and shook his head. "What are you doing? Get on your feet."

Guttman stood up, looking as if he was going to launch into a tirade, but he suddenly thought better of it. A group of people headed toward them, and Becker's mouth went flat, forming a grim line.

A tall, dark-skinned man strode over to them, followed by a group of armed men. He glanced at the *Novo*, and then his gaze slid toward the rather substantial amount of cargo on the hangar deck, but he didn't look impressed.

"Helsing," Becker said by way of acknowledgment.

"Looks like you've got yourself quite a haul here," Helsing said.

"It's not bad."

Helsing pursed his lips together and leaned toward Becker. "It's not great either."

Becker's gaze hardened. "Crowe will be fine with it."

Helsing bobbed his head to the side once. "We'll see. He hasn't approved of your team's performance lately," he said and gestured toward the offloaded cargo. "I don't know if this will even satisfy last month's quota."

Quinton watched, expecting Becker to attack the other man. Helsing also looked as if he expected it, as did the armed men with him.

Becker calmly regarded the man. "We'll see."

"Still, something is better than nothing. We'll do an accounting," Helsing said and looked toward the far side of the hangar. "Looks like that accounting will come sooner than we thought. Lennix is here now."

Quinton was irritated that he couldn't simply do what everyone else was doing. He wanted to see who this Lennix Crowe was. There was apparent deference being given, and among these dangerous people, that was saying something. But he had to keep pretending to be a simple robot, and robots didn't do things like look at the newcomer just because everyone else was.

He was able to twitch his head slightly and saw another group of people walking across the hangar. Everyone was centered on one man. Creases showed at the corners of his eyes and mouth, and his dark-eyed gaze regarded everything around him with professional calm. He had just enough gray to his black hair and beard to make him look distinguished rather than old. Quinton couldn't begin to guess his age, but he had something that no one else in that hangar had—command experience. He seemed to regard everything on that hangar deck with a comprehensive knowledge of how it served a higher purpose beyond its immediate value. Everything here served *his* purpose. He was a bit on the tall side—athletic but not excessively so. Lennix Crowe's strength was beyond that of his body. He had the bearing of a man who never changed his mind once he'd made a decision.

Quinton watched as Crowe looked around the hangar bay while listening to an older man speaking. The older man was referring to a report showing on a holoscreen above his wrist computer.

"They don't have the resources to keep up with projected growth for the mining operation," the older man was saying.

Crowe looked at him. "Nate," he said, and the other man became quiet, "the Grand Terra mining operation has to make scheduled payments just like everyone else. Just because they have something of value doesn't mean they get special treatment."

Nate considered this for a few moments and then the holoscreen minimized as he lowered his arm. "Understood."

"That's just it. *They* don't understand," Lennix said and rubbed a powerful hand over his thick ebony beard. He glanced toward Becker and Helsing and then purposefully strode over. His gaze flicked between them before settling on Helsing. "I need you to take a battalion of Union troopers over to the Grand Terra mining operation."

"Of course, sir," Helsing said. "Do you want me to just intimidate them?"

"Oh, I want more than a simple show of force. They need to be reminded of who reports to whom here," Crowe said and glanced at Nate.

The older man—some kind of advisor, Quinton guessed—regarded Lennix for a few seconds. "Applying the right kind of pressure will yield results in the short-term, but that doesn't take care of the bigger issue here."

"What are you talking about, old man?" Helsing asked.

Nate kept his gaze on Lennix, ignoring Helsing altogether.

"The Collective is increasing their influence over all salvage and mercenary operations. I'm not," Crowe said and gritted his teeth. Then he looked at Helsing. "Take the *Wraith,* along with a cargo container ship suitable for transporting organics."

"Yes, Commander Crowe," Helsing said.

Nate pressed his lips together in thought, and Crowe raised his dark eyebrows. "The appropriate pressure, you say. If they don't deliver on their promises, I'll remove a member of every household on every level of their pathetic colony until I've gutted a third of their numbers. See if they still try these stalling tactics when over 30 percent of their population is about to become slaves."

A rush of thoughts pushed through Quinton's mind. First and foremost was that he needed to get the hell out of there as quickly as possible. Second was that Lennix Crowe introduced a whole new level of ruthlessness that he'd never seen before. He didn't know what to think outside the utter revulsion he felt at what he'd just heard.

Quinton glanced at Helsing, and the man looked at Nate for a moment before turning back to Lennix. "I'll leave at once."

"Good," Crowe said.

Nate watched Helsing as he left. He seemed to arrive at some sort of mental calculation and simply shifted to the next topic.

What was wrong with these people? Quinton resisted the urge to shake his head. *This Lennix Crowe gives an order that if some mining operation can't deliver, he'll enslave a third of their population, and everyone on the hangar deck just takes this as a matter of course?*

Quinton opened the bot's comms and began scanning the station's systems for a data connection.

"I must advise against that," Radek said inwardly.

Though no one could actually hear his VI assistant, Quinton increased his frame rate. "I need to get out of here," he replied.

"Then allow me to interact with the station's systems."

"What for?"

"Because when machines interact, most monitoring systems aren't suspicious. If *you* do it, it might be detected, and an alert could be sent out. We don't want to draw attention to ourselves," Radek replied.

"What? That's nonsense," Quinton said and watched the scan session continue.

"You must stop what you're doing."

"Not without a good reason."

The scan finished, and he found a general communications system he could access.

"You're in more danger than you realize," Radek said.

Quinton paused his search. "What do you mean?" Nothing in his situation could be done without risk, but maybe the VI knew something he didn't.

"Interacting with computer systems poses a serious risk to you in particular because of the limited state of your PMC."

Quinton didn't understand. "PMCs by design are supposed to be superior to any other type of systems access, and you're telling me I can't do it?"

"Not exactly. I'm saying there is a high risk of detection if you do, more than your training would have accounted for," Radek said.

"What's the risk?"

"My primary objective is to ensure the PMC stays intact and operational. Part of that is to make sure you retain your current mental state."

"My mental state," Quinton repeated. "Well, my mental state is pretty damn agitated, Radek. I can be reasonable, but this is too much."

"What query do you want me to run on the station's systems?"

He needed to better understand the risk to his mental state, but he could worry about that later. "We need to find the source of the activation signal for starters. Then I need to get out of this unit and find a better body to use."

"Understood. Querying system for requested information."

Quinton brought his frame rate back to normal. His entire conversation with Radek had occurred in less than a second in standard time.

"Does this bother you?" Crowe asked.

Quinton tore his attention away from his depleting power core and looked at the person Crowe was speaking to. She was a beautiful woman—not a young girl who'd just attained adulthood, but a woman. She had brown, wavy hair, exotic almond-shaped eyes, and high cheekbones, and her skin was a medium olive tone that made her celestial blue eyes sparkle. She looked at Lennix Crowe with a surety born of confidence.

"I'm not here to judge the way you run your operation," said the woman.

Crowe regarded her for a few moments. "Most people don't have the stomach for it."

The woman arched an eyebrow. "You don't strike me as the type of person who cares what most people think. All that matters is what I can do." She pursed her lips for a moment. "To put a finer point on it, what I can do for you and the Union."

"Maelyn Wayborn," Crowe said. "I wouldn't expect such ruthlessness under so delicate a face."

Maelyn smiled. "You assume this is my real face."

Crowe's grin revealed genuine amusement but also something much darker.

"Back to the business at hand," she said. "Several of your teams have had a chance to observe my people in action." She gestured toward Simon.

Quinton had to stop himself from looking at Simon when everyone else glanced in the young man's direction.

Crowe gestured for Becker to come over to him. "How'd he do?"

"He was useful, sir. He spotted a few things that we might have overlooked," Becker replied.

"That's been happening a lot to your crew of late," Crowe said. Becker didn't reply. "But judging by all this, it looks like you managed to bring something of value back, so there *is* that."

Again, Becker remained quiet.

Crowe nodded. "That's what I always like about you, Becker. You're never one to fill the air with excuses. You stand by your work."

Quinton watched a data window on his HUD. Radek was accessing the station's system, and then he stopped. Klaxon alarms blared overhead.

Crowe's gaze narrowed, and he looked at Nate.

"Something is trying to access our systems," Nate said and looked at Becker. "Did you make sure these systems were secure?"

"Yes, we did," Becker said and looked at Simon.

"Never mind that," Crowe said. "Where's it coming from?"

Nate flipped through several menu options on his personal holoscreen, and then he frowned. After staring intently at the screen, he turned toward Quinton. "It's the bot."

Everyone nearby also turned toward him. Crowe narrowed his gaze and his mouth went flat.

"That can't be right," Simon said quickly. "I checked this unit out myself."

"Well then, you missed something because it has an active comms signal," Nate said. He made a snatching motion on his holoscreen and tossed it into the air. The holoscreen stretched and showed the comms session.

Quinton did the first thing that came to his mind.

"Malfunction," Quinton said and repeated himself. Then he turned and ran.

10

Quinton jacked up his frame rate, and his perception of everyone in the hangar bay came to a standstill. A power consumption warning flashed on his HUD, which he ignored.

"So much for trying things your way, Radek."

"I don't understand," Radek said. "They shouldn't have been able to detect my queries. I used the standard machine query protocols I observed being used by nearby systems."

"Great, that's just perfect," Quinton said derisively.

Another power consumption warning flashed on-screen. He needed to rethink his reliance on the virtual intelligence that was supposed to be helping him. He should've trusted his own instincts, but he couldn't keep his perception of time jacked up for long or else he risked doing more damage to the agricultural unit. He wanted to scream. He had these few precious moments to think of something other than running around like a malfunctioning machine.

Quinton glanced at Simon. The young man was frozen in mid-motion while he accessed his own wrist computer. He peered at the screen and saw that Simon was in the middle of typing a message. He couldn't read it, but it was meant for him because it had the agricultural unit's identifier on it.

He couldn't afford to wait around. He was mostly surrounded. Once he returned his frame rate to normal, he'd have seconds to get away. He glanced at the stacks of storage containers that had been assembled on the hangar deck.

Quinton reset his frame rate to normal and bolted toward the containers. He leaped into the air and climbed to the top, quickly scaling upward. After scrambling over the top, he jumped down on the other side and heard shouting from behind him. A group of workers looked in his direction, and he blew past them.

"Did you at least find anything on their systems?" he asked.

"Negative. I didn't have a chance to gain access to the communication logs," Radek replied.

Ahead of him, a group of armed salvagers was heading toward him. Quinton turned and ran toward a nearby ship, which was locked up good and tight. He had no chance of getting in there. Even if he could somehow escape, with all the armed security he saw coming, they would quickly shoot him down. Running away wasn't going to help him.

A message appeared on his HUD. It was a comlink from Simon.

I can help you. But you need to come back here. I know what you are. It's not safe.

Quinton heard more shouting from behind him, and white ionized bolts slammed into the bulkhead of the nearest ship. Ionized bolts would disable him, but he wasn't sure if it would damage his ESS; however, he didn't want to find out. What a mess this was. If he kept running, it was only a of matter time before they caught him. The young tech specialist was his only hope. But Simon had figured out what he was, and Quinton had no idea how he'd done that.

He ran back toward the others, who'd been following his progress, and saw Simon watching him from across the hangar deck.

Then another message appeared.

You need to let them capture you. Don't tell them what you are.

If Quinton had a stomach, it would have been sinking to his feet as if he'd leaped off the hangar deck into the abyss. He was out of options. He had to either trust Simon or take a chance and try to reason with Lennix Crowe.

Quinton didn't need to jack up his frame rate to take the time to consider that. Simon was the lesser of the two evils. There was no way he was getting off this hangar deck—not by himself and not without help.

He ran back toward the others, and the deckhands scrambled to get out of his way. They were afraid. They thought he was an out-of-control robot. Quinton realized that if he kept moving around erratically, they would certainly destroy him. He came to a halt and simply stood still with his arms at his sides, which was a miracle unto itself. Every instinct inside him wanted to run, to fight, to keep his destiny in his own hands. But this wasn't a fight he could win.

Soon he was surrounded by armed salvagers. They gathered around him, pointing their weapons.

"Wait!" Simon shouted as he ran over to Quinton. "Don't shoot it."

Becker pointed a hand cannon that was primed with a molten orange glow. The plasma bolt from that cannon would melt through the agricultural bot's chassis before Quinton would ever even register that the man had shot him.

"Becker," Simon said, "I've got it. Seriously, it's just a glitch. It's not dangerous."

"The hell it isn't," Becker said and looked back as Lennix Crowe caught up to them.

Simon stepped in front of Quinton and held up his arms. He looked at Maelyn. "Captain Wayborn, please. This is my part of the salvage."

Maelyn's brows pulled together in a thoughtful frown.

Simon looked at Becker. "Lower your weapon. It's just a glitch in this thing's programming."

Becker looked at Crowe, who gave him a single grim nod. "Simon, start making sense right now or I'm going to shoot you too."

"The bot was just trying to open a comlink back to its command-and-control unit. The system was reset, and part of the startup process was to check in. When it couldn't, it triggered a return to this bot's base of operations, but it couldn't figure out its location. The bot's interior systems are degraded and damaged. I can show the log data to your tech experts, and they can confirm it if you want, but that's what happened. It's on standby now. I have it under control. It'll do everything I tell it to. Want me to show you?" Simon asked.

Becker looked at Crowe, who glanced at Nate.

"Carradine, does that make sense to you?"

"I'll need to review the logs, but the alert did come from our comms systems," Nate said.

"Send them the logs, Simon," Maelyn said and looked at Crowe. "If Simon says it was an error, then that's what it was."

"That remains to be seen," Crowe replied.

"If you feel that strongly about it, destroy it. I assume you have another way to compensate my tech specialist," Maelyn said. Crowe gave her a questioning look. "You *are* a businessman, after all. Weren't you telling me earlier how you take care of the people who work for you?" she asked as she walked toward Quinton.

She glanced at Simon and gave Quinton a once-over. Then she turned back toward Crowe and the others.

Becker still had his hand cannon pointed toward them, and Crowe came to stand by his side.

"Why does this matter so much to you?" Crowe asked.

Maelyn's lips lifted into a half smile. "You're not the only one who takes care of the people you work with. You get more out of them when they're happy," she said and looked at Simon. "Why do you want this agricultural bot so much?"

"It has some good serviceable parts on there that I'd like to salvage. Particularly the haptic systems. I was also going to—" Simon said.

Maelyn held up her hand and Simon stopped speaking. "They understand," she said.

Crowe shook his head. "All right, in the spirit of cooperation and future business relations, I'll allow it."

Maelyn smiled, and Simon seemed to relax.

"I'll be in touch with you," Crowe said and looked at Becker. "Escort them back to their ship, along with whatever salvage they claimed."

Lennix Crowe left them, but his advisor gave Quinton a long look. Nate Carradine. He was an older man who almost seemed out of place among the other salvagers. He watched Quinton for a few moments and then followed the group. Quinton kept his eyes forward and walked with what he hoped was a dutiful robot stride under the control of one Simon Webb.

11

Lennix left the hangar bay. The heightened security protocols he had in place might generate a few false positives, but they were necessary for securing his operations. He'd built his salvage business from the ground up, functioning within the confines of the Collective. All companies in this galactic sector had ties to the Collective.

He rode up the service elevator, along with his staff. The bigger his operation had become, the more people he had to keep with him to ensure that it ran smoothly. He glanced at Nate Carradine, whose unfocused gaze meant he was working on something using his HUD. Nate was one of the few people Lennix trusted. He'd been part of Crowe's Union for a long time, but he had a mysterious past. Lennix thought the man had led a mercenary troop at some point in his past, but what he was looking for was Nate's extensive knowledge of pre-federation tech.

Nicos shifted on his feet, and Lennix could feel his insistent gaze upon his neck. He glanced over at him. "What's next, Nicos?"

"I just received a message that the Collective is sending a representative, along with an invitation for you to meet with them."

No wonder Nicos looked so uncomfortable. The invitation was a formality. This was a summons, and it was one that Lennix couldn't afford to ignore. The Collective had already been paid, but they wanted more. Crowe's Union had grown so large that it garnered the attention of Trenton Draven. Crowe had carefully built up his operations so as not to alarm the Collective, but there was a tipping point, and he must have gone past it.

"What was that about the Collective?" Nate asked.

Nicos looked at him. "They want to meet with us."

"There was a scheduled meeting for next month," Nate replied and frowned in thought for a moment.

Lennix had more freedom than most, mainly because Crowe's Union had several old federation warships at its disposal—nothing that would challenge the Collective in a direct fleet engagement, but it was something they couldn't afford to ignore either.

Lennix looked at Nicos. "Anything else?"

"Nothing specific, sir. Just a reiteration from the Collective on the importance of salvaging federation tech."

Lennix shook his head and snorted. They were always pressuring to keep their advantage. "Send a reply that we'll meet with the representatives at their convenience, and send them coordinates for a neutral-territory meeting location."

He saw Nate waving his hands as he navigated his own personal holographic interface, and he looked at him pointedly.

Nate caught the look and brought his hands to rest at his sides. The elevator stopped, and they headed toward the tram system that would take them to the far side of the station.

"I was reviewing the video surveillance footage of that robot back on the hangar deck," Nate said as their tram sped away.

Lennix sighed. "We've got the Collective breathing down our necks, and you want to worry about a malfunctioning robot?"

"The devil is in the details."

Lennix leaned his shoulder against the wall and folded his arms in front of his chest. "All right, what am I missing?"

"I'm not sure yet," Nate said and brought up the holoscreen for Lennix to see. The surveillance showed the agricultural bot springing into action, and Nate slowed the frames down. "The bot moves with precision, almost as if it anticipates what will happen to it."

Lennix peered at the holoscreen and then nodded. He could see what Nate was talking about. Thermal imaging revealed a secondary power source that was hidden in the chest cavity.

"What is that?" Nicos asked.

"It's some kind of secondary power source. Probably a redundancy," Lennix replied.

Nate shook his head. "I don't think so. You could see the power draw increase from the main power core at certain intervals . . ." His voice trailed off as he made a swiping motion and opened up another holoscreen. His eyes widened, and he looked at Lennix. "It's an Energy Storage System. Low power yield, but definitely detectable."

Lennix felt his eyebrows pull together as he peered at the image. "An ESS? But that means . . ." He looked at Nicos. "Find out where Maelyn Wayborn is right now."

"A Personality Matrix Construct. A PMC, and they said it came from Zeda-Six. That's a third-tier colony world," Nate said.

"What would a PMC be doing way out there? There's nothing of strategic value at that location."

"There is if you want to keep a PMC hidden. Regardless, we need to recover it. It's highly valuable," Nate said.

"You got that right. I'm not just going to give this to the Collective," Lennix said.

"Sir, they were heading to the secondary hangar bay where their ship is," Nicos said.

Lennix tried to open a comlink to Becker, but it wouldn't connect. "I can't reach Becker."

"They must be using a suppressor," Nate said.

"If they were jamming communications, it would have been detected," Nicos said.

"Not if it's small enough. They could have dialed in the suppression field to impact only targeted people," Lennix said.

"She betrayed you," Nate said.

"Maybe." Lennix shook his head. "It's more that she saw an opportunity and took it."

Lennix walked over to the console on the side of the tram car and tried to initiate a lockout that failed. He cursed.

"My access is restricted," Nate said. "She planted a suppressor on us as well."

Lennix had no choice but to admire Maelyn's tactics. "Clever, but she hasn't gotten away yet."

Nicos began rubbing his hands over his shirt, looking for some kind of device.

"Stop that. You're not going to find it," Lennix snapped. Sometimes he thought he was surrounded by idiots, with the exception of Nate.

"We'll have to wait until we get off the tram. Then we can disable the suppressor," Nate said.

"Why do we have to wait? Why can't we just disable it now?" Nicos asked.

"Because it's a microscopic nano swarm," Lennix said and shook his head. He looked at Nate. "She's good. I'll give her that."

Nate nodded. "It'll be close, but I think we can stop her before she leaves."

"We better."

12

QUINTON FOLLOWED THE OTHERS, leaving the hangar bay through a series of interconnected tunnels. Becker had Guttman and Oscar following behind Quinton and Simon.

Maelyn arched an eyebrow toward Becker. "We know the way from here. I'm sure you'll want to get back so you can monitor your deck crew."

"They won't try anything funny, if that's what you mean," Becker replied.

Maelyn nodded, managing to look amicable and unconvinced at the same time. Becker ignored her.

Quinton's sensors showed that Guttman and Oscar weren't keeping that close of an eye on him, and he was anxious to speak with Simon. The good thing was that Becker had set a quick pace for them to follow. Maybe Maelyn's comment about the deck crew had bothered him more than he let on.

The corridor opened to a smaller hangar deck, and Becker gestured for Maelyn to lead the way. When she flashed him a dazzling smile, Quinton felt a strange urge to frown. It was strange because he knew he couldn't frown, but these micro-habits were ingrained in his mind.

The smaller hangar deck was no less busy than the previous one they'd been on. Quinton heard snippets of conversations as they walked by, and a quick analysis from his VIs appeared on his HUD, highlighting a pattern of certain keywords and phrases. The people in close proximity all seemed to be commenting about a sudden loss of communications, a slight disruption that soon resolved itself as they walked past.

They walked toward a white shuttlecraft that displayed the sleek lines of a smooth hull, seeming to radiate speed and agility. There was a flash of blue as the loading ramp lowered.

"Nice ship," Becker said, and Maelyn looked at him.

"She gets the job done. Please inform Commander Crowe that I will be in touch with him soon," Maelyn said.

Becker looked away and listened to a couple of salvagers speaking, then looked down at his wrist computer. His gaze narrowed, and his hand shot toward his weapon.

"Don't," Maelyn said, holding something in her hand that Quinton couldn't see. Becker's hand was just above his hand cannon. "I was really hoping to avoid this."

"Whatever you're trying to do, it's not going to work," Becker said.

Quinton heard Guttman and Oscar mutter a curse.

Simon had his palm-sized blaster pressed into Becker's back. "Back off," he said over his shoulder and then looked at Becker. "Nothing personal."

The smaller man circled around to Becker's side and gestured for Quinton to keep going, but Quinton stayed put.

Becker clenched his teeth for a few moments.

"What are we waiting for? Let me take them out," Guttman growled.

"Becker," Maelyn said, "you'd better leash your dog. He might be able to get us, but I guarantee that *you* won't walk away."

Becker glanced behind him at Guttman and Oscar, shaking his head a little.

A high-pitched tone chimed overhead, followed by a klaxon alarm.

"Captain," Simon said to Maelyn, "we've gotta go. They're initiating a lockdown."

"I know. I was hoping we'd be on the ship before they figured it out," Maelyn said.

Maelyn and Simon kept their weapons pointed at Becker while backing away a few steps. Simon gestured for Quinton to join them.

"What are you trying to do? There's nothing here for you to steal—not when you've got a ship like that," Becker said and frowned, his gaze swinging toward Quinton. "What's so special about this robot?"

The ruse was up. Becker was putting the pieces together. The hangar deck was clearing as people began evacuating the area.

Quinton grabbed Becker's weapon from his holster, using the lightning-quick speed capability of the agricultural bot. Becker's eyes widened, and he reached for his weapon on pure instinct but came up short. Quinton pointed the hand cannon at Becker, and Guttman and Oscar flanked him, pointing their weapons at Quinton.

"It'll take them too long to explain," Quinton said.

"What the hell is that thing?" Guttman asked.

Quinton ignored him. "We don't have a lot of time," he said and gestured toward Becker. "How long do you want to be Helsing's lackey? I heard what he said to you. If you come with us, there might be something in it for you worth more than what you've got here."

Quinton took a few steps back and to the side. He glanced at Maelyn, whose mouth hung slightly agape, and then she looked at Simon.

"I told you. Somehow, it's got a PMC inside it," Simon said.

"Yes, yes," Quinton said quickly. "Now, if we're not going to shoot each other, let's get moving."

Maelyn pointed her weapon at him. "Not so fast. I'm not bringing them along."

"You'll never get out of here if you don't," Quinton said and gestured with the point of his weapon toward Becker. "Right now, he's trying to figure out how much Commander Crowe is going to reward him if he turns you over to him."

Maelyn narrowed her gaze and swung it toward Becker.

"It's nothing personal, Captain," Becker replied.

"What the hell is a PMC?" Guttman asked.

"Not now," Quinton replied. "Captain Wayborn, is it? We can sort this out away from here, but none of us wins if we stay."

"That's not how I see it," Becker said. "The longer I keep you here, the better it is for me."

Quinton lowered the hand cannon and squeezed the trigger. A plasma bolt charred the metallic alloy of the hangar deck near Becker's feet, proving more powerful than he had thought. "The next one is for you. Do you want to keep stalling, or do you not recognize an opportunity when it's staring you in the face?"

Becker gritted his teeth, and Quinton thought he was about to rush him. Becker shifted his gaze toward Maelyn. "He's right. I can help you escape. You won't get past the station's defenses without us. We're coming with you."

His henchmen began voicing a protest, and he told them to shut it.

"Captain," Simon said.

Maelyn regarded Becker for a few moments and then nodded once. "The PMC is right. We can sort this out away from here. I'll allow you to come along, but you keep your henchmen in line, or I'll take care of them myself."

The PMC . . . He had a name. He wasn't some mindless machine.

Maelyn turned around and headed toward the ship.

"Put your weapons away," Becker said to the others. "We're not going to shoot them."

"Fine," Guttman said, "but I'm not going on that ship. Do you have any idea what Crowe will do when he finds out?"

"Crowe is the least of your worries if you don't get on that ship right now," Becker said and looked at Oscar.

"I was getting tired of this place anyway," Oscar said and hastened toward the ship.

Simon followed, and Quinton was only a few feet behind. He held onto Becker's weapon.

Guttman considered it for a few seconds and then walked toward the ship, shaking his head.

Quinton walked up the loading ramp. Maelyn and Simon were in the cockpit.

"Have a seat, gentlemen," Maelyn said.

Becker and the others sat down. The seats weren't big enough for Quinton, so he stood.

"Becker," Maelyn said, "I need you to override the lockdown. I've opened a comlink for you to use."

"On it," he said and used his wrist computer to send in his authentication. "What would you have done if I hadn't come along?"

"There's more than one way to get past a lockdown," she replied.

Becker twitched his eyebrows. "That should take care of the defense cannons as well, but it won't last long."

"He's gonna come after us," Guttman warned. "He's gonna find out what you did."

Becker smiled. "That's why I used your credentials, Guttman. Now shut up."

Guttman sneered and shook his head.

Becker glanced toward Quinton and flicked his gaze toward the hand cannon.

"I think I'll hold onto it for a little while," Quinton said.

The shuttle's engines engaged and Maelyn swung the nose around, then flew out of the hangar. The defense cannons remained offline, and once they were clear, she increased the shuttle's velocity to maximum.

"How far away is your ship?" Quinton asked.

"It's not far," Maelyn replied. "Simon, let Kieva know we're on our way back."

"Yes, Captain," Simon replied.

"And we have a few extra passengers with us," Maelyn added.

Becker watched Quinton as if he wasn't quite sure what to make of him.

"Didn't anyone ever tell you that it's not polite to stare?" Quinton said.

Becker smirked. "I'm not. You're just an echo from a bygone age."

Quinton was about to reply when Simon spoke.

"Hang on back there. Looks like they've sent a couple of ships after us."

Guttman muttered incoherently and checked his seat straps.

"It's just comms chatter. They haven't located us yet," Quinton said.

The others frowned and glanced at each other. He'd patched into the shuttle's systems and was monitoring various data feeds. Simon would have noticed the same thing if he'd taken the time to look.

Maelyn flew the shuttle close to one of the cargo carriers to throw off the active scans from the space station.

Quinton looked at their current velocity. "The point is to get out of here alive."

"No one likes a backseat pilot," she replied.

A ship designation appeared on the nav computer's plot, but it was just a series of numbers—a ship without a name. It was supposedly bad luck to fly a ship without a name, but Quinton didn't want to point that out.

Becker continued to watch him, and it was becoming a bit uncomfortable. He'd called him an echo. What did that mean? Quinton kept a close watch on Becker and the others. They could have decided to come along, only to betray them later on. Guttman and Oscar didn't seem like they could pull something like that off without being completely obvious about it, but Becker was smart enough. He wasn't a mindless brute, despite his brutish appearance. Quinton had gambled when he'd brought up Helsing, but there was no love lost between

Becker and Helsing. He'd correctly guessed that Becker was tired of being beneath Helsing in Crowe's Union, and he'd have to keep that in mind. Once they reached the ship and were away from here, aggressive negotiations would open back up.

Becker knew what a PMC was, or at least was familiar enough with the concept. Judging by Becker's comment—bygone age notwithstanding—and the intense scrutiny of his unfaltering gaze, Quinton was under no illusions that the salvager wouldn't blow him out of an airlock if given a chance. He'd have to keep an eye on him.

Quinton monitored the shuttle as Maelyn waited until the last possible moment to slow down before docking with the ship. They attached to the vessel's outer hull, and Quinton saw a small docking tube extend to the cockpit.

Maelyn and Simon climbed out of their seats and gestured for the rest of them to follow to the forward airlock. Quinton did as directed and was soon followed by Becker and the others. There was a quick zero-g transition to the main ship, and by the time he landed, he was firmly in the artificial gravity field.

"Jump drive has been prepped, Captain," a woman's soprano voice said, coming from the ship's intercom system.

"Thank you, Kieva," Maelyn replied.

"Captain, we're being hailed by the station. We're not cleared to disembark," Kieva said.

"Understood. Ignore them."

They entered the bridge, and Maelyn went to the pilot's seat on the left. Simon took the seat on the right.

"You can't engage the jump drive here," Becker said.

"Watch me," Maelyn said and palmed the jump controls that had just become green on her holoscreen.

13

Quinton saw that a significant portion of power was being diverted to the engines. The jump drive was already charged and waiting for Maelyn to execute.

"What's she doing?" Guttman asked.

"Becker," Oscar said, "if she initiates the jump here, it could tear the ship in half."

"I know," Becker replied, and his gaze flicked toward the hand cannon that Quinton held.

"Don't do anything stupid. You're never gonna take it from me," Quinton said.

"I'm not listening to a damn robot," Guttman said and began unbuckling his straps.

"One, I'm not a robot. Two, do you honestly think she wants to die? Now sit tight and let her—" Quinton stopped speaking.

The ship's engines engaged at maximum, straining the inertia dampeners. He reached out and braced himself, nearly dropping the weapon. Guttman almost slid out of his seat, but Becker grabbed him and held him in place. The lights dimmed, and a shudder went through the floor and the walls of the ship. Quinton accessed the bridge computer and saw a countdown for the jump drive. They were increasing their velocity at an accelerated rate to reach minimum safe distance for an FTL jump.

Maelyn engaged the jump drive. The main engines cut off, and Quinton watched as the excess power was rerouted back into the jump drive as it began to fold space. Jumping through space and time didn't actually feel like anything. One moment they were in one place, and the next they emerged somewhere else. The transition folded space, creating a jump field around the ship. Once the ship reached the target coordinates, the jump drive powered down. The lighting inside the ship leveled off as the power fluctuations began to regulate themselves back to normal operating range.

"Jump is complete," Maelyn said. "In case anybody gets it into their head to try to take control of my ship, I've activated the lockdown protocols for unauthorized weapons use. Anyone who powers on or tries to use an unauthorized weapon will become the victim of the ship's countermeasures. You have five seconds to power your weapons down."

Quinton didn't think she was bluffing and quickly deactivated the hand cannon. He saw Guttman and Oscar do the same thing.

Becker stood up and held his hand out. "That belongs to me."

Quinton held onto the weapon and regarded Becker for a few moments.

Maelyn and Simon left the bridge, joining them.

"Give it back to him," Maelyn said.

"I don't trust him," Quinton replied.

"Don't make me take it from you," Becker said.

"I'd like to see you try," Quinton said and then held the weapon just out of reach. "Go ahead. Take it."

Maelyn sighed. "At least now we know you're a man."

Quinton looked at her. Becker inched closer to him, and Quinton snatched the hand cannon away.

"All of you are guests aboard my ship," Maelyn said. "I am the captain, and you will abide by my rules or I'll introduce you to the airlock. It's your choice, PMC. I can just as easily have the ship's countermeasures target you as them."

Quinton was already accessing the ship's systems and saw that they were now targeting him. The onboard stunners could release enough of a jolt to render even someone Becker's size into a drooling, ineffectual man-child on the floor. He rather enjoyed imagining it, but the effect the stunners would have on an agricultural unit made him hesitate. His host body wasn't designed to withstand the countermeasures. They could cause significant damage, including making the bot non-functioning, which he wanted to avoid at all costs.

"Fine," he said and flung the hand cannon back at Becker. The big salvager snatched the weapon out of the air and quickly checked it with the practiced efficiency of someone who knew how to maintain and keep a weapon operational.

"My name is Quinton. I'm a PMC," he said and saw Guttman and Oscar frown in confusion. "Personality Matrix Construct. Does that ring any bells? . . . No? All right, the quick version is that I uploaded my consciousness into an Energy Storage System—ESS—and it's here in my chest."

Becker looked at Maelyn. "You should disable this thing right now."

"I'm not a 'thing,' I'm a person. The governing body of PMCs defines them as living beings," Quinton said.

Becker grinned bitterly. "Governing body," he said and glanced at the others. They all shared a meaningful look that Quinton didn't care for. "Which governing body would that be?"

Quinton felt as if the knowledge was just beyond his reach.

"Do you even know?"

"Of course, I do. It's just . . ." Quinton said and paused for a few moments. "This agricultural unit isn't meant to house a PMC, so my access to the ESS is limited."

Becker looked at Maelyn calmly. "Do you want to disable him, or should I?"

"No one is going to disable me," Quinton said. He thought he could disable a few key systems before Maelyn did anything threatening.

"He's inside the ship's systems," Simon said.

"You're damn right I am. I have access to life support, artificial gravity, and maybe a few other systems right now," Quinton said.

"Good," Maelyn said. "If you do anything stupid, the lockout protocol will engage and erase everything, including the nav system. You'll be stranded out here with nowhere to go."

"Quinton," Simon said, stepping closer to him and raising his hands in a placating gesture, "I said I could help you and I meant it. I know that unit is in bad shape, and the power core is failing."

"Then you know how desperate I am," Quinton replied.

"That thing needs to be disabled," Becker said.

Guttman grunted in agreement.

Quinton crouched into a fighting stance, and the blade extended from his right forearm. Both Becker and Guttman regarded the weapon for a moment, as if judging whether they could subdue him.

"Back away from him," Maelyn said.

Much to Quinton's surprise, the two men backed off a few steps. He turned and saw that Maelyn held a sidearm in her hand. The polished alloy tip had a greenish glow.

"Quinton, is it?" Maelyn said. "I think there's a way we can all help each other."

Quinton retracted the blade back into his forearm and stood up straight. "All right, I'm listening."

"How did you come to be . . ." she said and gave him a once-over. "Why was your ESS put into that robot?"

"There was an activation signal, and Radek, my VI assistant, took control of a delivery drone while he tried to find an acceptable housing unit. This agricultural bot was the only thing available. I don't know where the activation signal came from, and I have limited access to my ESS, so my memory appears to be . . . limited," Quinton said.

Maelyn glanced at Simon. "Where did you find him?"

"On a light transport ship that came from Zeda-Six. According to the ship's logs, it had been on standby for at least forty standard years to preserve its power core. But this agricultural unit is quite a bit older than that—at least a century old," Simon said.

"Zeda-Six." Maelyn frowned.

"I didn't know where I was until I reached the space station," Quinton said.

"How did you get to the space station?" Maelyn asked.

"I used a planetary escape pod left over from an evacuation."

Maelyn's gaze flicked toward the damaged parts where he had fought the hunter mechs. "You look like you were in a fight. What happened on that planet? Wasn't there anyone there who could help you?"

"There wasn't anybody around."

"He's right about that. I checked," Simon said. "It was a third-tier colony world and has a classification of being unlivable. The population was evacuated over a hundred years ago."

"To answer your other question," Quinton said, "yes, I was in a fight. I was hunted by security mechs. They were following some latent protocol, and I couldn't override it."

Quinton watched as the others, including Becker and his henchmen, shared a knowing glance.

Becker cleared his throat. "Zeda-Six isn't part of any federation."

"What do you mean?" Quinton asked.

"We can't figure out what federation you came from."

"Why do we care what federation he came from?" Guttman asked.

"Because—" Becker began, but Maelyn cut him off.

"Simon, what was the last governing body of Zeda-Six?" Maelyn asked.

Simon pressed his lips together and brought up a personal holoscreen while he looked for the answer. "It looks like Zeda-Six changed hands quite a bit. At one point, it was part of the Jordani Federation, then part of the Acheron Confederacy."

"That thing is from Acheron?" Becker asked, cocking his head to the side.

Maelyn pursed her lips in thought.

Simon shrugged one shoulder. "Not exactly. Like I said, the system changed hands quite a bit. There are some references that show that the Dholeren United Coalition had a claim there, as well as the Castellus Federal Alliance. A lot of colony worlds changed hands on the outer rim territories, but the evacuation might've been organized by the DUC," he said and then added, "Dholeren United Coalition."

"They didn't have a PMC program or even the technology," Becker said.

Simon nodded. "No, not the DUC, but the Jordani had it for sure. And, of course, so did the Acheron. Maybe a handful of others. Since Quinton only has limited access to his ESS, we won't be able to answer the question out here."

Becker stabbed a finger toward Quinton. "That thing is a ticking time bomb."

Quinton was having trouble following the conversation. He kept running into invisible thought barriers. What were they so afraid of?

"You might be right about that," Maelyn said and held up a hand when Quinton's gaze swooped toward her. "Come on. Even you have to admit that there's something more going on here. Why would an activation signal suddenly come on now, and you don't even know where it came from?"

"I have information on how to track it," Quinton said.

"Let's not get ahead of ourselves here," Becker said. "It's not safe to travel with that thing."

Quinton was getting tired of being referred to as "that thing." He was not a *thing*.

Maelyn arched an eyebrow toward Becker. "I would've thought you could've figured this out. You *are* a salvager after all."

Guttman blinked his eyes rapidly and looked at Becker. "What's she talking about?"

Maelyn rolled her eyes and sighed. "What I'm talking about is that there's some tech that's only accessible via a PMC. You're worried about Lennix Crowe and what he'll do to you if he finds us. Well, with Quinton's help, you might not have to worry about Crowe ever again," Maelyn said.

"Yeah, but . . ." Becker paused.

"We can work out the details," she said.

"One of the details I'm interested in," Quinton said, "is how you can help me. I still have an issue with my power core. I have limited access to my ESS, so I'm not sure how I can help you access anything."

"Simon said he can help you. Let him examine you," Maelyn said.

"I can," Simon said. All eyes turned toward him. "At least I think I can. We don't have a power core that's compatible with you, so it's not a simple swap-and-replace, but I might be able to put something together that will at least keep you operational."

"Does that include a way for me to access my ESS?" Quinton asked.

Simon shook his head. "We can't tamper with an ESS, at least not here on the ship. It requires the use of a special interface and your cooperation. Everything ESS-related requires the cooperation of the PMC."

Quinton sent a message to Radek: *Is this true?*

That is correct. There are built-in safeguards to prevent unauthorized access into an ESS. However, there is the potential to find a workaround to force access, so I would be careful, especially with a tech expert.

Careful, Quinton mused. *Thanks.*

Quinton looked at Maelyn. "In exchange for your help, you want me to help you access what, exactly?"

"We'll get to that, but first let's get Simon to check you out and stabilize you. Once he's finished, we can talk," Maelyn said.

Quinton regarded her pretty face for a few moments. She had an agreeable tone that seemed to put everyone at ease. He couldn't afford to trust any of these people. However, he couldn't find any fault with what she'd said. He needed help and he needed it badly.

"Will you follow me, Quinton?" Simon asked.

"Oh, there's one more thing I want to know," Becker said. He was looking at Maelyn. "You jumped us out here in the middle of nowhere. How long will it take for the jump drive to recharge?"

"I was just about to confer with my chief engineer, Kieva. You're welcome to join me. She might have a few things for you to do to help out," Maelyn said and glanced at Guttman and Oscar.

Hints of a smile tugged at the edges of Becker's lips. "All right, after you."

They left the common area through one door, and Quinton and Simon went in the opposite direction.

"Radek," Quinton said sub-vocally so no one else could hear him, "I need you to monitor the ship systems."

"Of course," Radek replied. "What do you want me to monitor for?"

"Keep an eye on Maelyn and Becker. I don't think they're telling me everything."

"Understood. I'll monitor all references they make to you and PMCs in particular."

Quinton followed Simon. Radek hadn't been that reliable, but Quinton had to make use of him. He couldn't afford to watch everything himself, and he didn't think it was a good idea not to monitor his new associates.

"How did you figure out what I was?" Quinton asked.

"I wasn't sure at first," Simon said. He walked to a door and palmed the control unit so it hissed open. "I did detect a secure power source, which I now know is your ESS. The other thing that gave it away was your behavior. You didn't act like a robot, certainly not an agricultural robot. But when you gave Guttman some trouble, I knew for sure that there was something going on with you. The only thing it could be was a PMC, even though I honestly don't know how the hell you're functioning in that thing."

"So you've encountered a PMC before?" Quinton asked.

Simon shook his head once. "No, but I've read about them. I've seen virtual intelligences that are meant to mimic human behavior, but I didn't think you were one of those."

"All of you seemed worried about whether my origin was from the Acheron Confederacy."

Simon looked at him for a few moments. "Most people blame the Acheron Confederacy for what happened—the wars that followed their ascendancy."

"What wars?" Quinton asked.

Simon's eyebrows raised. "You really can't remember?"

"I'm not pretending, if that's what you're implying."

"I do understand if you're hiding what you are."

"Do you," Quinton said pleasantly. "Since I've been awake, I've been hunted and also shot at by an orbital defense cannon on a space station that was abandoned a century ago. Then I was picked up by you and your friend Becker, who wanted to claim me as property. And now I had to bargain something I don't even fully understand in order to get your help. But you want to tell me you understand why I'm hiding what I am."

They came to another door and Simon paused, his hand hovering over the door controls. "I didn't mean to upset you. But you don't know everything that's happened. There are good reasons why people are . . . Let's just say that people won't be overjoyed to learn that there are PMCs being reactivated."

"Have there been others? Have you encountered other PMCs?" Quinton asked quickly. His mind was beginning to race.

Simon palmed the controls, and the door hissed open. A familiar screeching sound came from inside, and Quinton looked over at a biological container in surprise. Inside, Stumpy was bellowing his dissatisfaction with his current living conditions.

"You brought it with you?" Quinton asked.

He walked over and peered inside the container. Stumpy stopped screeching and watched Quinton with wide eyes. His large flappy ears angled, as if he was trying to detect some kind of sound.

Simon walked over and stood next to the animal. "I figured you brought him with you for a reason."

"I didn't have a lot of time. It was more a last-minute decision," Quinton said. "Actually, the space station allowed me aboard because I had him with me."

"Is that right? I wonder why that was," Simon said.

The door to the workshop closed, and Simon opened the container. Stumpy hesitated for a moment and then bolted out, scrambling across the floor. He climbed a shelving system off to the side and perched on top of it, giving him a bird's-eye view of the entire room.

"I think the station's identification systems believed I was the creature's caretaker. It must've classified him as some kind of pet," Quinton said.

Simon made an *uh-huh* sound. "Did you name him—he got a name?"

"I called him Stumpy."

"Stumpy?" Simon said and cocked his head to the side, looking at the creature. "Really?"

"Yeah. His legs are short, so Stumpy."

Simon nodded. "I'll have to figure out what he eats."

"You don't need to keep him on my account."

"We'll see what happens."

Quinton watched him walk over to his workbench. "You never answered my question."

Simon looked over at him, his eyebrows raised. "What question?"

"Have you encountered any other PMCs?"

Simon shook his head. "No."

Quinton didn't believe him, at least not entirely. Simon could just be being cautious, or perhaps he wasn't allowed to talk about it. The young man deferred to Maelyn, who was clearly in command. But since Simon was going to help him, he didn't think it would be smart to make an issue of it right then. Simon was going to give him what he needed most, which was time.

"Let's get you checked out," Simon said.

Quinton walked over to the workbench, and Simon began to work on him.

14

Over the next few hours, Simon evaluated the agricultural unit that Quinton resided in. Quinton was impressed with how thorough Simon was with categorizing the damage to the robot. The power core needed to be replaced. The entire unit was beyond its original design specifications, even if it had been serviced on a regular maintenance schedule—which it hadn't.

"Stop doing that," Quinton said.

Simon was putting the shoulder assembly back together. He stopped and looked at him. "Huh?"

"Stop shaking your head and looking at me as if you expect me to . . ." Quinton said and stopped. He'd been about to say "die," but that wasn't right. If his power core suddenly stopped working, he would go into standby mode within the confines of the ESS. He'd be safe, but he'd lose all awareness of . . . everything—his sense of self, his surroundings, and his ability to influence his own life. He might as well be dead if that happened. But someone could also destroy the ESS, and then he'd be dead for sure.

"I'm sorry," Simon said and resumed his work. "It's just that—You know what, never mind. It looks like the power regulator was able to get your core up to 40 percent capacity."

"It's holding steady, but more than half of it is damaged or nonfunctional."

"Yeah, but the battery backup I made for you should help with the load," Simon said.

The battery backup was a square box that Simon had bolted to Quinton's back. "It looks older than this bot is."

Simon snorted a little and bobbed his eyebrows. "You're not wrong about that, but I've replaced the internal components and configured the inhibitor to prevent it from overloading your systems."

Quinton turned his humanoid metallic head toward Simon, doing his best to convey consternation into the insipid facial features.

"I know," Simon said quickly. "This body isn't you, but you know what I mean."

He finished what he was doing and stepped off the stepladder. "All right, see how that shoulder works now. I think that should do it."

Quinton raised his arm and found that he now had full range of motion without loss of motor control. He walked over to a storage container and lifted it up without any problems. He put it down and then did a handstand. Quinton pushed up onto his fingertips and switched from one arm to the other, showing a display of acrobatic skill.

"You're a miracle worker," Quinton said.

Simon grinned. "Nah, that's what they call my cousin, Scotty."

"Is he on the ship?"

Simon shook his head. "No, he's back . . . he's not on board."

Quinton looked down at his chest. It was all one piece again. Simon had used a regenerative nano-robotic blend to patch and repair the damaged areas, and it would also maintain the structural integrity of the exoskeletal system. It couldn't be used where the haptic sensors were on his hands and feet because it would interfere with the sensory receptors. Anything having to do with physical feedback by touch couldn't be fixed with the nanite repair systems. However, the stuff spread throughout the exoskeleton, and Quinton suspected that the agricultural unit could now move as well as it had when it was first built. Simon had staged the application of the nanites in sections and uploaded basic design functions, essentially giving the nanites instructions on what they were to maintain.

"Simon," Quinton said, "how long are we going to play this game?"

Simon looked away for a few moments, not meeting his gaze. "I'm . . . There are some things that I can't talk about with you. It's for our protection."

"What do you think is going to happen?"

Simon's mouth hung open a bit, and he bobbed his head to the side. Then he inhaled and sighed. "Look, I know it's frustrating, but I just can't, all right?"

Quinton thought Simon looked genuinely conflicted. "Not really. What happened that made all of you afraid of a simple PMC?"

"There is nothing simple about a PMC."

"All right, fine, but you act like I'm some kind of threat to you."

Simon turned away and put his tools back on the workbench. He moved methodically, like he was someone who returned things exactly where he expected to find them later on. When he was finished, he banged his fist gently on the open workspace for a few beats, ending decisively with the loudest of all. Then he turned around. "You *are* a threat, even if you don't realize it and even if you don't intend to be. Maybe that's even worse," he said and pressed his lips together. "Can you remember anything?"

"It's limited. Radek insists that it's because of this," Quinton said, gesturing toward himself.

"Is it still advising against direct interaction?" Simon asked.

Radek had told Quinton it was more or less up to him, and since trust was so limited, Quinton had chosen to wait.

"You're not the only one with trust issues," Quinton replied, then added, "or maybe your captain, I should say."

Simon shifted uncomfortably. "I still think your VI is keeping things from you, which I don't like."

Quinton had suspected the same thing, but Radek was in as fragile a state as he was at this point. "Why is it so important for you to know my origin?"

Simon arched an eyebrow. "I thought it was obvious, and it should be just as important to you."

The lights dimmed for a tick and then resumed. Repairs were being made to the ship while they waited for the jump drive to recharge.

"You see, this is what I think," Quinton said. "I think it will affect whether you help me or not. So, if I did really know, I might not tell you anyway until I knew more about what happened to make you all so suspicious of PMCs."

Simon pursed his lips and nodded once. "Fair enough, and I don't see us going any further unless I tell you a few things, so that's what I'm going to do."

Quinton walked over to him and stopped. "Don't you need to consult Maelyn?"

"She trusts me," Simon replied.

The door to the workshop opened, and Maelyn walked in. She glanced at both of them. "Talking about me?" She quirked an eyebrow, and Quinton wondered if she'd been listening to their conversation before making her timely entrance.

She smiled and walked over to them, eyes twinkling. But all the smiles in the galaxy wouldn't negate the simple fact that they were all walking on eggshells around him.

"I was about to tell Quinton a few things, and he asked if I should check with you first," Simon replied.

Maelyn turned toward Quinton and gave him a once-over. "I have to say, you're looking much better," she said and looked at the young man. "Simon, you're the best. I knew there was a reason I kept you around."

"I thought it was my charming personality."

Maelyn laughed a little, and Quinton liked how it sounded. She looked at him. "You wouldn't believe how shy he used to be."

Simon's face became serious with mock severity. "You said you wouldn't talk about it anymore."

Maelyn frowned. "I don't remember promising that."

Simon shrugged. "Of course, if you did, I could start talking about the things I know about you. For example—"

"That won't be necessary," Maelyn said quickly and looked at Quinton. "You must have a few questions for us," she said and leaned back against the workbench.

"Just a couple," Quinton replied. "But first I'd like to point out that I really loved the performance. The playful banter between the two of you, I mean. I really sensed a bond between you. It's very disarming, and it probably works on a lot of people, but I'm not one of them."

Maelyn eyed Simon for a moment and said, "He figured us out." She looked back at Quinton. "You're right. This was all a ruse to get you to open up to us. I'm just trying to get you to cooperate." She crossed her arms and regarded him. Quinton noticed the way her thick, wavy hair rested on her shoulders like they were blanketed in caramel, and his receptors detected the sweet citrusy scent of her smooth skin. "Or perhaps I'm just trying to be friendly. Maybe give you a reason to lower your guard a little. I believe there's a saying about it. You know, spirit of cooperation and all that."

"With *us*," Quinton repeated. "Aren't you the captain? So, I guess I just need to cooperate with you."

Maelyn smiled. "You're a witty one."

"Cut the act. I know you might seem friendly now, but how friendly could you really be? Not if you're willing to work with someone like Lennix Crowe."

Maelyn laughed. It was a jovial, musical sound that Quinton actually liked and probably would've joined in if she weren't laughing at him. She looked at Simon. "How old do you think he is?"

"He?" Quinton said. "*He's* right here, and you can ask me."

"But you don't even know. You have limited access to your ESS. What's the last thing that you remember?"

Quinton thought about it for a few moments. "I remember pieces of my training for my candidacy to become a PMC. I remember passing a series of tests, but I don't know who they were for. The memories are there, I know it, but I just can't get to them."

Maelyn looked at Simon. "The way his VI—" he said.

"Radek," Quinton interjected.

"Radek," Simon repeated, "explained it was because of the limited capacity for the agricultural unit to interact with the ESS. I think he had to decide between allowing Quinton to function in a limited capacity or not bringing the PMC online altogether. It's actually unprecedented. It means that the VI is choosing dynamic connections to allow access to Quinton's ESS, and it's happening in real time."

Maelyn pursed her full lips and inhaled softly. "Dynamic connections, you said. That would mean it has to expend precious cycles to make that determination on an ongoing basis. Isn't that less efficient?"

"I have no way to measure it. Not with what we have here on the ship. But Quinton can clearly interact with us, even with limited access. Whatever Radek has done is working, at least for now."

Quinton waved at them. "I'm still here. I'm not going anywhere. I know you're worried about something that I might be able to do, but unless you try to hurt me first, I really don't intend to do anything like that. You're just going to have to trust me."

"All right, Quinton," Maelyn said. "Let's see if we can get any of those suppressed memories to come up. Do you think Radek will cooperate?"

"He'll do what I ask him," Quinton said.

"Okay, good. Have you ever heard of the Dholeren United Coalition?" Maelyn asked.

"No."

"How about the Collective?"

Quinton shook his head.

"How about Castellus Federal Alliance? Tilion Empire, the Jordani Federation, the Acheron Confederacy."

"None of those sound familiar. I guess I should be relieved."

Maelyn's eyebrows raised. "Why would you say that?"

"Because it doesn't sound like . . . Judging by what's been said before, what if I was from one of those places? Would it affect our deal?" Quinton asked.

"It might, but it really depends," she said.

Quinton thought she was telling the truth. He felt he should have recognized some of those names.

"If he was from the Acheron Confederacy, then we'd—" Simon began to say when Maelyn cut him off.

"It wouldn't matter," she said.

"Yes, it would."

They were both silent for a few moments.

"Why does it matter?" Quinton asked.

Maelyn and Simon glanced at each other. "That could take some explaining," she said.

"Wait a second," Simon said. "Quinton, if Radek was operating under some kind of lockdown protocol, you would need to ask him before he could disclose it to you. This isn't something he would volunteer, but if you make the request, he'd have no choice but to tell you about it."

"What if the lockdown protocol forbids it?" Maelyn asked.

"Then, we'll still confirm that the lockdown exists and to what extent it can be influencing him."

Quinton considered it for a few seconds, then said, "Radek, I want you to show yourself to the others."

A moment later, a silvery orb appeared a few feet away from Quinton.

"Is there anything I need to know?"

"You'll need to make a more specific query," Radek replied.

Maelyn and Simon watched the hovering orb with great interest.

"Radek, are you operating under a lockdown protocol? Are you keeping things from me?" Quinton asked. There were a few moments of silence, and he suspected that Radek was stalling for time.

"Affirmative," Radek said.

Quinton felt a vague sensation of wanting to grit his teeth, but this was something the agricultural unit couldn't do. "I want you to end this lockdown immediately."

"I am unable to comply with this request."

"It's not a request. It's an order, and you will obey me," Quinton said.

"Apologies. I am unable to comply with this request."

Quinton growled.

"Hold on. Maybe there's a reason he can't comply," Simon said. "Radek, why can't you end the lockdown?"

The silvery orb spun but didn't reply.

"Answer the question, Radek," Quinton said.

"Conditions have not been met in their entirety. Between that and the limited capacity of this unit, I am unable to disclose the exact nature of the lockdown," Radek said.

"Let me get this straight," Quinton said. "There's a lockdown that's affecting my own access to myself," he said, gesturing toward his chest. "My own data. Information I need right now. Who instituted the lockdown?"

"I am unable—"

"For the love of—I don't want to hear what you're unable to do. Tell me what you *can* do."

"The lockdown affects what I am able to tell you," Radek said.

"That doesn't make any sense. No one has the authority to deny me access to my own mind," Quinton said angrily.

Simon's eyes widened, and he looked at Maelyn. "Wow. The VI itself is operating under a lockdown. Someone instituted a check against the VI itself. This isn't like the others."

"Others," Quinton said. "What others?"

Maelyn looked at Simon and shook her head.

"He was going to find out sooner or later," Simon said and looked at Quinton. "There were Federation Wars that happened probably around the same time you were uploaded. PMCs were used to enhance the combat capabilities of federation navies. That is, until they started going insane, but this was after the technology had spread."

"Insane? But the tech was proven. It was safe. PMCs were considered living entities with the same rights as the person they used to be when they had a human body," Quinton replied.

Maelyn cleared her throat. "He's older than we thought. Pre-galactic war age."

"What the hell does that mean?" Quinton asked.

"Things have changed since you volunteered to become a PMC," she said.

"You're right, this is pre-Sentinel fleet operations," Simon said and winced.

"Really, Simon," Maelyn scolded as her blue eyes flicked toward the ceiling. Then she looked at Quinton. "I think I know which federation you came from."

They both inched away from him, and Quinton became suspicious.

"Hey," he said, not liking that they were backing away from him. "Which one?"

Maelyn and Simon exchanged a few meaningful looks, trying to have a conversation without words, and they were utterly failing. Quinton accessed the door controls to the workshop and locked them. The overhead door indicator light shifted to red, and a soft chime sounded. Maelyn and Simon looked at the door and then back at Quinton.

"I need an answer right now," Quinton said.

Maelyn sighed. "All right," she said. "We'll be able to confirm this, but I think you are from either the Acheron Confederacy—the ACN to be exact—or the Jordani Federation. They were the earliest adopters of PMC technology."

Quinton cranked up his frame rate, which controlled his perception of time. Time didn't slow down for anyone else, but he was able to think much more quickly. Since he now had a direct connection to a power source, the familiar warning indicator did not appear on his HUD.

"Radek, is this true? Can you confirm any of this?"

As an answer, Quinton became aware of a new pathway to his ESS.

Acheron Confederacy naval lockdown protocol.

Condition seventy-four has been met.

Awareness confirmed.

Secondary protocols activated.

"I guess that's my answer," Quinton said.

He was from the Acheron Confederacy. He glanced at Maelyn and Simon, who were motionless. Maelyn's mouth was partially open, as if she was about to say something.

"Radek," Quinton started to say but didn't know how to finish. Radek was affected by the lockdown protocol as well. The VI was all he had to work with. "What just happened?"

"The lockdown couldn't keep you from the knowledge any longer."

"It couldn't? But that would mean I should be able to override the lockdown and get full access to my memories."

"Not entirely. The lockdown protocol functions as its own separate VI that can have a governing effect on you. It was added after the PMC load date," Radek said.

Great, he had some kind of Big Brother virtual intelligence watching his every move, but Quinton had no idea what its primary objective was.

"Can you tell me anything about the secondary protocols?"

"It's going to take me some time. The effects are intricate."

"Can it force me to do things I don't want to do?"

"Unknown," Radek said. "I can't say for sure with a great deal of probability whether it can or can't. If it could, that would violate core restrictions for PMC rights, rendering you no more than a machine. The greatest probability is that the secondary protocols are an influencer."

Quinton considered this for a few moments. "Either way, I'm being backed into a corner."

"I'm afraid I don't understand."

"You interpreted my question in specifics. It can't control my thoughts directly and force me to act accordingly. However, if it can influence me, then it can exercise some degree of control, the consequences of which might include cutting my access to my ESS."

"I see your point. I will devote some of my cycles to considering the problem."

Quinton wasn't sure how much headway the VI would make, but he guessed it was better than nothing. "You do that. I guess the question now is whether I tell the others."

"I would advise against that."

"Why?"

"Even though Captain Maelyn has narrowed the origins of your PMC, there still remains a doubt, which may work in your favor in securing their cooperation," Radek said.

"I wonder if it would make any difference," Quinton said and collected his thoughts for a few moments. "All right, don't volunteer any information to them unless I give the okay."

"Understood."

Quinton returned his frame rate back to normal.

"Are you sure you can narrow it down to just those two federations?" Quinton asked.

To Maelyn and Simon, no time had passed, and she took the question as a normal progression of their conversation.

"PMCs were invented by the Acheronians, but eventually the Jordanis had it," Maelyn said.

"It spread pretty quickly," Simon said. "I can do some research on it."

"Does it really matter? Would it change anything?" Quinton asked.

"Yes, it would," Maelyn said. "PMCs changed the way wars were fought across galactic federations—"

A comlink chimed overhead.

"Captain," Kieva said, her voice coming from the speaker by the door.

"What is it, Kieva?"

"I'm afraid Becker has found a stowaway in one of the cargo containers. You better get down to the cargo hold, ma'am."

"On my way," Maelyn said.

She looked at the door and then turned back to Quinton. "We'll finish this conversation, I promise, but Kieva isn't an alarmist, and I still have a ship to run. You can come with me if you want."

Quinton unlocked the door. "Lead the way, Captain."

Maelyn left the workshop, and Quinton and Simon followed her.

15

Quinton followed Maelyn down the corridor with Simon walking next to him. The young man kept glancing over at him, looking a little uncomfortable.

Quinton looked at him. "You're already in trouble. You might as well tell me what other PMCs you've encountered." He thought he saw Maelyn twitch her head to the side as if she hadn't quite heard what he said. "Don't worry about her. The cat is out of the bag. The drive signature has already been identified."

Simon shook his head. "You'd be an idiot to underestimate her."

"That's not what I meant," Quinton said. "I just want to know more about the other PMCs."

Simon looked pointedly at Maelyn's back for a moment. "We haven't encountered any PMCs, but we've heard some rumors."

Quinton expected Maelyn to interject a comment, but she kept striding forward. "Like what?" he asked.

"Just that there's been increasing Sentinel activity reported," Simon replied.

"What's a Sentinel?"

Maelyn turned back toward them. "We'll need to postpone the history lesson I'm afraid. Simon, make sure you keep an eye on Becker's team."

There was shouting from up ahead, and Quinton heard Guttman laughing about something, which couldn't be good.

"I'm not letting you anywhere near her. The captain is on her way here now," Kieva said.

"It's a Servitor," Guttman replied in exasperation. "I just want to have a look at her."

Quinton followed Maelyn as she strode into the cargo bay. Becker stood off to the side, his arms crossed as he leaned against the wall. He wore a mildly amused expression.

Kieva was on the shorter side. Her blonde hair was tied back into a ponytail and her button-brown eyes flicked toward Maelyn, looking relieved to see her. "Captain," she said, and Guttman and Oscar turned toward them.

Quinton saw someone hiding behind the stack of storage containers that Kieva was guarding.

Maelyn looked at Becker, who shrugged a shoulder. "What's going on here?"

Quinton saw that both Guttman and Oscar had elevated heart rates. There was a slight flush to their faces and, he suspected, their chests as well. The data showed itself on his HUD.

"We found a stowaway," Guttman said. The way he said it seemed to convey that he had some sort of claim on what he'd found.

"I see," Maelyn said. She looked at the storage container and activated her wrist computer, and her personal holoscreen appeared. "This came from Crowe's Union Station. This wasn't a mix-up. It's part of the resupply manifest."

"It's a Servitor. Do you know what they're worth? This wasn't an accident," Guttman said.

"He's right," Becker said, unfolding his arms and stepping away from the wall. "This isn't the kind of cargo that would go unnoticed by Crowe."

Maelyn looked away, seemingly unperturbed by Becker's comments. "Very well," she said, raising her voice slightly. "I want you to come out of there. I'm the captain of the ship, and I promise that no harm will come to you."

Kieva turned around. "Come on, it's okay now," she said and stepped out of the way.

Quinton didn't know what to expect when the Servitor stepped out from behind the storage container. It was a woman, but not like any he'd ever seen before. She was scantily clad, with dark lavender skin. There were hints of pink on her high cheekbones and full lips that were perfectly proportioned. She had legs that went all the way up, and she wore a formfitting shirt that only accentuated her remarkably firm and full breasts. The shirt ended, leaving her midriff bare, showing a flat stomach and hips that accentuated her womanly curves. Her dark eyes had violet in them, and Quinton couldn't help but gawk at the sight of her. He couldn't tear his eyes away, as if his mind refused to accept what he was seeing.

A few moments of silence passed while they all stared at her. He noticed that the other men all had similar reactions to the stunning beauty standing in front of them. She had long, silky white hair that seemed to glisten with silvery strands, as if they were enhanced by the lighting in the cargo hold. Quinton watched her with both admiration and a growing wariness that the person in front of him was designed for a specific purpose. She was meant to get a particular reaction, and it wasn't failing on any of them.

"What's your name?" Maelyn asked.

"Vonya Irani, Captain," she said. "I am a Servitor."

"Why are you on my ship?"

"The conditions of my employ were unacceptable, but I did not have the means to remove myself from the situation while maintaining good standing with my employer, so I added this cargo container to a manifest," she said and gestured with a long, slender arm, "destined for one of the independent trade ships that had come to the station."

Vonya's voice carried the alluring quality of silk sliding off smooth skin. Quinton wanted her to keep speaking so he could watch her full lips move as they formed words. Vonya kept her attention on Maelyn, but he thought she was well aware of the effect she was having on the men aboard the ship.

"Captain, please don't send me back," Vonya said simply and without a hint of pleading in her voice. "I would like to be of service to you and your crew in order to earn my place until I can make other arrangements," she said and glanced at the others for the first time. "Surely, I have some skills that could be of use."

Guttman cleared his throat. "I had a few thoughts on the matter," he said.

"Simon," Maelyn said, ignoring Guttman, "can you detect any tracer signals on this cargo?"

Guttman looked as if he was about to say something, thought better of it, and instead closed his mouth.

"Checking," Simon replied and brought up his own personal holoscreen. After a few moments, he shook his head. "No signal detected, Captain."

"What about the ship systems? Is anything broadcasting?" Becker asked.

And in one moment, the big man had proved to Quinton that he was more than a mindless brute.

"The ship's security systems would have detected it," Simon said.

Becker nodded, satisfied with the answer, but Quinton noticed that Maelyn was checking something else. Vonya simply stood there, looking stunning.

Becker looked at Maelyn's holoscreen and frowned. "I think you would have detected a subspace communication link broadcasting our coordinates."

Maelyn's eyes scanned the data on her personal holoscreen. "We would, but that's not the only way to track a ship."

"How else would someone track a ship way out in the middle of nowhere?" Guttman asked.

"A broadcast beacon is too obvious, but a short-range beacon would work," Quinton said.

Becker and Guttman looked at him doubtfully.

Maelyn closed the holoscreen. "They don't need to track us way out here. The three of you worked for Lennix Crowe, and you know how resourceful he is. No, he'll want to know where we check in, which means he doesn't need a subspace beacon tracker on the ship. All he needs is something small and undetectable that will come online the moment we check in to a space dock." She paused and her gaze took them all in. "We're going to have to make a sweep of the hull."

"You can't be serious," Guttman groused. "You want us to inspect the entire hull?" he asked and looked at Becker for support.

"I thought you wanted to avoid Crowe," Maelyn said.

Guttman looked like he was about to protest, but Becker silenced him. "She's right. It will be something small and unobtrusive, but it'll have its own power source," he said and looked at Maelyn. "Do you have any drones that can help with this?"

Maelyn's lips lifted in a wry smile. "I do have a few drones. There and right there," she said, looking at Guttman and Oscar. Quinton thought she included him in that all-encompassing look. "It will be a team effort. The more of us who get out there and search, the quicker we can be on our way."

Guttman exhaled explosively. "I'm not going out there to search the hull."

"Shut it, Guttman," said Becker. "We're guests on the ship, and like everyone else, we will contribute. Captain Maelyn has every right to request this of us."

Guttman's mouth formed the word "Captain" as if he'd never said it before. Then he shook his head and turned away.

"I'd like to help, Captain," Vonya said.

Maelyn frowned. "I didn't think Servitors were equipped to go on spacewalks."

"Not normally, but it sounds to me as if you need all the help you can get. I'm sure if I partnered up with someone—" Vonya said.

No sooner had the words escaped her lips that Guttman spun around. "She can partner with me. I'll keep an eye on her."

Quinton heard Oscar voice the same. He then glanced at Simon and saw the glint of anticipation at being partnered with Vonya.

"Gentlemen," Maelyn said, "I believe I overheard you speak about your preference to work alone. I think if you were out there with Vonya, you'd be too distracted, which negates the purpose of checking the hull," she said and looked back at Vonya. "You can help monitor our progress from inside the ship, along with Kieva."

Kieva smiled encouragingly at Vonya, who returned it in kind. "Come with me to the bridge, and I'll show you around."

Quinton glanced at Simon and noticed he was watching Vonya walk out of the cargo hold. His eyes had slid toward her lower back, but when he saw that Quinton was watching him, he immediately averted his gaze.

"What's a Servitor? And why was her skin purple?" Quinton asked. His question snatched the others' attention back to him. Becker's gaze narrowed, as if he'd just realized that Quinton was even there. "She looks human, but is she human?" Quinton asked.

"My God," Becker said, "you're a fossil. No, scratch that, you're just ignorant."

"I'm not the one standing there with my tongue hanging half out of my mouth like some beast in heat," Quinton replied.

Becker lifted his chin, and his lips formed into a smirk. "Already forgotten what it's like to be a man, I see."

Quinton stepped toward him. He knew he shouldn't let Becker get under his skin, but he was going on pure reaction in that moment. All he wanted to do was throw Becker through a bulkhead wall.

"That's enough of that," Maelyn said. She didn't raise her voice, but it carried a command authority that pierced his anger.

"Careful now," Becker said, goading him on. "I wouldn't want you to lose sight of what you are."

Quinton stood there. There were no telltale signs of the anger he was feeling inside. There was no explosive intake of breath or surge of adrenaline, but he yearned to knock that smug look off Becker's face. He was positive he could get there before any of them could react. There had to be limits to the ship's suppression systems. After all, he didn't have a weapon.

Maelyn turned toward Becker. "You're not helping. Are we going to have a problem?"

Becker stared at Quinton for a few more moments before turning his gaze toward Maelyn. "Of course not. I'm a professional. I'll take Guttman and Oscar, and we'll check the port bow area and work our way around." Becker gave her a small two-finger salute and then left the cargo hold.

"I'll start at the stern then," Simon said.

Maelyn nodded. "I'll take a group of drones and check midships. It shouldn't take us more than six or eight hours to do a thorough check."

"I might be able to cut down on some of that time," Quinton said.

Her eyes widened. "How?"

"The agricultural unit is equipped with sensors for detecting hidden power sources. It's actually quite sensitive and should be more than up to the task," Quinton said.

Maelyn frowned and looked as if she was trying to think of a way to decline his request without insulting him.

"I've been in the vacuum of space before. The unit can handle it," Quinton said. He felt an urge to prove that he was useful, like he had something to contribute. He didn't want to be idle.

"The unit can handle it," Simon said.

"All right, but you stick with Simon and stay away from Becker and the others," Maelyn said.

"Would it really be so bad if they were somehow launched into space and we couldn't rescue them?" Quinton said.

He'd hoped that Maelyn would be amused, but she wasn't. Instead, she left the cargo hold.

"Does she not like jokes?" Quinton asked.

Simon led them to the other side of the cargo hold, heading toward the stern of the ship. "I think she's concerned that there's a tracker on the ship."

"I get that, but she can't possibly like Becker or the others."

"It's not a matter of approval. You don't understand, but I can tell you about Servitors while we work."

"That would be nice, but about Becker and the others. Will Maelyn let them become a problem?" Quinton asked.

Simon paused partway through the doorway and looked at him. "You're asking if she'll be able to deal with Becker and the others decisively if things get bad?"

"Yes."

"I've known her for a while, and in all that time, she's never hesitated to do what had to be done when the going gets rough. You've met her for all of five minutes. Don't underestimate her," Simon said with a surety that Quinton couldn't question.

"I won't," he said.

Simon nodded and kept walking. Quinton followed.

"Servitors emerged as a species after the Federation Wars. I can't remember which colony world they came from, but they decided as a society to be subservient to other human factions. They modified their appearances, both the males and females."

"They genetically modified themselves to be beautiful?" Quinton asked.

"Yes, but there's more to it than that. They actually have other skillsets. Their reason for being, other than survival, is to bring peace wherever they are. They're pacifists. They seek to please people and believe this is the way to coexist in the galaxy," Simon said.

"They made themselves slaves? Are they owned?"

"No, they do have a choice, but they are bound by strict rules. They will never disclose the secrets of whomever they serve. They can be very insightful and make good advisors and confidants. If Vonya abandoned her employer before her contract was up, things must have been pretty bad. They might be subservient to other species, but they will run away if they feel that their life is threatened," Simon said.

"Yeah, but to genetically alter yourself so . . . I mean, the purple skin and all that looks great, but it just seems a little extreme," Quinton said.

Simon snorted. "If you think that's extreme, wait until you see some of the other species out there."

"Aliens?"

Simon shook his head. "No, just different variants of the human species. We've taken adapting to the galaxy to a whole new extreme."

"What do you mean?"

"Well, there are some groups that live on asteroids. They can survive with minimal atmosphere and some without oxygen at all. They don't look anything like us anymore, but they can communicate. They're actually pretty good at finding mineral-rich systems."

"What do they eat?"

"I don't remember. The point is that there are a lot of variants of the human race out in the galaxy now. The collapse of the federations caused us to drift further apart and find new ways to survive," Simon said.

Quinton was quiet for a few moments. "And most people blame the Acheron Confederacy for this?"

Simon inhaled and sighed. "A lot of people do, even if they don't talk about it."

Quinton was glad he hadn't told anyone about his Acheron origins. They were anxious enough around him as it was. "But they're just one star nation. It's not like they waged war on the entire galaxy," he said.

They walked into a room where there were several spacesuits off to the side. "No, they didn't," Simon said and walked up to one of the EVA suits. He brought it online. The suit opened at the front, and he stepped inside. "They just enabled everyone else to do it for them with the technology they brought into the galaxy."

Simon looked away from him when he spoke, but Quinton couldn't help but feel that he was talking about PMCs. He didn't know what to think about it, but he certainly didn't regret keeping his origins a secret. He couldn't imagine the others reacting well to that, so he wasn't going to volunteer the information anytime soon.

"Do *you* blame the Acheron Confederacy for how things are in the galaxy?" Quinton asked.

The EVA suit sealed itself, but Simon gave him a long look. "Yes and no."

"Well, which is it?"

"The fact of the matter is that there has been a lot of suffering since the Federation Wars. Planets capable of sustaining life are at a premium, but unless you have a powerful military, you don't stand a comet's chance of flying through a star at holding onto it. Maybe not even then."

"Why?" Quinton said. "Wait, what happened to federation core worlds? They haven't been destroyed, have they?" he asked, unable to keep the rising fear he felt inside from sounding through his artificial voice. Without full access to his memories, the implications were somewhat lost on him, but still, loss of life on such a galactic scale . . .

Simon walked into the airlock, and Quinton followed him. Simon stopped with his hand poised over the airlock controls and turned toward him. "I know this is a lot to take in. You seem to be someone from before the Federation Wars, and you've awakened to a galaxy that's changed considerably. I think it's best if we hold off on this discussion for the time being while we look for any tracer beacons on the ship."

Quinton knew he was being managed, and he didn't like it. They were giving him information piecemeal, and he wanted answers now. He needed to figure out who or what had sent out that activation signal. And what was even more important than that was *why* they'd done it. Simon had spoken about rumors of other PMCs being activated. Quinton needed answers, but he also couldn't rush into anything. He'd have to cooperate, and they couldn't go anywhere until they made a sweep of the ship's hull.

"All right, fine. Let's get to work then," he said.

Simon smiled, looking pleased.

"But sooner or later, you and Maelyn will have to level with me regardless of how you think I'm going to react," Quinton said.

The smile faded, and Simon nodded.

THEY SPENT the next several hours making a sweep of the ship's hull. Quinton was able to make the quickest progress because he was tapped into the ship's systems and could readily identify anything that wasn't supposed to be there. However, he was limited, like everyone else, to being in one place at a time. With Simon's permission, he took control of several repair drones, which helped them widen their coverage area. They were nearly done with their section of the ship when there was some sort of suit failure. Guttman was almost jettisoned into space because of a nozzle failure for the propellant. Becker and Oscar saved Guttman. The spacesuit's safety protocols isolated the damaged areas, but Guttman's leg had to be treated in the medical bay.

Quinton and Simon found themselves doing the bulk of the hull checks while everyone else was now inside the ship. Enough time had passed that Becker and Oscar should have rejoined the effort by now.

"This sector is clear," Simon said, his voice coming over the comlink.

"Same here," Quinton replied.

They'd split up and were covering different areas while bypassing the areas that had already been checked. Quinton was starting to think there wasn't any beacon, but they weren't finished.

He accessed the ship's comms systems with the intent of getting the others to come out to help. He saw that Oscar was heading back to a maintenance hatch airlock toward the bow, but where were Becker and Maelyn?

Quinton found them through the ship's life-sign detection sensors that monitored the ship. Vonya and Kieva were on the bridge, but Becker and Maelyn were still in the medical bay.

"He won't lose his leg," Maelyn said. "The damaged tissue will be replaced, but it'll take a few hours."

Guttman appeared to be unconscious inside a medical capsule.

"Nozzles don't just fail like this," Becker said.

"What are you suggesting?"

Becker stepped toward her. "I'm suggesting that that *thing* out there tried to kill him."

The only person on the ship Becker referred to that way was Quinton.

"He's been with Simon the whole time."

"Come on, Maelyn, you can't believe having a PMC running around is safe. Do you have any idea what they're capable of?"

"In fact, I do," Maelyn replied. "I checked the suit's systems, and it registered as a failure. No outside tampering occurred. Maybe you think Quinton somehow teleported to where Guttman was located and just yanked out the propellent nozzle assembly. Surely one of you would have seen that. Plus, there would be evidence of it on the suit." She tilted her head to the side. "There wasn't any."

An accident happened with Guttman's suit, and Becker's first thought was that Quinton tried to kill him? Guttman wasn't his favorite person by any stretch of the imagination, but murdering him was something else entirely. He'd joked about it, but he hadn't actually meant it. Not much anyway.

Becker and Maelyn left the medical bay.

"There's something you're not telling me. You don't seem surprised about encountering a PMC," Becker said.

Maelyn kept walking and didn't respond.

"Come on, we've got to work together. It doesn't cost you anything to tell me what you know about PMCs," Becker said, and Maelyn stopped. His tone was smooth, and they were standing close together in the corridor.

Maelyn regarded Becker for a moment. Quinton saw she had a pleased tilt to her mouth. "There have been rumors of others."

"Rumors," Becker repeated.

"Yes, rumors. Someone is doing this."

"Who?"

"I don't know, and we might never find out."

"Then what's your plan?" Becker asked, stepping closer to her.

Maelyn's mouth opened and she pressed her lips together. Becker leaned in and Quinton felt like his head was going to explode. Then Becker cried out and jerked away from her, shaking his arm. Maelyn held a palm stunner.

Becker shook his head and then grinned. "Can't blame a guy for trying."

Maelyn smiled. "This isn't going to happen."

Becker crossed his muscular arms in front of his chest. "You don't like what you see?" Maelyn glanced at his chest. "I can be pretty persuasive."

She chuckled a little. "Of that, I have no doubt. My plan is what I've already told you. Quinton is able to unlock tech that's been off-limits since the Federation Wars. I need that."

"Oh yeah, for whom?"

"That doesn't really concern you now, does it?" Maelyn asked and then said, "You're out of Crowe's Union and you want to start your own. Helping me can go a long way toward helping you achieve that."

"That's what you keep saying, but until I see it, I'm not going to accept anything at face value."

"Fair enough," she replied.

"But having that thing running around—it can turn on us at any time. It can seize control of the ship's systems before we have a chance to stop it. I don't see why we can't disable it—"

Maelyn shook her head, and Becker stopped speaking. "Even if you were to disable him, you'd effectively kill him, and we wouldn't be able to access his ESS. They go dormant forever. It's some kind of safety protocol."

"And you've seen this for yourself?" Becker asked.

"No, but do you really want to chance it?"

Becker was quiet for a few moments. Then he unfolded his arms, and there was a hardened glint to his gaze. "If it's between him and us, then it's going to be him. PMCs have caused enough problems."

"Why, Becker," Maelyn teased, "I didn't think such a cold-hearted salvager cared about things like that."

"I know what's been done, and the only way it stopped before was thanks to the Sentinel fleets."

"Sentinels aren't any less dangerous than PMCs. Quite the contrary."

"No, but they also stabilized the galaxy. As long as we stay out of their way, they'll leave us alone. That's the way it's always been."

"That's no way to live," Maelyn said.

Becker snorted. "Do you think you can take on the Sentinels now? Is that why you want this PMC around?"

"Hey, are you done here?" Simon asked.

Quinton was so startled that he severed his connection to the ship's security systems and didn't get to hear Maelyn's response.

He looked at Simon. "Yeah, this area is clear."

Simon nodded. "Good, same for me. We've got a few more sections to check, but I've been meaning to ask. How is the power regulator holding up? Is it still stable?"

"Power levels are holding for now," Quinton replied.

They continued onward. At least he knew why Maelyn was keeping him around. They needed him alive in order to access the ESS. It made sense, but he didn't understand anything they'd said about these Sentinels. He needed to find out as much as he could about them.

Simon began asking him more questions, and Quinton thought the young man was just trying to break up the monotony of the task they'd been given. Then Maelyn contacted them both, saying that they were coming back out to help with the search. Quinton needed to keep an eye on all of them. He wasn't sure if Becker had been convinced to go along with Maelyn's plan, and he would need to be prepared for it.

"Radek, have you made any progress analyzing the secondary protocols for the lockout?" Quinton asked.

"Still working on it. I will alert you once my analysis is complete," Radek replied.

Quinton engaged the bot's power detection systems and kept searching the hull.

16

After an extensive sweep of the entire hull of the ship, they found no tracking devices of any kind. Given the amount of time it had taken, Quinton was disappointed with the outcome. On the other hand, it had felt good to actually be doing something that wasn't life-threatening, although that concept was a bit of a misnomer where he was concerned. His power core continued to degrade despite being connected to the power regulator Simon had put together for him, though the power regulator did ensure that the agricultural unit's power core was connected to a readily available power supply contained in the box attached to his back.

"What are the current levels now?" Simon asked.

"30 percent and holding. I'll let you know if there are any changes," Quinton replied.

They'd made several space jumps, but Maelyn had not taken them to another habitable system. These were shorter space jumps, which allowed for quicker recharge times for the jump drive.

"Okay, where were we?" Simon asked.

There wasn't much they could do for the agricultural unit except finding a replacement power core.

"Genetic modifications," Quinton said.

Radek hadn't come up with anything insightful into the lockdown protocols and advised Quinton to try functioning as he usually would. He chose not to remind the VI that functioning normally would have required full access to his ESS.

"It's not as simple as that because of the side effects."

"Like what?"

"Sterilization, for one," Simon replied. "Or a complete loss of empathy."

"What good would that do?"

"The loss of empathy was intentional. The Sparns thought that if they could enhance their logical deductive reasoning, they could adapt to environments others didn't want," Simon said.

Quinton felt the vapid sensation of wanting to frown in thought, which the agricultural bot couldn't do. He found that he really missed being able to mirror the micro-expressions of the people around him. It had been a distraction to his thoughts, leaving him feeling less than what he should be feeling.

Maelyn walked into the galley, which had high countertops and stools for people to sit on. Simon was sitting on one of the stools, eating while Quinton stood there. He no longer experienced a sense of exhaustion, but sitting down and enjoying a meal would have lifted his mood.

Maelyn came over, carrying a cup of tea. She looked at Quinton. "What's the matter?"

"I was just trying to remember what the last thing I ate was," Quinton said.

Simon snorted a little and then frowned. "Can you remember?"

"No. I guess it's not essential," Quinton said.

"Or it's just Radek's way of looking out for you," Maelyn replied and sipped her tea after she blew on it for a moment.

"What kind of tea is that?" Quinton asked.

"It's from the Mozeyian Outpost. They get it from somewhere else . . . I can't remember where exactly," Maelyn said.

"Do you like it?"

"I wouldn't be drinking it if I didn't like it."

"How would you feel if something was controlling the knowledge of whether you even liked that tea. It might be mildly annoying at first, but then multiply that feeling by infinity, and then you'll understand how I'm feeling right now," Quinton said. His anger had sprung from nowhere.

Simon's eyes widened, and he looked at Maelyn and shook his head a little.

"Just . . ." Quinton said, holding up his hand and then bringing it back down to his side because the gesture could be interpreted by the ship's internal countermeasures as threatening. "Just don't," he said and stepped back. "Don't do that thing where you try and share some kind of unspoken conversation."

He turned around and walked out of the galley. Becker and Guttman were in the corridor.

"Careful now," Quinton said, shoving his way past them. "I might lose control."

He kept going without a backward glance. There was only so far he could go on the ship, but he just wanted to take a walk, even if it meant not having the physical release that came from moving actual muscles. At least he could see that he was moving, and perhaps his mind would use that to trigger some kind of release to mimic the endorphins that came from moving.

Simon had become his unofficial caretaker, and he was doing a great job, but Quinton didn't like being managed. He wasn't helpless. It wasn't supposed to be this way. He couldn't remember what he was thinking when he'd become a PMC, but this wasn't what was supposed to happen. He wasn't supposed to be brought online like this.

"Hey, hold on a minute," Maelyn said, running to catch up with him.

Quinton wanted to keep going. Some small part of him liked the idea of Maelyn chasing him, but he knew that was foolish. He'd already made enough of a fool of himself, so he stopped.

"It looks like you need to blow off some steam," Maelyn said.

"A new power core is what I need."

Maelyn nodded. "Our next jump is going to take us to the Mozeyian Outpost. It's an out-of-the-way trading outpost that might have what we're looking for."

Quinton stopped himself from making a hasty reply. "I didn't know that."

"Yes, I know. That's what I was coming to tell you."

"Well, I appreciate it."

"You know we have a weapons area. Do you want to get in some target practice?"

Quinton cocked his head to the side and regarded her. "You're handing out weapons now?" he asked.

Maelyn chuckled. "Only with target ammo. Nothing that could pierce the hull. Still, the sensation is the same," she said while taking a few steps ahead of him and turning around. "Come on, you might like it."

Quinton followed, and she smiled. "I don't know if it's going to help," he said.

They walked together.

"It might. I bet you're a good shot," Maelyn said.

"Why would you say that?"

"Since you have no knowledge of the Federation Wars, you must precede them. The earliest PMCs were taken from among military personnel. Regardless of which federation you served, I think it might help trigger more access to your ESS," Maelyn replied.

"It doesn't work like that," Quinton said. "My access to the ESS is limited because of this body. It's a resource issue and not a hidden-connection problem. Also, the gaps in my knowledge could be just that—gaps. The VIs are managing data access while balancing what I need to continue functioning."

Maelyn led him through a series of corridors that came to an open cargo hold. It was a long, narrow space. On the wall were several lockers. The doors on them opened at the same time, revealing an assortment of handheld weapons, but Quinton gravitated toward the assault rifles.

"Maybe it's a bit of both," Maelyn said. She walked toward a hand blaster. "Regardless, it might be fun. I come down here sometimes. It helps."

"Helps you cope with your worries and your fears?" Quinton asked.

She arched a dark eyebrow toward him. "Something like that."

Quinton was sure it wasn't anything like that.

He stayed outside the danger zone while Maelyn walked toward the entrance. She checked her weapon, and Quinton saw that she'd activated it. She pushed a button on the console in front of her, and the floor retracted. Beneath the opening was a subfloor that sported multiple barrier configurations. Some were hardly big enough to provide cover, while others were floating platforms.

Spherical combat drones flew in from the other side and took up positions throughout the course. Once they reached their designated area, a holo-image surrounded the drones, making them appear like soldiers in combat armor.

Maelyn sprinted toward the first barrier, firing a few shots from her weapon as she went. The combat drones immediately took action. They fired their weapons in quick bursts of suppressing fire meant to herd her, but she vaulted over the nearest barrier and dashed toward one on the right. Green bolts fired from her hand blaster, and she took out two combat drones. Once they'd been hit, the holo-images disappeared, and the drones dropped to the ground.

The combat drones quickly adapted their tactics and began working their way around to flank Maelyn.

"Anytime you're ready to join in, rookie," Maelyn said.

Quinton hastened toward the entrance and checked his assault rifle, setting it to three-round bursts. It wasn't an energy weapon. Instead, he preferred something that fired actual combat darts, even if they were just for target practice. He hadn't been aware of the preference until he'd selected the weapon. Maybe Maelyn was right about him.

Quinton ran toward the first barrier. A group of combat drones broke away from Maelyn and headed toward him. The agricultural bot wasn't exactly small, nor was it designed for combat, but it was agile. He darted out from cover and fired a few bursts at the drones with deadly accuracy, the ease of which surprised him. Recognizing the new threat, more combat drones were working their way toward his position.

Quinton glanced across the course and saw that reinforcements had arrived and were pressing toward Maelyn.

This is what she does to blow off steam?

He had the rifle, but he needed the high ground. He crouched and scrambled over to another barrier and was greeted with a barrage of weapons fire from the combat drones. Maelyn fired her hand blaster at the group of combat drones, causing them to cover their flank. Quinton used the distraction to race toward the elevated platform. An energy bolt clipped his thigh but didn't do any damage.

The assault rifle was strapped across one shoulder, and Quinton let it fall while he raced toward the elevated platform. He leaped into the air and grabbed the edge, then hoisted himself up, rolled away from the edge, and grabbed his rifle. He immediately started firing on the drones, cranking up his frame rate as time slowed down around him. He quickly scouted where the combat drones were located and tried to come up with a firing solution that would swing the odds in their favor. There were only two of them, and the sheer number of combat drones would overwhelm them eventually. The floor was littered with the drones they'd taken out. Quinton looked at them and saw that they weren't offline. They were still operational but in strict adherence to the rules of the simulation. He opened a comlink to them and took control.

He'd only cranked his frame rate up to about 45 percent, which meant that combat drones were coming toward him, and the glowing bolts from their blasters were even now blazing a path toward him. Quinton dove for cover as his frame rate returned to normal. He'd managed to take control of twelve combat drones that both he and Maelyn had taken out, and he reassigned their targeting protocols so they'd attack the other drones. Seemingly all at once, the defeated combat drones reactivated and flew up into the air, their weapons taking the others by surprise. The combat drones were thrown into complete disarray because they weren't supposed to attack other combat drones. More of them were taken out, and Quinton quickly recruited them. At some point, Maelyn stopped firing her weapon and simply watched as the drones "killed" each other until there were only his minions on the course.

Quinton stood up and surveyed the battlefield before leaping to the ground as Maelyn walked over to him. He relinquished control of his combat drone attack force, and they sank to the ground.

"Nice trick," Maelyn said.

"Thanks. I just came up with it," Quinton replied.

He heard someone clapping and turned to see Becker and Simon at the entrance.

"This is what you do for fun?" Quinton asked Maelyn.

"Sometimes. It's good to keep active, but I have to admit it usually lasts longer."

They headed back toward the entrance. Becker regarded Quinton for a few moments.

"You took control of the combat drones that had been shot down," Simon said. "Isn't that cheating?"

"If you're not cheating, then you're doing it wrong," Quinton replied.

Becker shook his head and looked at Maelyn. "Kieva says we're approaching the jump point."

"We'll be right there," Maelyn said.

Becker eyed her for a few more moments and then left.

They returned their weapons to the locker, and Maelyn looked at him. "Your reactions are really fast. It's almost as if you knew where the drones were heading before they got there."

"I'm able to adjust my perception of time."

Simon's eyes widened, and he grinned. "You can increase your frame rate?"

"Yes," Quinton replied.

"That's amazing," Simon said and looked at Maelyn. "He can adjust his frame rate, and his perception of time can either quicken or slow down." He looked at Quinton. "But isn't that resource intensive?"

"It is," Quinton agreed. "Without the power regulator, doing it would drain my power core."

Simon nodded. "That makes sense."

"I wonder what kind of soldier you were," Maelyn said.

Quinton had the strange sensation he'd get when trying to frown. "I don't know if I *was* one."

"You can't be serious. You certainly weren't a civilian, not with the way you handled the obstacle course. How do you feel?" she asked.

Quinton considered what she'd said for a few seconds. "I guess I feel better. I like doing something rather than waiting for this body to give out."

"Speaking of which," Simon said, "The Mozeyian Outpost should have what we need."

"Let's go to the bridge and find out," Maelyn said.

She headed for the door, and Quinton called out to her.

"Thanks for doing this," he said.

Maelyn regarded him, but there was something warm in her gaze. She nodded and walked through the doorway.

17

THE SHIP JUMPED into the star system where the Mozeyian Outpost temporarily resided. Maelyn had called everyone to the bridge.

"Why does the outpost move around from place to place?" Quinton asked.

"A couple of reasons," Simon replied. "Mobility allows for more salvagers and traders to use the outpost. It's also an information hub since outposts like Mozeyian draw in many frequent travelers. And last, but not least, it's more secure not to dwell anywhere for long periods of time."

Quinton looked at the main holoscreen. The video feed showed a massive space station that had taken up residence central to the system. It was close enough to the inner planets that it made resource acquisition easy enough for smaller ships to make salvage runs but was far enough away from the star's gravitational field to allow it to make an FTL jump.

"There're actually a dozen jump drives that have to be synchronized in order to ensure a successful jump," Simon said.

"How long have they—"

"You couldn't pick somewhere less conspicuous than here?" Becker asked Maelyn.

Quinton and Becker had been playing this game where they chose the most opportune moments to cut the other off in mid-sentence. It was irritating, but Quinton refused to show his frustration. He'd wear out the veteran salvager first.

"Feel free to stay aboard if you want," Maelyn said.

Becker shook his head.

"It's not ideal, but we have the best chance of finding a replacement power core here. We also need to resupply. After that, we'll plan our next steps," Maelyn said.

"The outpost is huge. Finding what we need is going to take forever," Guttman said.

"We'll need to split up, but it shouldn't be that difficult," Maelyn said. "Once we register with the docking authorities, we'll get access to their vendor systems. Then it's just a matter of narrowing down our search."

Becker shook his head again. "By now, Crowe will be monitoring for activity that has anything to do with our PMC friend here."

"You think Crowe somehow knows that my power core is failing and we need to replace it? That's a bit of a stretch, don't you think?" Quinton asked.

Becker pressed his fist against his mouth and puffed out his cheeks. "There is so much wrong with what you just said that I hardly know where to begin."

"It's still a stretch, but I'm sure if you continue to smash rocks together, you'll soon have a whole set to play with."

Becker glared at Quinton.

"Not Crowe," Simon said, drawing their attention toward him. "It's his advisor," he said while snapping his fingers, trying to remember. "Nate Carradine."

Becker nodded, and Guttman did the same. "Carradine probably figured out what he was," Becker said, gesturing toward Quinton, "before we got off the station. He would have reviewed all the video logs we had and has probably narrowed down the type of robot."

Simon looked at Maelyn. "All it would take would be a few enhanced images for a VI to recreate a model to identify Quinton. He wouldn't know about the power core, but if we're looking for replacement parts . . ."

"Crowe knows we have a PMC. He'll send out scout forces, and an outpost like this would be high on his list," Becker said.

"Yeah, but the Mozeyian Outpost moves around quite a bit to throw off regular traffic-tracking by people like Crowe or even the Collective. Don't get me wrong, they still conduct business with anyone who's willing to trade," Maelyn said.

There were a few moments of silence while they regarded each other.

"So we move fast," Quinton said. "I can access the outpost's systems easy enough and find what we're looking for. Then we just—"

"No!" Simon said and was quickly echoed by Maelyn and Becker.

That irritating frowning sensation registered itself on the agricultural unit's internal systems, and Quinton ignored it.

"Was it something I said?" he asked.

"Let me answer this," Simon said and looked at him. "Sorry about that, Quinton. You need to be careful, or you'll give yourself away. Most systems have better detection for unauthorized access."

"Yeah, but there are ways around that," Quinton said. He'd been accessing ship systems since he'd come on board. It wasn't particularly difficult, and no alarms had been tripped.

"I know there are," Simon said and rubbed the side of his neck, which made that soft scratching noise of fingers scraping the stubble of a few days' worth of beard growth. "We talked about the Federation Wars, but what you don't know is that during those wars, PMC-enhanced ships and weapons were used. These weapons systems, partnered with VIs, made them much more destructive than anything before. As the war went on, PMCs were used to take control of enemy installations wherever they were. In response to this, safeguards were put into place to help detect unauthorized access."

"Okay, but I still don't see what the issue is if I access the outpost's systems," Quinton said.

Becker exhaled forcefully. "You see, this is what I'm talking about," he said to Maelyn and the others, then looked at Quinton. "It always comes back to what you are. Constructs like you are the reason why the Federation Wars were so destructive in the first place. On top of that, most of them went insane, which made everything pretty un-fucking-stable. Get it now? There are systems in place to detect and safeguard against anything you try."

Quinton glanced at the others and then looked at Becker. "One, I'm not insane. Two, what do you mean by everything?"

"He literally means everything," Maelyn said. "Entire federations and star nations were toppled and scattered during the wars."

"What! That can't be right. There were risks in becoming a Personality Matrix Construct, but there were safeguards—stars. That's what the VIs were meant to do," Quinton said.

"Yeah, well somewhere along the line, they failed, and that's when things got worse," Becker said.

The agricultural unit was intended to cultivate exotic plant life, but those same systems were highly attuned to other living creatures. Quinton was able to see the biometrics of everyone on the bridge—most notably their level of agitation, even if they were temporarily working together for a mutual gain.

"What else? Tell me the rest of it," Quinton said.

Becker began to speak, but Maelyn cut him off. "Shut up. I'll do it, thank you very much," she said. Becker rolled his eyes, and Maelyn looked at Quinton. "Okay, look, we don't have time to go into the minutiae here, so this is going to be high-level. The galactic sectors had already been fighting for many years when the PMCs began to change. No one knows how it began. Reports are fragmented and, in some cases, unreliable. What we do know is that remnant militaries joined together to deal with the new threat," she said and paused for a moment before continuing. "You've heard us mention Sentinel fleets?"

"Yes," Quinton replied. "It's on my list of things to ask you about."

"They were created in response to the rogue PMC attack forces," Maelyn said.

"Rogue PMCs? What does that even mean?"

"They were the ones who went insane. Their safeguards didn't work. Millions died. It's what's going to happen to you," Becker said, and something ugly flickered far back in his eyes.

Quinton turned toward him, clenched metallic fists rising. "I'd be careful if I were you," he said in a quiet, deadly tone.

"Hey," Maelyn said, "look at me," and Quinton turned toward her. "You asked, remember. The fact is, Becker's right. There were large numbers of PMCs who went insane and just weren't human anymore. The safeguards *did* fail. Not all of them, though, but we're getting sidetracked. The Sentinels were created to fight the PMC fleets."

"But what are they?"

"They're a combination of VIs and PMCs, but with many more controls in place. Certain behavioral modifications were removed to make them obedient."

"Obedient!" Quinton shouted. "You mean they enslaved the Sentinels?" He spun around, his gaze taking them all in at once.

"Yes," Maelyn said, and he turned back toward her. "Yes. They were enslaved. They were the answer to a very dark time in our galaxy's history."

Quinton leaned back. "You're looking for a way to do the same thing to me," he said, taking a few steps away from them. "I almost fell for it too. I was willing to go along with it."

"No, that's not the plan," Maelyn said.

Quinton was constantly aware of all the ship's systems, including how they interacted and where their access ports were. They'd been cataloged by Radek and were available for his use. He'd done this in case Becker or any of the others tried to do something to him.

"I'm finding it hard to believe you," Quinton said.

Becker growled. "I should have known this was going to happen," he said and pulled out a hand cannon. It was fully charged and online.

Quinton accessed the combat suppression systems on the bridge, and a stunner bolt singed Becker's hand. Quinton closed the distance on the salvager and slammed him against the wall. "I told you that if you came at me, it wouldn't go well for you," he said and he turned his head toward Guttman. "Take another step and he dies. Then I'm coming for you."

Thick metallic hands squeezed Becker's shoulders, and he involuntarily cried out.

A stunner bolt struck Quinton's side, and a barrage of warnings appeared on his HUD. He wobbled on his feet for a moment.

"The next one will fry the power regulator," Maelyn said. "Now, put him down."

Quinton turned his head toward her. Gone was the pleasant, amicable, beautiful face. In its place was a hardened ship captain who meant what she said.

"Don't make me do it," she said. "I know you're in the system, but so am I."

Quinton turned back toward Becker. The salvager's hardened gaze was all anger, with the promise of retribution. Then Quinton dropped him to the floor and backed away. He walked toward Maelyn, ignoring Becker, but he monitored both of them through the ship's security systems.

"He threatened me," Quinton said.

"Indeed, he did," Maelyn replied.

"You can't trust him," Becker growled.

"The only thing that's not safe around here is you. If you want, I can leave you on the outpost. Do you want out?" Maelyn asked. She looked at Becker, Guttman, and Oscar in turn. They were silent. "I didn't think so. Next time you do something like that, our deal is off and you're off this ship. Do you understand?"

Becker clenched his teeth and looked at Quinton. "Fine."

"Don't mention it," Quinton said. "Next time, you'll have to be quicker."

Becker's mouth twisted into a partial sneer, and then he nodded a little.

"So, these Sentinels are still around?" Quinton asked.

Maelyn nodded. "Yes, they are."

"I thought the Federation Wars have been over for a long time now," Quinton said and looked at Simon for a moment. "Why are the Sentinels still around?"

"They're still performing their primary function—hunting down all PMC-controlled systems and class tech and destroying them," Maelyn said.

Quinton knew he shouldn't have been able to feel cold or shiver, but he definitely felt something. The truth was written on all their faces, a certainty that unified them all, even Becker, and it was impossible for him to ignore.

"So Becker's right," Quinton said. "Me being here puts you all in danger from these Sentinels."

Maelyn regarded Quinton for a few moments, her gaze calculating. Then she nodded. "There is always the risk of crossing paths with one of their fleets."

"Why are they still around? Why haven't they disbanded?" Quinton asked.

"Because no one is left to order them to stop. You have to understand that things were fragmenting. Groups were diverging, and people were just trying to survive long enough for the Sentinels to help establish some stability," Maelyn said.

"Yeah," Becker said derisively. "Except for the occasional case of mistaken identity, the Sentinel program worked wonders."

Quinton couldn't think of a snappy reply. He thought that if he had his physical body, he might have felt sick. But all he felt was an enduring numbness devoid of any of the emotions he should be feeling. What was wrong with him?

"Radek," Quinton said internally, "what's happening to me?"

"Emotional spike is being suppressed to keep system integrity," Radek replied.

"Damn it, Radek," he said aloud this time, startling the others. "Just stop it right now. I need . . . I need to feel." There was a rasp to his voice that hadn't been there before. He saw Becker look at the others with his eyebrows raised.

"Radek is his virtual intelligence assistant," Simon said quietly.

Quinton ignored them. He needed to process the information he'd been given, and his emotions were part of that process. He couldn't make smart choices if his emotions were dulled down to meaningless drivel.

"Everyone off the bridge," Maelyn said. "Give him some space. Go on. I'm serious. Get off the bridge now."

Quinton heard the others leave, and he looked up to see that Maelyn and Simon had stayed behind. Vonya lingered in the doorway, looking as if she wanted to say something. Maelyn gestured for her to go, and the Servitor left them.

Quinton tried to catch up with his racing thoughts as they spread out from him like rays of starlight, each one attached to a truth that he hadn't even considered, along with a promise that he wasn't ready to face. He'd woken up to a galaxy that he didn't recognize. He was a man out of time and without his own body. Why had he been brought online at all? What was he supposed to do? He felt the questions stack up, forming a huge wall that he was almost afraid to climb.

"Quinton, are you still with us?" Maelyn asked.

He didn't respond. He couldn't. He was still grappling with the harsh reality that had been thrust upon him. Now he understood Simon's reluctance to go into details. He'd been trying to protect him. Even Becker's contempt was making more sense.

"Quinton," Maelyn said. There was a note of concern in her voice. "Simon, can you do something for him?"

"I . . . I can't. We have to wait for him to respond."

"We can't lose this. There has to be something we can do."

Maelyn came to stand in front of Quinton. Her large blue eyes looked up at him, searching for some sign of life. "You said you couldn't remember anything. What's your full name? I just realized that you never told us. I'm Maelyn Wayborn."

Quinton still couldn't answer. It was as if he couldn't break free of this inner turmoil that surrounded him. As if he were standing in the middle of an explosion engulfed by flames, and the truth burned.

"Answer me," Maelyn said with a little bit of force behind her words. "You have to answer me. What is your full name?"

His name?

A vague impression of the agricultural unit's lack of frowning ability registered and was immediately dismissed.

"Quinton," he said softly, and Maelyn exhaled. "Quinton Aldren."

Acheron Confederacy Navy.

He tried to follow his thoughts to where this knowledge was contained in his ESS, but he couldn't reach it.

"Keep him talking," Simon said.

"Stay with me, Quinton. I can help you find out more about it. About who you are. I promise. I was never going to betray you. You've got to trust me on that," Maelyn said.

Quinton focused his attention on a couple of different things—the sound of Maelyn's voice, Simon speaking in hushed tones, and his own name. Names were powerful things. They anchored people to their identity, and he had his name. That was something that hadn't been kept from him. The inner storm raging inside him dissipated, and Quinton felt more focused and in control.

"I'm not going anywhere," he said. "You can trust me on that."

Maelyn smiled and looked at Simon.

"We were worried that as you learned more about what had happened, it would . . ." Simon said and paused for a moment.

"I know what you were trying to do. You were looking out for me," Quinton said. "But I still don't understand why it's so dangerous if I access the station's computer systems."

"Because the way you access systems is different than if we do it," Simon said.

"That's absurd."

"No, it's not," Simon replied. "Really, it's not. The rest of us have to go through authentication protocols. You can bypass them without even trying. It's part of the subspace comlink transceiver that you adapted."

"I didn't adapt—"

"Actually," Radek said, "it was part of the startup enhancements I made when I brought the agricultural unit online, and it interfaced with the ESS. It's part of the ESS core."

"Never mind," Quinton said to the others. "Radek just explained it to me."

"Good," Maelyn said. "So you understand why you need to stay aboard the ship while the rest of us go to the outpost."

"Uh, what," Quinton said. "Can you say that again?"

"You need to stay behind. We can't risk bringing you onto the outpost station. Too many things could go wrong. Becker's right about that too. Crowe will certainly have people monitoring all the trading outposts in this sector. I never did get access to his network of agents, but the reports are that they're quite extensive," Maelyn said.

"I'm not staying on the ship," Quinton said.

Maelyn frowned. She looked perplexed that he hadn't seen the wisdom of her logic.

"I said, I'm not staying on the ship. There's no way I'm staying behind. It's not going to happen," Quinton said. "Think of some other solution because I'm going to that station with the rest of you."

Maelyn and Simon exchanged a glance.

Simon pressed his lips together in thought. "I might be able to help," he said and looked at Quinton. "A disguise."

Quinton nodded. "That sounds perfectly reasonable. Let's do that."

18

QUINTON LOOKED at himself through the ship's security feed. He wore clothing —tan pants, boots, a shirt, and a long, thick jacket with the hood pulled up over his head. He glanced up at the camera and could see the faint glow of his eyes from within the dark folds of the hood.

He would appear more out of place than if he just went as . . . himself. "Ridiculous. This can't be what passes for incognito. I might as well walk in there carrying a sign."

Maelyn glanced at him and shook her head. "Nonsense. Most people's attention will be on Vonya."

Quinton looked at the Servitor, whose smile lifted her high cheekbones. She still had on a tight-fitting amber-colored shirt with much of her midriff exposed, and an ivory skirt that showed her smooth well-toned legs as she walked.

"You're okay with this? I thought you were going to check in with the other Servitors and get your own transport," Quinton said.

"Of course, I'm okay with this," Vonya replied. "I do appreciate your concern, but you really don't have to worry. I owe a debt to Captain Wayborn in exchange for my accommodations."

He wasn't worried. At least not that much. He just didn't want to wear these clothes.

"I'm sure both you and Toros Becker will dissuade any unwanted attention," Vonya said.

That was the other part of the plan Quinton didn't appreciate. Becker was coming with them. Both he and Quinton were posing as hired security. Quinton was pretending he was a Yezierian. Simon had explained that the Yezierians were from the former Tilion Empire. They'd enhanced themselves through cybernetic implants and exoskeleton replacement limbs. Yezierians hired themselves out, and once in a contract, they remained loyal until the contract was completed.

Quinton was a bit surprised by that last part because, based on his own observations from his somewhat limited interactions with other people, he'd just assumed that the Yezierians would function as mercenaries—no loyalty except for whoever had the most to trade. There wasn't a large population of them, but they were known. All he had to worry about— as if it was just one thing— was whether they'd run into any other Yezierians on the outpost. He doubted they would simply go along with someone pretending to be one of them.

Simon looked at Maelyn. "I wish you'd reconsider."

"I know you do, but the fewer of us going onto the outpost, the better," Maelyn said. She glanced at the others who were staying behind. "I can't leave them alone with Kieva on the ship."

Guttman and Oscar were also staying behind. They weren't happy with the decision either, but both men hadn't protested much after they learned that Becker was on the away team.

"Come on, let's get going so we can get out of here," Becker said, and looked at Quinton. "That is, of course, if there aren't any more outbursts."

"You never know what will happen," Quinton replied.

"I swear, if you give us away—"

"Yes, yes, I know just where the blaster will be pointed."

Vonya looked at them both and inclined her head. Becker's gaze softened a little.

"All right," Maelyn said. "Simon, monitor the info-nets for anything out of the ordinary."

"Will do, Captain," Simon replied.

They flew the ship to the Mozeyian Outpost, and Quinton withdrew his access to the ship's systems. When he had done so, Simon looked at him and gave him a curt nod. Quinton still didn't fully understand how any type of secure detection system could detect PMC access. While they were on their final approach to the Mozeyian Outpost docking platform, he cranked up his frame rate.

"Radek, I can't think of how they'd do it. Do you have anything?"

"Just theories. It would have to be something that we would need to test. But there must be some kind of pattern recognition where the detection protocols categorize and keep track of all data communications throughout the entire system," Radek said.

Quinton had come to rely on increasing his frame rate because it gave him some much-needed time to consider his options. The risk was that he was going to wear out the aged components of the agricultural unit. He tried to use the ability sparingly, but he just needed to think these things through. However, in real time, there would be less than fifteen minutes before the ship docked, and he wanted to have some idea of what he was walking into.

"I understand the theory, but I just don't think it's possible, not without severe degradation. They must be looking for something else. There's no way they can keep track of every single access point on their systems," Quinton replied.

"Perhaps, but how else would it work?"

Quinton felt an urge to sigh but knew he couldn't. If Radek was asking questions, then even the VI was perplexed. "Well, if I was trying to prevent . . ." He went quiet for a moment. "No, that's not correct. Simon and Maelyn never said that they were preventing access. They were simply detecting it, and then alarms would be raised. If the purpose of whatever monitoring systems they're using is only to detect certain types of unauthorized access, then they probably can't prevent it. At least not quickly. They must be looking for a pattern on even standard communication protocols. The first thing that comes to my mind is the ease with which I can access multiple systems."

"Also bypassing security measures."

"It makes sense, but it wouldn't lead to detection because I've been able to bypass any security measures I've found so far. Perhaps they monitor for multiple data connections that exhibit the same type of behavior at the same time," Quinton said, speaking slowly. "But that would mean they would need to be able to determine what's random and what's intentional."

"They must have perfected their method of detection because, according to Captain Wayborn and all the others, it's supposed to be extremely reliable," Radek said.

"I'm not sure how they'd know for sure since there haven't been that many PMCs around, although that fact could be evidence alone for its effectiveness. But there has to be a way we can know for sure," Quinton said.

"I don't think that's possible. What you're asking for is an early warning for an already sophisticated detection mechanism meant to prevent what you might try to do," Radek replied.

"Well, I haven't done anything yet, but I'm not—I need to have the option to access the systems that are around me. I can't simply cut myself off. There has to be some kind of middle ground."

"The highest probability for success would be to only access the system from one entry point at a time. Also, you must adhere to the protocols of the system you're on."

Quinton thought about that for a few moments. "You'll need to help me with that then. Can you do that?"

"It should be possible."

He supposed that this was as close to an affirmative as he was going to get from the VI.

"Has there been any change with the lockout protocols since we learned more about the Federation Wars and the Sentinels?" Quinton asked.

"Negative, but I do agree that these revelations are alarming. You should try to find out more about that."

Quinton must never underestimate Radek's propensity for stating the obvious. "Thank you, Radek."

Quinton returned the frame rate back to normal. Only a few microseconds had passed in real time.

"There's an issue with our clearance," Simon said.

Maelyn frowned for a moment. "Got it. Send out identification again."

"That worked," Simon said.

"What did they want?" Quinton asked.

"The ship identifier was stripped of its name, and I reauthorized it," Maelyn said.

"What's the ship's name?"

"The *Nebulon*."

Quinton nodded and waited.

"We're cleared for final approach to the docking platform," Simon said.

Maelyn led them to the portside airlock. Vonya watched the airlock doors with a bit of wide-eyed excitement. Quinton wasn't excited. He just needed to get a new power core.

"Let's say we do find this power core," Becker said. "How do we replace it without the ESS going offline?"

"The ESS has its own power supply, so I won't be offline," Quinton replied.

"Are you sure about that?"

Quinton wanted to reply that he was, but he couldn't.

"That's what I thought," Becker said.

Maelyn cleared her throat. "We have a list of potential places that will have what we need," she said and looked at Quinton. "Remember what we talked about. It's imperative that you stay out of the outpost's systems unless you use one of the designated consoles."

"I understand."

"Also, try not to overreact," Becker said.

Quinton knew he was being goaded. "To what?"

"Everything that you're about to see. If they're right and you predate the Federation Wars, then some of what you're about to see might . . ." Becker paused with a wide smile. "I'll just let you find out for yourself."

Maelyn rolled her eyes and opened the airlock. They entered the transit tunnel, which had an automated walkway that led toward the check-in counter, where she paid their docking fees.

Quinton looked around and saw that most people looked normal. They were all human. They weren't at all like what Simon had described. Becker watched him from time to time, and for once he was glad the agricultural bot had limited facial expressions.

They entered the transit hub and got onto a tram that took them to one of the Mozeyian Outpost's trading floors. The tram was a single sleek metallic tube that wasn't very long, but it moved quickly through the shaft. The trip was over in seconds, and they disembarked. That was when the freak show really became apparent.

The others started to walk, but Quinton stopped and looked at the wide-open multi-leveled inner sanctum of the outpost. Crosswalks connected the different levels above and below. He saw platforms with counter-grav emitters rise into the air, bringing patrons to the level of their choice. There were covered corridors that led to other parts of the colossal space station as well.

Quinton hastened to catch up with the others. Maelyn led them, Vonya followed, and Becker and Quinton brought up the rear. Their plan that Vonya would be a distraction to everyone they passed was right on the mark. Vonya strode with liquid grace, from her long platinum hair to her slender arms, as if she were a queen walking among her subjects. She occasionally made polite eye contact and gave a small nod of her head in acknowledgment of the people they passed, but otherwise, she followed Maelyn. No one gave Becker or Quinton a second glance.

Quinton looked around at the various storefronts they'd walked by. One thing that was almost immediately apparent to him was the fact that there was hardly anything new. Everything that was being traded was used, as if the galactic residents were living off the bones of the past, creating nothing themselves.

They stopped at one of the smaller storefronts that looked like it had third-hand rejects from some of the other traders. Quinton doubted any of the equipment inside actually worked. Why would anyone trade anything there? He was about to ask Maelyn when she walked in and headed for the counter.

Standing behind the counter were three men who appeared to be clones of one another. Their skin was pasty yellow, with small dark age spots on their bald heads.

"We have a customer," the centermost one said in a voice that was devoid of life and inflection. The other two men looked at them with that same dispassionate gaze.

Maelyn walked right up to the first one. "I have a list of things I'm looking for, and I'm hoping you might be able to point me in the right direction. I'll pay for the information, of course."

"Transmit your list," the man said.

Maelyn did. They'd put together a rather extensive list of things to be purchased, and within it was a power core that should be compatible with Quinton's agricultural unit.

The man quickly examined the list and looked at Maelyn. "First, you transfer credits, and then I will update your list with the appropriate storefronts that should have what you're looking for."

"Should have," Becker said. "For a paying customer, I expect better assurances than that."

The man looked at Becker. "You're paying for our intimate knowledge of the outpost. No one except the actual storefronts has the most accurate inventory of what they have in stock. You always have the option of trying to find what you need on your own, but I'm afraid that option takes the longest and carries with it a significant probability of failure."

"Time is important to us all," Maelyn said. "I've transferred the credits, as you requested."

The man looked over to one of his "brothers," who gave a single nod. Then he brought Maelyn's list up on his personal holoscreen, which immediately populated with corresponding storefronts for everything on the list.

"I've highlighted the storefronts that will have most of what you're looking for. Some of the things on your list are quite specific," the man said. He watched her for a few moments.

"Thank you. I'm sure it will help us greatly."

The man looked down at his holoscreen, made a passing gesture, and the data refreshed on Maelyn's personal holoscreen. She glanced at it for a moment and nodded, satisfied. Without another word, she turned around and walked toward the exit. Quinton glanced at the three men, who watched them with almost lifeless stares that he found unsettling. The whole encounter had felt as if they'd been interacting with people who'd had the life drained out of them. Simon had told Quinton that there were many groups of "humans" that had genetically modified themselves to adapt to surviving in the galaxy, but he couldn't come up with a practical reason why someone would forgo emotion and perhaps empathy in favor of pure logic. He wondered if the genetic modifications could be reversed.

Over the next several hours, they made their way through the outpost. There were more than a few people interested in purchasing time with Vonya. At first, Quinton had assumed that most interests were of a sexual nature, and there was plenty of that, but the vast majority of people desired a consultation for any number of situations. They sought comfort and reassurance that their troubles would lessen over time, that there were worlds left to discover where they could live. People would approach them, their gaze on Vonya, but the Servitor always deferred to Maelyn, who allowed Vonya to speak with them. Even Becker, who was impatient to keep moving, looked on with an expression between the harshness forged from an unrelenting galaxy and peaceful respite, but only for a few moments.

Quinton watched the encounters, wondering why anyone would seek comfort from a Servitor. Vonya had an angelic beauty—from the way she looked to the sound of her voice to the way she spoke. But Servitors lived to serve everyone else in whatever capacity was required. After a few gatherings, it finally started to make more sense. People were searching for an escape. They were looking for hope, but not everyone.

The Mozeyian Outpost had a mixed population of salvagers and mercenaries, as well as the people who hired them. It wasn't a safe place, but there was an order to it where people could conduct their business. The more Quinton observed, the more out of place he felt. It was a strange feeling to walk here, and the surroundings felt like they should have been familiar. The design of the decks, bulkhead doors, and some of the little things like tools, scanners, and even some of the service bots gave Quinton the strange sensation of being both familiar and foreign all at the same time, as if he were dreaming of a place he used to frequent, but it was a place he'd never been.

"It's time for us to move on," Maelyn announced.

Vonya looked around with an apologetic smile and empathy in her luminous gaze. The cluster of people began to disperse.

Quinton looked at Maelyn. "I didn't think they'd leave so quickly."

"It was expected," she replied.

"Captain Wayborn is my employer. She has the final say on how I am to execute my duties," Vonya said.

Quinton glanced at Maelyn, who shrugged.

They resumed their search. They'd been to a storefront that specialized in robot maintenance and repair. To throw off any of the data-sniffers monitoring for inquiries searching for an exact match for the agricultural bot's power core, they'd decided to look for similar cores but nothing exact. They needed something that was compatible, but it was proving to be much more difficult to find than they'd previously expected.

"We're running out of places to check," Becker said.

Quinton had chosen to remain as unobtrusive as possible, which included limiting communication with the others.

"I know," Maelyn said.

She checked her personal holoscreen and frowned. Becker and Vonya moved closer. They began discussing their options.

"The problem is that most of the available power cores are too damn powerful. Even with the regulators, we'd risk overloading his systems," Maelyn said.

His systems . . .

They weren't *his* systems. The agricultural unit wasn't Quinton. The others had the propensity to not make the distinction. Quinton wouldn't allow himself to think in terms of the agricultural unit and longevity. It was an unfortunate set of circumstances that had put his ESS into this robot body and nothing more.

"Can't we find something Simon could modify to keep him running?" Becker asked.

Quinton walked away from the others because he didn't want to listen to them anymore. This wasn't the time or the place. They were partway into a wide-open court with booths in the middle and shops along the edges. The area was filled with people. He put some distance between himself and the others. He hadn't accessed any of the Mozeyian Outpost's computer systems, but he could detect the multitude of comlinks and data feeds in the surrounding area without directly accessing them. The secure systems weren't broadcasting anything, but they were easy enough to find if he really needed to.

Quinton glanced at the others, who were still huddled over Maelyn's holoscreen, discussing their options. He walked over to a nearby storefront that looked filled with . . . a little bit of everything. There was no specialization at all. The storefront was home to everything that didn't have a home, and the equipment didn't appear to be in that great of shape. Quinton stood a few feet outside the entrance and saw that there were more than a few patrons inside.

After a few moments, he decided to enter. As he walked inside, several people glanced in his direction and quickly averted their gaze. Most of Quinton's face was covered by the hood he wore, but they also wore face coverings. The patrons were all armed, some more heavily than others. An older man walked out from behind the counter. The name "Rosevier" appeared near his face on Quinton's HUD. The man must have been broadcasting it.

Three men approached Rosevier and seemed to communicate with him, but without speaking. Quinton tried to listen by raising the sensitivity of his auditory systems, but it was no use. He saw that the group had entered a private comlink session. He glanced at the others inside the store, and they didn't appear to care about the private conversation going on around them. He accessed the storefront systems. They were open to anyone, and he was able to see the private session clearly indicated among the open comlinks. They weren't taking any steps to hide what they were doing beyond not wanting to be overheard. He watched the pattern of data that started out as indecipherable, but then it appeared in clear text.

"What rumors are you talking about?" Rosevier asked.

Quinton glanced around, almost positive that alarms were going to sound at any moment. "Radek, what the hell just happened?" he asked internally.

"It's the translator protocol VI. It can decipher encrypted messages. They're only using a basic form of protection."

"Is this going to alert any detection systems?"

"Not likely. They're using a closed system that isolates them from the outpost's main systems."

Radek's advice had been inconsistently reliable in the past, and he hoped his VI was right this time.

"Happenings on the galactic net. Sentinel activity. Several large salvager operations being more active," Solin said.

"There are always rumors about Sentinel fleet activity. Keep doing what the rest of us do out in the verse. Avoid them, and they'll leave you alone. Engaging them, even to open communications, is to invite trouble the likes of which no one is prepared for, not even the Collective," Rosevier replied.

Solin glanced at his silent partners before turning back to Rosevier. "The price I'm paying you should give me more than what's already common knowledge."

"You paid for the knowledge I can share. I can't help it if there isn't anything new."

"How about something else then? Another query, since the last one wasn't so informative."

Rosevier's gaze flicked toward their holstered weapons, and then he inclined his head once. "Ask."

"Crowe is paying for any leads to a salvager group that stole something from the Union."

"That's it? You're going to have to give me more to go on than that."

"He's particularly interested in an older agricultural bot—something that would have been used on one of the old colony worlds. Have you seen anything like that?" Solin asked.

Quinton turned away from them, pretending he'd seen something interesting on the other side of the shop.

"Have I seen anything like an old robot?" Rosevier said and then made a grandiose gesture toward his surroundings. "Take a look around. I'm surrounded by old robot parts. I've got all manner of cast-offs, pieces that belong to counter-grav emitters," he said and frowned. "Some might even work. Oh yeah, I've got a whole storage area of Jordani emergency docking clamp systems, which is great for shuttles navigating some of those ancient battlefields. That's where the real credits are."

"I didn't ask about Jordani docking clamps," Solin said, stepping closer to Rosevier.

"You don't like Jordani, that's fine. I've got a rare find you might be interested in," Rosevier said, and glanced conspiratorially from side to side. "Acheron made."

Solin's two companions hissed and closed in on Rosevier.

"Calm down. Geez. Everyone hates Acheron, but they made the best tech the galaxy has ever seen, and it's still in perfect working order."

Quinton had been so focused on the conversation that he hadn't noticed most of the other patrons heading toward the exit. There was a loud commotion coming from outside. He peered out but couldn't see anything. Still connected to the storefront's computer systems, he accessed the video feeds that covered the entrance. They were higher up and gave him a better vantage point. There was a heated exchange between several groups of people about five storefronts away. He panned the video feed across the court and saw Mozeyian peacekeepers heading over. They wore black helmets that covered their faces, along with armored mesh suits. Assault rifles were strapped to their backs, and they strode into the atrium with authority. Most were Becker's size or taller.

Quinton looked over to where Maelyn and the others had been and saw that they were surrounded by a group of mercenaries.

The private chat area became disabled.

"There's something going on out there," Solin said.

"Probably time for you to leave," Rosevier said. Solin peered outside but didn't move. "Seriously," Rosevier said. "Competing salvager clans are about to clash. I'm going to have to close up shop while the enforcers sort it out."

Quinton ducked down one of the aisles and opened a comlink to Maelyn. "I'm in one of the storefronts across from your position."

He saw Maelyn's gaze flick toward his location for a scarce moment before she refocused on the person she was speaking with.

"Wallace," Maelyn said, "I already told you I'm going to check in. Don't make this more than what it is," she said and looked over to where Quinton was located, giving a slight shake of her head. She'd left her comlink open so he could hear her, but then she closed it.

Sounds of footsteps came toward Quinton, and Rosevier looked around the corner of the aisle.

"You're not nearly as sneaky as you think you are," Rosevier said. One of his eyes glowed green from an artificial orb.

Quinton stood up, and Rosevier tried to see under his hood. Quinton looked away at the empty store. "I thought I saw something I was looking for," he replied.

Rosevier arched an eyebrow. "Is that so? Was it these used sanitation processors, or was it the private meeting room whose security measures you managed to make a mockery of?"

"You looked like you could use some help with those guys."

Rosevier grinned a little, his cybernetic eye gleaming. "Is that so? Are you some kind of guardian?" he asked and gave him a once-over. "I don't think so."

"You're right about that."

"Well then," Rosevier said and tilted his head toward the exit. "Time for you to leave."

The doors slammed shut, and Rosevier rolled his eyes. "Damn enforcers. Every chance they get they pull that security override to lock everyone down."

Quinton looked at the door, and Rosevier narrowed his gaze at him. "You're not a Yezierian."

Quinton considered denying it for all of half a second, then decided on a more direct approach to the problem. "Need me to prove it," he said, stepping toward the man.

Rosevier shook his head. "Don't do anything rash. Do you think you're the first person to come to this outpost wanting to hide their identity? This whole station is full of people not wanting attention drawn to them. It's why people come here."

Quinton regarded him for a few moments. "So, are we gonna have a problem?"

Rosevier held up his hands but didn't back away. "No."

"Good, then you'll help me get out of here."

"Can't."

"Why not?"

Rosevier frowned. "The lockdown."

Quinton was still connected to the storefront's video surveillance systems. He saw that the enforcers were going from storefront to storefront, opening the doors and making everyone come outside.

Not good!

"Do they normally search the area when they're trying to keep the peace?" Quinton asked.

Rosevier glanced at the door and walked over to the console behind the counter, bringing up the same video feed Quinton was watching. "They must be searching for someone," he said, and he arched an eyebrow toward him.

Quinton closed the distance and locked down the console. Rosevier looked at it, frowning, then lifted his gaze back to him.

"Now, don't do anything stupid," Quinton said.

"They're looking for you."

"I don't know about that, but I'd just as soon not be found."

"How did you turn off my console? Are you . . . All right, what's going on here? How the hell are you on my system?"

"You were the one who made a closed system. I just happened to have needed access to it," Quinton said.

"What do you want?"

That annoying frown-but-can't-frown sensation registered itself on the agricultural unit's systems. Quinton wondered if he could have Radek filter those unhelpful lapses so he didn't have to be aware of them. He couldn't take the time to explain it to Radek now though.

Quinton leaned toward the counter. "I need a new power core."

Rosevier's mouth opened partway, and he snorted. "A power core. Is that all? What kind?"

Quinton opened his personal holoscreen and showed Rosevier the specifications.

The shop owner looked at it and nodded. "That's odd. An old one too."

"Do you have it or something like it?"

"I might," Rosevier said. "For the right price, that is."

How about I don't kill you where you stand, Quinton thought and then chided himself for the harshness of it.

"What do you want?" he asked.

The enforcers were working their way closer. He also saw that Maelyn and the others were still speaking with the mercenaries. Becker looked ready to open fire, and Vonya smiled at everyone. Maybe it was better that he was in here.

"We'll get to that, but first I need to access this console so I can look at my inventory," Rosevier said.

Quinton didn't trust the man. He'd been too quick to seize the upper hand. If he was granted access, then he could raise an alarm, or worse. Quinton decided to find the inventory subsystem and run his own search, but the system was coded with a custom records-management process that he had no hope of deciphering quickly. He came around the counter to stand behind Rosevier and activated the console.

"Don't try anything foolish. I'm not violent by nature, but I'm getting backed into a corner here," Quinton said.

Rosevier gave him a curt nod and gestured toward the console. "Pesky thing, our inventory system. My business partner, Gervais, made us get it so that even if someone infiltrated our systems, they wouldn't be able to figure out what we actually have. The only way to decipher it is up here," he said and tapped the side of his head next to his artificial eye.

"How clever of you," Quinton said dryly. "Now get searching."

Rosevier nodded and accessed the console. A few minutes later, he brought up an image of a power core that closely resembled the one in Quinton's chest cavity. "It looks like I do have something similar to what you need," he said, sounding a little surprised that he'd found it. His eyes scanned the information. "Hmm, this is for older service bot models. I can see why you had so much trouble finding a replacement. The designers made the power core in such a way that you could only get it from the manufacturer. How greedy of them." He regarded Quinton for a moment. "I've got one in back. I can go get it for you, but I bet you'll want to follow me back there."

"I'm not letting you out of my sight," Quinton said and gestured for Rosevier to lead the way.

The shop owner led him to the back and palmed the security panel that granted them access to the storage room. The room was triple the size of the actual storefront, with aisles of freestanding shelving that were packed with various items. Rows of amber lighting lined the shelves, casting a soft glow in the dimly lit storage room.

Rosevier led him down one of the aisles toward the back.

"Where do you get all this stuff?" Quinton asked.

"Mostly by trade. Others are things that Gervais sought out. He'll go out and try to acquire the rare items that spacers are searching for while I handle the day-to-day operations of the storefront."

"Your partner."

"That's right. He's my sister's husband. We've been partners for over fifteen years. Started this business and built it up over the years by being smart and not overextending ourselves," Rosevier said.

They reached the back of the storage room where there was another console. Rosevier activated it.

"What are you doing?" Quinton asked.

Rosevier pulled his hands away from the console and looked at Quinton. "I have to bring the power core up from the warehouse."

"Where's that?"

"It's in the lower levels of the outpost. We all have a warehouse storage area. We use these consoles to deliver our products right to the buyer's ship. Oh, by the way, you'll need to transmit your ship ID to me so I know where to send the power core."

"Yeah, sure, that's not going to happen. I want that power core delivered right here," Quinton said, then added, "Who do you need to contact to get it?"

Rosevier frowned. "No one. It's automated. I can get it delivered here as well. I just thought you were in a hurry."

"Fine," Quinton said. "Proceed."

Rosevier nodded and went back to the console. He navigated through the interface and selected a few of the options. "On its way here now," he said and regarded Quinton for a few moments. "We need to discuss payment."

"I can get you paid."

Rosevier narrowed his gaze. "I've heard that before. No deal," he said and went for the console.

Quinton grabbed his arm and pulled back, and the shop owner's gaze slid toward Quinton's robotic hands. He wasn't even afraid. What would it take to make this guy squirm? He needed to get the upper hand.

"Definitely not Yezierian. No, no, you're something else," Rosevier said, his eyes slipping into a calculating glaze.

Quinton activated the cutting shears from his forearm. The darkened razor-sharp blade sprang from its holder, and he shoved Rosevier against the wall. He pressed the blade against the shop owner's throat. "You're focusing on the wrong thing."

Rosevier waggled his eyebrows once and smiled. "Am I?"

"What's wrong with you. You're not even—"

"Afraid," Rosevier said and grinned. "No, not at all. Endocrine suppression controlled by my implants. It's really quite helpful with negotiations." He frowned in thought for a moment. "Well, that and increased logical reasoning. So . . ."

Quinton cranked up his frame rate to maximum. He still had the power regulator Simon had made, but his power core was down to 23 percent. He couldn't intimidate the shop owner, so he had to think of something else to use as leverage. Strong-arm tactics weren't working, but everyone had a weakness, and he needed to figure out what Rosevier's vulnerability was. The shop owner's pale skin and white hair projected an impression of weakness, but he was clever. Quinton had to out-think him.

His gaze took in the console, and a few thoughts came to mind. Rosevier was business-oriented, almost to fault. There had to be something there that Quinton could use against him. He already had a data connection to the shop's systems. With his frame rate cranked to the max, Rosevier was neutralized, but computer systems didn't suffer from such restrictions. He supposed that if he had better equipment, he could process information faster than the shop's computer system. Regardless, he could still access the information he needed.

"Radek, I need your help."

"What do you need?"

Quinton brought up the accounting records on his data connection. "Can you run an analysis on these records and tell me if there's anything out of the ordinary?"

"Of course, but for future reference, if you just access the information, you can initiate a query on your own, and I will assist," Radek replied.

Quinton's awareness of the accounting records grew to encompass two perspectives—those of the observer and those of the analyst—at the same time. Both perspectives fed each other, allowing for logical leaps that brought him closer to what he needed. Then he found it—oh, did he ever find it.

He returned his frame rate back to normal.

"These intimidation tactics won't—" Rosevier was saying, and Quinton interjected.

"Your partner is cheating you," he said.

Rosevier frowned and cocked his head to the side, as if he hadn't heard.

"Gervais is cheating you. You're partners, right? Split everything down the line fifty-fifty?"

Rosevier nodded. "Yes, that's right."

"Well, he makes, on average, 20 percent more on everything than you do."

"That's impossible. I check every transaction myself."

Quinton stepped back and pulled his blade away from the shop owner's throat. "Look for yourself. There are two sets of ledgers. It's right there on the console. Go ahead. Have a look."

Rosevier looked at the console screen, peering at the data on it. He scrolled through a few pages, and then Quinton blanked out the screen. Rosevier frowned and looked at him.

"Do we have a deal?" Quinton asked. "You give me the power core, and I give you that report. There's fifteen years' worth of data there. Do we have a deal?"

Rosevier looked away and seemed to be considering it. He rubbed his eyes and shook his head, muttering Gervais's name. Then he looked at Quinton. "I'm afraid not. Um, don't get me wrong. This is huge and worth more than an old power core I'd have trouble offloading anyway, but I can't make a deal with you given this," he said, gesturing toward the console. "I'm truly sorry about that."

"You're sorry? What more do you want? I just . . ."

Alerts appeared on Quinton's HUD.

Power regulator . . . disabled.

Power core levels falling.

Twenty percent.

Eighteen percent.

Fifteen percent.

Twelve percent.

Quinton tried to move but couldn't. He looked at Rosevier, who gave him a knowing look. "What have you done to me?"

"I'm afraid you're worth more in trade than doing business with you directly," Rosevier said and inclined his head a little while pressing his lips together. "You can't move. Just a little suppression field that interferes with motor control."

Nine percent.

Quinton stopped trying to move in the hopes that he'd consume less power.

Seven percent.

Quinton began to panic. He knew he should try to conserve his energy, but he was about to go into standby. Rosevier must have guessed what Quinton was. He'd pull out his ESS and sell it to the highest bidder. Then Quinton would be enslaved.

He felt a mental shudder.

Enslaved.

Five percent.

A large panel next to the console opened, and a small storage container was deposited onto the ground.

"Oh, it looks like that power core you need just arrived," Rosevier said. He leaned down and opened the container. Inside was a cube that glowed in a faint yellow. He picked it up in one hand and regarded Quinton for a moment. Then he walked over, casually tossing the precious power core up in the air and catching it, and pushed back the hood covering Quinton's head.

"The suppression field drains that power core you have in your chest."

Three percent.

"There's something else I haven't told you," Quinton said.

Rosevier looked amused. "What's that?"

"Gervais has also been lying to the Mozeyian Outpost finance officer. You haven't been paying the proper fees based on your actual income."

Rosevier's expression faltered. "Then they'll take it up with Gervais."

Quinton laughed. "He's not here, so they'll come after the next best thing—you."

Rosevier's eyes darted from side to side while he considered the implications.

"I don't know as much as you do about this outpost, but my guess is that they take being cheated very seriously, and when they learn about you—"

"Stop."

"Turn off the suppression field."

Rosevier did, and Quinton's power core was holding at only 2 percent. There was no way he could make it back to the ship.

"Now replace the power core in my chest."

"You'd trust me to do that?"

"No, you idiot. I don't trust you at all, but you're all I've got. To keep you honest, I have a timed message waiting to be sent with all the incriminating evidence. And if you get any other ideas, I also tasked your automated delivery system to offload your entire stockpile as a generous donation," Quinton said.

Rosevier narrowed his gaze and sneered.

"You have less than two minutes. Now get over here and replace this thing," Quinton said, opening his chest piece.

Radek went on standby—not that he could actually do anything while the power core was being replaced, but he'd be the first to come back online.

Rosevier regarded Quinton for a few long moments and then nodded. He'd been beaten. All that was left was damage control. "You'll stop everything if I replace the power core, right?"

"I said I would. Now quit stalling."

Rosevier reached inside the agricultural unit's chest piece and initiated the shutdown-and-replace procedure.

Quinton's perception of everything around him went dark.

19

Quinton snapped back into consciousness.

System diagnostic running.

All systems operational.

Upgraded power core operating at 100 percent.

Veris initiation complete.

System startup complete.

Autonomous mode has been activated.

He remembered the last time he'd woken up. The agricultural unit had gone through a startup sequence that exposed a number of broken systems. Some were even critical, but somehow there were enough working that Quinton was able to keep going. This time, not only was the startup sequence quick, but systems were green across the board. He was still in danger, but at least he didn't have mechs hunting him. He couldn't expect to have everything go his way, but it was gratifying not to see a warning about the power core on his HUD.

Quinton raised his gaze and saw Rosevier standing a few feet away.

"I did as you asked. Now do your part," Rosevier said.

Quinton didn't respond right away. The agricultural unit's internal systems were all available to him, which hadn't happened when he'd first awakened. This improvement must have been due to a combination of having a functioning power core and the repairs Simon had done. Even some of the precision rodent-mitigation systems, which had the focused sonic generator, were now available for his use.

"We had an agreement," Rosevier said.

Quinton brought up the subroutine that was set to deliver the incriminating evidence to the Mozeyian Outpost's financial officer. He also accessed the command sequence that would offload all of Rosevier's current inventory. The timer was running out, but he hesitated.

"You were going to sell me," he said.

"I was," Rosevier replied. "Can you really blame me?"

Quinton stormed closer to him. "Yeah, I really can."

"We made a deal."

"We had a deal before, and you double-crossed me," Quinton said and put the countdown timer on the nearby console.

Rosevier's façade began to crack. "Don't do this. You'll ruin me. They'll kick me off the station, and I have nowhere to go. I did as you asked. I don't know who you are, but I think you're a man of honor."

Quinton laughed. "Trying to appeal to my good nature, huh? I think you're getting desperate. I think the moment I stop that timer is when you'll do something foolish."

He brought the sonic wave generator online, and a small cylinder raised from a hidden compartment on his forearm.

"Take your revenge then, but don't ruin everything I've built."

Quinton was taken aback by his reply. Somehow, Rosevier's logic had prioritized his life's work over his own life.

Rosevier's gaze darted to the timer and then back to Quinton. "You're right. You hear me?" he said, his voice rising. "You're right. I was going to—"

Quinton extended his hand and a focused wave of sonic power shoved Rosevier into the wall, hard. The shop keeper crumpled to the ground, unconscious.

Quinton glanced at the console and watched the timer run almost all the way down. Then he stopped the message and the inventory offload command.

A deal's a deal.

He glared at the man on the ground. Rosevier possessed logic to the point of being almost completely dispassionate, but not completely. Did that make him only partially human?

Quinton looked around at the things in the storage room. He needed to prevent Rosevier from interfering with his escape. He'd probably regain consciousness soon, and while slamming him into the wall again would give Quinton a certain amount of satisfaction, he didn't intend to stay there that long. He looked at the console and then walked over to it, accessing the inventory system. The console was unlocked, and it took him little time to find what he needed. When he stepped away from the console, he had the location of a bio-containment system. Rosevier didn't deal only with spare parts but anything from exotic plants to certain types of animals.

On the floor underneath a dark metallic shelf was a long capsule that looked to be large enough to accommodate Rosevier. It would be a tight fit, and Rosevier probably wouldn't be comfortable, but Quinton didn't really care about that. He retrieved the storage container and brought it back over to the console, opened it up, and forced Rosevier's body inside. It was more than a little cramped, but the double-crossing shop owner would live, which was much more than he deserved. Quinton activated the bio-containment protocols, which did a quick analysis of the container's contents, and then engaged the appropriate life-support option to ensure that Rosevier would survive through a short stasis period. He set the wake-up time for seventy-two hours. He should be long gone by the time Rosevier was released. The process was extremely quick.

Quinton opened the wall panel for the automated inventory system. He then lifted the storage container and pushed it into the cargo elevator that was used to transport containers to the warehouse. He selected the coordinates for a shelving unit in the warehouse far away from the exit. When Rosevier regained consciousness, it would take him even more time to find his way out of the building. Then Quinton closed the doors and watched as the cargo elevator disappeared from view.

He felt more than a little bit of satisfaction at extracting a small token of revenge for what Rosevier had tried to do to him. He needed to be more careful. The trouble was that he'd thought he *was* being careful. Now he needed to get out of there.

Quinton walked through the storage room and back into the storefront. He searched for another way out, but the only exit was through the front door. He glanced up at the vent above him, but it was much too small for him to squeeze into.

He pulled his hood over his head and accessed the storefront's video feeds. The enforcers had just walked over to the shop's door. Quinton hastened to the side and hid behind a stack of . . . He had no idea what the stack was. It looked like a pile of haphazard parts, but it gave him more than adequate cover.

The front door opened, and several Mozeyian enforcers walked inside. They called out for Rosevier.

"Activate his personal locator," an enforcer said.

"He's not here. It looks like he's on the warehouse level," replied the other.

"What the hell is he doing down there? Actually, never mind. Send a detachment down there immediately. He might be trying to hide contraband. Let's get out of here."

The enforcers left without checking the storefront at all. Quinton waited for them to move onto the next location and saw that, despite the enforcers' presence, activity in the open area had returned to normal.

Quinton came out from behind the stacks and went to the front door, peering outside for a few moments before opening it. The door split down the middle and pulled to either side, allowing him through. With a determined stride, he headed out into the most crowded area he could find. Then he went to where Maelyn and the others had been, but they were no longer there.

He shook his head. Things had just started going his way. He scanned the crowded area, looking for the others, but couldn't find them. He wasn't supposed to access the outpost's systems, but what choice did he have?

He brought up a list of the public systems that were on hand for anyone to use. He then opened a comlink back to the ship.

"This is the *Nebulon*," Simon said.

"It's me, Quinton."

"Quinton!" Simon exclaimed. "What are you doing?" he asked quickly.

"I don't know where Maelyn and the others are. We got separated."

There was a brief pause.

"We haven't heard from Maelyn either," Simon said.

"I think they're in trouble. The last time I saw them, they were surrounded by . . . Actually, I have no idea who they were. They weren't Mozeyian enforcers —I know that much—but they didn't look friendly either," Quinton said.

"All right, stand by. I'm going to try to reach her," Simon said. "And don't . . . just wait for me, okay?" he said and then added after a few seconds, "Wait a minute, did you find a power core?"

"Focus, Simon. I have a great story about that, and I'm fine for now," Quinton replied.

"Okay, stand by," Simon said.

Quinton glanced around, feeling out of place and that, at any moment, he would draw unwanted attention.

"She's not responding," Simon said.

"I can track her through the comlink."

"No, don't do that."

"Why not?" Quinton asked. "If this is because you're worried about it being detected, then don't be. I haven't been detected yet. I've been careful."

"No, it's not that," Simon said quickly. "You said she was surrounded by some people. If that's the case, then if we try to track her and they detect the signal, it might make things harder for her."

"So what do you suggest I do?"

"I'm trying to think of something," Simon replied. "No, I haven't heard anything yet. I know. I'll let you know as soon as I do."

Quinton assumed someone else had just come to the bridge and Simon was speaking to them. "Who was that?"

"Guttmann," Simon replied. "He's been checking in every fifteen minutes."

Quinton considered finding another biological storage container for Guttmann. Would anyone really miss him if he were gone?

"I think you should head back to the ship. It's what Maelyn would want," Simon said.

Quinton had no idea what Maelyn wanted. She made an outward show of keeping her motivations transparent, but he didn't trust her. He didn't trust any of them. Even if he returned to the ship, what would he do then? Now that his power core had been replaced, he could focus on finding the source of the activation signal or maybe even a better host for his PMC.

What if he just left? He could go back to Rosevier's store and see if there was a ship he could appropriate for his use. He could steal a ship and then he could do what he wanted, but how far would he really get if he did that? The galaxy had changed, and he was still finding his way. He couldn't do what he needed to alone, which meant he couldn't leave the others behind. He had a much better chance of succeeding with them than on his own.

"Quinton, did you hear me?" Simon asked.

"I heard you."

"Good. You should be able to find your way back to the *Nebulon*. Hopefully, by then we'll have heard from Maelyn," Simon said.

"That's not going to work," Quinton said.

He heard Simon sigh through the comlink. "What are you going to do?"

Quinton used the agricultural bot's power sensor to find the camera feeds in the area.

"Quinton?"

"Need a minute," he replied and then muted the comlink. He needed to concentrate. If there were enhanced detection systems capable of noticing what he was about to do, he'd need to get out quickly.

He followed the data connection to the video surveillance system, which cached recent footage before it was uploaded to the main system. He checked the feed from fifteen minutes earlier and saw Maelyn and the others being escorted out of the area.

Quinton began to follow the corridor they'd taken and reactivated the comlink. "I'm going to follow them."

"How?" Simon asked.

"I don't have much time, but the outpost's video surveillance system stores the video feed even after it's been uploaded to the main system. If I wait too long, it'll be overwritten," Quinton replied.

Simon was quiet for a few seconds. "That's . . . That's pretty smart."

"Thanks. I'll let you know when I find them. Oh, and we might need to make a quick exit."

"I'm already on top of that."

"Good," Quinton said and closed the comlink.

He walked through the corridors that connected the large open decks of the outpost. Whoever had taken Maelyn and the others seemed to be making their way toward another docking bay. Quinton quickened his pace, hoping to catch up with them. The last video feed he checked was only seven minutes old, so he wasn't far behind. Each time he checked, he didn't get the impression that Maelyn and the others were actually prisoners. Becker glanced back the way they'd come a few times, but that was it.

Quinton brought up the most recent video feed on his HUD. Becker kept watching their surroundings but didn't look as if he was going to make an escape from their captors anytime soon.

He increased his speed, weaving his way through the crowded corridors to the next open area. He must have reached the central part of the outpost because he'd emerged onto another massive plaza. There were eight crosswalks that connected to the other side. High above, he saw the edges of the semi-translucent shield, along with a wide expanse of the stars beyond. Aircars flew overhead, providing quick transport to the far side of the outpost.

He checked the nearby video feeds and saw Maelyn and the others enter the nearest crosswalk. Checking the timestamp, he saw that he was only thirty seconds behind them now. He hastened over to the crosswalk. Small booths were interspersed along the way, making a direct path across all but impossible. It would slow the others down as well. Most of the peddlers glanced in his direction with a practiced eye capable of determining whether he was an easy mark, but they soon averted their gaze. Quinton supposed that Becker's Yezierian disguise was good for something.

He crossed the middle of the crosswalk, and it was a straight-open shot to the other side. Spotting the back of Maelyn's head, he closed the distance as much as he dared without drawing any notice.

He opened a comlink to Maelyn. "Miss me?" he asked. "I'm a short distance behind you."

The men surrounding her came to a stop, and the rearmost turned toward him. A moment later, Maelyn and Becker turned as well, followed by Vonya.

Quinton froze, unsure what to do.

"Wallace," Maelyn said, speaking to the man nearest her, "I neglected to tell you that we left someone behind."

Wallace looked at Quinton and narrowed his gaze. "You're traveling with a Yezierian now?" he asked while trying to peer under Quinton's hood.

"Not exactly," Maelyn said. "I'm sure you can understand the need for discretion."

Becker cleared his throat. "I already told you that I spotted some of Lennix Crowe's people on the outpost. They're searching for us."

Quinton walked toward them without saying a word.

"That's close enough," Wallace said.

"Low profile, Wallace. Remember?" Maelyn said.

"I told you not to contact anyone, and instead, you called someone from your ship."

Maelyn rolled her eyes. "They sent him to look for me."

Wallace frowned and regarded Quinton for a moment. "How'd you find us?"

Quinton glanced at Maelyn, who gave him a small nod. "It wasn't that hard," he said and turned to address her. "Captain, Simon and the others became concerned when you didn't check in."

Maelyn nodded, and her gaze flicked to Wallace. "I was already on my way back. There's no need for you to provide an escort."

Wallace shook his head. "I have orders from Brandt himself."

Becker shook his head. "We don't have time for this. What difference does it make whether you bring us in or we meet you there? I already told you that Crowe isn't going to just let us go."

Wallace looked unconvinced. "We're on the outpost. There isn't much he can do to us here."

Becker's face deadpanned. "You don't know what he's capable of or what resources he has at his disposal."

"You should listen to him, Wallace. Becker was high up in Crowe's Union," Maelyn said.

Wallace shook his head. "You'll forgive me if I don't take the word of a turncoat salvager. And besides, what could you have done to Crowe that would make him hunt for you here?"

Maelyn regarded him for a few moments and frowned. Then, a klaxon alarm sounded overheard.

"Emergency jump will initiate in thirty minutes. Return to your ships immediately. This is not a drill," a monotone, dispassionate voice sounded after the alarm. The automated message repeated itself several more times.

General activity seemed to increase all at once as people began to leave the area.

"We have to get out of here," Becker said. "An emergency jump means there's an attack force on its way here now."

Maelyn stopped. Wallace's men watched them, looking ready to reach for their weapons if they thought it was necessary.

"From one ship captain to another, you can't ask me to abandon my ship," Maelyn said.

"I won't," Wallace replied. "I'll take you to your ship, and then we'll both get out of here."

They continued. Quinton walked next to Maelyn while Wallace led the way.

"Where did you go?" she asked.

"I was in one of the shops when the enforcers came."

"We got sidetracked by Wallace. We need to get you back to the ship. What's the power core reading at now?" Maelyn asked.

"It's fine. I found a new one."

Her eyes widened, and her gaze slid down to his chest. "But someone would have had to swap it out. You would've gone offline."

"I did, and don't worry about it. The shop owner won't be coming out of stasis for three days," Quinton said and explained what happened.

Maelyn shook her head slowly, and Quinton couldn't decide whether she was more concerned for him or the fact that she'd lose her big payday if something happened to him.

"Great," Becker said. "We got what we came for. Now let's get the hell out of here."

Maelyn opened a comlink to the ship. "Simon, I want you to move the ship to this docking platform. I need it done quickly," she said and was quiet for a moment, listening. "He's here."

Fifteen minutes later, they entered the docking area where Wallace's ship was located, and Wallace received a comlink from his own ship. He glanced at Maelyn for a moment and then closed the comlink.

"The *Nebulon* has taken up position nearby, I assume under your orders," Wallace said.

"That's right. We'll execute a jump once we're away and then transfer back to my ship. Is that acceptable?" Maelyn said.

Quinton admired her instincts. Moving her ship nearby meant that Wallace couldn't simply execute a jump without being followed. Maelyn seemed to be quite adept at neutralizing risks.

"Very well," Wallace said and led them to his ship.

Quinton walked with the others. He expected the patrons on the outpost to question why they needed to leave, but they didn't. They hardly took a moment to acknowledge the change, and business ceased. He was still connected into the outpost's computer systems. Reading the flow of data that traveled at the speed of light was becoming increasingly easy for him, and he could scarcely explain how he was doing it. It was as if he'd gained an awareness of which data streams to follow, and he wondered if Radek had had something to do with it. His VI assistant had been unusually quiet since the new power core.

The Mozeyian Outpost's power systems were being rerouted to the jump drive network and also the outpost's defenses. Quinton didn't know what the outpost had for defense, but whoever was in charge of them must've determined that there was a significant threat. Was Becker right? Did Crowe have warships with enough firepower to threaten the massive outpost?

Quinton glanced at Becker. The salvager wore the concentrated look of one determined to keep moving forward with each dogged step he took.

Wallace turned toward one of the access ramps that led to his ship. Every ship Quinton had seen so far looked to be designed for transporting cargo and defense, and Wallace's ship was no different. There were mag cannon turrets on top, as well as a few below. Their worn-looking barrels indicated many years of service, but there were a few empty turrets where the mag cannons should have been. It looked as if they hadn't been part of the ship's original construction but were an add-on, which meant their armament was less than that of an actual warship. Despite all that, the ship was much like everything else Quinton had seen in the galaxy—battle-worn but determined to survive. The ship might not be as pristine as the day it had launched from the shipyards, but it still had teeth and wouldn't go down without a fight.

They walked up the loading ramp and headed inside.

20

THE INTERIOR of the ship matched the exterior. As he walked the corridors, he noted dingy yellow metallic walls, and yet Quinton couldn't see a speck of dirt. He sampled the air with his sensors and noted that the atmospheric scrubbers kept the air fresh and free of contaminants. The ship was simply old and probably beyond its intended life cycle, but someone had kept it serviceable long past when it should have been scrapped for parts. Given the patchwork he'd seen on the hull, he thought someone must have cobbled together enough working parts to keep the ship serviceable, but he wondered if anyone was building ships anymore.

The loading ramp closed, and Wallace led them toward the center of the ship where the bridge was located. Their armed escorts stayed with them, but Maelyn didn't seem to mind. Becker strode behind her as if their armed escorts didn't matter to him in the slightest. Quinton wondered if it was for show, but perhaps Becker really didn't perceive them as a threat. He glanced at Vonya, and the lavender-skinned beauty smiled at him reassuringly.

The command deck had the standard workstation layout that was at once vaguely familiar to Quinton, though he couldn't remember why. The command chair was occupied by an older woman, who stood up.

"Sitrep, Elsa," Wallace said.

"We just got clearance to decouple from the docking platform, and we can be underway in a few minutes, Captain," Elsa said.

Wallace nodded and peered at the main holoscreen. There was a mass exodus of ships as they fled the outpost as quickly as possible. Quinton spotted the *Nebulon*, which had positioned itself on an intercept course.

"I see the *Nebulon*," Quinton said.

Wallace looked at him and frowned.

"Yes," Maelyn said. "We need to get back to our ship immediately."

Wallace shook his head. "You know I can't do that. Admiral Brandt's orders are that we bring you back to the fleet. Cantos signed off on the orders as well."

"Wallace," Maelyn said.

"I know what you're going to say, but I can't. Not this time. Brandt's orders are clear."

"I understand, but Brandt doesn't know everything," she replied, and Wallace pressed his lips together. "I claim captain's privilege."

Quinton glanced at the others. He had no idea what "captain's privilege" meant, but the others seemed to know.

Wallace regarded her for a few moments and stood up. "Very well, Captain Wayborn. Let's take this to my ready room. Elsa, you have the conn."

"Yes, Captain, I have the conn," Elsa replied and returned to the command chair. "Captain, what about them?" she asked, tilting her head toward Quinton and the others.

"Rosser, take them to the meeting room and keep two men posted outside," Wallace said.

"Understood, sir," Rosser said.

Quinton and the others were escorted off the bridge and taken to a meeting room a short distance away. They were left alone, and Quinton looked at Becker and Vonya. He couldn't help but think they were the extremes of who he could have been stuck with. By all outward appearances, Vonya was calm. She sat down in one of the chairs and closed her eyes as if she was meditating. Becker rolled his eyes and walked to the other side of the room.

"What's captain's privilege?" Quinton asked.

Becker looked at him for a few moments, his thick eyebrows pulled together, and then he shook his head.

Vonya sighed. "Captain's privilege is a courtesy between starship captains whereby they are granted a private meeting to discuss options for peaceful recourse."

"That's new, I guess," Quinton said.

"It's a waste of time," Becker said.

"Why?"

"Because it's just people pretending to be civilized. There's nothing to compel Wallace to let us go," Becker replied.

"Ordinarily, that might be true," Vonya said, "but they're both from the DUC."

"DUC?" Quinton asked.

"Dholeren United Coalition," Vonya replied.

Becker rolled his eyes. "They're a migrant fleet of refugees who dream of a galaxy that no longer exists."

"They work toward peaceful coexistence by welcoming anyone from the old federations to become part of the coalition," Vonya said.

"They're welcome to the galaxy's rejects," Becker said. He checked his weapon and returned it to its holster.

Quinton turned toward Becker. "What the hell happened to you that made you so bitter?"

Becker glared at him and Quinton watched him closely, expecting him to go for his weapon, but he didn't. "None of your goddamn business. Look, we're not friends and we'll never be friends. You're just a means to an end."

Quinton grinned. "I wasn't offering to be your friend, but you look like you have all this pent-up emotion about the galaxy. I figured you wanted to share your feelings. Get some of it off your chest."

Becker's mouth was partially opened. "My feelings," he rasped and narrowed his gaze.

Vonya stood up and walked between them. She moved with a feline grace that encompassed her entire body in such a way that was just pleasing to look at. Even Becker's gaze softened.

"Fine, I'll stop," Quinton said and looked at Becker. "How do you know Crowe tracked us here?"

"I know how he operates. He won't let this go. Not if he knows what you are," Becker said.

"Yeah, but how would he know that?"

Becker sighed. "Crowe has been around for a long time. You don't get to his position by employing incompetent people. Nate Carradine would be able to figure it out."

Quinton remembered the older man who'd been with Crowe on the hangar deck. He barely remembered that the man had been there but had no real impression as to what his capabilities were, so he'd have to rely on Becker's opinion. Despite his own opinions of Becker, the one thing the salvager was not was a bad judge of a situation. He had keen instincts for detecting a potential threat.

"Why go through the trouble?" Quinton asked.

"You don't even understand what you're worth," Becker said and held up a hand. "Now, before you say something stupid, let me finish. You know you can be controlled."

"So you've said. I don't know how, though."

"Neither do I, but Carradine would be able to find out how, and he's loyal to Crowe. I think they've been partners for a long time," Becker said.

"What does controlling me get him?"

Becker glanced at the door, and Quinton wondered if he was looking for a way to avoid answering the question.

"I can start guessing, if you want," Quinton said.

"You'd give him an unrivaled advantage, which is something he needs."

"What do you mean? Why would he need an advantage?"

Becker glanced at Vonya for a moment and then looked at Quinton. "Crowe isn't the most powerful salvager. There are others who are a lot more powerful, and none of them are willing to give up their relative positions and territories."

"Territories," Quinton said.

"Stepping on each other's toes goes with the business, but let's just say that Crowe might have overstepped and brought unwanted attention. That's why he won't let this go. He'll come at you any way he can."

Quinton considered this for a few moments, and Vonya returned to her seat. "Let him try."

Becker looked at the door. "I wish I knew what they were saying."

"Captain Wayborn is quite capable. I'm sure we'll be on our way soon," Vonya said.

Quinton figuratively frowned in thought and checked for open system access, immediately finding several that were available. Wallace didn't know what Quinton could do, so he should be able to listen to their conversation without raising any alarms.

He accessed the ship's systems and brought up the video feed for the captain's ready room.

"I already told you that it's dangerous to bring Quinton to any of the fleets," Maelyn said.

"Because you believe he's an actual Personality Matrix Construct from one of the older federations."

"Yes, either Jordani or Acheron."

Wallace exhaled forcefully. "Where did he come from? Has he been lurking around for a few hundred years?"

"No, he was recently activated, but it's complicated."

"Your propensity for finding trouble never ceases to amaze me. What am I dealing with here?" Wallace asked.

"You're not dealing with anything."

"He's on my ship."

"I told you we needed to get back to my ship."

Wallace rubbed his forehead and dragged his hand over his face and down to his beard. "Geez, Maelyn, stop mincing words with me. He could be in our systems right now."

She smiled a little. "He probably is by now. He's inquisitive by nature, I think. Like I said, it's complicated. None of which I need to delve into right now."

Wallace looked up at the ceiling for a few moments. "Do you really think he's listening to our conversation?"

Maelyn shrugged. "It's not important. No, seriously. Quinton is dealing with certain limitations, which might actually be helping him to retain his sanity."

Quinton's thoughts began to race. He supposed that if he'd been in his actual body, his pulse would have increased, along with a healthy release of adrenaline, none of which applied to his current . . . situation, but his mind was still human, equipped with years of conditioning, along with billions of years of evolution.

Wallace leaned forward. "This is supposed to reassure me."

"You asked for honesty. I'm leveling with you. We don't have a lot of time."

"You intend to bring an unstable PMC that inhabits an agricultural bot back to the migrant fleet. Are you insane? That's beyond reckless."

"Give me some credit, Wallace. That wasn't the plan."

"Oh, so you have a plan. This should be interesting."

"I'm thinking that you could actually help me," Maelyn said. Wallace raised his eyebrows. "I need you to contact Brandt and brief him. Then he can meet us away from the fleet. It'll be safer for everyone."

"I don't even know how Brandt will react to this. He might not want anything to do with it."

Maelyn pursed her lips in thought. "In that case, you'll need to bring Cantos into it. She'll at least listen to reason."

"Reason," Wallace said, and shook his head. "There's nothing reasonable about this. I have half a mind to toss that thing off the ship."

Quinton tried not to take it personally, but every person's reaction to the fact that he was a PMC was to immediately put as much distance as possible between them and him, and it was wearing thin.

"Don't do that," Maelyn warned.

"Do what?"

"Threaten him," she said. Wallace looked up at the ceiling again, which amused Quinton because he was listening and watching them through the comms system, which was located at the console on Wallace's desk. "He'll listen to me, but if you threaten him, there's no telling what he'll do. He's capable of much more than he knows."

He didn't know if Maelyn was building up his capabilities to get Wallace to cooperate or if those were her own opinions of him. She knew he was listening in and still said those things anyway.

"You're playing a very dangerous game, Maelyn," Wallace said.

She smiled and waggled her eyebrows once. "Those are the only ones worth playing. Now, before you say anything else, I have a deal with Quinton. It's mutually beneficial for both of us."

"What kind of deal?" Wallace asked.

"He helps us gain access to technology and resources we wouldn't otherwise be able to access, and we help him get a more suitable body. Ideally, we retrieve his DNA so his physical body can be regrown."

Wallace regarded her for a few moments. "You promised," he began and stopped with a slow shake of his head.

Maelyn held up her hand in a placating gesture. "Some chance is better than no chance at all. Someone activated Quinton. We have no idea who or why. Like I said, we don't even know for sure which federation he comes from."

"Jordani or Acheron." Wallace sighed. "There isn't a good choice either way. What are you going to do when he regains his memories and has full access to his ESS? Have you thought about that?"

"That depends on him."

A comlink opened from the bridge.

"Captain," Elsa said, "the Mozeyian Outpost has decreased their countdown to jump by more than half. They're going to jump much earlier than expected."

Wallace stood up. "Understood," he said and looked at Maelyn. "We're finished here. I'm on my way back."

Quinton was accessing the ship's communication systems, which covered a wide variety and was interlinked to every single system on the ship. He'd had knowledge of the outpost's broadcast moments before Elsa contacted Wallace.

"Why are you so quiet all of a sudden?" Becker asked.

It took Quinton a few moments to register that Becker was speaking to him.

Meanwhile, Maelyn said to Wallace, "Are we agreed then? Will you help me out?"

"Let's go see what we're dealing with first. Something must have happened for the outpost to move up its jump window. I don't like this at all," Wallace said.

They left Wallace's ready room, and Quinton returned his attention back to his immediate surroundings where he found Becker staring at him, his head tilted to the side.

"Didn't anyone tell you that it's not polite to stare?" Quinton asked.

Becker's lips lifted a little. He'd almost cracked a smile. Then he shook his head. "I wasn't sure if you were still there anymore. You might have just broken down. You know, you don't look so good."

"You're not getting rid of me that easily. Come on, Vonya, they're coming for us."

Vonya stood up and interlaced her long fingers in front of her.

Becker frowned and then his eyes widened a little. "You were listening to them? You were listening to them in the ready room."

If Quinton could smile, he would have. As it were, it was just a strange feedback from the agricultural bot systems of an expression that had no meaning for it. The bot's systems couldn't interpret the emotional data—in this case, a fair amount of satisfaction at the note of alarm in Becker's voice—packed into the response, or in this case, a smile. "How does that saying go? If you're not cheating, then you're not doing it right."

Becker chuckled and seemed a little surprised that he'd done so. The door opened.

Rosser stood outside. "They want you back on the bridge. Follow me."

They left the room and returned to the bridge. Wallace narrowed his gaze as if he preferred that Quinton wasn't there at the moment, but it was something he had to deal with. Maelyn gave him a confident nod.

Quinton turned his attention to Wallace. "I'm still here, Captain. Sanity still in check."

The others around them looked bewildered at his statement. Wallace winced. Now there could be no doubt that he'd listened in on their conversation.

Quinton looked at the main holoscreen. He had access to the ship's scanner array and noticed that the plot was crowded with ships fleeing the outpost.

"Elsa," Wallace said, "put us on an intercept course with the *Nebulon.* We'll be doing a high-speed pass," he said and looked at Maelyn. "The outpost is charging their jump drives. We need to make minimum safe distance and won't be able to slow down. You can make it to your ship by using one of our escape pods."

Maelyn smiled, looking as if she'd gotten exactly what she expected. "Thank you, Captain. I owe you one."

"You have no idea," Wallace said and glanced at Quinton. "But if your arrangement works out, then it could be good for us all. Safe travels, Captain Wayborn."

"To you as well, Captain, and your crew," she said.

She led them off the bridge, and Rosser escorted them to an escape pod. Maelyn went in first and the rest of them followed.

"It took you long enough," Becker said to Maelyn.

"Wallace took some convincing," Quinton said.

Maelyn arched a dark eyebrow. "I knew you were listening to us."

"I was, and I don't see how it changes anything." Even after he said it, he still didn't feel right about it. The constant suspicion of the people he surrounded himself with was wearing on him.

Maelyn regarded him as if trying to guess what his thoughts were. Quinton supposed that was one advantage to having a metallic, expressionless face—it didn't give anything away. A few moments later, she turned her attention to the escape pod systems. After a short wait, the pod was jettisoned from Wallace's ship, and they were on a direct path to the *Nebulon*. Maelyn opened a comlink to the ship. Simon, sounding very much relieved to hear from them, was only too happy to retrieve the escape pod.

Once they were back aboard the *Nebulon*, they headed to the bridge.

Simon smiled a greeting. "I'm glad you all made it back safely."

They were flying on a trajectory away from the outpost at best speed possible amid the other fleeing ships.

"Any trouble while we were away?" Maelyn asked.

Simon shook his head. "No problems here."

Quinton glanced at the main holoscreen, which showed a multitude of ships. At a casual glance, it looked almost chaotic, but then he spotted something peculiar. "That's odd. There's a group of ships on an intercept course with us."

The others turned their attention to the main holoscreen. It was difficult for the others to see because of the mass exodus from the outpost. Ships were jumping away as soon as they reached the minimal safe distance, so the plot on the main holoscreen was a bit confusing. Quinton highlighted the ships for them.

Simon hastened to the nearest workstation. "That isn't right. Scanners indicate that they're JFS warship design."

Becker cleared his throat. "It's Crowe. He's here."

Maelyn sat in the captain's chair. "We're not far enough away for a jump."

"You might not have much of a choice," Becker said.

The calculations appeared on Quinton's HUD. Maelyn was right—not much of a surprise there. The other ships were heading directly toward them, but they should be able to jump away before they reached them.

"It will be close," Quinton said.

"I suggest you all strap yourselves in. This is where it gets interesting," Maelyn said.

21

"WITH ALL DUE RESPECT, Captain, I think it would be best if I wasn't on the bridge," Vonya said.

Maelyn looked at her for a moment and then nodded.

"You two," Becker said to Guttman and Oscar, "we can't be here either. Go ahead and I'll be right behind you."

Guttman and Oscar left the bridge.

Quinton watched them go, and then looked at Becker. "Running away?"

Becker ignored him and looked at Maelyn. "I'll keep my comlink open, and if I can think of something that will help, I'll let you know."

"How very upstanding of you. You're with us in solidarity, but not on the bridge where someone can see you," Quinton said.

Becker gritted his teeth and inhaled, nostrils flaring.

"Quinton," Maelyn said, "it's for the best. No need for us to confirm anything for Lennix Crowe."

Since Crowe had managed to track them all the way here, they weren't going to hide the fact that they had escaped his space station with some help. Quinton thought Crowe was the type of person who didn't let small details slip past his notice, especially when those "details" were high-ranking salvagers in his organization. Becker turned around and left the bridge.

Quinton looked at Maelyn and shrugged. "I'm not going anywhere."

"I didn't expect you would, even if I wanted you to," she said, sounding mildly annoyed.

"It's because we're all so trustworthy," Quinton replied just as frostily.

Maelyn gritted her teeth a little and then exhaled softly. "Do you have to be so . . ." she said and paused, pressing her lips together.

Quinton waited a few moments for her to continue, but she didn't.

"Everyone here is looking out for themselves, so why should you expect anything different from me?"

Maelyn regarded him for a few moments, making him feel a little exposed. What did she see when she looked at him? Was it just an old service bot? Or did she see *him*, a Personality Matrix Construct that was the very essence of who he'd been when he'd resided in his human body? Quinton tried to recall his own face, and it was like trying to peer at a star map through a dense billowing cloud. He had enough to give him an impression but none of the details. Why was that fundamental knowledge kept from him? Was this part of the lockdown protocol? Did the others treat him like some kind of ghost in the machine because they wouldn't allow themselves to acknowledge that he was alive? They must know. They had to know. Quinton's artificial robotic eyes glowed a pale green. Maelyn had to know. He felt a sudden surge of longing for not just Maelyn but also the others to believe that he was more than a ghost from the past. He was more than what he could give them.

"Captain," Simon said, "we're being hailed. It's Crowe."

Maelyn held Quinton's gaze for another moment. "This isn't over," she said and then looked at Simon. "Understood. Patch the others in so Becker can observe."

"Yes, Captain," Simon said.

Quinton went to stand to the right of the captain's chair, and the vidcom came to prominence on the main holoscreen.

Lennix Crowe, wearing a black uniform, sat on the command bridge of a Jordani Federation destroyer. The crew was focused on their workstations, and their holoscreens glowed a pale green. Crowe lifted his dark-eyed gaze, and the video feed closed in so only his head and shoulders appeared.

"Captain Crowe. I didn't expect to see you here," Maelyn said.

On the upper-right side of the main holoscreen was a countdown timer for their jump drive to engage.

Crowe looked at her and arched one eyebrow. "Captain Wayborn, you've stolen something from me."

Quinton watched as Maelyn's eyes widened in mock surprise. "I don't think so. I'm sure it's just a simple misunderstanding."

"Is it though? I thought you were smarter than this. Did you think I wouldn't figure out what you've got there?" Crowe said, inclining his head toward Quinton.

Maelyn glanced at Quinton and laughed. "Imagine my surprise when we learned that the agricultural bot had something extra, but no, we didn't steal it from you. As you might recall, this agricultural unit was claimed by my sysops expert, Simon Webb, who accompanied your salvagers."

Crowe's gaze hardened, and he leaned forward. All pretenses of cordiality were gone. "I like you, Maelyn. You have a firm understanding of how things work. That's why I'm going to give you a chance to just hand it over."

"Excuse me," Quinton said. "Since you know what I am, then you'll also know that I'm not an 'it.' Furthermore, no one is handing any part of me anywhere without my say-so."

Crowe looked at Quinton for a moment and shook his head a little. "A PMC who believes they're still alive."

"A fool who believes they're in charge," Quinton said. Crowe glowered at him, his mouth forming a silent snarl. "I thought we were just stating the obvious here."

Crowe leaned back in his chair. "I'm really looking forward to meeting you in person."

"I can guarantee that this feeling won't last for long, but I'm afraid I'm also going to have to decline your offer to meet," Quinton said.

"It wasn't an offer, and besides," Crowe said, looking at Maelyn, "I think a suitable arrangement can be reached."

"But our business has already concluded. You're just trying to take what's rightfully mine," Maelyn responded innocently.

"Trust me when I say that you won't like it if you make me take him forcefully."

Quinton laughed. The countdown timer was almost finished. "Look who has a big bad warship. I bet you can't wait to use those weapons of yours. Are you really sure you want someone like me on there? You can ask the captain here for confirmation. I'm afraid I can't help getting into places I shouldn't be."

"Captain," Simon said, his voice going high, "they're targeting us."

Maelyn nodded once and looked at Crowe. "You'd risk losing access to the Mozeyian Outpost by firing weapons here in such close proximity to the outpost and all these other ships?"

Crowe shook his head. "Maybe I was wrong and you don't realize what you have, but if I can't take him from you, then no one will have him."

"Oh, I know exactly what I have, and you can be sure that you're never going to take him from me," Maelyn said, her tone becoming the hardest battle steel. Then she looked at Simon. "Execute jump."

Crowe leaned forward and smirked.

The *Nebulon*'s jump drives didn't activate, and Maelyn frowned. "Simon?"

"I'm trying, but we can't get a field lock. The calibration won't align. The nav computer has the coordinates, but it's like something is preventing an alignment," Simon said.

"I can override—" Quinton began to say.

"No!" Maelyn said with such command authority that he instantly stopped speaking.

Crowe laughed, drawing their attention back to the main holoscreen. "It seems that you're not going to get as far away as you originally thought."

"Simon," Maelyn said.

"I know. I'm looking, Captain."

"Don't bother. I'll just tell you," Crowe said and looked away for a moment, considering. "Never mind. I'll tell you in person when I get there." He closed the comlink.

Maelyn brought up her personal holoscreen. "The jump drive is online. So that's not it. What about the nav computer? Simon, run a diagnostic."

"Ship disablers," Quinton said.

"What?" Maelyn asked.

"Ship disablers. They're outside the ship. The JFS used them to prevent ships from making FTL jumps. Any kind of long-range drone could deploy them. Crowe hasn't been here long, so he didn't fire anything from his ship, but what if he had help? Someone on the outpost maybe?"

Maelyn looked at Simon.

"I hate to say it, but he's right," Becker said, his voice sounding over the comlink speakers on the bridge.

"It won't hurt nearly so much the more you say it," Quinton replied.

"Enough," Maelyn said. "Scanners aren't showing anything."

"They wouldn't," Becker said. "They're small, but they link up to form a field that you can't bypass. We'll have to go out there and destroy them."

"Are they attached to the hull?" she asked.

"I'm not sure. They could be, but they could also be maintaining position close by. We'll need our weapons for this," Becker said.

"Hold on a second," Quinton said. "Doesn't this ship have some kind of point-defense system?"

Simon nodded. "We do, but since the scanners didn't detect anything, we have no way to tell them what to fire on."

Quinton could just access the point-defense systems, along with any of the ship's other systems, but he didn't. Instead, he looked at Maelyn. "With your permission, Captain, I'd like to use the point-defense system on the ship."

"To do what exactly?" Maelyn asked.

"It's better if I just show you."

Maelyn considered it for a few seconds. "Go ahead," she said.

Quinton cranked up his frame rate, tentatively at first, expecting some kind of an alert to appear on his HUD, but none came. His new power core was in pristine condition and barely registered the additional draw as he raised his frame rate to the max. His thought processes sped up so much that time slowed down for everyone else. He was in the *Nebulon*'s computer systems, connected to multiple data streams that his army of VIs acknowledged. They awaited his commands. The strength of a PMC was the ability to simultaneously access multiple systems at once while being partnered with VI assistants that enabled the PMC to outperform any combat VI system alone. He unpacked a suite of VIs that took the aged scanner arrays and delved deeper into their detection capabilities, dialing them in to sense the tiny robotic swarm that surrounded the array. Without Quinton's augmentation, the ship's VI had rightfully classified the swarm as benign, given the fact that the ship was flying through crowded space. But the system didn't have the protocols required to make that determination. It wasn't designed for it. The protocols were for civilian use, and what he had access to was something much more capable.

There were two sets of point-defense cannons, each having kinetic and energy-based weaponry. They were lightweight, which wouldn't save them if they came within firing range of Crowe's JFS destroyers. He had to assume that Crowe had long-range missiles, which could reach them easily despite the other fleeing ships and the outpost, but Crowe wanted to take him intact. Quinton needed him to believe he could still do that.

He sent a new data feed to the main holoscreen, along with updated targeting parameters for the point-defense system. Then he slowed his frame rate back to normal time.

Maelyn glanced at the main holoscreen and did a double take.

Simon stood up, his mouth hanging open. "This," he said and looked at Quinton. "You did this?"

"Yes, now say goodbye to our pesky swarm," Quinton said and engaged the *Nebulon*'s newly enhanced point-defense cannons.

Both the kinetic and energy armament fired, sweeping their range of fire. Quinton engaged the maneuvering thrusters, and the ship rotated on its axis. The robotic swarm was beaten back. He was careful not to hit any of the other ships nearby. After a few seconds, the swarm was reduced to almost nothing.

Simon went back to his workstation. "I still can't get the jump drive to engage."

Quinton had the ship's sensors make another active scanner sweep, but nothing was detected. "There has to be something on the hull. I'm sorry, I can't do anything about that from here."

He withdrew from the ship's systems and felt a sense of emptiness from the loss of connection. For a few moments, he'd felt closer to "whole" than he'd felt since he'd woken up. Accessing the ship's systems had felt familiar and touched upon the very things those same VIs that had helped him also had to keep him ignorant of, locked away inside the ESS. He wanted to fully access the ship's systems again just so he could feel the complete immersion, chasing that feeling of wholeness. It was such a powerful urge that Quinton opened several data connections—not to do anything but just to feel whole again.

"Well then, we'll just have to go outside and take a look for ourselves," Maelyn said.

Quinton looked at her and nodded.

"Becker, Guttman, and Oscar, meet us at the rear airlock," Maelyn said. Simon stood up, intending to go with them. "Not you," she said to him. "You stay here and monitor Crowe's ships. As soon as we clear out the remaining disablers, I want you to execute a jump when we're back inside the ship."

Simon looked as if he was about to protest but didn't. Then he said, "Aye, Captain."

Maelyn turned toward Quinton.

"Lead the way," he said.

She nodded, and together they left the bridge. They headed toward the airlock near the middle of the *Nebulon*, which put them as close to the scanner array as possible. Quinton waited for the others to put on their EVA suits.

Maelyn grabbed a pair of boots with thick bottoms and tossed them toward Quinton. "Put them on. You need to wear them," she said.

Quinton glanced at the boots for a moment.

She gestured toward his feet. "You can't magnetize those footpads, yes?"

He checked the agricultural unit's feature list. "You're right, but the artificial gravity kept me attached to the ship before."

"Yeah, but we didn't have warships bearing down on us then."

Becker walked with the others inside the outer airlock, giving him a "get on with it" look.

Quinton quickly slipped on the boots, and the straps automatically adjusted to his metallic frame. He took a few steps, allowing the boots to self-adjust for maximum effectiveness, and they molded themselves to his peculiar foot shape. For the first few moments, it was like wearing two sets of shoes at the same time, but soon, the bot's motor control helped him compensate so he could walk normally, and he joined the others inside the airlock.

"About time," Becker muttered.

Oscar looked at Quinton, regarding him for a moment, and then said,

"Nice trick with the sensors and point-defense systems."

"Thanks," Quinton said.

"How did you do that?" Oscar asked.

The exterior airlock doors opened, revealing the Mozeyian Outpost's massive structure off to the side. Even though they'd put some distance from it, the outpost was still the largest thing in the area.

"Save it," Becker said.

"We've got work to do," Maelyn said.

"What are we looking for?" Guttman asked. He kept glancing around, and Quinton realized he was searching for the swarm.

"The swarm is gone," Quinton said.

"What's to stop it from coming back?"

"The swarm was part of the disablers attached to the ship," Becker said. The others looked at him. "I've never used them myself, but I've seen them before. Someone could have deployed them right from the maintenance airlock on the docking platform."

"That might have been useful to know earlier," Quinton said.

"Knock it off," Maelyn said. "We thought we'd outrun Crowe's agents. That's all there is to it. So, let's get the disablers off the ship and get out of here."

Quinton watched as the others nodded. Maelyn had a command authority that others had come to respect, even if this was only a temporary partnership.

She led them toward the sensor array, and they all engaged their mag boots. The artificial gravity field was weaker at this part of the ship, and Quinton realized that this was where the fields overlapped. Inside, the ship was fine, but here the weakness in gravity was enough that, with enough force, they could be jettisoned into space.

The scanner array was a series of sensors that were networked and located in different areas of the ship. The *Nebulon*'s navigation computer depended on the array to send the jump coordinates to the jump drive system. Quinton suspected that he could have found a way to override the safety systems and gotten the ship to jump anyway, but the risk was high that they wouldn't end up where they needed to be. It was no use getting somewhere quickly if they died in the process.

They reached the first in a series of sensors, which looked like tiny gray towers, a little bit taller than they were. Quinton scanned the sensor array for additional power signatures that didn't stem from the ship's power core. He filtered out everything else, and an object highlighted in red appeared on his HUD.

"I found one," he said and sent the targeting data to the others' suit computers.

The disablers were dark gray cylindrical-shaped devices that attached themselves to parts of the ship. A minimally charged plasma shot from a hand cannon or rifle was enough to destroy them, and they made quick work of removing the disablers on the nearby arrays.

Maelyn opened a comlink to the bridge. "Is the nav computer able to lock in the coordinates?"

"Negative, Captain, although it does take a few moments to cycle before it fails to lock on," Simon replied.

Quinton looked at the Mozeyian Outpost, and a series of massive maneuvering thrusters came online. The outpost was now moving away from them with increasing speed. He saw bright flashes from the other ships as they jumped away.

"Captain," Simon said, "I've detected a massive energy spike from the outpost. They're charging their jump drives. You need to get back inside."

"We can't. We have to clear out the last sensor array," Maelyn said.

"Now wait just a minute," Guttman said. "He's right. We can't be out here when that outpost jumps away. The gamma burst alone will kill us."

"Go back inside then," she said and started heading in the direction of the last sensor array.

Quinton caught up to her. "He's right. You need to get back inside the ship. I can take care of this."

Maelyn didn't slow down. "You're not shielded from gamma rays any more than we are."

"I know, but it won't affect me like it will you if you're caught out here. Let me take care of this for you," Quinton said.

Becker walked over to them. "The captain of the ship belongs on the bridge," he said. Maelyn shook her head and rolled her eyes. "Simon is as good as they come, but he's not the captain. We'll get this done."

She glanced at the others, who were already heading back to the airlock. Then she looked at Quinton. "All right," she said and handed him her rifle. "There's a maintenance hatch near that last array. I'll make sure it's unlocked for both of you."

Quinton took the rifle and gave her a quick salute by touching two metallic fingers to the side of his forehead. Then he ran toward the last sensor array.

Running with mag boots wasn't like running anywhere else. It took a lot of coordination, and even then, people couldn't do it well without the assistance of an EVA suit computer VI. He heard Becker following, and he wasn't that far behind. Becker knew what he was doing.

They made their way along the hull, approaching the last sensor array. It had a long shaft that extended ten meters from the hull. It was small in comparison to the ship, but they'd have to climb it. Quinton spotted a few of the ship disablers that had attached themselves to the shaft.

He glanced at Becker.

"I'm just protecting my investment," Becker said.

"I didn't think you'd taken a liking to me," Quinton said.

Becker looked at the shaft and walked over, preparing to climb.

"Wait. I can get up there faster. Why don't you go secure the hatch?"

Becker regarded him, then shook his head and smiled. "She *is* a beauty. I can see why you'd want to impress her," he said and raised his rifle. He shot the lowest disabler, leaving a slight scorch mark on the hull.

Quinton thought he hadn't heard correctly and checked his short-term memory.

Becker leaned toward him. "The thing is that I don't think she's into robots."

Quinton jumped up and grabbed the sensor. He swung around to the other side and shot the dark gray disabler. "I don't think she's into idiots either, so that rules us both out," he said, climbing higher.

Becker grinned and headed for the hatch. Quinton watched him go for a few moments, then continued his climb. The disablers seemed to have congregated on this particular array. The sensor wasn't just a solitary shaft but also had offshoots like the branches of a tree. At the top was a small dome about two meters in diameter. That's where he'd find the last disabler.

Quinton accessed the ship's systems and brought up the sensor systems. The readout nearly made him miss the handhold he was reaching for. He opened a comlink to the bridge. "Are you seeing this?"

There was a cluster of long-range missiles heading toward them, weaving their way through the fleeing ships.

"Yes," Maelyn answered. "Did you clear that last array?"

Quinton scrambled up to the shaft. "I'm working on it. It might be a good idea to bring the weapons systems online."

The point-defense systems were online, but he didn't know what kind of missiles Crowe had on those destroyers. Quinton reached the bottom of the dome and climbed toward the edge. The outpost's thruster went dark, and he saw the massive system of networked jump drives on the outpost reach the apex of their capacitor's capabilities. He glanced downward and saw that Becker had made it to the hatch and had just gone inside.

Quinton climbed over the edge and reached the top side of the dome. In the center was a ship disabler. He reached down and tore it from the hull, then threw it away from the ship. He scanned the area, looking for additional disablers, and none appeared.

"We're clear," Quinton said.

"Good work," Maelyn replied. "Now get back inside. We're charging our own jump drive now."

Quinton didn't respond. He hastened toward the edge and pulled himself down toward the hull, where he disabled the mag boots and pulled himself toward the ship. He then pulled his feet to his torso and pushed away from the sensor array. He'd pushed off at an angle that took him toward the hull.

The agricultural unit didn't have anything like the maneuvering thrusters that an EVA suit had, but he hadn't thought anything of it and had been in the middle of congratulating himself when he realized that he was "flying" headfirst toward the hull. The distance to the hull appeared on his HUD, and he quickly calculated his velocity.

A comlink opened from Becker. "Nice work. How do you plan on not bouncing off the hull?"

Quinton bit back a retort, and the bot's internal systems struggled to find a way to deliver his intentions but couldn't because it wasn't capable of conveying freaking facial expressions. He didn't know which made him more irritated—the fact that he couldn't make facial expressions or that Becker was right.

He increased his frame rate, and time slowed down. He secured the rifle to his back and did a few quick simulations for the best way not to bounce off into space. He extended his metallic arms in front of him, and if he'd been standing upright, his hands would have been over his head. The agricultural unit's hands were a composite alloy that was incredibly strong. He needed to redistribute the impact while propelling himself forward.

Even with his frame rate just above normal, Quinton was increasingly aware that he was rapidly approaching the hull of the ship. He'd done the calculations and tested them in a simulation. Now all he had to do was execute the maneuver and hope nothing broke on the agricultural bot's body that had been out of service for over a hundred years.

Why did I do this to myself?

Quinton executed his semi-controlled crash into the hull and skipped across its surface like a rock across a calm lake. He tried to reach for something to grab onto but couldn't. His feet dragged across the hull, and then he remembered the mag boots. He activated the boots and boosted them to maximum, which began to slow him down. Windmilling his arms, he tried in vain to push himself back toward the hull. It didn't work, and he imagined Becker was laughing at him. As he moved over a part of the ship where the artificial gravity field was stronger, he began to angle back toward the hull. That, in combination with the drag from his mag boots, allowed Quinton to come to an awkward stop. He regained his footing and looked around. He'd overshot the hatch by a good distance in the direction of the ship's engines.

"Get back inside!" Maelyn said, and there was no mistaking the urgency in her voice. She must have been monitoring him from the bridge.

"I'm on my way."

"Move it. You've got to run. Now!"

22

QUINTON SPUN AROUND AND RAN. He'd overshot the hatch by more than seventy meters. Even with mag boots and the aid of his VI assistants, he could only move so fast in near-zero gravity, which was nothing like an all-out run at the speeds he could maintain in a one-g environment.

The *Nebulon* lurched to the side, pulling Quinton off balance before he could push himself off. Only one of his mag boots kept him attached to the hull, and he scrambled to get his footing under control while grabbing onto a nearby handrail. His view of the Mozeyian Outpost twisted away. A bright flash illuminated the backdrop of the ship and momentarily overwhelmed his vision. Maelyn had angled the ship away from the outpost so that when it performed its colossal FTL jump, the *Nebulon* shielded him from the brief but intense wave of gamma radiation. She'd saved his life. An intense gamma wave could easily damage the internal components of the agricultural bot. He had no idea if his ESS was sufficiently shielded against the intensity he'd just observed and wasn't curious enough to push the limits, but he wasn't out of the woods just yet. He had to get inside the ship before they could execute their own FTL jump, and there were still long-range missiles on an intercept course with the ship.

Quinton ran, quickly closing the distance to the maintenance hatch. He rounded the corner, expecting the hatch to be open, but it wasn't. He peered through the rectangular window and saw Becker standing there. He had two fingers pressed to the side of his helmet near his ear, and his head was turned away as if he was having a separate conversation.

Quinton accessed the comms systems nearby and heard Becker speaking.

"Say that again, Guttman," Becker said.

They must have been using a private channel of their own because Quinton couldn't hear the reply. Becker's mouth hung open a little, and he looked at Quinton with his brow furrowed.

Quinton banged his fist on the hatch. "What are you doing? Unlock the door. Let me inside."

Becker inhaled deeply and glanced away from him for a few silent moments. Then he shook his head. "I can't," he said, his voice sounding thick.

Quinton glared at Becker with smoldering emerald eyes. "You can't?" he growled and jerked on the hatch.

He couldn't believe it. Becker wasn't going to let him in. He tried to access the hatch control systems, but they were offline.

Quinton opened a comlink to the bridge. "Becker won't let me in. He's locked out the controls. They're offline."

"Maelyn," Becker said, his tone calm and even. "You have to listen to me. We can't let him inside."

"I don't know what game you think you're playing, but you open that hatch right now," Maelyn said with a steely edge to her voice.

Quinton looked at Becker, who shook his head. Quinton studied him for a few moments. His shoulders were tight, and he stared off to the side without seeing. His heart rate was elevated. Becker was afraid—not of him or Maelyn but something else.

"You know I can't do that. They'll destroy the ship. We can't let him back inside," Becker said.

"Dammit, Becker," Quinton said and slammed his metallic fist against the hatch again. He wished he had the strength to tear it off the ship and force his way inside.

"Override his controls," Maelyn said. She must have been speaking to Simon.

Becker regarded him, his jaw set and his gaze hard.

"Why not?" she said.

"He can't override the controls," Becker said. "I've disabled all systems access. They're on manual. The only way they're getting open is if you come down here yourself, but there isn't time for that. You have to trust me."

Quinton wanted to punch the hatch again but didn't. Instead, he said, "Becker, look at me."

The salvager raised his gaze.

"Crowe is not going to get us. There's still time. Let me inside."

Becker sneered and rolled his eyes, shaking his head again. "You think I'm afraid of Crowe? He's here, but so are the Sentinels. They're here, and they're hunting for *you*."

Quinton glanced over his shoulder and then chided himself inwardly. The Sentinels weren't right behind him, waiting to pounce on him unsuspectingly.

"You don't know that," Maelyn said, speaking to them now. "If you don't open that hatch right now, our deal is off, and nothing will stop me from throwing you and the rest of your crew off my ship."

"I don't believe you. You know I'm right. I have to do this." Becker paused for a second. "You'll never get here in time, and he can't make it to another airlock." Becker scowled at him and gritted his teeth. "He's in the ship systems. They're going to scan us and detect a PMC presence. What do you think is going to happen then? You know how this is going to play out. They'll take out the ship without any hesitation or remorse, using weapons that will outclass anything available in this sector. Sentinels can't be reasoned with."

"I'll get out of the ship systems. They won't be able to detect me," Quinton said while trying to think of a way to get back onto the ship. Becker was right. This was the closest access hatch in the area.

"No, you won't. You can't help yourself," Becker said and then added, "You're in the ship systems. Look at the sensor feed. Look at Crowe's ships."

Quinton accessed the active sensor scan and saw that the JFS destroyers were now heading away from them. They'd altered course. He looked at Becker.

"You see it too. Even Crowe is running away from the Sentinels. This isn't personal, Quinton. But I'm not giving my life for you."

Quinton spun around and scanned the area. He couldn't see the Sentinels. He didn't even know what those ships looked like, but they were on the ship's sensors, and they were broadcasting their position. The sensors detected six ships, but they were too far away to determine what kind of ships they were. The Sentinels increased their speed, heading toward them. Quinton tried to think of why they would do that but couldn't come up with anything. He didn't know what scan they could do that would reveal his presence to them.

"Simon, are you there?" Quinton asked.

"I'm here."

"Have they scanned us? Have they already detected me?"

Simon didn't reply right away. "It's not that simple, but I don't think so."

Quinton looked through the hatch window and saw Becker watching him.

"You see?" Becker said. "He doesn't know."

"There has to be another reason they're heading toward the ship then," Quinton said.

He heard Maelyn begin to say something else, but he interfaced with the ship systems once again. Immediately, all the data streams were at his disposal, and his VI assistants waited for him to direct them. He felt an urge to turn them loose and take over the entire ship's systems, but he hesitated. Controlling the ship wouldn't help him.

"Radek, can you give me anything here? Any ideas?" Quinton asked inwardly.

An image of the plot appeared on his HUD, and it highlighted the long-range missiles that were still heading toward them at an unhurried pace. They'd likely increase speed once they got closer. They weren't close enough for the *Nebulon*'s point-defense systems to be effective, and the other ships would likely treat it as an attack. Crowe had been trying to intimidate them, but he'd also destroy the *Nebulon* to keep anyone else from using Quinton. Bargaining chip aside, Quinton didn't care for being treated like some kind of commodity.

He brought his attention back to the sensor plot. There were ten ships between the missiles and the *Nebulon*. The missiles had to be part of this. He just needed to figure out a way to use them or take them out of the equation.

Quinton accessed the *Nebulon*'s comms system and opened a broadcast subspace link to one of the other ships. The automatic comms systems that registered a ship-to-ship broadcast acknowledged it, and he was in. He bypassed their almost non-existent security measures, feeling as if what he'd just done was something he'd done many times before. He then opened separate comms channels to the remaining ships in the area.

". . . I don't know. He's broadcasting a signal," Simon said.

"Can't you lock him out?" Becker asked.

"No, I'm not going to lock him out," Maelyn said. "Quinton, tell us what you're doing. I want to help you."

Quinton cranked up his frame rate, allowing him to work with the world of data streams and subspace communications much faster than if he'd stayed in normal time. He was risking breaking the internal components of the agricultural bot that wasn't designed for such use, but he didn't have a choice. Becker wasn't going to let him back inside the ship, and he needed to convince him.

The other ships hadn't even detected the missiles in range. Their captains were too focused on jumping away from the system. He quickly calculated the highest probability of the trajectory the missiles would take to the *Nebulon*. Two of the ten ships on the path jumped away. Now he only had eight to work with. A quick query into their systems revealed that only five of the ships had some type of point-defense systems. He severed his connection to the other ships. They wouldn't be able to help. He offloaded copies of several VIs onto target ship systems because it would make what he was trying to do much easier by spreading the workload. Their access was tied directly into Quinton's ESS, which contained a data library for ship systems. The point-defense systems were rudimentary, with a solitary kinetic mag cannon that wasn't well maintained. A single small mag cannon couldn't provide adequate coverage, but these weren't warships. They were freighters meant for salvage and carrying cargo.

Quinton turned his attention to the maintenance records and winced inwardly. He'd be willing to wager that the captains of those ships mainly focused on maintaining the engines, trusting that running was a better option than relying on a nearly out-of-service point-defense system. Those systems had Cerberus protocols in their foundation, but given the state of the actual weapons, he could probably count on them being only 20 percent effective, and that estimate was generous.

He had five ships to work with that were in relatively close enough proximity to be effective. He put up their jump drive countdown timers while coming up with a firing solution that accounted for all the variables. He wouldn't test fire the mag cannons because that would alert the missiles' own sensors, and they would take evasive action. He needed to take them by surprise by having the mag cannons fire all at once.

Quinton uploaded his firing solution to the VIs he had on the other ships' computing systems, along with instructions for the VIs to delete themselves when the systems reset, which was the standard operating procedure for faulty systems. The captains would run a diagnostic on the faulty system, detect Quinton's VIs as anomalies, and then reset those systems.

The cluster of long-range missiles flew along their trajectory toward the *Nebulon*, increasing their speed. The mag cannons began firing a salvo at the missiles. Some of the mag cannons stopped firing after only a few seconds, while others increased their rate of fire, as if the cannons needed a bit of warm-up as they cleared their throats. The missiles' smart defense systems were taken by surprise and couldn't evade the sudden onslaught. They were destroyed without so much as a self-destruct protocol being engaged. Quinton ordered his VI assistants on the other ships to utilize the ships' sensors and search for any other missiles. He set the task to expire after fifteen minutes and withdrew from the other ships' systems, including the *Nebulon*'s.

Quinton returned his frame rate back to normal time. "It's the missiles," he said. "The Sentinels must have detected the trajectory of the missiles and were coming to investigate the ship. They haven't detected me at all."

Becker raised his eyebrows. "It's good in theory, I'll give you that, but I'm not letting you back on board."

As if to emphasize his determination, Becker sent a command to turn off Quinton's mag boots, and Quinton grabbed onto a handrail by the hatch. He could have taken control, but he waited. He could hold on for as long as he needed to.

"He's not in the ship systems anymore," Simon said.

Quinton put the comlink session on hold so he could think.

"Radek, you've got to give me something here. How can the Sentinels detect that I'm a PMC?" he asked.

"They must have protocols to detect the unique system access used by PMCs. Withdrawing all access, including latent subroutines, should erase all evidence of your manipulation of the system. Beyond that, they might be able to detect the leuridium power signature of your ESS, but sufficient shielding should prevent them from detecting that," Radek replied.

"Well, what would give me sufficient shielding?"

"It's hard to estimate because we don't know the scanning capabilities of the Sentinels' ships."

"For the love of—Take a damn guess," Quinton snapped.

"The highest probability for adequate shielding would be near the ship's reactor core. It's an area that must be shielded from the rest of the ship. Sensors in that area are designed for detecting containment breaches, not minuscule power core signatures," Radek said.

Quinton reconnected to the ship's systems and executed the cleanup protocol, which would theoretically erase all evidence of his activities in the ship's systems. Then he reactivated the external comlink that was connected to his shoulder and heard the others arguing. "I have a way to keep the Sentinels blind to me, but you need to let me back on the ship," he said and waited a few moments. "Becker, they're coming toward us right now, and if we jump away, they'll just follow us. We need to let them scan the ship."

"You're a damn fool," Becker replied and adjusted a setting on his assault rifle. "Maelyn, turn off the artificial gravity in this part of the ship, and I'll make sure the Sentinels won't detect us anywhere near Quinton."

Becker wasn't bluffing. A sufficiently charged plasma cannon would do the trick, and Quinton had nowhere to run. He didn't have time to fight Becker right then.

"I'm not in the system, and I removed all traces of being there. If I can get to the ship's reactor core, there's enough shielding there to prevent the Sentinels from detecting my ESS. Since I'm not in the systems, that's their only other way of detecting what I am," Quinton said and paused for a few moments. "Come on, Becker, think about it. You know I'm right. I thought you wanted to get your big payday. This is how you do it. This is your only chance."

Becker looked away from him, his dark-eyed gaze intense.

Quinton silently urged him to open the hatch. "It's the only way. The Sentinels aren't stupid. They're going to realize where I came from, and then they're going to come after the ship anyway. Your only chance is to help hide me from them."

Becker glared at him. Then he sighed and collapsed his assault rifle, deactivating it. The hatch opened.

Quinton stepped inside and closed the hatch. Becker had removed the control panel, which was why the hatch had to be manually opened. A few seconds later, the gray interior airlock door opened, granting them access to the ship. He brushed past Becker without saying anything. He knew the layout of the ship and began to run toward main engineering.

"Don't worry about the doors," Maelyn said. "I'll take care of them as you head to the reactor. Now run!"

That was all the confirmation Quinton needed, and he sprinted down the corridor to a maintenance shaft. He slid down the ladder to the lower levels, plunging down several decks, and only slowing his descent at the last possible moment. He emerged from the shaft and ran down a dimly lit, narrow corridor on the most direct path to the reactor room. Bulkhead doors shut behind him as he made his way to the rear of the ship. Since he'd withdrawn his access from the ship's computer system, he felt like he'd been submerged in a sea of darkness. He'd ignored it at first, but the longer he went without access, the more he felt like he was stumbling around in the shadows, cut off from everything.

Quinton knew the layout of the *Nebulon*, having committed it to memory when he'd first come aboard, but he checked the posted signs above the bulkhead doors and the faded remnants on the walls just the same. It was easy to get turned around in these maintenance corridors. All he needed was to get lost on a ship that wasn't overly monstrous by any stretch of the imagination.

He emerged from the maintenance path into the main corridor. Amber lights flashed outside the main reactor chamber as the doors began to open. Quinton bolted toward them. As soon as he was inside, the outer doors closed.

Quinton had a strange feeling that he should be breathing heavily. It had been a while since he'd felt the need to breathe. Stress and habits of the mind fueled well-established behaviors that he hadn't entirely put aside, and that was a good thing. Those habits reminded him that he was still human.

A nearby wallscreen flickered to life, and he saw Maelyn's face.

"All right, sit tight. I'll let you know when the Sentinels have done their scan."

Quinton nodded. "I guess if they've already detected something, none of us . . ." he couldn't finish what he'd been about to say. Maelyn had saved his life. He knew she'd had her own reasons for doing so, but he couldn't ignore what she'd done. She could easily have agreed with Becker, and then he would have been space dust.

Maelyn's lips lifted a little. It wasn't a smile or even the hint of one, but more of an acknowledgment. Regardless of what it meant, it reassured him.

"Thanks," Quinton said.

Maelyn looked away from the video feed toward what must have been the main holoscreen on the bridge. The image on the wallscreen Quinton watched split to show the bridge and the data feed on the main holoscreen.

A group of eight ships was highlighted. They were on an intercept trajectory that would bring them close to the *Nebulon*. A scout group. That must've been what they were—a Sentinel scout group—but who controlled them? They couldn't be autonomous, but Maelyn and the others had said they hadn't communicated when hailed.

"Jump drive is ready, Captain," Simon said.

"Understood," Maelyn replied.

If they jumped now, the Sentinel scout ships were close enough to determine where they'd gone. They had to wait, and Quinton hated it. Waiting to be scanned by the Sentinels went against every instinct he had. He glanced at the others on the bridge, seeing that Simon and Kieva were sitting at a pair of workstations. The doors to the bridge opened, and Becker walked in.

Maelyn ignored him, keeping her attention on the main holoscreen.

Quinton questioned the logic of just lying down and exposing their throats to the Sentinels. They were putting themselves at the mercy of something they didn't completely understand. He frowned inwardly. That wasn't entirely correct. Everyone else had more of an understanding about the Sentinels than he did. He needed to rectify that, but what could he do if he couldn't access the ship's systems or give away his presence in any way?

There was nothing he could do now. They'd taken their chances based on his plan—Maelyn most of all. She was the captain.

Radek, I hope you're right.

An idea came to mind, and Quinton spoke. "Can you record them? The data feeds from this encounter."

"We are," Maelyn replied in a hushed tone.

Quinton was glad she'd kept the comlink session open and a live data feed to the bridge. It was his only connection. Did she suspect that if she kept him in the dark, he would access the ship's systems even though he'd promised not to? He was tempted. He wanted to know what was going on, and he'd become accustomed to having information readily accessible. Perhaps it made up for having such limited access to his own ESS.

A data overlay came to prominence on the main holoscreen.

SN-DISCOVERY PROTOCOL INITIATED.

"They're scanning us now," Simon said.

Quinton was already still, but he wanted to hold his breath and be very still, or else he'd be detected. It was preposterous, but that was what fear was. For him, it was a fear of the unknown, but he'd also noticed anxiety in the others. Whatever the Sentinels were, they'd generated a universal dread among the ship personnel, along with a certainty of death if the Sentinels decided it was necessary. Becker had been willing to kill Quinton to save himself, which he understood. He didn't like the man, but Becker wasn't a coward. He'd thought they were all going to die if Quinton stayed. That was all there was to it. Quinton supposed he couldn't fault Becker for that.

He watched the wallscreen, feeling oddly exposed, as if something dark and sinister was lurking around the nearest corner. He resisted the urge to turn away.

"Oh my God! Did you see that?" Simon said.

Quinton saw that one of the Sentinels had accelerated past them with a sudden burst of speed, quickly followed by the others.

"They're attacking those ships," Simon said.

Quinton watched the data feeds on the main holoscreen and saw that Simon had highlighted the ships being attacked. If he had a mouth, it would have been hanging open in shock. The Sentinels' targets were the ships he'd used to destroy the long-range missiles.

"Why are they attacking them? It doesn't make sense," Simon said.

I did this, Quinton thought to himself. Those spacers were being murdered by the Sentinels, and it was all his fault. He sank to the floor, leaning heavily against the wall. He wished he could sink through the floor or become invisible. He was the reason those people were dying, all because he'd thought he was being clever. He'd left a few temporary VIs on those ships to provide protection should any other missiles be fired at them, thinking he'd protected them. The ships hadn't jumped away.

"Do you see the energy beam's power signature? I've never seen a magnitude that high. It melted through the hull in milliseconds," Simon said.

Becker came closer to Maelyn and then looked pointedly at the camera. "You're not so clever now, are you?"

Simon looked at Becker in surprise. "What are you talking about?"

"Those spacers are being slaughtered because of him," Becker said, jutting his chin toward the camera feed showing Quinton slumped against the wall in shame.

Kieva frowned. "I don't understand."

"Becker's right," Quinton said, and the others all looked at him. "I accessed those ship's systems and used their point-defense systems to take out the missiles. Then I left a temporary VI in place to scan for other incoming missiles. I didn't think . . . Those ships were moments away from jumping. They should've been gone."

"It's not your fault," Maelyn said.

Becker turned toward her. "You've gotta be kidding me! He's the reason the Sentinels destroyed those ships. Those spacers are dead because of him."

The last ship Quinton accessed had managed to execute a space jump, but a few moments later, several ships from the Sentinel scout force jumped also, no doubt in pursuit of them.

"You must see that," Becker continued.

Maelyn stepped toward him and thrust out her hand. A burst of energy came from her palm stunner, shoving him back. He tumbled several feet away.

"You," she hissed, striding toward him. She swung again, and another burst of energy threw Becker back toward the doors to the bridge.

He slowly stood and raised his hands.

"Get off my bridge before I throw you off this ship," Maelyn said and pulled out her sidearm. "Changed my mind. Throwing you off is too good for you," she growled and pointed her weapon at him.

Becker hastened backward, stumbling a little.

"Captain!" Simon said.

Becker held up his hands.

Maelyn sneered, her nostrils flaring. Then, through gritted teeth, she said, "Get out!"

He scrambled to his feet and fled. Maelyn headed back to the captain's chair. "Execute jump."

"Aye, ma'am, executing jump," Simon replied.

Maelyn sat in her chair and activated her personal holoscreen. Quinton glanced up to see her face still red with anger, but she tried to soften her features when she looked at him. "This wasn't your fault. You didn't know."

"Yes, it was. I should have listened. Becker was right," Quinton replied.

"He's an asshole. Unforgiving and rigid."

Quinton looked at her. "That doesn't make him wrong."

She started to speak again, and he shook his head. "I'd like to be alone."

Maelyn regarded him for a moment and then nodded. The comlink to the bridge disconnected, and Quinton saw the monitoring system for the reactor register a power spike as the *Nebulon* jumped away.

23

THE *NEBULON* HAD EMERGED from its jump some time earlier. Quinton made a conscious effort not to know how much time had passed. It actually required mental effort and assertion on his part to blank out his HUD, which was designed for ease of access. His HUD wasn't the agricultural bot's default interface. It had been altered when Radek adapted the bot's systems for PMC use. Quinton had his own HUD that was combined with that of the agricultural bot. All the data feeds normally within view were now invisible, and he didn't want to think about any of them. At some point, the heavily shielded doors to the reactor core opened, and he guessed that was Maelyn's way of urging him to leave the core.

Quinton stood up and walked out, leaving the reactor core behind. He tried to keep his mind blank, which was impossible. He wasn't even required to physically rest, so his mind was always active. There should have been something in his training to accommodate this, but those memories were unavailable—big surprise.

Those spacers had been slaughtered because of him . . .

Snippets of the events that had taken place a few hours before, along with Becker's condemnation, kept coming to the forefront of his mind—

Three hours and fourteen minutes.

Quinton stopped walking. He clenched one of his robotic hands into a fist, hoping the simple act of squeezing really hard would provide an outlet for his rage. He'd settle for feeling a strain or an explosion of breath, or even being able to grit his teeth, but he couldn't do any of those things. There was no buildup of corporeal pressure, but pressure was building in other ways. He hadn't wanted to know how much time had passed since he'd aided in the murder of spacers who were fleeing for their lives.

He glanced at dark gray walls of the corridor and focused on a blemish the maintenance bots hadn't been able to scrub clean. It wasn't the only imperfection evident on the old ship. He imagined striking the wall and feeling the force from his hands and shoulders dispersing throughout the rest of his body. He knew that if he struck the wall with enough force, he'd leave a mark . . . *his* mark. A few moments of heavy silence passed, and then Quinton resumed walking. The corridor walls had gotten off easy because a small part of him had cautioned against it. The agricultural bot was old. What if he broke something important? And for what?

He wanted to walk aimlessly and allow his feet to guide him, but that was impossible. Movement required a destination, so either he could spend his time picking obscure destinations on the ship, or he could go to the one place that made the most sense to him. It wasn't a logical kind of sense, but it was the only place he could think to go and not see anyone else.

Quinton walked into Simon's workshop and closed the door. The workshop was empty, with only the ambient glow of the amber lighting overhead. They were watching him. Maelyn would definitely be monitoring his location, and Quinton felt less inclined to try to hide it. He just wanted to be left alone.

He crossed the workshop toward a shelving unit on the other side and crouched. He was close to the shelves without making any contact. He could see the door to the workshop and stared at it for a few moments.

. . . slaughtered . . .

You're not so clever now . . .

Quinton was able to recall Becker's voice with stunning clarity. He didn't know what the Sentinels were capable of, and he hadn't listened to the others. They'd tried to warn him in their own subtle ways, while at the same time trying not to overwhelm him with information about a galaxy he scarcely understood.

The pitter-patter of small footsteps drew his attention, and Stumpy leaped down to the floor from some shelf he'd claimed as his own. The creature's sizable ears perked up, and his large round eyes regarded him with the vertical irises of a nocturnal predator. Then Stumpy walked toward Quinton, crouching on all fours. The creature vocalized at a high pitch that wouldn't have been heard by any of the others unless they'd augmented their hearing.

Quinton repeated the cadence of Stumpy's vocalizations, and the creature paused to peer up at him warily.

"Aren't we a pair," he said softly. Then he sighed inwardly. Here he was, sitting in a dark room, identifying with an animal slightly bigger than a rodent.

Stumpy leaped toward him, and he easily caught the creature in his hands, raising him toward his face. Stumpy cocked his head to the side and peered at him.

Quinton cocked his head in imitation. "Well, I'm not homesick for *your* planet. That's for sure."

Simon must have been feeding him because he didn't look as scrawny as Quinton remembered. The bare patches of fur were starting to show new growth. A few good meals and some rest in a safe place had done wonders for the little guy, but he had to be lonely. Quinton remembered the group of them that had climbed into the vehicle while he was fleeing from the hunter mechs. None of the others could have survived. The atmosphere was becoming toxic, at least in that region of the continent.

He lowered his hands to the ground, and Stumpy stepped off. He went a few feet away and sat on the floor, grooming himself. Quinton supposed that conveyed a certain level of trust. Stumpy was probably the only one on the ship who trusted him.

He spent the next few minutes watching the creature clean himself, doing a rather thorough job of it. Grooming must have been impossible on the planet because of the toxic nature of the fallout. He wanted to believe that not having access to the bulk of his memories was worse than being cut off from your species on a dying planet, but that would push the boundaries of his self-pity too far. He wasn't that far gone, and he decided not to dwell on it.

Quinton glanced at the wallscreen nearby and stood up. He wouldn't stay huddled in some dark corner. He didn't have to be inside the system in order to use it. He lamented the almost painfully slow access to information, but direct access seemed foolish to him right then. He increased the luminosity of the lighting in the workshop. He could see just fine in the dark, but he had the feeling that staying in the dark was the same as hiding, and he didn't want to hide anymore.

The wallscreen workstation was equipped with a holographic projector, and Quinton enabled several holoscreens. They were blank screens with a standard interface, waiting for him to initiate an action. He paused for a few moments, considering what he needed to do first, and then brought up the data recordings of their encounter with the Sentinels.

"Radek," Quinton said.

A holographic, semi-translucent sphere appeared.

"I need you to help me analyze this encounter."

"Analysis would be much quicker if you accessed the ship's computer system more directly than using this interface," Radek replied.

Had the VI expressed a note of disdain? Quinton dismissed it. VIs didn't have a preference for how they worked. Radek was merely pointing out the fact that working this way was suboptimal.

"Understood, Radek. Let's just work this way," Quinton replied.

He began querying the *Nebulon*'s computer system and realized that Simon had already pulled all data related to the Sentinel encounter into one place for him to review.

On one holoscreen, Quinton pulled up the communication logs that began with the initial broadcast from the Sentinel scout force. He compared that with the active scan data and tried to see whether the *Nebulon*'s systems had even detected the scout force jumping into the area.

"Radek, see if you can pinpoint the jump insertion of the Sentinels from this log data."

The shimmering orb turned his attention to the data on the holoscreen and seemed to study for only a second or two. "Impossible to predict to any degree of accuracy."

"That's what I was afraid of," Quinton said.

Thousands of ships had been fleeing the Mozeyian Outpost, and the *Nebulon*'s sensors hadn't been able to cope with all that information. All he had to work with was the initial broadcast detected by the ship's communication systems.

He studied the data on the screen. "The Sentinels arrived in-system and started broadcasting their presence. Why would they do that?"

"Are you asking me?" Radek asked.

Quinton glanced at him. "Well, no. I'm thinking out loud. It helps me organize my thoughts."

Radek was silent.

"Is there something you'd like to share about the Sentinels?" Quinton asked.

"I don't have enough data to establish a pattern, but in this instance, based upon the data, I believe the Sentinels were following their own established protocols."

"Destroying ships because their scans and systems access revealed a PMC presence?"

"That, too, but your question had to do with their initial broadcast. They announced their presence. Perhaps they expected compliance from whoever received the broadcast," Radek replied.

Quinton considered this and tried to think of what kind of compliance the Sentinels expected. A ship broadcasting its location was the best way to establish intent and avoid collisions. This was more of a concern when in close proximity. Compliance also meant that the Sentinels had a task to perform, and any ship within range of the broadcast was expected to just let them do it. Scanning ships and remote systems access to search for PMC activity seemed extreme, but according to the others, this activity was considered normal. The fact that successful detection of PMC presence resulted in an attack meant that the protocols were being followed irrespective of the lives aboard the ship.

"So much for rules of engagement."

Quinton looked at another holoscreen that was displaying the Sentinel attack data. These were warships, and they'd fired on civilian freighters. After destroying those ships, the Sentinels had moved on to scan the other ships. Even after two of the Sentinel scout ships had FTL-jumped out of the system to pursue a fleeing ship, the others continued. There was a certain level of detachment reminiscent of a VI control system. It had been almost a hundred years since the Federation Wars. Why were the Sentinels still around?

Quinton searched for other log data with previous encounters but couldn't find any.

"Your search for previous encounters with Sentinels in the ship's logs didn't yield any results, but this isn't your first encounter with them," Radek said.

"What do you mean? I think I'd know it if I had."

Radek opened another holoscreen. "These are the ship designations from the broadcast that came from the scout group," he said and brought up another screen. "This is the ship designation from the hostile ship encountered in the Zeda-Six Star System. The base designations are the same."

Quinton looked at the screens.

SN-Seeker-901 – Broadcast hail. Zeda-Six Star System.

The ship had changed course to pursue him while he was leaving the system. It had been a lone Sentinel scout ship.

Quinton looked at the designation for the scout group.

SN-Seeker-SF-301 – Broadcast hail. Mozeyian Outpost.

Seeker-SF . . . Seeker Scout Force.

It was a military designation. He recognized the hierarchical references, but which federation military had created the Sentinels?

If he'd allowed that ship to scan him when he was fleeing the Zeda-Six Star System, it would have destroyed him for sure. But why had the Sentinels been there in the first place? Had they tracked the activation signal to Zeda-Six and come to investigate? Had the hunter mechs on the planet been following some latent protocol that originated from the Sentinels, and was that the reason they wouldn't communicate with him in the first place?

Quinton stared at the two holoscreens, allowing his thoughts to explore the questions on his mind. If the Sentinels were hunting for him, then maybe he *should* leave the *Nebulon* and get a ship of his own to track the activation signal. How much could he trust the other people on this ship? Becker had been ready to hand him over to the Sentinels and flee the system. Guttman and Oscar would be sure to follow Becker's lead. But what about Maelyn, Simon, and Kieva? Maelyn had supported him, but could that change, and was it really fair for her to do so? Quinton thought Simon and Kieva would follow Maelyn's lead, but perhaps not as doggedly as Guttman and Oscar followed Becker's. Then there was Vonya. The door to the workshop opened, and he stopped in mid-thought.

Vonya entered. The Servitor had changed her clothing, which now covered significantly more of her smooth lavender skin but still didn't leave anything to the imagination. Her long platinum hair was tied back into a simple ponytail, accentuating her high cheekbones. Her gaze warmed at the sight of him, and she smiled a little as she closed the distance between them.

Vonya glanced at the holoscreens. "Am I interrupting you?"

Quinton wondered whether she had just happened to find him here or had been sent here by someone else. "I was just thinking about the Sentinels."

She came to stand by his side, looking completely at ease. He'd expected that the others would want to remain distant from him, except he hadn't realized it until just that moment.

"Time for quiet reflection is often time well spent," Vonya replied. She looked at the data on the holoscreens. "What's so special about Sentinel ship designations?"

Quinton wasn't sure how the others would react if they learned that the Sentinels were more aware of him than they'd originally thought. It wasn't that he intended to hide it from them, but he hadn't decided whether he wanted to share it with them yet.

"That's what I was looking at. I don't have any memories of Sentinels."

Vonya regarded him for a few moments. "It must be frustrating for you."

He knew she was trying to soothe him, perhaps lull him into a sense of confidence, false or otherwise. "It is," he said, and was glad to have someone acknowledge it. "Radek was just pointing out to me that we'd encountered a Sentinel when we left the planet I was activated on."

Vonya's eyes darted back to the holoscreen. "Really!" She pursed her full lips, which drew his attention. "That can't be a coincidence."

"Only if my luck changes," Quinton replied, and she chuckled.

"You'll need that. Constant vigilance is exhausting. Being able to regard the situation you find yourself in with a bit of dry humor allows for relief."

"It doesn't change anything. Are you going to keep trying to counsel me?"

Vonya looked at him. "Not if you do not wish me to."

Quinton didn't reply. He didn't know what he wanted.

"It's what a Servitor does."

"What's that exactly?"

"We attend to people's needs and provide advice when desired."

Quinton wondered just how many things could be grouped under "attending to people's needs."

"And what do you get out of it?" he asked.

Vonya arched a platinum eyebrow toward him. "The satisfaction of knowing I've touched the lives of others in a meaningful and positive way."

Quinton made an unintelligible sound.

Vonya frowned a little and then smiled. "Do you find it amusing?"

"Would it offend you if I did?"

"No. There are many people who don't fully appreciate our ways."

"I bet there are a lot of people who try to take advantage of you."

"Many *think* they do," Vonya replied.

There was something in her gaze that Quinton hadn't seen before. It was like a comfortable knowledge of one's place in the galaxy, but there was also a certainty that she was playing a game at a higher level than most people comprehended. He had dismissed the Servitor out of hand, but perhaps she was much more dangerous than he'd initially thought. He just didn't understand in what form Vonya's particular brand of danger would manifest. Did she even know?

"Interesting," Quinton said. "So did Maelyn ask you to check on me?"

Vonya quirked an eyebrow at him, and her eyes twinkled. "Would it bother you if Captain Wayborn sent me to you?"

"You didn't answer the question."

She exhaled softly, managing to make even that look graceful and alluring at the same time. He might be stuck in a robot body, but he wasn't dead. Vonya was a beautiful woman if one preferred the utter perfection of female symmetry—from the deliciously feminine features of her face, to her long slender arms, and down to the tips of her fingers.

"Yes, she did," Vonya said finally. "She believed it might make you feel better if I spoke to you."

"Did she send you to Becker too?" he asked and almost immediately wished he hadn't. Almost, but not quite.

Vonya drew herself up, looking neither annoyed nor offended. "I prefer to get to know the entire crew. It helps the captain if I contribute in this way."

"That's just it. We're not a crew. We're passengers on Maelyn's ship, along with a whole lot of promises."

Her eyebrows pulled together in concern, and a small part of him liked the attention, the comfort in the illusion that he wasn't alone. But it *was* an illusion. This was just another of Vonya's tricks.

"We share a common goal that will benefit all involved," she said.

Quinton glanced at the holoscreens. "I don't know if it's going to work out the way you think it will."

As she regarded him for a few moments, the door to the workshop opened and Maelyn walked in.

Quinton glanced at her as she strode into the workshop, coming toward him. She was a formidable woman, the bearer of a fierce beauty that was at once at odds with Vonya's stunning perfection. But her beauty was real. She had thick dark brown hair, tanned skin, and subtle blue eyes that blazed when one was lucky enough to be caught in their crosshairs. He'd seen her raw anger as she handily removed Becker from the bridge. She was a woman who was used to command. He hadn't seen it when they'd first met, and he wondered how he could have missed it. He'd seen her as strong and kind, and very much a product of the harsh realities of this galaxy, but Quinton didn't really know who she was. She was tenacious and seemed to keep to herself and a trusted few. But what did she really want?

Maelyn looked at him with a coolness that was reflected in her blue eyes. Quinton studied her and then cranked up his frame rate, slowing down his perception of time and elongating the moment. On second thought, he'd been sure her eyes were pale green. He checked his memory and found that the color of her eyes had changed. On the deck of Lennix Crowe's hangar bay, Maelyn had had eyes of celestial blue. Then, sometime after they'd escaped from Crowe and were on the Mozeyian Outpost, they'd been a pale green with hints of brown in them. Now they were a blue that was as intense as the largest star burning the hottest.

Quinton lowered his frame rate back to normal. She blinked, and there was a calm set to her mouth. Her jawline was on the square side but not in any way masculine. Where Vonya was tall and slender, Maelyn had an athletic body that was properly proportioned and no less perfect than Vonya's engineered physique. Quinton had never taken the time to admire it. He'd only sneaked a few glances during their time together. He was a man, after all, and if he wasn't looking, then there had to be something wrong with him. Becker had detected something in the way Quinton regarded Maelyn.

She looked at Vonya for a moment. "Thank you, Vonya," Maelyn said and turned toward Quinton. "I asked her to check on you."

Quinton nodded. "Well, it would have been her or Simon."

Maelyn tilted her chin down and sighed.

"I know what you're doing. You send in a friendly face and then we can gloss over the fact that this situation—me being on this ship— is spiraling out of control."

She smiled widely, her eyes gleaming with amusement. "You really don't think much of us, do you?"

"Would you? Since I met you, it's been all about what I can do for you. I'm so valuable that Crowe is willing to commit vast resources to capture me. Are you saying you would do any less?" Quinton asked and then added, "No, you're always much more subtle than that. Why use a blaster when you can use empty promises?"

"Quinton, that's not fair," Vonya said.

Maelyn raised one of her hands in a placating gesture. "On the contrary, Quinton is being very fair."

He felt the annoying urge to frown, which came with the added bonus of an error about not having a mouth to hang open.

Maelyn pressed her lips together for a moment, but there were still hints of a smile around the edges. "However," she said, "the promises I made to you aren't empty."

Quinton looked away from her toward the holoscreens—not because he needed to see the information on them but to buy himself a few moments to think. He turned back to her. "I don't think this arrangement is going to work out between us."

"Are you breaking up with me?"

He felt the urge to frown yet again, along with the irritating feedback on non-capability. He leaned away from her. "What?"

Maelyn laughed, and despite himself, it was a sound he found soothing to his artificial ears. "Will you at least hear me out and then make a decision?"

Quinton's guard went up immediately. *Are you breaking up with me? What did that even mean*, he thought. Aloud, he said, "What? That's it? You'd just let me go? I wouldn't have to bargain for it or take more direct action to secure my freedom?"

Maelyn's eyebrows rose for a quick second. "Are any of us really free?" she asked and held up her hand. "Never mind, don't answer that. But to answer *your* question, yes, I'd let you go. You're not my prisoner, Quinton."

"What about Wallace?"

Maelyn inhaled deeply and arched a dark eyebrow. Vonya watched them both with keen interest. "That's not something you need to concern yourself with. I can take care of myself."

"I know you can take care of yourself, but I thought—"

"I know what you thought, but look, I'm going to level with you. That's what you want, isn't it?" Maelyn asked.

Quinton nodded.

"First, you're right. I'd considered sending Simon to check on you. You two have a rapport. You obviously wanted to be alone, but when I saw that you were working in here, I thought it would be best for you to see a friendly face. Vonya was nearby and said she thought she could help you," Maelyn said.

Quinton glanced at Vonya, who nodded once.

"It was highly manipulative, and I offer my heartfelt apologies for being concerned for your well-being."

He grinned and shook his head. "All right, fine. There wasn't some nefarious motivation on your part, and I appreciate your concern. Thank you."

Maelyn inclined her head in a small nod. "I said I was going to level with you, and I am. You want to track the activation signal and get out of that body."

"Preferably into my own body based on my biological scan data."

"I don't understand," Vonya said.

"As part of the upload process for becoming a PMC, biological scan data was always retained as a backup," Quinton replied.

Vonya frowned. "But it's been so long. Are any of those records still around?"

"I don't know for sure, but I do have access to resources that might help," Maelyn said.

Quinton didn't respond. He waited for her to continue.

"You always have the option to wander the galaxy on your own, but I'm not sure how successful you'd be."

"I don't know. I'm pretty determined," he said.

"Of that I have no doubt. Let me tell you why coming with me is your best option. I'm from the Dholeren United Coalition. There are several large nomadic fleets that form the coalition, and it's made up of people from multiple federations. They were displaced during the Federation Wars, as well as in the aftermath. There were many roaming groups just looking for safety."

"Nomadic fleets? Why didn't they resettle on a habitable world?"

"Some did. Actually, a lot of them did, at least initially. Then various salvager groups and pirates raided those areas. Why work to build a permanent settlement when someone else was just going to come and take everything you own?" Maelyn said.

"Couldn't they defend themselves?" he asked.

"It's not an all or nothing, Quinton. People did try to defend themselves, and some succeeded for a little while. But eventually, defending a habitable world wasn't a viable long-term option. You see, not only were they the victims of remnant militaries, but the worlds were also visited by Sentinel scout fleets. You've seen what they're capable of. There are records of them visiting the same devastation on newly minted colonial worlds. So, what would you do?" she asked with raised eyebrows. Quinton was silent. "Moving around was their best option. And the DUC is more accepting of people from all federations than other groups."

"Okay, I'm with you. Keep talking," Quinton said.

"Since the DUC accepts refugees from all over, we have access to a pretty robust knowledge base. There might be someone with knowledge about PMCs and that signal used to activate you," Maelyn said.

"Is that before or after they try to enslave me? I don't know if I can go along with this without full access to my own memories. I mean, there seems to be a common hatred of the Acheron Confederacy. What if you learned that they were the ones who activated me or somehow there's a connection there? What would you do then?" Quinton asked.

"I don't know how people would react to that," Maelyn said. "I don't even know how the DUC leadership would react, but I don't think it would matter because you're the key to unlocking technology and access to data that we simply don't have right now. It's been locked away from us. So regardless of people's prejudices, they will *need* you, just like you need us. Whether you want to admit it or not, your best chance at surviving is with me."

Quinton regarded her for a few moments. No matter how he tried to dissect it, Maelyn made some very good points. He wanted to find a flaw in her argument, but he couldn't. She'd already acknowledged the risks associated with going with her.

"I'll do everything I can to help you," she said.

"Why? Why would you make a promise like that? I don't know if I can trust you, and you don't know if you can trust *me*."

"Eventually, you'll have to trust someone. That is, unless you plan to remain alone."

He didn't need Radek to tell him what the probability for success was if he decided to go off on his own. Whether he liked it or not, he needed to stay on the *Nebulon* and see this through.

Quinton gestured toward the holoscreens. "Since we're being honest, I think you should know that I've encountered the Sentinels before, but I didn't know what they were," he said and told her what had happened during his escape from the Zeda-Six Star System. "What do you think?"

Maelyn peered at the data on the holoscreens and then looked at him. "You're right. They might be hunting for you. I think we should assume that they are."

"So, you still think bringing me to the DUC nomadic fleets is a good idea?" Quinton asked.

"Our options are limited, but I'm not bringing you to the civilian fleets. We're going to meet at a neutral location to protect the fleet," Maelyn said.

"I just don't know how the Sentinels could have tracked me here."

"It could just be coincidence. It's certainly not the same scout ship, but they must have a central command that they report in to."

"Central command—COMCENT," Quinton said. "Maybe we can find out what they know?"

Maelyn shook her head. "No way. It's too well protected, and you saw what they can do. That was only a scout force."

"Okay, but when the scout force reports to COMCENT, that means there will be more Sentinels looking for me," Quinton said.

"Not just you. I wasn't—There've been other reports of PMC activity."

"What kind of reports?" he asked.

Maelyn shook her head. "I don't know, other than the fact that there have been rumors, and it's something that would be quite concerning if it was true."

Quinton considered this for a few moments—more than a few moments to be exact, thanks to his internal clock. "You're worried that another war will happen. The Sentinels will increase their activities and maybe become more aggressive. That's what you're afraid of."

"That's what *you* should be afraid of," she replied.

There was something in the certainty of her reply that made him think he would be foolish not to listen to her. Yet, he wasn't sure how he could go on avoiding the Sentinels, and he said so.

"Everyone avoids the Sentinels. You wouldn't be alone in that," Maelyn said.

"I can't promise that I won't access computer systems when I come across them. I can try and limit my footprint, so to speak, but I can't stumble around any more than I already am," Quinton said.

Maelyn looked at him for a few long moments and then nodded slowly. She didn't like it, but what choice did he have? He thought about the salvager ships that had been destroyed by the Sentinels. There had to be a way for him to mask his presence.

"So, are we still on to meet with the leadership of the DUC?" Maelyn asked.

She wasn't going to take anything at face value or she wouldn't have asked. She didn't demand or expect his cooperation.

"Yes, let's see what we can find out," Quinton replied.

She smiled a little. "Good. I'll make the arrangements."

"Do those arrangements still require the presence of Becker, Guttman, and Oscar?" he asked.

He really didn't have any problems with Oscar, but he doubted Oscar would leave Becker.

Maelyn's gaze hardened. "We have a deal," she said, as if that explained everything.

"I'll never trust Becker."

She inhaled and sighed. "You don't have to trust him, and he doesn't have to trust you."

Quinton couldn't help but detect the warning note in her voice. Becker had challenged her authority and come up short. She could use the blaster, but Quinton thought she preferred mutual cooperation. He decided he'd play along for now. He'd much rather work with Maelyn than against her. But regardless of what anyone said, he would keep a close watch on Becker and his men.

24

THEIR MEETING with the Dholeren United Coalition leadership was delayed. There were concerns that the meeting would draw attention from the Sentinels or even Lennix Crowe, so extra precautions needed to be taken. Maelyn explained that the additional security measures were because of her report that had been delivered by Captain Wallace. A DUC admiral by the name of Severin Brandt had sent Maelyn a recorded message. The DUC admiralty didn't want to chance an open connection with Quinton on the *Nebulon*. From a security standpoint, Quinton approved of the precautionary steps being taken, but he was still impatient to get on with it. Vonya had commented about a saying that referred to "idle hands opening the way to mischief."

Quinton had some free time on his hands, so he stayed busy by analyzing the current data from the Sentinel attack. The standard protocols they followed were extreme, as if the entire galaxy were in one big interstellar war and the Sentinels retained some kind of emergency powers that allowed them to violate just about every pre-Federation War law to protect people.

Spacers had always scanned each other. It was the only way to determine what kind of ship or other installation they'd encounter in a given star system. But the Sentinels accessed ship systems and then determined whether they were going to obliterate those ships, colonies, space stations, or just about any settlement found across the galaxy. It was a gross abuse of power, and it had led the survivors of the Federation Wars to take extreme measures of their own in order to avoid combat with the Sentinels and each other. Genetic augmentation had always been practiced, but Quinton's limited memory of it indicated that it had been highly refined to fit unique circumstances, such as adapting to a habitable world. But post-Federation War, people had taken genetic manipulation to a whole new extreme where they could almost scarcely be called human anymore.

Quinton looked at Simon expectantly. They were alone on the bridge.

"What you're asking is impossible for me to duplicate," Simon said.

"It's not impossible."

He'd been directly interfacing with the *Nebulon*'s computer systems while conversing with Simon at the same time. Multitasking was actually getting easier for him, but it did require increasing his frame rate, so sometimes his conversation with Simon was a little off-kilter.

"Do you know how to do it then?" Simon asked.

"That's the point. Radek has helped create cleanup routines that effectively mask my presence in the system and will remove all traces that I can think of, but that's the problem. What if we missed something? We need a way to test it," Quinton said.

Removing traces of his presence on the ship's computer system was simple in theory but had proven to be frustratingly difficult to implement. In all instances, Quinton had to disconnect from the computer system to avoid detection. That was the easiest thing to do, but it severely limited what he could do.

"You can't go around making changes to the system, even if it's less efficient. You also access information quicker, which leaves a trace, and no, telling the *Nebulon* to stop logging activity won't work either because there are limits to how many processes the ship's computing system is able to monitor," Simon said.

"That's the part I don't understand. What if you'd made the improvements or found another way to do what I can do, but without being a PMC?"

"Then any Sentinel we encountered would become hostile."

"That would mean that there haven't been any improvements to computing systems since the Federation Wars."

"I wouldn't go that far," Simon replied. "That's an oversimplification. There have been changes and improvements, but innovation has slowed down, and anything we do requires that we consider how the Sentinels would react."

"I know you told me that there have been multiple war efforts to stop the Sentinels, and they were all put down hard, but I just don't believe that all the options have been explored," Quinton said.

Simon shrugged one shoulder. "Regardless, I can't guarantee that even with Radek's improvements for hiding your presence you wouldn't be detected by the Sentinels. Think about it. They're not dumb machines that keep doing the same thing over and over again. They adapt too. Based on the reports of every encounter we know about, the Sentinels aren't stagnant in the methodology they use."

Quinton was quiet for a few moments while he considered. "I just want to be thorough. There has to be a way to fool them, but we can't wait to encounter a Sentinel to test out our ideas."

Simon pressed his lips together while he peered at the data on the holoscreen in front of him. "Much of our detection capabilities for PMC activity stem from what the Sentinels use."

"They shared it with you?"

Simon snorted and shook his head, grinning. "We had the capability beforehand. It came out during the Federation Wars when multiple federations were producing their own PMCs, so the ability to detect PMC activity was born of necessity."

"I see," Quinton said. "How long do you think they'll delay the meeting?"

"Not that long. They'll want to keep it a secret, but they also can't sit on this for any great period of time," Simon replied.

The door to the bridge opened and Maelyn entered, along with Becker.

"Any word from Brandt?" she asked.

"Not yet," Simon said.

Maelyn nodded and looked at Quinton. "It shouldn't be too much longer."

"Let's hope not," Becker added.

The salvager had gone back to treating Quinton as he'd done before—slightly indifferent with the occasional proverbial jab.

"What I'd like to know is how Lennix Crowe was able to track us to the outpost," Quinton said.

"He has an effective network of informants," Becker replied.

"We were only there for a few hours. Can they normally track someone that fast?" Quinton asked.

Becker leveled a look at him. "You think it's me. That I somehow informed Crowe of our location."

"You did work for him. Maybe you decided that changing sides . . ." Quinton paused, choosing his words, ". . . ending your employment was a hasty decision, and how else could you rectify such a decision but by offering me up to Crowe?"

Becker chuckled and then nodded. "It's tempting, and I can see why you'd think that, but you'd be wrong."

"Am I?"

"You don't get it. Crowe doesn't offer second chances."

"Is that so," Quinton replied. "Apparently, I'm pretty valuable. He must want what I can do in the worst way. I can see him making an exception in this case."

Becker glanced at Maelyn and rolled his eyes. "There are rumors that Crowe is in trouble with the Collective. That's why he'd like to get his hands on a PMC."

"The Collective?" Maelyn said. "Draven is after him?"

Becker arched an eyebrow, then nodded once. "These are just rumors."

"What kind of rumors?" Quinton asked.

Becker scratched the stubble of his beard. "Crowe tried to claim something that didn't belong to him, or he failed to deliver on a big promise, and Draven plans to absorb Crowe's Union."

"That's it? One bad deal and Crowe's entire operation is at risk?" Quinton asked.

"There's also a rumor that Crowe tried to steal something important from the Collective. It doesn't really matter," Becker said and glanced at the main holoscreen for a moment. "All I know is that demands were increased across the board. They wanted us to bring in as much salvage as we could. Crowe became obsessed with resource allocation."

Maelyn pursed her lips. "If he had the Collective breathing down his neck, that would explain a few things."

Quinton looked at her.

"I'd thought Crowe wanted you in order to sell dumbed-down versions of you, or he'd use you to help his operation run more efficiently, but I might have been wrong. He needs you to survive, or . . ." She stopped speaking and looked at Becker, and then they both looked at Quinton.

"Why do I get the feeling I'm not going to like where this is going," Quinton said, dryly.

"Crowe needs you in order to take on the Collective," Maelyn said.

"Wait, what?" Quinton began and stopped. "I'm assuming he has a way to enslave me, but how does that mean he can suddenly take on the Collective?"

Maelyn and Becker didn't look at each other, but there was some kind of deference evident between the two of them.

"I thought we were done hiding things from each other," Quinton said.

Maelyn tapped her fingertips on the nearest workstation and then turned toward him. "You could give him a tactical advantage in space combat. It would be enough of an advantage that Crowe could start nibbling away at the Collective."

Becker exhaled explosively and shook his head. "That would be a huge power play," he said and frowned. "That would really shake things up."

Maelyn nodded.

Becker regarded her for a few moments. "One day, I'd like to find out what you were really doing trying to infiltrate Crowe's organization."

"Who said I was trying?" Maelyn said dryly.

Becker snorted.

"I understand this is important, but how much of an impact would this have?" Quinton asked. He was getting tired of being in the dark about . . . everything.

"The Collective is a known entity," Maelyn said. "We avoid them whenever possible, but sooner or later you have to deal with them. They're one of the largest purveyors of just about anything you can think of, but at a cost." She pressed her lips together. "The dominant faction of the Collective came from the remnants of the Tilion Empire Fleet. They had one of the most intact military fleets at the end of the Federation Wars. The Tilions had already been quite militaristic. They sought to fill the void the Jordani Federation left after both they and the Acheron Confederacy destroyed themselves. I'm afraid there's a lot of history here that you'll need to learn about in order to understand."

"What a surprise," Becker said. "Quinton needs another history lesson."

Quinton looked at Becker with what he hoped was a menacing glare. The agricultural bot's facial features weren't meant to convey much in the way of emotion, but he thought he could change the eye color to something more menacing.

"There are a few lessons I'd like to teach you, Becker," Quinton said.

Becker's smile didn't reach his eyes. "Anytime."

"Not now," Quinton replied. "I think I'll take a page out of your book and wait for . . ." He glanced at Maelyn and didn't finish.

"Now that we have that out of the way, I think we can move on," she said.

"We still don't know how Crowe was able to find us," Quinton said while making a quick change to Becker's wrist computer configuration. "We checked the ship for trackers and didn't find any, so that was a dead end. I checked the subspace communication logs and didn't see anything out of the ordinary."

Becker frowned and looked down at his wrist for a moment.

Maelyn nodded. "I think we'll be safe for the time being. Crowe's not going to know where the DUC leadership wants to meet us, and even if he did, he might get more than he bargained for. Admiral Brandt isn't going to take any chances where that's concerned."

"Crowe's too smart for that," Becker said.

"How so?" Simon asked.

"He won't attack unless he thinks he has a tactical advantage. He's not above sacrificing some of his ships, but he won't commit to an all-out assault against anything the DUC has in their arsenal," Becker replied. He looked down at his wrist computer and then let out a startled yelp, tearing it off his wrist and rubbing the area where it had been.

"What's wrong?" Simon asked.

Becker looked at his arm and then at his wrist computer, which was now on the floor. "I don't know. It just started burning," he said and bent down to retrieve it. Then he glared at Quinton.

"You gotta watch those configuration settings. Sometimes you can overclock them, and who knows what can happen?" Quinton said.

Simon looked at Maelyn, his eyebrows raised and mouth partially open. Becker turned away, grumbling while he accessed his wrist computer's configuration settings.

Quinton thought it would be too much for Becker to handle if he actually laughed, but inside he felt a wave of satisfaction at Becker's frustration. Sometimes a little bit of payback could go a long way.

Maelyn looked as if she was about to speak, but a comlink registered on the main holoscreen. Simon looked at Maelyn, who gestured for him to acknowledge it. A brief message appeared on-screen that contained a meeting time and a set of coordinates for them to follow.

"It looks like we've gotten our invitation, gentlemen," Maelyn said.

Since Quinton was already in the *Nebulon*'s computer system, he had access to the navigation computer, and the destination appeared on his HUD.

"That's not right," he said.

Simon frowned. "What do you mean? The message is definitely from the DUC."

Quinton saw Maelyn's lips curve slightly.

"Oh, the message looks authentic, but the coordinates take us to the center of a star system. And I mean inside the actual star. That's not right," Quinton said. He looked at Maelyn and waited.

Becker followed his gaze. "What is this? What's going on?" he asked.

"It's just a security measure," Maelyn replied. "Trust me when I say that we're not going to jump into the center of a star."

Quinton thought she sounded confident, but he didn't like not knowing where they were going. "What are the real coordinates then?"

The edges of Maelyn's lips lifted a little. "Captain's privilege," she said. Then she walked over to the captain's chair and opened a ship-wide broadcast. "We'll be jumping to a neutral location for our meeting with the DUC leadership. Kieva, I need you to report to the bridge."

Maelyn closed the comlink.

Quinton looked at Becker, who didn't seem bothered by not knowing their coordinates, but Quinton didn't believe that for a second. He studied the coordinates, hoping Radek might see something he couldn't.

"It irritates you not knowing where we're going," Becker said.

"And you're not?" Quinton said. "At least *I'm* not pretending to be fine with being kept in the dark."

Becker smirked. "Shouldn't you be able to figure it out? I mean, I thought PMCs were supposed to be highly capable of this sort of thing."

Quinton knew Becker was goading him, but that didn't mean it wasn't working. It was. He hated not knowing where they were heading. There were millions of possibilities based on the coordinates alone, but he could reduce those if he kept their potential destinations within jump range. However, that still left them with too much data to predict the meeting's location with any degree of accuracy. So, no, he couldn't figure it out.

"You do have limits. That's good to know," Becker said smugly.

Quinton made a mental note to come up with creative ways to frustrate Becker. The man had a temper. He could make that work for him, but he had more important things to consider at the moment.

He didn't think Maelyn would tell him, even if he asked. If Admiral Brandt was really concerned about security, then this could be just the first in a set of coordinates until they arrived at the actual meeting place.

In thirty minutes, Quinton would find out. He couldn't help but think that if Crowe was willing to do everything in his power to control Quinton, then what would stop the DUC from doing the same? Any fleet admiral worth their stripes would see the tactical advantage of what Quinton offered. Wouldn't he want that for himself? He needed to be prepared in case this meeting went sideways. He chuckled at the thought, which drew a few inquiring glances in his direction.

"It's nothing. I just thought of something funny," he said.

Becker looked away from him, and Maelyn arched an eyebrow.

"It's not worth repeating," he said. He then added, "Quinton's privilege."

Maelyn leaned back in her chair and smiled. "Very well. Enjoy it."

He wouldn't go so far as to believe his little play on words had been clever, but he did like her smile. He walked over to Simon's workstation on the bridge.

"How capable is the DUC fleet?" Quinton asked.

Simon's expression faltered.

"I'm not looking for specifics," he added quickly. "But if Crowe somehow found this meeting place, how safe would we actually be?"

Quinton's biometric sensors showed that Simon's heart rate had increased. The young engineer looked away from him for a few moments.

"I . . ." Simon said, drawing out the word. "The DUC does have defensive capabilities, but there's a higher priority for threat detection and avoidance."

Quinton considered this for a few moments, hoping he'd misheard what Simon had said. "Threat detection and avoidance . . . Are you saying that running away is standard fleet doctrine for the DUC?"

He heard Becker chuckle.

Simon swallowed hard, his expression serious. "Sometimes it's the best option. You keep moving around and you live. Stay and fight, or even attack, and a lot of people will die."

Quinton turned toward the main holoscreen. It was clear that Simon wasn't comfortable with that answer, and he'd accidentally touched on a sensitive subject.

"I wasn't judging."

"Yes, you were," Simon said.

He waited a few seconds before responding. "You're right. I, um . . ." Quinton didn't know what to say. He didn't want to offend one of the few people on the ship that he actually liked and respected. Simon had helped him, both with repairs to the agricultural unit and as a companion.

"It's okay, you're from a different place and a different time. A place I wish I could have seen," Simon said.

Now Quinton really didn't know what to say. "I'm going to go stand over here," he said, gesturing behind him.

Simon nodded and focused his attention on the workstation holoscreens in front of him.

He'd been standing off to the side for a few minutes when he heard Maelyn clear her throat. When he turned, she gestured for him to come over.

"Is asking what you're thinking about part of 'Quinton's privilege'?" she asked.

"It might be."

"I'm sorry, but I can't disclose the actual meeting location. You don't have to worry about it though."

There was a flurry of sensation errors as the agricultural bot's internal systems failed to interpret the spike of Quinton's emotions. He really hated that.

"I want you to trust me," Maelyn said.

Quinton let out an audible sigh. "I'd like to, but it's not just . . ." He paused for a second, reconsidering. "Don't worry about it. Let's just get through this part in one piece."

Maelyn nodded. "Fair enough," she said.

It took several jumps for the *Nebulon* to reach the star system for the meeting with the DUC. Admiral Brandt had put them on a tight schedule, but Maelyn was familiar with standard DUC protocols, even for a secret meeting. Once they entered the star system, there was a subspace communications beacon that gave them the coordinates for the next star system. Once the beacon transmitted its message, it engaged the self-destruct protocol. Quinton suspected that it also contacted the DUC to keep them apprised of the *Nebulon*'s progress. However, he didn't try to access the communications beacon to confirm this.

"We're here," Maelyn said.

The confirmation showed on the main holoscreen, along with the star map of a binary star system that was about the most unfriendly place Quinton had seen yet. When they formed, a binary star system gradually stabilized after billions of years. The binary star system they were in now was the result of when two individual solar systems collided. The two stars were in a celestial tug-of-war until, eventually, one absorbed the other. This process could also take billions of years. But what Quinton was seeing was that the individual star systems had once had a system of planets with them, and all that was left of the rocky planets were massive asteroid fields. One day, a long time from now, they might re-form into new planets, but Quinton would never be around to see that. The larger Jovian planets hadn't even settled into a stable orbit yet.

A video comlink registered with the *Nebulon*, and Maelyn acknowledged it.

On the main holoscreen, the head and shoulders of an older man appeared.

"Captain Wayborn, I'm glad you made it."

"Thank you, Admiral Brandt. I've come as you requested."

Brandt shifted his gaze toward Quinton. "I'm looking forward to speaking with you when you come aboard the *Astra*." He looked at Maelyn. "Captain, your shuttle is cleared to board, and be advised that security measures are in place."

"Understood, Admiral," Maelyn said.

The comlink severed, and the main holoscreen went blank. They set a course for the waypoint.

Quinton looked at Maelyn. "What security measures do they have in place?"

Becker looked at him. "It means don't go poking around."

Quinton glanced at him and then turned back toward Maelyn, waiting.

"Becker's right. They'll have additional security measures in place that are specifically designed to detect and prevent PMC access. So please, show some restraint," Maelyn said.

Quinton had suspected that the DUC would take precautions against him, but he couldn't help but be a little curious as to what they had in place and whether he could bypass it. The temptation began to build up—

"Quinton," Maelyn said.

"I'll play nice as long as they do," he replied.

Maelyn nodded and had Simon set a course for the waypoint.

Quinton had already hardened the communication capabilities of the agricultural bot. Communications could work in a number of different ways. Data communications between computer systems required that one party send information while the other received it. However, even the most hardened security systems had to account for the vulnerability of the initial communication. Neither sender nor receiver was totally secure. This was why he had effectively sealed off every conceivable way for a comlink to register with him unless he approved it. Furthermore, he had routed all comlinks to a virtual sandbox that was controlled by Radek. It was an additional layer of security that gave Quinton some comfort. He couldn't get around the fact that he was vulnerable, and the odds were stacked in everyone else's favor because of his ignorance of the galaxy. He'd have to improvise if the situation called for it.

A short while later, they boarded the shuttle and Maelyn flew them to the

Astra. The DUC *Astra* was a Tilion Empire cruiser that had been heavily modified during its lifetime. Quinton could still see the original design elements, which pointed to a heavy cruiser design. He supposed he should be thankful that it was an actual warship and not some kind of converted freighter. According to the shuttle scanners, there were two more cruisers and a civilian transport ship.

No one was left behind on the *Nebulon*. Becker kept looking in Quinton's direction, as if there was something he wanted to say. Quinton was sure it was nothing he wanted to hear, so he ignored him.

The shuttle flew through the hangar bay shields, and Maelyn landed the shuttle. After opening the side doors, the loading ramp extended to the ground. Quinton was closest to the door, but he waited for Maelyn to lead the way. She was the captain, after all, and as he was almost constantly reminded, this was her ship.

She looked at him for a moment and then exited the shuttle. Without a backward glance, Quinton followed her.

He hadn't known what to expect when he got out of the shuttle. He thought there would be an escort of some sort, and definitely armed soldiers. There was a large group of them, but the hangar deck was essentially empty. They were the only ship in attendance. He glanced around and thought this would've been a good ambush site.

Rows of black-armored soldiers held their assault rifles in front of them. Power signatures appeared on his HUD, showing that the armor and rifles were fully charged. A DUC delegation walked through a break in the rows of soldiers. Quinton recognized Admiral Brandt as he strode over to them. Walking next to him was a woman with blonde hair and a mixture of mature and youthful features. Quinton found that he couldn't estimate her age, but if her eyes were any indication, she looked to be of an age of experience and intelligence. There were other people who followed them, but he assumed the most important people were the two in front.

Maelyn came to a stop and said, "Director Cantos, Admiral Brandt, I'd like to introduce you to Quinton."

"Severin Brandt," the admiral said. He paused for a moment, taking in Quinton's appearance. "I have to admit I didn't expect . . ." his voice trailed off.

"I didn't expect it either," Quinton replied, breaking the awkward silence.

Director Cantos laughed. "Well met, Quinton. Sherilyn Cantos, one of the elected leaders of the Dholeren United Coalition."

Quinton felt an urge to stand up straighter. Maelyn introduced the rest of the crew.

Brandt looked at Quinton after the introductions were concluded. "My understanding is that some kind of activation signal was sent to the Zeda-Six Star System and that's how you came to be here."

"That's the long and short of it," Quinton replied. Then he added, "The reports you've no doubt read are accurate. I have limited access to my Energy Storage System. This body was the best of the extremely limited choices available."

Brandt chuckled without humor. "I can identify with that—the limited choices, I mean."

Brandt looked at Cantos, his eyebrows raised. She gave him a small nod and then looked at Quinton. "We also heard about the Sentinel attack near the Mozeyian Outpost."

"Crowe's Union ships were there as well," Maelyn said. "He opened hostilities against my ship. Quinton was helping to defend the ship, but he didn't fully understand the capabilities of the Sentinels."

The rest of the delegation looked at Quinton, as if trying to somehow peer past the rough exterior of the agricultural unit. Maybe they were trying to find his ESS.

"Captain Wayborn said we might be able to help each other," Quinton said. He figured that if they were being formal, he should address Maelyn by her title.

Sherilyn Cantos interlaced her fingers in front of her and regarded Quinton calmly. "Yes, we'll get to that, but I'm interested in your intentions."

"My intentions," Quinton repeated, "are that I'd like to get out of this body. I'd like to be put back in my own body so I can have access to my own memories. You have no idea what it's like to be so close to who you once were and have it kept from you."

"That's just the thing. We don't know who you are," Sherilyn said.

"I'm happy to get to know you, if that's what it will take to get your help, but I don't have a lot of time," Quinton said.

The barest hints of a smile lifted Sherilyn Cantos's lips. "You misunderstand me. We cannot find any record of a Quinton Aldren at all in our records." She looked at Maelyn. "We've checked all of our data repositories."

"Surely there must be some kind of mistake," Maelyn said.

"I'm afraid not," Cantos replied.

"So what if you can't find a record of me. Aren't your records incomplete?" Quinton said.

"They might be," Brandt said. "But it could also be that your records were erased. We've compiled documentation over the years from all the old federations. They came from all the refugees that joined the DUC and have been pieced together for a century. So you must understand that our records are probably the most intact you'll find."

Quinton was quiet for a few moments. "Does that mean you're not going to help me?"

"That's what we're trying to decide," Cantos said.

He didn't like where this was heading.

"We think Quinton is from either the Acheron Confederacy or the Jordani Federation. He predates the Federation Wars," Maelyn said.

"If he's from the Acheron Confederacy, that may complicate things. This could be some kind of latent ploy from Grand Admiral Browning. If that's the case, no good can come of this," Brandt said.

"Hold on a minute," Quinton said. "I don't even know who that is, so I'm not anybody's ploy. I came here because I needed help. Maelyn said you were my best option and that we could help each other. You need access to technology and resources that only I can give you. Do all those wants go away because you suspect some kind of connection to this Admiral Browning from the Acheron Confederacy?"

The others around him went into a stunned silence, which wasn't the response he'd been hoping for. The environmental detection systems in the agricultural unit showed him the nearest data access points, and he wanted to access the *Astra*'s systems to find out who Browning was.

Brandt stepped closer to him, and Quinton noticed that the nearby soldiers watched them intently. "Browning was a monster. He's the reason the Federation Wars lasted as long as they did. He's responsible for trillions of deaths. The Acheron Confederacy is gone. We've taken in refugees from there, but they've cut all ties to their former federation. And it's a good thing too. Their contributions are the reason this galaxy is in the state it's in. Entire worlds have been destroyed. Entire civilizations are gone. And all of this has given rise to anarchists in the form of warlords wielding old federation military might. I realize that your memories are an issue for you, but trust me when I tell you that I would love to forget the things I've seen. And I'm not the only one. So please don't act high and mighty, flippantly challenging our concerns."

Brandt had spoken evenly and coldly, which was much more effective than if he'd been yelling. Quinton looked at Director Cantos and saw the same battle-steel resolve in her gaze. In addition, there was general agreement from everyone who was standing nearby. He saw the same haunted bitterness in their gazes, although some didn't shine quite so brightly.

Quinton looked back at the crew of the *Nebulon*. Simon gave him a small nod and a look of encouragement. Becker merely looked at him impassively. Kieva and Vonya watched with keen interest, as did Guttman and Oscar.

He turned and started to walk back toward the shuttle. Every soldier in the area readied their weapons, pointing them at him in a seemingly single fluid motion. He halted. The soldiers carried kinetic-style rifles that had computing systems he could access. "So you don't intend to help me, but you're not going to let me leave. Is that right?" he asked.

Brandt looked at Cantos.

"Who's in charge here? Because I'm not sure if it's you, Admiral Brandt, or if it's you, Director Cantos. Who should I be speaking with?" Quinton asked.

Brandt looked over at his soldiers. "Stand down."

The soldiers lowered their weapons but didn't look any less dangerous because of it.

"Leadership is shared in the DUC," Cantos said.

"Are you authorized to help me? Maybe I should have started off with that, because right now, I feel like I'm wasting my time. And as you can clearly see, my time is limited," Quinton said, putting as much edge in his voice as he could.

"We are authorized to negotiate," Cantos said.

"Okay, what do you want?"

"We have other ways to confirm your identity, but it will require your cooperation," she replied.

"I can be reasonable," Quinton said. He thought he heard Becker mutter and clear his throat. "What do you have in mind?"

"We have in our possession a data relay console that was frequently used by PMCs during the Federation Wars. They were part of the subspace communications network relays," Cantos said.

"And you want me to access them as a way of confirming my identity," Quinton replied.

Cantos nodded.

"Before I do anything, I'm going to need some assurances from you."

Brandt exhaled explosively. "I don't see how you're in any position to request assurances."

"Don't you even want to hear what they are before you make your decision?"

Brandt regarded him coolly.

"I'll take whatever test you have for me, but regardless of the results, I want your assurance that you won't try to stop me from leaving here," Quinton said.

"That is a reasonable request," Cantos said. He looked at her and waited for her to continue. "You mentioned before that you would like to get back into your own body. That means Maelyn told you about the DNA vaults."

"That's right. The DNA vaults have the genome of all PMCs ever uploaded," Quinton said.

Admiral Brandt shook his head. "That was the practice before the end of the Federation Wars."

"The vaults were often attached to military outposts, but most are no longer around. The ones that remain are guarded by Sentinels. I'm telling you this so you'll understand that what you want might not be possible for us to deliver," Cantos said.

"I understand there's a risk. Let's get on with it," Quinton said.

Cantos brought up her wrist computer and accessed her personal holoscreen. "I'm authorizing you to use this data access module to access the console."

A data connection comlink initialized, and he accessed it. A challenge protocol presented itself, and something in Quinton's ESS responded with the proper authentication codes. This back and forth went on for almost a full minute before he was granted access.

Confirm PMC identity.

Quinton Aldren, G class.

Acheron Confederacy Navy – SP.

Quinton cranked up his frame rate to the max. The act of authenticating with the PMC communication console had activated more parts of his ESS than ever before. Data windows appeared on his HUD.

Data update available. Commence download.

The PMC console was following a standard set of protocols that were included in the update file. Quinton brought up a secondary interface and queried for the activation code used to initialize his PMC.

ACN – PMC recovery protocol.

Activation code trace running.

A long list of coordinates appeared in front of him, and Quinton copied it for future reference.

There was very little doubt that he had been part of the Acheron Confederacy Navy, but the information available didn't indicate a rank or anything like that. His classification was *G class*. He didn't know what that meant either.

Quinton then queried for DNA vaults that contained his unique genome. As the list appeared on his internal HUD, he wondered how many of those installations would still be intact.

His session with the PMC console closed before he was ready. They must have set some kind of time limit for access in anticipation that he could increase his frame rate to quickly access data.

He returned his frame rate to normal and looked at Director Cantos. "It worked, although I would've preferred a little more time."

"A precaution on our part. What did you discover?"

"There is a record of my genome, and I saw my identity. I'll transfer the data to you. I'm from the Acheron Confederacy Navy, although there was no record of anything more than that. There's no rank or ACN identification for me other than a PMC classification," Quinton said.

Cantos looked at Brandt. His eyes narrowed. "It could be some kind of special project. I'll have it investigated."

"Here are the lists of the coordinates for the DNA vaults. I assume you can compare these locations to your own star charts," Quinton said.

Director Cantos regarded him for a few moments. "Thank you for sharing the information with us. I also want you to know that we don't hold the fact that you are from the Acheron Confederacy against you, but for our own protection, we do need to confer with the rest of the DUC leadership before we agree on a way forward."

Quinton looked at Maelyn, who gave him a small nod. "All right."

Director Cantos smiled. "Thank you for understanding. I invite the rest of you to take your ease. We have a place for you to wait, and refreshments will be served."

Quinton didn't have any need for refreshment, but he certainly had plenty to think about. He'd been able to decipher the activation code, but there was a strange reference in it. He needed time to do his own analysis of the DNA vault locations. It wasn't just a simple list of the coordinates. It looked like there was other information in the data upload he'd received.

They were escorted out of the hangar bay. Simon glanced at him a few times. Maelyn walked behind Brandt.

Director Cantos turned toward Maelyn. "Captain Wayborn, there are several things we'd like to discuss with you away from your crew."

"I'm at your disposal," she replied.

The group split and Quinton wanted to go with Maelyn, or at least listen to their discussion. No doubt they were going to be discussing him.

Maelyn looked at him before she joined the others. "It's fine. I'll regroup with you in a little while. At that point, I'll tell you everything I'm authorized to tell you."

He leaned toward her and said quietly, "I don't think they're going to help me."

"They're concerned, Quinton, and with good reason, but I'll convince them that this is our best option."

Maelyn rejoined Director Cantos and Admiral Brandt, and Quinton went with the others.

25

Refreshments were indeed served. Becker, Guttman, Oscar, Kieva, and even Simon immediately went over to the food and drink that had been set out on a table for them. Quinton supposed they were getting tired of the food available on the *Nebulon*, but he couldn't be sure about it. Any table of delicious food in a room full of hungry people was sure to make them swoop down for a meal. Quinton's gaze slid to an assortment of fruits in a wide variety of colors.

Vonya looked at him with a pinched expression.

"You better join them before there's nothing left for you," Quinton said.

She glanced at the others before turning back to him. "Do you miss it?" she asked and gestured toward the others.

Becker noticed them and looked pointedly at Quinton before he took a hearty bite of his food, chewed it, and then swallowed, looking content.

Quinton hadn't thought about eating. Somehow, he'd managed to avoid it. Simon sometimes snacked while they were working, but it was nothing like the spread here. The agricultural unit had highly sensitive receptors equipped for scent, but he'd disabled them. He was tempted to turn them back on so he could smell the food. The others kept commenting about it.

He looked at Vonya. "Sometimes," he said and meant it.

She nodded with a sympathetic expression and then joined the others.

Quinton couldn't remember why he'd volunteered to upload himself into a Personality Matrix Construct. He must have been part of an Acheron Confederacy Navy project, but none of the records he'd found indicated what. At least he'd found the coordinates to DNA vaults that had his identification. He could become human again, as long as the vault was intact. The vaults had been established to offload PMCs who had decided to end their artificial existence.

His thoughts turned to the activation signal. He was able to decipher it, which meant he could trace it back to its origins, but what if Brandt was right and the activation signal was just some kind of latent protocol? He'd forgotten to ask them about the rumors of PMCs getting activated and whether there was increased Sentinel activity concentrated in a particular sector of the galaxy.

Both of Quinton's choices were dangerous. Tracing the activation signal to its origins ran the risk of the agricultural bot breaking down permanently, and trying to find a DNA vault established for the Acheron Confederacy Navy was risky for everyone.

"Quinton," Radek said inwardly, "you asked that I check Becker's activities according to the *Nebulon*'s computer systems."

Quinton was pulled from his thoughts. "Oh yeah, that's right. What did you find?"

"I believe Becker was conducting an investigation of his own."

"So he was watching me while I was watching him?"

"Not entirely," Radek replied. "He was checking ship maintenance logs."

A report appeared on his HUD, and Quinton looked at the log data. Becker had spent a lot of time reviewing the ship's automated maintenance routines, particularly trash and waste removal, which struck Quinton as odd because those systems were automated. The only time people actually checked those activities was when they stopped working or when those systems were due for manual inspection, which, according to the logs, Simon had done several months prior.

Quinton glanced at Becker. "What were you looking for?" he asked subvocally and then returned his attention to Radek. "Was there anything else he was doing?"

"Nothing out of the ordinary. He'd been trying to see what you were doing, but with the cleanup VIs you have running on the *Nebulon*'s systems, that effort has halted."

"Thanks, Radek. Good work," Quinton said.

His comms session with Radek ended. He thought about Maelyn and wondered what she was discussing with the DUC leadership. The *Astra* had security measures in place to detect whether Quinton tried to access their systems. He didn't want to risk it, but he wanted to know what was going on.

He had turned his attention to Simon when a tauntingly logical idea pushed to the forefront of his mind.

I shouldn't do this. I told her I'd play nice, Quinton thought.

Simon's comlink was active and ready to receive a connection to Maelyn. He was her second-in-command, and it was probably their standard protocol that contact was maintained, if possible. Now that Quinton had noticed the comlink, he couldn't stop thinking about it.

Simon, Simon, why are you doing this to me?

There must've been other comlinks in whatever meeting room Maelyn was in, but would it have something that could prevent subspace comms? Something that worked from ship to ship, but with personal comms? It could be done, but there was only one way to find out.

Quinton used Simon's comlink to open a data connection to Maelyn's comlink and set the priority to the lowest level so it wouldn't generate an alert.

He nearly grinned when Maelyn's comlink accepted the connection. When it was this easy to gain access, how could he *not* do it?

He brought up Maelyn's comlink interface and engaged the microphone so he could listen. He thought about activating the vidcom capabilities, but that might be noticed by the others. The only way he was going to see what was going on in that room was if he accessed the *Astra*'s systems, which would surely be detected, unless they were bluffing about their ability to detect PMC activity.

No, no! Focus, he chided himself.

Maelyn's comlink microphone became active, and he immediately heard someone speaking.

"You asked for options. I'm giving you options," Brandt said.

"The options aren't even plausible," Maelyn replied.

"We don't need this kind of trouble. We have enough to deal with considering the heightened Sentinel activity. We need to manage the migration of the entire fleet, and we need to do it by reducing our risk exposure," Brandt replied.

"You just don't like the fact that he's from the Acheron Confederacy. You're letting it cloud your judgment," Maelyn responded.

Quinton wasn't sure if Maelyn was answerable to Brandt. He wasn't even sure if she was in the DUC Navy despite being a ship captain. She seemed to hold a post that was answerable to multiple groups or leadership types.

"I do have a bias, and rightfully so. Any time we've conducted operations that had something to do with the Acheron Confederacy, it cost us in lives and loss of ships. Sherilyn, we don't need this," Brandt said.

"Yes, we do. What about the recolonization effort? The Acheron Confederacy had a detailed record of habitable systems that they kept secret from the rest of the galaxy. They used automated terraforming systems," Maelyn said.

"She has a point, Severin," Cantos said.

"I'll give you that," Brandt replied. "It's not like I wouldn't want to get my hands on the alleged resources kept at an Acheron military facility, but I've chased these leads before, many times—not just for the Acheron Confederacy but for any other federation that had a military. Many times, they'd been picked clean or destroyed, or there was a Sentinel monitoring station in the area."

"You've seen the reports of overcrowding on migrant fleet ships. The answer to our problems is not to simply acquire more ships. People need a home. We'll never have a second chance if we don't have a safe place for people to go," Maelyn said.

"Your heart is in the right place, Maelyn," Cantos said. "But whenever we've tried to colonize, even in secret, eventually the raiders come. It's a never-ending cycle."

"I understand that, and eventually, the secret would get out. But we would have a head start. No one else has this knowledge. No one else is working with a PMC. Quinton could help us do this if we helped him in return. It's the only way this is going to work," Maelyn said.

"I think we should wait and see if we can find somebody who has expertise with PMCs. They could probably help Quinton. He's stuck with limited access to his ESS. We don't know what will happen if he gets access to all his memories," Cantos said.

"Agreed. We should wait," Brandt said.

"Quinton doesn't have a lot of time," Maelyn said. "Simon has done the best he can with maintaining the agricultural unit, but we don't have any place to move his ESS to."

"That's hardly a reason for us to move faster than we choose to. My understanding is that if the agricultural unit were to cease operating, then Quinton would be forced to withdraw completely into his ESS. He'd be less dangerous that way," Brandt said.

"That's not fair to him," Maelyn replied.

"This isn't about being fair. This is about ensuring our survival. You'd put our fate into the hands of a PMC?" Cantos said, then added, "I know you want to help him, but there are bigger things at work here. The DUC needs our protection."

"Then don't give us any resources. I can take the *Nebulon* and scout a few of these locations. I could report back, and you could make a decision after that," Maelyn said.

"And we just overlook the fact that Quinton could take control of the *Nebulon* any time he chooses?" Cantos said.

"He could. And he could have done it way before now, but he didn't."

"Does he trust you?" Brandt asked.

"A little. Maybe more than a little, but he's become increasingly aware of the precariousness of his position. How would you be?"

"I've been backed into a corner before," Brandt said.

"I'm surprised you've allowed yourself to get caught up in something like this," Cantos said.

"Should I have just ignored the situation? No, I don't think so," Maelyn replied.

"Do you trust him?" Brandt asked. "When it comes right down to it, do you think Quinton will act like any other PMC ever encountered?"

"He hasn't exhibited any signs of losing his sanity. He's remarkably strong-willed and stubborn. I think those were traits the ACN looked for in its PMC candidates," Maelyn said.

"That's because he was recruited to help fight a war. I've never heard of the G class PMC," Cantos said.

"I can do some checking into that to figure out if we even know what the designation means," Brandt said.

"I think if we treat Quinton fairly, he'll reciprocate," Maelyn said.

"Thank you for your assessment. We're going to leverage our extensive resources to see what our next step should be. Please inform your crew," Cantos said.

There were a few moments of silence before Maelyn replied, "Understood, Director Cantos. I'll see to the maintenance of the *Nebulon*."

Quinton severed the connection to Maelyn's comlink. They were going to make him wait because they wanted to consult with PMC experts. They might be looking for the best way to control him. He kept reviewing what he'd heard. Maelyn continued to defend him. It was both gratifying and reassuring, and it made him not want to disappoint her.

A few minutes later, Maelyn joined them in the conference room. She walked over to Quinton and told the others that they needed to talk. They moved to the other side of the room.

Quinton looked at her. "I was listening," he said.

Maelyn frowned and then looked down at her wrist computer. Then she glanced at Simon, figuring out how Quinton had overheard her conversation.

"What are you going to do?" he asked her.

"I'm going to help you. There's too much at stake if I don't," Maelyn said.

"Was the Acheron Confederacy really terraforming worlds in secret?"

"That's one of the oldest rumors in the galaxy. Some people say it's just a foolish dream that gives spacers hope. It makes them continue to explore, but no one's ever found one."

"Well then, we might be the first," Quinton said.

Maelyn smiled.

"Why are they so hesitant about this?"

"Brandt and Cantos have been alive for a very long time. They were young when the Federation Wars began. I guess you could say they've witnessed the great collapse and the dark times that came after. They might appear harsh to you, but it's not without reason," Maelyn replied.

Quinton considered this for a few moments. "And you're going to disobey them to help me?"

Maelyn frowned. "No, I'd disobey them to find the DUC refugees a homeworld. Someplace safe from the Collective and people like Lennix Crowe. Some spacers thrive without setting foot on solid ground, but most people don't. We need our terrestrial roots planted on a homeworld that can be defended."

She wanted to find a home for the migrant fleet, and judging from Director Cantos's response, it wouldn't be the first time. Quinton wondered how many times they'd tried to colonize a new homeworld before giving up on it. Still, he'd thought there might have been other reasons for what Maelyn had in mind.

"Oh," Maelyn said with a playful glint in her eyes, "and there's you, of course. Can't forget about that."

Quinton chuckled a little, feeling relieved. "I grow on you after a while. It's part of my charm."

26

MAELYN WENT over to the table and began selecting food to eat. Quinton noticed that she seemed quite deliberate with her selection and only took small amounts. He glanced at the others and saw that they'd exhibited the same behavior. He'd expected Guttman and Oscar to pile on the food with exuberant proportions of debauchery, but they hadn't. Quinton supposed they were on their best behavior.

Maelyn sat and began eating while Becker joined her. The two spoke quietly. He didn't want to stand there staring at them, so he decided to shift his attention elsewhere. The rest of the crew was farther down the table. Guttman and Oscar were speaking with Vonya and Kieva. Simon waved him over.

"I never got a chance to ask you about how it went accessing that PMC console."

"Authentication took longer than expected, but after that, things went much more smoothly. The session didn't last very long," Quinton said.

Simon nodded. "They're just taking precautions, but they might let you access it for longer next time."

"If you say so," Quinton replied, unconvinced.

He glanced toward Maelyn, and a HUD overlay appeared on his internal heads-up display. The thermal analysis suite showed that the skin temperature on her cheekbones had increased. She was still speaking with Becker, and the two of them seemed completely at ease with one another. He didn't need a wide array of sophisticated sensors to inform him that there was some level of attraction shared between them, and he wondered when that had happened. *Had* it happened, or was he simply seeing something that wasn't there? Why did he care anyway? It was as if Becker didn't remember Maelyn throwing him off the bridge using a palm stunner and then threatening him with her sidearm.

"I *do* say so," Simon said, interrupting Quinton's thoughts.

He looked at Simon. "What?" he asked.

Simon finished chewing his food and swallowed. "I said that I do think they'll let you have another crack at the console. Did you learn anything else from it?"

Quinton looked down at the table and saw a few large nuts. "Do you mind?" he asked.

Simon glanced down at the table. "No, go ahead," he said, gesturing to the nuts.

Quinton picked up a couple and peered at them. "The authentication process accessed parts of my ESS that I hadn't known were there."

"What do you think it means?"

Quinton tossed a nut up in the air and deftly caught it. He tossed it up again. Then snatched it out of the air again and allowed it to glide across the back of his metallic fingers. He switched hands and did the same with both of them. "There was also an update."

Simon watched Quinton's finger dexterity with open appreciation. "Impressive," he said, inclining his head once. "Did the update affect the lockdown?"

"That's a good question," Quinton said. He hadn't thought to check that. "No, at least not as far as I can tell. I don't have any more access to my ESS than I did before. However, I'm able to retain the knowledge gained from the PMC console."

He saw Becker lean back, grinning. Quinton flicked the nut, and it darted across the room and clipped Becker on the back of the neck. Becker's hand came to his neck, and he turned toward them.

"Sorry about that. It must have slipped," Quinton said, gesturing with his hand.

Simon frowned. He'd seen what Quinton was doing and knew that he hadn't slipped. Becker shook his head, and Maelyn stood up.

Quinton looked at Simon, but before he could say anything, the door to the room opened and Admiral Brandt walked in. He headed straight toward Quinton.

Maelyn joined them, and Becker followed her.

"We've checked the vault locations against our current star charts," Brandt said. "It looks like there were indeed facilities at these locations, but many have been destroyed. Here, look for yourself."

The DUC fleet admiral activated his personal holoscreen and made it bigger, showing a galactic representation of the nearby sectors. "It looks like Sentinel fleets have discovered the vaults and cleaned house."

Quinton looked at the galaxy map. Radek ran a quick comparison of the list of vaults from the PMC console and compared it with the locations on the map. Brandt was right.

"Are you sure they've all been destroyed? Maybe some of them have been left intact or at least partially operational," Quinton said and looked at Maelyn. "Could we go look at a few of them? Maybe the data here is wrong."

Maelyn shook her head, and several of the others did the same. "The data is accurate. Salvagers would have picked those locations clean a long time ago. They have exploration drones that scout the old federation star systems. Also, the Sentinels wouldn't have left any of the infrastructure they found operational if it was designed for PMC use."

Brandt nodded. "Those systems would have been the first ones targeted."

Quinton looked at the galaxy map and tried to think of a solution. How destructive were the Sentinels? How well hidden were the vaults? Despite what the others had said, he still believed there must be something the Sentinels had overlooked. Star systems weren't inconsequential. There were lots of places to hide things. Usually, the best place to hide something was in plain sight, but the others were unwilling to even scout out some of these systems.

"It was a long shot at best, but we'll keep searching," Brandt said and shut down his personal holoscreen.

Quinton had committed it to memory, so he didn't need it on display.

"He's right," Maelyn said. "We'll keep searching. We can also find a more suitable body for you to use. There are several groups that specialize in androids, which will give you more access to your ESS."

She was just trying to help, and Quinton appreciated it, but he didn't want to find another cobbled-together android body to stick his ESS in. That was no way to live. He wanted to feel what it was like to be human again and not some shadowy reflection or memory. He'd gotten his hopes up when they'd shown him the list of vaults.

Maelyn looked concerned and glanced at Simon.

Quinton focused his attention on accessing the ESS. He didn't try to access his memories, but there were parts that had been activated when he'd authenticated with the PMC console. He brought up the deciphered activation signal used to bring him online. He then used the key to authenticate to his own ESS.

Access granted.

Mission parameters updated.

Quinton studied the message that appeared on his HUD.

"There's another vault," Quinton said finally.

The others became quiet.

"Where?" Maelyn asked.

He projected an image of the galaxy map, along with the coordinates of a star system that had been locked away in his ESS.

Brandt peered at the coordinates. "It's not in our data repositories."

"That's good. That means no one has been there," Quinton replied.

"There's no way you can know that," Becker said.

Quinton ignored him and looked at Brandt. "If I was in the ACN, then this could be a military installation. There could be things there that you could use. Didn't you say that ship upkeep is a huge issue, with more things needing repairs and not enough parts being fabricated?"

"That's true," Brandt said. Lips pursed, he looked at Maelyn.

"I think it's worth looking into," she said.

"Will you send ships to help scout the area?" Becker asked.

Brandt peered at the galaxy map and then looked at Quinton. "How do you know there's a vault there?"

Quinton had hoped this detail would've escaped the fleet admiral's notice. "I don't. When I authenticated with the PMC console, I received an update, and the lockdown protocols lessened. These coordinates have to do with the activation signal that brought me online."

Becker exhaled explosively. "The truth is you have no idea what could be at those coordinates."

Quinton was quiet for a moment while he squelched his irritation. "No, I don't," he said finally. "But there has to be something there. My ESS was in a hidden storage facility on Zeda-Six. I don't understand why there was a lockdown protocol used in the first place, and this unit is insufficient to find that out. But the fact that there are Acheron Confederacy military installations hidden out there and that I happen to have a set of coordinates associated with the activation signal is too much of a coincidence. None of you have to go with me. Lend me a ship and I'll go scout it myself."

Brandt shook his head. "Ships are among the most valuable commodities in the galaxy. We're not going to just give one to you."

"I'll take him," Maelyn said, and Brandt looked at her. "We need this, Admiral. We both know it, even if Cantos doesn't want to admit it."

Quinton thought Brandt had the look of a man who didn't approve of the current situation, and nothing was going to change that.

The DUC admiral inhaled deeply and sighed.

"I'll need your authorization to leave the ship," Maelyn said.

"This is ridiculous," Becker said, rounding on Maelyn. "There could be anything at those coordinates. Send a recon drone, and if none of those are available, then wait. The Sentinels targeted all Acheron Confederacy star systems for a reason. Browning was the most cunning officer before he turned against them. The man was a butcher. None of you have questioned whether Quinton is part of something Browning set in motion all those years ago."

Maelyn glanced at the star map. "Those coordinates are nowhere near the Acheron Confederacy. They're not in any claimed territory. It's just another red giant star system with minimal resources."

Becker shook his head. "This is more dangerous than you're letting on. I've led countless salvage missions in the verse, and there's a reason my team survives. We may not get the biggest bounties, but we more than make up for it by living to salvage another day. There's a right way to do this, and going recklessly to these coordinates is the surest way to die quickly."

"You don't have to come, Becker," Quinton said.

Becker scowled and turned back to Maelyn.

"Quinton's right," she said. "You've helped us get this far. Admiral Brandt can see that you're suitably compensated."

Brandt nodded. "That won't be a problem, and based on Captain Wayborn's recommendation, I'd even offer you a position in the DUC fleet."

Becker looked down at the floor for a few moments and then looked at Maelyn. "That's not what I want."

"I've led more than a few missions myself. I promised Quinton I would help him, and I intend to do that. I see no reason for you to remain aboard my ship," she said.

Quinton wanted to cheer or pump his fists in triumph, and he couldn't decide which, but the expression on Becker's face almost made him feel sorry for that reaction.

"I'll need some time to coordinate things on our end," Brandt said to Maelyn. "But I can give you clearance to leave."

She regarded Brandt, and something unspoken passed between them.

Brandt left the room.

"What just happened?" Quinton asked.

"The DUC leadership could relieve him of duty. He's sticking his neck out for this," Maelyn said. "But the potential gains outweigh the risks. Having said that, Quinton, I want you to know that if the situation is too dangerous to proceed, we'll regroup with the DUC and decide our next move."

"That sounds more than fair," Quinton said.

She looked at the others. "None of you are compelled to go. Service on the *Nebulon* is voluntary."

"I wouldn't miss this," Simon said.

Kieva nodded. "I'm with you, Captain."

"I'd like to go with you, if that's all right," Vonya said.

Maelyn nodded once and looked at Becker and the others.

Becker glanced at Guttman and Oscar. Guttman was shaking his head, muttering something about dying.

Becker sighed and looked at Quinton. "This better not be a waste of time."

Maelyn looked at Guttman and Oscar.

"We'll go," Guttman said.

She smiled. "All right, then. We leave at once. We'll need to do some planning on the way."

Becker arched an eyebrow. "You're not sure how long Brandt will give us clearance."

"Something like that," Maelyn said and headed for the door.

Quinton followed her. "Thanks," he said.

She gave him a small nod. "Don't thank me yet."

"You and Radek have a lot in common."

Maelyn looked at him and frowned. "Your VI?"

"Yeah, he doesn't know what to make of someone conveying appreciation either," he said.

She smiled a little. "In that case, you're welcome."

Quinton snorted, and they headed back to the main hangar bay where the *Nebulon* waited for them. He glanced back at Becker, thinking about what the man had said. He was right. They didn't know who had sent the activation signal or why, and it could be true that he was merely being used as a pawn in someone else's game, but Quinton was determined to control his own destiny. And that included finding his DNA so his body could be regrown and he could finally get out of this damn agricultural bot.

27

THEY REACHED the main hangar bay, and a deck officer spoke with Maelyn for a few minutes. The rest of them headed to the *Nebulon.* Quinton walked behind Becker.

The loading ramp extended from the *Nebulon*'s shuttle, and he heard Vonya speaking with Simon, asking him about preflight checks. The others climbed aboard, and Becker turned toward Quinton.

"I didn't think you'd decide to come with us," Quinton said.

Becker was cradling something in his hand that Quinton couldn't see. He shrugged one shoulder and tilted his head to the side in a so-so kind of gesture. "You were right about one thing—we don't know what we'll find."

"Don't tell me I've made a believer out of you."

Becker regarded him. "No, I still think you're an idiot."

"The feeling is mutual, but I have to know. Why are you coming?"

"Do you want to know if I'm coming for her?" Becker said and jutted his chin toward where Maelyn stood talking to the deck officer.

"That doesn't matter to me," Quinton said.

Becker laughed a little. Then he flicked whatever he was holding in his hand straight toward Quinton's face. Quinton caught it easily. It was a thick oval-shaped nut that looked exactly like the one he had thrown at Becker earlier.

"Quick reflexes," Becker said and walked up the loading ramp.

Quinton followed him, and Maelyn soon came on board.

They prepped the shuttle for launch and flew away from the *Astra.*

Everyone aboard was quiet, and Quinton felt an urge to break the silence, but he couldn't think of anything to say.

"Radek," Quinton said inwardly, "do you know anything else about those coordinates?"

"I have the same level of access that you do. Again, if I knew more or thought I could offer some insight that would assist you, I would notify you," Radek said.

Something in the VI's response pulled at his curiosity. "Why do I get the feeling you're not telling me something."

"I am not deliberately omitting information that you need."

"Or perhaps I'm not asking the right question," Quinton said and considered it for a few moments. "Do you have any further information about the coordinates based on your analysis? Something out of the ordinary, perhaps?"

Radek didn't respond right away, and the seconds seemed to accumulate. Then he said, "You've mentioned several times that the coordinates became available from your ESS after you authenticated with the PMC. This is inaccurate."

"How?" Quinton said, ignoring the agricultural unit's error message about not being able to frown. "How is it inaccurate? It's perfectly accurate. I was able to get the coordinates after I authenticated with the PMC console and received the update from it."

"Neural patterns indicate that the coordinates became available while you were focused on the activation signal and the locations of the DNA vaults the DUC representative had. It could also be that these thought patterns in your construct might have influenced the lockdown to change behavior."

If Quinton had a mouth, it would have been hanging open like a fish out of water. "Are you saying that my thought process can influence the lockdown protocol?"

"Unknown, but as part of my analysis capabilities, I have to note all the variables in order to reach an accurate theory on what changed. As a VI, to ignore your thought processes at the time would be negligent on my part. However, I don't feel comfortable estimating the probability that all variables influenced the result. The process would need to be repeated several times in order for a pattern to be established."

Sometimes Quinton felt like the two of them spent a lot of time going around in circles when they spoke, but he thought about Radek's response for a few moments. He had asked the VI for it, and it was clear that Radek hadn't volunteered his idea because he didn't think it would help. Radek might've been right, but Quinton wasn't so sure. VIs handled the PMC interface with . . . well, with everything. They could probably monitor things that he wasn't even aware of, so why not his thought process. The way the brain worked in the matrix construct was intricate and stretched the limits of any intelligence, be it virtual or otherwise. People were always trying to figure out how the mind works, such as why some ideas seemed to spread like beams of light bursting from a pulsar, and others just didn't seem to generate any momentum.

"It's interesting, I'll give you that. I don't know what to think about it. Either way, we'll both understand more about this lockdown once I get out of this body and have full access to the ESS," Quinton said.

The shuttle docked with the *Nebulon*, and they returned to the ship.

Maelyn looked at Becker. "Are you familiar with the munitions systems on the ship?"

Becker nodded.

"We were resupplied by the *Astra*. Can you check them? I'd like a visual inspection," she said.

"Will do, Captain," Becker said, smiling. "Oscar, Guttman, you're with me."

Quinton went to the bridge with Maelyn and Simon. Kieva and Vonya headed to the main engineering section to check on an automated maintenance hatch that was putting errors in the logs.

Simon sat at his workstation. "Updates from the *Astra* are complete. Navigation computers processed the updates, and we're ready to go on your orders, Captain."

"Thank you, Simon. Set a course for the closest jump point. I'll have coordinates for you momentarily," Maelyn said and went to the main holoscreen.

Quinton joined her.

The screen showed a star map of the current system, and she inputted their destination coordinates.

"It looks like we'll need a minimum of six jumps to get there," Quinton said.

"That's right, and the closer we get, the more updated our information will be on our destination," Maelyn said.

Calibrating the jump capacitors for the jump drive systems was required as part of routine maintenance. The fastest they could reach the coordinates was forty-eight hours, and that just brought them within the vicinity.

"We need to talk about something," Quinton said.

Maelyn arched an eyebrow, intrigued. "All right, what do you want to talk about?"

"I need to . . ." he began and stopped. "I'm going to need to be in the *Nebulon*'s systems, fully integrated. I know you're all worried about this."

"If there are Sentinels there, then . . ."

"Then we should execute emergency jump procedures and leave. The reason I need to be integrated is because we might get a challenge protocol from the Acheron military facility that's likely at our destination. We might have only one opportunity to communicate," Quinton said.

Maelyn inhaled and sighed, then glanced at the star map.

"I'm expecting that there'll be some kind of challenge protocol, and I'm hoping there's something in here"—he tapped on his chest piece where his ESS was housed—"that I'll be able to respond with like I did with the PMC console."

Maelyn crossed her arms in front of her and tapped two fingers on her full lips, considering. "If we're wrong, whatever is there might just decide that we're hostile and attack us. I don't want you integrated with the system when we jump in. We don't know what's on the other side, but if we do receive a challenge protocol, I'll give you permission to interface with our comms systems. Not before. We need to scout the system, which means we'll be doing passive scans until we're confident of what's there. Then we'll go for a closer look."

Quinton would rather have been integrated with the system before they jumped to their destination. It was just more efficient, and he could react much quicker to the information that would be available. He tried to think of a scenario where delaying his integration with the *Nebulon* would increase the risk, but the fact of the matter was that he just wasn't sure.

"All right, we'll do it your way. You are the captain, after all," Quinton said.

Maelyn smiled. "There's only one captain." She paused for a moment. "I know it's a struggle for you when you integrate with ship systems."

"The struggle comes when I need to pull out of them. Working within them makes me feel whole, like it's what I was meant to do."

She nodded. "There's a reason for that."

"What do you mean?"

"Helping PMCs cope with their new environment required a certain manipulation. VIs help bridge the connection, but they also engage brain patterns for reward centers of the brain. This helps condition PMCs to function more efficiently," Maelyn said.

"We're conditioned to enjoy it," Quinton said while considering the implications.

"It's what I read. It was one of the reasons PMCs became disassociated with who they were and became more machine-like."

"So, are you saying that Radek is manipulating me?"

Maelyn nodded. "To a certain extent, but not with malicious intent."

"I don't understand what you're trying to tell me, so why don't you just come right out and say it."

"Think of it like an addiction. Have you noticed that you continue to look for excuses to interface with ship systems or any computer system, for that matter?"

Quinton shook his head. "It's what I'm supposed to do. It's what I was trained to do."

"It's one of the reasons the Federation Wars consumed the old federations. You need to be aware of the danger. I'm not trying to tell you not to utilize your capabilities. I'm trying to warn you that there are consequences of which you might not be aware."

Quinton regarded her for a few moments. "You know, this isn't who I am," he said, gesturing toward his body.

Maelyn's eyebrows pulled together. "I know, Quinton," she said.

"And I know it's easy to forget. This is all anyone sees."

"If there *is* a DNA vault at those coordinates, we'll be able to regrow your body, and you can offload out of your ESS. Everything will work out," Maelyn said.

He looked at the star map, unsure what to say to her.

"I *am* curious to see what you really look like. I've tried to imagine it, but I really have no idea."

Quinton looked at her. "You've tried to imagine it? Were you dreaming about me?" he asked and chuckled.

She looked at him with an almost deadpan expression. "Wouldn't you like to know," she said, her eyes gleaming as she walked away from him, heading toward the captain's chair.

Quinton laughed. "You're right. I *would* like to know."

She didn't answer him.

He studied the star map on the main holoscreen, thinking about what Maelyn had said. He was aware of his PMC training, much like he was aware that he could walk. He couldn't remember learning how. He could just do it. Sometimes when he thought about what he could do, those skills felt like being able to walk. He couldn't remember being conditioned or predisposed to want or need to integrate with computer systems, but he couldn't rule out Maelyn's warning either. The knowledge was likely within his ESS. Maybe Becker was right and they should wait—try to find a better android that was more capable of housing his ESS, but he'd gotten the impression from Admiral Brandt that these weren't readily available. He supposed that made sense. Why keep highly sophisticated androids around if the Sentinels would just determine them to be PMC technology and destroy them, despite the collateral damage. A century of such behavior would severely limit Quinton's options for finding a more suitable replacement body. Pursuing the DNA vaults was his best option. Traveling the galaxy in an old agricultural bot wasn't a long-term solution.

A lot of what Becker had said now had Quinton thinking. He had perfect recall of all their encounters, and he was able to simultaneously review everything Becker had said since they'd first met.

Quinton stayed on the bridge until after the *Nebulon* executed its FTL jump from the star system. Now, they were on a recharge cycle. The ship was capable of making continuous jumps, and the length of time required to recharge the capacitors was dependent upon the distance they traveled. They didn't need to push past the red line because it wasn't safe. The farther they jumped, the greater the risk for computational errors for their destination. Even with their best sensors, when dealing with interstellar distances, they were still looking back in time. That was why after each FTL jump, they did a sensor sweep, which updated the navigation systems. There were also navigation stations deployed throughout the galaxy that were connected through a subspace communication net. These were the most reliable way of getting a nearly up-to-date picture of their target destination, although this only got them part of the way. Navigation stations were only in sectors that spacers traveled to. Before the Federation Wars, they'd been maintained by the governing federation, and the sensor data was shared throughout the galaxy.

Quinton left the bridge. He needed to talk to Becker, which wouldn't be easy because the man became irritable whenever they were in close proximity. The feeling was mutual, but Quinton wouldn't let that stop him. Becker was a seasoned salvager who'd spent years delving into the skeletons of a bygone age to retrieve anything useful.

Becker and his crew were inspecting one of the *Nebulon*'s smaller kinetic point-defense turrets that was in a storage bay. Hiding turrets in this way gave them a small advantage in dicey situations. Point-defense turrets weren't meant to dissuade an aggressor, so there was no need to advertise a ship's defensive capabilities. The *Nebulon* also had point-defense masers, which resided on the outer hull of the ship. The *Nebulon* was a small freighter meant for speed, maneuverability, and combat avoidance, with limited long-range combat engagement capabilities.

"I'm telling you, Vonya's massages are the best thing I've ever felt," Guttman said.

Quinton slowed down as he came near the storage bay doors and saw Guttman standing near the base of the mag cannon. He was accessing the console and running a diagnostic.

"Is that only because she won't sleep with you?" Oscar asked.

Quinton glanced up and saw that Oscar was standing on a counter-grav maintenance platform hovering near one of the ammunition loaders that fed the cannon.

"I'll get there, don't you worry," Guttman replied. "It's still showing a degradation for the actuators at anything above half speed."

"I'll take another look," Oscar said. He lowered the counter-grav platform and moved to the other side of the loader.

"She's been training me on giving massages too. Her skin is amazing. I don't know if it's all Servitors or just hers, but it's the perfect combination of smooth and firm," Guttman said.

Oscar grinned and stepped back from the loader, leaning on the handrail to peer down at Guttman. "Let me get this straight. Our resident Servitor is rewarding you by letting *you* massage *her*?"

"Well, it's give and take," Guttman said quickly.

"Riiight," Oscar said, drawing out the word as long as possible. "It's never gonna happen, my friend."

"Keep telling yourself that. What is it *you* do with her? Calibrations?"

"I just enjoy talking to her. She's interested in piloting, so I've been running her through simulations," Oscar replied.

Becker exhaled explosively from the other side of the turret where Quinton couldn't see him. "Enough! I'm tired of hearing about it. You're both stuck in the friend zone. Move on."

Guttman laughed. "Is that why you keep trying to sweet-talk the captain?"

Quinton had heard enough. He walked into the room. "Is this what you guys talk about while you work?" He looked up at Oscar and studied the loader. "The angle of the loader is a little off. That's why it keeps underperforming."

Oscar turned back toward the munitions loader and studied it. "It's not showing up for me."

Quinton quickly climbed up the turret. "Looks like something hit it pretty good and knocked it out of alignment."

Oscar frowned. "I get that, but I can't see it with the scanner."

"Oh. The sensors I have are highly accurate for this fine-tuning kind of work, although the designers probably didn't have this in mind," Quinton said, gesturing toward the turret.

He told Oscar the adjustments he needed to make, and Becker circled over to their side, riding his own counter-grav maintenance platform.

"All right, Guttman, run another test," Oscar said.

Guttman initiated another test that fed ammunition through the loader on one side of the turret and into the loader on the other side. He increased the speed. "That's good. We're able to get to 70 percent now."

Quinton studied the loader, looking for anything else out of alignment, but couldn't find anything. He wanted to get it to 100 percent.

Becker chuckled. "If you're looking for perfection, it's not going to happen. Guttman's right, 70 percent is really good for these old turrets."

Quinton looked at him and then glanced at Oscar, who nodded.

"That does it for this one," Becker said. "Guttman, let the bridge know that they'll be able to run a live fire test in a few minutes."

Becker and Oscar lowered to the ground, and the counter-grav platforms sank seamlessly into two depressions on the floor.

Quinton leaped down and landed nearby.

"Thanks," Oscar said.

"No problem," Quinton replied.

Becker looked at him for a moment. "What do you want?"

"I wanted to talk to you."

Becker rolled his eyes. "I'm a little busy."

They cleared the turret platform, and the airlock doors closed. The turret began to rise, moving out of view.

Guttman and Oscar walked ahead of them.

Quinton suppressed a flash of irritation, thinking that this was going to be even harder than he'd initially thought.

"I need your help," he said.

The three men stopped in the middle of the corridor and turned around to look at him.

"I know. It's shocking," he said.

Becker recovered first. He turned to Guttman and Oscar. "You guys go on ahead."

The two men shrugged and continued onward. Becker raised his eyebrows and waited for Quinton to speak.

"Look, I understand why—you know what, never mind that. I don't care about what happened. All I know is that we need to work together so that we can both get what we want," Quinton said.

"What is it that you think I want?"

"Come on. Do I need to spell it out for you?"

"I'm genuinely curious."

"You want to set yourself up with a star union of your own, running different salvage operations with ships and all that," Quinton replied and paused for a moment.

"You've got me all figured out."

"I know that you're above and beyond your comfort zone for a man who takes risks regularly."

Becker turned around and walked away.

Quinton hastened to catch up to him. "You asked."

Becker shook his head. "You said you need my help."

Quinton nodded. "I do. Did you know I have perfect recall? Believe me, it's not all it's cracked up to be. There are some things I'd like to forget, but lately I've been thinking about some of the things you've said, and I'm beginning to think that your issue with me is a lot more personal than you let on."

Becker stopped, and steel entered his gaze.

"I'm not here to talk about your past. I'm just telling you what I think. I need you to keep an eye on me."

Becker snorted. "I never intended not to."

"You don't get it," Quinton said and told Becker about what Maelyn had explained to him about the behavior modification that came with PMC interfacing with computer systems. "I'm not going to be anyone's pawn, but I realize now that I might not be the best judge."

Becker frowned. "What do you want me to do?"

"Just what you wanted to do before. I want you to terminate me if I . . . you know," Quinton said and stopped.

"Does Maelyn know about this?" Becker asked.

"No, and while I think if push comes to shove she'd do what's needed, I do think she'd hesitate. You wouldn't, and that's what I need."

Becker crossed his arms and leaned back against the corridor wall. "This is something," he said and chuckled without any humor. "How do you know I won't just do it, you know, for fun?"

"I don't."

"Uh-huh."

"I don't know what we're going to find. I know what I want to have happen, and I'm going to do everything I can to make sure that it does, but I need . . . There are things I don't understand."

Becker unfolded his arms and stood up straight. "Even if I agreed to this, how would it even work?"

"You mean you haven't already thought up a way for me to meet an early demise?"

"Oh, I have. It usually involves explosives."

While Quinton didn't like the thought of being blown up, he couldn't fault the logic.

"It would never work. You'd be able to stop a remote detonation in any case."

"Then you'll have to stay close." Quinton watched as Becker thought about it. "To be honest, I didn't think you'd hesitate."

"I'm just trying to figure out how I'll know if it needs to be done. I'm thinking about the aftermath. I don't want to do this and have the DUC try to hunt me down for taking you away from them," Becker said.

Quinton considered it for a few moments and then transferred a file to Becker's wrist computer. "This is a recording of our conversation. It's unalterable, and they can verify it. That should get you out of any trouble with the DUC."

Becker opened his personal holoscreen and examined the file. Then he closed the session. "You're serious about this."

"I am," Quinton replied. "Why would you think I'm not serious?"

Becker pursed his lips and then shook his head. "It doesn't matter," he said quietly.

"The next thing I need is for you to tell me more about the Federation Wars," Quinton said.

"We already told you about them," Becker replied and began walking down the corridor.

"You gave me an extremely high-level version of events, but I need to know more. I need any advantage I can get, so don't hold anything back."

Becker sighed. "This could take a while."

"We have two days until we get to that system. I'll help you with whatever Maelyn has you guys doing."

Becker considered this for a few moments. "All right, I'll tell you. But if you do anything to irritate me, like overclock my wrist computer so it burns me, flick something at my neck, change the shower settings to suddenly become ice cold, or make stupid comments, then that's it. I'm serious. The nonsense stops now."

Never before had Quinton wanted so badly to take a proverbial jab at Becker. It was a good thing the agricultural bot couldn't show facial expressions. "I'll be the absolute vision of cooperation."

Becker glared at him and kept walking.

Yeah, this is going to be tougher than I thought.

28

OVER THE NEXT TWO DAYS, Quinton learned a few things about Toros Becker. The man had a tireless work ethic. He simply stayed on task until the job was done. They had to use stimulants to stave off weariness while they went through the *Nebulon*'s systems. Even with the stimulants, Maelyn tried to make them rotate for a few hours' rest. Not everyone complied.

Quinton had spent much of his time with Becker, the most time the two had spent together since coming aboard the *Nebulon*. He thought that if Becker could ever get over his hatred of machines and all things related to PMCs, they could actually work well together. Well, he hadn't actually thought that. It had been more or less suggested by Maelyn, but the notion was wishful thinking on her part. Quinton was satisfied that Becker wasn't trying to kill him, which meant that he had to do the same. He didn't want to kill the man . . . at least, not anymore, but if Becker pulled another airlock stunt, then all bets were off.

"What is it, Quinton? I can hear you thinking," Becker said.

They were in the galley, and Becker was wolfing down his breakfast. He swallowed his food and stifled a yawn.

"Take a second to chew your food. I don't need you choking here in the galley," Quinton said.

Becker continued to take enormous bites. His dimpled chin bobbed up and down quickly while he chewed.

Quinton had received a crash-course in the recent history of the galaxy. They'd had to do their best to estimate when he'd been uploaded into an ESS.

"I just don't get it," he said. "The Acheron Confederacy goes from breaking the Jordani Federation's tyrannical control to an all-out conquest of every other star nation and federation alike? It doesn't make sense, and I'm not saying that because I'm from there."

Simon sat across from Becker. He leaned forward. "What's so hard to understand? We've seen many star nations rise up to become the dominant force in the galaxy. That's how the Jordani came to prominence. The Acheron Confederacy was just next in line."

"Maybe," Quinton said.

"Browning was the first," Becker said.

Grand Admiral Elias Browning, along with several galactic fleets under his command, had begun waging war against star systems almost seemingly at random. The Acheron Confederacy disavowed Grand Admiral Browning, but there was a general agreement that the Federation Wars started with Browning's betrayal of the ACN. Many atrocities were attributed to him.

"From war hero to war criminal. I don't understand how that happens," Quinton said.

"Maybe you'll understand better once you get your memories back," Simon said.

Becker gulped down his water. "It's not that far of a stretch. Lennix Crowe increased the Union's influence and reach, which brought him in direct opposition with the Collective. Draven wasn't just going to sit by and let Crowe keep challenging the Collective. He needs to put them in their place, or else other unions will rise up and challenge them."

"Browning was truly awful," Simon said. "He butchered space stations and colonies. And that was *before* the problems with PMCs started happening."

"I've heard you say that before, and I guess you're right. I just think there's more to it. Who controlled the Sentinels?" Quinton asked.

"Sentinels were created from remnants of federation militaries banded together to combat PMC-controlled systems and fleets," Simon said.

They'd talked about this before, and Quinton didn't see any advantage to circling back to discuss it again. Galactic history had been cobbled together through reports of fleeing survivors as they sought to avoid being pulled into the desolation. Quinton also noticed that there seemed to be discrepancies in what the crew members recalled as the "history" of the galaxy, but they were unanimous in the fact that Admiral Browning's exploits had plunged the galaxy into all-out war the likes of which had never been seen.

Simon checked his comlink and then looked at the others. "We're nearly to the jump point. We should get to the bridge."

Becker nodded while taking one last mouthful of food and then stood. They left the galley. Quinton had believed that learning more about galactic history would help him with what they were going to find, but he wasn't so sure anymore. The more he learned, the more questions he had.

They did a long-range sensor sweep as they headed to the target star system, hoping that they could learn more about it as opposed to jumping in blindly.

The red giant was an old star, but they'd recently discovered that there was a singularity in orbit around it. In galactic terms, it slightly outmassed the star that was still slowly consuming it. Because of the singularity, they had to jump farther out in the star system.

Simon went to his workstation. Maelyn sat in the captain's chair, and Quinton and Becker stood nearby. Kieva sat at her workstation next to Simon.

The others were in a common area midship, but they were comlinked to the bridge.

"Execute jump," Maelyn ordered.

The *Nebulon* jumped to the outer edges of the target star system. Passive scanning systems came online, and they set a course to the interior of the star system, believing that this was the most likely place for an ACN facility to be located.

"Not the most peaceful star system we've ever been to," Simon said.

Quinton looked at the data on the main holoscreen. He wasn't integrated with the ship systems yet, so he was reliant on the *Nebulon*'s computers to make the data being gathered available. The singularity in this system must have been a recent event—in galactic terms. The other planets in-system had an orbit that hadn't completely stabilized yet.

The star system was lifeless. No planets here could support anything remotely livable. Perhaps with hundreds of years of terraforming it could be different, but there were much better systems available for supporting life.

Quinton looked at Maelyn. "Passive scans are only going to get us so far."

He was impatient to be integrated with the *Nebulon*'s systems, but he'd promised Maelyn he would wait for her permission.

"No other ships detected in the system," Simon said. "In fact, I don't see anything that indicates anyone has ever been here."

But it was too soon for them to conclude that there was nothing there. Quinton needed to broadcast a specially crafted comlink.

"You're up, Quinton," Maelyn said finally. "Interface with the *Nebulon*'s systems and broadcast your signal. Let's see if anything's waiting for us out there. Simon, I want the emergency jump coordinates ready to execute."

Quinton accessed the *Nebulon*'s computer systems and saw that the emergency jump coordinates were already loaded into the navigation computer. He cranked up his frame rate and then took control of the communications array, uploading a modified protocol for a broadcast signal that included the activation signal used to bring him online. He then initiated an active scan of the system. If they were going to broadcast a communication signal, there was no reason not to initiate an active scan.

"Broadcasting now," Quinton said, then added, "I'm adjusting to juggling multiple frame rates." His voice sounded even more monotone, with less emotional inflection. It felt strange, as if he were in two places at once. His perception of time was at once normal, like everyone else's, and as fast as the agricultural bot's internal systems would allow. It was a risk because, despite their best efforts, the agricultural bot's internal systems weren't designed for this kind of computational capacity. They were being pushed beyond their limits, but he had to push them. If this was some kind of Sentinel trap, he'd need to react quickly.

A response came via a subspace comlink, which contained a challenge protocol similar to what he'd encountered with the PMC console, but it was more complex, comprised of multiple layers of protocols requiring a response. Since he was directly interfacing with the ship systems, the response protocol authentication came from his ESS. He provided a vast array of authentication codes that he hadn't even known were inside his ESS, as if it were responding autonomously.

Quinton pinpointed the location of the subspace comlink to a large moon that orbited a Jovian planet. He focused an active scan pulse at those coordinates and could detect only a comlink array there. There was no other facility detected. The array probably had another subspace comlink to a facility that managed the challenge protocols. They could still execute an emergency jump, but he suspected it would be close. If they ended up in a dampening field, they couldn't simply jump away.

He'd sent the last authentication code and was waiting for a response.

"I received a reply and am working through the authentication protocol. So far, it's just like the PMC console," Quinton said.

"Where did the reply come from?" Maelyn asked.

He updated the main holoscreen with a flashing icon to indicate the location.

"Simon, set a course for those coordinates," Maelyn said.

"Are you sure you want to do that?" Becker said and then held up his hands in a placating gesture. "I mean, he hasn't received a response yet. There hasn't been an all-clear invite."

"Whatever's over there could just be coming online, and that's taking some time," she replied.

Becker turned his attention to the main holoscreen and didn't say anything else.

Quinton was tempted to send another transmission but decided to wait. A few minutes passed before a reply finally came. "We're authorized to approach. They sent us a secondary set of coordinates. I'll put it on the main holoscreen."

The coordinates were located on the other side of the star system.

"We can get there quicker with a micro-jump," Maelyn said.

"Initiating micro-jump," Simon said.

Becker looked at Quinton and appeared as if he wanted to say something.

"That was the only reply I got. It's an invitation," Quinton said.

Becker inhaled deeply and sighed. Then he nodded.

The *Nebulon* jumped to the other side of the star system where a small asteroid field was located.

Several warnings appeared on Quinton's HUD. The agricultural bot's internal systems were wearing out. Power levels from his core were fluctuating, and he returned his frame rate back to normal time.

"System resources aren't meant for the excess load. Recommend avoiding overtaxing the system," Radek said sub-vocally.

Quinton quickly acknowledged the list of warnings. "Understood," he replied.

"Quinton," Simon said with concern in his voice. He had the agricultural bot's status report on one of his holoscreens.

"What's wrong?" Maelyn asked.

The power fluctuations returned to normal. "It's fine. I just overdid it," Quinton replied.

Maelyn looked at Simon. He refreshed the report, then nodded at Maelyn.

"Erratic orbital patterns are being reported for our destination," Quinton said. A few moments later, the warning appeared on the main holoscreen.

"No weapons systems detected," Simon said.

Quinton looked as if he was peering at the main holoscreen, but he was interfaced with the *Nebulon*'s sensor array and accessing the data in real time before the *Nebulon* put the data through its own analysis. He could have deployed his VI assistants into the *Nebulon*'s systems, but they might be detected by a Sentinel scan. Even though he was in the system, he was simply using it by inserting himself into key areas that didn't require actual manipulation. It was one of the protective measures he and Simon had come up with to limit their risk exposure should the Sentinels suddenly show up.

"The trajectory suggests a pattern of ships docking with one another," Quinton said.

A high-res image appeared on the main holoscreen.

"Would you look at that," Becker said.

"It's a station, all right. They've just kept it hidden," Maelyn said.

"Quinton's signal must have caused it to activate," Simon said.

"I thought the activation signal had come from here, but how can that be if the station is only coming online now?" Quinton asked.

He glanced at the others.

Maelyn shook her head. "I don't know. Maybe the signal was relayed through here."

It was possible. The coordinates were unlocked from within his ESS, which meant that someone had put them there. They had wanted him to come here.

Another window appeared on the main holoscreen, which had a series of images on them. "These are archival images of the stations that contained the DNA vaults for the Acheron Confederacy," Maelyn said.

They were cylindrical in appearance, with only a few docking ports. When compared with the live video feed from this star system, the station was much larger. Multiple sections of the station had docked together, and its overall length was over three thousand meters.

Simon leaned back in his chair. "Look at the size of it."

"Captain," Kieva said, "I've received a remote autopilot request from ACN starbase Endurance."

Maelyn looked at Quinton.

"I've had no other contact from them," he said.

"There can't be anyone there. Not if it's been hidden all this time," Becker said.

Maelyn nodded. "Authorization granted."

The *Nebulon* flew toward the middle of the massive station. Quinton peered at the high-res image, and his own analysis appeared on his HUD. Entire sections of the station's walls had a rocky outer layer that made it appear as if it were just another asteroid. He easily picked out point-defense turrets that, upon first pass, looked to be in pristine condition. The surrounding asteroid field shifted, and rays of starshine gleamed off the battle-steel plating.

The *Nebulon* was guided into a central hangar bay. Thick armored doors opened as they made their final approach.

"Is this like anything you've seen before?" Quinton asked.

Becker studied the live video feed on the main holoscreen. "It looks like a standard station design, but they've usually been destroyed by the time we find them. This one looks operational."

Quinton looked at the others as they watched the holoscreen. Simon kept shifting in his seat as he tried to keep track of the data streams on his workstation, but he couldn't stop himself from gazing at the main holoscreen. There had to be a DNA vault there.

The *Nebulon* landed in a vast but empty hangar bay.

Quinton glanced at the others and then opened a comlink to the station. He connected immediately, feeling as if he'd been pulled inside a massive computer system that had been specifically designed for PMC access. He wasn't sure if he was more relieved to be accessing the station or if *it* was just enthusiastic to have someone who'd finally answered its call.

"Systems are still coming online. There is an atmosphere. Life support is functioning normally," Quinton said and paused for a few moments. He chuckled a little. "There's a lot of information."

"Can you throttle it down so you don't get overwhelmed?" Maelyn asked.

"It's being throttled down. The VIs are working on it. I don't know where to begin. There's so much here," Quinton said.

"Focus on what we came here for first. You need to find out if there's a DNA vault, and can you authorize data access so Simon can access the station?" Maelyn said.

The station was managed by its own VI that was less sophisticated than Radek. Quinton requested station access for Simon, and it was immediately granted. Then he began a search for a map of the interior layout.

"I'm in," Simon said.

"Good. Begin searching for a world database. We need to find out where their secret colonization projects were located," Maelyn said.

"And ships. Don't forget to look for ships. There are more hangars than this one. They can't all be empty," Becker said.

"I have the schematics for the interior. Making them available to everyone now," Quinton said.

Maelyn nodded and stood up. "Let's get the away team ready. Kieva, I want you to monitor our progress from the ship. Send a comlink to Admiral Brandt giving the all clear, and include our current coordinates."

Becker looked at Maelyn. "Brandt was following us?"

"Of course. I kept them apprised of our progress," she replied.

"I guess I expected him to be a little bit more cautious."

"Ordinarily yes, but . . ." Maelyn said and gestured toward the main holoscreen.

Becker nodded in agreement.

The others were leaving the bridge, and Quinton hastened to catch up. They met up at the main airlock where Guttman and Oscar distributed weapons to everyone.

"I don't think we'll need those," Quinton said.

"That's why you're not in charge," Becker said. Guttman and Oscar grinned.

"It's just a precaution," Maelyn said. "Sometimes, these places have automated defenses."

Vonya glanced at the sidearm that Guttman was trying to hand to her and shook her head.

"Take it just in case," Maelyn said, and then Vonya slowly reached out for it.

Quinton looked down at the gauss rifle he'd been handed and slung it onto his back. An analysis of the station's atmosphere didn't reveal any foreign contaminants. The station was as pristine as the day it had been fabricated.

He opened the airlock and walked down the loading ramp. The nearest wall displayed a massive black and gold emblem of the Acheron Confederacy Navy—two golden triangular halves that angled away from a sphere on a black background. Beneath were the words "Perseverance. Endurance. Fortitude. Readiness."

The others joined Quinton, and he watched them take in their surroundings in silence. Every ship and space station he'd been on since he'd been reactivated had had a long service record. They'd been patched up and were well beyond their design specifications. He glanced at the others again. Becker and Guttman had the beginnings of a scowling expression. Vonya calmly took in the sight of the ACN emblem as if she was studying something she hadn't seen before. Maelyn had a tightness in her eyes that bordered on resentment, as if she'd been betrayed. Simon and Oscar looked at the emblem with a thoughtful frown but nothing more. Quinton wondered if this was how the members of the DUC would react once they got here.

Quinton made a clearing-his-throat sound. "I wouldn't go around commenting on how much you hate the Acheron Confederacy here. Just a little advice."

Becker shook his head and then strode toward the hangar bay doors that led to the station's interior. Quinton and the others quickly caught up with him. The sensors detected their presence, and the automatic doors opened.

"Has anyone or anything tried to contact you?" Maelyn asked.

"No, there are a lot of systems still coming online. There's a tram system a short distance ahead of us. Maybe we should split up to explore this place," Quinton said.

"He's right," Guttman said. "We'll cover more ground that way. There are a few other hangar bays, smaller than this one, but I want to check them out to see what's inside."

They reached the end of the corridor, which emptied into a small plaza where a tram system was online. There were several trams waiting to be boarded.

Guttman and Oscar headed toward a tram on the left. Guttman turned around. "Becker, are you coming?"

Becker shook his head. "Negative, you guys go ahead and report back in. I'll catch up with you."

Guttman's lips formed a thin line. Then he shrugged and nodded. They walked onto one of the trams and left the station with just a slight hum as the counter-grav plating sped the tram away.

Maelyn frowned. "I'm surprised you didn't go with them."

Becker almost glanced at Quinton but covered it up with a slight shake of his head. "I thought I'd stick with you and see what else the station has for us."

"We need to look for a bio lab. That's where we'd find a DNA storage vault, along with a medical capsule and material to grow Quinton's new body," Simon said.

"I like the sound of that. We should always do what Simon says," Quinton said.

Simon smiled, and they climbed aboard a tram. "I think that used to be a game a long time ago."

"What game?" Becker asked.

"Never mind that now," Maelyn said. "We need to take this tram . . . Oh, it's a combination elevator system as well. We just input the bio lab destination."

Quinton had already selected the destination before anybody could use the interface. "You sound surprised by the elevator system."

"I am, only because . . . I just hadn't expected it to be here, that's all," she said.

She looked around the gleaming interior of the tram as if she expected to see something that wasn't actually there. Quinton noticed the others doing the same.

The tram slowed down and then stopped, and then they began to rise. They ascended forty decks before the tram came to a stop again, and the rear doors opened.

The corridor beyond began to light up as they walked off the tram. The interior lighting had a tinge of yellow to it, reminding Quinton of the light of a yellow main sequence star. The agricultural bot's sensors detected trace amounts of ultraviolet radiation, which people needed in order to stimulate production of essential vitamins, but it also had a positive psychological effect on spacers who spent long periods of time away from a planet.

As they walked the corridor, Becker looked at Quinton. "Do you even know how you transfer back into a body?" he said and frowned. "And don't give me any flack because I don't know the technical terms. You know what I mean."

Quinton searched the data available on his ESS for the procedures and couldn't find anything. "I don't know, but why would I need to know? They'll have the procedure here. They'd be prepared for it since these DNA vaults were so widespread. Or I just need full access to my ESS."

Becker nodded and didn't say anything else.

The bio lab revealed bright white walls and amber-colored holoscreens that flickered to life as they walked inside. There were several medical capsules farther inside.

Simon whistled. "Look at how many of them there are," he said and looked at Quinton. "As long as we have the right stock of materials, these are capable of regrowing a body for you."

Internally, Quinton laughed with anticipation. He was so close.

Maelyn received a comlink from Kieva. "Go ahead, *Nebulon*."

"Captain, I received a response from Admiral Brandt, and they'll be at the station within two hours. He'd like you to have an update ready for him when he arrives," Kieva said.

"Understood," Maelyn said.

"Ask her if she's detected any broadcast signals from the station," Becker said.

Maelyn asked.

"None detected," Kieva replied.

"Very well. I'll be in contact," Maelyn said and closed the comlink.

Quinton accessed the bio lab systems and began a search for his DNA profile.

Simon sat down at one of the workstations. Quinton looked at the others. "I've given you all access to the station's computer systems, including Guttman and Oscar."

Vonya sat next to Simon and watched him work while Becker opened a comlink to Guttman and let him know.

Quinton put the status of his search on one of the nearby holoscreens.

"I didn't realize there were so many of them," Maelyn said as she looked at the screen, her face etched with sorrow.

"Neither did I," Quinton said quietly. There was a long list of DNA profiles, and each one of them had been a person like him. All at once, he felt a profound sense of emptiness. Most, if not all, of the people on this list were dead. They had died during the Federation Wars. Even though their DNA profiles were here, they couldn't regrow their bodies because they lacked the minds to go with them. A PMC was required—otherwise the body that was regrown would be lifeless.

"We should take a copy of this back to the DUC in case they find any other PMCs," Quinton said.

Maelyn nodded soberly. "We will," she promised and looked at Simon.

"I have a data uplink to the *Nebulon* already online, and I'm moving information across."

Quinton tried to focus on something else, but he kept watching his search window, unable to do anything else. Then the search stopped.

DNA profile match.

Quinton read the status window a few times before he believed what he saw. "That's it! That's me! I'm in there. Do you see it? I'm in there!"

Maelyn smiled and nodded enthusiastically. Even Becker tilted his head in an acknowledging nod.

"Oh boy," Simon said. "I just found the procedure to get Quinton back into a body. It's complex, and there are risks involved."

"What kinds of risks?" Maelyn asked.

"Based on this," Simon said, pointing to the data on the screen, "it's almost like they'll be scanning his consciousness again before it will be allowed to be transferred back into his body. There's a risk of rejection."

"What?" Quinton asked. "My body isn't going to reject my mind. The two go together."

"No, I understand that, but I'm just telling you what's here. There *is* a risk.

Also, there's some kind of integrity scan to confirm that the PMC is stable," Simon said.

Becker chuckled. "And here I almost regret making all those instability jokes."

"Ha, ha, very funny," Quinton replied. Then he looked at Maelyn. "I don't care what the risks are. I can't stay in here," he said, gesturing toward the agricultural unit's chest cavity.

"I know," Maelyn said. "Are there any other androids on the station that would be a suitable match for him?"

Quinton balled his mechanical hands into fists. "No!" He backed up a few steps. "I'm not going into another android. We're going to bring one of those medical capsules online, engage the restoration protocol, and follow the procedure. Enough is enough."

Maelyn gave him a long look, and Quinton knew that her concerns were justified, but he had to get out of this body. Maybe it wouldn't have been so bad if he had full access to his ESS, but he didn't, and he'd had enough. He finally had everything he needed to make this happen, and he wasn't going to lose this opportunity.

Maelyn looked at Simon. "What do you need?"

"We need to transfer his ESS into one of those chambers. There's a cradle inside that's designed for it. We just need to place it there," Simon said.

Maelyn looked at Quinton. "We need to access your ESS."

Before she finished speaking, he had ripped the chest plate from the agricultural unit's body, exposing the ESS. The decagonal shape of the ESS glowed pale blue, and its surface pulsed from the lcuridium core.

Maelyn looked at it, and her eyes widened a little. She leaned forward to get a better look.

"Wait! You can't touch it," Quinton said.

"Why can't we touch it?" Becker asked.

"I was going for some heightened drama," Quinton said.

Becker frowned at him.

"I was just joking. It has defense capabilities that will neutralize anyone who tries to tamper with it. Either it will knock you out or your heart will stop beating. Either way, it's not worth the risk." He looked at Maelyn. "I need to have Radek initiate the release, and the ESS will disconnect from the agricultural unit. Then you can use an anti-gravity field to transfer it into the cradle. Will you do that for me?"

Maelyn nodded and smiled. "Yes, of course I will."

"I don't know," Becker said. "It would make for a nice decorative piece on the *Nebulon*'s bridge."

Quinton was so excited that he wasn't even annoyed. "Once I'm done with it, you can do whatever you want."

Becker received a comlink from Guttman. "Looks like they found a couple of ships that they want me to see. Everything seems under control here," he said and looked at Quinton. "I'm going to go meet up with the others."

Quinton looked at him for a few moments. "Thanks," he said.

Becker gave him a nod and left the room.

"What was that about?" Maelyn asked.

"Just a contingency plan."

She glanced at the door Becker had used and then back at Quinton. "For what?"

"It's really not important. We didn't end up needing it," Quinton said and gestured toward his ESS. He felt oddly vulnerable. Maelyn arched an eyebrow. "He was going to do something for me in case things got out of control."

She tilted her head to the side a little, waiting for him to continue.

"It's not important," Quinton said and looked at Simon. "Are we ready? Can I give Radek the go-ahead?"

Simon nodded. "Yes, we can start the upload process now. That will give us time to get the other things in place."

Quinton thought Maelyn looked annoyed, but he didn't want to get into it right then. She grabbed the small handheld gravity field emitter used for transferring dangerous substances and powered it on. Two prongs ejected from the end and began to glow.

"Here goes nothing," Quinton said. Then he had Radek initiate the release protocols that would detach him from the agricultural unit.

Quinton had to withdraw from the station's systems, as well as those of the *Nebulon*'s. Being cut off from everything made him feel diminished, less alive than he'd been mere moments before, but it would only be temporary. He probably wouldn't even notice the missing time. Just as Radek was initiating the release protocols, he remembered that he'd forgotten to ask how long the process was going to take. He probably should've asked that, but it was too late to . . .

29

QUINTON DIDN'T WAKE up like he expected to. He'd thought that when he woke up, the others would be looking down at him as he regained consciousness in the medical capsule. He'd be inside a newly grown body that was his own, taking his first breath, and he'd have full access to his memories. Instead, he just sort of became aware, but even that wasn't the right way to say it. He wanted to frown and tried to organize his thoughts. He felt an increasing sense of awareness, as if he'd been floating in an empty void, and now he was being pushed toward an invisible barrier.

An image of a video feed appeared in front of him showing the bio lab, which was empty. The agricultural unit he'd been housed in stood to his left. Its chest panel had been torn open. The bot's metallic alloy had splotches of a white filmy substance that, at first glance, one would think could be scrubbed off, but Quinton knew better. The bot had been exposed to a harsh atmosphere for a very long time. He hadn't taken time to look at the agricultural bot's appearance because it was more upsetting than comforting. Now that he was no longer trapped inside, he wanted to destroy it because if he didn't, there was a chance that his ESS would somehow end up inside it again. Quinton knew it was foolish, but that didn't change how he felt.

Turning his attention to the medical capsule, he tried to peer inside, and the video feed zoomed in closer. His body was inside. He could see his legs—*his* legs—and his body up to his chest. His head and shoulders were blocked from view because they were inside some kind of chamber. The capsule was filled with a liquid that had a yellowish tinge to it.

A silver sphere appeared in the video feed. The sphere looked like liquid mercury—silvery and highly reflective.

"Quinton?" Radek asked. The sphere flashed along its edges.

"I'm here," Quinton replied. "What's going on? How come I'm not in my body?"

"Regrowth is only 65 percent complete and requires a full reanimation check for adequate muscle stimulation and response," Radek replied.

He glanced at the agricultural unit again. "Where am I?"

"Your ESS is still active and is undergoing an integrity check as part of the revival protocols."

He felt an urge to shake his head, except he didn't have one, which made having the urge highly distracting. "Something's wrong. You wouldn't have awakened me otherwise. I was supposed to wake up inside my own body. Where is everyone? How much time has passed? What's going on?" He tried to access the station's systems and couldn't, which increased his anxiety about the situation to whole new levels.

"Wait," Radek said. "I have you restricted for your own protection. Please don't override it until I've explained a few things to you."

Since Radek was asking him not to override his restriction, it meant that Quinton *could* exert some level of control over his situation. He calmed down a little. Radek was afraid of what Quinton would do and was trying to protect him.

"Endurance Starbase system utilization is extremely high because of a massive data dump to a DUC ship called the *Neseverous*."

"The DUC is already here? How long have I been out?"

"It's been five hours since you were taken offline. I've been monitoring the process the entire time."

"Why would the DUC try to do a massive data dump? It would be quicker to just query the system for the data they wanted. Simon knows this. He would have told Maelyn if she didn't already know it," Quinton said.

"I'm unaware of the communication between Maelyn and the DUC fleet."

"What do you mean 'unaware'? You're in the station's computer systems. It's just a matter of monitoring comlink activities. Maelyn wouldn't have blocked access," he said.

"I'm not actively inside the station's computer system. I reside within your ESS, which is inside the cradle awaiting transfer into your biological form."

"Then how could you know that the station's computer system is being highly utilized?" Quinton asked.

"Because the computer system told me."

Quinton couldn't fault the logic. The extremely limited VI that managed Endurance Starbase had probably reprioritized, or more likely was given a high priority for the data transfer, which was making his own analysis and download take even longer.

"Then why did you wake me up?"

"Too much time had passed, and no one from the *Nebulon*'s crew has returned to check on your progress," Radek said.

Quinton considered this for a few moments. The only way to find out what was happening on the station was for Radek to wake him up. "I understand. Remove the restriction. Let's see if I can figure out what's happening here."

"Done," Radek said.

Quinton's awareness shifted to a phalanx of holoscreens that represented his interface with Endurance Starbase's computer system. Radek helped to organize the data feeds Quinton could now access so he wouldn't be overwhelmed by the sheer volume of information available. Instead, he was overwhelmed by the fact that the station's sensors detected two opposing fleets locked in an engagement. He saw that the *Astra* was among the DUC ships engaging the other fleet. He opened a tactical workstation holoscreen and designated the second fleet as hostile. He didn't know who they were.

Quinton opened a comlink to Maelyn.

"Wayborn here."

"Maelyn, it's me, Quinton."

"Quinton!"

He located her position near a residential section on the other side of the station. Simon and Vonya were with her.

"Who's attacking us?" Quinton asked.

"Wait a second, I'm going to patch Becker in," Maelyn said.

Becker joined them. "The transport shuttles in this hangar aren't space worthy. I have no idea why. They look like they've been cannibalized for parts."

"Becker, Quinton is awake," Maelyn said.

Quinton heard something loud from Becker's comlink connection, and then an impact alert came to prominence.

"Who's firing on us?" Quinton asked.

"Becker, are you all right?" Maelyn asked.

Becker exhaled explosively. "Yeah, we're fine. That was close."

"The DUC fleet is fighting Union ships," Maelyn said.

"Crowe is here?"

"Are you in a body yet?" Becker asked.

"No, it's not ready."

"How are you awake?" Maelyn asked.

"Radek woke me up. He was monitoring the integrity check for my ESS and received an alert from the system because of the data dump to the *Neseverous*. It's degrading the entire system."

"I told you that you shouldn't have given Brandt your access codes for the station," Becker said.

"Never mind that," Maelyn said. "Quinton, how much time is left for the transfer?"

"The body regrowth is now at 72 percent. How did Crowe find us so fast?"

Another impact alert came from a different part of the station. Someone was using kinetic artillery and was taking shots at the station.

"Hey, since you're just wasting time, can you make yourself useful?" Becker said.

"He's right, Quinton. Are you able to help us?"

"How?"

Becker cursed. "How about engaging the station's point-defense systems for starters. Does this place have anything that can shoot back? The DUC isn't going to last long against Union ships. I bet Crowe brought everything he had here."

Quinton winced inwardly. He accessed the station's point-defense systems and brought them online, assigning targeting priority to Union ships.

"How did Crowe find us?" he asked.

The tactical holoscreen showed the two fleets pounding on each other with mag cannons and maser beams. It appeared that both sides had ships fleeing the battle, and several were now going offline. Becker was right—Crowe's Union ships were outmaneuvering the DUC fleet ships.

"You guys need to get back to the *Nebulon*," Quinton said.

"Tell us something we don't know," Becker said.

"The tram system is down," Maelyn said.

Quinton accessed the station's transport systems. After the station had been hit, it must have initiated safety protocols that precluded the use of the tram system.

"I think I can override it," Quinton said. "Maelyn, follow the maintenance corridor to your left. It will take you to an emergency transport station that should get you most of the way."

He heard Maelyn speaking to Simon and Vonya. "Why won't the bulkhead door open?"

"I don't know, but she said she'd meet us farther..." Simon said, and Quinton ignored him while he tried to find a way to help Becker. Then he paused.

"Becker, it's time to come clean. Did you tell Crowe our location?" Quinton asked.

"What? Not this again. No, dammit! Telling Crowe where we are is a death sentence."

Quinton still had his perfect recall from their time on the *Nebulon*.

"Why were you so interested in the *Nebulon*'s maintenance logs? You kept reviewing their activity."

"Look, we can talk about this or you can help us get out of here. We're stuck in a small hangar bay with ships that can't take us anywhere," Becker said, scowling.

"What was so interesting about the automated maintenance systems?" Quinton asked.

"Maelyn, he'll listen to you. Can you tell him to help us?" Becker asked.

"No, I don't think so, Becker. Answer the question," Maelyn replied frostily.

Becker cursed and lowered his voice. "I was trying to find out if someone on the ship was giving away our location to Crowe."

"What does that have to do with the maintenance systems?" Quinton asked.

"What did you find out?" Maelyn asked.

"Nothing. I couldn't find anything firm, and I knew that if I made an accusation, I'd be on the top of everyone's list of betrayers. Maelyn, I'm telling you that I did not do this," Becker said.

"I'm not convinced," Quinton said. "In fact, I think I'm going to vent the atmosphere in that hangar bay."

"Wait!" Becker cried out. "Guttman and Oscar are with me."

"It could be any one of you," Quinton replied and accessed the life-support systems for Becker's location. He heard Guttman shout in the background about the ventilation system flushing out the atmosphere.

"Stop it! I was checking the maintenance systems because sometimes you can schedule a subspace comlink to coincide with the ship's automated systems used to manage repair drones. That's what I was checking for. You can look for yourself," Becker said.

Quinton opened a comlink to the *Nebulon*'s systems and checked the logs. Becker was right. Someone could have done what he'd suspected, but they hadn't.

"Quinton, I know you're in the *Nebulon*'s systems. What did you find?" Maelyn asked.

"He's right. Becker is right. Someone could have done it, but they didn't try to mask a subspace comlink. However, unless jump drones are part of routine maintenance, I think whoever was feeding Crowe information was using them," Quinton said.

He heard Becker gasp and then begin to cough. Either Becker was caught in an elaborate lie and had become the leader of all deceivers, which Quinton didn't believe he would do, or he wasn't the traitor. He restored life support to the hangar bay.

Becker inhaled several lungsful of breath before he could speak. "I told you it wasn't me."

"Then who the hell was it?" Maelyn asked.

"I don't know," Quinton replied. "Since the drones were operating under an automated maintenance system, there isn't a clear identification of who added them. Whoever did this is subtle, capable, and able to . . ." he paused for a moment, his mind racing. "Maelyn, is Vonya with you?"

"No, we were separated. Do you think it was Vonya?" Maelyn asked and then scowled. "It has to be her. Neither Kieva nor Simon would do this. Vonya has spent time with everyone, 'finding her place and getting to know the ship.' She fed me a Servitor's sad story, and I ate it up like a fool," she said bitterly.

"Not for long," Quinton said and began searching for Vonya.

Maelyn wasn't the only one who'd been fooled by Vonya. She'd fooled them all. His perfect recall brought up every interaction with the beautiful Servitor, looking for some kind of sign that she had been lying to them. Why had she done it? Was she just loyal to Crowe, or was he somehow coercing her to work for him? He'd find out soon enough. There was nowhere on this station that she could hide from him.

Quinton accessed the station's life-sign tracking system and was able to locate everyone on the station except Vonya.

"I can't locate her. She doesn't appear to be anywhere on the station," he said.

Maelyn opened a comlink to the *Nebulon*. "Kieva, did Vonya return to the ship?"

"Negative, Captain," Kieva replied.

"Understood. If she returns to the ship, don't let her come aboard," Maelyn said.

"Captain, what's going on? Vonya has been such a great addition to the crew—"

"Kieva, she's been using jump drones to inform Lennix Crowe of our location and who knows what else. I don't have time to go into it. We're on our way to you. Prep the ship for launch," Maelyn said.

"Aye, Captain," Kieva replied and closed the comlink.

Since the bio-detection systems on the station couldn't locate Vonya, Quinton started checking for door-access control systems, which included the airlocks. "How did you get cut off from each other?"

"Can we focus on getting off this station?" Becker said. "Can you use your illustrious access and find us a ship to escape on? I don't know that we could make it back to the *Nebulon* if we had to run."

The tram systems were offline due to damage from a mag cannon blast that had penetrated the station's armor. Emergency bulkhead doors sealed off the damaged sections, and Becker and the others were stranded. He accessed the stations logs for any ship that had been left there.

"There might be something, but you'll have to head away from the central station. There's a dark hangar bay that was sealed for storage. You'll need to restore power and then see if the ship inside is space worthy," Quinton said.

"Can't you restore the power?" Becker asked.

"No, it's entirely cut off from the station, but it might be your best bet. It's closer than trekking all the way back to the central hangar," Quinton said.

Becker growled in disgust and disconnected the comlink.

"What's the status of the regrowth?" Maelyn asked.

Quinton checked it. "Ninety-seven percent complete," he replied and felt a surge of anticipation. "I think Vonya is off the station. An exterior airlock was accessed shortly after you were cut off, and a repair shuttle's been taken."

"Can you contact the shuttle?"

"I can't. There's no response. She could have taken the comms systems offline in order to prevent me from accessing it. I can't track her," Quinton replied.

Maelyn sighed heavily. "Okay, we'll deal with her later. Will the station's point-defense systems stay online after you begin the transference protocol?"

Quinton glanced at the holographic sphere that hovered nearby. It bobbed once. "Radek says it will."

"Good—" Maelyn said as an alpha priority alert appeared on all of the holoscreens around him.

The alert was for unauthorized access to the station's computer systems.

"What the hell," Quinton said as more alerts appeared.

"What's wrong?"

"There's been unauthorized access to the station's systems. Someone has bypassed the security systems," he said.

"Can you block their access?"

He was trying that, but the first thing the infiltrator had done was to create alternative access points, and as Quinton blocked them, they appeared somewhere else from an entirely different subsystem. "I'm trying, but they keep coming back."

"Quinton, I think you're in danger. You need to get out of the station's computer systems."

He raced to block the unauthorized access and tried to think of a way to stop whoever it was. If he took the entire system down, then the point-defense systems would be taken offline, as well as internal systems. Maelyn was right. They were all in trouble.

"Crowe wouldn't come here unprepared. He wants to capture you, and there are infiltration protocols that can be integrated into a system to do just that. They already have access. You need to pull back and begin the transference protocol. It's the only way to avoid being taken over," Maelyn said.

Quinton had multiple holoscreens up, and he was furiously trying to eradicate the rogue VI that was infiltrating the station's computer system. It was a race, but he thought it was one he could win.

"Quinton, you need to listen to me," she said.

The rogue VI began spawning even more copies of itself at a rate he hadn't thought was possible.

Maelyn called out to him again.

"What about you and Simon? You haven't made it back to the ship yet."

"Don't worry about us. We can take care of ourselves. I've redirected the tram to take us to the bio lab. We'll leave the station together."

Quinton looked at the status for his new body.

Regrowth complete.

He hesitated.

It was all right there for him. All he had to do was to order Radek to begin the transference protocol, and his PMC would be merged with the brain of his new body. He'd be whole again. This was what he wanted. This was why he'd come here. He looked at the bio lab through the video feed and saw the medical capsule. His body was in there. He could have a new life. This was it.

"Quinton," Radek said, "shall I engage the transfer protocols?"

He wanted to tell Radek to do just that, but the words wouldn't come. He glanced at the tactical workstation holoscreen that showed Union ships pushing back the DUC fleet. Inside the station's computer systems, a vicious infiltrator VI was attempting to assert control. What would it do if it couldn't get to him? Would it simply stop what it was doing, or would it turn its attention toward taking control of the station's computer system? He didn't know. Maelyn and Simon were on their way to the bio lab, and Becker and the others were trying to find a ship to escape in.

But what was he doing? The enemy was closing in all around him, and what was he going to do?

He could engage the transference protocol, and if it worked, wake up in a new body of flesh and blood. He'd have access to all his memories. All the answers he'd sought would be his, but what good would that do if they all died? What good would it do for him to survive here while everyone else died around him?

Quinton looked at the two fleets battling for control of an Acheron Confederacy Navy space station. Who'd hidden it here? Why had the coordinates been in his ESS, and why was he here?

The holoscreens rearranged themselves in front of him—the tactical holoscreen, a video feed of the tram that Maelyn and Simon rode, the central hangar bay where the *Nebulon* waited, and a holoscreen where he saw Becker, Guttman, and Oscar running down a corridor, racing for a safe way off the station. Rising above the other holoscreens was a video feed of the interior of the bio lab. He still couldn't see his own face that was hidden inside the capsule. And here Quinton was, at the cusp of ending this ordeal. He'd fought for this, risked his life for this. He glanced at the other video feeds. Theirs was a harsh galaxy, but in rare moments he glimpsed the older ideals when things hadn't been so dire.

He dismissed the video feed of the bio lab, and it disappeared.

"No, Radek, there's been a change of plans," Quinton said.

30

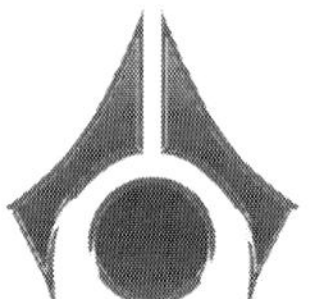

"I MUST ADVISE AGAINST THAT," Radek said.

"I'll take it under advisement."

He needed time. He was in a virtual holding area where he could use the station's computer systems but not directly interface with it the way a PMC was meant to. Quinton pulled up the central computing core location and opened a direct connection to it. He needed to interface with the computing core if they were going to have a fighting chance.

"The body can wait," he said.

He uploaded his own VI suite into the computing core, and his assistants began a quick assessment of the new environment. Then they facilitated additional connections to his ESS.

G Class PMC Access Level.

Quinton became aware of the access level seemingly before the curious thought had formed in his mind. He was a Galactic class Personality Matrix Construct, which carried the highest level of access and interface with ACN computing systems. Radek raced to unload the concepts that hadn't been available to him while he'd resided in the agricultural bot. Quinton hadn't fully understood just how feeble a connection to living the bot had provided. It was like using the flimsiest material to hold the weight of a Titan-class battleship. He brought up the specs of the ship of the wall that formed the foundation of the Jordani Federation Navy. He knew its armament, as well as the kind of fleet deployments that made the best use of the interstellar fortress.

Quinton cranked up his frame rate, and his perception of time sped up while virtually no time at all passed for the others. He was no longer bound to the pitiful hardware of a decaying old robot, and it was glorious. He didn't need to worry about hardware that was about to fall apart. He was in an ACN Starbase Alpha meant for picket duty, protecting strategic star systems on the fringes of federation territories. The starbase had the armament equal to that of a small fleet. There were weapons systems that had never been brought online. He'd only engaged the point-defense systems, but the starbase was designed to deal out significant punishment to any who sought to destroy it. It was technology meant for fighting a war, and Quinton was the only one who could command it.

He tasked a VI with the sole purpose of blocking the infiltrator VI that had been unleashed by Lennix Crowe. Quinton's VIs were capable of learning and adapting through the use of Sapient Combat Simulations. They essentially took action while running countless simulations to help sway the outcome to achieve his objective. As they engaged the advanced rogue VI, they tried to adapt to tactics that were taking place on a virtual battleground of the station's computing system. They'd slow the rogue VI down, but it would eventually adapt.

Quinton shifted his focus to the space battle occurring dangerously close to the starbase. The DUC fleet ships were being pushed back by the Union ships. Because his frame rate was so high, he was looking at a snapshot of the situation that was in the midst of progressing. The DUC fleet hadn't been defeated, but his own analysis indicated that it couldn't fight the Union ships for much longer. He knew what Admiral Brandt was fighting for—habitable worlds that they could keep hidden from Crowe's Union and the Collective. The DUC migrant fleet was made up of galactic refugees and comprised the migrant's most capable warships. They were enough to make any aggressor think twice before engaging in hostilities, but Crowe would never relent until he either had what he wanted or destroyed it.

Quinton checked the status of the station's weapons systems. Several missile silos were coming online, but it was going to take time for the autoloaders to bring actual missiles to the silos. Safety protocols required that the missile tubes go through an integrity check before being cleared for duty. The starbase wasn't combat ready. He needed a faster response. Then he found it. The station had twin particle cannons that wouldn't take long to charge. They were designed for a quick response, unloading a devastating attack that could tear through kinetic shields and the reinforced multi-alloyed hull of a Jordani warship.

Quinton instructed the starbase's combat VI to divert power to the two particle cannons.

The starbase also had heavy mag cannons along its underside. They'd immediately passed the startup protocols, and Quinton received a green status for them before he moved on.

While interfacing with an advanced computing core like the ACN station, he wasn't limited to the physics of normal time as observed by humans. He found that he could multitask and partition his focus, but there was a cost. The more he partitioned his attention, the less focus he was able to apply to a complex problem. That's where his VI assistants helped because they handled the technical aspects of his orders.

There were physical limitations. The particle beam cannons needed time to prime before they were able to fire. The more powerful the beam, the more they needed to prime, but he was impatient. In normal time, it would take mere seconds to prime, but for Quinton, it seemed to take significantly longer.

He created a virtual Sapient Combat Simulation, leveraging the combat VI to come up with a firing solution that would be sure to get Lennix Crowe's attention. Once he had his firing solution, he authorized the combat VI to execute.

Twin particle beam cannons came online, fully primed, and fired a devastating beam at the Union ships. His targets were along the edge of the Union ship deployment. He hit one destroyer-class vessel directly in the main engines, and the other one was hit midship, where the bridge would be located. The main engines of one destroyer went offline, and it began spinning out of control. The closest ships in the area evaded it, thanks to the quick thinking of their captains.

The particle cannons fired again, this time focusing on one ship. The particle beam shredded through its shields and hull, devastating its defenses. Then Quinton fired his mag cannons at the target. The particle beam exposed the ship's interior, and kinetic artillery tore through the rest. The ship broke apart as its main reactor failed.

Union ships shifted their targeting priority to focus on the starbase's weapons, and a bombardment from kinetic weaponry slammed into the starbase defenses. Point-defense turrets unleashed the fury of their armament, barely holding back the bombardment.

Quinton opened a comlink to the DUC ship *Astra*.

"This is *Astra* actual," Brandt said.

"Admiral Brandt, I've taken the pressure off your ships. If you regroup, you'll have a chance to make another attack run while I have their attention," Quinton said.

There was a long pause.

"Admiral, I have control of the starbase," Quinton said.

"Quinton, where is Maelyn? The last I heard, you were getting a new body," Brandt said.

"I still am. I'm just delaying it. Can you regroup?"

"Understood. Give us some time to regroup, and we'll hit them with everything we've got," Brandt said.

Quinton closed the comlink. The point-defense systems were belching out artillery, trying to hold off the Union fleet's bombardment, but some were penetrating through his defenses. He analyzed the Union fleet. They had two JFS heavy cruisers that were protected by smaller destroyer-class ships, along with several squadrons of light attack craft. He needed to give the DUC fleet time to regroup, but that didn't mean he had to take a beating from the Union ships.

Quinton opened a broadcast comlink to the two cruisers. Two of the five missile tubes in the station had failed their integrity check. He diverted missiles to the other three tubes. Autoloaders rushed to deliver missiles to their silos.

Union ship *Devastator* acknowledged his comlink. "Who is this?" a man asked.

"Well, who's this?" Quinton asked in turn.

"This is Lieutenant Henderson of the Union ship *Devastator*."

"That sounds very impressive, Lieutenant Henderson. I'll make sure I target your ship first. Now put me on with the commanding officer."

"You haven't told me who you are."

Quinton sent a data packet through the comlink. "Henderson, do you recognize the coordinates I just sent you? They are for the precise location of the command bridge that you're actually sitting in on that ship. In essence, I know exactly where you are. I know just where to point my weapons. If you don't put me on with Lennix Crowe right now, I'm gonna unleash the full armament of this ACN Starbase Alpha."

Quinton was bluffing. Oh, he knew exactly where the bridge was located on that ship. That wasn't a ruse, but particle beams wouldn't be enough to destroy the bridge. They were too far away, and it would take a sustained blast for a bit longer than it had taken to destroy the smaller ships.

A video comlink came online and showed Lennix Crowe's face. "Captain Wayborn, are you going to beg for your life?"

"Close, but you got the wrong person. I'm Quinton. I'm the PMC you're trying to capture. That infiltrator VI was a nice touch. I have to admit I didn't see that coming. Courtesy of your lavender-skinned spy, I presume."

"Are you going to stick with a voice-only comlink? Don't want to show me your face?"

"That's a bit difficult right now because I don't have a face," Quinton said. Instead, he opened a video channel but used Crowe's face, tweaking his appearance by giving him a man bun, horns sticking out of his forehead, and painted lips. "There. How do you like that? I think it's some of my best work yet."

If he'd been in Crowe's position, he probably would've just kept firing on the starbase. However, the bombardment from the Union ships slowed down.

"I'd rather take that starbase intact. The armament stores alone are worth a fortune. Can we come to an arrangement?" Crowe asked.

"You could retreat to minimum jump distance and then get the hell out of here. Would that work for you?"

Crowe smiled a non-smile with a smoldering gaze. "I'm sure you've analyzed the tactical data. The DUC can't win and neither can you. I'm going to take that starbase. You see, I think you have minimal weapons available to you, and you're just trying to buy yourself some time."

Sometimes Quinton got tired of people not doing what he wanted them to do. "Believe what you want."

Crowe nodded. "I will. I know the DUC is regrouping. We've got something special planned for them. As for you, well, that's a problem that will resolve itself."

If Quinton had teeth, they would be clenching right now. His mind raced. He'd underestimated Crowe's determination. The man could not be bluffed. He had all the cards, and he definitely had the upper hand.

"We'll see about that," Quinton said, his own voice sounding raspy. "You might take the starbase, but I'll see to it that it costs you everything."

Crowe laughed, and Quinton was about to sever the comlink when Crowe spoke again. “My infiltrator VI is based on Sentinel technology. It’s the technology that was designed to destroy you. There’s no way you can beat it. All I have to do is outlast your attack. Then, I’ll come aboard, retrieve your ESS, and you’ll be mine.”

Quinton severed the comlink. He wished there was a panel in front of him for his hand to smash, but at the same time, he felt a tugging sensation at the edge of his thoughts. It was as if there were something he should be remembering, but he couldn’t quite get it. Without warning, it blazed like a beacon to the forefront of his mind. He froze, unable to do anything. Radek and his army of VIs demanded direction, but he couldn’t give it.

Please be wrong.

He turned his attention to the communication systems of the space station and felt as if the ground was falling away from his feet. The infiltrator VI had taken control of a communications array and was broadcasting a subspace comlink. There was only one intended recipient, and Crowe didn’t even realize what he’d done.

Quinton opened a comlink back to the *Astra*. “Admiral Brandt, you have to break off the attack. You need to get out of here. Leave the system immediately!”

“Impossible. We’re about to regroup for our attack run.”

“Break off the attack, or all your ships will be destroyed. You’ll lose everything.”

Active sensor readings from the station detected new FTL jump emergent points into the star system not far from their location.

“Now isn’t the time to give up,” Brandt said.

“You don’t understand. The Sentinels are here. Check your active scans. They’re still jumping into the system. It’s a fleet. It’s too much for you. Get out of here,” Quinton said.

31

A FEW SECONDS DRAGGED BY, and while Quinton waited for Admiral Brandt to acknowledge the inevitable, he ordered his VI henchmen to bring up every weapons system operational on the ACN starbase. Sentinel ships continued to jump into the star system, swelling the number of ships beyond those of Crowe's Union ships. But that was just it. Space fleet engagement wasn't just a numbers game. Classes of ships and their capabilities in combat greatly influenced the outcome of any fleet engagement. The starbase scanner array included the ability to run active scans through subspace. Quinton's curiosity spiked for nanoseconds, and Radek quickly provided him with the knowledge framework that surrounded FTL scanning. He didn't know if either the DUC ships or the Union ships could run active scans through subspace, but the Sentinels could. They were already adjusting their trajectories to put them on an intercept course with the starbase.

"They're coming up on our sensors now," Brandt said. "How'd they find us?"

"It was Crowe. He's trying to use an infiltrator VI to take control of the starbase, and it's based on Sentinel technology. My guess is that it has a few extra capabilities that he wasn't aware of and couldn't account for. They sent out a broadcast that brought the Sentinels here."

Quinton heard Brandt order his astrogator to plot a new course for the DUC fleet.

"It's not too late for you to get away," Quinton said. "You can micro-jump to the edge of this star system and then retreat. I'll hold them off as long as possible."

Admiral Brandt was quiet for a few moments. "I don't know what to say."

"Save it for later," Quinton said.

The comlink to the *Astra* closed, and he saw that more and more ships of the DUC fleet had altered course.

Union ships were still on an intercept course for the starbase, and he wondered if they hadn't detected the Sentinels yet. Quinton focused his attention on the Union ships. Their fleet was comprised of older Jordani Federation ships that had probably been repurposed or abandoned in a shipyard. The JFS fleet used to coordinate their fleet engagements with what the Jordanis thought was secure communications, but the starbase was able to detect the subspace signals used by the Union ships. Quinton sent out a broadcast of his own, disguising his signal as an acknowledgment from the two Union cruisers, except his signal uploaded a very precise and very deliberate data signature unique to when a PMC was prevalent on a ship's computer systems. The effect was almost immediate. A portion of the Sentinel fleet altered course, heading for the Union fleet.

Quinton felt a moment's satisfaction imagining Crowe scrambling to figure out what had happened. But he didn't have a lot of time to relish the thought and turned his attention to the starbase.

Becker, Guttman, and Oscar had found a ship inside the hangar bay that had been offline, and they'd restored power to it. Quinton didn't recognize the kind of ship it was, but the designation indicated it was some kind of prototype.

Quinton opened a comlink to Becker. "You need to leave."

"I know that, but we're still trying to access the ship here. It looks like it has a jump drive, but it's been on emergency standby for a really long time," Becker said.

"You know all this, but you can't access the ship yet?"

"It's not like we're standing around here doing nothing. I got the data from the console here in the hangar. Can you access the ship?" Becker asked.

Quinton opened a comlink to the ship and received a PMC challenge protocol. Authentication was done quickly, but he detected that it had required access to his ESS. He really needed to figure out what else was stored there beyond his unique PMC.

ACN *Wayfarer*.

A loading ramp opened from the sleek outer hull, and Quinton heard Becker call out to the others. Quinton initiated the ship's startup protocols.

"Thanks," Becker said. "It sounds like the bombardment stopped."

"Not for long. As soon as the engines are ready, get out of here and meet up at the emergency jump coordinates," Quinton said.

"Where's Maelyn? Last I heard, she and Simon were heading to you."

"They're next on my list. Look, the Sentinels are on their way here right now, and they're going to attack. You don't want to be here when that happens."

Becker began shouting orders to the others and then said, "Quinton, thanks. I'll see you at the rendezvous."

He severed the comlink. Becker had almost sounded like he'd meant it. Maybe the salvager wasn't so bad . . . Who was he kidding? Becker was still a pain in the ass, but that didn't mean Quinton was going to abandon him.

He opened a comlink to Maelyn.

"The tram just stopped," she was saying when she acknowledged the comlink.

"I stopped it," Quinton said. "And now I'm sending you back to the *Nebulon*. I'm overriding the safeties because there isn't a lot of time."

The tram began heading away from the bio lab, but it slowed down after a short distance and came to a stop. He sent another override to force the tram to return to the central hangar bay where the *Nebulon* would be, but the tram wouldn't respond.

"What did you do?" Quinton asked.

"You think you're the only one who knows how to override a system?" Maelyn replied.

The tram began heading back toward the bio lab, and there was nothing he could do to stop it. The only thing he might be able to do was to shut down the tram system altogether, but that would leave Maelyn and Simon stranded, which wasn't what he wanted.

"Dammit, Maelyn, stop it. The Sentinels are here, and they're coming to destroy the starbase. Brandt and the DUC fleet are in full retreat. They're getting out of here, and that's what you need to do."

"I'm not going to leave you here."

"You have to."

"No, I don't. You don't get to tell me what to do," Maelyn said.

The tram's velocity increased. She must've been guiding it on manual control.

"Maelyn, you have to listen to me. I have a plan for getting out of here."

"You're just saying that. You don't have a plan."

"Yes, I do. My body is waiting for me. I'm going to download my PMC into it. There's an escape pod not far from the bio lab that's capable of micro-jumps. I can get out of here, and then you can pick me up in the *Nebulon*. Look, I'll show you," Quinton said and sent her the location of the escape pod.

"It could work," Simon said.

Maelyn sighed. "You better be there," she said.

Quinton saw the tram come to a halt, then begin speeding back the way it had come. "I will be. I promise."

His awareness was surrounded by all the systems that were connected to the computing core. With the starbase's resources at his disposal, he was able to slow down the infiltrator VI significantly but not completely.

He received an alert that the hangar bay doors where Becker and the others were had opened. A quick view of the video feed showed the ship flying out of the hangar. Becker, Guttman, and Oscar had escaped.

The tram had just arrived at the plaza near the main central hangar. Quinton urged Maelyn and Simon to run. The starbase's combat VI showed that Union ships were now engaging the Sentinels while retreating. A large group of Sentinel ships had broken off from the main group and were now heading toward the starbase.

Hyper-capable missiles were loaded into tubes. Those were new. At some point, Radek had made the knowledge of them available. He executed a firing solution, and missiles with high-yield antimatter warheads flew from the tubes. Once clear of the starbase, they went into hyperspace, shifting from normal space for less than a second before returning almost on top of the Sentinel fleet ships. Antimatter explosions tore through even the Sentinel warships, causing massive destruction. At the same time, twin particle beam cannons fired on the Sentinels ships, and he devoted all mag cannons to targeting them as well. Quinton had unleashed the full combat capability of the Acheron Confederacy Navy starbase. The Confederacy might've been gone, but Quinton was still here. He wasn't sure what that meant, but he knew the Sentinels used lethal force at the slightest detection of a PMC, and he wanted to make them suffer.

"Quinton," Maelyn said, "we've reached the *Nebulon*."

"Good. Launch immediately," he said and heard the monotone intonation of his voice because he was stretching himself entirely too thin.

The starbase's main central hangar had two hangar bay doors on each end of the starbase, and he opened the doors away from the battle.

"Execute a micro-jump as soon as you're clear of the hangar bay doors," Quinton said.

He was ready to take over the *Nebulon*'s systems if Maelyn didn't cooperate, but the *Nebulon*'s engines engaged, and the ship sped toward the exit.

"We're on our way. What's the status of the transference protocol?" Maelyn asked.

"Transfer has begun," Quinton lied.

The *Nebulon* flew through the hangar bay doors and executed a micro-jump. A second later, it appeared on the fringe of the star system.

"We'll maintain our position here in case something goes wrong with the escape pod," Maelyn said.

There was something in her voice that clued him in that she had caught on to what he was doing.

"Quinton," she said.

The first wave of powerful spinal-mount particle weapons that were fired from the Sentinel battleships slammed into the starbase. It quickly burned through the shields and began melting through the armor, destroying a missile tube. One of the missiles exploded, but it hadn't been armed, so the damage was minimal.

A barrage of alerts appeared in front of him. Sentinel ship weapons were powerful, and he adjusted his analysis of their capabilities. The tactical plot still showed Union ships fleeing the area. One of the Union cruisers had been destroyed, but it wasn't Crowe's. His ship was still making best speed away from the battlefield.

Run, you bastard. Run away.

Maelyn called out to him.

The recent battle developments wouldn't reach the *Nebulon* scanners for another fifteen minutes, so she couldn't know what was happening.

"No need to wait around," Quinton said.

The last of the Union ships jumped from the system, but they weren't followed by the Sentinel ships. Those ships changed course, heading for the starbase. He didn't know if they had somehow figured out what he'd done to trick them or if they'd decided he was the bigger threat.

"What do you mean? The transference shouldn't take that long. You need to pull back into your ESS," Maelyn said.

Quinton felt all kinds of urges for muscle movements he wasn't even capable of, but they were ingrained into the human psyche. He was a physical being and needed to release the tension from his emotions. They rooted him into his own humanity.

He pulled back from ordering his VIs. They were frantically trying to come up with a superior firing solution against the approaching Sentinel fleets. His combat VI focused the starbase's firepower on the support craft and then began shooting their heavy hitters. The Sentinel ships looked like they were an amalgamation of multiple federation militaries. The information he had on hand was for specific federation militaries, which helped but wasn't exactly conclusive.

"I'm sorry," Quinton said.

"What did you do?" she asked and paused for a moment. "Just get to the escape pod. It's all you have to do. Complete the transfer. Then get to the escape pod. Just do it!"

Quinton looked at the video feed from the comlink to the *Nebulon*. He saw Maelyn sitting in the captain's chair. Her shoulders were drawn up tight, and her face was almost rigid.

"I can't do that. I have to stay here and take care of this."

"Yes, you can. You can do this," Maelyn said almost pleadingly.

Quinton added a video feed to the comlink and showed her his face—the face of his human form inside the medical capsule. His eyes were closed, and the body floated in amber liquid.

"I figured you'd want to see this at least once," he said and created an avatar that resembled his face for the comlink.

Maelyn swallowed hard and leaned back into her chair for a moment. Then she slammed her fist down. "Just get to the escape pod!"

Quinton shook his head, and his makeshift avatar mimicked the movement. "There isn't an escape pod. I lied."

Maelyn's eyebrows pulled together, and her face became a tight frown. "I thought you weren't a hero."

He chuckled. "I'm not. I just don't like to lose."

Her full lips lifted in a sad smile. "Neither do I," she said, her voice sounding thick, almost strangled with emotion.

"I know," Quinton replied. "Tell Brandt that at least this part of the Acheron Confederacy didn't fail."

"Is that why you're doing this? Because everyone blames the Acheron Confederacy for the Federation Wars? Do you think this will make everything better? It's not your fault," she said.

Quinton looked at her and felt a stubborn gleam in his eyes. Then the comlink severed.

The Sentinels had destroyed the comms array he'd been using and overwhelmed the starbase's point-defense systems. They weren't trying to preserve their numbers. They were playing a logistics game, and their objective was clear. Quinton threw himself into the fight by using every weapon that was still operational and overriding any and all safeties for critical systems. Wreckage from the Sentinel ships formed a small debris field. He kept at it, trying to take as many of them out as he could. At least he could make the bastards pay.

The general condemnation of the Acheron Confederacy bothered him. At first, he'd been indifferent to it largely because he hadn't had access to his memories. But when he'd learned that he was from the Acheron Confederacy, coupled with his perfect recall of recent events, he found that he wanted to learn more about it. The more he learned, the more he questioned the general consensus, at least in part. There was sufficient historical evidence to support that, for some reason, the ACN had begun fighting with the other federations, but it wasn't clear why. There'd been no formal declaration of war. At the center of it all was a rogue grand admiral by the name of Elias Browning. Quinton couldn't put all the pieces together because he didn't have enough information, and now he wouldn't get the chance. Maybe Becker was right and he was someone else's pawn in a war that was no longer being fought.

He looked at the tactical plot and heard his avatar sigh. He turned his attention toward it and wanted to glare at it, but he couldn't because glaring required . . . Despite having access to every type of sensor throughout the starbase, he felt detached. A body grown using his DNA was in the bio lab, and it was going to die, just like he was about to. The Sentinels pushed forward, firing their superior weaponry at the ACN starbase. He'd destroyed many of their ships, and the Sentinels' rate of fire had diminished. There were limits to even their technology.

Quinton pulled back from the weapons systems, trusting his VIs to do the best they could against an unwinnable battle. The Sentinels had been created to hunt down and destroy PMCs, but what if there was a way he could convince them that he wasn't a threat. Would they even listen?

He found a backup comms system that was still operating and sent out a broadcast, which included the challenge protocol he'd encountered on the PMC console.

A response was sent.

Authenticate.

Quinton had expected that the stored information in his ESS would offer up his clearance codes as part of the authentication process, but it didn't.

"Quinton Everett Aldren, Acheron Confederacy Navy."

Unknown Personality Matrix Construct.

ACN Rank.

He didn't know his rank, but the knowledge became available from his ESS. "Commander," he said.

His ACN commander's identification transferred from his ESS to the comlink and then to the Sentinels.

Confirmed.

"I'm not a threat. You can stop trying to kill me," Quinton said.

Threat anomaly confirmed.

Prevention of spread is required.

He didn't understand, and he wondered if the Sentinels were nothing but a malfunctioning, overpowered virtual intelligence that needed to be turned off. He sent a series of commands through the commlink, ordering the Sentinels to cease all hostilities.

Security override has failed.

Hostile PMC host detected.

Probability of spread 100 percent.

Targets confirmed.

Several Sentinel destroyer-class ships began to maneuver away from the rest in the direction that the DUC and Union ships had gone. Quinton detected a surge of energy to their jump drives and targeted those ships. His remaining particle beam cannon fired first, and he spiked the energy levels past critical. The Sentinels were attempting to hunt down the others. He wasn't going to let them.

The particle beam burned through the Sentinel destroyers, piercing one ship's hull and tearing into the next ship in the formation. The remaining Sentinel ships refocused their fire on the starbase. They were closing in on his position, but they weren't moving fast enough. The starbase had limited maneuvering that any ship could outrun, but he engaged the engines, heading *toward* the Sentinel fleet.

Pieces of the starbase began to break away under the heavy fire from the Sentinel ships. Mag cannons went offline. Point-defense systems became inoperable. He'd expended most of his stockpile of missiles, with the exception of those that he'd lost from enemy fire. Then his remaining particle beam cannon stopped firing.

Those were all the weapons available. He'd given everything he had, and now he was going to die—alone.

"Quinton, I've done as you've asked. The body has been destroyed," Radek said.

"Was it painless?" he asked.

"The body remained in a comatose state and never achieved awareness."

"Collapsing stars, Radek! Your bedside manner still sucks."

Radek didn't reply for a few moments. "No pain was felt."

Quinton chuckled. "That's good. I'm going to join him in a few minutes," he said while giving his authentication for the self-destruct sequence, which would also destroy a large number of Sentinel ships.

"Look at them, Radek. They're trying to run," he said.

Radek didn't reply.

The good thing was that when the starbase blew up, he wouldn't feel a thing. The bad thing was that he'd never get a chance to feel anything again. Why was he so afraid? He felt it there, deep inside—irrational and primal. In the short time he'd been reactivated, hadn't he done something? Had it been worthwhile? He didn't know, but at least it was something. He would have liked to have seen more of the galaxy, but the Sentinels . . . The blast radius of the starbase was enough to get most of them. He wasn't sure how many would escape. Perhaps some of the damaged ones would, but they wouldn't recover enough to follow Maelyn and the others. He used the time he had left trying to find his records in the ACN starbase's computer system. He'd found his DNA record, but what about his service record.

There wasn't one. There wasn't anything listed. He didn't need to check more than once. Why didn't he have a service record? He had an ACN rank. Why wouldn't his service record be here? Someone had activated him. But maybe it had only been some latent protocol from an automated system. If that was the case, perhaps it was better that he never regained his memories.

Quinton's thoughts halted. The starbase's self-destruct timer was reaching critical mass, but he could still access his ESS and access the knowledge of who he was. With his frame rate cranked as high as it was, he'd have time to take in all the memories that were locked away. He just wasn't sure if he wanted to. He'd pulled back from the starbase's computer core. There was no need for him to be aware of all the systems going offline and the damage reports anymore. He knew what was about to happen.

He wondered what he would find in his ESS, but at the same time, he was afraid of what he'd find. Maybe he was fortunate not to have to remember a lifetime of experiences and people who were all gone. Why go through so much pain and loss when he was about to die?

Quinton thought about the people he'd encountered, the friends he'd made. They were enough for him. He didn't want to spend his remaining time remembering a world that no longer existed and instead chose to think about the people he'd met. The variants of humans he'd encountered perplexed him because of the lengths the people had gone to survive in this galaxy. He thought about Simon and how he'd been the first person to figure out what Quinton was. Simon was the only person who had tried to help him without demanding something in return—some last vestige of decency, or perhaps Simon hadn't aged enough to be as pragmatic as someone like Becker. Then he thought about Maelyn. She was something else. At least he'd been able to show her his face. It had been important to him that they all saw him for what he was and not that damn agricultural bot body he'd been trapped in. He was relieved that he wasn't in there anymore.

Quinton brought up the video feed of the bio lab and looked at the agricultural bot, standing stone-still like a lifeless husk. Then he closed all the data feeds, even the timer for the self-destruct. He'd had enough of being connected to everything.

32

THE *NEBULON* WAS on the fringe of some nameless star system. The one thing that Maelyn actually liked about being captain of her own ship was that there was very little opportunity for idleness. There was always something that required attention, but now the ship felt empty.

She headed to the bridge to meet with Simon and Kieva. They'd been in this star system for ten hours, and passive scans had shown that there was no one else there.

Kieva entered the bridge and walked over to Maelyn and Simon. "Have we heard from the others?"

Simon shook his head. "Nothing."

"Becker got what he wanted, and that's all," Maelyn said.

Kieva frowned a little. "I really thought he meant to join us. They all said they couldn't rejoin the Union."

Maelyn wasn't surprised, at least not much. She shrugged.

"I keep thinking we're going to hear from Quinton," Simon said and held up his hands in a placating gesture. "I know. I just thought he would've found a way to— I thought he would've found a way off that starbase."

"So did I," Kieva said.

Maelyn's throat became thick, and she swallowed. Quinton had been struggling to find his place and make sense of the galaxy. She thought about their last conversation, trying to glean some kind of insight, but it was a waste of time. "He's gone," she said.

Simon nodded, and his shoulders slumped a little. He looked away from her. "I know. I just don't want him to be," he said and smiled a little. "I liked having him around."

"Me too," Kieva said. "He was quite charming. It must've been hard for him being trapped in that agricultural bot."

"Can we just move on? No sense wasting time kicking a broken jump drive," Maelyn said a bit more harshly than she meant to.

Simon and Kieva shared a glance.

"Vonya covered her tracks too well. I've been over the system, trying to figure out how she did it. Quinton and Becker were right. She used the automated maintenance schedules and just added a jump drone to the routine maintenance and waste-disposal system. We probably would've figured it out eventually," Simon said.

Maelyn felt a spike of irritation. Vonya had fooled her as well, and she hated that. "You mean we would've eventually noticed that our stock of jump drones had dwindled? She must've known she was on some kind of time constraint. I'd love to get my hands on her again."

"I spent the most time with her," Kieva said. "She seemed so convincing. I've never heard of a Servitor being a spy."

Maelyn scowled. "Because she wasn't a Servitor. She was just in disguise."

"Well, it was a pretty convincing disguise," Simon said. The two women looked at him, and his eyebrows raised as he shrugged.

"We'll need to be more careful in the future—more secure with who we allow to access our systems, and . . ." Maelyn said and paused, clenching her teeth. "I'm the one that usually does the misdirection. I really want to find Vonya."

"If that's her real name," Simon said. "Probably not, and we don't even know if that's what she really looks like."

"She could have gone anywhere," Kieva said.

"Not anywhere," Maelyn said. "She'll need to report back to Lennix Crowe."

"Captain," Simon said, "it's not that I wouldn't want to go on another hunt with you, but we should probably report to Admiral Brandt. He might have different plans for us, especially once they've reviewed all the data they got from the starbase."

Maelyn felt the muscles in her shoulders loosen. Simon was right. Hopefully, there'd be some clue to where the Acheron Confederacy had hidden the colony worlds. "We will, and we'll do it now. There's no point waiting here any longer," she said.

Kieva went to her workstation and brought up the astrogation interface.

Simon looked at Maelyn. "Are you all right?"

"I'm fine," she said probably a little too quickly. She sighed. "I'm annoyed. I thought things would've gone differently."

He nodded and touched her shoulder, then went to his own workstation. Maelyn sat in the captain's chair. She was eager to be away from the star system. She wanted to believe they'd gotten actionable data from the starbase, but there were no guarantees. If they hadn't, she still had a mission. Crowe's Union wasn't going to stop. One thing she knew about Lennix Crowe was that he wouldn't quietly disappear. The Collective wouldn't let him.

"Coordinates are in the nav computer, Captain," Kieva said.

"Let's go," Maelyn said.

Lennix Crowe sat in his ready room near the bridge of the Union ship *Devastator*. He leaned back heavily and rubbed the tension from his forehead.

The door chimed, and he glared at it. He just wanted five minutes alone.

The door chimed again and opened. Lennix scowled.

"We need to talk," Nate Carradine said.

"If you were anyone else, I would . . ." He let the thought go unfinished. "What couldn't wait? The Sentinels haven't found us."

Carradine shook his head. "No, I don't think they were as interested in us as they were in that starbase."

"The infiltrator VI needs a lot of work. Who cleared it for use?" Lennix asked. He wanted to know who he was going to severely punish.

"Let's not be too hasty with the consequences. The infiltrator VI did its job. We needed something that could help us capture a PMC. I believe if we'd had more time, it would have succeeded," Carradine said. He sat down on a couch and leaned forward, resting his elbows on his knees.

"It also broadcast a signal to the Sentinels and brought them there. I wouldn't necessarily call that a success. Quite the opposite," Lennix said.

"It needs refinement. That doesn't mean we should execute the person most capable of fixing it. Wouldn't you agree?"

Lennix inhaled deeply and stood up. He didn't reply. He didn't need to.

"Have we heard from our asset?" Carradine asked.

"She hasn't reported in yet."

Carradine nodded. "I'm sure she will when she's able. None of us are where we expected to be right now."

"My friend, you have a serious knack for making an understatement, but I agree. I didn't think she was up to the task."

"Does this mean you've reconsidered her capabilities?"

Lennix tilted his head to the side once. "We'll see. She hasn't shown up yet. Anyway, the PMC is gone, so we'll have to move forward with our contingency plans."

Carradine stood up. "You sure about this? Trenton Draven can be negotiated with."

Lennix shook his head. "Not this time. And I'm not gonna watch everything I've built be absorbed by the Collective. We'll simply need to move our operations."

"Understood. I think we should look for more PMCs. It stands to reason that there might be others being activated."

Lennix regarded him for a few moments. "That's a big 'if.' Hoping for something to fall into our collective laps isn't a good strategy."

"Given the losses we've sustained, it might be our only strategy," Carradine said.

Lennix clenched his teeth. If that damn infiltrator VI had done its job properly, he would have been on that ACN starbase and in control of a powerful PMC. It wouldn't have mattered that he'd lost so many ships. He could replace ships. He'd have to anyway.

Lennix stood up, and Nate joined him. No more sitting around.

33

QUINTON WOKE UP, which was at once perplexing and unexpected. He should've been dead. The self-destruct had destroyed the starbase and all the attacking ships in its vicinity. That was his last memory, and yet here he was.

System diagnostic running.

The words appeared amid the darkness of his thoughts. Where was he?

Veris initiation complete.

System startup complete.

Autonomous mode has been activated.

"Hello, Quinton," a familiar voice said.

His eyes opened, but he narrowed them as he saw the curve of a nearly transparent ceraphome ceiling in front of him. There was a circular room beyond that was dimly lit with the azure glow of ambient lighting. He'd never seen this room before in his life, and he took in the smooth white walls bathed in a bluish light with the clarity of enhanced optics.

"Radek," Quinton said and was startled to hear his own voice with such clarity. "What happened? How'd did I get here?"

A status window appeared on his HUD.

Energy Storage System integration with cybernetic avatar complete.

Personality Matrix Construct integration optimal.

"I'm just as surprised as you are. I went to active status at the same time you did," Radek said.

Quinton looked down. He was in some kind of storage container, which he'd think about in a minute. He raised his hands. They looked like his own hands but for the chrome-colored "skin" of the advanced composites that comprised his musculature. He had a full-sensory interface. He could see, smell, and feel. He glided the tips of his fingers along the smooth walls of the cool storage container.

As he did so, he noticed the muscles in his arms move in a perfect copy of true flesh and blood.

He wanted to see his face but was only able to see an obscure reflection in the ceraphome window.

"I have a partial log from the starbase," Radek said. "In its final moments, a subspace comlink request opened to this place. A data transfer occurred, and your PMC was integrated with the ESS in this cybernetic avatar."

Quinton frowned and actually felt the artificial muscles of his face contract. "That shouldn't have been possible. There wasn't enough time to transfer that amount of data."

"Correct," Radek said, "but the data was compressed. Are you sure you didn't initiate the transfer?"

"Me? How would I even do that? The last thing I remember thinking was how much I didn't want to die," Quinton said.

"Perhaps if you initiate a connection to the ship, there'd be more information available to help us figure out what happened."

He connected to the ship's computer system. The ship was called the *Wayfarer* and was a star-class jumper. There was a brief PMC challenge protocol that ended quickly. He could crank up his frame rate to review the particulars, but something else caught his attention.

"We're not alone," Quinton said.

"The biosensors indicate three people are aboard this ship."

He opened the storage container and stepped out. This body was so easy to use. It felt just as natural as an artificial body could feel. He looked at the ship's identifier and chuckled. He knew who was on the ship.

"We'd better get to the bridge before they break something," Quinton said.

He thought about opening a ship-wide broadcast but decided not to. He wanted to see the looks on their faces, so he walked toward the door and left the room.

The lighting in the corridor dimmed for a few moments before returning to normal. Quinton's first thought was that they'd already broken something. He headed to the bridge and found Becker, Guttman, and Oscar arguing.

"What did you do?" Becker asked.

"Nothing," Guttman replied. "Ever since we got that crazy data burst, nothing's been right."

"Well, just reset the system then," Becker said.

"We can't," Oscar said. "We don't know where we are. The jump drive isn't like anything I've ever seen, and the navigation system contains star charts that are seriously outdated. We're lucky to even be here."

Becker growled. "The ship's computer system keeps bumping me off."

"Same here," Guttman said. "Wait a minute, you don't think this is happening on purpose."

"On purpose?" Oscar asked.

"Yeah, like Quinton sent us here as a joke to get revenge," Guttman said.

Becker sighed and shook his head. "Doesn't matter," he said. "What? It doesn't. I'm the captain, so we'll just need to figure out what's wrong with the ship and then be on our way."

Quinton smiled, and it felt so good that there were no annoying errors thrown up in response. He walked onto the bridge, and the others went silent.

"I loan you a perfectly good ship, and you're out here stranded in the middle of nowhere. You're lucky I happened to be around," he said.

Becker narrowed his gaze.

Guttman's mouth hung open, and then he shook his head. "You see, I told you he wasn't helping us."

"Quinton, is that you?" Becker asked.

"In the flesh," Quinton said and frowned a little. "Sort of anyway." He laughed. Becker and Guttman didn't. Oscar laughed but looked uncomfortable. "Hey, I didn't expect to be here. And no, I didn't do this on purpose."

Becker inhaled and sighed. "How did you get off the starbase?"

Quinton held up his hands. "I'm not sure, really. I'm still piecing things together."

He strode to the captain's chair and sat down.

"What are you doing?" Becker asked.

Quinton arched an eyebrow toward him. "This is my seat."

Guttman and Oscar looked at Becker, who continued to watch Quinton. His brow furrowed, and his gaze went cold.

"You're welcome to try to take command," Quinton said and stood up, but that didn't convey what actually happened. He had moved so fast that he was in front of Becker well before a second had ticked away on the ship's clock.

Becker's eyes widened, and he tried to step back. Quinton didn't let him. "I have a few enhancements, but look, I don't want any trouble," he said and let Becker go.

"All right," Becker said.

Quinton regarded him for a few moments. "I need to hear you say it."

Becker looked away and shook his head. "All right, Captain."

Quinton glanced at Guttman and Oscar, who immediately called him captain. Then he looked at Becker. "Now that we've gotten that out of the way, I'm hoping we can help each other. This ship wasn't meant for you. It was designed for someone like me."

"Why?" Becker asked.

Quinton returned to the captain's chair and sat. "I'm not sure, but I'll figure it out—with your help, that is."

"What are you going to do with us?" Guttman asked.

"Well, that depends on you. I'm hoping we can come to some kind of agreement—you know, like a temporary alliance. I could actually use your help," Quinton said.

Becker pursed his lips in thought. "What do you need?"

Quinton rubbed his hands together and glanced at the outdated star charts that Oscar had on the main holoscreen. "There's a whole galaxy out there. Help me fix the ship, and we'll take it from there."

Becker looked at Guttman and Oscar. The two men nodded, and Becker turned back to Quinton. "You've got a deal."

"Excellent. I've got a good feeling about this," Quinton said.

"What about our rendezvous with Maelyn?" Becker asked.

"We're not going to make it, but I'm sure we'll catch up with her sooner or later."

He considered sending Maelyn a message but decided not to—at least not yet. There were still too many unknowns, and he needed some time with his new ship. He was better off if people thought he was gone. He glanced at Becker.

"You're probably right."

"I'm glad you agree," Quinton replied. "All right, we've got some things that need immediate attention, one of which is the food replicator." He looked at Guttman. "I thought you'd find that one important if you'd like to eat anytime soon."

At the mention of food, Guttman's glower vanished in the face of more mundane needs.

"We'll also need to check the life-support systems as well. The ship's been offline for a very long time," Quinton said.

Becker nodded. "And the nav system."

"He's right. The data hasn't been updated in forever," Oscar said.

Quinton nodded and smiled inwardly. He'd learned a few things since being brought back online, such as the importance of keeping people on task so they didn't get into trouble. He needed their help to explore the galaxy, and they needed time to get used to him being the captain.

Guttman left the bridge, and Becker walked over to Quinton.

"This new body. Does it give you full access to your ESS?"

"It does."

"And?" Becker said with raised eyebrows.

Quinton smiled. He'd been expecting this. "Captain's privilege."

ACHERON SALVATION

1

QUINTON and his crew rushed their sleek shuttle past a field of decrepit, broken-down spacecraft, searching for anything remotely intact enough to be worth investigating.

"I still say we could make do finding what we want out here," Guttman said in a voice that was always a tad too loud for normal people.

"That's why you're not a scout," Becker replied, keeping his gaze on the main holoscreen.

Oscar snorted a little.

"You think that's funny?" Guttman asked.

"As a matter of fact, I do," Oscar replied.

Quinton heard the sounds of a quick scuffle from the two men who sat at the rear of the shuttle.

Oscar laughed while Guttman growled.

"Okay, seriously. Stop," Guttman groused. "You always gang up on me. I've had it!"

The two salvagers wrestled for control, with Guttman using his short, stocky frame to its fullest advantage. Oscar managed to slip away with a grin, but Guttman spun around and his gaze zeroed in on Oscar.

Becker looked behind them and shook his head, pressing his lips into a thin line as though he were considering whether he was going to have to get out of the copilot's chair. Too much time in the shuttle meant tempers were at an all-time high.

"Okay, Guttman," Quinton said, "we'll do it your way."

Guttman stopped advancing on Oscar.

"There, you see," Oscar said, gesturing toward the front of the shuttle.

Guttman frowned and scratched the patchwork of a beard that grew over his flabby jawline. His belly stuck out beyond his chest, and he narrowed his protruding eyes suspiciously.

"But do me a favor first," Quinton said. "If you can detect whether or not any of these ships have a working power core *and* their main engines are operational, I'll take us there immediately."

Guttman bit his lower lip, shook his head, and glanced at the holoscreen next to his seat.

"Go on, take a look," Quinton said.

Guttman slid forcefully down into the chair and reached toward the holo-interface. Then, he banged his fist on the side panel. "I can't."

"Why not?"

"You know damn well why not."

If any of the ships had active power cores, they would already have detected them. The ships had been out there for a long time, waiting for the people of Three Moons Shipyards to either bring them in for refitting or scrap them altogether. Bringing depleted power cores back online took time they didn't have and required equipment they hadn't brought.

"What about the engines?" Quinton asked. He twisted around and looked at Guttman.

Guttman sneered and glared at his holoscreen. "You're not as smart as you think you are. There are some good prospects out there, like that HK light freighter over there. That one could work for what we need."

What we *need*, Quinton thought derisively. His three passengers had, over the past few months, helped him get the *Wayfarer* space worthy. This whole operation was his way of paying them back.

"You won't do it. You won't take a look."

Quinton glanced at Becker.

"We don't have time for this," Becker said.

"I knew it," Guttman groused.

"Why don't you do us all a favor and just shut up."

"Come back here and make me!"

Becker shot to his feet. "My pleasure," he growled.

Quinton grabbed Becker's thick, muscular arm, stopping him from going anywhere. Becker was tall and liked to fight, but he was no match for the cybernetic avatar that Quinton was housed in. No amount of implants or strength enhancements could compete with the enormously powerful, advanced composites of his avatar. Despite superior strength, speed, and intellect—something the others might question, but Quinton did not—frustration could get the better of them. They'd been cooped up together for a long time without shore leave, and they all needed a break but had decided they'd much rather steal a ship. Becker, Guttman and Oscar wanted to get whatever ship they could find to get away from him, and Quinton tried not to take it personally.

"Let me go," Becker said, his deep bass voice deadly quiet.

"Calm down, this will only take a second. What if Guttman's right?" Quinton asked.

Becker glared at Quinton's hand and then his gaze slid back to Quinton. When Quinton let go, Becker sat back down in the copilot's seat.

"You shouldn't encourage him," Becker said.

"What the hell is that supposed to mean? I'll tell you what, Becker, I'm finished. I'm finished with all this. We're done," Guttman said.

"Hey, come on," Oscar said quietly. "Calm down."

"No, I'm serious. All of you walk all over me, and I've had it. I went along with it because in the Union we had each other's backs, but not anymore. There isn't any Union for us, and I don't have to take this crap from anyone."

"We just have to get through this one last thing and then we can take a break," Oscar said.

Guttman shook his head. "It's always one more thing. Then it's, 'Shut up, Guttman. You're an idiot, Guttman.' Well, I've had it. I'm not doing it anymore."

Quinton used the maneuvering thrusters to change course, bringing the shuttle toward the HK. Tempers had been flaring for weeks, and this was just the latest in a long line of escalating blowups.

"Will you be satisfied if I take us to the HK?" Quinton asked.

Guttman crossed his arms. "I don't care what you do."

"Well, I'm going to take us to the HK—the ship *you* picked. If you think it's good enough to salvage, I'll leave you on it. Deal?"

Guttman raised his eyebrows.

"I'm serious. I owe all of you. If you want out that badly, then here's your chance," Quinton said.

Guttman licked his lips and his eyes gleamed. He nodded. "All right," he said and looked at Oscar and Becker. "You guys are going to miss me when I'm gone."

Quinton altered course to give them a better view of the HK. Guttman's grin died, and a bout of laughter bubbled from Becker's mouth.

"Oh, she's a good ship right there. What do you say, Oscar? Think you can fly her?" Becker asked.

Entire sections were missing from the light freighter. It appeared that salvagers from Three Moons Shipyards had decided to scrap the ship for parts, but it had looked nearly intact from their initial approach vector.

Becker stopped laughing. "Okay, are we done? Now can we stick with the plan?"

Quinton changed course. "Sticking with the plan."

Guttman slammed his fist onto the holoscreen controls and they went off.

"Hey, don't worry about it," Oscar said. "You've still got us, and we love you."

Guttman jerked his head toward Oscar, who was holding out a bottle of Sangorian Bourbon.

"Peace offering," Oscar said, raising the bottle as the liquid sloshed around lazily.

Guttman smiled and grabbed the bottle, popping it open to take a long pull. Then he offered it to Oscar. They passed the bottle around and even Becker took a drink. He glanced at Quinton.

"Keep it. It would just be wasted on me," Quinton said. He could taste the bourbon. In fact, he could smell it and knew it was worth all the sighs of pleasure from the others. He could take a drink and his sensors would report on the chemical components of the bronze liquid, but he couldn't enjoy it. It wouldn't take the edge off. That was just the way things were.

Becker handed the bottle back to Guttman and gave him a nod.

Then just like that, there was peace once again on the shuttle.

Quinton could have flown the shuttle by integrating with its computer instead of the physical flight-control systems. Personality Matrix Constructs—PMCs—were capable of direct machine interfaces, among other useful skills, and his prototype avatar was designed for the PMC interface. It was radically more advanced than the Consciousness Driven Android—CDA—he'd trained for in the Acheron Confederacy Navy. Quinton had been a commander in the ACN, which caused no shortage of friction with Becker and the others. They hated and mistrusted anything that had to do with the Acheron Confederacy, and it didn't matter to them that the confederacy had been gone for almost a century.

The outdated star charts on Quinton's ship had designated this sector along the Castellus Federal Alliance expansion route. For a century, Quinton's PMC had been in storage on a third-tier colony world. He didn't know how he'd come to be on that world, and he had no idea who had activated his PMC. His knowledge of the interworkings of the galactic region was woefully out of date. It would take time to put the pieces together, and his arrangement with Becker and the others had helped, but that deal was coming to an end.

"I never know what to think when you're quiet like this," Becker said.

"I was just checking the status of the *Wayfarer*."

They couldn't risk flying the *Wayfarer* into the shipyard's region where they might be detected by automated defenses. Although Quinton had his doubts about this, Becker was sure this was the case, and it wasn't Quinton's mission. Becker was calling the shots. Instead, they'd opted for a fifteen-hour journey on a shuttle—fifteen hours to breach the protected interior of the Three Moons Shipyards and fifteen hours of the bickering that came with being confined to small places. This didn't bother Quinton so much. Then again, he didn't have to put up with the smell. Three men in a small space… There was going to be a smell eventually, and there was plenty of ripeness in the shuttle. Quinton could just ignore his highly sensitive smell receptors. The others had no such luxury.

They flew toward a large installation that was built into the side of an oddly shaped asteroid. Thousands of docking ports covered the outside of the asteroid, and automated tugger drones guided various ships in for inspection and evaluation. The larger ships were docked along the perimeter and other designated docking ports. Small to mid-size freighters were escorted to open hangar bays. Quinton saw that the hangars were designed for certain ship types but not others. Some hangars held ships that were in various states of either repair or breakdown—he couldn't decide which.

"The shipyard's name doesn't resonate with this place," Quinton said.

Long-range sensors had detected six asteroids nearly the size of small moons.

Becker looked at him and shrugged one shoulder. "Are you surprised? Three Moons Shipyards is just a cover name."

"It looks more like a junkyard."

"It probably was at one point."

Quinton nodded. "Are you sure about this?"

"About what?"

"This," Quinton said, gesturing toward the video feed on the main holoscreen. "There have to be better ships out there than this."

"Oh, there are, but they'll also have more security measures in place to protect them, as well as trackers."

"I can deal with trackers."

"We'll find something. By the looks of things, we'll have our pick and can probably get more than one ship from here."

"If you say so," Quinton said, not convinced.

"You haven't been salvaging as long as we have. Ships like the *Wayfarer* are few and far between. More often than not, it takes the parts of multiple ships to get one in good working order. By that time, it'll have a new identification and won't show up on any rogue registry of stolen property."

Salvaging, or something directly tied to it, was the way of life in the post Federation War galaxy. Quinton didn't point out that they used to build things—ships, stations, colonies. Exploration and expansion were what galactic residents had striven for. Now, it was just this—salvaging for scraps.

"Does it bother you?" Becker asked.

Quinton shook his head. "It depends on who we're stealing from. The original owners of these ships are long gone, so is it really stealing?"

"So pragmatic."

"It's the least I can do," Quinton said.

He flew away from the larger docking ports. They couldn't fly the bigger ships with such a small crew. But that wasn't exactly right. Quinton could fly those ships with the help of his VI, Radek, but the point of getting a ship for Becker and the others was so they could part ways with him. PMCs were dangerous and sometimes unstable, and they experienced Quinton differently now. Despite months aboard the *Wayfarer*, their fear had dulled only a little. He'd even updated his appearance to look human down to the finest detail, but that had created more problems than it solved. Now they believed he was just pretending to be something he wasn't.

"Take us down near the maintenance access area," Becker said and then craned his neck toward the others. "All right, pay attention. From here, we'll explore the nearby hangars. We're looking for ships that've had some work done to them. The priority is the most intact ship we can find. With any luck, we'll find a few of them."

Quinton glanced at the layout of the central complex. "How do you know the ships in these hangar bays are any better than somewhere else?"

Becker smirked. "Trade secret."

Quinton made an *uh-huh* sound and plunged the shuttle toward an older Kappa freight ship, which still sported large bronze cargo containers that looked more like canisters. He increased their velocity, and the cargo carriers blurred past the video feed.

Becker went quiet, his mouth forming a grim line.

Proximity alarms sounded inside the shuttle and a warning flashed on the main HUD.

"You're going to kill us all!" Guttman said.

"Come on, Quinton, pull up," Oscar said.

Large shipping containers were mostly smooth walled except for the junction points where both interior and exterior sensor towers were located. These were essential for protecting the cargo and the shipping container.

The shuttle sped toward an island of towers.

"I don't know, I'm feeling a little unhinged," Quinton replied. "You know, there are several open comms channels." He updated the HUD to show the Three Moons Shipyards secure transmissions, as well as the command-and-control comlinks used for their drone workforce. "I'm sure I can tweak the control signal and find out why this area is so important."

Becker shook his head and Guttman shouted for him to stop.

"Do you think their comms systems can detect a rogue PMC interference if I attempt system access?"

"For the love of—Just answer him," Guttman pleaded.

Seconds went by while the shuttle sped toward the towers.

Becker looked at Quinton. "Go ahead. See what happens."

Damn it, Quinton thought. Becker was calling his bluff.

Quinton's tactical VI presented a course for him to fly through the towers. Becker watched, his face deadpanned. Guttman and Oscar's groans became louder but then were cut off as Quinton cranked up his frame rate. His perception of time accelerated so quickly that it slowed down for everyone else. Seconds in normal time dragged out while Quinton executed evasive maneuvers that narrowly avoided the towers. The inertia dampeners squealed, throwing up alarms as the shuttle jerked through the plot Quinton had programed. Maneuvering thrusters fired in concert with the mains that were beyond anything a mere pilot could execute, making use of systems—including artificial gravity—to assist with obstacle avoidance.

Quinton's frame rate returned to normal and Guttman's scream was cut short. They'd made it through, but the maneuver had pinned everyone to their seats. His passengers were jostled but would otherwise be okay.

Becker shook his head to clear it. "And you wonder why we can't wait to get our own ship."

"That hurts. You could have just answered the question."

"You're right. I could have."

"You still can."

"Maybe."

"I'm still waiting."

Becker's lips lifted. "You can't stand not knowing."

Quinton sighed inwardly. Becker was right. He didn't want to give the former salvager the satisfaction of knowing that, but Becker's smirk meant he already knew.

He was being foolish. He thought he'd gotten his impulse response under control, which had been a real issue when he'd been trapped in an old garden bot.

The limited systems access had so severely reduced his capacity that it had been a miracle he'd survived. But his current avatar was designed for a PMC. He had full access to his memories, but there were still questions he couldn't answer, although this was no time to charge down that particular wormhole.

Quinton flew them to the maintenance hatch and deployed the docking clamps. The others activated their EVA suits and secured their helmets. Quinton didn't have a need for protective outerwear since the avatar could function quite well in temperature extremes that included a vacuum. And he didn't need to breathe, so oxygen wasn't an issue for him. However, in order to conceal his identity, he updated the avatar's configuration to make it look like he was wearing an EVA suit as well.

Becker led them to the hatch and gestured for Quinton to join him. Guttman and Oscar waited behind them.

Quinton accessed the door-control systems. Bypassing the pitiful security of the access control system was beyond easy; however, in order to cover their tracks, he brought up an access list of the previous systems that had used the door to gain entry to the hangars. A quick analysis filtered the entries by time stamp, and he picked the user or system that would most likely be used to access the door.

Quinton yanked the hatch open and they all went inside the complex.

"No alarms," Oscar said.

Becker looked at Quinton and nodded. "Good job." He then looked at the others. "The layout should be familiar."

Guttman nodded. "It looks like a Union layout."

"Where do you think Lennix Crowe got it from?"

The others shared a knowing look, and Quinton finally understood why Becker seemed to know where he was going.

Becker accessed his wrist computer, and both Guttman's and Oscar's highlighted with the data he'd sent them.

"You know, I could just access the system and probably find suitable ships quicker," Quinton offered.

"You know we can't risk that," Becker said.

Guttman and Oscar headed down the corridor away from them.

Becker went in the opposite direction and Quinton followed him.

"The security here's pitiful. They'd never know I was in the system."

"You're right because I don't want you in the system. Quinton, you told me you'd cooperate. We do this my way. If I don't need you to access the system, then I don't want you to do it. If we come up short, we'll try it your way. All right?"

They weren't concerned about whether Quinton could access the system. They were more concerned about whether his access would trigger alarms. Quinton wasn't sure he wouldn't trigger any of the PMC fail-safes that seemed to be in just about every computer system they'd come across. It was easier to hide his presence on the larger and more complex systems, but that wasn't the case here.

They spent the next few hours exploring the hangar bays that contained ships in various states of disrepair. Some of the ships had massive hull breaches while others were missing critical systems from main engine pods, life support, or the power core, and sometimes all three.

"Doesn't this bother you?" Quinton asked.

"Actually, it's kind of encouraging."

"How?"

"Because those components were removed to rebuild something else. We're looking for the ship they were rebuilding," Becker replied.

The salvager had removed his helmet because an atmosphere was being maintained. Quinton found this interesting since there was very little life on this part of the station. The air was cold, which was evident whenever Becker breathed.

A comlink registered to both of them.

"I think I found a good one," Guttman said.

A few moments later, Oscar joined them on the comms channel. "I'm not having any luck at all. I keep finding breakdown projects. No intact ships at all."

"It's all right, Oscar, I found one. You should head to my coordinates," Guttman said.

"On my way," Oscar said and left the comms channel.

"What did you find?" Becker asked.

"A Stellar Gypsy that has all the critical systems intact. Looks like it was going to be cleared for auction in another month or two. The modular layout is for carrying cargo," Guttman said, his voice high with excitement.

"That's a good find. Keep checking the systems and see if you can bring it online. Have Oscar do a double-check with you."

"Roger that," Guttman said and disconnected.

They headed to another hangar bay, and Quinton was starting to feel that his time with these people was just about up. He would help them get away from here if the ships they found were in working order. Then that would be it. That was the end of their arrangement.

"It looks like you've got what you wanted," Quinton said.

"Not yet. I know there's another ship over here."

"You know what they say about wanting more."

Becker frowned and shook his head. "No, what do they say?"

"Sometimes it's better just to accept what you have."

"One ship does not a fleet make."

"Is that what you want—a fleet of ships?"

Becker tilted his head to the side and peered into the hangar. He mumbled a response, and a subspace comlink opened from the *Wayfarer.*

"Go ahead, Radek," Quinton said.

Radek was his virtual intelligence assistant that actually resided within his Energy Storage System—ESS—but Quinton had left the sub-VI on the *Wayfarer* to monitor the ship systems.

"A massive broadcast signal has just reached this star system," Radek said.

"From where?"

"From the communications buoy in the system. The origin of the broadcast is unknown."

Becker looked at Quinton. "What's going on?"

"The *Wayfarer* detected a broadcast that came from outside the star system."

"I have analyzed the signal and confirmed that it's a PMC activation signal similar to the signal that activated you on Zeta-Six."

Quinton's thoughts scattered for what felt like long moments as seconds dragged by. Radek sent him a data dump of the signal detection and the VI's analysis. This contained standard comms initiation protocols, but it was looking for a particular acknowledgment before the rest of the data inside the signal could be reviewed. Quinton was a PMC and could provide the special acknowledgment but wouldn't risk it. There was no way for him to determine what else was inside the signal. There could be block protocols that could initiate changes in him and in Radek. It was too risky to do further analysis here, even if he increased his frame rate to maximum. He needed the computing resources aboard the *Wayfarer*.

The signal was almost here, and that meant there must be a PMC somewhere nearby.

Quinton looked at Becker. "We've got a big problem."

2

BECKER WAS STANDING inside a hangar bay and had just turned on the overhead lights when he suddenly went still and a wide smile lit up his face.

A golden hull nearly gleamed in the light. Heavy robotic arms were frozen over the rear of the ship, and it looked as if several large sections of the hull plating had been completely replaced. The ship almost completely filled the entire hangar bay.

Becker raised his wrist, reading his amber-colored holoscreen, and grinned. Quinton cleared his throat and Becker tore his gaze away from the ship. "What did you say?" he asked, his eyes sliding back to the holoscreen.

"I said, we've got a big problem—"

"Yeah, baby!" Becker pumped his fist and looked at Quinton. "Critical systems are all intact. Someone even restocked atmospheric filters for the life-support systems. There's enough fuel in the power core to take us away from here. Jump drive," Becker paused and whistled. "It's got a Paxton Series 15 drive—"

"Becker! You're not listening to me. We've got a big problem," Quinton said. Becker raised his eyebrows and looked at him questioningly. "Radek detected a PMC activation signal heading this way."

Becker blinked several times and leaned forward. "What? Heading this way, or…"

Quinton brought up his own holoscreen and showed Becker the trajectory of the signal. It would reach them in less than ten minutes.

Becker's gaze darted to the ceiling, his lips pressing into a white slash. Then he looked over at the ship with longing eyes. "Yeah, but that doesn't mean there's a PMC here. Right? The signal that activated you went through thousands of star systems before you were reactivated."

"That's true, but activation signals aren't sent out randomly. At some point, there was an ESS in this star system," Quinton replied.

Becker swore and took a few steps toward the ship, then turned back toward Quinton.

"Think about it. This system was used for scrap. It's a good place to hide something, especially during the Federation Wars."

Becker bit his lower lip a little and then sighed explosively. "Can you help me with the ship?"

"I don't think you understand."

"I do. Can you help or not?"

"That signal is going to trip the security protocols for the entire area. Then, Three Moons security teams are going to swoop in after they initiate a lockdown. No one can afford to have a PMC roaming around their operations, especially if the Sentinels are tracking the activation signal."

"Have any Sentinels been detected?"

Quinton couldn't believe Becker was being like this. Normally, the spacer was much more cautious. "Not yet," he said finally.

"So we have time. Have they initiated a lockdown?"

Quinton rolled his eyes, then licked his index finger and held it in the air as if trying to gauge the way the wind would blow. "How should I know? I told you I wasn't in their systems. What the hell, man? We've gotta get out of here."

"No!" Becker said and stomped toward the ship. "It's a damn Diamondback Trailblazer. There's no way I'm going to…" He raised his hand to his ear and opened a comlink to the others. "What's your status?"

"I've just begun the startup sequence for the Red Sun freighter. Oscar found a Mercury class star jumper a few hangars away from me," Guttman replied.

"Things are heating up. Can you switch to emergency startup sequence and use maneuvering thrusters to get to the waypoint?" Becker asked.

Quinton heard the atmospheric scrubbers running through a cycle overhead. Radek was still feeding him updates via the subspace comlink. By all outward appearances, no alarms had been raised.

"Guttman," Oscar said, "you don't need to wait for the power core to come online if you've got emergency backup power. You can bring up minimal systems while the power core comes online."

Becker ran toward the Diamondback and initiated the maintenance override to gain access to the ship systems. Quinton walked away from the gleaming hull and headed back to the corridor. Not directly interfacing with the station's computer systems was keeping him in the dark, and he walked over to the access terminal near the hangar bay entry. The interface came right up and there were no alarms. What was taking them so long? The activation signal must have been detected by now, but he couldn't confirm it because he wasn't patched into the station.

Overhead, the atmosphere scrubbers cycled again, sending a gust of air into the hangar.

Quinton squatted and placed the palm of his hand on the floor, increasing the sensitivity of both his auditory system and his sense of touch. He began cataloging the sounds and subtle vibrations through the floor, increasing his frame rate slightly to give himself an edge in analysis and reaction time. He couldn't increase it too much, or detecting anything out of the ordinary would be all but impossible. He just needed a slight edge.

Becker shouted an impressive stream of curses and hastened away from the ship. From Quinton's perspective, Becker wasn't moving very fast. He partitioned his efforts so he could interact with Becker while still doing his analysis. Multitasking like this made him more reliant on his VI assistants, which could sometimes be a challenge.

"Who the hell rips out the entire backup system?" Becker said and frowned. "What are you doing?"

"I'm listening."

"For what?"

"To see if anyone's coming."

Becker shrugged. "Oh that. Don't worry about it," he said and walked past Quinton.

Quinton stood up.

"I'm patched into the system," Becker said, waving his arm up and down, and the amber holoscreen flashed. "No alarms." He grinned.

This was too much. Quinton was often accused of being reckless, but seeing Becker's flippant reference to station security was downright alarming. "Wait a second."

"Can't wait, Quinton. There's another hangar this way. Thanks for the ride. We'll take it from here. You can head back to the shuttle."

Guttman and Oscar paused their own conversation.

"Goodbye, Quinton. It's been great," Guttman said, and then a bout of laughter bubbled out over the comlink.

Oscar grinned. "Woohoo! Thanks for the memories."

Quinton shook his head and hastened to follow Becker.

"I thought we'd never be rid of him. We're almost free, boys," Becker said and started jogging down the corridor. Without warning, he lost his balance, as if the floor had dipped heavily to one side.

"What the…" Quinton muttered and blocked out the jeering from the others.

He heard a faint humming sound far down the corridor that sounded more like an echo. A soft breeze blew overhead again, and Quinton glanced at the vent. Becker stumbled ahead.

The others were laughing uproariously and spouting random words.

"I could never leave my body. Women would miss me too much," Oscar said.

"They'd have to get past your bad breath," Becker quipped.

This led to them all speaking at once.

"Hey, morons!" Quinton shouted. "Put your helmets back on. You're being gassed."

He had to repeat himself two more times before his inebriated companions acknowledged that he'd spoken.

"I got your helmet right here," Guttman said mockingly.

"Wait a minute. Is that why I'm feeling so good?" Oscar asked with a long sigh. "God, I really needed this. Just needed to cut loose and be still. I couldn't handle being on that smelly shuttle anymore."

Quinton bet they were just sitting on the floor, taking it easy.

The hell with this, Quinton thought. Becker stumbled and fell, and Quinton quickly caught up with him. He pulled him forward and palmed the helmet controls on Becker's spacesuit. The helmet protracted, and clean air began pumping into the spacer.

Becker groaned for a few seconds, and Quinton spared a moment's satisfaction, knowing the headache that awaited him. There were still no alarms, which Quinton no longer believed was possible. Time to break his promise. He cranked up his frame rate to the max and infiltrated the Three Moons' computer systems. One of the advantages of being a PMC was the ability of directly accessing any computer system. Energy-state data storage meant that he could access the data at the speed of light. Quinton's PMC actually resided inside an ESS. Essentially, he was a being of light with the strong perception of being human. The leuridium core could power his ESS for a thousand years. Quinton's VIs helped manage the brain-to-machine interface, which also included accessing external computing systems. The risk of accessing the current systems was the enhanced detection capabilities for PMC infiltration. Those capabilities hadn't been well developed when Quinton was uploaded into an ESS. A century and several brutal wars later, he'd awakened to a galaxy vastly different from the one he remembered. Memories of his old life stirred, as if sensing his attention, but he ignored them. No use dwelling on the past. Whatever the past was, it was gone. At least that was what a friend had told him once.

Quinton blew past the pitiful security protocols. Civilian-grade security was no match for his capabilities, nor were they designed to be, and he obliterated the PMC detection protocols for anomalous activity before the system had a chance to detect him. Computing limitations could always be tied to the system they resided on. Quinton's platform had been created through the Acheron Confederacy Navy's advanced research projects initiative. The Acheron Confederacy hadn't been the most powerful federation in the galaxy, but its technical base was ahead of the curve with research and development it had carried out in secret. Quinton's cybernetic avatar outclassed most computing systems he'd encountered. His VI henchmen infiltrated and confirmed that the station's automated defenses *had* been engaged.

The lockdown protocols were designed to function even in the event of successful infiltration. This made things more complicated. Initiated security measures, which included atmospheric contamination, functioned on isolated systems that were now offline, and he couldn't simply kill the lockdown protocols. They'd have to be physically reset. They functioned as such for the purpose of remaining undetected and thus able to operate in isolation. Those systems had their marching orders and there was no central command authority to stop them.

Clever.

Quinton brought his frame rate back to normal. Becker was breathing deeply.

"I said to put your helmets on," Becker snapped.

"I'm already on the bridge," Guttman said. "You should see this thing. This is it. This is my ship. I think it was going to be someone's luxury ship. Not anymore. The carpets feel amazing. I just need to take off my other boot."

Becker pushed his brows forward in frustration.

"I bet it's good," Quinton said.

Becker glared at him.

"Quinton, you have no idea. My bed on the *Wayfarer* was nice enough, but this is amazing," Guttman said while letting out a moan of pleasure. "Heh, there's wetness on my cheek."

Quinton tried not to imagine Guttman stripping off his spacesuit.

"Hey, have you closed off the ship? Are you ready to take your new ship out for a ride?"

Becker glared at him. "Are you trying to get him killed?"

Guttman groaned with effort. "Yeah… No. I'm not sure."

"You'd better get to it if you want to keep that ship."

"You're right. Is someone coming?" Guttman asked. He sounded like he was climbing into a seat.

"Yup. They're on their way. I'm sending you a set of coordinates. Enter those into the navigation system and switch to the ship's life-support systems," Quinton said and muted the comlink to Guttman. "He probably doesn't have his helmet or his spacesuit on, for that matter. The only way he's gonna make it is to escape on that ship. His head will start to clear once he's off the station's umbilical."

"Hey, there's lights outside," Oscar said.

Quinton accessed the video feed. Oscar was sprawled on the floor, looking as if he'd just rolled on the ground. Quinton traced the source of the flashing and saw three oval-shaped security drones flying through the corridors. He accessed the door-control systems and closed off the corridor.

He looked at Becker. "Security drones."

Becker unholstered his blaster and Quinton did the same.

A comlink broadcast came through the station's communication systems.

"What the hell was that?" Becker asked.

Quinton recognized it immediately, even though he didn't want to believe it. It was the acknowledgment of a PMC activation signal. Somewhere in this facility, a PMC was coming online.

3

"WHAT'S HAPPENING?" Becker asked. He kept his gaze down the corridor with his weapon ready. Ribbons of flaxen light radiated from both sides of the corridor, separated by adjoining sections that were locked together.

"There's a PMC coming online," Quinton said and tacked on, "I think."

"What do you mean 'you think'? Don't you know how it works?"

Quinton brought up the standard operating procedures for PMC reactivation on his HUD.

"We're slightly more complicated than the standard computing core."

There was a loud clang against the bulkhead door farthest from them. Several more clangs reverberated through the corridor, followed by a bright flash as the security drone began cutting through the door. The video feed showed that an armored unit with eight legs, like a spider, had seized the door while it used a plasma cutter to slice through it. As if sensing it was being watched, one of the drone's crimson optics spun toward the camera. Then the video feed went dark.

Quinton and Becker hastened away from the door.

"That's right, you're a sophisticated piece of—"

"Be careful how you finish that statement," Quinton warned. "Right now, I'm trying to keep all of us safe. Oscar is staring at the back of his hand like he's never seen it before, and Guttman has stripped off his spacesuit down to his underwear. Geez, there's a stain on his belly. Does he ever not get food everywhere? Not to mention the security drones that are converging on our location. If you want to take your chances without me, I can live with it."

Becker glanced behind them.

"Eyes front. We're turning here," Quinton warned.

They increased their pace and ran past another set of bulkhead doors. Quinton tried to close them, but they wouldn't respond to his commands.

"They won't shut."

Becker slowed down. "We'll have to close them manually."

A metallic slam echoed down the corridor. The drones were through, and Quinton saw them race through the opening at breakneck speeds.

"Come on, it's too late for that," he said.

They ran along the corridor, Quinton matching Becker's pace.

Guttman's cough sounded through the comlink. "We're green across the board."

Becker cursed. "Guttman, hang on a second."

"It's all right. I locked out the console he's sitting at," Quinton said.

"How?"

"Comlink. I've uploaded the waypoint coordinates to the nav computer."

"What's with these straps? I can't move!" Guttman shouted.

"Sit still," Becker ordered.

"Guttman, guess what?" Quinton said as they ran. "There are a group of female Servitors on that ship, and they're heading to the bridge right now to help you out."

"Really?" Guttman asked with awe in his voice. He sounded like he was twisting in his seat to look for them.

"Yup, there are six or seven of them on their way right now."

"But no one is supposed to be on the ship."

Becker shook his head. "They come with the ship. It's part of the luxury package. Enjoy it. They can't wait to meet you."

"I will," Guttman said, sounding like he was drifting off to sleep.

Quinton muted the comlink so Guttman couldn't hear them.

"Good thinking. That ought to keep him occupied for a while," Becker said.

Servitors were genetically enhanced humans that exemplified physical beauty, and their services extended beyond primal pleasures to nurturing psychological and emotional wellbeing. Quinton had yet to actually meet one. They'd encountered an agent who had disguised herself as a Servitor and had had no shortage of admirers, with Guttman first and foremost among them.

Quinton pulled Becker to the side just as a red particle beam singed the wall where his head had been and returned fire with stunning accuracy. Two of the flying security drones tumbled out of the air and crashed. The third dropped toward the ground and flew near the wall. Quinton couldn't get a clear shot at it.

"Where's the other one?" Becker asked.

That was a good question. The big spider-drone should have been with the others. More and more of the video feeds were cutting out and going offline, blinding him. How could a glorified scrapyard have such a comprehensive response for intruders?

"I don't know."

They kept running.

"Are we close to Oscar's location?" Becker asked. He was starting to breathe heavier.

"Hey, you don't have to worry about me. I found a ship," Oscar said.

The pilot had been quiet this whole time. The video feed of the hangar bay showed Oscar sitting in a small, two-person aircar that rested on a raised maintenance platform. The entire engine was in pieces on the floor, and it looked as if it had been in the process of being gutted for parts. Quinton saved a quick recording of Oscar sitting in the aircar, attempting to engage the flight controls. He was acting as if the vehicle was actually moving.

"He's not going anywhere," Quinton said, bemused, and sent the video feed to Becker.

Becker grinned for a few moments and then frowned. "The bulkhead doors are closed— the video feeds just dropped for the surrounding corridors."

Charging into the area where several spider-drones were attempting to reach Oscar wasn't a great idea. They were armed, and Quinton wasn't sure their blasters could penetrate the drones' armor.

"We have to get to him," Becker said. "We can't leave him like that. All they have to do is vent the hangar bay and he's dead."

Quinton used the comlink channel to Oscar's wrist computer to access the aircar's computer systems. It still had emergency power, which was fortunate for Oscar. He engaged the canopy and a protective shield protracted over Oscar's head, sealing the inside. The aircar's life-support systems came online, and Oscar stared at the roof of the vehicle with a mixture of awe and bewilderment.

"Now sit tight," Quinton said. His voice boomed over the aircar's sound system. "Don't touch anything."

"I wasn't… I wasn't going to," Oscar replied.

"Can you lock him out like you did Guttman?" Becker asked.

"I can't, but I did enable the first-time-user preference interface." If Oscar accessed the aircar's controls, he'd spend twenty minutes answering new-user prompts.

They raced to the end of the corridor, where it split into two different directions. A spider-drone sped toward them and Quinton cranked the bulkhead door shut. The drone slammed into the door with enough force to put a sizable dent in it. They moved fast, but Becker continued to breathe heavily, and Quinton wasn't sure how long the spacer could keep up the pace. He was certain Becker wouldn't appreciate an offer to carry him.

There was another broadcast from the PMC being activated. It was broadcast on all comlink channels, and Quinton was able to pinpoint its source.

"Why is it doing that?" Becker asked.

"It's not the PMC. It's the VI that's sending out a general broadcast. It's probably because the ESS is unable to be installed into a host, so the VI is requesting information on how it should proceed," Quinton said.

"Well, can't you tell it to shut up? Tell it this was an accident and it should shut down."

Quinton felt a flash of irritation ignite amid his thoughts. The utter disdain that Becker and the others had for PMCs sometimes rubbed Quinton the wrong way. PMCs were alive. They were actual people. They weren't machines that should be shut down until it was convenient. The fact that they were being used as pawns was the source of growing irritation for Quinton. He'd been in the same situation when he was brought online. He'd been hunted as a result, and he was very lucky Radek had taken matters into his own virtual hands or he wouldn't be alive.

"I'm not doing that."

"What? Why not?"

"Because it's not a machine. How would you like it if I knocked you out every time you wanted to wake up? Dose you up with drugs to make you unconscious just because you had the audacity to wake at an inconvenient time." The words came out harsher than he intended them, and Becker was taken aback.

"All right, I get it," he said evenly, "but we've got to save Oscar."

Quinton opened the control interface for the maintenance platform where the aircar was located. He ordered it to lower one side so the top of the aircar faced toward the hangar doors. The hangar bay door-control systems were still online, so he ordered them to open. The hangar bay quickly depleted its atmosphere and Quinton initiated the aircar's emergency egress system. The passenger compartment of the aircar was also an escape pod. Its thrusters exerted enough force to carry it beyond the hangar bay doors and out into space.

Becker watched the video feed, his eyes wide. "What have you done?"

"Oscar is safe. He's got thirty-six hours of O2, which is more than enough time for us to pick him up. I'm not leaving without that PMC."

Becker knew better than to argue with him.

Quinton scanned the walls and found a maintenance access tunnel. He bypassed the security mechanism for the door, and they entered, having to bend over a little to fit inside the small space. Quinton closed the door and waited for a few moments, hearing the security drones race by, none the wiser.

"We're clear," Quinton said quietly.

Becker led the way since they didn't have room for Quinton to squeeze ahead.

"Straight on for a hundred meters. Then left," Quinton said.

Becker quickened his pace. Quinton noticed that he kept glancing toward the ceiling.

"Minimal monitoring in here. They're probably reliant on drone check-ins rather than monitoring these tunnels," Quinton said.

Becker nodded. "How'd you know these tunnels were here? Did you see it on their system?"

"This isn't the first time I've done something like this."

"Now there's a story I'd like to hear."

"Later," Quinton said. Despite Becker's disdain for the pre-Federation War galaxy, he was keenly interested in what Quinton had done for the Acheron Confederacy Navy.

"How are we getting this PMC out of here?" Becker asked.

They reached an intersecting tunnel and Becker gestured for Quinton to lead.

"You don't want to take the long way back to the shuttle?"

"Not really."

Quinton heard the clatter of the security drones as they went by in the corridor, detecting four of them. He tried to detect a comlink session being used by the drones, but there wasn't any. They must be coordinating using a line-of-sight comms, but without any video feeds in the area, he had no way of confirming his hunch. Whoever designed the security response for Three Moons had taken their job quite seriously.

"How far do we have to go?" Becker whispered.

"Just a little farther," Quinton replied and then added, "The fun part will be going back into the corridor."

"Why do we have to go back?"

"Because it's the only way to get outside."

"You didn't say anything about going outside."

"You didn't think the PMC was in here?"

"Yeah, I kinda did. I figured it was on a ship that had been brought in or in some kind of cargo stored here. Nothing goes to waste in places like these," Becker said.

"Not a bad guess, but still not right."

"You told us the activation signal propagates through a star system's communication infrastructure, so it didn't need to know precisely where a PMC was stored."

"That's right, but this one came directly here. To this asteroid, in fact," Quinton said.

Becker didn't reply because they were nearing the maintenance hatch that would let them back into the corridor. Quinton leaned toward the hatch and listened for a few moments. He looked at Becker. "Okay, it sounds clear. There's an exterior hatch and airlock a short distance from here. We'll take that to the asteroid's surface. Then it's just a few hundred meters away."

Becker nodded.

Quinton opened the door and they stepped into the dark corridor. The security protocols must have switched off the lighting, but Quinton could see in the dark and Becker's HUD could compensate for low-light conditions. They quickly ran toward the exterior hatch.

Quinton opened the hatch and saw an airlock a short distance from them. He stepped through the hatch, but something slammed into him from above and knocked him back into the corridor. As he was crashing into the wall, he cranked his frame rate up to maximum in order to quicken his perception of time and slow everything else down. Becker was just starting to flinch away from the doorway, and the spider-drone that had been hidden on the ceiling of the airlock was coming through the door. Quinton lowered his frame rate and aimed his blaster. At this point, his perception of time was still way above normal, but it wasn't at a standstill for everyone else. Plasma bolts shot from his blaster. His back hit the wall as the bolts hit the spider-drone's armored chassis. Quinton fired his weapon again as the spider-drone closed the distance. Becker was turning toward him. The jagged ends of the spider-drone's legs also had grabbers, which meant they probably performed maintenance, as well as security. The plasma bolts scorched the armored chassis but didn't penetrate it. He angled his fire toward one of the oncoming legs and blew the end off the body. Then the spider-drone was on top of him.

Quinton grabbed the nearest leg and twisted to the side. He jumped toward the ceiling, yanking the spider-drone's leg hard. Becker fired his blaster at it but missed. The spider-drone's leg bent at an awkward angle and Quinton let go, but it still had six legs. It stabbed him, and the hardened alloy penetrated his own armored torso. Quinton didn't feel pain, but he did register that the spider-drone could do some serious damage to him. The drone slammed him to the ground, and he rolled to the side, breaking the jagged foot off the drone's leg as he did.

The spider-drone tried to stab him again, but Quinton was too fast. He scrambled out of the way and stood up. More spider-drones were heading toward them from farther away.

"Go out the airlock!" Quinton shouted, making sure his speech came out in normal time so Becker would understand him.

Becker spun toward the hatch. He was sure Becker was moving as fast as he could, but he still appeared to be moving in slow motion. The spider-drones were able to move quicker than an unenhanced human, but Quinton's avatar had the advantage now that the trap had been sprung. He increased the power output of his blaster and took out three of the spider-drone's legs. With only one left, it couldn't do more than flail about. Quinton ran past it and into the airlock. He slammed the hatch shut and was through the airlock before the other spider-drones reached it.

The asteroid's terrain wasn't as uneven as he expected. Becker waited for him outside, and Quinton looked at him incredulously. Why wasn't he moving?

"I don't know which way to go."

Quinton shook his head. "Sorry about that," he said and closed the distance. He grabbed Becker by the back of his suit. "We've got to move."

They were at the edge of the artificial gravity field, but it was still half the standard one g. He took several steps to gain momentum and leaped. Becker used his suit thrusters to level them off and extend the jump.

The brownish, roughened terrain sped by as Quinton jumped into the air again. The PMCs location was on his HUD, and they were closing the distance.

"We've got company heading our way. Where's the shuttle?"

Quinton had had their shuttle on standby since they first arrived. He hadn't been convinced they wouldn't need to find another way off the asteroid.

"It's coming," Quinton replied. He'd tasked a VI to manage the autopilot so the shuttle would head to their location.

Quinton peered into the distance and saw what looked like an escape pod that had crash-landed onto the surface of the asteroid. It looked to have been there a long time.

"We're going to have to hold them off. Aim for the legs. They're vulnerable there," Quinton said.

As they closed the distance, they noted patches of bronze amid the blackened walls of the pod, which easily blended with the asteroid's surface. If there hadn't been an active comms signal coming from it, Quinton was sure he'd have missed it.

Quinton opened the escape pod's hatch while Becker fired his weapon at the spider-drones, but they dodged out of the way. Inside the pod was an ESS core suspended in a counter-grav cradle that had been designed for it. The decagonal shape of the leuridium core glowed with a bluish light that pulsed lazily.

"Why don't they send out a body with it? Seems short-sighted to me," Becker complained.

"I'll bring it up at the next PMC governance review meeting about improving their services," Quinton said.

He couldn't reach inside and just snatch it out of the cradle. There were defenses in place. He initiated a comlink using his own PMC protocols.

PMC offline.

VI designate Greta.

Quinton observed the spark of communication from Radek to Greta. Radek had to conduct the initial greeting, or Greta might not communicate with him.

PMC Quinton Aldren – G-Class.

Greta, we're here to retrieve you.

Understood. Clearance given to transport PMC Nash Harper into an acceptable host.

No host available. Hostile forces in the area. Need to transport.

Must confirm with COMCENT.

PMC Nash Harper will not be moved without a host.

"Damn it," Quinton said.

"What is it?" Becker asked.

"It won't allow me to retrieve it without a host."

Becker's mouth opened a little and he frowned. "We tried. Let's just leave it."

Quinton wasn't going to leave it. Greta was just following safety protocols, but he didn't have time for this.

"I see the shuttle," Becker said and then fired his weapon at a spider-drone. He hit one of the legs, but it hardly slowed down.

Guttman's comlink became active. "Someone's firing weapons at my ship," he said. His voice was clear. The euphoric effects must have worn off. "Quinton, what did you do? I can't control the ship."

Quinton sent a command to end the lockdown via comlink on Guttman's ship.

"Head to the waypoint," Becker said.

"I'm trying."

"Do the best you can. We're a little busy down here," Becker said.

"Fine," Guttman grumbled.

Becker kept firing his weapon at the two spider-drones as they continued to push closer to their position. They darted out of the way of incoming fire, staggering their approach.

Quinton glanced at them. "Hold your fire."

"Why?"

"I have an idea. I need one of them intact."

Becker glanced at the escape pod and his eyebrows raised. "You can't be serious. You're going to stick that thing into one of those drones?"

"Do you have a better idea?"

"How the hell are you going to do it?"

Quinton watched the spider-drones racing toward them, their legs propelling them across the uneven terrain with ease.

"I have no idea."

4

"You only need one of them," Becker said and fired his weapon.

Quinton did the same, focusing his fire on the drone that had taken the most damage. The spider-drone's legs were built in sections, so unless they shot them out near the body, the thing could still move.

The other drone stopped and shot its particle beam toward them. Quinton took out its leg, cutting off the deadly beam, but Becker cried out in pain. The spacer went down and dropped his weapon. Quinton ran over to him. He had seconds before the spider-drone reached them. He'd taken out the drone's weapon so it would have to come in close. The fact that it wasn't retreating meant that it expected reinforcements soon.

Becker clutched his shoulder. His suit was venting atmosphere. The suit's self-repair functions began working, closing the hole, but it would do nothing for the pain.

Becker would live.

Quinton turned toward the drone. "Now it's your turn."

He scanned for any comlink signals and didn't detect anything. The drone was cut off from whoever had activated it. It still had six of its legs, and he needed to disable it without destroying it. Quinton increased his frame rate and searched for an access panel. The elliptical armored body had ridge lines, so it was difficult to see every surface. He ran a quick tactical analysis, which gave him two possible locations for the access panel, neither of which were easy to get to.

Quinton reduced his frame rate but kept it high enough that his own reaction times were faster than the drone's and then rushed toward the creepy critter. Its crimson optics blazed as it darted toward him. Had he surprised it? He darted to the side and fired his weapon, obliterating one of its legs. The spider-drone dropped off-balance, and Quinton took out another of its legs. Then he slid underneath its body, grabbing its underbelly. The drone spun around, trying to find him, and then slammed its body onto the ground in an attempt to knock Quinton lose. When that didn't succeed, the drone dragged its underbelly along the rough terrain. Quinton glanced up and saw that the drone was heading toward a deep crater.

Quinton saw the access panel, which required special tools to open. How thoughtful of them. The nanorobotic alloy that comprised his "skin" hardened, and Quinton pierced the armor. He tore off the panel and shoved his hands inside. The spider-drone might not have had an active comlink, but it couldn't protect against the physical access that Quinton now had. He quickly found the command-and-control subsystem and overrode it. The spider-drone stopped struggling, but that was the easy part. The hard part was that they were both sliding toward the edge of the crater. Quinton pushed his feet toward the ground, trying to slow them down, which didn't help in the slightest. The low gravity hampered his movement. Rather than slowing down, he was flying over the surface.

Quinton muttered a curse. More Three Moons security forces were on their way, and Guttman was getting attacked on a ship with only emergency power. Oscar was in an escape pod waiting to be rescued. Becker was hurt, there was a PMC coming online, and he was soaring toward a deep crater. Maybe he needed to rethink his life.

The spider-drone's body jerked to a halt and Quinton's legs flung out from underneath it, but he held on.

"I've got you," Becker said.

His voice came over the comlink. He'd shot a grappling tether, which attached to the armored body of the spider-drone, and Becker quickly reeled him in. Quinton felt a slight increase in gravity as he was brought back into the field.

"Thanks. I owe you one," Quinton said and dragged the spider-drone back to the escape pod. The shuttle had landed nearby.

Becker's suit was blackened at the shoulder and the spacer grimaced in pain. "I can't stop you, but this isn't a good idea," he said, jutting his chin toward the escape pod where the PMC waited.

Quinton didn't reply. He walked back to the pod and peered inside. "Greta, I have a temporary body available for the ESS."

Unacceptable.

"We don't have a lot of options. It's got a sensor interface that should help. I've got extensive materials back on my ship, but you've got to trust me."

The VI seemed to consider this for a few moments and then the shield protecting the ESS core powered off. Quinton used the cradle to transfer the core to the open panel of the spider-drone. The core burrowed deeper into the chassis and began the PMC startup sequence.

"Come on," Quinton said.

They went to the shuttle and Quinton secured the spider-drone in the rear cargo hold.

"Radek," Quinton said sub-vocally so no one else could hear, "restrict access from that PMC until we know more about what we're dealing with."

"Understood, sir."

Quinton engaged the shuttle's flight controls and they rose upward. He swung the shuttle around so its cannons were locked onto the escape pod and fired. It blew apart. If anyone came to investigate, they wouldn't find much evidence of what had happened here. Swinging the shuttle back around, he spotted the last spider-drone limping back toward the station. He fired the mag cannons again and destroyed it.

Quinton updated the main holoscreen with both Guttman's and Oscar's comlink locations.

"How you holding up?" Quinton asked.

"I'll live," Becker said while studying the holoscreen. "Oscar is closer."

Quinton nodded.

Becker activated Oscar's comlink. "Hey, Oscar, are you awake?"

Becker had to repeat himself.

"Yeah," Oscar answered. "Ouch. Yeah, I'm here. I guess they gassed us," he said in a quieter tone.

Quinton flew toward the escape pod. It didn't take long to catch up with its slow speed.

"We're almost to you. Is your suit intact? Do you have your helmet?" Becker asked.

"No," Oscar answered irritably. "Damn it! No helmet."

"We don't have enough room for that escape pod in here," Quinton said. "We'll need to tether it to the cargo holder."

Oscar groaned and there was a sound of him checking the compartments. "I've got something—Yes! They've got an emergency head covering in here. I can open the hatch and make it to the shuttle. Just let me know when."

"Stand by," Becker said and looked at Quinton. "I'll go back to the rear airlock."

"Like hell you will," Quinton said and stood up. "With that shoulder of yours, I'll end up losing both of you. Sit tight."

Becker clamped his mouth shut and didn't protest any further. "Release the controls. I can still fly the damn shuttle."

Quinton waved without turning around as he headed to the rear airlock. "All yours."

About a minute later, Quinton was in the airlock, facing the deep dark. An automatic tether was attached to the back of an EVA utility belt that had suit thrusters. The aircar escape pod was a short distance away.

"All right, Oscar. Time to open up," Quinton said.

Oscar chuckled. "I didn't know you cared, but this isn't the time or the place for us to confess our truest feelings for each other."

Quinton smiled. "You know what I like."

Oscar laughed, and the hatch to the escape pod popped off with a puff of atmosphere. Quinton deployed a tether toward the open hatch and Oscar attached it to his suit. He pulled himself out of the pod and Quinton retracted the tether.

"Gotta move it," Becker said.

Quinton increased the speed of the retractor, then caught Oscar and pulled him into the airlock.

"We're secure. Go," Quinton said.

They went inside the shuttle and Oscar sat in one of the rear seats. "Thanks, Quinton," Oscar said with a heavy sigh.

Quinton gave him a nod and returned to the pilot's seat.

A message from Radek appeared on Quinton's internal HUD.

"The PMC would like to speak with you," Radek said.

"Tell him we're in the middle of a situation and I'll talk to him after it's resolved," Quinton replied. It was disorienting enough for a PMC to be brought online, and the experience was going to be compounded by the fact that whoever was stored in that PMC was stuck inside a spider-drone.

"I'm afraid he's insisting— He's overriding my control."

"What is the meaning of this! You can't keep me in the dark. Who is this?" the slightly modulated voice asked.

Quinton should have anticipated that Radek might not be able to keep their new guest in the dark.

"Ready to take over?" Becker asked.

"Not yet," Quinton replied.

Becker glanced at him.

"Hey, I asked you a question," the PMC said.

Quinton muttered a curse. "Calm down. My name is Quinton Aldren. I'm the one who saved you."

"Saved me? Did something happen to the transport ship? What happened to the *Kendrick*?"

"What's your name?"

There was a pause for a few seconds. The PMC was still coming online.

"Nash Harper."

"Okay, Harper, call me Quinton. What's the last thing you remember?"

Becker flew them toward Guttman's comlink signal.

"Deployment orders… I can't remember. I should be able to. The *Kendrick* was taking us to a major offensive with… Wait. I don't know who you are. I shouldn't be talking to you," Harper said.

Harper had limited access to his memories. Ordinarily, Quinton could sympathize with that, but right now he just didn't have the time.

"Harper, I don't have time to go into this with you. I need you to be patient."

"I don't have to listen to you!" Harper exclaimed.

The PMC tried to seize control of the shuttle's computer systems, but Quinton had anticipated that and locked him out.

"I can't let you do that."

"How did you do that?"

"I promise I'll answer all your questions," Quinton said. He wasn't going to share his complete identity because he wasn't sure which federation Harper was from. Even though he hated to keep Harper ignorant of that information, it was for his own good.

Quinton initiated a comlink with Harper's VI. Then he initiated a PMC integrity check via the stored procedures that were part of the VI suite.

"Hey, I don't consent to this. I'm going to stop—" Harper went quiet as he was brought offline. The integrity check would take a few hours to run. It was unlikely that it would improve Harper's mood, nor would it make him less suspicious of Quinton, but he had no choice.

"Okay, I've got it," Quinton said, and Becker returned control of the shuttle's flight systems to him.

"What happened?"

"Nothing. He's just a little confused," Quinton replied.

Becker's gaze darted toward the interior cargo hold, and his hand went to his blaster. "Are we in danger?"

"What? No, put that thing away before you hurt someone," Quinton said.

Becker looked unconvinced.

"I told you I took care of it," Quinton said.

The *Wayfarer's* shuttle was a fast ship, capable of greater speed than the luxury ship Guttman was so keen on keeping.

Guttman was flying through a scrap region, attempting to lose the Three Moons security force that was chasing him. He wasn't doing a bad job of keeping them at bay. Becker activated Guttman's comlink and they heard him spouting a steady stream of curses. He was talking to himself, questions and all.

Quinton heard Oscar chuckle from behind him and he snorted. Even Becker cracked a smile.

"Hey, Baby New Year," Quinton said, "we can hear you."

Guttman stopped speaking. "Oh good, now you've got something else to make fun of me about."

"Well, you're the one who stripped off your suit so you could be…" Quinton paused a moment. "I think you said you just wanted to be free."

Oscar laughed and Quinton joined him as Guttman growled.

"All right, that's enough. Guttman, were you able to charge the jump drive?" Becker asked.

"Charge the jump drive! Why didn't I think of that? Of course, I did. And it was the first thing those damn security forces shot."

"Are they the ones…" Quinton began to say and then stopped.

"What! Go ahead and say it. Have a nice laugh. You idiots are going to miss me when I'm gone. Do any of you know how to cook? Enjoy plain old nothing from now on."

Quinton glanced at the others. "He does have a point. I think we should save his ass. Let's put it to a vote."

"A vote! I swear, Quinton, I'm going to find a way to get you back. So help me, I'm going to find a way."

"Right, then," Quinton said. "A vote. Oscar?"

"Yeah, let's save the little guy."

"That's one for yes. But he just threatened me, so I've got to give it a hard no. What about you, Becker?"

Becker shook his head. "Stop messing around."

Quinton mimed disappointment. "Looks like it's your lucky day. I guess I'm in the saving mood today. Guttman, we're coming up on your six. When I tell you..." He paused.

"Say again, Quinton, you cut out," Guttman said.

"Oh, sorry about that. When I tell you..." Quinton said and paused again.

"What? What did you say? What do you need me to do?" Guttman asked. After just a few moments, he said. "You're messing with me? Damn it! I'm going to kick—"

Quinton flew a trajectory that kept Guttman's ship in his line of sight most of the time. Guttman was weaving his way through space junk, as were the two ships pursuing him. Radek put up a flight path that Guttman and his pursuers would most likely take.

Becker tried to answer Guttman, but Quinton muted his comlink and fired the shuttle's mag cannons in controlled bursts, hitting the partial hulls of ships that were in the area and altering their trajectory, which put them in the paths of the security ships. They had elongated snouts like a dart and only had single occupants. One of them managed to avoid the space debris, but the other crashed into it and tumbled off course. The damage to the ship must have been severe because the pilot used his escape pod.

The remaining security ship executed a tight maneuver that swung the front of the ship, pointing it in the shuttle's direction. Quinton fired the mag cannons again and altered course, removing them from the path of the security ship's return fire.

They both missed.

"Guttman, you're in the clear. We've given them something else to chase," Quinton said.

"Nice of you to finally show up," Guttman replied.

Becker looked at Quinton. "You know he's not going to let this go."

"I know."

"Don't you think you pushed things just a little too far?"

"We all have a flaw. Several, in fact."

The security ship was on an intercept course, and Quinton initiated a comlink to it.

"Something isn't right," Guttman said.

"What's wrong?" Becker asked.

"I'm not... I can't. Nothing is responding. Did you lock me out?"

Quinton shook his head. "That's not me."

"Shit," Becker said. "Listen to me. Head for the nearest escape pod."

"What! No! This is my ship!"

"Listen to me, or you're going to die. They triggered a dead-stick remote override, but it won't affect the escape pods because they're on a closed system," Becker said.

Guttman cursed. "Core containment is failing," he said. He sounded like he was running.

The security ship was trying to angle its approach to the shuttle to get a clear shot, but Quinton wouldn't let it. When the ship's comms system acknowledged his broadcast, Quinton got into the security dart's systems. He quickly shut everything down and then jettisoned the escape pod.

The luxury light transport ship flashed as the core containment went critical and the ship exploded.

"Guttman, are you there?" Becker asked.

Silence.

Quinton executed an active scan sweep, but there were too many objects for the shuttle's scanners to identify an escape pod.

Becker called out to Guttman two more times, but there was no response. He leaned forward, peering at the video feed on the HUD.

"Guttman, please respond."

"Ha ha! How do you like it? Now come and get me," Guttman said.

They were able to track the escape pod using Guttman's comlink; however, there were no emergency supplies aboard, and Guttman had to ride the entire trip back to the *Wayfarer* in the pod. No one was too disappointed, though. Undergarments notwithstanding, there were just some lines that shouldn't be crossed unless absolutely necessary.

Oscar brought Becker the first aid kit and applied a healing pack to his shoulder.

"No signs of pursuit," Quinton said.

Becker frowned. "That doesn't seem right."

Quinton had the shuttle going max speed, so the trip out would be much faster than the way in had been.

"I thought so too. I have Radek monitoring their communications from the *Wayfarer*. He'll let us know if he learns something we need to know."

As they traveled back to the *Wayfarer*, a brooding silence descended on the others. They were leaving empty-handed despite all their preparations, including picking the target that was both the most likely place to find a ship worth stealing and with a small enough operation that it wouldn't bring the ire of any major players in the galaxy.

Quinton was just as perplexed about how the events had unfolded as the rest of them.

"You didn't know anything about this activation signal?" Becker asked.

Oscar looked at him. Both he and Becker were thinking the same thing—that he had somehow known about it.

"No, I didn't know."

Becker pursed his lips while he considered Quinton's response.

"I'm serious. I had no idea that an activation signal was coming. You can review the communication logs on the *Wayfarer* if you want, but I'm telling you the truth. This wasn't me."

Becker nodded and Oscar relaxed. "The timing is suspicious."

Quinton exhaled. "I don't know. I guess you're right."

Oscar cleared his throat. "I just want to put this out there. Whatever you might have seen me doing in that aircar, it wasn't me. I mean, I'm not responsible for that, so let's just keep it between us."

Quinton put up the video recording of Oscar pretending to fly the aircar. "I don't know. This is pretty compelling stuff."

A grin bubbled up from Becker's mouth. He leaned toward the holoscreen as if taking a closer look. "Certainly looks like Oscar to me."

Oscar's cheeks reddened. "So, any chance I can persuade you to delete that recording?"

Quinton paused in thought. "There's one thing I've learned from all of you—that everything has a price. Make me an offer."

Oscar bit his lower lip and looked away.

"It had better be good," Quinton said.

5

THE SHUTTLE's maximum speed would have cut their travel time to the *Wayfarer* in half, but they hadn't accounted for Guttman's incessant humming. Guttman was alone in an escape pod and had hours to entertain himself. When he worked, he hummed a lot, along with muttering snippets of conversations or anything he was thinking about at the time. This was occasionally broken up by singing, which would crescendo where he inserted the names of random objects into whatever song he was singing. Becker had muted Guttman's comlink a few times, but then the trapped spacer would get lonely and reinitiate a new comlink session to bypass the muted one. Quinton didn't have the heart to remove that capability. Too much isolation wasn't good for anyone, and they were in this together, even if it meant enduring the colorful nuances of Guttman's personality. They all had them, but that didn't mean he couldn't lessen the duration of their travel time. Quinton uploaded an intercept course to the *Wayfarer's* nav computer, and the star jumper was on its way to them.

"Not that much longer," Quinton said.

Guttman stopped humming. "Thank God," he said and looked at the holoscreen.

"Can I ask you a question?"

Guttman leaned away from the comlink video feed with suspicion. He had the look of someone who'd been a frequent victim of playful baiting and wasn't eager to be the target again. But he also had an insatiable need to take the spotlight. He enjoyed the attention.

Guttman looked away from the camera and sighed. "I'm really not in the mood."

"Headache still bad?" Quinton asked.

Guttman nodded and massaged his temples.

The escape pod hadn't been stocked with supplies, and Guttman made sure everyone knew about it. There was also no food in the pod. Guttman had been lucky that its life-support systems were operational, but the pod was far from being suitable for anything like sustained occupancy for more than a few hours. Waste disposal was a real concern because the pod had been stripped of its management system. Whoever had been refitting the ship must have been working on the life-support system and had been in the process of replacing key components.

"All right, what is it?" Guttman said. "Go on, ask me what you were going to ask me."

"Oh, that. Don't worry about it. It's not important."

"Quinton, don't you do that. I hate it when you start to ask a question and then don't. It's annoying."

Quinton experienced an immediate urge to remark about Guttman's singing, but both colossal restraint and sympathy for someone who was cut off from everyone else made him decide not to.

"Okay," Quinton said.

Becker and Oscar didn't look over at him, but they were definitely listening. There wasn't enough room in the shuttle to avoid it.

"Why strip off your space suit? Why did you do it? I mean, what was going through your mind when you decided that enough was enough—get this thing off me?"

Guttman snorted a little and then shrugged. "It was the inhibitor. Trace amounts of—"

"I know all that, but what I'm trying to understand is why after achieving the point of 'I feels so good' you'd take off your clothes?"

Oscar swung around in his chair to face the video feed. "That's a good question."

"I don't know."

"Come on, think about it. I genuinely want to know," Quinton said.

Guttman didn't reply right away, and the seconds ticked by for two full minutes. "Freedom," he said quietly.

Quinton's eyebrows knitted together in a thoughtful frown. "Freedom? I'm not following."

Guttman looked at the camera. "You wouldn't, but *they* know what I mean."

Quinton glanced at the others. Becker didn't look at him, but Oscar looked away and nodded a little.

"We're always stuck in a ship or space station," Guttman said. "We've got to wear our safety gear because everything is old. You never know when something is going to break. We've only got entertainment modules to remind us of the open sky."

"Why don't you just go planetside somewhere?" Quinton asked.

"Where?"

Quinton looked at Becker. "You told me there were habitable worlds out there."

Guttman forcefully exhaled through his nose, and it sounded like the pressure release of an environmental system purge. "Yeah, right. They're tightly controlled with more restrictions than you'd have off-world if you wanted to change your mind. I told you I want freedom—swim in a lake without seeking a permit and swim naked if I wanted to," he said and pointed a finger at the holoscreen. "Just don't. You asked and I'm answering."

Quinton raised his hands in a placating gesture. "I'm pretty sure we can find something like that. Maybe not a planet, but surely one of these space stations has a module that offers the same thing."

Guttman banged his fist down beside him and leaned toward the camera. "No, you don't get it. I don't want to pay an hourly credit wage to buy an illusion for a few hours. I want the real thing, whenever I want it. I don't want to swim in water that's been recycled. I want hot springs. I want a lake with a mountain range nearby. On a planet without anyone breathing down my neck about it."

A somber silence settled on the others that Quinton couldn't help but notice, and he wouldn't attempt to cheapen it with a snarky comment. Guttman had given him a real answer, and the sentiment was clearly shared by the others. They probably didn't want the same things, but they shared the spirit of the desire for what they wanted. It reminded him of Maelyn. She'd been after information about colony worlds that the Acheron Confederacy might have kept hidden from the rest of the galaxy.

Becker turned toward him. "We need to talk."

"I'm not going anywhere. Talk," Quinton replied.

"That—PMC," Becker began. Quinton was sure he'd been about to say 'thing,' but instead he said, "Harper. Is he stable?"

"I don't know. The integrity check is still running, and it'll help repair him if there's degradation," Quinton said.

"If those measures really worked, the Federation Wars wouldn't have happened."

"I'm not going to disable him because you're afraid."

"Damn it, Quinton, this is serious. These are real concerns. You might have beaten the odds, but that doesn't mean he will," Becker said and tilted his head toward the rear of the shuttle.

"I told you I'd keep an eye on him."

Becker tapped his fingertips on the console in front of him. "I know you're trying to do the right thing, but you need to trust what I'm saying—what we're all saying. There are reasons PMCs are shunned."

Quinton eyed him. "That hurt my feelings."

"I'm serious."

"So am I. You think I like that you guys have this deep-seated fear that I'm about to go insane?" The others went still. "Sure, I joke about it. Sometimes it's even funny, but I haven't done anything to deserve it. And PMCs were more than stable..." He'd been about to say, "where I came from," but that wasn't as accurate as "*when* I came from."

Becker pursed his lips and nodded. "Like I said. You beat the odds, but that doesn't mean everyone else can. And," he said, holding up his hand when Quinton tried to speak. "And, even with your experience, it wasn't a sure thing. The *Wayfarer* doesn't have another one of those bodies in it."

A proximity notification appeared on the HUD. The *Wayfarer* had finally reached them.

"It doesn't, but that doesn't mean I'm not going to try to help Harper."

"You stuck him in a security bot," Becker said.

"It's more of a combination maintenance and security bot. Three Moons Shipyards were quite practical about the whole thing," Quinton said. Becker glared at him. "Look, you can check out the bot when we get back aboard the *Wayfarer*. It'll take Harper time to acclimate to a new body. I removed the more dangerous limbs from it. Also, we'll need to explain to Harper what he's woken up to."

Becker leaned back in his seat and scratched his chin. "The fact remains that you don't know who we're dealing with."

Quinton didn't reply.

Oscar leaned forward. His short, dark hair had blond tips. "Quinton," he said, calmly, "we just need to be careful. What if Harper tries to take control of the ship?"

Quinton thought about how Harper had circumvented Radek's control to speak with him. "I understand."

"We need more than that. We need a plan," Oscar said.

"What do you mean?"

"He means," Guttman said, "we need a way to stop Harper from killing the rest of us if he decides we're a threat."

"He's right," Becker said. "The fact of the matter is that we're vulnerable. We can't access the ship's systems the way you can."

"But I wouldn't let him do anything like that. And besides, what do you propose? One of you guard Harper at all times with a weapon?"

"I thought about it, but it's not practical. We need a fail-safe. Something that can disable him if we need it," Becker said.

"I don't believe this. Harper isn't even awake yet and you want me to strap a bomb to the spider-drone to address the possibility that he might do something to you? Does that sum it up?" Quinton asked and looked at all of them. "By that logic, we should all be sitting here with our weapons pointed at each other. How does that behavior build any trust or even cooperation?"

"Do you think it was any different on the *Nebulon*?" Becker said and gave him a long look. "Maelyn had a security system on her ship that would have disabled the agricultural bot you were in if you'd proven to be unstable."

"She did, but she also gave me some time to process the situation, which is what I intend to do for Harper. The *Wayfarer* doesn't have a suppression system like what was on the *Nebulon*, so we'll just have to do the best we can with what we've got."

Becker looked as if he wanted to press the issue, but Oscar spoke first. "All right, let's just table this discussion for now. Okay. Let's get back on the ship, get cleaned up, and have a bite to eat. Then we can come at this again after we've had some rest."

"I, for one, could go for some food," Guttman said. "But I could probably hold off on a shower."

"No!" Quinton, Becker, and Oscar shouted at once.

Guttman looked at the video feed innocently. "If you guys are sure."

"Yes!" They said in unison.

Guttman chuckled. With the exception of Quinton, they had all achieved a certain level of ripeness that could only be cured by some vigorous scrubbing.

"I'll make sure Harper is under security lockdown with restricted access to the ship," Quinton said.

He was the *Wayfarer's* captain, so the decision was up to him. Everyone else was a passenger, but Quinton knew the value of crew cohesion.

Becker brought up the scan feeds from the *Wayfarer* and put them on the shuttle's HUD.

"They let us go," Quinton said.

"I know. What I can't figure out is why," Becker replied.

Shipyard security had chosen not to send more ships after them beyond the initial pursuit.

"Were there other pirates in the star system?" Oscar asked.

"That's what I was looking for," Becker replied. "Nothing has been detected, and we're too far out to see what they're doing now."

Oscar shook his head. "It doesn't make sense."

"No, it doesn't," Quinton agreed. "I had Radek record their comms chatter. There might be something in there. Can you guys take a look? You might see something I'd miss."

Quinton could access data faster than anyone else on the shuttle, but what good was that if he didn't know what to look for. He needed their expertise. "The only thing I keep wondering about is why their security measures were so good. I mean, it was well thought out—almost military in their response."

Becker nodded. "It was better than I thought it was going to be for an independent shipyard."

"Maybe it's not independent anymore," Oscar said.

Quinton considered that for a few moments. "There was nothing to indicate it's a Union shipyard."

Becker shook his head. "It's not Crowe's Union."

"The Collective, maybe," Oscar suggested.

"I'll have Radek compile a list of names based on the comms data. Maybe something will jump out at you," Quinton said.

The others agreed. The lack of response from shipyard security bothered Quinton. It meant that they were more worried about something else than they were about being robbed. It could be that the PMC activation signal had thrown their response teams into disarray. It was definitely worth considering.

Later, Quinton stood before the main holoscreen on the bridge of the *Wayfarer*. Shortly after they'd returned to the ship, he executed an emergency jump that had taken them out of the star system. He'd also moved the spider-drone into the maintenance workshop where Greta continued running the integrity check of Harper's PMC. Since coming aboard the ship, she had partnered with Radek and leveraged the *Wayfarer's* computing core to quicken the check.

The door to the bridge opened and Becker entered. He'd expected Becker would be joining him. The man was a workhorse and would make a good ship captain.

Quinton gave him a once over. "I thought you wanted to get cleaned up?"

Becker looked at the information on the holoscreen. "I'm more interested in figuring out why they let us go."

Quinton nodded.

"The only reason I can come up with is that they were worried about something else. I'm not sure what, though. Is this all Radek has been able to find out?"

"Yes. It looks like they were expecting—at the very least—a Sentinel scout ship to survey the area," Quinton said.

Becker peered at one of the data windows and expanded it. "They recalled all their ships and shut down operations."

"Is that how Crowe's Union would've handled it if the activation signal had gone to one of their operations?"

"I'm not sure. There was no standing protocol on what we should do in that eventuality. Contrary to what just happened, PMC activation signals aren't that common."

Quinton considered it for a few moments. "Maybe the activation signals are more common than we thought."

"Or maybe this is a recent development. We've been out of contact for a while."

"True. I'd like to know if a Sentinel scout ship *did* show up in that star system. It wasn't worth the risk of sticking around, but I am curious. Based on this information, I have to think that whoever was running Three Moons Shipyards had expected the Sentinels to show up. Maybe they were prepped by somebody."

"Like who?" Becker asked.

"The Collective."

"Three Moons was an independent operation. The Collective doesn't prioritize the successful operations of independent companies."

"Unless they were recently acquired by them," Quinton said and shook his head. "It's just a thought. You know more than I do about how the salvager operations mesh together."

"Well, for one, they don't all wear a badge that makes it abundantly clear they're with the Collective. So, if there *is* a partnership, it might be kept secret."

"Why?"

"There's competition between different salvager operations. It's not uncommon for someone to create opportunities from the misfortune of others."

Quinton nodded. "All right, no giant sign that says who their affiliation is.

We might not be able to figure this out from this data. I thought you might have had an insight into it since you picked this target."

"I thought so, too, but I'm coming up short."

"Well, there's nothing that matches Crowe's Union, so we know Lennix had nothing do with this," Quinton said.

He noticed that bringing up Becker's former employer didn't make him as anxious as it used to.

"I'd recognize Union data transmission, so we're covered on that."

"So where do we go from here?" Quinton asked.

"I was thinking that we need to go to… Find some place to get some current news, but I'm not so sure that's a good idea right now."

"Harper?"

"Harper," Becker agreed. "I don't think it's a good idea to bring him anywhere he could be detected."

"We can't stumble around in the dark forever. Remember, I'm trying to fulfill my end of our agreement. You, Oscar, and Guttman all helped me put the ship back together."

"It looks like we won't be rid of each other as fast as we thought."

"You say that like it's a bad thing."

Becker shrugged a meaty shoulder. "We have different goals, Quinton. It's not personal."

"I know it's not," Quinton said but suspected otherwise. "We agreed to keep helping each other out to get you a ship. As for Harper, you don't have to be involved in that."

"As long as we're all on this ship, we're all involved in it. When is the integrity check going to finish?"

"In another hour."

"Is that normal?"

"That's what the analysis should tell us." Becker considered this for a few moments and Quinton continued. "You've got time. Go get cleaned up and I'll meet you in the workshop. We can question Harper together."

"Won't that take longer?"

"That depends on Harper, doesn't it?"

Becker nodded and left the bridge.

Quinton studied the data on the screen. Sentinels were the product of the Federation War. They were the answer to the PMC menace that was infecting the galaxy. Something had made PMCs unstable, and Quinton had no idea what that was. When he was uploaded before the Federation Wars began, becoming a PMC had been highly revered. They'd been necessary to the survival of the Acheron Confederacy Navy.

Sentinels roamed the galaxy in groups, hunting for PMCs and any type of technology that was remotely related to them. If the Sentinels determined that there was a PMC presence on a ship or space station, it was destroyed. There were no communications, and any inquiries were ignored. But Quinton had communicated with a Sentinel once, and it wasn't an experience he was eager to repeat. The best thing for him to do was to find another DNA vault and regrow his body. The only problem with that plan was that he had no record of his DNA. But one problem at a time. He'd given Becker the impression that Radek was overseeing Harper's integrity check of his PMC, but that wasn't entirely true. Quinton was also monitoring the results as they came in. There'd been a degradation of the PMC that he was in the process of trying to repair, and that was why the integrity check was taking a bit longer than normal.

Quinton left the bridge and headed toward the workshop.

6

THE ESS that stored Nash Harper's PMC must have been damaged, but Quinton couldn't figure out how. He stood in the workshop where the spider-drone sat in a maintenance cradle.

"The ESS is intact and operational, so how come PMC stability scores are so low?" Quinton asked.

Radek was the lead interface of Quinton's own virtual intelligence and had taken the form of a holographic sphere hovering in the air. "In the absence of detectable damage to the ESS, the stability scores are only indicative of the PMCs current state but don't demonstrate what those scores would have been when it was first created."

Quinton bowed his head. No one else was in the workshop. "Is that just a fancy way of saying that Harper could have been unstable when he was uploaded?"

"That is one possibility. According to Greta, there was an update to Harper's ESS that was only processed once he was activated."

"Do the logs indicate when they received the update?"

"Negative. It could have been queued for the entire time the escape pod resided on the asteroid."

"What did the update do?"

"Specifics are unknown, but it did use the mergence protocol," Radek replied.

Quinton wanted a triple shot of that Sangorian Bourbon Oscar had on the shuttle. Maybe the ship's VR could reproduce the whole bourbon experience for him.

Mergence protocol was used to provide PMCs with updated mission data and skillset augmentation. "Does Greta know if that's causing the instability?"

He preferred to speak with Greta directly, but the VI was focusing all her resources on mapping Harper's PMC so she could keep him functioning.

Mergence protocol, once initiated, couldn't be undone. Quinton knew the theory of how it was supposed to work. It was meant to build upon the experiences of other PMCs to increase their functionality. It required thorough personality mappings, and only PMCs that had similar mappings could be integrated without affecting the original host's identity.

Harper's stability scores were borderline concerning. The only way to make a better assessment would be to bring Harper out of the maintenance routine, which Quinton intended to do once the others arrived. Harper might just need some time to adapt to his situation.

Quinton was integrated into the ship's systems, which included knowing the locations of the crew for emergency purposes. This data was available to anyone, and Becker and the others insisted on having an area of the ship where they could have privacy. This included their quarters, as well as one of the common areas, and allowed them to meet without worrying about whether Quinton would be monitoring them. He understood the need for privacy, but sometimes he did wonder what they talked about. He respected their wishes, even though it was his ship—unit cohesion and all that. They didn't exclude him from those areas of the ship, but they had certainly relaxed more now that barriers had been established.

Quinton glanced at the spider-drone. Harper was going to have to learn how to use it until they could find a better host for him. No doubt the others were discussing this among themselves.

The biometric readings on the ship indicated that Becker, Oscar, and Guttman were on their way to the workshop. A short time later, the door opened and the three men walked in. Guttman and Oscar carried assault rifles while Becker had decided to keep his heavy blaster holstered on his side.

"Armed and dangerous, I see," Quinton said.

"Just in case," Oscar said and took up a position that gave him tactical coverage of the maintenance cradle.

Guttman—fully clothed, thankfully—rested his stocky russet frame against a countertop on the other side of the workshop.

Becker walked over to Quinton's side. "Ready when you are."

Quinton looked at the others. "How about we don't have itchy trigger fingers."

Oscar adjusted the strap of his rifle so it swung behind him. Quinton knew that Oscar could have that rifle ready in seconds, but the show of faith wasn't lost on him.

Guttman shook his head. "I'll hold onto it," he said. He wasn't pointing his weapon at the spider-drone, which was Guttman's idea of "good enough" cooperation.

Quinton thought about his own reactivation. Harper was lucky they'd found him. At least there weren't any hunter mechs trying to kill him. He'd just have to deal with a little mistrust.

"All right, the maintenance cycle is going to expire," Quinton said.

The spider-drone's legs spasmed a few times, and Quinton stepped toward it. "Harper, can you hear me?"

There was no response.

"Harper, you're coming out of an extensive maintenance cycle. Give yourself a few minutes to get acclimated."

The spider-drone's ocular units on the armored torso moved. The others went still. Guttman lifted his rifle a little, but Becker gestured for him to lower it.

"It's just a mobility startup check. The same thing happens on any bot or mechanized suit," Quinton advised, and the others relaxed.

"Where am I?" Harper asked. His voice was tight, as if he was straining.

"You're aboard my ship, the *Wayfarer*."

The ocular unit was able to spin, so Harper could see the room while his body was still locked in the maintenance cradle.

"Your movements are restricted. This is as much for your own protection as it is ours."

"This isn't a humanoid avatar. Why have I been installed here?"

Quinton frowned. They'd gone over this before Harper had agreed to go through the integrity check. "Your ESS was stored on an escape pod we found on an asteroid. There wasn't anything else for us to use."

"This doesn't make any sense. This bot feels strange. Why was I activated then?" Harper asked, sounding slightly less strained.

"Let's take this one step at a time. What do you remember?"

The spider-drone's body jerked as Harper tried to move. "Get me out of this thing. I need to move."

"Not yet."

"Why not?"

Quinton stepped closer. "You already know this. You're in the wrong kind of body and it's going to take some practice to get used to it. I promise I'm going to let you out of the cradle, but I need you to cooperate. One step at a time."

A sound that seemed to be a mixture of a sigh and a growl came from Harper.

"I know it's frustrating. Remember your training."

"I do," he replied. "I do remember."

"Okay, let's start with your name and rank."

"Nash Harper, Lieutenant, Acheron Confederacy Navy. Tactical engagement specialist."

"Thanks for that. I'm Quinton Aldren, Commander in the Acheron Confederacy Navy. I'm a G-class PMC."

"Commander," Harper said. "G-class. Have I been assigned to your command? What fleet?"

"What do you mean?"

"Commander, you should already know. Galactic class PMCs were designed to utilize other PMCs as part of their command structure. Which battleship cruiser are we on? Is it the flagship ACS *Javelin*?"

Quinton considered Harper's response for a few moments and could guess what Becker and the others were thinking.

"Another one," Guttman said softly, but not quietly enough.

The spider-drone swung its gaze toward him. "Who are you. Are you a civilian?" Harper asked and looked at Quinton. "Why are civilians aboard an ACN warship? They don't have clearance."

"Clearance? You don't even know what kind of ship you're on," Guttman said.

"That accent," Harper said, and the spider-drone jerked toward Guttman. "Jordani!" he snarled. "Why isn't he shackled. Is he an intelligence asset? He doesn't look like it, but it could be a disguise."

Quinton was starting to think that he should have met with Harper alone.

Guttman chuckled, and Quinton glared at him. "Not helping."

"Commander, I need the mission briefings for our fleet deployment," Harper said.

Becker exhaled and looked at Quinton. "This is going to take a while. Maybe we should give you guys a few hours."

"Appreciate the backup," Quinton replied.

"I think you've got this, *Commander*."

The spider-drone's head turned toward Becker. "Insolence is not to be tolerated in the ACN."

Becker inclined his head. "Oh, I apologize."

Guttman laughed and walked toward them.

Harper shifted his focus to Quinton. "You're out of uniform."

"A lot has changed," Quinton replied.

The others started heading for the door.

"Must have. Admiral Browning wouldn't tolerate such lapses," Harper said.

The others froze mid-stride and turned around.

"Did he say Browning?" Oscar asked.

Guttman grumbled a reply.

Grand Admiral Elias Browning had been a war hero with accumulated victories over the Jordani Federation. Then he, along with several fleets, had broken away from the Acheron Confederacy to start a deadly campaign that spread across multiple federations. Browning went from the most renowned war hero to the vilest war criminal and was directly responsible for the Federation Wars. Quinton had tried to locate historical records to find out what had happened, but there wasn't much left. The Federation Wars had spread so rapidly that much of the old federations were gone, leaving mere shadows of what they'd once been. The galactic consensus was that Admiral Browning had unleashed his armada of PMC-enhanced ships on an unsuspecting galaxy. The lines of enemy and ally had been dissolved. Quinton had been uploaded into a PMC before all this, predating the Federation Wars, so he'd been prepared to fight the Jordani. Now the question was: when had Harper been uploaded?

"Have you served Admiral Browning?" Quinton asked.

The ocular units tilted to the side in what was reminiscent of an incredulous stare. "Of course. The battle of the Darcaya Star System brought the Jordani to their knees, breaking their hold on the galaxy."

Guttman spoke quietly to Becker, but Quinton ignored him.

Harper turned toward them.

"Never mind them for a second," Quinton said. "What do you remember?"

"Commander, this is highly irregular. All the ACN had been committed," Harper said and paused. "You're not an officer in the ACN."

"Yes I am. You've seen my credentials."

"That doesn't explain how you don't know about the single most important fleet engagement in the history of the confederacy."

"That's because I was uploaded before the campaign."

Harper considered this for a few moments. "You're one of the early ones. Why haven't you received a mission update?"

"I don't know. What I need to know is the last thing you remember. What were your orders?" Quinton asked.

"My orders?" Harper said. "I haven't received them."

"But did you have an—"

"Wait! There was a recruitment recall notice. Those were my last updates."

"What was the recruitment for?" Becker asked.

Harper regarded the spacer for a moment.

"It's fine. I want to know, too," Quinton said.

"It was for a major offensive, something more dangerous than the Jordani. Admiral Browning was assembling a new task force."

"Do you know what the objective was?"

"No, those details would be given after."

Quinton glanced at the others. Becker opened his mouth as if he were about to speak, but he didn't say anything. Then he looked at Quinton, his mouth forming a grim line.

"Do you know what this means?" Becker asked.

Quinton nodded once. "I do."

"I'm glad you guys do, but I don't," Guttman said.

"I agree with my friend here. I'm not following," Oscar said.

"Harper was uploaded just before the Federation Wars. He served that bastard Browning," Becker said.

The spider-drone's legs jerked as it struggled against the maintenance cradle's restraints.

"I don't know who you are," Harper snarled, "but I'll strip the flesh from your bones if you say another word against Admiral Browning." The last of that utterance came out in a deadly whisper—the kind of tone that men killed over. Harper wasn't making an idle threat. He meant what he said.

Guttman and Oscar raised their weapons.

"Don't," Quinton said. "He doesn't know. Lower your weapons. Now!"

Guttman and Oscar still held their weapons but weren't pointing them at Harper.

"I'm going to bring Harper up to speed. It's best if you guys weren't here," Quinton said.

"Sounds good to me," Guttman said and headed for the door.

Oscar and Becker stayed where they were. Then Becker looked at Oscar. "Come on, we need to find another place to get a ship of our own," he said and looked at Quinton. "We'll be on the bridge."

Becker headed for the door, but Oscar gave Quinton a sympathetic look. "Good luck," he said and followed Becker out of the workshop.

Quinton turned toward Harper.

"Commander, permission to speak freely."

Quinton was really going to have to do something about the military protocol Harper was clinging to—though not *exactly* clinging to. It was representative of the world he'd known, and now Quinton got to take it from him. Lucky him. He thought about Simon, the young technical specialist who had helped him understand that the galaxy he remembered was no longer around. Then there was Maelyn, captain of the *Nebulon*. He'd been impatient to find out the state of the galaxy, but she'd been quite deliberate in how that information had been revealed to him. It wasn't the first time Quinton had been managed. His career in the military had made him familiar with operating on a need-to-know basis, but when he'd been reactivated, the situation had been different. His access to his own ESS—his memories—had been restricted. There had to be something similar going on with Harper, but Quinton wasn't sure to what extent. There was only one way to find out.

"Go ahead, say what you will," Quinton said.

"You can't trust those men. They should be off your ship immediately."

Quinton leaned back against the workbench across from the cradle. He regarded Harper, and his hands came to rest on the cool metallic countertop. "They're not so bad. You'll understand more when you hear what I've got to tell you."

"Understood, Commander."

Quinton sighed. Time to pull the healing pack off the wound before it was ready. This was going to hurt.

"That's the first thing. There isn't an ACN anymore…"

7

MORE THAN TWELVE hours had elapsed while Quinton gave Harper a crash course on the galaxy he'd awakened to. He tried to be as patient with Harper as possible, but the news that the world Harper thought he knew was gone couldn't be processed over the span of mere hours. They hadn't spent the entire time talking. Quinton had unlocked the maintenance cradle from the spider-drone, giving Harper some time to get acclimated to it.

There were obvious shortcomings to using the spider-drone, but Harper was adapting well to the new body. He was aware of the danger that prolonged use of the spider-drone meant but seemed to bounce from subject to subject. He'd focus on what had happened to the ACN for a while and then shift his attention to how to make the best use of the spider-drone.

Harper regarded him. "How long do you think I'll have to stay in this?" he asked and raised one of the legs. The spider-drone's legs had multiple joints, and Harper was able to not only wave the leg as a gesture for attention but also pivot the joints. On the ends of the legs were grabbers that Harper made mimic a human hand. The fingers seemed to meld into one another to form three elongated appendages that were capable of latching onto things. Quinton ought to know because several spider-drones had tried their best to dismember him.

"We'll try to find you a replacement as soon as we can."

"Good, because it doesn't feel right. I can use it, but Greta says there's some diminished capacity from the ESS interface into the drone's onboard central processor."

"What does it feel like?"

Harper took a few steps around the workshop. The spider-drone had four legs, which were enough for it to move around with. Quinton wondered if mobility would have been more of a challenge for Harper if the drone had retained all its appendages. The agricultural bot Quinton used had been humanoid and had a few useful capabilities. Its main problem had been that it was ancient and not designed to have a PMC installed into it.

"Like I'm wearing someone else's shoes that don't fit right," Harper said. "It's not all bad. The mobility interface is actually pretty good. I don't need to focus on moving each individual leg. I can focus on where I want to go, and it does the rest. There are interface errors, though. I'm working my way through them. I guess it's going to take some time and practice."

"Let me guess—you get an error whenever you try to make a micro expression."

"Micro expression?"

"Facial expressions—some quirk or habit that is unique to you—but the bot is unable to fulfill the request. That really used to annoy me," Quinton replied.

Harper paused for a moment. "I just added those errors to the ignore list."

Quinton had done the same, but he recalled that they still had a way of sneaking to the forefront.

Harper walked toward Quinton and seemed to regard him. "They didn't have anything like what you're using when I was uploaded."

Quinton's cybernetic avatar was made from advanced composites that were incredibly powerful but duplicated natural human musculature. The skeletal structure was a duplicate of a human skeleton, but again, was many times stronger. The bones were hollow to allow for molecular circuitry and power transmission. Nerve impulses moved literally at light speed, which was around a hundred times as fast as the chemically transmitted impulses of the human body. But despite all the advances, no computer could fully match the brain's interconnections. The ESS was the means by which much of the "thinking" ability of a PMC worked. Quinton's and Harper's personalities and experiences were stored in an energy-state, the limitations of which were expressed in how the ESS was able to integrate into a host machine.

"I wasn't expecting this. The ship was on the Starbase Endurance and had been designed for PMC use," Quinton said.

"Lucky for you."

Quinton remembered his battle with the Sentinel fleets. He'd thought he was about to die. At the time, he'd felt as far from lucky as one could possibly get, but he didn't correct Harper.

"You're the lucky one," Quinton said.

"How?"

"Virtual environment for one. The *Wayfarer's* computing core has plenty of capacity for you to function within a virtual world. There are some configurations already set up. I haven't…" Quinton paused. He didn't want to tell Harper that he hadn't tried them because he didn't need them. "There hasn't been time for me to try them out."

"Why would you?" Harper said and was quiet for a few seconds. "I'm sorry, sir. I know you're trying to help. I just… They really blame Admiral Browning? Everyone hates him?"

"There isn't a lot of love for him out there."

"Still, how can one person be responsible for the Federation Wars? Do you know how crazy that sounds? We were fighting the Jordani and winning. Victory was all but assured. There were going to be Federation Accords for peace. That was what was going to happen."

"It doesn't make sense to me either, and the records are lacking. The facts are that, for whatever reason, Browning began raiding strategic targets across the galaxy. That much is clear."

"I don't believe it."

"Did you know him personally?"

"No, but… He took care of the people who served under him. He was ACN to his core."

Quinton had never served under Browning, but he'd known him by reputation. He thought he would have been transferred under Browning's command, but this was unclear. He remembered the selection process for PMC candidates. They wanted experienced naval officers. He hadn't been the highest-ranking officer to go through the selection process, but he had made it through all the qualifiers to be in the final pool of candidates. He didn't remember anything after that. Presumably, this was when he'd been uploaded into an ESS. How he ended up on a fringe system hidden away on a third-tier colony world was anyone's guess.

"I keep calling you 'sir,'" Harper said.

"It's all right."

"I don't know if I can stop, Commander."

"Harper, it's going to take time. You've been awake for less than a day. Give yourself time to get acclimated."

The spider-drone didn't move, and this bothered Quinton. There were very few people who could remain completely still for any length of time. Movement was part of being human, and he was tempted to query Greta for a diagnostic review of Harper.

The drone's ocular units looked away from Quinton. "I know, sir."

Quinton moved so he was standing in front of Harper. "The war we were meant to fight is over. We missed it."

"What's left for us then? What are we supposed to do? Everyone we knew. Our families. All those people are just… gone," Harper said. His voice sounded thick. "How did you deal with that?"

"I had restricted access to my memories. It wasn't until I'd integrated with the starbase that those memories were even available."

"I… I can't ignore it like you can."

"I didn't ignore it. It wasn't until I ended up here that I accessed those memories. Greta can help regulate them to help you cope with it. Radek did the same for me. I gave myself time."

"You increased your frame rate."

"Yes, but after a while, I decided that longing for a world that was gone wasn't going to help me. I haven't forgotten them. If you remember fighting the Jordani, it's not the first time you've lost people."

"I'll have to try that," Harper said. "Commander… Quinton. Thank you for helping me. I'd like to be alone now, if you don't mind."

"You're welcome. It's fine. I'll be on the bridge. Come join us when you're ready."

"About the others—they don't trust me. They think I'm like those other PMCs they've been taught about."

"You're right; they don't trust you," Quinton confirmed. "Your access to the ship's systems will be restricted for the time being."

"You don't trust me either?"

Quinton regarded him for a few moments. "I want to trust you, Harper. This is my ship, and the lives aboard it are mine to protect. We'll take it one step at a time and go from there. Try not to take how the others react to you personally. They have real reasons for their prejudices. I don't agree with them, but they've spent a lifetime learning to survive in this galaxy, and we're the newcomers."

"When you put it like that, it makes much more sense. I'll remember what you said, sir."

Quinton left the workshop and headed for the bridge. He walked past the galley where Oscar and Guttman were eating. Guttman's voice echoed through the corridor. The man had one volume to his booming voice.

Quinton glanced inside the galley as he walked by.

"How many times do I have to tell you? Say it, don't spray it," Oscar said.

Guttman leaned back. "Sorry, but you should have seen it."

Quinton walked onto the bridge and found Becker standing in front of the main holoscreen.

Becker looked at him and then glanced at the clock. "How'd he take it?"

He'd put on a fresh set of clothing—all black, as if the spacer had some sort of aversion to anything that had color to it. He looked as if he'd gotten a few hours of sleep; however, his deep-set eyes were still tight with stress, same as Oscar and Guttman. They were wound up too tight. Something was going to break.

"He wanted to be alone for a while."

Becker titled his head to the side once. "I guess he has full access to his memories."

"Most of them."

Becker nodded and crossed his muscular arms over his chest. "That's… something else. You were out of it in the beginning, but Harper was ready for action. Is that normal?"

Quinton snorted and shook his head. "Normal," he said and sighed. "Yeah, you could say that. We were fighting a war. We needed to be ready to get up to speed quickly, sometimes in the middle of a fleet engagement that was already in progress."

"Sometimes I forget that you were an officer."

"It's all part of my disguise."

"You don't fit the profile."

Quinton looked at him, slightly amused. "What profile is that? Ramrod straight with a giant pole shoved up my ass? Come on, we're not all the same, you know."

Becker arched an eyebrow. "Did I hit close to the mark or something?"

Quinton was irritated and it surprised him. "Something like it."

"Get over it. I've met former military before—the old-timers who managed to survive and the ones who'd been trained by people who'd actually been in the military when there were real federations and star empires around. They all had a certain command authority."

"Oh, you want me to be more decisive. My way or the airlock," Quinton replied.

"Something like that."

"You know how you told me that agents of the Collective don't roam around advertising who they work for? Well, it's something like that."

"You were a commander in the ACN. You commanded a ship and perhaps a battle group—maybe even something approaching an actual fleet. You know how to fight."

"What's your point?"

"Just that you don't act like an officer."

Quinton simply stared at him for a few moments. "Noted. Thanks for that. Would you like me to tell you what you act like?"

"Harper really has you twisted up inside. Maybe you need some downtime."

"Maybe."

"Before you go, what's Harper's status?"

"His access to the ship's systems is restricted."

Becker nodded. "Good," he said and glanced at the holoscreen. "We've been trying to find a secondary target."

"Any luck?" Quinton asked, thankful for a change in subject.

"No."

"There are star systems in the nav computer that might have ships. We could try one of those."

"That's the problem. The nav computer's astrogation charts are decades out of date. They need to be updated. We'll need to find a data beacon and then choose a target from there," Becker said and looked at the main holoscreen again. He shook his head, annoyed.

Quinton moved to stand in front of him. "You know, speaking of command experience, you—everyone—needs to calm down. A data beacon isn't a bad idea, but what about heading someplace where we can get off the ship for a while?"

Becker's gaze slipped into some sort of calculation while he considered it.

"I know you want to get your own ship and get off of this one, but think about what just happened. You're all so desperate to move on that it almost cost you everything. What good is finding a ship if you're not alive to enjoy it?"

Becker unfolded his arms. "I'll talk about it with the others."

Quinton grinned. "You think Guttman and Oscar are going to pass up shore leave?"

Becker rolled his eyes. He knew Quinton was right. "What about you? What are you going to do?"

The door to the bridge opened and Harper walked in. The spider-drone's armored chassis was the same height as Becker's chest. The spacer looked at him, and Quinton noted that he'd positioned his hand near his blaster.

"What about the activation signal?" Harper asked.

"What about it?" Quinton replied.

"We should trace it. Figure out who sent it."

Quinton shook his head. "No one sent it."

"How do you know?"

"It's just some latent protocol from a remnant facility that the Sentinels are likely destroying right now to make sure it doesn't happen again."

Becker looked at him but didn't say anything.

"We need to be sure," Harper said.

Becker walked toward the door. "I'll leave you two to work this out."

Quinton resigned himself to a long conversation that would ultimately end up increasing Harper's frustration, and Quinton couldn't blame him. At one time, he'd also wanted to track the activation signal.

8

Colo Jakin stepped onto the elevator and the doors shut, blocking out the crowded common area of the residence deck that served as the premiere living space on Chiba Station.

A bubble of space surrounded Colo, which he hardly noticed. A woman on the elevator regarded him curiously. She wore a spacer's pale gray flight suit, and her dark hair was cut short. She whispered something to her companion, another spacer, and Colo ignored them. They must be among the latest tours from the temporary habitation deck for frequent visitors of the station. Colo glanced at the woman. She had either been owed a favor by some higher-up in Chiba Station Affairs, or she'd found a valuable claim that warranted a tour of what the good life meant on Chiba.

The elevator chimed as it reached the central terminal, which was the heart of the station. Colo stepped out of the elevator and set a brisk pace.

"Excuse me," someone called out from behind him.

Colo ignored them. He didn't have time for this.

Hastening footsteps followed him, and then there was a tap on his shoulder. Colo glanced behind him.

The woman from the elevator looked at him evenly. "Are you the dockmaster?"

Here it comes, Colo thought. "In about fifteen minutes."

The woman frowned as she kept pace with him.

"I was told that you're the dockmaster."

"I'm off duty."

The woman nodded. "I'm Captain Waymire—"

"Let me just stop you right there, Captain," Colo said. Why did these ship captains always start with their rank, as if that carried any weight on the station.

"Official inquiries into salvage licenses have to come through the Chiba Ministry of Affairs."

Captain Waymire's thin lips lifted in amusement. "I already have my salvager rights for Kizu Star System and the cluster, for that matter. I'd like to talk to you about expanding those to include more of my employer's ships."

Colo's eyebrow arched with curiosity. "Who do you represent?"

"Okan Consolidated."

"I've never heard of them."

"We seek to expand our operations here."

There was always someone looking to jump to the front of the line. "Talk is cheap. Who's your backer?"

"My backer?" she asked, feigning confusion.

Colo rolled his eyes and quickened his pace. "That's all the time I have," he said, heading toward the security checkpoint for Chiba personnel.

"We're funded by Esperon."

Colo stopped and gestured for her to come closer. "Anyone can throw out a name. Give me the ID of the signatory."

Waymire inclined her head and made a passing motion from her wrist computer toward him. The signatory's ID appeared on Colo's wrist computer and he was able to determine the authenticity with the data he had on file.

He looked at her and shook his head. "Next time, lead with this."

"I didn't want to appear pretentious."

"But ambushing me at central was fine," Colo said and sighed. "Okay, you'll still need to take this through central processing. I'm sending you a guest pass to get you through security."

"I appreciate your help, but that process will still take many weeks or more."

Colo pursed his lips. Waymire knew her stuff. Going through official Chiba channels *would* take months. Meanwhile, she'd be limited to the common claim regions for salvage runs.

Waymire stepped closer to him. "Perhaps a few sessions at the pleasure dome."

Colo laughed. "Planetside? Are you kidding me? No."

"What is it you want?"

"Ten percent of your claims for the next year."

"Three percent for six months."

Colo shrugged and began to walk away.

"Five percent for ten months."

Colo turned toward her. "Make it seven and you've got a deal. Otherwise, enjoy the next few months of minimal profits."

"Six percent," she said, and Colo started to walk away, "with a signing bonus of twenty-five thousand."

Colo regarded her for a few seconds. She was serious. She likely had several leads to a salvager's treasure trove. "All right, you've got a deal," he said. Then he transferred a different contact from Chiba's regulator office to her. "Welcome to the Collective, Captain Waymire."

Waymire inclined her head and transferred the credits into his account.

Colo headed to the Chiba's Docking Authority control center. He stifled a yawn as he walked through dingy corridors that no amount of maintenance cleanup crews or atmospheric scrubbers could fix. He thought about his encounter with Captain Waymire, wondering who else she'd sought out as she started up her operations. Colo had walked away, suitably compensated for fast-tracking a new request through bureaucratic channels. He made a mental note to add Waymire to the list of contacts he needed to keep an eye on.

The doors opened to the wide expanse of Chiba's Docking Authority, which was the gateway for any ships that wished to conduct shipping and salvaging operations in the sector.

He glanced toward the massive viewport that showed Boros's grimy, fungus-laden atmosphere. The colony world was fifty years into a substantial terraforming effort that still required more than twenty-five years before the atmosphere was even breathable. The planet looked like an old stain. Colonists crammed together to scrape out a living in dome-covered cities. Spacers came to Boros when they had nowhere else to go. Colo hadn't been anywhere near the immigration offices in years. Once had been enough. He had no need to look at the putrid desperation of people clamoring for a living wage that only guaranteed they wouldn't starve. Of course, they hadn't realized that when they committed to helping build a better tomorrow.

Colo glanced at an image of Boros before the terraforming initiative had begun. Instead of a sickly yellow, the atmosphere had been a reddish brown from an overabundance of carbon dioxide. The image was meant to show how the colonial populace was helping the terraforming effort. This also included a data overlay, with real-time feeds from atmospheric sensors deployed across the planet.

Other than the influx of desperate spacers on Chiba Station, eager to trade in an existence aboard a ship for a cramped HAB unit, there were colonists who had managed to scrape up enough credits to return in hopes of finding work that would get them a ticket to another star system. The risk was that if they couldn't find any work or couldn't afford to wait on the station for a ship captain in need of additional crew, they were taken back planetside to start the process over again —a process that could take years. Outgoing communications from the standard colonist was monitored and altered before it was routed into the star systems communications network. There was a price to pay for their ignorance.

A tall, narrow-shouldered man hastened over to him.

"Welcome back, Dockmaster Jakin."

Colo frowned and gave the man a once-over. He noted the stim-induced intensity to the man's gaze. "Malachi, have you been at it again?"

Malachi pressed his virtually nonexistent lips together, and his pale cheeks colored. "I was ahead. There were ups and downs, but I was so far ahead."

Malachi was a Chiba Station coordinator who had become somewhat obsessed with wagering on various sporting activities sponsored by station authorities. "Sounds like you should have quit while you were ahead."

Malachi sighed. "I was so close. It just kept getting better and better."

"How much were you up before you lost it all?"

"How do you know I'm not still up?"

"Because you showed up to work today, and you're wearing the same uniform as yesterday," Colo said and gestured to a stain near the Chiba Station patch.

Malachi glanced down and began scrubbing the stain with his fingers. "I thought… Never mind."

They walked to the control center. "How much?" Colo asked again.

"Five thousand."

"You lost five thousand credits?"

Malachi shook his head. "No, I was up by five thousand. I lost closer to eight."

"Taking a hyperlane to Boros, I see."

Malachi blanched. "I might have a problem."

"Might?"

Malachi shook his head. "I'll stay away. I'll even take a different way home."

Colo didn't think Malachi was going to be successful. The adverts had a way of finding almost anyone. Just a little nudge during a journey and sure enough, Malachi would be back gambling away wages he hadn't even earned yet. A week or two at most, and his assistant would come to him, desperate for help. Colo wasn't sure if he'd help him or not. His last assistant had been much more pleasing until… Well, he let go that line of thinking. Assistants were easy enough to replace, and the good ones never stayed long. Malachi had potential, but he also had a lot of flaws.

"I have a couple of updates for you. One, there's a station-wide alert limiting broadcast communications."

"Another lockdown?"

Malachi nodded and sent the briefing to Colo. "Yes, but they've given this a top-tiered severity."

Colo opened the briefing on his wrist computer and quickly scanned it. "All right, all ship comms will be monitored for outbound broadcasts and routed to station security. What's next?"

"Inspector Ko Ji is looking for you," Malachi said.

Colo walked inside the command center. Thirty-six members of his staff waited at their workstations for him to officially take the handoff from the current command center staff located several decks below them. He headed for the raised platform where he oversaw operations.

"Did he say what he wanted?" Colo asked.

"He's upset about the cargo inspections schedule. He says he needs more staff for the increased workload."

Colo snorted. "Negative, the staff he has is capable of fulfilling the workload. And tell him there's no approval for overtime. If he doesn't like it, he can take it up the chain."

Malachi nodded. "Got it. Tell him to stop complaining and get to work."

Colo chuckled and regarded his assistant for a moment. Then he gestured for Malachi to come closer. "I'm sending an application to your wrist computer. It's an inhibitor for your finances. It'll force you not to exceed your budget allocation in the entertainment ward."

Malachi raised his eyebrows and his wrist computer beeped when it received the special program. "Thank you! Thank you so much. I don't know how I can repay you."

"Oh, you *will* repay me. We'll come up with something," Colo said.

Malachi swallowed and nodded.

Colo forwarded his credentials to Chiba Station's central computer. All Dockmaster duties now cut over to him and his staff. An instant later, there was a flurry of activity as docking requests filled up the queue, as well as flight plans for ships heading out. They needed to be reviewed and approved before the ships could leave.

Colo leaned forward in anticipation. One of the things he loved about his job was that sometimes a salvager managed to find something truly remarkable and valuable. For the next standard cycle, no ships could leave or dock without his permission. He loved his job.

The hours flew by, and Colo was busier than normal. The workload efficiency meter was high enough that he had to take part in more of the day-to-day part of operations, which meant fielding special requests that came in to his staff.

An unknown ship request entered his queue and a message appeared on his personal holoscreen from Malachi.

I think you need to take this one ;)

Colo's lips curved at the winky smiley face that also included the galactic credit symbol. Maybe keeping Malachi around was going to be a good idea.

Colo selected the comlink session for the unknown ship. "Welcome to Kizu Star System. This is Dockmaster Actual for Chiba Station. Transfer your ship registration and credentials now."

"Greetings, Dockmaster Actual," a woman replied, and a video session was added. "I'm Captain Mercy Gentry of the *Gypsy Clipper*."

Captain Gentry looked barely old enough to process an astrogation update to a ship's navigation computer. She had long, dark hair, and her pale skin was nearly covered with body artwork that Colo couldn't make sense of, but it was her eyes that drew him in. They were alluring and dangerous, all wrapped up into one naughty-looking package.

Colo received the data he'd asked for and informed the "captain" of his name. "What is the purpose for your visit to Chiba Station?"

"Why does anyone come here? I'd like to file a salvage claim."

Colo nodded. "I see," he said. The ship was on an intercept course with the station. "There's a problem."

"What kind of problem. You do accept freelance claims?"

"We do for registered ships, which yours is not. You lack the proper permits to salvage anything in this sector."

"You're right; I don't have the proper permits. I'm transferring the data on our salvage claim to you now. We happened upon a derelict ship on our way to you. It didn't make sense for us to leave the cargo for someone else to find just so we can file paperwork that can clearly be done now."

Colo winced. "About that, Captain Gentry."

She narrowed her gaze and her mouth formed a grim line. "Is this where you give me some kind of bureaucratic red tape that robs me of fifty percent of the value of my cargo?"

"There is a hefty penalty for salvaging without a permit."

"This is ridiculous. I'm going to turn my ship around and head to the nearest jump point. I'll find somewhere else that's willing to deal with me."

"No, you won't."

"Excuse me?"

"You heard me, Captain. You're not leaving."

"How do you intend to stop me?"

"Oh, I don't need to stop you. You're running low on fuel and supplies."

Her eyes widened. Colo didn't believe she was the real captain of that ship. More likely, she'd killed the original captain.

"Here's a tip for you, *Captain*. You contacted us using an unsecured comlink, which basically gave us access to your ship's systems. Now, we can't actually affect any of the systems, but we can query them for status, which I've done. So, forgive me if I find your bluff—excuse me—*assertion* in regard to leaving this star system bordering on the fringe of hilarity."

Gentry snarled a curse.

"Now, Captain, I can clear your ship to dock, and after an inspection of the cargo, we can calculate your penalty responsibility for salvaging without the proper permits."

"You're going to take half the value of our find."

"Look at it this way: at least you'll get to keep half."

She looked angry enough to spit plasma. "Fine."

"Excellent. Sending clearance for a secure docking bay. The inspectors will meet you at the airlock," Colo said and looked at her for a moment. "I wouldn't keep them waiting."

"Understood. *Gypsy Clipper* out," Gentry said and closed the comlink.

Colo laughed. Welcome to the Collective. Looks like his own bank account was about to get another credit bonus. As an incentive for enforcing the regulations, Chiba Station staff received a percentage of the value of the cargo, which could add up over the course of a pay cycle.

Colo's workload lightened as the hours went by, and he checked the video feed of the docking bay where the *Gypsy Clipper* was undergoing a lengthy interior inspection by Ko Ji. The inspector liked to complain, but he was quite thorough at his job. Colo wouldn't put it past Gentry to try to hide the most valuable items they'd "found," but Ko Ji would find those too.

Malachi caught his eye and smiled, and Colo gave him a nod. He looked back at his holoscreen at an alert that appeared moments before a klaxon alarm screeched throughout the command center.

A comlink from Chiba Station's defense minister, Jocasta Sable, appeared. "Jakin! What have you allowed on the station?"

"I don't know what you mean. All docking requests have been filed to the central office, and broadcast comms are being monitored as you requested."

"I don't care about—Look at the damn system plot and tell me what you see!"

Colo brought up the system plot, which showed six additional ships. They must have just entered the system, but they were so close to the planet! No ship could have done that. He felt the blood drain from his face, and he looked at Jocasta in alarm.

"You brought a damn Sentinel strike force down on us!"

"That's not possible," Colo said and brought up the docking security dashboard on his personal holoscreen. It was filled with broadcasts. "This can't be right—"

Jocasta snarled. "There are broadcasts coming for practically every ship that has docked during your shift."

Colo accessed the space dock monitoring system and initiated regression analysis to figure out which ship had started broadcasting first. How the hell had he missed this? "I, I, don't know how this happened," he said and stood up. His mouth went dry.

The analysis finished running and a single ship name appeared.

Gypsy Clipper.

"I found where it started but—"

"But it's already spread, compromising other ship communication systems." Jocasta looked away and began barking orders to bring up the station's defenses.

People began fleeing the command center. They'd seen the ships that were heading for the station, and there was only one thing they could do. Malachi ran over to him. "The Sentinels are here!"

"I know," Colo said and gritted his teeth. What had Gentry found that started all this? He should have paid more attention to it. He'd known there was something wrong, and he should have trusted his instincts. "The ship you gave me began broadcasting a signal."

"A signal? Can't we shut it down?"

"Station security has been trying, but it keeps popping back up. It's spread to the other ships. It brought the Sentinels here."

"Can we send our own broadcast to the Sentinels? Tell them it's a mistake?"

"You're welcome to try," Colo said.

Malachi's gaze darted to a workstation and then he shook his head. "I'll stick with you."

They ran out of the command center. All Colo could hear was Jocasta's bitter assertion that there would be no escape for any of them. He glanced at the wallscreen that showed a live video feed from Boros. Already, there were thousands of escape pods en route to the planet's surface.

"We need to get to an escape pod," Malachi said.

"You think those people are gonna live, think again. There isn't enough room down there. All of them are choosing a slow death."

Colo ran down a corridor and stopped at a bot maintenance hatch. Malachi was right behind him.

Colo entered a special access code and waited a few seconds for acknowledgment. The hatch opened to a darkened interior.

He looked at Malachi. "I have a shuttle. This shaft is the quickest way to get there. Keep your arms close."

Colo didn't wait for Malachi to reply. He stepped into the maintenance shaft with one foot on each side of its darkening walls. Inhaling deeply, he leaped down, and air began to rush past his face. Indicator lights for each deck flashed by him in an orange blur. He plummeted downward at startling speeds. His heart started to race, he felt an ache in his gut, and his body became rigid. Then, the artificial gravity slowed his descent and his feet lightly touched the ground.

Colo heard Malachi screaming above him, and he hastened out of the way. He quickened his pace and glanced behind him. Malachi was crouched on the ground, panting.

"No time to waste," Colo said.

He ran to the end of the corridor and stopped at a hatch, quickly entering his access code. Malachi caught up with him and waited. Colo watched the status window shift to green once the atmosphere was cycled into the small docking bay beyond.

"I had no idea this was even here."

The door opened, revealing a small platform where a shuttle waited. Colo raced to the other side and entered through the access hatch. The shuttle was small. It only had two seats and a small storage compartment. Colo sat in the pilot seat and began the preflight checks. Malachi sat next to him and closed the rear hatch.

As the engines powered up, Colo sent the command to open the docking bay doors.

"How do we get out of here?" Malachi asked.

Colo jutted his chin toward the ceiling and grabbed the flight controls. "We go up."

The shuttle rose upward, and after a few seconds, they were outside Chiba Station where Boros's poisoned atmosphere came into view. Thousands of escape pods were streaking through it. Colo swung the shuttle around and increased the mains to the maximum, pressing them back into their seats until the inertia dampeners were able to compensate.

They flew along Chiba Station's massive structure. The shuttle's onboard flight computers helped him navigate through the station's outer structure. Colo set a course, and the flight plan appeared on the main holoscreen.

"You have a star jumper on standby?" Malachi asked.

"Always have a way out."

The star jumper was essentially an interstellar support module used for small shuttles to escape star systems. He updated their course, and they flew away from the station.

"My God!" Malachi said.

Colo saw two huge ships flying toward the station and noted massive weapons mounted center mass on each of those ships—spinal mounts, which were powerful weapons that needed to be part of a warship's superstructure or the ship would be torn apart when it was used.

Chiba Station had point defenses that were reliant upon smaller, rapid-fire mag cannons. He wasn't a weapons expert, but he was certain that Chiba Station was minutes from being obliterated.

Several bright, bluish flashes came from the Sentinel ships, as if a lightning storm had erupted from their powerful weapons. The bolts blew through the station and seemed to spread along the outer hull. There were several more flashes, building up in intensity, and then large sections of Chiba Station began to break apart and collapse in on itself.

Colo watched in horror as the bolts spread to the nearest escape pods, destroying them almost as soon as it reached them. The last thing he heard was Malachi whimpering, and then there was nothing. No last word. No last breath or even a thought. He felt nothing. Colo Jakin was nothing.

A GUNNISON FREIGHTER lingered at the edge of Kiva Star System. The captain and crew watched the Sentinels annihilate Chiba Station with grim satisfaction. Chiba Station had no strategic importance, but it sent a powerful message to its powerful backers—a message that was being sent throughout the sector. They watched as the wreckage of Chiba Station spread amid the destructive forces of Sentinel weaponry, forming a vast debris field that would orbit the planet. The Sentinels patrolled the area, systematically destroyed anything that crossed their paths, even after the broadcast signals that had drawn them into the star system went silent.

"That's enough," the captain said. "Execute jump coordinates delta. We've got more messages to send to Trenton Draven and the Collective."

9

QUINTON STARED AT THE SPIDER-DRONE. He wanted to act like he'd misunderstood, but there was absolutely no chance of that, and Harper knew it.

"There has to be something," Harper said. One of the drone's legs tapped the ground, seemingly an outlet for a mental tick.

Guttman and Oscar pointedly looked away, as if suddenly finding the last swallow of Angorian ale worth further scrutiny.

"No, there is," Quinton said, trying to think up a response that would smooth things over.

"I've gone over the ship's diagnostic reports for most of the systems. The weapons systems and point defenses are all fully functional. All of you have done a thorough job with it," Harper said and looked at Guttman and Oscar, the latter of whom threw a nod his way.

Quinton thought a bit of deflection was in order. "Guttman, do you need any help with—"

"Nope, I've got it covered."

Quinton quirked an eyebrow. "Really, because I seem to recall several complaints on your part about the physical checks of systems as part of routine maintenance."

Guttman stood up and made a show of stretching his arms. "I did, but then —Oscar, yeah, Oscar brought up that it's good exercise. Movement is essential for optimal health," he said as he tried to suck in his gut.

"I'd be happy to help out," Harper said. "I've been checking those systems anyway."

Guttman's eyes went wide, and Quinton couldn't tell if the spacer was more shocked or afraid that he'd missed it.

Harper looked at Quinton. "You said I should make an effort. I'm making an effort, but this is ridiculous. Look at him." The spider-drone surged toward

Guttman, who nearly jumped out of his skin. "Seriously, what are you afraid of?"

"I know," Quinton said. "If you wanted to murder poor Guttman, all you'd have to do is wait for him to go for his middle-of-the-night galley raid."

Oscar grinned a little and shrugged when Guttman threw him a scathing look. "You do have a pattern. We all do." He stood up. "Let's make it a group effort."

Guttman blinked several times. "Cross training, yes! That will work."

The two spacers headed out of the galley.

Harper looked at Quinton, who nodded his head toward the door. Without another word, the spider-drone followed them into the corridor.

Becker walked in and glanced at Quinton. "Where are the others?"

"Communal maintenance check. Strength in numbers."

Becker nodded and went to the meal console. He scrolled through what the fabricator could make with the supplies aboard and shook his head. "We need supplies."

Quinton didn't need to eat—or sleep, for that matter—but he still enjoyed the smell of food. He could consume food and even taste it, but it was wasted on him.

Becker made a selection and a few seconds later, some kind of brownish gruel squirted into a bowl. Quinton was able to smell a faint odor of cinnamon.

"It's not that bad. You could have chosen something else," Quinton said.

Becker sat down and began eating the protein-paste meal. "I'll live."

"We need a supply run," Quinton said. They'd let the supplies run low because Becker thought they'd be on their own ship by now. "You know, we could send a message to the DUC."

Becker finished eating and chased the paste down with some water. He then rubbed the top of his lip and stood up. "Too many strings."

"They owe you."

Becker shook his head. "No, they owe *you*. Anyway, how would it look if after all these months I sent a message to the Dholeren United Coalition requesting payment?"

"That doesn't change the fact that we were part of the mission."

"Oh, so it's okay if I tell Maelyn you're alive?"

That hit home. Quinton hadn't wanted to contact Maelyn for the same reasons Becker didn't want to get involved with the DUC. The DUC was always recruiting. Keeping Maelyn in the dark about their survival of the starbase's destruction had been Quinton's decision. Becker was right. They couldn't contact the DUC because by all accounts, Becker had gotten a ship—the *Wayfarer*. But Quinton had taken it with the promise of helping the spacer find a ship of his own.

"It's complicated."

"It's a big galaxy."

"The DUC probably doesn't have what you're looking for anyway."

Ships were among the most valuable commodity in the galaxy for anyone who wanted to be independent.

"Don't bite my head off," Quinton began, and Becker's eyes narrowed. "I know you want off this ship. Why not take an interim job in someone else's operation?"

"Listening to our conversation last night?"

"Give me a break. I don't have to spy on you guys to figure out what you were talking about," Quinton said.

Harper had done it for him and reported it, but Becker didn't need to know that.

"I've already done that. I put in ten years in Crowe's Union. Worked my way up. I had multiple crews under me," Becker said.

Quinton nodded. "And then I showed up."

Becker looked as if he'd swallowed something sour. "You don't get it."

"What don't I get?"

"I had things in the works."

"Really," Quinton said dryly. "I wasn't there for long, but it looked to me as if Dante was going places and you were waiting for Crowe to let a few scraps fall your way."

Becker glared at him. They'd been through this before.

"You took a chance."

Becker grabbed his plate and threw it in the washer. Then he stalked out of the galley.

Quinton followed him. "You took a chance. You saw an opportunity to get what you've always wanted, and you took it. But it's proven to be much harder to reap the rewards, and you're going to stand there and tell me you'd rather go back to where you were."

Becker quickened his pace, heading to the bridge. He slammed his palm against the door controls.

"Plus," Quinton said, following him inside. "You fell for it, too."

Becker spun around. "For what?"

"We're men. She had a pretty face. You do the math."

Becker stepped toward Quinton. "I didn't do it because of Maelyn."

"Maybe not, but that's part of it—the promise of a big payout and, come on, she was… *something*."

"When we're done, you can go find her."

He'd considered it, more than once, but he always wound his way back to it being a bad idea. The more time that passed, the more that idea was reinforced. That, and now he had his memories—Nope, he wasn't going to do it. Mental trap avoided.

"Look, we can't keep going at this in the dark."

Becker spun around and brought up the main holoscreen.

"It's not going to work," Quinton said.

Becker ignored him and brought up a star chart.

"You're smarter than this. We need information. There has to be someone we can go to that has a lead for what you need," Quinton said.

Becker flipped through a few more star systems and then swiped them off to the side. He rolled his shoulders, stretched his neck, and let out a long sigh.

"You're right, Quinton. This isn't working."

Quinton felt his lips lift in a tentative smile.

"I was hoping we could hit a few of the places I knew about, but we need better odds."

"Now you're talking! I had Radek query for sector comms buoys to give us a starting point."

Becker grinned. "Yeah, those are unreliable. News travels by ship. The buoys get the fluff."

"I know, but it'll give us the highlights. At the very least, we'll know if there are other reported instances of the activation signal."

They needed to avoid those systems so as not to cross paths with the Sentinels. They'd nearly killed him, and Quinton wasn't in any rush to repeat the experience. In fact, he preferred to avoid it altogether, and he'd get no arguments from Becker or the others on that front.

An audible chime overhead signaled a ship-wide broadcast. "Quinton, we need your help down in engineering," Oscar said.

They heard Guttman shouting in the background, which was answered by Harper.

"Now would be great."

"We're on our way," Quinton replied.

Both he and Becker ran out of the bridge, quickly making their way through to the belly of the ship.

"He's coming," Oscar said. "Hold on, he's right here."

Quinton rounded the corner. Harper had Guttman pressed against the sidewall of the reactor core. If the spider-drone pierced the sidewall, they'd have some serious problems.

"Guys! Is five minutes of peace too much to ask?" Quinton said.

"Tell him to put me down!"

The spider-drone's head spun toward Quinton. "He tried to deactivate me," he said and turned back toward Guttman.

Becker stood behind him. "Quinton," he said in a tone that said he'd better deal with this.

"Harper, what exactly happened?"

Guttman growled. "All I did was try to help."

Harper had one of the spider-drone's legs raised as if he were getting ready to skewer Guttman.

"Hey, look at me," Quinton said.

Harper didn't turn around, and Guttman continued to try to get free. His sidearm was on the floor nearby.

"Harper," Quinton said. Getting no response, he then spoke more forcefully. "Lieutenant Harper, you are a guest on my ship! If you'd like to remain aboard, you'll put Guttman down now!"

His combat HUD overlay measured the distance to Harper and gave Quinton several options with which to disable the spider-drone, but none of them guaranteed that Guttman wouldn't get hurt.

Harper cleared his throat and then stepped back from Guttman. The spacer sagged to the floor.

Quinton relaxed a little. "What happened?"

Harper backed away from the others. "He tried to access my control panel."

"Wait," Guttman said, rubbing the area where Harper had held him. "Hold on a second. An alert flashed on the panel and I was just trying to get a better look."

"After you said we'd all be safer if I went into standby."

"Until we found you a better body, is all. That's it. I was just making a suggestion."

"What's the matter? Don't you like spiders?" Harper said and tapped each of his legs in rapid succession on the floor.

Guttman's eyes became wide. "That's beside the point." He shook his head and glared at Quinton. "I want off this ship. As long as this—Harper is here, I'm not going to be."

"I can take you to the nearest airlock if you want," Harper said.

"That's enough," Quinton said. "What am I supposed to do here?" Guttman opened his mouth to reply. "It's a rhetorical question. We're stuck here. We *are,* and I expect a little more cooperation from all of you," he said and looked at the others. "You think getting off the ship at the next resupply depot is going to get you where you want to be?"

"I won't be *here*."

"Yeah, you'd be burning credits, hoping for another ship to arrive that'll take you with them. And that's only if they overlook the fact that all of you are on the run from Crowe's Union," Quinton said. He glared at Guttman and the spacer looked away.

"All right, you made your point," Becker said.

"I don't think I have," Quinton said and walked toward Guttman. "He's not going anywhere," Quinton said, gesturing toward Harper. "He didn't ask for this. He didn't choose to be here. Something turned him back on. It's like being born again, except you know a lot more."

Guttman backed up against the wall.

"Look at him!"

Guttman's eyes darted to Harper. The spider-drone remained perfectly still, and Quinton had no idea what he was thinking.

"You go on and on about how we should treat you with more respect. Isn't that right? How about treating Harper like he's a guy who's stuck in a bad situation? Maybe instead of treating him like he's about to go insane, you can find a way to help him out, or God forbid, make him feel a little bit welcome," Quinton said and looked at the others. "We weren't part of the history you know. I don't know what happened that caused the PMC degradation that gave rise to the Sentinels. I don't doubt that it happened, but this," he said, gesturing to all of them, "this constant mistrust and animosity stops now. You want off this ship so bad, fine. I don't care anymore." Quinton looked at Becker. "Go have your little meeting that's sure to follow and then get the hell off my ship. Good luck. See you later. I'm through with this bullshit," he said and exhaled. "Harper, come with me to the bridge. Now."

Quinton turned and left the others behind, Harper following without saying a word. They made it back to the bridge and Quinton glanced at the main holoscreen, which still had Becker's star system search on it. He inhaled deeply and rested his hands on his hips.

"Thank you, Commander."

Quinton winced and shook his head.

"I'm sorry. I keep doing that."

"It needed to be said," Quinton replied.

"I might have overreacted. I don't like how they look at me."

Quinton turned around. "Guttman can be a little overdramatic, but it takes two. You can't lose control like that. The only reason things didn't get worse was because of Oscar. He could have shot you. He chose not to. They're not a bad group if you get to know them."

"Why do you defend them? They just want to leave."

"I owe them."

"But it's still not right."

Quinton regarded Harper for a few seconds. "It's complicated," he said. He didn't want to discuss how PMCs were almost universally mistrusted and outright scorned.

"I'll do better, sir—uh, damn it."

Quinton ignored the lapse. "There *is* something I need from you."

"What do you need?"

"You need to be honest with me."

"I haven't lied about anything," Harper said, the tone of his voice rising a little.

"I mean by omission. That drone isn't meant to hold you. You know the rules. Greta is going to help you as much as she can, just like Radek does for me, but you can't lose control. Neither of us can."

"That's easy for you to say."

Quinton leveled his gaze at him. "You've been reactivated less than two days. Are you saying you can't handle the current situation?"

One of the spider-drone's legs tapped the ground in rapid succession. Did Harper even notice it?

"There could be others like me."

"And."

"We should be looking for them."

"No, we shouldn't."

"The Sentinels can't be that much of a threat."

"Harper, do me a favor. Never say that again. You don't know what you're talking about, and this is exactly what worries the others. There's a price to pay for ignorance. I know. I paid, and now you don't have to. Just trust me. If you can't do that, then at least be cautious."

"What happened?"

"Not right now. I'll tell you if you stick around long enough. I need a promise from you that you'll stay in control, and if you think you can't, then you'll back off."

The spider-drone's armored torso was tilted downward as if Harper was looking away. "I don't think I can make that promise."

"Why not?"

"I need to be able to trust myself."

"Yeah, and I need to be able to trust *you*."

"But you're worried that I'm not stable."

"All our lives are on the line if you're not."

"I don't understand."

"We're going to have to resupply. There are built-in security protocols that can detect PMC access. If you trip those alarms doing something you think isn't going to be noticed, it will invite unwanted attention and could give away our location to the Sentinels. Trust me when I say that you don't want that to happen."

Harper was quiet for a minute. "I promise I won't lose control with the others, but like you said, it goes both ways."

Quinton wanted to believe him, but he couldn't. This might have been because of the PMC integrity check he'd run on Harper, or the fact that he'd seem completely in control one moment and then would ask an obscure question in the next. He just needed Harper to stay in control long enough for them to find another body, or better yet, a DNA vault.

"Thank you, Harper."

10

SOMETIMES QUINTON REALLY MISSED SLEEPING—LAYING down on a comfortable bed and slipping off into oblivion only to wake up hours later refreshed and ready to take on the day. He didn't need to sleep in the traditional sense, but there was a rest cycle built into the upkeep schedule that Radek tried to make him adhere to. A quick frame rate increase when less than a second had passed in real time meant that he'd gone through his own rest cycle. Apparently, the human mind needed downtime to process information and to just wander on its own. Quinton knew the science behind it. The knowledge and importance of it had been drilled into him as part of his training, but the rest cycle was tied to having a normal human body. Most creatures had evolved to go through a rest cycle for the recuperation of the body and also for the brain.

Harper required at least ninety minutes for his rest cycle because of the limitations of the spider-drone. The drone's computer systems and hardware only allowed for increases in frame rate in a limited capacity. Even though Quinton could go through days without a rest cycle that took only seconds to achieve, Harper required it every eighteen hours.

A sound of exaggerated static came from shipboard comms. "Now hear this," Oscar said. "Captain, your presence is requested on the bridge immediately. All nonessential personnel should stay away. Guttman, the galley is off-limits—" Oscar's voice cut off. "Captain, hurry! Angry spacer is closing in."

Quinton chuckled. The star class jumper should have had a larger crew if he was concerned with routine maintenance and anything like maintaining a standing watch. They traded off duties and Quinton carried most of the slack. Over the last thirty-nine hours, Harper had helped them maintain the ship, and there hadn't been any more incidents.

Quinton walked past the galley on his way to the bridge, and Guttman nearly collided with him.

"We're not going to leave without you," Quinton said.

"Oh, I know it. Club Ranstead, here I come," Guttman replied.

The clipped cadence of the spider-drone came from farther down the corridor. Guttman glanced behind them for a moment.

"Good morning," Quinton said.

"Good morning, Captain," Harper replied. "It went better this time. I think the VR needed a little bit of tweaking. Greta has got it much better tuned."

The ship had a VR interface that had a pretty extensive library available. Quinton had never even tried it. Becker and the others hadn't been too keen to use it either.

Guttman looked at him for a second.

"The VR is available to anyone, Guttman. You can use it," Quinton said.

He shook his head, which surprised Quinton. Of anyone on the ship, he'd thought that Guttman would have embraced VR, but he'd always refused.

"There's a training VR that shows you how to use it," Harper said.

"I know how to use it," Guttman said and then added, "Thanks anyway."

Quinton felt one of his eyebrows twitch. Guttman had been almost civil in his tone toward Harper.

They went on the bridge and joined Becker and Oscar.

"Nice 'all hands,'" Guttman criticized.

"All we need is the captain," Oscar replied.

Quinton looked at the main holoscreen, which showed a rather small resupply depot. "It's a little underwhelming. Are you sure you'll be able to find an information broker here?"

Becker nodded. "These are the best places."

There was a small interface window waiting for Quinton's input. He had to transfer his captain's credentials, which would authorize payment to put in at Club Ranstead.

"It looks a bit run-down. Are you sure someone isn't going to try to steal this ship?"

"They might try," Becker replied.

"They won't succeed," Harper said.

"Pay the fee and no one asks questions. That's exactly what we need," Becker said and raised his hand, gesturing for Guttman to wait.

"I'm going to pay the fee. I can't wait to see what this place looks like on the inside," Quinton said.

"Are you sure that's a good idea?" Oscar said. "You coming with us, that is."

"Are you afraid I'll embarrass you or something? You're making me feel like your goofy cousin."

Oscar considered for a few moments, looking uncomfortable, and then looked at Becker.

"Let's get one thing straight—I'm coming," Quinton said.

"*We're* coming," Harper said.

That brought a few raised eyebrows.

"Harper, you need to stay aboard the ship. I'm pretty sure a spider-drone would garner attention we don't need," Quinton said.

Harper was silent for a few moments, and then he started laughing. "If you could see the looks on all your faces! Woo!" He shifted on his feet and a couple of his legs tapped the ground. "I know. I get it. I'll stay here and monitor communications. Maybe I'll find something interesting."

Quinton knew that the best way to get someone to cooperate, especially on a ship, was to give them something to do, and not something meaningless. That wouldn't work for anyone beyond basic intelligence. He glanced at Guttman for a moment. Harper had been a tactical officer trained in the Acheron Confederacy Navy, which had had one of the best trained navies in the galaxy. He might be a little biased when it came to that, but nothing he'd seen so far had changed his mind. Monitoring comms chatter among the locals was well beneath Harper's skills, but it could prove valuable if the effort paid off.

Quinton's outward appearance was human—dark hair, two meters tall, athletic, with a handsome smile. He had Radek engage the life-sign protocols that allowed the cybernetic avatar to simulate a live human. His body mimicked breathing that would increase if he exerted himself. His eyes blinked. He could even produce sweat if required, and he gave off body heat.

Quinton opened a sub window on the main holoscreen, which showed the ship's life-support system. On the bridge were the biological markers of four humans and one spider-drone.

"Good enough for you guys?" Quinton asked.

The others peered at the main holoscreen.

"That ought to work," Becker said.

Guttman walked over to him, peering at him as if he were trying to see through a facade. "That's creepy. Look at him. I would never have guessed."

Quinton held out his arm and Guttman touched it. "It's warm. That's impressive. It's actually warm to the touch," he said, looking at Becker and Oscar.

Oscar walked over and gave him a nod, then raised an eyebrow. "We need a few more of these."

Quinton glanced at Harper. "I wish."

"Impressive," Becker said. "How long can you maintain it?"

"I'm actually not maintaining it. It's part of the onboard programming. I've just activated it."

"Nothing can interfere with it?"

"Like what?"

"I don't know. That's why I'm asking you."

Quinton snorted and gestured toward the image of Club Ranstead. "Yeah, like anything in there is going to have the ability to detect something wrong with me."

Becker shrugged. "Don't underestimate them."

"It looks like they cobbled together a few old mining platforms and installed several industrial HAB units."

"It's nicer on the inside," Guttman said.

Quinton authorized the credit transfer and received docking clearance. Oscar returned to the pilot's workstation and set a course.

"Have you been there before?" Quinton asked.

Becker shook his head. "Not Ranstead, but there are plenty of mobile resupply depots that travel throughout the sector. The reason this one is so far out in this star system is because of the Ashanti mines here."

"Never heard of them."

"They don't like visitors. Club Ranstead must have gotten clearance to be here; otherwise, a squadron of gunships would've convinced them of the error of their ways."

"I didn't realize these were Ashanti mines," Guttman said and looked at Quinton. "No visitors to their mines ever. They only use their own freighters to transport the exotic gases that they mine out of the star system—even if it's to transport to a larger freighter that has been contracted to bring it somewhere else."

Becker nodded. "They're one of few mining operations that know how to extract the gases. They operate throughout the sector. How they extract and refine the material is a closely guarded secret. Others have tried to figure it out, but it's a pretty lethal process."

"Okay, so no courses through the internal star systems unless we want to start trouble. Got it," Quinton replied and frowned. "How do the Ashanti bring people into their operation if everything is so secretive?"

"Carefully," Becker replied.

Quinton gave him a look.

"I don't know. They probably have multiple layers of operation, and only so many people are privileged to know the inner workings of their method of operation."

"What if someone wants to leave?"

"They're not allowed."

Becker's face was deadpanned, but Quinton didn't believe him. "Right, then. Time to go find an information broker. I, for one, can't wait to question them. Do we pay them for a session, or do they charge by the question? We don't have endless credits." Technically, they didn't have credits at all. Quinton had secured their funding from a Union creditor who had unknowingly transferred several transactions to them. It was nice of the Union to bankroll them like that.

Becker sighed. "I'm not sure of the inner workings of the Ashanti mining corporation. It depends on their role in the company and the level of knowledge of their operations. Now stop messing around. I don't need you to scare off any broker contacts."

Quinton had gotten what he'd wanted, which was an answer to his question, and nodded.

"Why would a broker be based here?" Harper asked.

"They're not here," Becker replied. "Contacting info brokers isn't the same everywhere. We're here to get a way to contact them."

"I didn't know that. I thought we'd be meeting them here," Quinton said.

"You thought wrong. They're secretive, and why take the risk if you don't need to with an in-person meeting?"

Quinton couldn't fault the logic, but he still didn't like it.

"I won't know the contact methods available until we go inside."

Oscar flew the ship to the docking platform. Once the docking clamps were attached to the hull, refueling hoses extended to the receivers.

Quinton authorized payment of the refueling operations and then looked at Oscar. "You didn't even scratch the paint on the hull."

Oscar pursed his lips and nodded once. "Would you expect any less? We're all professionals here."

A memory of Oscar pretending to fly an aircar that was secured to a maintenance platform came to his mind and he smiled. "I'll buy you a drink."

Oscar grinned and shook his head. "I think I owe you several."

Guttman was peering at his personal holoscreen with a look of intense concentration. He grunted a few times as he navigated the interface, then tapped the confirmation button. "Resupply order has been put in. Standard resupply for this class of ship."

"When are they going to deliver it?"

"It won't take them long. Probably within the hour."

Quinton looked at Harper. "You'll need to open the secure hatch and allow them to unload the order there." That way, they wouldn't have access to the interior of the ship.

"I can do that. Do you want me to store the supplies after they deliver them?"

"I'd appreciate it, but if something comes up, we'll get to it when we get back," Quinton said.

"Understood, sir," Harper said.

Quinton and the others went to the forward airlock. His biometric sensors showed the slightly elevated heart rates that signaled their anticipation and excitement at finally getting off the ship. Oscar and Guttman were chatting about where they would go first. Even Becker wasn't immune, and neither was Quinton, for that matter. He felt a slight pang of regret that Harper had to stay behind, but given his current form, there wasn't even the option of a disguise.

They all wore enviro-jackets that had hoods, which could serve as an emergency helmet should the need arise. One thing Quinton had learned since being reactivated was that most people in the galaxy had a general mistrust of their surroundings. There were redundancies built into any space structure, but this preparedness had spread to the individual level. This wasn't exactly new to Quinton. His experiences in the ACN had been full of preparedness plans, but warships were designed for going into dangerous places, and a state of readiness was expected. Civilians had never needed to bring that kind of preparedness into their daily lives. Merchant fleets experienced this to a lesser extent than federation militaries, but as they entered Club Ranstead, it was just another stark reminder of how the galaxy had changed.

The resupply depot's rounded design brought visitors into a central promenade. Ranstead's interior looked old. Small maintenance bots scurried around, performing maintenance tasks throughout the multileveled area. The interior wasn't overly large, less than a kilometer. Becker led them past various shops and eateries. The smells of cooked food sent out an enticing aroma.

Becker led them to a dimly lit place called Nunu's. There were plenty of spacers inside, and much of the foot traffic outside brought them to the restaurant and bar. They walked inside where multiple bars were located throughout the different zones, which seemed to follow a certain theme. Neon holographic themes lit up the walls and ceilings with such vividness that it was almost easy to forget where you were. Quinton thought this was the purpose.

Guttman inhaled deeply and sighed. "I need a drink."

Oscar agreed.

"You guys go on ahead. I've gotten a few nibbles on my initial inquires," Becker said.

"Do you want backup?" Quinton asked.

Becker shook his head. "Nah, it'll be fine. I'll call you if I need you."

Quinton nodded once and followed Guttman and Oscar. They headed for a warmly lit bar and sat on the stools. The patrons in the area glanced at them and then went back to their meals. Cheers erupted from a crowd of people that surrounded an area Quinton couldn't see.

A good-looking bartender, nearly covered with intricate body art, came over and took their meal orders. Guttman opted for an extensive sampler, while Oscar chose some kind of delicacy Quinton had never heard of. The bartender looked at Quinton expectantly.

"Got any local brews?" Quinton asked.

The bartender arched an eyebrow. "Really? I had you pegged for an import," she said with a wink and nodded. "I have just the thing for you, hon."

For the better part of the next hour, they watched Guttman devour plate after plate of "succulent delights," as he liked to call them. As if their jovial mood drew like-minded company, the spacers were soon swapping stories shared by people who lived and worked in the deep dark. There were cautionary tales or insights into sectors where there was salvage potential, which Oscar and Guttman seemed to lap up eagerly. More than a few times they looked in Quinton's direction. He'd give an acknowledging nod and raise his glass in a toast, but he didn't participate much, preferring to observe. There were others who also quietly observed. He kept an eye out for Becker, but he was nowhere to be seen. He considered contacting him through comlink but didn't. If Becker needed help, he'd contact them.

Quinton stood and gave up his stool to someone else, walking over to the outskirts. There was a cheer as Oscar and Guttman bought another round of drinks for their new friends. Quinton kept having the urge to move, as if he needed to expend some nervous energy. Being here triggered memories of shore leave when he'd been part of the ACN. The accommodations had been nicer, but the ambiance was the same. Spaceports had a commonality, as well as the people who frequented them.

Oscar and Guttman eventually yielded their places at the bar and moved toward the gaming section. The small crowd joined them. Quinton took another pull from his drink, which was more of a habit—something to do that came from a lifetime of practice. He found that he kept looking for the familiar faces of friends who were long gone, casualties in a war he'd never gotten to fight. The artificial biological imperatives he'd activated as part of his human appearance were also reactive to his inner yearnings, and he inhaled deeply. He looked around at the spacers who came and left. Some navigated the sections, unable to find a place to temporarily occupy. Standing there alone holding a nearly empty drink made him feel borderline pathetic. With a shrug, he put a stop to the slight pang he felt for a life he hadn't gotten to live and focused on where he was. He took one last pull from his drink and set the empty glass down on the bar.

Quinton turned and decided to make his own circuit through Nunu's. Maybe he'd even find a place to occupy for a little while. He passed various iterations of the name Nunu's where the typography was altered to fit the theme of the area. There must be a history to the name of the place, but he doubted it was all that complex—probably someone who'd once owned the place, or maybe it was just easy for people to remember.

He smelled a familiar and complex floral scent that reminded him of summer nights and outdoor gardens. Glancing toward his right, he saw someone looking at him from beneath the cowl of a hood. Music saturated the area with a rhythmical beat. There was something familiar about her, even though he couldn't see her face clearly. He glanced down and saw lavender skin extending from her neck to the soft edge of her white blouse.

Quinton strode toward her. It was too much of a coincidence if it was who he thought it was, but he was going to find out, regardless. She considered him from beneath the hood for a few moments and then pushed it back.

Quinton was pretty sure the temperature of the room hadn't gone up, but he couldn't have sworn to it. Violet eyes, deep and mysterious, regarded him. Some women have a quality about them, something completely intangible and indefinable, which gets called a lot of different things. Quinton thought of it as heat, fire. It wasn't always about sex, but it often was, and it definitely was with the Servitor.

Quinton was extremely aware of her body and eyes. Her soft lips lifted only slightly, and then she removed her coat. Long, silky black hair seemed to shimmer in the warm light from above. She sat in a tall chair, and her long legs crossed beneath a dress that seemed to part, showing swaths of smooth skin. Her expression told him that she knew exactly what effect she was having on him.

"I was wondering how long it was going to take you to find me," she said.

"You look like someone I met before. I'll leave you to it."

"You don't have to leave," she said. Dark eyebrows raised and she tilted her head slightly. "Yes, you've been among my kind before."

"I wouldn't go that far," Quinton replied. He'd intended to walk away. Becker should be done with what he was doing by now.

She smiled a little and extended her hand. "I'm Kandria Pavond."

Quinton felt his lips lift along the edges. He wasn't going anywhere, and they both knew it. He took the proffered hand and introduced himself, but then didn't want to let her hand go because of how her skin felt. For lack of a better description, she was perfectly proportioned. His avatar was fully equipped, and Quinton felt a rush of purely physical hunger that hit him suddenly. It was unexpected and perfectly natural.

"Would you sit with me?" Kandria asked, gesturing toward the seat next to her.

"Does anyone ever say no to that?" Quinton sat down.

"You looked disappointed when you first noticed me."

"Occupational hazard?"

Kandria simply stared at him, unperturbed by his quip.

"Like I said, I thought you were someone else. They pretended to be one of you."

Kandria lifted a dark eyebrow, and her face took on a thoughtful frown while she considered what he'd said. "Not something the average person could get away with. What name did she give you?"

"How do you know it was a she?"

Kandria smiled, and Quinton grinned. She had him there.

"Vonya Irani."

"I don't know her. You said she fooled you?"

"Not just me but a lot of people. A whole space station, in fact."

Kandria looked troubled. Several spacers walked by, watching them for a few moments, but she kept her attention on him. He was the lucky one.

She pursed her lips in thought.

"I guess it doesn't happen often?"

Kandria shook her head. Even that was done with an allure that made him forget where he was. "We go through a lot of training, which isn't easily replicated by the uninitiated," she said and then smiled at him. "Thank you for telling me about her."

"You're welcome," he replied. "I'm surprised you don't want to know more."

She shook her head. "No need, unless there's more you think I should know."

With that, Quinton wanted to tell her everything he did know, but he remained quiet for a few moments. "What kind of training do you go through?"

"Years of education that covers a wide range of subjects, in addition to our physical conditioning."

"When does the genetic modification happen?"

Kandria seemed amused. "When we've been initiated. About halfway through our training."

Quinton pursed his lips. "Are the changes permanent?"

"Some."

"I see."

"She betrayed you, this woman who pretended to be a Servitor?"

"How do you know it wasn't a Servitor?"

"It wasn't."

Quinton knew he was being manipulated. He was easy to read. Kandria knew her craft well and had the instincts to go with them. Betrayal wasn't a strong enough word for it. Vonya had tried to kill them. All of them.

"I didn't mean to upset you," Kandria said.

"It happens when people try to kill me."

Kandria looked away. "I see. Violence is too easy an option."

Quinton chose not to respond.

"I watched you over there," she said and gestured toward where Quinton had been with the others. "Your companions seemed to be enjoying themselves, but you, not so much. Why is that?"

"Does everyone just spill out their feelings to you?"

"Only if they want to."

"Yeah, I don't need to."

"That's fine as well. What else would you like to talk about?"

Warm violet eyes regarded him.

"Why are you here? Is Club Ranstead a preferred scouting grounds for Servitors?"

"I'm likely here for much the same reason you are. This was a convenient place to resupply, but I doubt that's the only reason you're here."

"I was told that Servitors seek to bring harmony to the galaxy."

"That's one thing we do."

"Right. Then why does it feel like you're trying to squeeze me for information?"

"I thought we were having a conversation," she said, and as if on cue, a ringlet of hair detached itself, coming to rest on her firm breast.

"Does it bother you that someone is out there doing a pretty good job of pretending to be one of you?"

Kandria considered it for a moment. "It's something that will need to be addressed, but this is hardly the first time it's happened."

"I'd like to find her."

"Then what?"

"That depends. Many people lost their lives because of what she did."

"You intend to murder her?"

"She deserves it. It's not something that's going to change."

"I understand the desire for justice."

"But you don't approve."

"There is always accountability. I regret that this person utilized a Servitor's likeness in order to achieve her deception. It undermines what we're trying to do."

"Great, so would you be willing to help spread the word about her and then inform the DUC?"

Kandria shook her head and sighed with a saddened expression. "The Dholeren United Coalition welcomes all the wayward spacers. I will do what I can."

Quinton hadn't been expecting that response. Servitors were sometimes hard to figure out. He made Vonya's data profile available and sent it to Kandria.

"There, you have it."

Kandria opened her personal holoscreen and peered at the image of Vonya. She frowned. "The resemblance is remarkable."

"Could Vonya have been a Servitor and…" Quinton pressed his lips together for a moment. "Quit or something."

"No one ever leaves."

Quinton frowned. "I don't believe that."

"I understand why you'd think that. It takes years of training and dedication, especially if you're not born into it. Anyone who lacks dedication will leave long before they become a Servitor."

Quinton still wasn't convinced. "What if you wanted to?"

"I don't want to."

"But what if you did? What if you decided that you'd rather be in the company of one person and then elected to settle down, as it were."

"Are you inviting me to travel with you?"

Quinton chuckled. It was tempting, especially now that the question had been raised. "I don't think so. I've been down this road before, and it's not one I'm eager to repeat."

Kandria leaned toward him, and a slight blush appeared on her delicate cheekbones. "You stand apart. Men like you are rare."

Quinton felt the heat gather under his shirt. "You don't get rejected often, do you?"

Kandria giggled, sending wiggles everywhere. "Don't be silly. You didn't reject me."

She wasn't entirely wrong about that. She might not have really offered to travel with them.

"You're not like the other spacers. I don't know what it is exactly, but I get the feeling that you don't know what you want."

"I know what I want," Quinton assured her.

"You misunderstand. Most people think they know what they want, but they're often wrong."

"So, what's next for you?"

"Deflection is a normal tactic," she said and placed her hand on his forearm. "I hope you find what you need. Very often, it's not what you think."

"I guess I can say the same about you."

Kandria tittered a small laugh. "What do you think I want?"

"Honestly, I wish I could say it was me, but…"

"I have no doubt it would be a pleasant way to spend a few hours," she said, watching him.

He felt like an idiot. What would it hurt if he spent some time alone with Kandria? She was willing and there was a mutual attraction between them, so what was the problem? It wasn't as if he hadn't had the casual encounter before, and this avatar seemed more than willing and capable of rising to the occasion.

"I can't," Quinton said, imagining Guttman screaming at him for what he'd just done.

"Our time comes to an end, then?"

A comlink from Harper registered on Quinton's HUD.

"Are you trying to broadcast something?" Harper asked.

"No, why?"

"It's strange. I'm monitoring communications and there isn't a broadcast, but Club Ranstead has intrusion signatures that are actively scanning for your identity. They've enabled a communication-dampening field around the station. Pretty interesting method actually. It looks like something based off an old Til signature," Harper said.

"Wait a minute. You said my ID? Do you mean my description?"

"Nope. How would they know what you looked like anyway? No, they've got ID signatures."

"Wait, are you in Ranstead's systems now?"

There was a long pause. "Yes."

"Harper," Quinton began.

"Not from our ship. I'm using a neighboring ship's access."

Quinton closed his eyes.

"Is something wrong?" Kandria asked.

His entire conversation with Harper had occurred sub-vocally.

"You know that moment when a friend does the exact opposite of what you needed him to do? That's what I'm dealing with now."

Kandria smiled, her eyes glistening. "It can't be that bad. Maybe they had good reason."

"She's right," Harper said.

Quinton stood up. "Whatever reason he had isn't good enough," he said, and then added sub-vocally to Harper, "Get out of Ranstead's computer system right now, and erase any footprint you left behind."

"But Quinton, they have your identification."

"I know. I'll look into it. Do as I say," he said and cut off the comlink.

Kandria stood up. She leaned toward him and kissed the side of his face. "I've enjoyed speaking with you."

Quinton smiled. "I wish it could have been longer."

"Maybe some other time. What is your ship called? In case I learn anything about Vonya," Kandria replied.

He couldn't tell her, especially now considering what Harper had just discovered. "The DUC will be much easier for you to contact."

"You are correct," she said. "Perhaps our paths will cross again someday."

They parted ways. Quinton was heading back toward the others, and the Servitor was walking in the opposite direction. She had pulled her hood up, and in the dim lighting, she blended in with other people walking in the same direction. He saw Oscar watching him, his eyebrows raised in an unspoken question.

Quinton shook his head and held up his hand, making a circular motion with his fingers. Oscar nodded and spun around to get Guttman.

Quinton opened a comlink to Becker. "Are you close to being done?"

"Yeah, I was just about to come back to Nunu's."

"Don't. Just head back to the ship."

"What happened?"

"Harper detected a comms-dampening field around the depot, and they're looking for my identification."

"How the hell would they have that?"

"I have no idea. We've got to go."

"I'll meet you back at the ship," Becker said and closed the comlink.

11

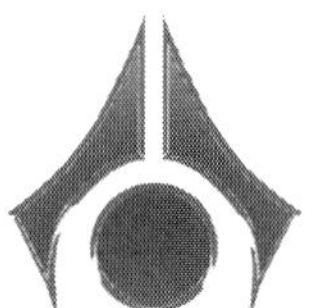

QUINTON WAITED for Oscar and Guttman outside of Nunu's. He looked around, watching the spacers walking by. None of them gave him a second glance.

Oscar walked toward him. "Guttman won't leave."

Quinton blinked several times. "What?"

Oscar sighed. "He's not coming back to the ship now."

Quinton stepped toward Nunu's, and Oscar grabbed his arm. "Don't do that," he said.

"We've gotta go," Quinton insisted.

"What's happening?"

Quinton told him about what Harper had discovered. "I don't want to leave without him, but I might have to."

"Listen, why don't you go back to the ship, and I'll get Guttman."

"You'll get Guttman?" Quinton repeated, sounding unconvinced.

Oscar nodded. "Yes, you don't get him. He likes to sound off and stand his ground, and I get it. We were hoping for a whole day here. He needs to blow off some steam."

"You think Becker will go along with that?"

"Yes, he gets it. If you go in there and drag him out, you'll cause a scene. You'll do the exact opposite of what you want and draw attention to yourself. I'll go in there and reason with him, but it might take a few more drinks."

Quinton glanced through the entry of Nunu's. The darkened interior had warm, ambient lighting, and the sounds of the patrons' lively conversations spilled out into the corridor.

"I'll get him to come. It's just going to take a little while. I'll let Becker know," Oscar said.

"Do you want me to stay?"

Oscar shook his head. "Not necessary. I've got this," he said and went back inside.

Quinton stood there for a few minutes, not knowing what else to do. Then he started walking back to the ship.

"Radek," Quinton said sub vocally, "what do you make of this? Are the ship's systems compromised? Is that how they got my ID?"

A small holographic sphere appeared on the upper right side of his internal HUD.

"Negative, the *Wayfarer's* systems have not been compromised, and the captain's identification you provided to Club Ranstead's systems is completely different. There are no associations with it."

"Then why do they have an intrusion signature based on my PMC identification?"

"Unknown. Perhaps if you accessed the signature, it would reveal more information," Radek replied.

Quinton had been thinking along those lines. He'd been trying to avoid accessing the depot's computer systems, but he didn't have much of a choice. Either they knew who he was and had reason to believe he'd come to the depot, or someone was casting a very wide net in hopes of finding him. Neither explanation sat well with him. How would whoever was doing this know he'd survived the Sentinel attack on the starbase? There might be another reason, something he couldn't think of yet. Radek was right. He needed to access Club Ranstead's computer systems.

Quinton considered his options for infiltrating their computers. He needed to access the security monitoring systems that were analyzing all communications on the depot. He could use a subspace comlink and insert a session, but they might detect it and he'd give himself away. He needed to be smarter than that. The best way to hide what he was doing on anyone's computer system was to utilize a system that was already connected. There were plenty of existing communication sessions that were near constant. He'd take control of one of those and use that, but he didn't want to be physically anywhere near his point of entry. He wanted nothing that could be traced back to him or his ship.

Quinton opened a comlink to the *Wayfarer* and accessed the communication systems. He found that Harper was still using a neighboring ship's access and killed the session. He sent Harper a message telling him that he was looking into it.

Since Club Ranstead's security had enabled a communication-dampening field, they were more than concerned that someone with Quinton's identification would begin broadcasting. This meant that they would be monitoring for it on any comms systems and not just outbound ship broadcasts. This might be easier for him to track than he'd thought.

Quinton looked around as he walked through the depot. Club Ranstead was just a resupply depot, and not a very large one at that. There were limited shops, but mostly it was designed for a temporary break from shipboard life. He spotted a general info terminal that anybody could use. The info terminal would certainly be monitored, but that was exactly what he was looking for. He created a specially crafted message that was an invitation for free drinks at Nunu's and then uploaded it to the info terminal. As people walked by, they were sent the fake invitation, which created a comlink session to the personal wrist computers that everyone wore. How best to hide than simply becoming the most average asteroid among a field of them? When people responded to the invitation, the comlink was confirmed, which gave him a valid communication session that could not in any way be traced back to him. He had a limited amount of time before the fake invitation would be purged from the info terminal, so he had to work fast.

"Okay Radek, let's see what we can find out."

Quinton unpacked an infiltration program that he uploaded into Club Ranstead's internal communication systems. He didn't need to take control of the security systems to determine what they were scanning for. In order for any intrusion signature to work, it had to analyze all communications that passed through it. All Quinton had to do was run his queries to the normal comlink sessions and allow himself to be scanned. This also allowed him to collect a snapshot of the intrusion signatures Club Ranstead security was using. He took a data dump of the entire signature set.

Quinton was still within view of the info terminal he had commandeered, and groups of people were checking their wrist computers as they came into range, many of whom headed in Nunu's direction. He grinned sub-vocally, thinking about all the people who were going there expecting a free drink.

Quinton did a quick analysis of the intrusion signatures, and it was just as Harper had said it was. Based on a Til signature, it was more a wildcard that could pretty much look for whatever anyone wanted to input. The intrusion signature wasn't anything particularly special, other than the fact that it had Quinton's PMC identification. He still had no idea how they had gotten it.

Becker opened a comlink to him. "Where is everyone?"

"I'm heading to the ship now. I had to take a slight detour. But Oscar and Guttman—" Quinton began.

"Oscar contacted me. I'm not seeing any alarms that indicate they're looking for us—you, that is—so I told them it was fine to stay where they were for a few more hours," Becker said.

Quinton made his way through the throng of people and then said. "Are you going to join them?"

"No," Becker said.

"I'll meet you back at the ship then," Quinton said and closed the comlink.

Quinton returned to the ship, and Becker was already on the bridge, sitting at a workstation that had multiple holoscreens up.

He glanced at Quinton. "What did you find out?"

"Somehow, they have my ID, and they're looking for any broadcast with it."

"What do you mean your ID?"

"Do you remember when the DUC had me do that automated challenge protocol?"

Becker nodded.

"They have that ID, the one that's associated with my PMC."

Becker frowned in thought and then rubbed his chin. "I don't know. It doesn't make any sense. The only people who would have a copy of that are the DUC and Maelyn. Can you check if the *Nebulon* has been to Club Ranstead?"

Quinton shook his head. "Don't you remember? Club Ranstead doesn't keep those kinds of records. No questions asked, and your visit will be purged. And even if Maelyn had a copy of my ID, there's no way she'd make it available."

"What if she was looking for you?"

"Even if she was, she's way more subtle than this. This is like using a quad-barrel mag cannon to take out a hatch. Sure, you'll open the door, but you'll destroy whatever's on the other side."

Becker considered it for a few seconds and then nodded. "You're probably right."

Quinton smiled. "And that admission didn't even hurt this time."

Becker rolled his eyes.

"This is reactionary. I don't think we're going to figure it out here."

The door to the bridge opened and Harper joined them. "What's reactionary?"

Quinton raised an eyebrow.

"The auditory systems of the spider-drone are pretty sensitive," Harper said by way of explanation.

"I was just telling Becker that the intrusion signature seems like a reactionary response to something."

"Tactically, that makes sense. But we don't know why it's appeared here," Harper said, then added, "Who uses an old Tilion security system anyway?"

At that, Becker sat up straight and spun his chair around. "What did you say?"

"I said the intrusion signature was Tilion, based on the Tilion Federation," Harper replied.

Becker looked away, glancing at the main holoscreen for a moment. The screen was displaying a live video feed of the docking platform and an exterior view of Club Ranstead. He shook his head and looked at Quinton. "It's not the Tilion Federation."

"Yes, it is. I've seen this type of security before," Harper said.

"I'm sure you have, but that was either before or shortly after the Federation Wars began. The Tilion Federation, or what was left of them, was absorbed into the Castellus Federal Alliance," Becker said.

"But you told me that both of those star nations are no longer around," Quinton said.

"They're around, but they're known as the Collective."

"The Collective?" Quinton repeated. "*The* Collective? The group Lennix Crowe was so worried about?"

Becker nodded once. "The Collective—Trenton Draven—wasn't happy with Crowe's Union."

"The Collective? Crowe's Union? Who are these people?" Harper asked.

Becker sighed and turned away from them. He opened a comlink and began speaking to Oscar.

"They're powerful organizations that were built upon the remnants of the old federations," Quinton said.

"How powerful are we talking about here?"

"They have fleets from whatever ships were still around after the Federation Wars," Quinton said, remembering that Lennix Crowe had attacked him on the starbase with several Jordani cruisers.

Becker closed the comlink and turned toward them. "Oscar and Guttman are almost back to the ship."

"Really?" Quinton said. "I thought they'd be a lot longer."

"I didn't ask, and they didn't say," Becker said.

Quinton started the preflight checks for the *Wayfarer*. If the others were on their way back, there was no reason for them to stay after they were aboard. The preflight check process wasn't entirely automated, but he could get it to a point where Oscar could take over once he was back. Quinton thought about Nunu's. There had been quite a few drinks consumed. If Oscar wasn't able to finish preflight checks, he'd have to do it himself.

"So, Club Ranstead is somehow tied to the Collective," Quinton said.

"At least in part, or they based their security protocols off a service that's a subsidiary of them. There isn't one big charter that joined them all," Becker replied.

"Have you been to any of the Acheron Confederacy core worlds?" Harper asked.

The question caught Quinton off guard. He hadn't been expecting anything like it. He shook his head.

"Maybe we should go back there. Maybe there's something we can use," Harper said.

"There isn't anything there," Becker said.

"How do you know? You just said you haven't been there," Harper said, his voice sounding a little defensive.

"No one goes there because there isn't anything left. Those worlds, like much of the old federation core worlds, were destroyed in the wars," Becker replied.

"I want to go there. I think we should go there next."

Becker glanced at Quinton and then looked back at Harper. "You think we should go there?" he said, unable to keep the incredulity out of his voice.

"Harper, I'd like to see it for myself, too, but now isn't the right time," Quinton said.

The spider-drone turned toward him. "It's never the right time. When will the right time be? I'm serious. When will the right time be?"

"Not today," Quinton replied. He wasn't going to be lured into Harper's longing to return home. It was contagious, and Quinton knew it was one of the things they couldn't do now. "We need to focus on finding you a new host or a DNA vault."

"This spider-drone isn't so bad. I'm repairing it," Harper said and gestured toward several of the damaged armored panels that had been patched up. "Why is it so hard to find a suitable host?"

"Harper, we've been over this. Many of the technologies that were developed for PMC use were destroyed by the Sentinels. We might be able to find something that's better suited for you than the spider-drone, but a DNA vault would be better. Then we can regrow your body and offload you into it. I want the same thing," Quinton said. He'd almost had a new body, but it was gone, as well as any record of his DNA.

"Do you think there are any more ACN starbases out there?"

It wasn't the first time Harper had loosely indicated that he was envious of the cybernetic avatar Quinton resided in. He wished there were a second one aboard that Harper could use, but he wasn't about to give his up. "I wish I knew."

"I still say the core worlds are our best chance—" Harper began and stopped. The door to the bridge opened, and Oscar and Guttman walked in.

"You won't believe what just happened," Guttman bellowed and then continued without waiting for a response. "Nunu's was overrun by a bunch of people seeking free drinks. There were hundreds of people in there. I don't know what's gonna happen. When we left, there were security forces en route."

"It was getting pretty rowdy," Oscar agreed.

"You're lucky you escaped," Quinton replied.

Guttman agreed, but Oscar gave him a sidelong glance.

"Oscar, I started preflight checks for you. Can you take over for me, please?"

Oscar stifled a yawn and walked to the pilot's workstation.

"I don't know about you guys, but I'm going to take a nap," Guttman said.

"That's going to be a hard negative on that nap," Quinton said.

Guttman turned around. "Why? What now?"

"We had a resupply delivery. All that stuff needs to be stowed or we'll lose it all. Unless you don't want any of that food and the other things you ordered," Quinton said.

"He's right," Becker said. "The rest of us will give you a hand."

Quinton feigned surprise, and Becker shook his head. "It'll go much faster if we all help," he said and then added, "Harper, come with us. You can help too."

As they headed off the bridge, Quinton stuck his head back. "Oscar, as soon as the preflight checks are done, we're out of here."

"I'm on it," Oscar said.

Over the next hour or so, they brought in the standard resupply cache from Club Ranstead. If Quinton hadn't been so concerned that the depot's delivery personnel would react poorly to seeing Harper, he would've had him bring it in. Once they were done, they headed to the galley, and Quinton and Harper watched Becker and the others drink some coffee.

"I miss coffee," Harper said.

"Me too," Quinton agreed.

"At least you can taste it."

"It's not the same," Quinton said and looked at Becker. "So, what did you find out about an information broker? Do you have any contacts?"

Becker sipped his coffee and sighed contentedly. "Yeah, I've gotten the contact protocols for five brokers. I need to review them to see which one would best fit the bill."

"Contact protocols? Why do you need to use that?" Quinton asked.

"Direct contact with an information broker never happens. We use these contact protocols as a way to establish temporary communications with someone else who has direct contact with the information broker. Actually, there're probably several levels more than that, but you get the gist," Becker replied.

Quinton considered this for a few moments. "All this to find a ship for you."

Becker glanced at the others. "Not just a ship for me. I want to go independent. I want to start my own salvage operation. Oscar and Guttman are going to join me. We'll be partners."

"It's not like we have much of a choice," Guttman said.

"I don't understand," Harper said. "Why wouldn't you have a choice?"

"They burned quite a few bridges helping me," Quinton replied.

"I was getting tired of it anyway," Oscar replied. Then he raised his mug to the others. "Partners."

"Everyone wins," Quinton said, and the others looked at him. "There's something I'd like to ask the information broker."

Becker set his mug down and crossed his muscled arms in front of his chest. "The session is limited. This is for everyone's protection."

"Please," Quinton said in an exaggerated tone. "How long will it take to get a few targets for ships?"

"I intend to get targets for ships, but I'm also looking for potential sellers."

"Either way, it shouldn't take too long. Would the broker have information about Sentinel activity?"

The others became still.

"Why do you want to know about that?" Becker asked.

"We should also ask about the activation signals. Maybe they can help us find where they're coming from," Harper said.

Becker shook his head. "It's too dangerous."

"Maybe for you, it is," Harper said.

"Hold on a second," Quinton said. "It can't be that dangerous. We're just asking if there've been reports of more signals being detected and if there's been an increase in Sentinel activity. If there has been, we need to know where so we can avoid those places. Those seem like reasonable questions to ask an information broker, especially if we're in the market for a new fleet of ships to start our new salvage operations," he said and paused for a moment. "I'm speaking figuratively here. I don't want to join your salvage organization."

Becker considered it for a few seconds. "You've got a point. I think that'll be fine."

"That's twice in one day. A few more, it might become a habit." Quinton smirked.

"You wish," Becker said.

12

"Oscar, execute emergency jump coordinates," Quinton said.

"Executing emergency jump coordinates," Oscar replied.

The *Wayfarer* slipped out of the compromised location in their third attempt to contact an information broker.

Quinton looked at Becker. "You still think I'm being too cautious?"

Becker peered at the main holoscreen. On it were the final moments of the communications drone they'd used to wait for the Angry Pilot to contact them.

"That's two no-shows and one attempted capture," Quinton said.

Guttman cleared his throat, hands clasped behind his neck. "What did you expect? This is the risk we take for using a broker. High risk. High reward."

Becker had gotten five contact protocols for different information brokers. Dagan and the Phantom Node hadn't even shown up. The Angry Pilot tried to capture them. That left two more.

"I expected them to take their fee and give us what we paid for. Now, I just want to hunt down the Angry Pilot," Quinton replied.

Becker's glare had more frustration than malice to it, but he had this way of making Quinton think it was his fault, that the things that had gone wrong for Becker were somehow Quinton's doing.

"Guttman's right," Becker said.

Quinton gave him an exaggerated head nod. "That's right, I forgot everyone's an opportunist here. If you knew this going in, then why was the original plan just for us to put the ship right on the coordinates where anybody could ambush us? And you say *I* play fast and loose. This is downright reckless."

They'd decided to use communication drones to give them a layer of protection, which had paid off just now. Becker argued that those drones were the reason they'd had two no-shows.

Becker glared at Quinton. "Are you done?"

Quinton regarded Becker for a few seconds. The spacer was normally more cautious than this. He must really want off the ship. Quinton glanced at the others. Guttman gave him a can-we-get-on-with-it look.

"Right, good talk. Where to next?"

Becker looked at Oscar. "Set a course for Mortis."

Oscar looked at Quinton.

"Do it."

They would travel to the rendezvous coordinates and deploy another sacrificial comms drone. Hopefully, Mortis would be different from the other brokers they'd tried to contact.

"Fifteen hours' travel time," Oscar said.

Becker left the bridge and was soon joined by Guttman and Oscar.

"You shouldn't let them treat you like that, sir," Harper said.

Quinton looked at the spider-drone. "We're not in the ACN anymore."

"I still don't like it. They should be restricted to their quarters," Harper said. "Would you like me to initiate a lockdown?"

"No, Harper, that will not be necessary."

"Are you sure?"

"Yes, I'm quite sure," Quinton replied.

"Fine," Harper said, cramming a good bit of disapproval into one word.

Fourteen hours and forty-five minutes later, Quinton was still on the bridge. Harper had gone to the workshop to continue repairing the spider-drone. For the moment, he had accepted that there was a severe shortage of consciousness-driven androids out there that were capable of holding his ESS.

Becker walked onto the bridge and came toward Quinton. "It'll be better today."

Quinton snorted softly. "Only if our luck changes."

Becker chuckled.

Before the fifteen-hour mark, the others had joined them on the bridge. A secure comlink registered with the ship's communication systems.

"All right, here we go," Becker said.

They'd agreed earlier that Becker would take the lead communicating with the information broker.

A voice-only secure comlink channel opened, and a countdown timer appeared next to the comlink session. They had ten minutes.

"You're go for Mortis."

"We're in the market for a new ship," Becker said.

"You and everyone else. What kind of ships are you looking for?" Mortis asked.

"A freighter class, either light- or medium-bulk transport will suit our needs."

"What's your first choice?"

"A former auxiliary ship would be perfect. Something along the lines of a Proteus or Endeavor class," Becker said.

"Querying," Mortis said. After a full minute had run on the clock, he continued. "Compiling list and coordinates. Do you care if they have ship-launch fighters?"

"They're nice to have but not essential. We can acquire those elsewhere."

"Adding that to the query. What else do you need?"

"Can you also include a list of transport ships in this sector? I don't want to be traveling all over the galaxy for these things."

"Understood. I have the list available. Once credits are transferred, I will send it to you," Mortis said.

A data window appeared from within the comlink session. Quinton thought the price was rather high for just a list of information, but Becker quickly acknowledged it.

"Payment has been sent," Becker said.

A few moments later, Mortis replied. "Confirmed. What else?"

"Wait a second," Quinton said. "How do we know this list is any good?"

"The data provided is current as of right now. What happens after this is not my concern. It's yours," Mortis replied impatiently.

Harper put a text message up on the main holoscreen. *Comlink trace running.*

"Is there anything else?" Mortis asked, sounding as if he'd like to end the transaction.

"Yes, there is," Becker said. "We've been hearing rumors about rogue PMC activation signals. Do you have any confirmation about that? Is there a particular sector we should avoid?"

"I'm surprised you're not asking about the increased Sentinel attacks."

Becker glanced at Quinton for a moment. "We've been out of touch."

"You must have been. Have you been living on an asteroid somewhere? Never mind. Ships are in short supply, so I'd move quickly on the highlighted ships on the list I gave you. There isn't a lot of time."

"Thanks, Mortis. What about those attacks?" Becker asked.

"There's been increased hostility between the Collective and Crowe's Union. There's a lot of credits to be made if you've got any information the Collective is looking for," Mortis said.

"What kind of information?"

Mortis grinned. "That kind of data comes at a cost."

As if on cue, another charge appeared on the comlink. Becker acknowledged it.

"Confirmed payment," Mortis said. "The data we're seeing is that there have been increased Sentinel attacks, but they seem to be targeted at organizations associated with the Collective. Locations are coming to you."

"How are the Sentinels being used?" Quinton asked.

"The Sentinels respond to a broadcast with a PMC identification protocol."

Quinton's eyebrows shot up, and he looked at Becker, who had a similar expression. Lennix Crowe had figured out how to lure Sentinels by using Quinton's identification.

"So, if you have any information, I can broker the deal with Trenton Draven personally. It's a lot of credits. Enough to buy that whole list of ships if they were all available. What do you say?" Mortis asked.

Everyone on the bridge of the *Wayfarer* became extremely still. Harper turned to look at them. The broker had essentially promised Becker and the others enough credits to set them up for the remainder of their lives if they were to take him up on his offer. Quinton knew they wouldn't do it. If the offer sounded too good to be true, then it probably was. That, and he was right here. A betrayal would end their association with a deadly finality.

"I don't have any current information," Becker said.

"Understood," Mortis said. "One last bit of parting advice before our time runs out. Make sure that whatever ship you get, you have adequate amounts of ammunition. Federation War tech is coming back online. There have been a lot of reports on it. There are also rumors that another incursion is going to start soon."

Quinton didn't know what that meant, but Becker seemed to.

Becker looked at Harper and gave them a nod.

The comlink session was severed, and Oscar executed a micro-jump. The trace hadn't reached the ship, but Quinton didn't want to take any chances. He'd given Oscar orders to leave the area as soon as they were done.

"Oh man," Guttman said, breaking the silence.

Quinton looked at them. "You know that feeling when there's an asteroid on the landing pad? That's all I'm getting right now."

Becker shook his head.

Quinton continued, "I would've been tempted by all those credits. I mean, you could get your own salvage operation."

Becker looked at Quinton. "We had a deal."

"We did."

"I don't understand," Guttman said. "How did Crowe get your ID?"

"Yeah, I don't understand that either," Oscar said.

Becker looked at Quinton and waited for him to reply.

"It must be from the starbase. Crowe used Sentinel tech to infiltrate the system through Vonya." Quinton stopped. "Vonya," he said and shook his head. "It's just the gift that keeps on giving," he said through gritted teeth.

"Who's Vonya?" Harper asked.

"She's a spy for Crowe's Union," Quinton replied. He was silent for a few moments. "I need to be alone. Go on. You've got a list of ships to look through and systems to review. You don't need to do that here."

Becker gestured for the others to go. Then he looked at Harper. "Hey, would you give us a minute alone?"

The spider-drone followed the others off the bridge.

Quinton cranked up his frame rate. He needed to think about this now and wanted to do it before he spoke with Becker.

"Radek, is what Mortis said possible? Can Lennix Crowe be using my PMC ID to lure the Sentinels into an attack?"

"In order for this tactic to work, Crowe's Union must know the location of a Sentinel Scout ship unless they have monitoring posts deployed. An alternative to this is that he has some kind of agreement with the Sentinels," Radek replied.

"I don't know about that. Interactions with Sentinels are usually one-sided."

"Agreed, if the Sentinels show up to a star system based on a broadcast with your PMC identification, they're already traveling with hostile intent."

Quinton knew what that meant. Sentinels would destroy anything to prevent an outbreak of what they called PMC spread. If they detected a trace of PMC activity on ship computer systems or even space stations, they would destroy them to prevent the spread.

"Do we have any data from the attack on the starbase that can confirm whether..." Quinton began and stopped. That wouldn't help. The intrusion signature had his PMC ID, so he didn't need to confirm that Crowe was actually using it. He was. Now, all he needed to decide was what the hell he was going to do. "Stand by, Radek."

Quinton slowed his frame rate down so he could speak with Becker. "What's an incursion?"

Becker frowned for a moment. "You just did that thing with the frame rate, didn't you?" Quinton nodded. "An incursion is when the Sentinels send out all their fleets to check inhabited star systems, looking for... anyone like you."

Quinton gritted his teeth. "Damn it!"

"That's not all, Quinton. If another incursion happens, a lot of people are going to die. There's no safe place. The Sentinels can misinterpret any advance in computing as being manipulated by a PMC."

Quinton turned away and paced across the bridge.

"What are you going to do?" Becker asked.

"Lennix needs to stop this. Does he know what he's doing?"

"He might not care. If Draven was hunting for him, he'd look for a way to take the pressure off."

"And having Sentinels attack Collective installations would take the pressure off?"

Becker nodded. "Yes. To anyone on the outside—meaning whoever didn't know what we know—the Sentinels are targeting the Collective. That can bring pressure from all kinds of former federations, as well as anyone who has a grievance with them."

Quinton considered this. He couldn't fault Lennix Crowe's logic. His back was against the wall, and he'd lost the one thing that would've given him an advantage, so he'd chosen the next best thing. Until a few moments ago, the galaxy had been completely open to him, and now it was being cut off.

"You can't run from this," Becker said.

"I know," Quinton replied.

"What are you going to do?"

"I don't know. What if the Sentinels thought they had me? What if they thought they'd gotten me? Would they stop attacking?"

"You want to give yourself up?"

Quinton shook his head. "No, but if I could find a DNA vault, I could put myself in a body and send my ESS to the Sentinels. Wouldn't they back off?"

Becker shook his head and raised his gaze to the ceiling. "That's the stupidest thing I've ever heard. What are you thinking? That's not going to get them to stop."

Quinton swore. "Because the Sentinels are also looking for copies of PMCs.

Damn it. Who the hell came up with such an all-or-nothing solution? Who thought this was a good idea?"

"They were desperate."

Quinton laughed bitterly. "I know the feeling. What the hell am I going to do? We have to get Lennix to stop this."

Becker shook his head. "I don't know if he will. I don't think he will."

"He'd risk an incursion?" Quinton said and shook his head. "That's obvious. Wouldn't someone like the DUC and the other federation remnants try to get the Collective and the Union to stop their little shadow war they've got going on?"

Becker thought about it for a moment. "Maybe."

"Maybe! Are you serious? Aren't any of these governments proactive?"

"It's not that simple. I mean, they wouldn't even know where Crowe's Union is. Hell, I don't even know where their operations are anymore. Lennix might've taken everything away and hidden it."

"I need to find Lennix Crowe and get him to stop. Wouldn't the Sentinels realize they're being used? I wonder if this is related to more PMC signals being detected. That's like releasing antimatter on a ship. We've got to do something. Maybe we need to do all of those things," Quinton said.

"Quinton," Becker said mildly.

"Maybe we can reach out to the other… DUC, or Trenton Draven, and tell him what's going on. Then we can—"

"Quinton."

He looked at him. "What?"

"We had an agreement."

"You help me repair the ship and I help you get your own."

Becker nodded. "That's right. We have leads to a ship now. That's enough for us. We can't help you take on Lennix Crowe, the Collective, and the Sentinels."

Quinton stared at him for a few moments. "That's it? You're just going to leave? You got what you wanted, so it's good luck, Quinton. Wish you the best. Is that what you're telling me?"

The door to the bridge opened and Harper ran inside. "Cowards!" he bellowed. "You should toss them out the airlock."

The spider-drone hastened toward them and Becker pulled out his heavy blaster, pointing it at Harper. The tip glowed orange. "You come any closer and I'll melt that thing you call a body. Do you understand me?"

Harper came to a stop. A panel opened from the armored torso and a micro-blaster used for demolition extended, primed and ready. "It doesn't change what you are. You're a coward, just like the others. You cut and run when things get tough. You're weak and pathetic. I bet you've never stood for anything in your entire life."

Becker snarled and shoved his blaster toward Harper. Quinton darted over and grabbed his wrist. A plasma bolt melted through several layers of the floor.

"Enough of this," Quinton said. Becker's blaster dropped to the floor. "Back off, Harper."

The spider-drone took several steps back, and his micro-blaster retracted back inside the armored body.

"Let go of me," Becker said.

Quinton let him go.

Becker held his wrist to his chest. He flexed his hand a few times and then retrieved his weapon.

"I'm going to take us to the nearest star system. You can make your own way from there," Quinton said.

Becker's lips compressed to form a grim line. "Fine," he said and walked off the bridge.

"Go on," Harper said as he left. "Scurry on back to the others." Then he walked back to Quinton. "I'm with you, sir."

Quinton threw a nod to Harper. He meant well. Harper was a soldier, and Becker and the others were survivors. Harper was willing to stand and fight, while the others seemed to know the price to be paid for making a stand. This might not be a fight Quinton could win. He hated it. All of it. And he had no idea what he was going to do next.

He'd expected more from Becker. They'd been through a lot. And Oscar and Guttman would more than likely follow Becker's lead. So much for loyalty. When loyalty and survival collided, survival won. It was time for him to part ways with Becker, Oscar, and Guttman.

Quinton accessed the navigation interface and looked for the nearest star system that had a space station. They'd head there straight away, and then he'd have to come up with a plan.

13

"I SAY we take out Harper before Quinton can do anything about it," Guttman said.

"Guttman, come on," Oscar replied.

"What? He attacked Becker! He's got a weapon!" Guttman kept looking toward the door, his eyes wide as if he expected an attack to come at any moment. "I knew this was gonna happen. I just knew it."

"Yeah, right. You did not."

"Oscar, I'm telling you. I've had my doubts about Harper ever since Quinton brought him on board. He's not stable."

Oscar leaned forward, resting his elbows on the table. "Becker, what happened? Why did Harper attack you?"

Becker kept one of his hands by his blaster and sneered. "He called me a coward. He said we're all cowards."

Guttman stood up. "That's it. I say we go down to the bridge and teach that thing a lesson. I'm no damn coward. Who the hell—all of us are cowards?" he laughed bitterly and rolled his shoulder, stretching his neck from side to side.

"You need to calm down," Oscar said.

"You need to calm down," Guttman mimicked. He pressed his fists onto the table and leaned toward him. "You can't smooth-talk your way out of this, hermano."

"Because your 'storm the bridge and teach them a lesson' plan is so much better. Get real."

"You know what you can do, Oscar," Guttman said with a snarl as he stepped around the table.

Oscar glared at Guttman and inhaled explosively as he stood up. "Is there something you wanna say to me? I'm right here. Go for it."

Becker stepped between them, planting a beefy hand on each of their chests. "Guys, enough. Knock it off. We can't do this."

Guttman glared at Oscar for a moment then backed away, jerking his head from side to side. Oscar held his hands up in a placating gesture and then rested them on his hips.

Guttman jabbed a finger in Becker's direction. "Why are you so calm about this?"

Becker gritted his teeth. "You think I'm calm?"

Guttman nodded. "I've seen you upset. Hell, I've seen you go after an entire crew, numbers and odds be damned."

"What do you want me to do? We can't stop Quinton."

"The hell we can't."

Becker leveled a gaze at him. "We can't, and he's not going to let us do anything to Harper."

"Guys," Oscar said, "Quinton doesn't deserve this. He's done everything he could to help us, and we made a deal with him. So, no, I'm not going along with anything that puts us against him. You can count me out of this."

Guttman scowled. "At least we know where you stand."

Silence settled between the three men for a few long moments.

"Oscar's right," Becker said, finally. "I've got nothing against Quinton. I just want off this ship. I want to move on. Don't you?" he asked, looking at each of them in turn. "I'm tired of all this. I'm just… sick of it."

Guttman seemed to gather himself up, getting ready for another outburst, but then he sighed, and his shoulders slumped a little. "I'd love to get off this ship and go somewhere quiet. Wait for this whole thing to blow over," Guttman said.

"Cowards," Becker said, acidly.

"What if he's right?" Oscar said, drawing their attention. "Harper. What if he's right? The whole 'cowards' thing. We're just going to run away. No, I mean it."

Guttman shook his head. "I'm not a coward."

"Not just you," Oscar replied. "All of us, and it doesn't stop there. What have we always done? We've seen it in the Union and even with others outside Crowe's Union. We wait for the upper hand. We strike when others are vulnerable, and we run when we know we can't win."

"I call that surviving," Guttman said.

Oscar nodded. "Yeah, but it doesn't make us brave. Maybe we are cowards. Not," he said, drawing out the word before Guttman could interrupt, "without good reason. We need to survive, but what if it's not enough?"

Guttman rolled his eyes toward the ceiling. "You're starting to sound like a DUC recruiter."

Oscar shrugged.

"What do you want us to do?" Becker asked.

"I don't know; but doesn't leaving Quinton on his own seem wrong?"

"Wrong," Guttman scoffed. "Not everything is about right or wrong. The longer we stay here, the more likely we're going to die on this ship. Did you forget what happened on that starbase?"

"You mean the one where Quinton defended all of us against a fleet of Sentinels? That one? The same where he got us to this ship so we could escape. Yeah, you're a real piece of work." Oscar shook his head.

"Oscar," Becker said, "I don't like it any more than you do. But we've got to be realistic here. There's nothing any of us can do about the Sentinels, Crowe, or the damn Collective. Nothing," he said and looked away. "Nothing we can do."

Oscar slipped his hands into his pockets and looked away.

"If I could think of something, I'd tell him. I'd even help him, but there isn't. Guttman's right. We're dead if we stay here."

Oscar took a few steps and then turned back to face the other two. "Harper might not be stable. We even thought Quinton wasn't for a while, but there's something in both of them, something we've lost. The way he looks at us… as if he's the only one to realize it. He's not."

Guttman glanced at Becker. "What's he talking about?"

Oscar walked toward the door. "I need to get some air."

"Watch out for Harper," Guttman said.

Oscar paused at the door for a few moments.

"He's right," Becker said. "We've got to watch our backs. Quinton stopped Harper this time, but we can't rely on him always being there."

Oscar exhaled explosively. He turned around, walked to his quarters, and closed the door.

"What the hell was that all about?" Guttman asked.

"Salvager's remorse."

Guttman glanced at the door to Oscar's room and sighed. "We need to keep an eye on him. That remorse can make you do stupid things," he said and looked at Becker. "So, what happens now?"

"He'll be fine. Quinton is going to drop us off at the nearest star system that has a station or resupply depot. From there, we'll have to make our own way," Becker said.

Guttman grumbled and sat down. He opened a holoscreen and began looking at star charts.

A few seconds later, Becker joined him.

Quinton watched the video feed of the passenger lounge on his internal HUD. Both he and Harper were still on the bridge. Harper had entered a rest cycle a short time earlier, and he'd be out for a few hours.

Quinton disconnected the video feed. Forget crew cohesion now. Maybe he'd be better off with the others off the ship. He still wasn't sure what to do. Should he try to stop Crowe? How was he supposed to do that? Did that mean hunting him down wherever he was? He'd have to find him first, but the *Wayfarer* wasn't that kind of warship. It had teeth, but there were limits to what he could do with one ship. Would somehow taking out Crowe stop the attacks, or would his second-in-command take up the same fight? A Sentinel incursion sounded bad for everyone, so why would Crowe risk it happening? There were risks, and then there were risks someone takes when they think they have nothing left to lose, but still, Quinton couldn't figure out what Crowe wanted to achieve. What was his endgame? If Crowe's back was against the wall, he had no choice but to fight. If Lennix Crowe was simply trying to get the Collective to back off, these attacks would be limited. Crowe would just be trying to prove a point and the attacks should stop.

Quinton glanced at the comlink control on his workstation. He needed Becker for this. Becker knew Lennix Crowe. He'd been part of Crowe's Union for years. But then he looked away and shook his head. Only a few hours ago, he'd told Becker he was going to drop them off at the nearest spaceport, and he doubted Becker or any of the others wanted to speak to him. He considered bouncing ideas off Radek but dismissed it.

The door to the bridge opened. Becker stepped inside and stopped. "We need to talk," he said and looked over at Harper for a moment. "Alone."

"He's in a rest cycle, so we can talk here."

Becker walked toward him, his blaster holstered on his hip. Quinton did a quick query for the others. Guttman was in the galley, preparing a meal, but he also had a weapon nearby. Oscar was in his quarters.

"All of you are armed now?" Quinton asked.

"I don't want any trouble."

"Right."

"None of us feel safe around Harper. That's just the way it is."

"Unacceptable," Quinton replied. "Argh—It's my turn. I'm not going to allow everyone to walk around my ship armed and moments away from a fight. That's no way to live."

"I'm not giving up my weapon."

Becker didn't change his posture at all. He was simply stating a fact.

"Put your weapons back in the armory. Argh—again, it's my turn. There are palm stunners available. Use those for self-defense while on the ship."

"Palm stunners."

Quinton nodded. "Yeah, palm stunners. I tweaked them so they'll have no problem with… They'll work. That's all you need to worry about. I'm not going to have people blowing holes in my ship."

Becker considered this a few moments. "Do they work on you?" he asked, his tone light.

Quinton lifted his lips.

Becker snorted. "All right, fine. I'll let the others know," he said and paused. "Quinton, things got out of control."

"You think?"

"I do."

"What did you want to talk about?" Quinton asked, preferring not to kick the old drive coil.

"Iskevian Spaceport," Becker said and gestured toward the main holoscreen. A star chart appeared, showing the *Wayfarer's* coordinates and a plot to the spaceport. "It's not associated with the Collective, so it should be relatively safe. From there, we can find our own way."

Quinton looked at the coordinates. He hadn't actually picked a spaceport to leave them at yet. "Sounds good," he said and sent an update to the nav computer.

The data on the main holoscreen refreshed, showing the updated destination. Twenty-nine standard hours and they'd be at the Sunta Nebula where Iskevian Spaceport was located.

Becker nodded a little and a thoughtful frown appeared.

"There's something I'd like to run by you," Quinton said.

"All right."

"It's about Crowe. Do you think he realizes what he's doing?"

Becker pursed his lips in thought. "Yes. Even if he didn't, Carradine would know."

"Who's that?"

"Nate Carradine is Crowe's advisor. They've been partners for a long time. He keeps his head and is strategic. Crowe wouldn't do something like this without Carradine's input," Becker said.

"Okay, I'm just trying to understand what Crowe's doing."

"There's been increasing tension with the Collective."

"I understand that. He could just be doing this to get them to back off."

"Maybe."

"You're not filling me with a whole lot of confidence. If Crowe's ambitions are to rival the Collective, then he could push his advantage. Meaning that he'll continue to lure Sentinels to Collective targets and eventually force Draven to surrender."

"He could just be doing enough damage to the Collective to get them to back off."

"True," Quinton said. "But Crowe is also ambitious. If he's got someone like Carradine advising him, then I think whatever he's trying to do is more elaborate."

"What do you mean?"

"You know more about sector politics than I do, but there are power players out there. These attacks are public. Crowe isn't making a secret of what he can do. He's only hitting Collective targets, but the risk is shared by everyone if the Sentinels begin another incursion. Draven must be getting pressure from everyone else to negotiate with Crowe."

Becker nodded slowly. "I see where you're going. Yeah, I think that's accurate." He pressed his lips together and nodded again. "Yeah, that makes a lot of sense."

Quinton arched an eyebrow. "You don't have to sound so surprised."

Becker grinned a little. "I'm not… not really. But then these attacks would stop. Crowe would account for this in his overall plan."

"Precisely," Quinton said. "At first, I thought I'd need to find a way to stop him, but now I'm just thinking that he'll stop on his own once he gets what he wants."

"You mean you hope he stops."

"Well, yeah. If a Sentinel incursion is as bad as you say it is, then Crowe can't want that. What good is a power grab when the end result is much worse than the current state of affairs? He's proving a point."

"And locking in a target on his back. This isn't going to sit well with anyone."

"They don't have a choice."

Becker sighed and shook his head. "What are you going to do?"

"About Crowe, I'm not sure. I need to find a CDA for Harper."

"A CDA?"

"Consciousness Driven Android. They were designed for PMC use. It's either that or another DNA vault."

"I've never come across a CDA. My guess is that the Sentinels destroyed them first, as well as anyone who made them."

"Maybe they missed a stockpile somewhere."

Becker looked away a few moments and then turned back toward Quinton.

"This isn't your problem, Becker. That much is clear."

Becker looked as if he were going to say something but decided against it and walked away. "We'll store our weapons in the armory," he called out over his shoulder as he left the bridge.

Quinton didn't reply. He looked at their destination on the main holoscreen, feeling a spike of irritation at the thought of Crowe using his identity. How could he stop him? Harper didn't have time for Quinton to hunt down Crowe and stop the use of his ID. Crowe would no doubt have redundancies in place. Sometimes the best course of action was simply to do nothing, but it went against his instincts. He wanted to do something about it. There had to be a way to take away Crowe's ability to use Quinton's PMC credentials to lure the Sentinels.

"Radek, there are some things we need to work on."

14

EVERYONE on the *Wayfarer's* bridge became quiet. They'd just made the final jump to Iskevian Spaceport located near the Sunta Nebula. The advantage of building a spaceport away from any star systems was that ships were able to jump in relatively close proximity to the spaceport. Even a jump drive with the tiniest of range could jump within a day's journey. The *Wayfarer's* jump drive could bring them nearly on top of it, which is exactly what Quinton intended to do. Becker advised against it. No need to irritate spaceport security. They wouldn't be there long. The others would fly the shuttle to the spaceport and Quinton would remote-pilot the shuttle back to the ship.

"You can't be serious, Oscar," Guttman scoffed.

Oscar ignored him and looked at Quinton, raising his chin. "I'm saying that I'd like to stay on and help you. It's the least I can do. You've saved my life more than a few times. I owe you."

"You don't owe me anything," Quinton replied.

Harper stood on the other side of the bridge near an auxiliary workstation. He'd connected to the ship's systems using the data port.

"Don't do this," Guttman said and gestured toward Becker. "We're going to be partners. The three of us. We need you with us. Stick with the plan."

"He's right," Becker said.

"We can still be partners. I'll catch up with you guys later," Oscar replied.

Becker looked at Quinton.

"This is news to me."

Becker considered Quinton's response for a few moments and looked at Oscar. "Anytime, Oscar. You're always welcome to fly with us. I mean that."

"Thanks, Becker," Oscar said and looked at Guttman. "You two take care of each other."

"You're insane," Guttman said and gave Oscar a playful shove.

Becker walked over to Quinton and extended his hand. Quinton shook it. "Good luck, Quinton. Take care of yourself."

"You, too."

Becker and Guttman left the bridge, heading for the shuttle.

Quinton walked over to Oscar. "Are you sure about this?"

Oscar smiled. "Already trying to get rid of me?"

"No," Quinton chuckled. "It's not that," he said and glanced toward the doors to the bridge. "They're not wrong. It's going to be dangerous. You're probably better off with them, keeping down low until all this stuff blows over."

"Maybe, but then again, maybe not."

Quinton nodded once. "All right, Oscar. Thanks for sticking around."

Quinton returned to his workstation and sent a standard check-in to Iskevian Spaceport to inform them that they wouldn't require docking services. Then he sent a flight plan for the *Wayfarer's* shuttle where two passengers would disembark.

The docking clamps released the shuttle and Becker flew them to the spaceport.

He put a video feed of the traffic heading to the spaceport on the main holoscreen. They weren't far from the port, but The Eye of Sunta filled the view. It was a nebula that resembled an angry red eyeball amid a gas cloud that spread hundreds of lightyears across. The fringes were wreathed in pale gold that gradually became an expanse of blue until finally giving way to the crimson central region. Millions of years would need to pass before it might actually become a star, or possibly a brown dwarf. Either way, Quinton wouldn't be around to see it. Still, it made for a stunning backdrop for the spacers who lived on the spaceport.

"You know, I could have flown them there," Oscar said.

Quinton snorted. "Are you a glutton for punishment?" Oscar's eyebrows raised a little. "For the next half hour, you'd have had to endure Guttman's comments about how you just made the biggest mistake of your life."

"And that I should reconsider… yeah, I know."

"I can get the shuttle back to the ship."

"Where do we go from here?"

"I was thinking of Seginus Prime," Quinton replied.

"Seginus Prime?" Harper said, speaking up for the first time. "I thought we were looking for a DNA vault."

Quinton had a list of coordinates for possible DNA vault locations he'd gotten from the DUC. When he'd been aboard the *Nebulon*, they hadn't checked all the locations. Instead, they'd gone to a set of coordinates that had been locked away in his ESS.

"Not yet," Quinton replied. "Seginus is home to Golden Taos. They specialize in refurbished droids."

"Do you think they'll have CDAs there?" Harper asked.

"CDAs?" Oscar asked.

"CDAs are short for Consciousness Driven Androids. They were designed to host PMCs," Quinton said and then looked toward Harper. "Probably not, but you never know. What they will have is a service bot that will be a better fit to store your ESS. Then we can search for a DNA vault."

"How far away is Seginus Prime?" Oscar asked.

"Just a few jumps from here. It won't take long, which is a good thing."

"Why is it a good thing?" Harper asked.

Quinton wasn't going to mislead Harper. "Keeping you in that spider-drone isn't healthy."

"It's not so bad. I'm getting more used to it. Having access to my own VR helps. I've made it like I'm remotely operating this old drone," Harper said.

"Still, Greta's diagnostic reports are concerning. Operating a spider-drone for the short term is fine, but not for ongoing usage. Degradation is highly probable."

"I know. I've seen my VI's reports. She doesn't let me forget it. Degradation leads to instability and the eventual breakdown of the PMC."

"What about finding Crowe?" Oscar asked.

"I don't know, Oscar. I spoke to Becker about it. I think Crowe is playing a dangerous game, but I don't think he intends for it to get out of control," Quinton said and paused for a few moments. "I'm not sure how to find him. I thought about sending a crafted message through sector comlink channels, but who knows how long that could take."

"You couldn't use your credentials, so how would he hear about it?" Harper asked.

"I wouldn't use mine," Quinton said and glanced wryly at Oscar. "I could always use Guttman's." They shared a laugh. "To answer your question, Harper, by the time any data made its way back to me, Crowe would be long gone."

"There are higher priorities, such as tracing the activation signals," Harper said and stopped.

Quinton's gaze darted to the main holoscreen. The tracking signal for the shuttle disappeared, quickly followed by all inbound and outbound ship traffic from Iskevian Spaceport.

"The ship broadcasts are gone! Where the hell did they all go?" Oscar asked.

Quinton initiated a subspace scan pulse and found the shuttle, but there was a delay and a lot of interference. "It's still there," he said and activated the direct laser communicator since subspace was unavailable. "You have to abort. Turn the shuttle around. Come back to the ship. The spaceport is under attack."

"Can't get a signal lock. You're breaking up. Repeat. You're breaking up," Becker replied.

Quinton increased the laser comms output and repeated himself. Then he followed up with a data packet and received confirmation of receipt.

The plot on the main holoscreen changed.

"Disruptor field is active, sir," Harper said.

Several bright flashes came from the spaceport. Someone was attacking it.

"Oscar, get us on an intercept course with the shuttle. We need to close the distance before we jump out of here," Quinton said and began activating the *Wayfarer's* weapons systems.

"Course laid in, but the nav computer won't let me execute emergency jump coordinates after. It's like I'm locked out," Oscar said.

"It's the disrupter field. We'll need to breach it before we can jump," Quinton said and engaged active scans.

"Sir, let me run the scans. I can narrow the scanner range for the field disrupter generators," Harper said.

Quinton handed off control of the active scans to Harper. "Update the tactical plot as soon as the generators are detected."

"Radek, run analysis on scan data."

"What priority?"

Quinton looked at the tactical plot on the main holoscreen. Disruptor field generators had been deployed within the vicinity of the spaceport, and more appeared, which meant they'd been in hyperspace before the field had gone active.

"Sentinel ship signatures," Quinton answered finally.

When he'd last engaged the Sentinels on the Starbase Endurance, the tactical data had become part of his ESS before being transferred to the *Wayfarer*. PMCs were designed with knowledge sharing in mind, which included the retention of tactical data from engagement with enemy forces.

Outbound ships weren't able to engage their jump drives because they were caught in the disrupter field. Instead, they flew as fast as they could, hoping to breach the field long enough to execute a jump. It's what Quinton intended to do but doubted the civilian ships had the capability of detecting the field generators. They'd be flying blind. Civilian ship captains might not even know to look for the field generators.

Quinton heard Oscar speaking with Becker over a direct communications link. The disrupter field affected subspace comms.

"Tell him to get a move on it or I'll leave him behind," Quinton said.

The tactical plot updated with enemy ships—two destroyer class ships and five scout class ships. Not the best odds, but it could be worse.

"Sir, the hostiles are focusing their bombardment on the spaceport. They're not targeting the fleeing ships at all," Harper said.

"That's good. It'll give them a chance to get away then," Oscar said.

"Wouldn't be so sure about that," Quinton replied.

Powerful particle beams punched into the spaceport, cutting through escape pods and small ships that couldn't get out of the way fast enough. Quinton clenched his teeth. They didn't have the firepower to take on the Sentinel scout force, and there was nothing he could do for the spaceport. In a short time, it would be completely destroyed.

"Radek, were there any broadcasts detected with my identification?"

"No broadcasts detected by our comms systems."

Something had brought the Sentinels to the spaceport.

"Harper, give me a firing solution for field generators. We'll need to take out enough of them to escape the field," Quinton said.

"It will be difficult, sir. New field generators keep appearing on the plot."

"Standard blanket ambush tactic. Pick a direction heading away from the fighting and then we'll use best speed."

"Understood, sir," Harper replied.

"Where are they coming from?" Oscar asked.

"They're deployed in hyperspace. Once they transition to normal space, they disrupt communications and prevent ships from using their jump drives."

"How long can they keep this up?"

Quinton frowned. "Long enough," he said.

"What about the other ships? The spacers are trying to run away. Isn't there something we can do to help them? Can't you disable the field generators somehow?" Oscar asked.

The only way to disable the field generators was to destroy them. Not even the Sentinels could disable them, at least they shouldn't be able to. The generators would complete their scheduled run before going dormant. He couldn't destroy all the field generators. There wasn't anything he could do. They were outclassed but not nearly as bad as the freighters that were trying to escape.

"The shuttle just docked. Becker and Guttman are back aboard," Oscar said.

Quinton looked at the main holoscreen, and at the same time, he'd integrated with the ship's systems. He became aware of the data even before his cybernetic avatar could register that he'd seen the information on the holoscreen.

The Sentinel destroyers had split up, each attacking the spaceport from different vectors. The scout ships were scattered between them, focusing on destroying the spaceport's point defense systems—a task they'd soon be finished with—and then they'd begin focusing on the fleeing ships.

Quinton altered course to give him a clear targeting vector of the destroyer.

"Commander," Harper said, "that's the opposite course I've already laid out."

"Targeting priorities have changed," Quinton said and activated the *Wayfarer's* main weapon. A new holoscreen appeared in front of him.

Becker and Guttman came onto the bridge.

"Let's get out of here…" Becker said, his voice trailing off. "Wait, why are you attacking?"

"You better strap yourself in," Quinton said.

"We were better off in the damn shuttle," Guttman growled and hastened toward the nearest seat.

Quinton kept their speed constant. No need to give away what he was doing.

"They're going to detect us," Guttman said.

"No, they won't," Quinton said. "That's the unfortunate effect of using disrupter fields. It blinds them as much as it does us."

"Unless they've figured out a way around that limitation," Becker replied.

"They'd have to have invented a whole new field of physics if they have."

Quinton flew the *Wayfarer* along a trajectory, using the spaceport to prevent the Sentinels from noticing them.

"Commander," Harper said, "the design of those destroyers is based on ACN Leviathan class."

As Harper shared the information he had on the destroyer, Quinton merged the data with his own knowledge base and updated his firing solution.

"So that's what's on the upper deck," Becker said.

"What's on the upper deck?" Guttman asked.

"It's a tachyon lance," Quinton said.

"Oh, that explains it," Guttman said.

A secondary reactor came online, and its status appeared on the main holoscreen.

"I was wondering where the power draw was going to come from," Becker said.

"You've seen this before?" Harper asked.

"Not on a ship this size. Crowe was trying to get a lance working on one of the Jordani cruisers they'd found."

"That's never going to work. Jordani Federation ships didn't have the capability of producing the power required," Quinton said.

"And this ship does?"

Quinton didn't reply. He authorized the power tap and tasked a VI to manage the power flow. It had to be carefully monitored or it would overload the ship's power systems.

"Field is stable," Harper said.

"Prepare to route the power to the lance," Quinton replied.

He aligned the ship to be within targeting range and then fired the lance. The focus emitter arrays locked into position and the lance became active. High energy-focused particle beams more powerful than what the Sentinel destroyers were using pierced the armored hull of the ship. Quinton kept the tachyon lance active while it burned through the interior of the destroyer, making its way to the computing core.

"Oh my God, you're using a power tap, but that's prone to—" Becker said and was cut off.

Klaxon alarms blared and red flashing lights came on. Power levels from the tap spiked to critical levels. A shudder could be felt throughout the ship.

"Closing the tap," Harper said.

The tachyon lance stopped. The system had overloaded and needed a cool-down cycle.

"You've disabled their ship," Oscar said. "Look, it's not firing anymore. It's on a collision course with the spaceport."

"Hot damn," Guttman said. "I didn't know this ship could do that."

"Not for long. We can only sustain the lance in short bursts," Quinton said.

The power tap was still drawing power.

"I can't get the tap to close. There are fluctuations on the other end keeping it open," Harper said.

Quinton altered course and engaged maximum thrust. The reactionless drive kicked in and they began flying away from the spaceport.

"Can't we finish them off?" Guttman asked.

"We can't," Quinton replied.

"Then why did you attack in the first place?"

"To cause confusion. They weren't expecting anything like what just happened."

"Yeah, but if you can do it once—"

"No, Guttman," Becker said. "He just gave the spacers a fighting chance to get away."

Quinton tried to disrupt the power tap, but it wouldn't disengage. Siphoning power from higher dimensions ran the risk of erratic power surges that could force the tap to remain active. There was only one way to dislodge it.

"Go to your own life support," Quinton said.

The others engaged the emergency life-support systems from their seats. Emergency helmets protracted over their heads.

The power tap wouldn't disengage because there wasn't enough negative energy to disrupt the field. Quinton sent a burst of negative energy into the tap, and the ship's main power reactor began to drain. He quickened his frame rate exponentially. Capacity alerts sprang into his consciousness, which he had to ignore or he'd lose the ship. His army of VI assistants each made their analysis of the power tap available to him. It was as if he'd become aware of hundreds of analyses at once, and within the multitude of data he found a pattern. There was always an order to the universe, even if he was incapable of understanding it without Radek's help. Quinton siphoned off more negative energy from the ship's main power core and then ordered his VIs to insert the negative energy in bursts into the power tap. The effect was instantaneous. The field to the higher dimensional energy began to lose its hold and then the channel closed.

Quinton's frame rate snapped back to normal. The main engines stopped and they went to emergency power throughout the ship. Becker shouted his name.

Quinton held up his finger. "Harper, get ready to execute firing solution alpha."

"Firing solution ready."

The entire system had to be reset, which was mostly automated on the *Wayfarer*. At least it was supposed to be.

Quinton cursed and stood up.

"What can we do to help?" Becker asked.

"Follow me," he said and ran off the bridge.

Becker and Guttman followed him. Harper and Oscar stayed on the bridge.

Quinton made it to the maintenance hatch and slid down two decks. He opened a comlink to Becker and Guttman. "We have to restore main power before we can do anything else. The whole system is overloaded. I had to use up most of the core to sever the power tap."

"Okay, manual reset," Becker replied.

Quinton assigned a set of power relays to each of them. The *Wayfarer* wasn't a huge ship, but there were six relays spaced throughout the ship. The purpose of the relays was to route power away from the core in the event of an overload. Quinton was pretty sure the reqs had meant something along the lines of catastrophic overload. Even as fast as he could move, he couldn't physically be in more than one place at a time.

He ran to the relay, which was in the overload position, looking like an exposed cylinder a meter across. He rotated the cylinder, shoved it back into place, and continued. By the time he got to the fourth relay, Becker and Guttman had gotten to theirs.

Quinton initiated the power core reset. A violent shudder vibrated the walls and floor around them.

"Sentinel scout ships are firing on us," Harper said.

Quinton brought up the tactical plot and saw that the scout ships had launched a kinetic bombardment. They were just out of point defense range and were maintaining the distance.

Clever.

Quinton routed emergency power to missile tubes and granted Harper access to the missiles so he could directly interface with them. Small swarmer missiles launched in large volleys. That ought to buy them some time and overwhelm the scout ships' point defense systems.

Systems began to come back online, and Quinton started to head back to the bridge.

"Quinton, the jump drive coils won't align," Oscar said over comms.

"On my way," Quinton said. "You should get main engines back soon… There they are."

"I'm on it," Oscar said and began initiating the main engine restart.

Quinton stopped in the middle of the corridor. "Radek, I need a jump coil diagnostic."

"Complete," Radek replied. "The ship has taken damage near the jump drive."

"Can we bypass the damaged coils?"

"Negative, there are too many coils out of alignment, and there are whole sections that would breach safety protocols."

Jump drives required a minimum number of coils in order to fold space. Since none of them wanted to be obliterated while they tried to make the jump, he'd have to come up with a solution.

"Show me the damaged sections," Quinton said.

Radek showed him a schematic of the jump drive and the sections of coils that surrounded it. One section had overloaded. He studied the schematic and an idea came to mind. There was a part of his brain that sought to solve problems regardless of survivability. It simply presented a solution, and some chance of survival was better than no chance.

"I'm sorry. It's impossible for the ship to jump until the coils are repaired. Time to replace the damaged sections will take repair drones a minimum of twenty-two hours. Shall I begin the repair cycle?" Radek asked.

"Negative," Quinton said and started running toward the drive core.

He passed Becker and Guttman.

"Where are you going?" Becker asked.

They weren't able to match his stride.

"I'm going to kick the jump drive. You should head back to the bridge," Quinton said.

As he ran down the corridor, he checked Harper's status. His utilization was near the limits of the spider-drone, even with the help of the ship's computer system.

He opened a comlink to Oscar.

"Main engines are online. We're moving. Harper won't respond to me," Oscar said.

"He's busy. Just make sure the ship stays on course."

"Oh good. Disrupter field generators are going offline. The scout ships are falling behind, or at least I think they are. Without scans, I'm not exactly sure of their location. They're not firing on us anymore. The jump drive is still offline."

"I'm going to take care of it. You'll need to act quickly."

"Me? Won't you be able to initiate the jump from where you are?"

"I might not be able to," Quinton said. "I don't have time to go into it. Just be ready as soon as the jump drive status changes."

Quinton closed the comlink. One thing that had been drilled into him since he'd first served aboard a warship was that shipboard diagnostics, while very informative, couldn't solve the mechanical problems on a ship. They were advisors and could only function amid a rigid set of controls. This limitation was one of the founding principles that PMCs had been designed to overcome.

Quinton hastened through the bulkhead doors and into the jump drive chamber. The coils' housing units were mounted to both the floor and the ceiling with enough space for Quinton to squeeze through, though the space was normally occupied by maintenance drones.

"One Sentinel scout ship disabled," Harper said, "but the other one is on its way. It disabled the remaining swarmer missiles. It must have analyzed my attack pattern. I can't spare any more missiles."

"It's fine. Focus on the disrupter field generators."

"Yes, sir," Harper said and paused for a moment. "Sir, what are you doing—"

"Focus, Harper."

"Right, sir."

The comlink severed.

Quinton quickly made his way to the interior of the jump drive coil system. The entire jump coil housing units were offline, but Quinton couldn't see any visible damage. He took control of several maintenance drones and sent them to do a physical inspection. They'd initiate repairs if they could. Quinton continued forward and stopped at the sections that couldn't be bypassed. The Sentinel mag cannons had penetrated the outer hull and into the chamber. They weren't venting atmosphere because emergency shields had been initiated to compensate until the hull was repaired.

Quinton severed the jump coils' housing units so they were no longer part of the jump drive system. Between doing that and overriding all the safety protocols, he forced the ship's computer system to report a green status for the jump drive. That was the good part. The bad part was that he had to stay here with the jump drive to physically bridge the connections between the damaged sections. The avatar was capable of withstanding a significant but brief power surge. He just needed to hold on long enough for the drive to work.

"I don't know how you did it, but jump drive is green."

"What are you waiting for?" Quinton asked, then checked the tactical plot on his internal HUD. They were seconds from breaching the weakening disruptor field. Active scans showed the Sentinel scout ship pursuing them.

"Initiating jump," Oscar said.

Quinton detected the power spike in the jump drive as it spooled up. The jump drive distorted space surrounding the ship and then folded it, allowing the ship to travel to the emergency coordinates. The initial folded space from the drive was so intense that the jump drive had to be shielded from the rest of the ship. As folded space expanded to fill the distorted space, it became less dangerous. Quinton felt as if his entire body was being disassembled on the molecular level, every atom stripped away. His last thought before being pulled into darkness was that maybe he should have sent Harper to fix the damn jump drive.

15

SYSTEM DIAGNOSTIC RUNNING.

The words appeared amid the darkness of his thoughts. Where was he?

Veris initiation complete.

Cybernetic repair cycle has completed successfully.

Leuridium power core stable. Irreparable damaged sections have been removed.

Energy Storage System functioning nominally.

Personality Matrix Construct has passed all integrity checks. Integration optimal.

System startup complete.

Autonomous mode has been activated.

"Hello, Quinton," Radek said.

Quinton opened his eyes. He saw the curve of an opaque ceraphome door less than a meter in front of him and heard Becker and the others speaking in the room beyond.

"What happened?" Quinton asked Radek sub-vocally.

"Over seventy percent of the cybernetic avatar had been damaged beyond the capacity of the onboard repair capabilities of the unit."

"Seventy percent!"

Quinton looked down to see that he was in the avatar's storage container aboard the *Wayfarer*. He raised his hands. They looked like his own hands but for the chrome-colored "skin" of the advanced composites that comprised his musculature. His full sensory interface was working, which meant he could see, smell, and feel. He rubbed his thumb and forefingers together, noticing the muscles in his arms moving in a perfect copy of true flesh and blood.

"Seventy point four eight zero one—"

"I get it," Quinton snapped. His leuridium power core had been damaged by the jump drive.

His avatar provided the most protection in the chest area where his ESS was stored. The cybernetic avatar's design was based on a human body and, much like evolution, had developed the skeletal framework of musculature to protect the most critical parts of a person—the brain, heart, and lungs. The avatar was similar.

He'd almost died. Really died, as in utter destruction to the point of never being able to come back. Death. Finality. Quinton felt a shiver sweep down his spine. He'd known it could happen, and he understood the risks when he'd gone into the jump drive chamber to fix the coils. He thought there was a good chance he would survive, but seventy percent damage to the avatar… It had been more than a mere close call. Death had torn open the door, and the only thing that prevented it from claiming him was the design of the avatar whose built-in safety protocols were part of the base system his PMC used.

Quinton blinked his eyes several times while he considered his mortality. If he'd died, would he have felt anything? He doubted his death would be like when a flesh-and-blood person died and a bunch of chemical reactions occurred in the brain as the body shut down. What would his last moments have been like? Would he experience all the thoughts and feelings as one's life flashed before their eyes at the moment of death? This was the second time he'd almost died, and neither time had he experienced any of the things he'd expected to feel. He hadn't thought about his life or anyone, remaining focused on what had to be done. It was a hollow and empty feeling, and it worried him. He didn't like it. Maybe the engineers who designed PMCs had overlooked something.

"I've detected a severe spike of emotions," Radek said.

Damn VI, monitoring everything about him. He cursed inwardly.

"You think! How the hell should I react?"

Radek didn't reply, and Quinton heard Guttman speaking.

"If we'd gotten to that spaceport an hour earlier, we'd be dead," Guttman said.

"Yeah," Becker said in agreement.

"Makes you think," Oscar said.

"What? That leaving might not be the best option right now?" Guttman asked.

"You tell me."

Guttman sighed.

Quinton heard someone walking toward the holding container where he'd been rebuilt.

The outline of Becker's large, dark shadow came closer, as if he was trying to peer inside. "Is this going to work?"

"How should we know?" Guttman said.

"I don't know," Oscar said. "I know it's not just a storage container, and the menu options indicated that it could repair the damage."

Becker stepped away. "I don't know what else to do."

"There's always Harper."

"No, thanks," Becker replied. "I wish we had someone like Tolman or Fisher with us."

"Geez, Tolman," Guttman said. "He thought he could crack any secure system."

"All tech experts are like that," Oscar said.

"I know. We could use their help."

"Tolman had the worst breath. He could smell up a room with stink, it was so bad," Guttman said and grinned a little.

"Fisher had that head tick where he almost constantly nodded when he was working. It was distracting to be on runs with him," Oscar said.

Becker chuckled. "Yeah," he said. "What about that kid... Simon?"

"Oh yeah," Oscar agreed. "Webb. Simon Webb. He was good. Really good. Figured out that Quinton was a PMC before anyone else did."

"Yeah, but he's loyal to the DUC," Guttman said.

"He was, but I think he was more loyal to Maelyn Wayborn," Becker said.

"The boy had a crush, you think?" Guttman asked.

"Probably," Oscar replied.

"She was... impressive," Becker said.

Quinton updated the avatar's configuration so he looked like his normal self. Skin tone, hair, and even his eyes were all back to normal. He commanded the door to open and the others looked at him.

Quinton stepped out of the container and regarded them. "I almost died, and you ladies are talking about who likes who. What are you, a knitting circle?" He grinned and the others joined in.

"Good to have you back," Becker said.

"I guess I have you guys to thank for that."

Becker glanced at the others. "Yeah, we carried all the... pieces and assembled them in the chamber."

Quinton winced. "I guess I owe you all around."

"Shit," Guttman said, exhaling forcefully. "You pulled all our asses out of the fire again."

The others nodded in agreement.

"Maybe leaving isn't the safest choice after all," Quinton said.

Becker's eyebrows raised, and then he shook his head. "You were listening to us."

Quinton snorted. "Well, yeah. Wouldn't you? I mean the conversation was just so fascinating." He smiled and then added, "It wasn't that long. I'd only just come out of it and Radek was bringing me up to speed. Where's Harper?"

"He's in the middle of a rest cycle," Becker replied.

Quinton made an uh-huh sound. "And is everyone getting along?"

Becker's expression went flat, as did Guttman's.

"We've been repairing the ship," Oscar said. "There was significant damage in certain areas. Harper and the repair drones were able to fix the coils' housing units. They've made a lot of progress on that front."

"How come you never told us that this ship had a power tap or a damn tachyon lance?" Becker asked.

"It didn't seem relevant," Quinton replied. Becker and the others frowned.

"I'm serious. You remember the condition the ship was in after… you know. But it wasn't essential."

"I've never heard of a power tap on a ship this size," Becker said.

Quinton nodded. "Evidently, there's a reason for that."

"Yeah, but you were able to disable a Sentinel destroyer!" Guttman said.

"Only because we took them by surprise. Once they report in, they'll be ready for it," Quinton said.

"Still," Becker said, leaning back against a workbench and crossing his arms. "It would have been nice to know."

Quinton shrugged. "Now you do. Consider yourself on the inside track now," he said and regarded the others for a few seconds. "Iskevian Spaceport was supposed to be independent, as in not part of the Collective."

Becker nodded. "They're not." Guttman and Oscar agreed. "They're run by the Omicron Coalition. No ties to the Collective at all."

Quinton's eyebrows pinched together. "Then why did the Sentinels attack? What were they doing there?"

"I have no idea," Becker replied. "I've checked the ship's communication logs and there weren't any broadcasts."

"We might not have been there long enough."

Becker nodded. "That's what I was thinking, too."

"Then why would Crowe target the spaceport? Is there any strategic advantage that I don't know about?"

"I can't think of anything," Guttman said.

"Same here," Oscar replied.

"Only if Crowe was trying to make the rest of the galaxy aware that he could hit them, as well as the Collective," Becker said.

Quinton considered it for a few moments. "In order to get others to pressure Draven and the Collective to give Crowe what he wants."

Becker pressed his lips together for a second and tilted his head to one side. "I don't know. I mean, that's pretty ruthless, even for Crowe. He still needs to continue his business after this shadow conflict with the Collective is resolved. What good does it do him if instead of creating pressure for Draven, people started going after Crowe?"

"Who do they hate more?"

"Good point. Crowe could be banking on the perception that the Collective left him with no choice but to do these things."

"That's still pretty damn ruthless. It's too much," Quinton said and looked at the others. "He's gone too far. How many people have to die before they stop?"

"I agree," Becker said. "The other groups aren't going to take this lying down. There's probably already some mobilization going on, but the problem is the Sentinels."

"What about them?" Quinton asked. "Besides the obvious, I mean."

"If groups of spacers start mobilizing for a fight—and there's already increased Sentinel activity—Crowe would be the least of our worries. Once an incursion starts, there's no stopping it," Becker said.

Quinton needed to know more about the previous incursion. He wanted to question it because he didn't want to believe it was as bad as the others feared, but he'd be wrong. The certainty of it was written on the faces of Becker and the others, and he had to trust that.

"Then we need to stop Crowe."

"How the hell are we gonna do that?" Guttman asked.

"We find him."

"Yeah, and then what?"

"That depends on where we find him. We take him out ourselves, or we get others to help us do it," Quinton said.

Crowe was using Quinton's PMC identification to lure the Sentinels into attacking unsuspecting targets. He still needed to help Harper, but he couldn't ignore this. If he could figure out how Crowe was doing it, he could come up with an effective countermeasure. But if he could find Crowe, he could stop what he was doing at the source.

"We can't do this alone," Becker said.

"I know, but we can't advertise what we're doing either."

"Agreed. We'll need to come up with a plan," Becker said.

"We?" Quinton regarded them all for a few moments.

Becker looked at Guttman, who gave him a nod. "Looks that way," Becker said.

Oscar cleared his throat. "For the record, I was already going to help Quinton with this."

Becker looked at Oscar with mock severity. "And your point is?"

Oscar smiled. "I'm better than both of you. You just wanted to leave, but I stayed." He looked at them, nodding his head in a self-satisfied way. "I think you both should tidy up my quarters for the next month, for starters."

Becker rolled his eyes. "Yeah, you win, buddy. Oscar is the winner."

Hearty laughter bubbled out of all of them.

"It's about time someone acknowledged it. Don't you feel better now that you did?"

These were the moments Quinton liked the most—the camaraderie and surety of purpose. It reminded him of his time in the Acheron Confederacy Navy, but at the same time, it was different. These were different men than the spacers he'd served with.

"You're right. I'm getting all weepy-eyed," Becker said.

"Now you've done it. The big guy does care," Quinton said.

Another round of chuckles. Then Becker gave him an appraising look. "Are you back to normal now?"

"As normal as can be expected."

"I'm serious. You were in bad shape."

"Well, I don't want to repeat the process. Spare materials were used to patch me up, but it was a close thing," Quinton said. "Were you worried you'd be stuck with Harper?"

Becker looked at him solemnly. "I'd be lying if I said I wasn't concerned. I think you need to keep a closer eye on him."

"Unbelievable," Quinton replied. "He helped defend the ship and you still don't trust him."

"I don't, and I'm sorry it bothers you," Becker said. Quinton looked away, but Becker stepped in front of him. "I'm not trying to cause trouble. All I'm saying is that you need to keep a closer eye on him."

"I do. He has restricted access to the ship's systems."

"So did you on the *Nebulon*, but you still found a way around that," Becker said and held up his hand in a placating gesture. "I know this is different. I've been checking some of the logs."

Quinton looked at him for a long moment. Becker knew what he was doing when it came to ships. He'd figured out that Vonya had betrayed them to Crowe. "All right, you've got my attention. What did you find?"

"Nothing."

"Nothing," Quinton repeated.

"That's right. Nothing. He's covering up what he does in the ship's systems. Not completely. There are some log entries, but something isn't right."

Quinton thought about it. Oscar and Guttman were silent.

"I figured you'd know more about it or might be able to check into it. You know, watch out for it," Becker said.

"You mean spy on him."

Becker shrugged. "If he's got nothing to hide, you won't find anything, but if you do find something, wouldn't you rather know before it escalates into something dangerous?"

"We're just asking that you check into it," Oscar said.

"All right, I will," Quinton said.

16

LENNIX CROWE HAD SPENT MORE time on *Union Cruiser Savage* than he had any other ship in a long time. Pragmatism had become the need, which required his presence in leading offensive operations against the Collective. He glanced around the conference room. The faded glory of a blue and gold crescent star adorned the walls, and smooth, gleaming surfaces surrounded a holotank in the middle of the room. He shifted in his seat. These chairs weren't nearly as comfortable as the ones on his previous flagship. *Savage* was a warship through and through, which provided very little in the way of creature comforts.

Multiple holoscreens were sourced above the holotank, showing the people who were essential to the Union. Crowe's Union was more than just another assembly of extensive resources fueled by salvage, mercenary, and shipping operations. It was very much his Union, but it was also theirs. No amount of compensation could guarantee loyalty. Belief in the mission was what held the Union together, which was more crucial now than it had ever been.

There was a shift in movement along his peripheral vision that tugged at his attention. Carradine leaned forward, peering intently at his personal holoscreen.

Lennix looked back at the speaker highlighted on the holoscreen. "Continue, Captain Nakada."

"Our scouts have confirmed that the Sentinels are no longer in the Kizu Star System, and Chiba Station has been destroyed. A few of the domed cities of Boros Colony were damaged from the battle, but the Sentinels ignored them for the most part."

"Have the salvage teams begin recovery operations immediately," Lennix said.

"Understood, sir. We've alerted newsnets about the attack and expect the Collective to send recovery teams," Nakada said.

"They'll be too late, I think," Lennix replied, the edges of his lips lifting a little. "Excellent work, Captain. Convey my congratulations to your crew."

"Thank you, sir," Nakada said.

Carradine cleared his throat and looked at Crowe. "I'm sorry to interrupt, but I've just received the latest intelligence briefings."

Lennix regarded him with eyes of burnt almond and nodded. Then, he turned toward the holoscreens. "Senior captains remain. Everyone else can go. Resume normal daily operations."

Many of the holoscreens disappeared, leaving a dozen senior Union captains.

Crowe looked at Carradine. "What have you got for us, Nate?"

"Operation Undermine continues to be highly successful. Draven has become preoccupied with protecting his assets, but he's still scouting for Union operations in multiple sectors. The losses we've sustained were expected, but the damage to the Collective has been much worse. For anyone else, it would have been catastrophic."

The Collective was the single largest independent salvage, mercenary, and trade conglomerate in the galaxy. They rivaled the remnant federations and star empires throughout the galactic sectors.

"No doubt Draven is feeling the pressure," Lennix said.

"But there have been some alarming developments," Carradine replied. "We'll need to confirm some of these, but there have been reports of Sentinel attacks on unauthorized targets that have nothing to do with the Collective."

"Could someone else have found a way to copy our attack?"

Carradine shook his head. "I've reviewed the mission reports. Our method is contained. In fact, the only thing Draven's intelligence agents have been able to figure out is the initial broadcast that's tied to the attacks. They've pushed out security updates in an effort to block it, but they're still blind to our tactics and methodologies. It'll be easy to circumvent their security measures, but we need to address the issue of these other places being attacked by the Sentinels."

"Where else has been hit?"

Carradine gestured toward the holoscreen where a new sub-window appeared.

Lennix's eyes widened. "This many? Are you sure about this?"

Carradine nodded. "We need to validate some of these accounts, but they're only the attacks we know about. There could be more."

"The primary risk always was that the Sentinels would increase their patrols in known population centers."

"That's true, but the attack patterns are almost exactly the same as our methodology. We'll be blamed for all of them."

Lennix cursed. He stood up, clenched his teeth, and interlaced his fingers atop his head. "We've been double-crossed."

"It would seem so," Carradine agreed.

Lennix released his hands and peered at the report again.

"They're going to blame us for these attacks," Captain Nakada said, and the other senior captains agreed.

Their goal had been simple. They had to get the Collective to back off and allow them to keep building up the Union. He hadn't meant for the Sentinels to begin widespread attacks. Their operations, while it had risks, were designed to be precise within a wide range of targets to convey a clear message to the Collective, as well as anyone who supported them. The Collective maintained their operations through populated galactic sectors right alongside everyone else. They'd been careful to avoid the most populated star systems.

"Should we continue with Operation Undermine?" Nakada asked.

Lennix inhaled deeply, holding his breath for a few long moments before he released it and looked at the others. "Continue with existing operations. Hold on any new targets until we get more information."

The senior captains acknowledged their orders and the various comlinks disconnected, leaving Lennix alone with Carradine.

"It doesn't make any sense," Lennix said, finally.

Carradine knew to wait him out while he gathered his thoughts. "Desher delivered exactly what he promised us, but we were nearly there on our own. We only needed him to get us across the finish line by using that PMCs identity we pulled from the starbase, but he never promised anything else."

Lennix shook his head. He'd never liked dealing with information brokers, and Admen Desher wasn't any different. "This is what happens when we go into business with someone we don't really know."

"Desher gave us what we needed to survive."

"It has to be him," Lennix said and paused for a few seconds, considering. "What I don't understand is why. Why would he do this? What does he gain by it?" Lennix asked and shook his head. "We need to find him. He needs to be neutralized."

"We could release his identity. Let Draven hunt him down for us," Carradine said.

Lennix thumped his knuckles on the edge of the holotank a few times. "No one will believe us, and too many questions would be asked. Our shadow war with Draven hasn't been as clandestine as we'd hoped. We need to circulate a profile of Desher's ship and then broadcast an anonymous bounty for any information about it."

Carradine frowned in thought. "He'll know it's us looking for him."

"That's fine."

Carradine nodded and looked away for a few seconds.

"That look," Lennix said. "I'm not going to like this, am I?"

"It's just a thought."

"I've learned long ago to trust those instincts of yours. Let's hear it."

"The same instincts that advised you to deal with Admen Desher?"

"Nate, just get to the damn point. The sooner you tell me about this idea of yours, the sooner we can do something about it."

Carradine sighed. "What if—and I stress *what if*—Desher himself is a PMC?"

Lennix's thoughts flatlined as he contemplated. "Can't be. There's no way."

Carradine raised his eyebrows. "Consider the possibility for a moment."

"Fine. Consider away for me then."

"All right. Desher understood exactly what we were trying to do."

"That makes him clever, not a PMC."

"He's familiar with Sentinels and their protocols."

Lennix shook his head a little. "Still not conclusive."

"I'm not going for irrefutable. However, if I'm right, there's more at work here than an information broker gone rogue."

Lennix frowned in concentration. "That still doesn't explain what he's trying to do."

"What if he just wants to agitate the Sentinels? Maybe even trigger an incursion," Carradine said.

Lennix's eyes went flat. "All the more reason for us to find him. Lay a trap of our own and get rid of him. But I still think we're only seeing a partial picture here. We need more information."

"Agreed on all counts."

Lennix placed his palms on the edge of the holotank and rocked back and forth a few moments. All communications with Desher had been secured to protect both their identities. He glanced at Carradine as his mind made mental leaps of logic. "Nate, I really hope you're wrong."

Carradine swallowed hard. "I do, too, for both our sakes."

If they weren't wrong, they might have encountered a PMC from the Federation Wars, but unlike Quinton Aldren, Admen Desher could be the kind that the Sentinels were meant to hunt down and destroy.

"We need to proceed carefully," Lennix said, "as much as we can."

17

"A SUCCESSFUL JUMP," Oscar said.

Quinton read the report on his personal holoscreen. Oscar was right. "Run a full diagnostic on the drive and coils. We need to make sure we've worked out all the issues."

"The preliminary reports look good. Coils are properly aligned and are operating within acceptable safety parameters," Harper said.

"And the bypass?" Quinton asked.

"No errors reported."

They'd had to reduce the number of jump coils, which affected how far they could travel. The *Wayfarer's* range was still vastly superior to most ships, according to Becker, but what did he know? He'd only spent the bulk of his life on ships.

"That's good. We're still operating without any spares, which isn't ideal. Our effective range is going to diminish if we don't get more. That is, unless any of you know how to make some and have been holding out on me," Quinton said and eyed them all for a moment. "Couldn't hurt to ask, I guess. Let me know if the diagnostic turns up anything else."

"Understood," Harper replied without including "sir" or "commander."

Quinton wasn't sure if this meant that Harper was beginning to accept the circumstances as they were, or he'd simply forgotten. Quinton had given him more to do on the ship, which he knew worried the others, but Harper needed to be invested in what they were doing. Relegating him to the background was only going to hasten the degradation of his PMC. Quinton understood the struggle, although Harper dealt with it in his own way. It was going to have to be enough.

Quinton looked at Becker. "Once we confirm that the drive is good to go, we can go after your old boss. How do we find him?"

"You're not going to like it."

"If you say we have to go to another information broker, I'm throwing myself out the airlock… and I'm taking you with me."

"It's the quickest way to get information. They compile it from multiple sources. You want to find Crowe fast, then this is the way," Becker replied.

"No, it's not. It's convenient at best. I'll grant you that."

Becker's mouth twitched in annoyance. "I hope you've got a better idea."

"I might. I was thinking we cut out the middleman and go for the source."

"How do you propose we do that?"

"How about I make him an offer he can't refuse?" Quinton said, and Becker simply stared at him. "Send him a message—a specially crafted message that can only be opened by him."

"How would that work?" Oscar asked.

"It's simple," Harper said without looking away from his workstation.

"Yes," Oscar prompted.

The silence stretched, and then Harper turned the drone's optics over toward them.

Quinton nodded encouragingly.

"Yeah, it's simple. Just have him authenticate the message in such a way that confirms his identity. I imagine with your intimate knowledge of the Union, this task shouldn't be that difficult," Harper said.

Quinton smiled and looked at Becker. "There you have it."

"Okay, that could work, but—"

"We'll send a bunch of messages to all the old Union contacts you guys can think of. I expect that at least some of them are still being monitored by Crowe," Quinton said.

Becker glanced at Oscar. "Maybe," he said, sounding unconvinced.

Quinton frowned. "What do you mean 'maybe'? Crowe is a businessman. He needs resources even as he strikes at Collective targets. There's no way he can do this without a supply line of some sort from multiple sources for redundancy. We'll give him a way to contact us."

"You can't be serious. We can't just wait for him to reply."

Quinton gave him an incredulous look. "Duh. No one said anything about sitting here doing nothing. We've got plenty of other things to do. But I want to know how you plan to get him to authenticate."

Becker leaned back and his seat reclined a little. He rubbed his chin while he thought about it. "Crowe has likely increased security, so trying to slip past those measures might be more trouble than it's worth."

"Okay," Quinton said slowly.

"If the message came from me, that might make it through the chain," Becker said.

"Becker, are you sure about this?" Oscar asked.

Becker shrugged and then nodded. "We left. Crowe knows it. We're not dead, and sure, maybe we can keep operating under the scanner and not get noticed by the Union, but I'm starting to not care. That doesn't mean I would put myself on Crowe's tactical plot, but I think he's got enough going on that wanting to get revenge on a couple of former employees is a little beyond him right now. Like Quinton said, Crowe is a businessman."

Quinton stood up and clapped his hands slowly. "Wow," he said. "You finally realized that Crowe doesn't own you."

"I never thought he owned us, but it was more profitable and safer if we stayed away. At least until your sorry ass came along," Becker said.

Quinton remembered how scared Becker and the others had been about leaving the Union on the promise that it would be worth their while. It had taken a lot longer to collect on it, but this was the first time any of them had mentioned that moving on from Crowe's Union might not have been as detrimental to their health as they'd previously thought.

Becker looked at Quinton and smiled—not just a companionable smile but one he recognized.

"You're going to make me pay for this, aren't you?"

Becker nodded. "Duh," he said, mimicking Quinton. "With interest… a whole lot of interest."

"And here I thought we were working for the good of the galaxy."

"That doesn't mean we have to go broke doing it. Plus, I'm providing you a valuable service. My connections are going to help you get past all the standard bureaucracy and go right to the source."

Quinton snorted. "You're laying it on kinda thick, aren't you? I mean… what if you can't deliver? That would really be… hmmm, what's the word I'm looking for? Ah, yes—unfortunate." He smiled. "I'd need to be reimbursed," he said, "with interest. A whole heck of a lot of it."

"You won't be sorry you made this deal."

Quinton grinned.

"Enough already," Oscar said. "Quinton, what are you going to include in the message?"

"A strongly worded letter advising him to stop or else," Quinton replied.

Oscar blinked several times, and Quinton continued. "A couple of things, actually. Definitely a message from yours truly, but also a few things to infiltrate his communication systems."

"Don't broadcast a signal to the Sentinels," Oscar said.

Quinton nodded. "Of course not. That goes without saying. No, I thought I'd utilize a tactic that Vonya released on the starbase. Something persistent. Something that will seek out exactly how they're signaling the Sentinels and either remove it altogether or change the targets. I haven't decided what I'm going to do. I might do both of them, maybe more… You know, use a randomizer, so the options are always different. Their security systems will have trouble tracking that."

"You can do that?" Becker asked.

"Yeah."

"I guess I'm a little surprised. Who'd have thought that a commander in the Acheron Confederacy Navy could do that," Becker replied.

"What do you think we do? Roam the decks barking orders when we're not on the bridge stating the obvious or being tyrants to our officers?"

Harper's chuckle blossomed into a hearty laugh, and after a few moments, Quinton joined him. Then he looked at Becker.

"All right, there was some of that. I know *I've* served under my fair share of those commanders. But there was more to the ACN than simply having the most capable weapons. We lacked ships, so we had to make the ones we did have more capable than other federations, empires, or star kingdoms. This included data warfare. Infiltration systems were something we were the best at."

Harper looked at Quinton. "I'm so glad to hear you say that, sir. I was beginning to think you'd forgotten."

Quinton *couldn't* forget, and sometimes it was a curse, but not always. "I didn't forget," he said and looked at Becker. "Anyway, yeah, we're multi-talented. I'll have it ready by the time we jump within range of a galactic comms net."

"I never really thought about it. That you also could do that stuff," Becker said.

"Me either," Oscar agreed.

"Yeah, we're all full of surprises," Quinton said.

The temperature in the room seemed to decrease a little, as if the mood had shifted as it sometimes did when they were all faced with the fact that they were from two very different worlds—one of which had existed before the Federation Wars that devastated the galaxy Quinton had woken up to where the survivors of the Federation Wars limped onward in a struggle to survive and rebuild what they could.

They went back to their workstations and Quinton sat in the commander's seat, beginning to craft the message he wanted Lennix Crowe to receive. He drew from his brief experience aboard one of Crowe's space stations when he'd been stuck in an old agricultural bot. He added a few extra options for the worm to be more reactive once it infiltrated Crowe's Union ships. He'd had to draw from his experience as a tactical officer where he'd specialized in cyber warfare. The standard communication and systems protocols hadn't changed that much since the Federation Wars. The Sentinels were part of the reason for the stagnation, but PMC detection systems had been more developed since he'd been uploaded. He could have crafted a message that embedded a specialized version of one of his VIs, but he didn't want to risk detection. He'd settled for a dumbed-down reactive version of the worm and hoped for the best. He had Radek check his work to make sure the outcomes he expected were the ones that would actually happen. Radek did this by creating virtual environments and testing thousands of outcomes in seconds.

"Quinton," Oscar said.

Quinton turned in his seat to look at him. "Yes?"

"I have a list of coordinates that will put us in range of a galactic comms net. Do you want to check them over?"

"Pick one," Quinton said.

"You got it."

The ship made another successful jump without any issues with the drive coils or the drive itself, and it was reasonable to believe that the jump drive would continue to work reliably moving forward. If only they could guarantee everything else would go as smoothly.

"Are you ready yet, Becker?" Quinton asked.

"Just finished. You can upload at any time."

Quinton authorized the upload to the comms net. He also allowed various updates, including navigational data and other data from the lone comms buoy.

"Radek, analyze the data we've just received and let me know if there's anything we need to take a look at," Quinton said.

Oscar laughed, reading something on the holoscreen in front of him. He looked at them and shrugged. "They're still broadcasting messages about ship warranties backed by—you're going to love this—Three Moons Shipyards!"

Quinton grinned, as did Becker.

"I don't understand," Harper said.

"Three Moons Shipyards was where we found you," Quinton replied.

"I know that, but why would ships need a warranty?"

"They don't," Oscar said. "It's just another way for someone to scam credits from spacers."

Harper went back to his work.

"When do you want to go to the next buoy?" Becker asked.

"I have Radek running a few queries," Quinton said and twitched his chin toward Harper.

"I can see that, you know," Harper said. "I thought you realized that the spider-drone has an option for omnidirectional viewing."

"So, we can't sneak up on you. Got it," Quinton replied.

"Don't you get disoriented if you enable that option all the time?" Becker asked.

"I do, but that's why I have Greta monitor it for me," Harper replied.

Quinton glanced at Harper thoughtfully, experiencing an urge to test that omnidirectional viewing option of his but filed that away to try later. He wondered how much of the spider-drone's onboard computer was being devoted to giving Harper the peace of mind that he wasn't going to be attacked.

"Yeah, we need to find Harper a better body," Quinton said.

"What about the DNA vaults?" Becker asked.

"Yeah, well, we'll look for both, but stopping Crowe from starting a Sentinel incursion is the top priority," Quinton said.

"Quinton," Radek said, "I've found something that I think you should see."

"Put it on the main holoscreen."

"It's a recent distress beacon," Radek said, and a data window appeared for them to review.

"Looks like an automated message," Quinton said and frowned. "That can't be right. Radek, are you sure about this?"

"The distress beacon is authentic. It's an Alari Star Council outpost."

Harper walked over to them. "An Alari message here?"

"Who are they?" Becker asked.

Quinton looked at Becker for a moment. "I guess they're not around anymore. They were a small star nation that the Acheron Confederacy had trade pacts with."

"More than that," Harper said. "They were our allies."

"That must have been after I was uploaded," Quinton said. He accessed the other communication logs from the comms buoy and nearly stood up.

Becker looked at him. "What? What is it?"

Quinton put the data on the main holoscreen. "There was another PMC activation signal. Short burst. Source unknown. It was just recorded about forty hours ago," he said and frowned. "The distress beacon became active shortly after."

"It's not active anymore," Becker said.

Quinton checked the coordinates of the distress beacon. They were within jump range.

"Quinton, the beacon is no longer active," Becker said.

"The outpost could be old and it malfunctioned."

"Yeah, or the Sentinels have already taken it down."

"Who… not it," Quinton replied.

"I meant the signal."

"We're going to check it out," Quinton said. "Oscar."

"Right, plotting a course," the pilot said.

"Not right on top of it. Let's be a little cautious with our approach. Just in case," Quinton said.

"I'll let Guttman know," Becker said.

The jump drive status appeared on the upper right corner of the main holoscreen.

"Hey, Oscar, also—"

"Have an emergency set of coordinates ready to execute in case there are hostiles in the area."

"I knew there was a reason I kept you around."

"That's because I'm the best."

"I won't forget it."

Becker closed his comlink and looked at Quinton. "Guttman is heading to main engineering."

"Good idea," Quinton replied. They'd been reliant on maintenance drones that Quinton and the others could control, but considering their last encounter with the Sentinels, those measures weren't enough.

Becker rubbed his forehead and squeezed his eyes shut.

"What's wrong?"

Becker shook his head. "It's nothing. Just a headache."

Quinton looked at him for a moment. Becker had taken a blow to the head during the Sentinel attack. He was lucky that a headache was all he'd walked away with.

"Ready to execute jump," Oscar said.

"Make it so," Quinton replied.

The ship emerged into the outer fringes of a star system with a blue giant main sequence star. Initial scans revealed a few rocky planets orbiting extremely close to the bright star. The planets' compositions must be highly dense with extensive deposits of metals, or the star's gravitational forces would have prevented those planets from forming in the first place. There were three gas giants in the system, each with an assortment of moons, but the star system was otherwise unremarkable. Quinton had expected to detect a few mining installations on the interior planets, but there weren't any. Not a bad place to station an outpost.

The plot refreshed on the main holoscreen as new scan data was brought in. Quinton traced the distress beacon to one of the gas giants.

"That can't be right," Becker said.

"That's the source of the beacon."

"The outpost could be on one of the moons," Oscar said.

"It's not," Quinton replied.

"Did the beacon use some kind of repeater like how we tracked the ACN starbase?" Becker asked.

"That's a good point," Oscar said. "They probably wouldn't want to give away their position."

"Are you guys finished guessing?" Quinton asked. "I can just tell you if you give me a chance." He looked at them, and Becker gave him a get-on-with-it look. "It's a distress beacon. Unless someone is trying to ambush us, the location of the outpost is fine. Yes, by the gas giant is probably right. They could move the outpost into the upper atmosphere if they needed to. It's not unheard of, depending on what the outpost is used for."

"Why don't we do an active scan of the system, just to be sure?" Oscar said.

Quinton refreshed the passive scan data on the main holoscreen. "Because we're not the only ones here." Someone had entered the system ahead of them.

"Sentinels?" Becker asked.

"I don't know," Quinton replied. "It's just one ship. We'll need to go in quietly."

Quinton accessed the communications system and there were no broadcasts coming from the outpost. The star system was already quiet.

"Then it's not an ambush," Becker said.

"Yup," Quinton replied.

If there had been other ships in the star system waiting to see who investigated the emergency distress beacon, they would have already closed the trap for the other ship. The beacon and the outpost were real, and there was at least one PMC who'd come online.

"Oscar, take us in," Quinton said.

"Aye, Commander. Taking us in," Oscar replied.

"Harper, monitor for other ship activity."

"Aye, Commander," Harper said.

Someone had reached this star system ahead of them and weren't giving away their position. They'd have to get closer to the outpost to see if they were there.

18

THE *WAYFARER* FLEW on a direct intercept course to the Alari Star Council outpost. They needed to make up for lost time. Rather than spending the better part of twenty-seven hours to reach their target destination, Quinton executed a micro-jump that closed the distance. The gas giant's colorful belts of pale green to yellow with a few brownish reds filled the view on the main holoscreen. The planet was surrounded by a few large, distinct rings where several of its natural satellites carved a path through the dust, ice, and rocks.

Quinton deployed a reconnaissance drone that would maintain its position beyond the atmosphere and passed control of the subspace session over to Harper, who would continue monitoring it.

A HUD overlay appeared on the main holoscreen, which showed their best guess as to where the distress beacon had come from. Quinton activated a focused active scan pulse through subspace toward the targeted region. The scan widened until they received a positive scan result.

"The outpost is in the thermosphere in one of the darker belts," Quinton said.

"Won't it be crushed?" Oscar asked.

"No… well, it can if it goes deep enough, but the darker belts are older and less dense than the lighter regions."

Becker cleared his throat. "This ship wasn't designed to fly into the interior atmosphere of a gas giant."

"You're right, but we only need to reach the outpost and then we'll be protected by its artificial gravity field. It's gotta be massive if it's positioned here," Quinton replied.

"It had better be, to compete with a planet that size."

"They were designed for it."

"Assuming the outpost hasn't been damaged," Becker said and then held up his hands, palms up. "I know. I know. Let's just get on with it."

"Take us in, Oscar," Quinton said.

He continued to review the scan data of the Alari outpost as the ship flew toward it. They couldn't actually see it, but the sensors detected it several hundred kilometers inside the atmosphere.

Quinton opened a comlink to engineering and Guttman answered. "Expect a power spike to the inertia dampening system."

"Understood," Guttman replied.

Quinton closed the comlink, and Becker looked at him quizzically. "Nothing, I just haven't heard Guttman use so few words before."

"Yeah," Becker said and turned back toward the main holoscreen.

The live video feed was replaced by a three-dimensional schematic rendering of the outpost from the incoming sensor data. Quinton diverted power to the ship's artificial gravity field, creating a bubble of resistance to the gas giant's powerful gravitational pull.

He checked the ship's communication systems. They hadn't received anything from the outpost. He'd initiated several broadcast hails to the outpost, but they hadn't been answered yet.

The Alari outpost was built into the bottom of a metallic asteroid that had likely been mined out for that purpose. The bottom was essentially a large, cylinder-shaped habitation unit, two kilometers wide that narrowed toward the bottom.

"I'm not detecting any active weapons systems," Harper said.

"Understood," Quinton said. He had access to the same scan data, but Harper was speaking the updates aloud for the benefit of Becker and Oscar.

"I guess the fact that they're not shooting at us is as open an invitation as we're likely to get, but how are we going to get inside?" Becker asked.

Quinton looked at Radek's analysis of the sensor data. "A docking port isn't ideal. I'd rather find a hangar bay… There, I've found one," he said and updated the waypoint.

Oscar flew them toward it.

More scan data revealed that the outpost's lower decks were significantly damaged, but the upper decks still had power. They hadn't received any response to their hails, so Quinton scanned subspace frequencies for a data connection within the vicinity of the hangar bay doors. He found one almost immediately and accessed the door-control systems. A quick analysis of the doors showed that they weren't secure. He sent a docking request. The door-control systems would only engage the open-door protocols if they were authorized by the outpost's central command. Quinton inserted an override that put his data session between the door-control systems and central command, which allowed him to grant his own docking request. Their lack of security was his gain.

"Hangar bay doors are opening now," Quinton said.

Oscar flew the ship toward them, and in a few moments, they were safely within the outpost's artificial gravity field. The ship's power draw returned to normal.

Oscar deployed the ship's landing gear and set the ship down. The hangar bay doors remained open so he enabled the atmospheric shield, which worked, but the hangar bay didn't fill up with a breathable atmosphere.

"Looks like we'll need suits for this one," Quinton said.

"I won't," Harper said.

"Harper, I need you and Oscar to stay with the ship."

"I thought I was coming with you. There could be PMCs on this outpost. There might be a body for me to use."

"Yes, we'll look for that, but I need you to monitor the recon drone for Sentinel ships, and we also don't know where the people who arrived before us went. I need you to stay here," Quinton said.

Harper was quiet for a few moments and then said, "Yes, Commander."

Becker stood up. "Guttman is on his way to the airlock."

"Oscar, you're in charge while I'm gone," Quinton said.

"Harper and I have got this, but don't take too long," Oscar said.

Quinton and Becker left the bridge.

"I saw what you did there," Becker said.

"We need an established chain of command; otherwise, everything just falls apart," Quinton replied.

They met Guttman at the portside airlock, and Quinton waited for them to put on their EVA suits. They'd opted for plasma assault rifles instead of their hand blasters.

Harper contacted him through comlink. "I'd like to deploy a few more recon drones to see if there are any other ships docked with the station. I'll have them fly close enough to the outpost that they'll stay in its gravitation field."

"Good idea. Let me know if you find anything," Quinton said and closed the comlink.

They entered the airlock and waited for it to cycle. When the outer airlock doors opened, Quinton walked out first and glanced around. The hangar bay was empty except for their ship. He gestured for Becker and Guttman to follow.

"You know what I don't get," Guttman said.

"I don't even know where to begin with that one, but I guess I'll have to start somewhere," Quinton replied.

Guttman snorted. "I'm serious. Where'd everyone go? Why would they abandon this place?"

"They were probably recalled by Alari High Command," Becker said.

They walked across the hangar toward the deck officer's office a short distance down the corridor.

"That's what we always assume," Guttman said. He walked over to the nearest workstation and brought it online. "I want to know why. Were they attacked, or did they just …? I don't know, leave or something."

"I'm not able to access their computing core, so I don't know why they decommissioned the outpost," Quinton said.

"That's just it. If they decommissioned it but left it intact, they might have expected to come back," Guttman said. The workstation holoscreen powered on. "You're right about the computing core. The alerts say it went offline," he said and frowned. Both Quinton and Becker peered at the holoscreen. "It went offline when the beacon stopped. It looks like someone tried to bring this outpost back online."

"That's good enough for me. That means they're still here," Quinton said and headed for the door.

Becker followed him and then stopped in the doorway. "You coming?" he said to Guttman.

Quinton stopped and looked through the clear ceraphome window to the office. Guttman stood near the workstation. He started walking toward them and then went back to the workstation.

"I know the computing core is down," Guttman said, "but the workstation has local storage. I'm going to see if I can find some supply caches nearby. There might be a good find there, especially if they really planned on returning."

Becker nodded. "Let us know if you find anything."

The adjacent corridor was lit by emergency lighting.

"Think he'll find anything?" Quinton asked.

"If there is something to be found, he'll find it," Becker said. "He's got a good head for finding valuable cargo."

"I doubt there will be any ships here."

"Agreed, that would be too convenient. Even if there were any, I doubt they'd be in good working order. Certainly not space worthy," Becker replied.

They made their way through the outpost, and a short while later, they entered a central section where there were elevators that actually had power to them.

They entered the elevator.

"Destination?" a modulated voice asked.

"Central operations," Quinton replied.

The elevator doors shut.

"I guess these are on an isolated system," Becker asked.

"Evidently."

The elevator sped upward.

"You don't know?" Becker asked.

"Of course, I know. Do you really think the elevator needs to be in contact with the computing core to operate?"

"Yeah, I did."

Quinton considered it for a few moments.

"What?" Becker said, annoyed.

"I was just thinking that this is what it must be like for you to explain to me how things work," he said and nodded a little. "It's a great feeling. I could get used to it."

Becker rolled his eyes and shook his head. "Sometimes… sometimes you're a real ass, you know that? Just answer the damn question."

Quinton just looked at him.

"You don't have to be such a jerk about it." Becker gritted his teeth and stepped toward him.

Quinton grinned. "All right. All right. I'll stop. Geez, that's some kind of temper you've got there."

Becker backed up to the other side of the elevator and glared at the wall. "Never mind, I don't want to know. The sooner…" He mumbled the rest.

"Okay, Becker, come on. I'm just kidding around. It's what we do."

Becker swung his gaze toward Quinton, gritting his teeth.

"Some military bases are different. They have systems that can work autonomously if they need or as part of a complex system. The designers built in redundancy in the event of being cut off from critical infrastructure. It's how the ACN designed their starbases. That's why the base we were on could still function, even though it had suffered from severe weapons damage."

Becker's gaze softened a little. "Thank you. That's all you had to do."

"What's the matter with you?"

"Did you ever check into Harper's use of the ship's computer system?"

Quinton hesitated and frowned.

"I don't believe this. You never checked."

"I meant to. I just haven't gotten around to it yet."

Becker leaned toward him. "You don't forget anything."

But Quinton had forgotten. "I'll do it as soon as we get back on the ship."

"Do you need me to remind you?"

"No. I said I'd do it and I meant it."

"I don't believe you. Radek, are you there?" Becker asked. Radek's holographic sphere appeared. "Great. Can you remind Quinton to check on Harper's use of the ship's computer system for me, please?"

"Reminder is set," Radek said.

"Excellent. Make it daily until the task is done," Becker said.

"Acknowledged. Reminder preferences updated."

Quinton's gaze darted between Becker and Radek. Then he chuckled. "Thanks, Radek," he said.

Becker smiled, white teeth gleaming amid the dark skin inside his helmet. "You brought this on yourself."

Quinton laughed. "I guess I did."

He received a comlink request from Harper. Quinton answered it.

"The drones were unable to locate any other ships docked with the station," Harper said.

"What about the other hangar bays? Does anything look like they've been recently used?"

"Negative, Commander. I've recalled the drones."

"Understood. Thanks for the update," Quinton said and told Becker.

"Maybe they already left or weren't able to get inside the outpost," Becker said.

"Come all this way and just give up?"

"If they're salvagers, they might. Whoever came here knew what they were getting themselves in for. I wouldn't risk my ship to come here, and with news of increased Sentinel activity, they might have decided it wasn't worth the risk either."

"Unless the ship didn't stick around."

Becker frowned. "Boarding party."

Quinton nodded.

"That's a hell of a risk to take. We should warn Oscar."

"They're already monitoring for any ships that enter the area," Quinton said.

The elevator chimed as it reached the central operations deck. He tried to access the outpost's security system to see what was beyond the elevator door, but the system was offline.

Quinton's reactions were startlingly fast, well beyond the capabilities of even the most enhanced human. As the doors opened, he had a little over a second before a barrage of plasma bolts rapid-fired at them. Quinton threw himself toward Becker, knocking him into the wall. Then he leaped off the wall, propelling himself to the other side of the elevator. He'd caught sight of two automated defense turrets that had risen from the floor in the middle of the corridor beyond.

Quinton increased the power output of his assault rifle and fired a quick three-bolt burst. One of the turrets exploded. The other turret pinned him into the corner.

Becker recovered from being shoved into the wall and looked at Quinton, nodding his head toward the remaining turret.

The turret stopped firing and Quinton burst from the elevator, firing his weapon in a suppressing spray. His shots were accurate, but they didn't need to be. He was the distraction. Becker destroyed the second turret.

Central operations was a few dozen meters away. No other defense turrets appeared, and Quinton couldn't detect any power cables that led to more turrets on standby—not under the floor or hidden inside the ceiling.

"Why don't you hang back while I scout ahead?" Quinton said.

Becker nodded and kept a pace several meters behind him. Quinton peered through the clear ceraphome doors and saw several rows of workstations beyond. He scanned for local computer systems and they were offline, but someone had enabled the defense turrets. He reached the door first and took up a position just outside the doorway.

"See anything?" Becker asked.

A few metallic storage containers sat beneath several large holoscreens.

"Yeah," Quinton said. "Cover me from here while I go take a look."

Becker hastened to the other side of the wide doorway and kept out of sight.

Quinton palmed the door controls and walked into the operations center. The interior was a large round room that was more akin to a command center. The black Alari Star Council emblem shone from the holoscreens.

Quinton scanned the layout and didn't detect anyone inside. He walked toward the storage containers. They looked familiar. He went to the onboard controls and brought up the status interface. They were CDA storage containers. Inside each of them was an android designed to house a Personality Matrix Construct. There were two of them here. If they had an ESS inside of them, then there were two PMCs here.

Quinton detected a PMC broadcast that seemed to be coming from the other storage container. He walked over to it but didn't acknowledge the broadcast. The contact protocol wasn't one he was familiar with. The storage container lurched forward hard, knocking Quinton several meters back.

"Stay away from it!" a deep voice boomed.

Quinton bounced off the workstation and stumbled to the floor. Before he could regain his feet, something heavy and mechanical bounded toward him, fast. Quinton lifted his rifle. He glimpsed a pair of CDA red robotic eyes in battle mode as it grabbed the end of the rifle and tried to yank it out of Quinton's grasp. He held on as the CDA pulled him off the ground and flung him toward the wall. He spun in the air and his shoulder bore the brunt of the impact.

Quinton regained his feet. "Wait!" he shouted.

The CDA charged. "You can't have them, Agent of Harding!"

Quinton had just enough time to see Becker coming through the doorway, weapon raised. Quinton threw his rifle at the CDA's face and slid forward, tripping the android and scrambling onto its back.

"I'm here to help you, dammit!"

The android spun and pushed himself up, trying to knock Quinton off.

A plasma bolt hit the wall behind them.

"Hey!" Becker shouted. "Either you stop moving, or I start shooting at those storage containers. Which is it gonna be?"

The CDA craned its neck toward Becker and stopped.

"Becker?" said a familiar feminine voice.

Quinton stood up. Two spacers came out from behind the storage container. Both held a hand blaster, but neither of them was aiming at anyone. The leader looked at Becker and then at Quinton. From inside a clear face shield, celestial blue eyes widened in recognition.

"Quinton?"

"Hello, Maelyn."

19

THE NERVOUS SHIFTING of Quinton's feet revealed his discomfort as he looked at Maelyn. She lowered her hand blaster and stepped toward him, stabbing him with a poisonous glare full of fury and betrayal. It was the betrayal that Quinton felt in his gut. If he had to choose between a hand blaster and the look in her celestial blue eyes, he'd choose the blaster.

"You're alive," she said, sounding as if she couldn't believe it. Then she glanced at Becker. "You're both alive."

"Guttman and Oscar are fine, too," Quinton said, and her gaze swung back to him.

The second spacer approached and stood next to Maelyn. Quinton recognized Simon as the face shield became translucent.

Simon's eyebrows raced upward, and then he smiled. "Quinton, is that really you?"

Maelyn raised her hand blaster, pointing it directly at Quinton. "That's a good question."

"It *is* me. I realize this is probably a shock to you both," Quinton replied. Maelyn didn't lower the hand blaster, and Simon looked as if he couldn't believe what he was seeing. "I can prove it to you. Simon, you helped me when I was stuck in that agricultural bot from Zeta-Six," he said and looked at Maelyn. "Were you able to find those colony planets from the data repositories on the Endurance Starbase?"

Simon stepped forward and took a good look at Quinton. "I… How did you survive? Where did you…? You look so real, like flesh and blood, but that body must've been destroyed."

Quinton nodded. "It was. My PMC was transferred via subspace into an ESS in this cybernetic avatar."

"You can't trust him," said the CDA that attacked him.

Becker still had him covered with his plasma rifle.

Quinton looked at the CDA. "I think we've gotten off on the wrong foot. I'm Quinton Aldren."

The CDA regarded him. "You could tell me you were Admiral Elias Browning, and I still wouldn't believe you, Agent of Harding."

Quinton frowned and glanced at Maelyn and Simon for a moment. "I don't even know what that is. What's an Agent of Harding?"

The CDA looked at Maelyn. "You said you came here to help me. If you mean that, you'll shoot him. You can't trust anything he says. Agents of Harding are the enemy."

Quinton shook his head and grinned. "She's not going to shoot me," he said and looked at Maelyn. "Right?"

For a few moments, Maelyn appeared as if she was seriously considering it.

"Walsh," Simon said, "this is Quinton Aldren. He's not an agent of anything."

"Walsh," Quinton parroted, quickly exploiting the advantage of a name, "I came here because of the PMC activation signal. I'm actually here to help you. Simon is right; I'm not anyone's agent. How can I prove it to you?"

Walsh regarded him for a few seconds. "PMC authentication. You denied my initial request, but it's the only way. Then you'll know who I am, and I'll know exactly who you are," he said and looked at Maelyn. "Be ready to act."

Quinton was a little bit amused but also annoyed at the same time. Whoever Walsh was, he was deadly serious. Quinton looked at Maelyn. "It's me, Maelyn. Don't shoot me."

She smiled, but it didn't reach her eyes. "Go on, Quinton. Prove it."

Quinton inhaled deeply and sighed.

"Would you look at that!" Simon said excitedly. "You can mimic our behaviors. You didn't need to take that breath. It's a mental stimulus for releasing tension. That's amazing. I'd really like to know more about this avatar."

Quinton smiled a little and then looked at Walsh. "Here it comes." Opening a data comlink to the CDA, he transferred his PMC authentication. PMC authentication protocols drew upon unique identifiers that were encoded into his ESS. They went well beyond a simple data handshake that conveyed credentials. It was something that couldn't be forged. This was to prevent anyone from impersonating another PMC.

Walsh's credentials appeared in his HUD.

Walsh, Corvax, Alari Navy.

Specialization—defense tactical command.

Walsh frowned for a few moments and then stood up straight. "Commander, please accept my apologies. I had no idea that you were a Galactic class PMC of the Acheron Confederacy Navy. I have an update for you, sir, when you're ready to receive it."

Becker snorted and lowered his weapon a little. "Oh my God, not another one."

Maelyn lowered her blaster and returned it to the holster on her hip. "What do you mean 'not another one'?"

"We've encountered another PMC who believes Quinton is his commanding officer."

Maelyn regarded Quinton for a few moments. Her expression gave nothing away beyond the fact that she was furious with him.

Walsh cleared his throat. "Commander, I must insist."

"All right, what have you got to tell me?" Quinton asked.

Walsh gestured to one of the storage containers nearby. "The PMC in this container is of vital importance."

"Who is it?"

"This is Commander Isobe Misako. She's an ACN intelligence officer who has a mission briefing to give us when she's brought back online," Walsh said.

Quinton nodded and gestured toward the other storage container. "And who's in this one?"

"That's Lieutenant Chloe Bradshaw, also in the Alari Navy."

"Are there any more PMCs here?"

"I don't think so. I knew I was going to be stored with Lieutenant Bradshaw and that Commander Misako was going to join us. But that was before..." Walsh stopped and frowned for a moment. "The Federation Wars," he said. "Agents of Harding were everywhere. We are preparing to make a major offensive."

"Were," Quinton said. "The Federation Wars were a long time ago."

"But that's not possible. We were to be part of the vanguard."

"Who's we?" Becker asked.

Walsh looked at him for a moment and then turned back to Quinton.

"Go ahead. It's all right," Quinton said.

"You don't know..." Walsh said. "You don't know about the offensive? You've never heard about the Agents of Harding?"

"I was uploaded before the Federation Wars. I was supposed to serve in Grand Admiral Browning's Freedom Armada for the final assault in the Wildner Sector in the Jordani Federation."

Walsh looked away and considered this for a few moments. "You're one of the early ones. Before the Agents... Before Harding."

"Before Harding did what? And which Harding are we talking about here?" Quinton asked.

"Miles Harding, the original PMC. The one who paved the way for all of us," Walsh said.

"Miles Harding," Becker said. "*The* Miles Harding, the hero of the Federation Wars?"

Walsh turned toward Becker so fast it seemed like his body had simply jerked in one direction. "Harding was no hero," he snarled.

Becker glanced at the others. "Boy, have you got a lot to learn. And you think Browning—"

"Becker!" Maelyn said. "Not now. This isn't the time."

Becker's mouth hung open a little, as if he'd been about to form a word but didn't.

"No, don't stop," Walsh said. "What were you going to say about Admiral Browning?"

"Maelyn's right," Quinton said. "We can sort this out later. This isn't the safest place for us to be right now."

Walsh looked at Quinton and nodded. "Understood, Commander. There's a lot you must be brought up to speed about."

Becker shook his head. "He's not the only one. You really think whatever mission you had all that time ago still applies today? Don't you realize you've been on standby for five or six decades? Whatever your mission was, it's over."

"This is one of the contingency plans. The mission parameters might've changed, but the mission hasn't," Walsh insisted.

Quinton looked at Becker. "Come on. We don't need to do this right here. We can sort this out later." He looked at Maelyn. "We can sort everything out after we're off this outpost. Agreed?"

"Fine," Maelyn said. "We have a shuttle."

"We have a ship in the hangar bay. You sure your shuttle is going to survive the trip? The outpost is barely maintaining its altitude," Quinton said.

Maelyn rolled her eyes and shook her head but didn't respond. Instead, she walked over to Becker. "I need to talk to you," she said and headed for the door. Becker looked at Quinton, shrugged, and then followed her.

Walsh walked over to one of the storage containers and activated the counter grav option from the controls. The storage container began to hover above the ground, and he did the same thing for the other one.

"Are there any unoccupied CDAs here in the outpost?" Quinton asked.

"There should be some spare units, but the computing core is down," Walsh said.

"That was me," Simon said. "I had to take it down because there were hundreds of systems bleeding power. I had to reroute them into other systems or disable them to keep the outpost here. Actually, I was trying to get it to go back to its original orbit but couldn't. The outpost did have an orbit well above the atmosphere before Walsh tried to bring it back online."

Quinton nodded. "Did you also enable the defense turrets in the corridor outside the operations center?"

Simon flinched. "Whoops. I'm sorry about that. We thought the Sentinels might try to board this place."

"The Sentinels send in boarding parties?"

"Sometimes."

What would be the point of that? The Sentinels that Quinton had encountered had simply destroyed their targets. He hadn't thought they were capable of carrying out other kinds of missions.

"You almost got us," Quinton said.

"To be fair, we didn't know you were here, and we didn't know you were alive. Why didn't you contact us?" Simon asked. He'd been about to say "her," meaning Maelyn, but he'd switched it at the last second.

"It's a long story, Simon. It really is. Becker and the others helped me get the ship running, and then it's just been one thing after another," Quinton replied.

Simon regarded him for a few moments. The spacer's boyish looks had thinned out some, giving way to the more mature man he was becoming.

Experience had aged him, and Quinton realized he wasn't going to accept such a shallow response.

"Can we talk about this later?"

Simon swallowed hard. "We thought you were dead. That you sacrificed yourself. It was hard on all of us, but it was especially hard on her. She deserved better."

Each of his words was like a concussive blast directed at his chest. He *had* sacrificed himself. At least he'd meant to. He'd thought it was better to just leave well enough alone and everyone could move on.

"Fine, I'm the bad guy," Quinton said. "But what I need now is a CDA unit because we rescued another PMC that's stuck in a spider-drone. Will you help me with that? His name is Nash Harper, and he's on my ship. Remember how it was with me? How hard was it to keep it together? He has access to his memories…most of them, but he's stuck in a damn spider-drone. I'll let you beat up on me for the length of one voyage, but first, we help him. Does that work for you?" Quinton asked bitterly.

Simon brought up his personal holoscreen, and Quinton watched as he accessed the outpost's local computer system. "There's another unit in storage. I can have it sent to the hangar bay where your ship is. You just need to tell me which one."

Quinton transferred the hangar bay's location.

Simon watched the screen for a few moments and then nodded. "It's on its way.

Quinton looked at Walsh. "All right, let's get these guys out of here. I'll help you with the storage containers."

As they guided the containers out of the operations center, Quinton glanced toward Maelyn and Becker speaking quietly by the elevator. Becker looked like he was doing most of the talking. His avatar had a highly acute auditory system, and he could have listened in on their conversation, but he didn't bother. He could guess what was being said.

Quinton received a comlink request from Oscar.

"Harper asked me to contact you. A Sentinel scout force has entered the system. They're on their way here. I hope you found what you were looking for," Oscar said.

"We did," Quinton said and quickly filled him in. "Tell Harper that we have a CDA unit on its way to the ship. We can begin the transition once we get out of here. We're on our way back."

As they reached the elevator, Maelyn and Becker became quiet.

"Sentinels have entered the system. They're on their way here now," Quinton said and looked at Maelyn. "Where's your shuttle?"

Maelyn looked as if she were about to say something but the elevator doors opened. She walked inside and the rest of them followed.

Quinton positioned himself next to Maelyn. "Are you going to ignore me?"

"No, I'm trying not to shoot you," she replied. Then she moved to the other side of the elevator.

Quinton shook his head and glared at the status window in front of him.

20

Quinton's head tilted to the side. He'd done nothing wrong. Nothing. He resisted the urge to look in Maelyn's direction. She could stare at the elevator doors for as long as she wanted.

Shoot him?

He didn't owe her anything, so why did it feel like he did? He'd delivered on his end of the bargain. The DUC had gotten what they wanted, and he'd been under no obligation to remain in contact.

Focus, dammit, he chided himself. The Sentinels were in the star system. It was only a matter of time before they figured out where the distress beacon had come from, and that would lead them here.

He hadn't been able to contact Maelyn after the battle on the ACN starbase. They'd needed to repair the ship, which had required more time than any of them thought it would. After that, he'd decided to put off contacting her and the DUC. She was jumping to all kinds of conclusions. He shook his head and ignored another spike of irritation.

"Simon," Quinton said.

"Yes?"

"Where is the *Nebulon*?"

Maelyn looked at him. "It's on the other side of the system with the star between the ship and us."

"The plan was for you to recall it when you'd left the outpost?"

"Seemed like a good idea at the time."

"The Sentinels will probably focus their efforts here," Quinton said. But it was understood that it wouldn't be safe for the *Nebulon* to jump anywhere near this area, and they couldn't escape the Sentinels on the shuttle. "You can dock the shuttle with the *Wayfarer*, and we can rendezvous with the *Nebulon* after."

Maelyn didn't have any other options, and they both knew it.

"Unless you've got a better plan," Quinton added.

Maelyn shook her head. "No, I don't," she said and looked at him. "Thank you."

Quinton thought he kept the surprise from his face but couldn't be sure.

"Awkward," Becker snorted. "Couldn't resist."

"Thanks, buddy. Glad to know you always have my back."

Becker tapped the side of his head, giving him a two-finger salute. He glanced at the elevator's destination. "I didn't see a hangar bay at that location."

"There isn't one," Simon said. "It's more of a maintenance bay. The shuttle is small enough to fit inside."

Quinton watched as Becker glanced at the storage containers and Corvax. "You'll be able to fit all this in the shuttle?"

Simon frowned.

"We'll be going with Commander Aldren," Corvax said.

Maelyn looked at him. "You have an open invitation to come with us if you want."

"Thank you for your assistance, but the situation has changed."

"Of course," Maelyn said.

Becker leaned toward Quinton and raised an eyebrow. He nodded a little by way of acknowledgment.

The elevator reached its destination and the doors opened. There was a long corridor beyond, with emergency lighting flickering in some places along the way.

Quinton looked at Corvax. "It might make more sense for us to split up. The key is to get everyone safely out of here, including them," he said, gesturing to the storage containers. "They'll fit on the shuttle, and you can come with Becker and me to the ship. This way, when the Sentinels attack, we'll know they're safe."

Corvax's artificial jade-colored eyes considered this from the metallic chrome-colored alloy of the CDAs head. "Yes, Commander."

Quinton hadn't meant for it to be an order but didn't argue the point. "Let's get them to the shuttle."

They exited the elevator and guided the storage containers down the corridor.

Oscar opened a comlink to Quinton. "The Sentinels took out the recon drone and have just micro-jumped. They're on their way here."

"Understood," Quinton replied and closed the link.

The Sentinels were definitely within weapons range. They quickened the pace. The door to the maintenance bay was still a long way. They should just turn back to the elevator and head to the *Wayfarer*. Maelyn wouldn't like sacrificing the shuttle, but he didn't think she'd be opposed to the idea.

"Hold on. Stop," Quinton said. "We should turn back—" He stopped speaking.

A broadcast appeared on almost all comlink channels seemingly at once. His frame rate increased to maximum, and a cyber-attack alert appeared on his HUD. Radek had increased Quinton's frame rate.

"Remote hack attempt buried in the broadcast. The highest probability is that this is of Sentinel origin," Radek said.

To protect himself, Quinton had changed his avatar's communication protocols to route all message traffic through a virtual sandbox. The analysis occurred so fast that there was hardly any kind of discernible latency—certainly not for general commlink-type attempts.

Quinton reviewed the report. The Sentinels were trying to exploit a vulnerability that existed in the mere acknowledgment of an initial comlink request. They were also trying to broadcast on multiple subspace frequencies in order to overwhelm the receiving system in hopes of bypassing standard security protocols. He didn't know what the remote hack would do if it succeeded, and he didn't have time to fully investigate it now, even with his frame rate set to maximum. He initiated a data comlink to the others and uploaded a set of instructions to disallow all outside communications. This would effectively sever existing outside comlinks and prevent new connections from being made.

He received an almost instantaneous response from Corvax. The CDA's communication configuration was to deny all comlink attempts until they were deemed safe and the PMC accepted.

Quinton turned his attention to the storage containers that held the PMCs on standby. They both had active comlinks to the Sentinels. He cursed inwardly and raced to sever their connections. He was able to sever one of them quickly, hopefully before the Sentinels were able to execute whatever payload they'd included in the message.

He was too late for the second one. He knew it. Corvax knew it.

The Sentinels' malicious code was even now running its exploits on the vulnerable PMC in standby. Quinton tried launching a trace to protect the PMC inside, but the Sentinels had gotten their foothold and they wouldn't be dislodged. The PMC was being reactivated and there was nothing he could do to stop it. He tried to think of a solution but couldn't. Any attempt he made to stop the PMC from coming online was overridden. This entire confrontation had occurred at the speed of light, and less than a second had elapsed in normal time.

Quinton grabbed the container before anyone could react. He saw the occupant's name on the status window.

Commander Isobe Misako—Acheron Confederacy Navy Intelligence.

Quinton shoved the container toward the maintenance bay doors where the *Nebulon*'s shuttle waited. As the container began its journey, he uploaded new security protocols to the *Wayfarer,* hoping he'd been in time. He couldn't wait for the acknowledgment. As soon as the updated protocols had been delivered, he forced a communication reset for the *Wayfarer's* systems. Oscar would probably freak out, but Harper would be able to explain it to him.

Quinton lowered his frame rate back to normal time. The others were about to look at their wrist computers.

"What have you done?" Corvax asked. He'd taken several steps down the corridor, chasing the container with Misako inside.

"There isn't anything I can do for her. The Sentinels have corrupted the PMC," Quinton said, and sent him Radek's detection report for the remote hack attempt.

Corvax received it and looked at the container. "The mission."

"I know," Quinton said. "We have to go back. We can't go that way."

Simon peered down the corridor. "Wait. What happened? That container is coming online. The PMC is being reactivated."

"I'll explain," Quinton said. "You need to trust me."

He urged them back toward the elevator.

Becker came to his side. "Guttman is back at the ship. The Sentinels are positioning themselves to begin their assault."

No sooner had the words come out of his mouth than the emergency lighting in the corridor dimmed.

"Run!" Quinton shouted.

Corvax pushed the storage container with Bradshaw inside toward the elevator. Simon jumped on top because the CDA could move much faster than they could run. Becker did the same. Quinton scooped Maelyn up and carried her to the elevator.

The floor shook beneath his feet as the Sentinels began their bombardment of the outpost.

21

Corvax pushed the container through the elevator doors, and both Becker and Simon leaped off. Quinton and Maelyn were right behind them. He set her down, and the doors closed. Quinton accessed the elevator control system via the local data port and initiated an override of the safety protocols to accelerate the elevator.

The deck numbers flashed overhead while the elevator raced to the upper hangar bay. If he hadn't altered his own security protocols under advice from Radek, he might have been in some serious, irreversible trouble.

Maelyn looked at him with a curious expression. "What happened?"

Quinton had to sever all comlinks from the *Wayfarer* while the communication system reset.

He looked at Maelyn. "What is it about us and elevators?"

She regarded him for a few moments, and then he saw a flicker of recognition in her eyes. Her lips lifted a little, showing hints of a smile.

"The Sentinels attacked us," Quinton said, gesturing toward Corvax and the storage container. Becker held his plasma rifle raised slightly. "Radek detected it, and I was able to stop it before they could do anything."

Becker glanced at Corvax. "What about him?"

"Commander Aldren warned me before the attack came."

Becker frowned. "This is from the increased frame-rate thing."

"It allows him to process information much quicker than we can. His perception of time is orders of magnitude above ours, and probably theirs," Simon said, inclining his head toward Corvax.

Maelyn glanced at the storage container. "What about them?"

"I wasn't fast enough," Quinton replied. "The comlink for PMCs in storage is open to receiving information. I was able to disconnect the comlink sessions for Bradshaw, but by the time I got to Isobe Misako, it was too late."

"Couldn't you reverse whatever the Sentinels did to her?" Simon asked.

"Not without corrupting the PMC," Quinton said.

The elevator slowed down a few moments before it stopped at the deck with access to the upper hangar bay. He'd had to tweak the artificial gravity field so the rapid stop didn't slam them all through the metallic ceiling.

"Comms are still down on the ship," Becker said. He looked away for a moment. "I've got Guttman. I let him know we're on our way. He says there's a problem with the reset you did."

Several loud pops sounded progressively closer to their position, and Quinton accessed the recon drones Harper had deployed. He could see the Sentinel ships through the atmosphere of the gas giant. Particle beams penetrated through the atmosphere and sloughed through the outpost's armor. The pops came from rapid decompression as the particle beams penetrated the armor. The beams were heading toward them. Either the Sentinels had guessed where they were, or they were just luckier than everyone else.

The emergency lighting dimmed, and station-wide alerts boomed from overhead. *Unable to maintain orbital locations. Main engine failure for units twelve through eighteen. Outpost will reach crush depth in fifteen minutes. Abandon the outpost. Proceed to the nearest escape pod or egress point for transport. Abandon the outpost.*

The announcement ended as they ran out of the elevator and down the short corridor that led to the hangar bay.

"Simon," Quinton said and gestured inside the deck officer's office. He turned to the rest of them. "Go on. We'll be right there."

Simon joined him in the office. Corvax headed to the ship, guiding the storage container. Maelyn and Becker waited outside the office.

"Doesn't this outpost have any weapons?" Becker asked.

"No, decommissioned outposts don't have weapons on standby," Quinton said and gestured for Simon to go to the workstation. "Did the CDA unit make it to the hangar bay?"

Simon accessed the workstation. "Yes, it's waiting for pickup. It's on the far side of the bay," he said and stood up.

"Not so fast," Quinton said. He heard more pops coming from below the elevator. They were fainter, as if smaller. "You took the computing core offline. Did you leave yourself a way to bring it back?"

Simon frowned. "I can, but we need to get out of here."

"We can't leave yet. If we do, the ship won't last long," Quinton said.

Becker looked down the corridor and cocked his head to the side. "Do you hear something?"

Quinton walked toward the doorway and listened. Then he looked at Simon. "Can you set up remote access to that workstation?"

Simon nodded.

"Good, do it and head to the ship."

A sound of metal being torn apart came from the elevator. The lights flickered inside and the doors closed.

Quinton lifted his plasma rifle and stood next to Becker.

"What do you want me to do?" Simon asked.

"Divert power to the remaining engines. Overload them. We need to get all the thrust we can to break through the atmosphere," Quinton said.

Something slammed the elevator doors, causing them to bend outward, straining against the metallic frame.

"Holy shit," Becker said and backed up.

They backed down the corridor and into the hangar bay. The elevator doors burst open, bending outward as a CDA forced its way through. Crimson eyes gleamed through the flickering amber lighting. It was the CDA that housed Commander Isobe Misako of ACN Intelligence, except it wasn't her anymore. She meant to kill them. The Sentinels must have corrupted her PMC and were controlling her. It was either that or she was one of those Agents of Harding Corvax had accused Quinton of being.

Quinton fired his rifle and Becker did the same. Maelyn and Simon ran toward the ship.

The CDA leaped up, scrambling along the ceiling before dropping back to the ground. Then it bounced from one side of the corridor to the other while propelling itself forward. It moved so quickly that they couldn't get a clear shot.

"Go!" Quinton shouted and increased his frame rate. This wasn't a fight Becker could survive.

Quinton darted to the side and fired his weapon, anticipating where the CDA would go next. Radek enabled a multitude of combat VIs, all with sapient combat simulations active. Misako must have had hers engaged, which was why she'd been able to dodge the rapid fire of their weapons.

Misako tried to alter course as she received the glancing blow of a plasma bolt from Quinton's rifle. The damage only blackened the metallic alloy of the CDA's protective and apparently armored skin. The standard Consciousness Driven Android that Quinton had been trained to use wasn't a battle-bot. It had been designed to give the PMC a sensory experience akin to that of their original human body. At some point during the Federation Wars, this had changed.

A violent shudder went through the outpost's floors and the walls, as if the entire structure was experiencing extreme turbulence. Sudden rises and drops made fighting the CDA all but impossible. The others should have reached the ship by now. All Quinton had to do was make it there so they could leave.

Quinton turned and ran out of the corridor. Misako would be close behind him. The floor pushed upward at a nearly constant rate, causing him to lose his balance temporarily.

"Need more time before the ship can safely leave the outpost," Radek said.

Simon had been able to divert power to the engines, and they were pushing the outpost upward. If Quinton went inside the *Wayfarer* now, leaving Misako outside, she could cause more damage and possibly disable the ship altogether.

Quinton veered off course, running away from the ship. He either needed to keep the CDA busy while the outpost reached a safe altitude for the ship's escape, or he needed to stop it for good. What if he could disable it? Misako must still be inside the CDA. She must be fighting against what the Sentinels had done.

Quinton came to a stop and turned around, initiating a comlink broadcast to the CDA like he'd done with Corvax earlier. He included his PMC authentication and identity. Corvax had responded to the fact that Quinton was a Galactic-Class PMC with command authority.

Misako stopped coming toward him. The red gleam of the CDA's machine eyes seemed to take on more of a human-like cast to them. It was working. Misako must be fighting back.

"Commander Misako, what is your mission?" Quinton asked.

He stepped cautiously toward her.

Misako's gaze jerked toward him. "Stop the spread!"

The CDA lunged toward him, knocking the barrel of the plasma rifle to the side as Quinton fired. She shoved him backward and Quinton flew through the air. He landed near the atmosphere shield, coming dangerously close to the crushing depths of the gas giant's atmosphere beyond. The shield could only contain the atmosphere. Ships and any other objects, including him, could go through the weak shield with almost no resistance at all.

Quinton looked at his plasma rifle. The barrel was bent, and the status window showed a great big failure message. He hastened away from the shield.

Misako hadn't spoken to him; that was the Sentinels. He'd communicated with them before. The CDA slowly approached him, as if each step was a struggle.

"Commander," Misako said. "I can't stop them."

A data comlink to the CDA became available and Quinton uploaded his own VIs to help fight the Sentinel hack. He tried to think of something else he could do. He'd been able to counter the Sentinels that had infiltrated the starbase's computer systems, but he'd gradually lost control, and it appeared that Misako was losing the same battle.

The CDA lunged toward him, but the attack was slow and the movements were off, as if the inner battle with the Sentinel was spilling over into the physical struggle. Quinton easily blocked the movement but stepped back.

The data comlink disconnected and Misako grunted with effort, as if she were trying to lift something heavy. Quinton stood there, unsure how to help, but a dark knowledge was growing inside him that insisted he knew what he had to do. He couldn't bring Misako on the ship. She was lost to them. The Sentinels had taken her away, and yet he couldn't make himself leave. He didn't know Isobe Misako, but her authentication confirmed that she'd been in the Acheron Confederacy Navy.

Misako stepped toward the shield in short, jerky movements. She wasn't trying to survive anymore. She was trying to die. She knew she was lost and didn't want to be an instrument of the Sentinels.

A bright flash raced past the area outside the shield. The Sentinel scout ships had resumed their bombardment. Quinton gritted his teeth and glared upward where the Sentinel ships waited. He couldn't stop them. Not like this. Not here.

"Commander," Misako said. She was right at the shield. Her arms flailed as if she'd lost control of them. "Polaris Op," she muttered and then lunged through the shield.

Quinton saw the CDA fall away, and he screamed with the primal defiance that came when facing predators. He calculated the rate of her fall and tried to imagine the last moments she'd feel as the gas giant's crushing gravity squeezed the CDA with the PMC inside.

He flung his broken rifle through the shield, then turned around and ran toward the rear loading ramp of the ship. More bright flashes from the Sentinel's bombardment lit up the hangar bay. They were targeting the last location where their agent had been.

Quinton ran up the loading ramp, and it started closing as he reached the top. He headed for the bridge.

"Oscar," Quinton said, "take us out on my mark." He'd reconnected to the ship's computer system and used the ship's sensors to detect the Sentinel attack pattern. "Now!"

The ship's engines engaged, and Oscar flew them out of the hangar bay. He maintained altitude while the outpost continued to ascend and then flew away while the Sentinels continued to bombard the outpost. They hadn't detected them. Once the outpost breached the gas giant's atmosphere, the Sentinels would destroy it, if they hadn't managed to do it before, and that was the *Wayfarer's* narrow window of opportunity to escape.

There was no minimum safe distance because they couldn't keep the ship inside the gas giant's atmosphere. The Sentinels might not detect when they left the atmosphere, but they would almost certainly detect the jump.

The others on the bridge were quiet, which was both sobering and appreciated.

"Breach the atmosphere and execute emergency micro-jump," Quinton said.

"Aye, aye," Oscar replied.

The *Wayfarer* increased its altitude amid the gas giant's atmosphere, and tumultuous storms were beginning to tax the inertia compensators. Their power core had to balance the need between the jump drive charging and the increased velocity.

The ship emerged from the gas giant's atmosphere, and Oscar increased their velocity, accelerating their distance from the planet. Then he executed the micro-jump that took them away from the planet, the Sentinels, and the ghosts of the past.

Quinton uploaded a second set of coordinates into the navigation computer. He looked at Maelyn. "Send these to Kieva. She'll be able to meet us there."

Quinton remembered the *Nebulon's* capabilities. It would take them a little bit of time to catch up with them, but at least the Sentinels wouldn't be anywhere near them when it did.

Once Maelyn had sent the message to the *Nebulon*, Oscar executed the first in a series of jumps.

Maelyn walked to Quinton. "I need to speak to you."

"And I need to check on my ship," he said and began to walk away from her.

"Captain's Privilege," Maelyn said.

Quinton came to a halt and glanced around the bridge. Becker, Oscar, Guttman, and Simon looked at him. They expected him to comply. Captain's Privilege was a practice of cooperation among ship captains in this post-

Federation War galactic society. He was expected to have a private meeting with the visiting ship captain while they agreed on an acceptable outcome. It was meant to be a civilized negotiation, but he suspected Maelyn had something else in mind. She was still angry that he hadn't contacted her or the DUC after the destruction of the starbase, but he was thinking of Misako and how the Sentinels had infiltrated and corrupted the PMC. If he hadn't acted so quickly, they might have overwhelmed all of them. He'd been in a fight like that before, and it was like slowly suffocating while the world closed in around you.

Quinton looked at Maelyn. "Fine then. Follow me," he said and left the bridge.

22

QUINTON ENTERED the ready-room that was just off the bridge. He hardly ever came into this room. There was a clear ceraphome desk with a small half-dome holoscreen projector on the left side. He walked around the desk and glanced at the charcoal-colored couch on the far side of the room. Two lounge chairs with gray memory foam were positioned across from the couch. There was an empty coffee mug on the desk. Becker used the office occasionally and must have left it.

Maelyn followed him inside and closed the door.

He was inside the ship's systems and quickly read through the most critical of alerts. Repair bots were already at work patching the hull. The damage was from the previous encounter with the Sentinels while they destroyed another space station. The life-support systems were in need of attention, particularly the atmospheric scrubbers. The cartridges needed to be replaced. He thought he'd asked Harper to take care of that. Quinton couldn't misremember anything. Becker had been right about that. However, he could ignore certain things. He'd need to find out why Harper hadn't performed one of his assigned duties. The spider-drone was on its way to the rear cargo hold. No doubt that Harper was excited to be transferred into the CDA from the outpost.

"Quinton," Maelyn said softly, and he looked at her.

He hadn't forgotten how beautiful she was. He couldn't forget the curve of her magnificent jawline as it met her neck and then down to a set of collar bones that he'd sometimes imagined kissing. He'd first seen her through the optics of an old agricultural robot and then from the video feeds of the *Nebulon* and on the ACN Starbase Endurance, which included the last comlink where he thought he was about to die. Quinton wasn't sure what it was about the shape of her eyes, her mouth, the soft skin of her cheekbones and the adorable dimple that presented itself when she laughed. He was well past the time in his life when the attention of a beautiful woman made him stammer incoherently, but he'd been powerfully attracted to her. Maelyn was athletic, with a woman's curves that his cybernetic optics drank in the sight of, whether he wanted them to or not. On the starbase, he'd tried to imagine what it would have been like to see her with his own eyes in a freshly regrown body based on his DNA. He'd memorized every curvature of her body and the natural curl to her long, thick, chestnut hair. His smell receptors reported the familiar chemical breakdown of the floral scent of her preferred soap. Quinton could ignore his memories but not forget them, and seeing Maelyn in her pale flight suit that hugged her curves reignited all that attraction.

The sophistication of the mapped consciousness into a PMC was such that it included things beyond behavioral patterns. Quinton wasn't a scientist, but he knew what he felt, even without the biological chemistry that would have been present if he'd been in his own body. He didn't know how it worked. Perhaps it was a function or interpretation of his VI assistants to help him retain his humanity. He wasn't sure, and it probably didn't matter.

Maelyn's eyes took in the sight of him, and her biometrics showed a slightly elevated temperature from her lips and face, even her hands. This could be because she was angry with him or hurt by the fact that he hadn't contacted her. Quinton could access a plethora of biometric data, but none of it could tell him what she was thinking.

"Can we sit down?" she asked.

Quinton gestured toward the seat on the opposite side of the desk.

She glanced at the seat but then shook her head. "I was thinking over here," she said and walked over to the couch near the wall.

Quinton walked around the desk and sat in the plush chair near the couch. "How does…" he began. He'd been about to ask how this was supposed to work, but that wouldn't have gone over well. He shook his head a little. "I know you want to talk, but now might not be a great time."

One of Maelyn's eyebrows twitched up a little, but her expression was guarded. "The ship is safe. Oscar is piloting through the set of jump coordinates you gave him. Becker and Guttman are going to check on critical systems. Simon is probably helping them as much as he can. So, I ask you, why put this off?"

This was his ship, and he wanted to do it himself. He looked away from her. "I don't know. It could be that there are three PMCs aboard my ship, and I really need to talk to them. There would have been a fourth, but she got infiltrated by the Sentinels." Quinton sighed and swallowed hard, lifting his gaze toward her. "And there's you."

She leaned forward a little. "We'll get to that. What happened to Commander Misako?" she asked.

Quinton gritted his teeth. "I didn't get to her in time," he said and told her how the Sentinels had successfully initiated a remote hack that gave them access to Misako's ESS, which led to the corruption of the PMC residing there.

Maelyn pursed her lips for a few moments. "So, your security measures saved not only your own life, but the lives of three more people. Not to mention that you protected the rest of us when they attacked, but you're full of fury because there was one casualty instead of five, including a PMC you'd already rescued before," she said and waited for a few moments. "You need to cut yourself a little bit of slack, Quinton."

Quinton's eyes went skyward. "When you put it like that, it sounds… heroic. I was so close to stopping it. With this avatar and my frame rate so high, I should have been able to prevent it."

Maelyn shook her head. "God, you're so arrogant."

Quinton frowned. "What?"

"Arrogant! Your ego is as big as an entire star system. Would you listen to yourself? You didn't even know the Sentinels could do this. No one knew they had this ability, and yet here you are beating yourself up about it. I'm calling rubbish on the whole damn thing. Misako's death is tragic, and I'm not making light of that, but the fact remains, Quinton, you aren't perfect. You just don't like—"

"To lose," Quinton finished. His lips lifted a little. He wasn't sure which was more frustrating, the fact that she'd just thrown his own words at him or that she was right. Dammit, she was right. "I understand what you're saying. I do. But the Sentinels…"

"They're the real enemy."

"Misako was an intelligence officer, you know. She had a mission briefing she was going to deliver. She had answers."

"I know. I was there when Corvax told you."

He'd been close to getting some answers. Was there a mission or a purpose for PMCs being reactivated? He'd been prepared to just let go of those questions, but knowing he'd been about to get some answers gave rise to a molten frustration deep inside him—frustration that was tied to the reality that everything he'd known was gone. He wanted to make the Sentinels pay for that and much more. And now, Lennix Crowe using some form of Quinton's identity to lure them into becoming his own personal strike force meant that Quinton couldn't just walk away.

He stood up. "I need to speak with Corvax. He might know more about the Federation Wars and Admiral Browning. Maybe he can shed some light on this whole mess. I know I sure as hell can't."

He took a few steps toward the door.

"Why didn't you contact me?" Maelyn asked.

Quinton stopped with his hand stretched toward the door controls.

"After the battle. You survived. Why didn't you meet me at the waypoint coordinates? We waited for Becker and the others, too. We waited a long time," she said.

The way she said "we" was synonymous with the word "I." She'd waited there. She'd waited for him.

Quinton turned toward her. "The ship wasn't as space worthy as we thought. Becker, Guttman, and Oscar helped me repair it. In exchange, I was going to help them get a ship of their own."

Maelyn stood up. "Was the communication system malfunctioning?"

Quinton regarded her for a few moments. "Maelyn," he began.

"Don't," she snapped. "Answer the question."

"I intended to contact you, but I knew you thought I was dead, and so did the rest of the DUC. I started thinking that maybe contacting you wasn't the smartest thing to do."

Maelyn glared at him. "The smartest!" she snarled. "The smartest… Are you…What kind of idiotic, flawed logic led you to that? I really want to know."

"You got what you wanted—colony worlds for the DUC to start settling, rebuilding and all that, including whatever tech you managed to get off the starbase before the attack."

Maelyn closed the distance between them. "You're unbelievable. You think that the only reason I helped you was to get access to the Acheron Confederacy's secret colony worlds project? Did you forget the fact that I got as close as possible to disobeying orders from the DUC admiralty to help you? Did you forget that part? I convinced Admiral Brandt that it was worth helping you not only so I could help the DUC, but to help you, you idiot. I stayed at the waypoint for weeks, hoping that maybe you'd found a way off that damn starbase. Then I spent months trying to find other PMCs who might have been reactivated and lost in a galaxy they didn't understand. PMCs like you."

Quinton's thoughts flatlined. Her words seemed to strike him with tiny molten bolts of plasma. Individually, they didn't kill, but together they knocked him off his proverbial feet. He'd really stepped in it. She'd been something he'd really needed at the time, and he'd rewarded her friendship with nothing. It was worse than that. He'd abandoned her. "I didn't know you did that," he said. "You thought I was dead, right?"

"I did, but I also thought that maybe… maybe you'd found a way to escape."

Quinton opened himself up to a star system full of second-guessing the decisions he'd made since first waking up on the *Wayfarer*. Every path had led him to this moment—him feeling like an idiot for hurting someone who cared for him.

Great job, Quinton, he said sarcastically to himself.

He kept trying to think of a way to make it up to her. Simon was right. Maelyn deserved better, and he should have known that. As he looked at her, he realized there wasn't anything he could say that would undo any of it.

"I'm sorry," he said. "I'm really sorry."

The edges of Maelyn's lips tugged downward in a grim, hurtful line.

All the reasons he'd used to convince himself that not contacting Maelyn was the right decision were shallow and worthless. He could hear his father's words echoing from a lifetime ago: *Quinton, when you're right, you're right, but when you're wrong, admit it. Be man enough to admit it, and you'll be a better man for it.*

Quinton exhaled deeply. "You're right, Maelyn. I should have contacted you and let you know I was alive. What I've done is inexcusable. I promise to return you to your ship, and after that, you can do whatever you want."

Maelyn's tongue quickly glided over her lips, and her head tilted to the side. Her celestial blue eyes stabbed him in the chest. "You avoided me because you thought that once I found out you were alive, I'd try to get you to do something else for the DUC."

Quinton frowned, feeling like he was about to be ambushed, but there was no avoiding it. Sometimes he had to just take his blows as they came, and this was no different. "Yeah, I did. Am I wrong?"

Maelyn looked away, disappointed. "No, I would have tried. And you could have said no if I had."

That stung him. She was right to be furious with him. Hell, he was furious with himself. He was better than this. Now he just felt like a coward, which he wasn't. He'd made a mistake, and he wouldn't repeat it.

"What else do you want me to say? I said I was sorry. I meant it. I'll take you to your ship and then you don't even have to see me again."

Maelyn shook her head. "It's not that simple."

Some foolish part of his brain came up with the idea that making a stupid little joke in an attempt to deflect from the situation would be good, but he banished that idea to a black hole in his mind that he set aside for his truly awful ideas, never to be heard from again.

"Okay," Quinton said. "Do you want to sit back down?"

"No!"

Quinton flinched a little. "Okay then."

Maelyn gritted her teeth and balled her hands into fists. "You're such a jerk." She used an angry tone, but there was also a hint of something close to amusement in spite of her fury. It was a long way from forgiveness, but it was something.

"I am," he agreed. "I'd let you use a palm stunner on me, but I don't think it'll have an effect—"

Everything else Quinton had been about to say he couldn't because he'd dropped to the ground. He couldn't move his arms or legs. Multiple alerts snapped to existence on his HUD, demanding his attention.

Maelyn smiled sweetly and squatted down next to him. Something silver flashed in her hands, and she regarded him for a few moments, appraisingly. "Did that hurt?"

He hadn't felt pain, but the cybernetic avatar did register the disruption of the molecular bonds that made his cybernetic musculature work. There wasn't any damage, other than to his pride because he was helpless. He felt like he was floating in a pool, but he couldn't move.

Maelyn waved the palm-sized disruptor in front of him. "I wasn't sure it was going to work on you."

She adjusted the disruptor field and he could move his head.

Quinton grinned bitterly. "All right, now that you've had your fun, turn it off."

Maelyn pursed her lips in thought, and her eyes flashed playfully. "Oh dear, I don't know if I can. This is so much fun. Maybe I'll just keep the field engaged while I go take a walk."

"You wouldn't—Maelyn!" Quinton shouted as she headed for the door.

He quickly disabled the door controls, locking her into the room with him.

Maelyn spun around and grinned, enjoying this a little too much. She glanced at the door, and he thought she was deciding whether to leave him or not. He'd disabled the door controls, but he was also sure she could figure out a way to override them.

"You deserve much more punishment than this," she said.

Quinton glared at her, but it had no venom in it. "Maybe a little more, but let's not get away from ourselves here. You've had your fun. Now turn off the disruptor field."

Maelyn sashayed over to the couch, sat down, and crossed her legs, looking at him with indifference.

"What more do you want? I already said I was sorry," he said. "You know, being trapped on this ship with Becker, Guttman, and Oscar was no picnic. Most of the time, they're complaining. It never ends. They're worse than a bunch of first-year cadets on training rotation. If I could have exchanged them for you, I would have. I know it was wrong now."

Maelyn's lips twitched, this time in a good way. Maybe she'd even forgive him… eventually. As the minutes dragged by, he began to wonder how long she was going to keep him like this. He wasn't going to ask.

Maelyn nodded to herself. "Now we can negotiate."

"Negotiate?"

"You owe me," she replied.

Quinton chuckled. "And you say *I'm* unbelievable. I'm not negotiating anything until you turn off that disruptor."

Maelyn considered this for a few moments. "You should consider installing a ship-wide suppression system like I have on the *Nebulon*. It would have prevented something like this from happening."

"Maybe you can give me the name of a few reputable installers who can be trusted to upgrade my ship."

Maelyn nodded again and then turned off the disruptor field. The alerts on Quinton's HUD vanished as the avatar's cybernetic musculature returned to normal. He stood up and eyed her warily. Then he sat down.

"I didn't see that coming."

"I know," she replied and just looked at him for a moment. "Let's set the personal stuff aside for now."

"Okay." Quinton nodded.

"You're aware of the increased Sentinel activity throughout occupied sectors of the galaxy?"

"We knew they'd become more active, but it's because of Lennix Crowe and the Union's conflict with the Collective."

"That's part of it, but it's getting worse. Sentinels are targeting places that have nothing to do with the Collective."

"Why?"

"I haven't received an update about what DUC intelligence has uncovered in their investigation."

"Is this an incursion?" Quinton asked and then quickly added, "Becker told me about them."

Maelyn ran her fingers through her hair, brushing it away from her face. "It could be the beginning of one, yes."

"The only way I can think of how Crowe got my identification was from the Sentinel code he used to take over Endurance Starbase. It lured the Sentinels there. He must have figured out a way to make it work, then came up with a deployment protocol to use against the Collective."

"He must have had help."

Quinton frowned. "You mean from outside his organization?"

Maelyn nodded.

"So he hired someone or forced someone to figure it out. Does it really matter how?"

"Yes, it does. If we can figure out who helped Crowe, then we can also figure out a way to reverse what's been done."

"We've been working on stopping Crowe," Quinton said and told her about the specially crafted message he had spreading through galactic communications channels.

"Crowe wouldn't want an incursion to happen."

"I wouldn't be so sure about that. We hunted for a Jordani battle group that was wreaking havoc across inhabited star systems. They were commanded by a real brutal bastard. He'd conduct raids among civilian ship traffic using them as shields, knowing full well that our ROE prevented us from engaging them."

"How did you stop them?"

"The civilian ship captains used their ships as weapons. They flew them into the Jordani warships, freeing us to engage. The point I'm trying to make is that sometimes the person leading doesn't care about the damage they're doing. Crowe might have reached his limit."

"Or he might be in over his head. What was a tactical advantage is now out of his control."

"Maybe," Quinton said. "He still needs to be stopped."

"Take a look at these intelligence reports gathered over the past few months. There has been increased Sentinel activity and also PMC activation signals," Maelyn said. She activated her personal holoscreen and a galactic star map appeared. "These icons are where Crowe used the Sentinels to target Collective installations. Now I'm adding in the other star systems where the Sentinels also attacked." Quinton watched as more star systems were highlighted, and they were equal to the number of systems Crowe had attacked. That couldn't be a coincidence. "Now, here are the reported sightings of Sentinel scout ships throughout the region, and keep in mind that these are only the ones we know about."

The star map updated again, showing vastly more sightings of Sentinel ships.

"I take it that this is more than what's normally reported?"

Maelyn nodded. "They're hunting for PMCs."

"I don't suppose you've found a way to log activation signals."

Maelyn chuckled. "Funny you should ask." The star map updated again with dozens of signals. "There's a clear correlation between increased Sentinel presence and an increase in PMC activation signals."

Quinton peered at the data on the holoscreen. He had Radek conduct his own analysis, which also concluded the high probability that these activities were interrelated.

"Do you see the correlation?"

Quinton nodded. "A correlation exists, but we still don't know what it means."

"They're in response to one another."

"How?"

"The Sentinels have always searched for PMCs and the remnant tech associated with them. Their activity increased after Crowe started using them as a weapon."

"Right, so if we stop Crowe, then the Sentinels should stop."

"What about the activation signals? Something triggers them in response to the increased Sentinel presence."

"What if it's just the Sentinels triggering the activation signals?" Quinton said. "As a way of exposing people like me."

"If that were the case, the Sentinels would be present wherever the activation signals go, and that's not happening."

"Have you been able to trace the activation signals?" Quinton asked.

"Some, but not to the source. We've been trying to beat the Sentinels to the locations in hopes of rescuing the PMCs before they're killed."

"And."

"It's complicated," she said.

"Complicated?"

"Yes, it wasn't just danger from the Sentinels that we had to be concerned about. We didn't know if the PMCs being reactivated were stable. The Alari Outpost was the closest we'd gotten. It was touch and go even before you showed up. Corvax was a bit on edge when we arrived."

Quinton remembered how disorienting it was when he'd been reactivated. "What is it you want from me?"

"Something is triggering the reactivation signals after decades of silence. Don't you want to know who or what it is?"

"I'm more interested in stopping Crowe."

"That might be harder than you think."

"I'll find him, and I can guarantee you that he won't enjoy the experience."

"Quinton, spaceports, stations, refueling depots, colonies and the like are all closed off to you. You can't go to any of them."

He looked at her and frowned. She was serious. "I'm pretty sure I can provide the local authorities or governing bodies a set of credentials that they won't second-guess."

Maelyn shook her head. "I'm sure you can, but your ship is unlike anything that's registered. That's something you won't be able to fake. They're not allowing anything that doesn't match up in their data repositories to come anywhere near a docking port. Security forces and measures are in full operation. I've seen them fire on ships to prevent them from reaching them. No one wants to give the Sentinels a reason to destroy what's left."

"We'll have to agree to disagree on that."

"Come back to the DUC. You can help us track the PMC activation signals."

"No," he replied.

"That's it? No, 'I'll think about it?' Just, no?"

"Yes," he said and held up his hands in a placating gesture. "Hear me out and stop fingering the disruptor. You're making me uncomfortable."

Maelyn interlaced her fingers and rested them on her lap.

"I volunteered for the PMC program to protect the Acheron Confederacy, to help Admiral Browning defeat the Jordani Federation and its allies. Now you think that because I woke up years after those battles have been decided I should just take up another cause and fight for that? That's what you're asking me to do."

He regarded Maelyn for a few moments and she nodded.

"Yes," she said.

"I don't want to. In fact, I'm choosing not to. Wait a second," he said as she was about to interrupt. "I just want out of this. The galaxy wants people like me gone, and looking at the aftermath of the Federation Wars, I'm a little inclined to agree with them. If I could help the others get out of this and back into a human body, then that would be all right with me."

Maelyn inhaled and sighed. Then she stood up. "You've made your point."

Quinton stood up. He was a little surprised that she wasn't belaboring the point.

"You said you wanted to talk to Corvax. Let's go do that. Do you mind if I come along?" she asked.

Quinton eyed her suspiciously, and she looked innocently back at him. Why did it feel like she'd given in too easily?

"Fine with me," he said, and they left the room.

The *Wayfarer's* entry to both the armory and the workshop was located in the cargo area, where the weapons were stowed and locked in their cabinets. The workshop walls were lined with storage cabinets and two metallic tables for equipment maintenance and repair. The workshop, like most of the ship, sported pale, sleek lines with burnished copper accents.

Quinton slid down the ladder between decks and saw Walsh Corvax standing near the CDA storage container, which hovered several feet off the floor. The CDA looked more robotic than Quinton's avatar, as if it was a much earlier model. The chassis was humanoid in appearance and roughly the average size of a human. Corvax's CDA had a masculine physical appearance, but the exterior was chrome-colored with green accents. Quinton wasn't sure if the accent colors were a user preference or not.

Corvax looked at him, and his optics glowed a brilliant green. The CDA was a similar model to that which Quinton had expected to be reactivated in.

"Your ship is quite impressive. I knew the ACN loved their ship designs, but this star class jumper has capabilities beyond anything we had in the Alari Navy," Corvax said appreciatively.

Corvax's entire demeanor had changed after they'd authenticated with each other and he'd learned that Quinton was a Galactic class PMC.

Quinton was about to reply to Corvax when shouting erupted from the other side of the cargo area.

"What do you mean it's not here!" Harper shouted.

"It didn't make it to the ship; otherwise, it would have been in the hold," Guttman replied.

Quinton hastened past a row of cargo containers.

"You did this on purpose," Harper said with a scowl. The spider-drone's legs tapped the ground in irritation.

"I didn't sabotage the delivery. The cargo never even made it to the hold. You better back off," Guttman growled.

Quinton saw Guttman glaring at Harper. Several of the spider-drone's legs shook, as if they were getting conflicting signals from Harper.

"Harper," Quinton said, "what happened?"

The spider-drone was poised like a coiled spring, ready to explode.

Guttman looked at Quinton. "He's barely keeping it together."

"There was a CDA for Harper that made it to the hangar," Quinton said.

Guttman nodded but kept an eye on Harper. "I know. That's what I'm trying to tell him. It never made it to the ship."

Quinton winced inwardly. Damage from the Sentinel bombardment must have prevented the cargo drones from bringing it to the ship. There had been so much happening at the time that Quinton hadn't checked before they left.

"Harper, it's not his fault," Quinton said.

Harper didn't respond. He didn't move at all, which Quinton found more disturbing than if he'd begun shouting.

Becker and Simon came into the cargo area.

"What's going on?" Becker asked.

Quinton stepped toward Harper. "It's not his fault," he said.

Guttman exhaled explosively. "This is bullshit! I don't have to stand here and take this from him. I'm getting out of here," he said and stomped his way past Harper.

Quinton heard a faint muttering coming from Harper. It was so soft that he doubted anyone else could hear it.

"Yes, it is. Yes, it is. Yes. It. Is," Harper said in a harsh whisper.

Quinton opened a comlink to Harper, but it was refused. Harper had closed himself off.

"Harper," Quinton said softly. "Are you still with me? We'll find you another body."

"I had a body," Harper replied, finally. He turned around slowly, and the spider-drone's optics seemed to regard the others.

Quinton turned toward the others. "Give us a minute."

Maelyn corralled the others into the workshop. He heard Corvax say that the integrity check of Chloe Bradshaw's PMC was nearly complete.

Harper looked at Quinton and said, "I should have gone out and retrieved the CDA myself."

"You were doing what I asked you to do—monitoring the Sentinels and making sure the ship was ready to leave," Quinton replied.

"I could have done it. I should have."

"No, you couldn't have."

"Why! Is it because you don't trust me either?"

Quinton drew himself up. "You're not giving me much of a reason to. Now knock it off."

Harper didn't reply.

"First thing," Quinton said, "no one is trying to prevent you from getting a body. Guttman may be… well, he's Guttman. He may not like you, but he's not out to get you. Is that understood?"

Harper remained silent.

"Is that understood, Lieutenant?"

"The ACN doesn't exist. Remember? I'm not a lieutenant anymore," Harper replied.

Quinton watched the spider-drone very carefully. Dissociative disorder was a prevailing cause for PMC failure. It led to insanity.

"All right," Quinton said.

The spider-drone's optic bobbed up and down as it regarded Quinton. "It's just Nash. No, I'm just Nash Harper. Quinton, I don't think I can stay in this drone much longer."

Quinton knew what it was like to hold on to your sanity by your fingertips. If Harper lost it, then it wouldn't matter if Quinton forced him into standby because Harper would be gone.

"I promise I'll get you a replacement. The next place we're going to will be a station that will have something for you, even if I have to steal it. I just need you to keep it together. Can you do that?"

Harper was silent for a few long moments. "I believe you. I think it might be better if I go into a long-duration rest cycle. The ship's VR helps, but it's not perfect."

"I understand," Quinton said. "Just stay away from Guttman for a while, okay?"

He watched as the spider-drone left the cargo area. He felt helpless. He should have made sure that the unoccupied CDA had made it to the damn ship. After he'd gotten confirmation that it had reached the hangar bay… The attack.

He heard the others speaking in the workshop and joined them.

Another CDA stood in the room. The exterior chassis had adjusted to being more feminine. Artificial azure eyes shifted toward him. A PMC authentication comlink registered with Quinton, and he acknowledged it. There was a brief exchange of data to confirm their identities.

"Commander Aldren," she said.

"It's just Quinton."

"Negative, Commander. I can't do that," Bradshaw replied.

"This isn't… Never mind. We'll bring you up to speed."

Bradshaw looked at Corvax, and her metallic lips lifted in wry amusement. "You really thought he was an Agent of Harding?" she said and shook her head a little. She turned back to Quinton. "I've been brought up to speed, sir. Walsh filled me in."

Quinton glanced at Corvax for a second. "She just woke up."

"Yes," Corvax said, understanding. "As part of the PMC integrity check, I uploaded what I'd learned so Bradshaw could hit the ground running."

Quinton glanced at Maelyn, Becker, and Simon.

"It's knowledge-sharing. In short increments, it's safe."

"What about larger increments?" Becker asked.

"Not safe," Corvax explained. "There is a high risk of corruption with mergence protocols."

Quinton frowned. "That's news to me."

Corvax looked at Bradshaw. "He predates the Federation Wars."

Bradshaw nodded. "Oh, I see," she said and looked at Quinton. "Mergence protocol was expected of you, right?"

"In my training, it was encouraged, but Radek just informed me that those protocols had been disabled by the time I was reactivated."

"That must have been Admiral Browning's work then," Corvax said.

"What makes you say that?" Quinton asked.

"Because if you were an Agent of Harding, we'd all be dead."

Becker cleared his throat. "Now, wait a second. You said this before about Harding being the enemy. Are you talking about *the* Miles Harding?"

"Are there any others?" Corvax replied.

Simon glanced at Maelyn, and she gave him a nod. "Miles Harding created PMC technology. He was the first PMC ever."

Becker nodded. "Yeah, if my galactic history is right, Harding was pivotal to the ACN defeating the Jordani Federation."

"That is true," Corvax said.

Becker looked at Quinton with raised eyebrows.

"Why do I get the feeling that our whole world is about to get turned upside down," Quinton said and looked at Corvax and Bradshaw. "As far as I'm concerned, everyone in this room has clearance to whatever information you're going to share."

Corvax looked at Bradshaw. "You might be better at this than I am."

Bradshaw nodded. "Works for me. It's really quite simple. Everything you think you know about the Federation Wars is wrong."

Quinton watched as the others exchanged pointed looks. Maelyn looked the least surprised. He'd long suspected that there was significant misinformation about the Federation Wars. Maybe Maelyn believed the same.

"This is crazy," Becker said. "You've only just gotten here. We're the ones who've lived here. We know more about what happened in the Federation Wars than you."

Bradshaw grinned. "That's where you're wrong. Walsh and I were there at the beginning of the Federation Wars, although they didn't call it that at the time." She gave them an appraising look. "First of all, thank you, Simon, for providing Corvax and me with your historical records. They'll really help us make this easier for you."

Becker looked at Simon. "When did you do that?"

"Just a few minutes ago," Simon replied.

Becker looked at Quinton.

"They can do the same things I can," Quinton said. "They adjusted their frame rates to give themselves time to review the data."

"That's only partially correct, sir," Bradshaw said. "But we'll get to that. Your history tells you that Admiral Browning went rogue and took all his followers—about a dozen fleets under his command—and began attacking the other federations, coalitions, empires, what have you. He was credited with the most egregious war crimes ever committed. I'm here to tell you that this is all a lie. Browning didn't do those things. He tried to stop them from happening." Becker opened his mouth to say something, and Bradshaw gestured for him to be quiet. "The massacres and attacks on civilian targets, colony worlds, and military installations *did* happen. But they were because of Harding. Miles Harding Prime, to be exact."

Becker shook his head. "You're wrong. There were PMC lockdown protocols that would have kept Harding from doing those things."

"There were. He figured out a way to break free of them," Bradshaw replied. "And this is where it gets a little unclear. We think—or Browning's intelligence apparatus thinks—that the mergence protocol that allowed PMCs to build up the intelligence and experiences of other PMCs is what led Harding Prime to betray the ACN and every other galactic civilization."

"Harding went insane?" Quinton asked.

Bradshaw shook her head. "That's the thing. We don't know. All those attacks that Admiral Browning was accused of were orchestrated by Miles Harding. We tried to stop them. We succeeded in the beginning, but that's when Harding got creative. He was too methodical to be insane." Bradshaw paused for a moment, considering her words. "He's different."

"You've encountered Miles Harding?" Simon asked.

"Yes, and no," Bradshaw replied. "I'm an operations officer and logistics are my specialty. PMCs who came into contact with Harding's forces had to be isolated, but I never came into direct contact with Harding."

"They were compromised," Quinton said and frowned. "Harding could infiltrate other PMCs! That means that he could've... Did he create the Sentinels?"

Becker's mouth hung halfway between denial and indignation.

"That's where we're unclear. Harding may have had a hand in their creation, but he didn't need to be actively involved. He might have provided remaining federation navies with the tools to create them."

"You don't know for sure," Maelyn said.

Bradshaw shook her head.

Maelyn pursed her lips. "If the galaxy was already uniting against Admiral Browning, there was no way he could defeat Harding."

"Harding had somehow spread himself among the other federations," Bradshaw said. "They were eager to get their hands on PMC technology. It was a huge tactical advantage. We can compartmentalize ourselves to function in any computer system. Warship weapons systems became much more efficient with PMCs than they had been with virtual intelligences alone."

"He gave it away to everyone and they lined up to get it," Quinton said bitterly. "But he also included a way for him to take control later on." He looked at the others. "Browning must have seen it first. The Federation Wars were some kind of elaborate plan of Harding's."

"He tried to warn them," Corvax said. "In the beginning, he tried to warn the ACN and then anyone who would listen."

"But he was discredited and chased away because he couldn't stop it," Simon said. His eyes were wide.

Becker grunted. "You all sound like conspiracy theorist nut jobs. This is crazy. Why would Harding do any of this?"

"He's got a point," Quinton said. "Did Browning figure out Harding's motivation?"

"I don't know," Bradshaw said.

"Me either," Corvax replied. "That's why Commander Isobe Misako was crucial to our mission."

"Who?" Becker asked.

"The CDA that attacked us," Corvax said. "Communications had become impossible to secure, so we'd started using PMCs to carry mission briefings for combat operations, but Misako was different."

"How?" Quinton asked.

"Because…" Corvax began but paused, thinking. "Browning had come up with a way to stop Harding. I think it has to do with you."

Quinton blinked several times. "Me?"

"Him?" Becker asked almost at the same time.

Maelyn nodded. "You predate the Federation Wars, Quinton. You're a Galactic Class PMC. As I recall, you weren't sure what that was, so it must have come after you were uploaded."

"I didn't know. That wasn't part of my training."

Becker looked at him and narrowed his gaze. "It sounds like *they* don't know either," he said, gesturing toward the two CDAs.

"We'd know more if Misako had survived," Bradshaw said and looked at Quinton. "But you do have command authority, sir."

"Because of his rank?" Becker asked.

"That, too, but also because of the type of PMC he is," Bradshaw said.

All of them looked at Quinton. "There are quite a few assumptions being tossed around."

"There are also a lot of good points. It makes sense," Maelyn said.

"Just because we like an explanation doesn't make it right," Quinton replied.

Becker's shoulders slumped a little and he sighed. "I'm glad you're at least questioning this."

"I'm gonna need some time to think about it."

"No, you don't," Maelyn said. "Increase your frame rate. Have Radek run his analysis and you'll see that there are a lot of kernels of truth."

Quinton frowned. She was right… again. It was beginning to be a habit. "I'll get to that, but first, Harper needs a body."

"Quinton," Maelyn said and stepped closer to him. "You're meant to command them. Browning had a plan. You're part of it. It all makes sense."

"Yeah, a dead man had a plan to continue fighting a war that ended long ago," Quinton said. "I'm not saying there wasn't a plan, but that doesn't mean I have to drop everything and take up his cause."

Maelyn opened her mouth to reply but then pressed her lips together. "What are you going to do then?"

"I'm going to help Harper. We have a list of space stations in the Sector that will have what we need. That's first. Then Crowe has to be stopped," Quinton said.

Maelyn rolled her eyes, and Quinton could guess what she was about to say. He couldn't dock at any spaceports because they're afraid of a Sentinel attack. But he'd failed to help Harper before, and he wasn't going to ignore him because of what they'd just learned.

"We'll dock with the *Nebulon* in a few hours," Quinton said and left the workshop.

No one followed him.

This was his ship. If they didn't approve of where he was going to fly it, they could leave.

23

It was easy to get lost in the vastness of the galaxy, which was why Quinton wasn't too concerned that they'd been tracked. With most of the passengers gathered near the portside airlock, the bridge of the *Wayfarer* wasn't as crowded as it had been a few moments ago.

The *Nebulon* was about to dock with his ship, and Quinton resisted the urge to look over at navigation. Oscar wouldn't be sitting there. Becker, Guttman, and Oscar were all going to the *Nebulon*. He didn't know what Maelyn had offered them, but it wasn't too hard to guess.

"The *Nebulon* has docked," Bradshaw said.

Quinton stood up. "I'm going to see them off. Corvax, you have the conn."

"Aye, Commander. I have the conn," Corvax confirmed.

Quinton left the bridge and headed toward the portside airlock. He could hear the others talking from all the way down the corridor.

"You can't be serious," Guttman said. "You still have that creature aboard ship?"

"Yeah, you're going to be bunkmates," Simon replied and grinned.

"Like hell we are. What was its name again… Thing?"

"Stumpy."

"That's right. It's got gimpy little legs. If it comes near me, I'm going introduce it to the wrong end of my blaster."

"That would be unwise," Simon said.

"Yeah, right," Guttman replied.

"No, seriously. Captain Wayborn made Stumpy an official member of the crew. You're just visiting, so…"

"Official member of the crew?" Guttman said. "Is that true, Captain?"

"Quite true," Quinton heard Maelyn reply.

He'd forgotten about the furry little creature that had hitched a ride with him. He was glad Simon had kept him.

"Come on, you're joking with me."

"Nope," Simon said. "His official title is pest control. He scampers all over the ship."

"I'm still not bunking with that creature."

"I'm sure it wouldn't be able to stand the smell," Becker said.

Oscar stepped into the corridor. "Quinton," he said.

"Are you ready to go?" Quinton asked, hoping Oscar wouldn't reveal that he'd been listening to their conversation.

"Just about. Listen, I wanted to talk to you."

"Don't worry about it, Oscar. You stayed when it counted, and you don't owe me anything."

Oscar eyed him for a few moments, then nodded. Without another word, he headed back inside.

Quinton followed him in and looked at the others. They were gathered around the airlock doors. They all looked at him. Simon appeared as if he had something to tell him but couldn't seem to pick the right moment. Guttman kept checking his gear and the same pockets a few times, then gave Quinton a nod. Becker regarded him, as did Maelyn.

Quinton sighed at the awkwardness. "I guess I lost all the kids in the divorce."

The airlock doors opened and Kieva stood on the *Nebulon* side. She was short, blonde, and cute. "Hello, *spacer*," she said approvingly.

Guttman frowned. "You know this is Quinton."

Kieva's lips lifted. "Oh, I know," she said. "You're cleared to come aboard."

"Thank you, Kieva," Maelyn said.

Kieva gave her a two-fingered salute, waved to Quinton, and started to head back through the airlock.

"It's a shame we didn't have more time," Quinton said.

Kieva's laugh echoed down the corridor.

Quinton looked at the men who'd been his companions for the past few months.

Guttman's face became serious. "Be careful."

"One step ahead. Right?"

Guttman nodded. Then he went onto the *Nebulon*.

"Quinton," Simon said, "I made a navigation update available to the *Wayfarer*. You'll need to acknowledge it."

"Thanks, Simon."

Simon nodded and went back to his ship.

Becker walked over to him. "Are you sure about this?"

"Harper needs help. This is something I have to do," Quinton said. Becker nodded. "But if I hear about any ships for sale, I'll send you a message."

Becker shook his head. "If it's up for sale, it's probably not worth flying."

"That's right. You want to find the ones that are about to come on the market."

Quinton watched him for a second, then looked at Maelyn. "So, this is it."

Maelyn regarded him. "For now."

"If I learn anything that could be useful to you, I'll reach out. I promise," Quinton said. It was all he could do. She thought he was making a mistake, and he saw the resignation in her gaze.

"I would welcome it, Captain Aldren," Maelyn said.

Quinton smiled. "Safe travels, Captain Wayborn."

She walked through the airlock and Quinton watched as she secured the *Nebulon's* airlock. She looked at him through the small window. Then, the *Nebulon's* docking clamps released and the two ships separated.

Quinton walked back toward the bridge but stopped at the galley. All the food and supplies had been stored away, and the galley looked abandoned. He'd spent hours in here with the others. It was their meeting place.

As he watched the *Nebulon,* he wondered if he was making a mistake. But he wasn't second-guessing himself—at least not completely.

The door to the bridge opened.

"Ready to execute jump, Commander," Corvax said.

Quinton walked to the captain's chair and sat down. "Very well. Take us away."

MAELYN WALKED AWAY from the airlock where Becker was waiting for her.

"What do you think he'll do?" Becker asked.

"Exactly what he said he'd do," she replied.

Guttman let out a long sigh of relief and smiled. "Thank you, Captain. I don't think I could have taken being on a ship with a crew of PMCs for much longer."

Maelyn looked at him with a surprised expression.

"Quinton is fine," Guttman said quickly. "It's the others. Especially Harper. There's no saving that one."

"Indeed. We'll see."

Becker looked at her and frowned. "I can't figure out what you're doing."

Maelyn smirked. "You could just ask."

"I think I just did."

"You can follow me to the bridge," she said.

Guttman left them, heading toward the crews' quarters.

"Now, don't be like that," Becker said, speaking to Oscar.

Maelyn raised her eyebrows, and Oscar shrugged. "It still doesn't feel right. We're abandoning him."

Maelyn nodded. "Oh, I see."

"I get why you're mad at him, but he's—"

"Going to do exactly as he thinks best," Maelyn said. They reached the bridge, and she looked at Oscar. "For what it's worth, getting you guys off that ship is probably for the best."

"Why?" Oscar asked.

"Because Quinton has a black hole's worth of stubbornness. Once he's made up his mind, there's no convincing him to do anything else."

"He's just trying to do the right thing for Harper."

Maelyn nodded. "I know," she said gently. "I understand why he's doing it."

"But it's not what you want him to do," Becker said.

Maelyn shook her head. "It's not what you think. I'm going to show you what I shared with Quinton."

"This has to do with increased Sentinel activity," Becker said.

"And the PMC activation signals," Maelyn confirmed. "I don't think it's the last we'll see of Quinton. He's stubborn, determined, and sometimes irritating, but he's a good man. Sometimes even the best of us have to learn things for ourselves. The sooner he realizes he's pursuing the wrong goal, the better off he'll be."

"The wrong goal," Becker said and frowned. "You mean Lennix Crowe?"

Maelyn nodded. "Crowe might be part of all this, but he's not the real problem."

"Who is?"

"I don't know."

"Then what are you going to do?"

"We're going to look for PMC activation signals," Maelyn replied sweetly. "Don't look so alarmed. It'll all make sense soon."

Becker snorted. "Guttman is going to flip out. He's gonna lose it when he hears what I think we're going to be doing." He leaned back on the nearby workstation and gestured toward the main holoscreen.

Oscar crossed his arms and did the same.

Maelyn had hoped she could convince Quinton to go with her. She never expected to see him again. She'd thought he'd died on that starbase, and seeing him on that outpost, alive, and in some kind of prototype body… She gritted her teeth. He seemed genuinely sorry. Regardless of her own feelings, they all needed Quinton. She just hoped he learned it quickly enough that the real players of the Federation Wars didn't catch up with him first.

Becker held up his hand. "I'll get Guttman up here. He's going to want to hear this, too."

Maelyn nodded. "All right, gentlemen. Get ready to blow the airlock doors wide open."

24

TERACOM INDUSTRIAL SPACEPORT was just under five astronomical units from the *Wayfarer*.

"They're firing on us," Harper said.

"Warning shots only," Corvax replied.

Quinton activated the comlink. "Captain Alina, I thought we were going to be friends."

A squadron of Conda scout ships on patrol had swooped to their location almost as soon as they'd jumped into the system.

"Transfer your ship registration and your credentials immediately, or I'll order my squad to fire on your ship," Captain Alina replied in a no-nonsense, trigger-happy voice.

"I have a firing solution," Harper offered.

"Negative," Quinton replied.

"Have it your way then, Captain," Captain Alina said.

Quinton hadn't muted the comlink when he'd replied to Harper. "Wait a second. I wasn't talking to you. I'm sending our registration and credentials to you now."

"Hold your position," Alina said.

Quinton muted the comlink.

"Sir," Corvax said, "we're within range of the Conda's frag-cannons."

Frag-cannons were capable of firing three-round bursts, which could penetrate the armored hull.

Quinton looked at the tactical plot on the main holoscreen. The squadron of Conda Fighters had staggered their approach. They were agile and could get up to speed quickly.

The comlink went active again.

"Star class jumper *Wayfarer*," Captain Alina said. "Your ship is unregistered with any of the common ship registries in the sector. Teracom Industrial Spaceport is closed to you. You will leave this area immediately, or we will destroy your ship."

"Captain," Quinton said, "as I already included in the data I sent you, this is a prototype ship that we salvaged from wreckage on an outpost. That's why it's not on any of your registries."

"Oh, is that all?" Captain Alina said mockingly. "Well, why didn't you say so?"

"Captain, I can tell that you're a formidable woman. We'll leave immediately as ordered, but is there anyone who could deliver what we need?"

The comlink went dark.

"Weapons systems are powering up on all of them. I have point defense systems on standby," Corvax said.

Quinton cursed. This was the fourth spaceport they'd been to and the receptions had all been similar. Spaceport security was operating at the highest severity.

"I have a firing solution," Harper said.

"I already said no," Quinton snapped.

He engaged maneuvering thrusters and throttled up the mains, and the ship quickly increased its distance from the Conda Space Fighters.

"We could have made a run for the spaceport," Harper said. "We could have slipped past their defenses. There's no way they can secure every docking platform."

They'd already tried to gain access to four other spaceports. They'd even come close to reaching a docking platform with two of them. Maelyn was right. The spaceports in this sector were in tight lockdown.

"We can't take out civilian security forces," Corvax replied.

"I was just going to disable their ships. They can survive on life support until a repair ship arrives," Harper replied.

"The moment we fired on them, they would have alerted the spaceport and the rest of their security forces," Quinton said.

He watched the tactical plot. The Condas hadn't left. They were making sure the *Wayfarer* departed the area, so he engaged the jump drive and did just that.

"We could try raiding a warehouse facility," Harper said. "I could reprogram a few drones to break in and retrieve what we need."

Quinton looked at him. "We don't have drones that can do that. Warehouse facilities are huge. We wouldn't know where to look even if we were able to get inside one. We tried scouting before and were detected."

"So, we're giving up?"

"No," Quinton replied. "Never, but I don't want to keep doing the same thing and failing. That's just a waste of time."

A message indicator appeared on Quinton's personal holoscreen. He frowned. They hadn't received any comlink requests, but the message had made it through his own security measures, so he knew it was safe. He opened it, and a recorded message from Simon came to prominence.

"Simon," Quinton said quietly. He put the recorded video up on the main holoscreen. "I just got this. I don't know what it is, but I think all of you should see it too."

"Quinton," Simon said, "I put this message on a conditional subroutine to be presented after the ship made a certain number of jumps," he paused and lifted the edges of his lips a little. "I know you're determined to help Harper get a more suitable host for his PMC. Sounds familiar, doesn't it? Anyway, I wanted to give you another option. I've cleared this with Maelyn, and chances are you might have already thought of this. But, just in case you haven't, I'm hoping you'll carefully consider what I'm about to say." He paused again as if wanting to give them a moment to take in what he'd said. "Okay, here it is. We—or Maelyn, that is—have copies of your DNA data and also the entire DNA archive from Endurance Starbase. It was one of the first things we transferred when... Well, you know when. Harper's or even the others' DNA might all be in there. It's an option if you want to pursue it. That's all I wanted you to know."

The video recording ended and the screen became dark.

"I see what he did. How he stored the message," Bradshaw said. "Quite clever, actually."

"Simon is one of the good ones," Quinton said.

"They have copies of our DNA?" Harper asked.

"Mine for sure," Quinton said and smiled a little. He leaned back in his chair and shook his head a little.

"What are you smiling about?" Harper asked.

"Because sometimes people know you better than you give them credit for," Quinton replied. "Never mind. We have a choice to make."

"Why didn't they just tell us about it then? Why wait?" Harper asked.

"Also," Corvax added, "what good is having the DNA data if they don't have the means to grow the body?"

"They can't do it on the *Nebulon,* but the DUC has the resources for it. Simon wouldn't have sent this if they didn't have the transference protocols to offload our PMCs," Quinton replied.

"I still don't see how this helps," Harper said.

"Really? You don't?" Quinton asked and paused for a moment, giving Harper time to consider it. Harper didn't reply, so Quinton continued. "Because, if they have your DNA on record, we can safely get you out of the spider-drone. If they don't, they have mine. I can offload this avatar and you can use it."

The spider-drone's optics regarded him. "You'd do that?"

"Of course. That's what I was going to do anyway, but I was hoping to do it without help from the DUC."

"You can't do that, sir," Corvax said, and Bradshaw echoed the same. "You're a Galactic class PMC. Admiral Browning must have had plans for you. If you give that up, we might not be able to find another."

"Maybe he did, but there might not be any other option."

"He's right," Harper said. "I can't let you do that."

Quinton regarded his new crew for a few moments. "It might not even be an issue."

"It's not, because I'm not going to let you do that," Harper said.

Quinton glanced at the others. Sometimes a CDA's facial expressions could be so deadpanned that they might as well not exist. He thought he saw some kind of understanding pass between them that Quinton could only suspect, and he certainly didn't like where this was going.

"Fine, let's move on, but before we do, there's something I need to show you guys," Quinton said.

He showed them the Sentinel tracker data Maelyn had given him.

"Where did the data come from?" Corvax asked.

"Dholeren United Coalition. The DUC. They have an extensive network of ships and contacts."

"That makes sense since they're a nomadic civilian space fleet," Bradshaw said.

"Multiple fleets, outposts, and hopefully a few colonies by now," Quinton said.

"This data is old," Corvax said. "Without more current updates, all we're seeing is that these Sentinels exist. Albeit, there are more of them now than before."

Quinton nodded. "And these new data points are from PMC activation signals."

"This is what we should be focused on," Corvax said.

"Could this be Polaris?" Quinton asked.

"Maybe," Bradshaw replied. "We can't be sure, but if Misako told it to you, then it must be important."

"I was thinking the same thing, but it could also just be the Sentinels trying to trap us," Quinton said.

Corvax cleared his throat. "Commander, if you're looking for our input on what we should do next, then mine is that we pursue these activation signals. One of them could lead us to the source."

"I agree with Walsh," Bradshaw said. "Browning had a plan. We should trust it."

"They're right, Quinton," Harper said. "This is more important than finding me a better host."

Each time Harper used the ship's VR during a rest cycle it performed a PMC integrity check. Quinton had added this command without Harper being any the wiser. Since he'd first rescued Harper, there had been a steady decrease in the stability of his PMC. The VR helped slow it down, but the trend was going in the wrong direction. Harper didn't have a whole lot of time before the damage was irreversible.

"There could be more Galactic class PMCs. I can't be the only one," Quinton said.

The others remained quiet.

"Don't you think so?"

Bradshaw nodded. "Of course. Browning wouldn't have hinged a way to defeat Harding on so slim a chance."

"True," Corvax said. "But we can't know that until we find out what's triggering the PMCs. Wherever the activation signals occur, these Sentinels aren't far behind."

"That can't be a coincidence," Quinton agreed. "We can't do this on our own. We're going to need help."

The others agreed, and Quinton sent a subspace comlink to the *Nebulon.*

25

THE MAIN HOLOSCREEN showed a video comlink of the bridge on the *Nebulon*. The *Wayfarer* had just emerged at the waypoint. Quinton looked at Maelyn.

"Captain Wayborn," he greeted.

"Commander Aldren," she replied, choosing to use his ACN rank in acknowledgment that he was more than just an independent ship captain.

Becker stood nearby Maelyn and tossed a nod his way. Oscar waved, and Guttman was sitting next to Kieva.

Quinton looked at Simon. "I got your message. Top marks. We all agreed."

Simon tilted his head to the side a little by way of acknowledgment. "I had help."

Quinton's gaze flicked back to Maelyn. "You were right."

Maelyn raised a dark eyebrow, and the hint of a dimple appeared next to one of her delicate cheekbones. "About what?"

Quinton chuckled and leaned forward. "You already know. We had a hell of a time trying to reach any spaceports in the sector. I'll save the details for another time."

"I'll look forward to it," Maelyn replied.

He just bet she would. "Do you have the DNA data?"

"I do."

"Is Harper listed in it?"

"I don't know, and I can't search for it. The data isn't aboard the ship."

One of the spider-drone's legs began tapping the floor, but Harper remained quiet.

"Time is an issue here, Maelyn. If we have to negotiate with the DUC for access to the data…"

Maelyn shook her head. "No, it won't come to that. I promise you. They have their own copy, and I have *my* own."

That was as much of a confirmation as he was likely to get from her, but it was enough. Maelyn wouldn't lie to him. "I trust you," he said.

Her lips lifted and her eyes gleamed. "Thank you, Quinton."

The spider-drone's leg stopped tapping the floor.

"I've shown the others the Sentinel tracking data and the PMC activation signals that've been reported or detected by the DUC," Quinton said. "Can you send us updates for it? If we're going to track the PMC activation signals, I'd like to target a system farthest away from Sentinel activity."

"Of course," Maelyn said. "We've been working on this. Simon can give you an update."

A data burst was added to the comlink channel and Quinton authorized it.

Simon stood up. "We've been trying to track the activation signal since the starbase attack. The signals occur more frequently than ever before, but the pattern seems to be random. We think this is by design," he paused and glanced at the others. "I'm just going to say that this is Admiral Browning's design instead of referring to it as something else. If this is incorrect, then I'll adjust accordingly." Simon turned back to the holoscreen. "So, the activation signal is random, at least by our analysis, but I think yours might be different."

"We tried this before," Quinton said, "the first time around."

"We didn't really pursue it before," Maelyn said. "The coordinates for the starbase came from you."

"Let's not get sidetracked," Simon said. "Time is of the essence, right? Okay, here's my theory, but I'll need you—all of you—to confirm it. I think the pattern of the activation signals also contains coordinates for finding the source."

"How would that work?" Guttman asked.

"The pattern itself contains an encoded message that they can decipher," Simon replied, gesturing toward Quinton and the others.

"I think the Sentinels would be able to figure this out," Becker said.

Quinton considered it and agreed with Becker.

"I know what you think," Simon said to Becker. "I want to know what *they* think."

Becker didn't reply.

"What do you think of Simon's theory?" Maelyn asked.

"I hate to say it because it's Becker, but I have to agree with him," Quinton replied.

"Knowing a pattern exists is a lot different than understanding what it means," Corvax said.

"I agree with Walsh," Bradshaw said.

"If the Sentinels had already figured it out, none of us would be here," Harper said.

Quinton chuckled softly. "This is what I get for making snap judgments. You all make good points. All right, let's have a look at what you've got, Simon."

"Great," Simon replied. "The data is time-lapsed, so you can try and see the pattern."

"No need. Just send all of it. Radek and the other VIs will take that into consideration," Quinton said.

A new data link became available. Quinton routed it into the *Wayfarer*'s computer systems and gave access to Corvax, Bradshaw, and Harper. Then Quinton increased his frame rate and began an analysis of the PMC activation signals. First, he focused on where they appeared on a galactic star map. The pattern was random and completely unpredictable. He then shifted his attention to the frequency of the signals as they were detected.

"Some of the signals are reactionary," Bradshaw said.

"I see it, too. Filter those out," Corvax added.

Quinton created a filter that ignored PMC activation signals that occurred after an initial signal was detected. Radek presented multiple iterations of data subsets because some of them filtered out so much information that there was nothing left.

The reaction from the other PMCs was almost immediate. The advantage of PMCs was their ability to create predictive algorithms that had any number of applications. There was a pattern to the PMC activation signals. Each of the PMCs aboard the *Wayfarer* contributed to the refinement of the filter until they couldn't break it down any further. Quinton saw the beginnings of it first, but then the others added their own interpretations.

Quinton and the others returned their frame rates back to normal time. Less than a minute had passed.

"Simon, you're a genius," Quinton said. "There *is* a pattern that contains information for us to find the source."

"That was fast. Are you sure you've got it?" Becker asked.

Quinton nodded. "It was a team effort. We all contributed to it. I think that might have been a requirement."

"There were also a great many false activation signals," Corvax said.

"Yeah, someone is triggering them," Quinton replied. "There's a strong correlation between those and Sentinel activity."

"Are the Sentinels capable of doing this or not?" Maelyn asked.

"I don't think so," Quinton replied. "They only respond after the signal is triggered. If they could do this on their own, there would be no length of time between the activation signal and when the Sentinels showed up to investigate."

"That makes sense," Maelyn replied.

"So how do we find the source of the activation signals?" Becker asked.

"It's complicated," Quinton said and looked at Maelyn. "Captain Wayborn, is your jump drive charged?" he asked and sent a set of coordinates to the *Nebulon*.

"Of course," she replied.

"Wait a second," Becker said. "We're just going? No discussion?"

Maelyn looked at Quinton.

"Trust should work both ways," Quinton said.

Maelyn gave him a slight nod. "It does."

"Good. I have a request."

"What do you need?"

"I need a pilot. Do you happen to have an extra?" Quinton asked and looked at Oscar. "I need your help."

"That won't be necessary, Oscar," Maelyn said before Oscar could answer.

"It's fine. I'll go back over there," Oscar said.

"I'll take care of it," Maelyn replied. Quinton looked at her and frowned. "I'll be coming to your ship, along with Simon. Becker can help Kieva look after the *Nebulon*."

Quinton wasn't sure what to say. "If you're sure, then welcome aboard."

Becker stared at Maelyn for a few moments. "*I'll* go with Oscar back aboard the *Wayfarer*. We already know the ship. You should stay here."

Quinton hadn't anticipated any of this. He just needed a backup pilot in case he was preoccupied with something else. "He's got a point."

Maelyn smiled. "That he does. We'll do it your way, Becker."

Quinton had to hand it to Maelyn. She certainly knew how to motivate people to do exactly what she needed them to do. They shared a knowing look as he watched Becker and Oscar leave the bridge.

Quinton looked at Simon. "Next time."

The young spacer nodded. "I'm picking my moment."

Once Becker and Oscar were back aboard the *Wayfarer*, Quinton executed a jump to a nearby star system. The binary star system was uninhabited and showed no signs of anyone having ever been there.

The pattern Quinton and the others had deciphered showed them how to find where the PMC activation signal was going to occur next.

"Nothing detected on the scanners," Corvax said.

"Understood," Quinton replied. "Starting broadcast."

Quinton accessed the ship's comms systems and initiated a data comlink broadcast. A challenge protocol presented itself, and authentication codes contained within Quinton's ESS responded with the proper authentication codes. This back and forth went on for almost a full minute before he was granted access.

Confirm PMC identity.

Commander Quinton Aldren, G-Class.

Acheron Confederacy Navy, SP.

Quinton increased his frame rate, and multiple data windows appeared on his HUD.

"I'm accessing the comms drone," Quinton said.

PMC conditions have been met.

Access granted.

Data update available.

Provide Activation Code.

Quinton sent over the data he had for his own activation, then received the following reply.

Multimode authentication required. Provide additional activation codes to proceed.

Quinton requested the data from Corvax, Bradshaw, and Harper. All three replied with the data and Quinton sent it to the comms drone. The comlink interface showed him that the comms drone had been recently constructed, so this wasn't some remnant tech left over from the Federation Wars that was simply being reactivated.

Multimode authentication granted.

Stand by for updated configuration.

Quinton had put the data session on the main holoscreen, which was also mirrored on the *Nebulon* so the others could see what was happening.

Polaris Operation authorized.

Salvation initialized.

A set of coordinates appeared in the data session, along with a thirty-six-hour countdown timer.

The comms drone then began broadcasting a series of subspace comlinks, and a few moments later these were acknowledged by the other comms drones. Then the comms drone went offline.

Quinton returned his frame rate to normal. "I think it initiated a self-destruct protocol. I'm not able to reach it."

"What happens in thirty-six hours?" Becker asked.

Quinton reviewed the data upload he'd received from the comms drone. "It's the Polaris Operation," he said and looked at Corvax and Bradshaw. "We have to get to those coordinates."

"What's there?" Maelyn asked.

"I think I just triggered the broadcast of PMC activation signals everywhere. In thirty-six hours, it'll spread to enough drones that they'll begin broadcasting at the same time."

The drone hadn't self-destructed. It simply wouldn't accept another comlink from him.

Becker leaned forward. "Are you sure? Why would Browning do that?"

"It's a recall for PMCs," Quinton said and updated the star map on the main holoscreen. "This is a tracker for the subspace signal that came from that comms drone. See the spread? It's contacted all comms drones in range. Then the process repeats. We have to stop this."

"Why?" Corvax asked.

"Because if all those PMCs come online at once, this will cause another Sentinel incursion. They'll be slaughtered before they can be recalled."

"What's at those coordinates?" Becker asked.

"Hopefully, a way to stop the broadcast," Quinton said. "I've uploaded the coordinates to the nav computer. You should be receiving them now."

"Confirmed," Maelyn replied. "Synchronized on your mark."

"Execute," Quinton said.

The two ships initiated a space jump at precisely the same time.

26

ADMEN DESHER SAT in the command chair on the bridge of the stealth star-class jumper. The CDA he occupied was perfectly still. His specialized protocols had negated the micro habits that maintained the illusion that he was human. The comlink session to the comms drone linked to Browning's Polaris Operation had just been authorized. He was rarely in the same star system that the hyper-jump-capable comms drones traveled to. They never stayed anywhere for long, and in the mere months since he'd been reactivated, neither had he.

Admen had been triggering PMC activation signals from these drones since he'd been brought back online. He glanced over the storage container full of spent leuridium ESS cores of the PMCs he'd questioned. They hadn't known anything. Browning had kept all his PMCs ignorant of his plans. If there was a PMC in his vicinity, he'd retrieve it, but things were seldom that convenient. If any of the Sentinels found a PMC worth pursuing, he'd be informed.

Admen knew his own activation hadn't been the product of some random occurrence. Browning's Polaris Operation had begun to be initialized with the destruction of an ACN starbase brought back online by a Galactic class PMC. All of Admen's own predictive algorithms put him on a direct intercept course with the G-class PMC known as Quinton Aldren. None of the records that he had access to contained any information about that PMC. He was outside of Admiral Browning's last known command structure. Admen wondered how many of the PMCs Browning had scattered across the galaxy had been detached from his original fighting force. Admen was as likely to find a PMC created from Browning's original command as he was to find a completely new one, and he'd spent quite a bit of time considering how it had been done. Browning must have found a way to modify PMCs under his command, and they'd been altered so they couldn't be traced by the Prime.

The comms drone received a massive subspace broadcast. If Admen hadn't infiltrated the drone's systems, he'd never have detected the occurrence. Dozens of realizations stemmed from that one data session. He stopped his own scheduled broadcast to allow the comms drone to carry out its own protocols initiated by the broadcast it had received.

Polaris Operation authorized.

Salvation initialized.

The comms drone prepared a new data broadcast and Admen copied it. Within the broadcast were a set of coordinates. His predictive algorithms indicated the highest probability that these actions were by Browning's design. Admen carried a subset of the Prime's VIs that authorized him to investigate these coordinates. His alpha priorities were updated.

The ship's scanner detected several gamma bursts as warships entered the system. Admen had their ship signatures on file. Tactical alerts came to prominence as his own scans reported the active weapons statuses of the Union warships.

Admen had anticipated the chance that he'd encounter Union warships. They were hunting for him. He'd used Crowe's Union to help trigger Sentinel activity throughout the galaxy. He could have engaged his jump drive and escaped, but there was an opportunity being presented to him, and he wasn't going to let it slip through his fingers.

27

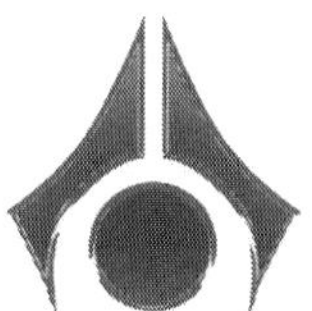

QUINTON HAD EXPECTED the jump coordinates they'd received from the comms drone to lead them to some far-off star system on the fringe of the galaxy. Instead, it was the opposite. They traveled along one of the spiral arms of the galaxy that led them to a much more volatile and dangerous region of space. These star systems weren't inhabited by anyone because galactic expansion hadn't exhausted the most habitable star systems. The great diaspora led to the creation of multiple federations, star unions, imperiums, and just about any other words where a group of people settled into the galactic sectors of known space. There was still room to grow, and there were plenty of mysteries left to discover in the galaxy.

Quinton had limited the range of his ship's jump drive so that the *Nebulon* could stay with them. They were under a time constraint, but they would arrive well before the countdown timer for Polaris expired. The *Nebulon's* jump drive had an impressive range, but because the damage to the *Wayfarer* from their encounters with the Sentinels limited their effective jump range, it brought the disparity of capabilities between the two ships to something they could work with. They had tens of thousands of light-years to cross and very little time to do it.

Another reason for traveling across the deep dark with another ship was to displace the risk of solitary traveling. They were pushing both ships hard to cross the vast distance to the source of PMC activation signals. Data communications via subspace could cover much greater distances quicker than any starship could travel, and Quinton thought the initial thirty-six-hour countdown hadn't been an arbitrary amount of time. It must have been based on their location relative to the coordinates they'd been given. He could appreciate the subtle nuances of a plan that tried to account for an awe-inspiring number of variables. Browning couldn't have done this on his own, but regardless of how many people had been involved, it was an impressive feat.

Each jump disrupted the comlink channel between the two ships, so they'd re-establish communications, perform a quick diagnostic of critical systems, and then execute another jump that brought them ever closer to their final destination. More than thirty hours had passed, and they were finally about to execute their final jump. To reduce the likelihood of an encounter with hostile forces, Quinton had chosen to avoid populated star systems. Maelyn had received updates from the DUC's Sentinel and PMC activation signal trackers. There were increasing reports of Sentinel ships in populated star systems even as the PMC activation signals had decreased. Quinton surmised that the decrease in detection wasn't because all of the specialized comms drones had gone dormant; it was because they'd stopped broadcasting activation signals as part of the Polaris Operation. He had no idea what Salvation meant, but since it had been part of the data he'd received from the comms drone, he knew it was significant.

"The nav computer is giving us the green light, but that star system is a mess," Oscar said.

Quinton glanced at him.

"I'm just saying we need to be careful."

Quinton nodded. "Be careful. Got it," he said and looked at Maelyn. "Ready, Captain Wayborn?"

"At your discretion, Commander Aldren."

Quinton checked the jump coordinates for the umpteenth time. "Execute Jump."

The two ships' jump drives engaged, folding the distance and they emerged on the other side. A few seconds went by while scanners raced to map out the star system. They had been two thousand light-years from the star system, so the data they had was out of date, but it did indicate volatility. Navigation systems on both ships had the benefit of a huge data repository to compare the visible galaxy against. Those systems took the scan data, as well as the high-resolution images of their destination, and attempted to match them up for known star-system types. They weren't blind going into an unexplored star system, even though they could never be fully prepared for what they would find. A couple of thousand years in galactic terms was less than the blink of the eye. It had taken humanity thousands of years to expand out into the galaxy, and they weren't finished. However, what the scanners reported was the mashup of multiple star systems. Each of the galaxy's spiral arms became denser as they drew nearer to the galactic core. Stars, both common and rare, planets, and vast nebula-forming clouds made the area within twenty thousand light-years of the galactic core rich in materials but not stable enough to allow for life to evolve for very long.

The data from the scanners were funneled into a map of the star system and displayed on the main holoscreen. Three separate star systems were merging to form a new singular star system. The process would take a long time. Two of the star systems were binary, but they were being devoured by a blue giant star. The five stars were in a celestial tug of war as they orbited each other. The system of planets orbiting each of those star systems had become the near chaotic mess that was only just beginning to form a new system. Remnants of over a hundred rocky planets were in the process of colliding while trying to re-form, only to begin the cycle all over again. They stretched out over eighty light-minutes from stars battling to the death. Beyond them were dozens of gas giants, some of which had an elliptical orbit that pulled them closer to the dueling stars, only to be flung far away. Some of them would never return, but they wreaked havoc on the star system's already chaotic interior.

"Not the safest place to fly," Quinton said.

"It's no place to take a ship," Becker replied.

Quinton peered at the main holoscreen. "And shockingly, that's exactly where we need to go."

Becker didn't offer any more comments.

The waypoint had them going to a mass of former planets that had clumped together amid the scattered remnants of even more planets.

"The nav is going to struggle with this," Oscar said.

"We're going to help it," Quinton said. "Be ready to take over, but don't hesitate to input course corrections after we micro-jump."

"Won't that interfere with what you'll be doing?" Becker asked.

"We can account for it," Quinton replied, and looked at the video comlink to the *Nebulon*. "Keep that data link open. I'll make sure a course is uploaded to the *Nebulon,* but if the link goes offline, you'll have to take over."

"Understood," Maelyn replied.

Quinton increased his frame rate, and so did Corvax, Bradshaw, and Harper. They only increased to a point where they could multitask but still communicate in real time with the human crew. Quinton's avatar was the most capable of the four of them, but the CDAs were doing extremely well. Harper did the best he could within the capabilities of the spider-drone.

All of them were fully integrated with the ship and the scan data that came in from both ships. Integrating with the ship in this way meant there was no latency in accessing the data. With the assistance of Radek, who was the primary VI for Quinton, as well as the others' own virtual assistants, information overload was offset. Multitasking in this way was what PMCs were designed to do. It was what they excelled at.

Quinton accessed the flight controls for both the *Wayfarer* and the *Nebulon* and executed a micro-jump. When he emerged farther into the system, they immediately flew on an intercept course that would take them to the waypoint.

A data comlink broadcast was detected, and the ships' scanners quickly identified another ship in the system.

No sooner had Quinton brought up the signal analysis of the broadcast than an alert appeared. It was a PMC broadcast, but it had the same infiltration code that the Sentinels had used.

"It's an Agent of Harding. It must want control of Salvation," Corvax said. Whoever that other PMC was, Quinton had to agree with Corvax's assessment. It wasn't one of them. For the first time, Quinton had to categorize another PMC as the enemy. It was one thing to know about a potential enemy, but it was another thing to come face-to-face with one.

"Targeting enemy ship," Harper said.

The unknown ship executed a micro-jump. They must have detected them.

"We need to get there first," Quinton said and kept them on course.

"The ionized gas cloud is interfering with our scans, but I'm able to detect a power core signature. Multiple power cores. There's something huge in there," Corvax said.

The Agent of Harding was trying to get access. The only thing Quinton could do was try to beat him to it.

"There isn't a way to fly through that mess," Bradshaw said.

"I'm going to try to communicate with it," Quinton replied.

They couldn't see what it was. The scan data and the high-res images all showed only a mass of remnant chunks of former planets that had clumped together, but something in there was generating power. This is what they had come for. It was certainly enough power to generate a massive broadcast that could spread to all the Galactic sectors.

Quinton broadcasted his own comlink and received the same challenge protocols he'd gotten earlier from the comms drone. He sent his PMC identification and rank, and then invited the others to do the same along his comlink. The authentication to Salvation pulled codes from each of their energy storage systems.

A data update became available, and Quinton acknowledged it. It was a flight plan that took them right into the heart of a crushing debris field. Quinton hesitated. If he was wrong about this, both ships would be destroyed. But if he didn't go inside, the enemy would control whatever was on the other side. He couldn't be sure how many fail-safes Admiral Browning had put in place. Not going at all meant that the timer for Salvation would expire, which would activate every PMC scattered throughout the galaxy. This would trigger a Sentinel incursion, and the galaxy would be thrown into chaos. Quinton put the new course into the nav computer and pushed both ships' throttles up to maximum.

28

QUINTON HAD ENABLED the *Wayfarer's* point defenses to help protect the ship from the debris field they were flying into.

"I suggest you enable your point defense systems," Quinton said to Maelyn.

"Already engaged."

She knew her stuff. Quinton had access to the *Nebulon's* navigation system, but not any weapons systems.

"We still don't know what's inside," Becker said. "What do you think is in there?"

"We're going to find out," Quinton replied.

Simon cleared his throat. "Power core readings are incredibly high, but there are multiple sources, some of which are large shipyards. If there's a tech base, there could be a fleet."

"A massive factory for creating warships?" Becker asked.

"Could be," Quinton said. "There's certainly enough material here to use. Don't forget, whatever's in there has been around for a while, considering the secret location, an abundance of materials, and time enough to do something constructive with it all."

"It's a miracle it's still there," Becker said.

"That's a good point," Maelyn said. "Look at the destruction. How could anything survive here for long?"

"Polaris Operation," Corvax said. "This is a place to coordinate Polaris Operation."

"This is where we stop whatever Salvation is," Quinton said.

"Multiple ships detected entering the star system," Corvax said.

"Jordani class heavy cruiser design," Harper said. "I have a firing solution."

The others glanced at the spider-drone in bewilderment. Harper was becoming too eager to shoot first and ask questions later.

"How many ships are there?" Quinton asked.

"Twenty-two—make that thirty-two ships, sir," Harper replied.

"We're not going to engage those ships," Quinton said.

On the main holoscreen, he could see Guttman's 'I told you so' look. Becker frowned, and Quinton gestured for him to take it easy.

"I'm sorry," Harper said. "That was foolish. I'll work on a firing solution in case we need to make a hasty retreat."

"Understood," Quinton replied.

"They're Union ships," Maelyn said.

"Crowe!"

"How the hell did Crowe end up here?" Becker asked.

Quinton's mind raced while he considered it. How had Lennix Crowe even learned about this place, much less made it here at virtually the same time they had? "It can't be a coincidence, so it must have to do with that other ship we detected."

Corvax looked at him. "If this Lennix Crowe is involved with an Agent of Harding, then he's a pawn, willing or otherwise."

Quinton nodded. "Someone desperate enough to figure out a way to use the Sentinels as his own personal attack force."

"You think Crowe had help luring Sentinels to attack Collective targets?" Maelyn asked.

"It makes the most sense. Crowe had Sentinel code to help capture me on Endurance Starbase, and he must have gotten help with adapting it so he could use it for something else."

"Why is he here then?"

"He's in over his head," Quinton replied.

"What do you mean?"

"Would an Agent of Harding hesitate to create the conditions for a Sentinel incursion if it meant flushing us out?" Quinton said, gesturing toward the other PMCs, as well as himself.

"That would mean they were the ones attacking other targets besides the Collective," Maelyn said and nodded.

"Like I said," Quinton replied, "he's in way over his head. I have no idea why he came here, but it must have something to do with the Agent of Harding."

Quinton heard Maelyn reply, but it sounded distant, as if he were listening to her speak from another room. He also heard the others shouting, and he thought he heard Becker call his name, but he couldn't reply. The data comlink to whatever Salvation was had suddenly become active, and it pulled him inside an abyss that had taken him away from the bridge of the *Wayfarer*.

Something was doing an analysis of Quinton's ESS, and he thought it must be an integrity check. Even though he recognized the access and flow of information, it didn't seem to be taking anything away from him, but Quinton felt as if it was reviewing his actions. Within moments, the utilization of the data comlink lessened and he regained more control.

"It's all right," Quinton said. "I'm fine."

"What happened?" Maelyn asked.

"It was a data connection to them."

"Them?" Becker said. "Who?"

"Not a 'them'—it. Whatever's on the other side," Quinton said.

The two ships flew through the dense asteroid field. Some of the asteroids were the size of dwarf planets, and even though they flew quickly, they gave themselves enough time to alter course if needed.

"Simon," Oscar said, "are you getting an automated guidance request?"

"I just got it," Simon replied.

The same request had appeared on Quinton's internal HUD. "Give it access. We're being guided inside. We must be close enough for an automated docking procedure."

Oscar hesitated for a few moments, then acknowledged the request.

"Do it," Maelyn said to Simon.

Simon also acknowledged the request, and both ships' flight control systems were handed off to the Acheron Confederacy Navy installation they were heading to. Quinton recognized the ACN protocols used for guiding visiting ships to space stations, starbases, and even large warships.

Their velocity increased, which confirmed what Quinton was thinking. "They must already have a course planned for us."

Becker groaned. "I just wish I knew who *they* were. Has there been any other contact?"

Quinton shook his head. "No."

Becker looked at the others. "Anyone else?"

No one else had been contacted.

"Our scanners just went dark," Oscar said. "They're operating normally, but we can't see anything."

"We must be inside a dampening field," Quinton replied.

Both ships were on their own now, and there was no going back. They had to see this through. The ships' engines throttled down, but their velocity increased, and the motion wasn't even registering on the ship's inertia dampeners. The ships raced at such speeds that Quinton could only track their progress by increasing his frame rate. They flew between dwarf-planet-size asteroids, some of which had molten cores with deep fissures along the surface. They flew toward an area that was completely devoid of light, as if all the light had been swallowed, but the scanners still reported data of their immediate vicinity. They were flying into a mighty tunnel that was a good two hundred meters across and lit by a brilliant strip of lights. As it enveloped them, they noted stone walls that glittered with an odd sheen, as if they'd been fused glass-slick, but before long the tunnel walls became suddenly metallic. It was a gray metal, gleaming with a bit of yellow in the light, stretching so far ahead that its mighty bore dwindled to a gleaming dot with distance.

Their speed dropped, and Quinton was able to make out the shapes of hatches sliding past—dozens of hatches, with most as large as the one they'd flown into. The occupants of both ships' bridges were silent as their minds reeled at the structure's sheer size. This was beyond anything they'd ever experienced.

One huge hatch suddenly flicked open, and both ships were guided toward it. They slipped neatly through the open hatch, and the *Wayfarer* settled onto a floor comprised of the grayish-yellow alloy. Quinton watched as the *Nebulon* followed.

The image on the main holoscreen showed that they were in a dimly lit metal cavern more than a kilometer across. Nearby were rows of neatly parked combat spacecraft with the ACN's black and gold emblem on their sides. Quinton peered at the floor and saw the two golden triangular halves that angled away from a sphere on a black background. The letter of the first word was underneath.

"Perseverance," Quinton said quietly. He stood up and walked toward the holoscreen.

Corvax joined him. "Endurance," he whispered.

The lighting in the massive hangar increased.

"Fortitude," Bradshaw said.

Rows of combat fighters gleamed under the lights.

"Readiness," Harper said.

Quinton glanced at Becker and then Oscar. Both men watched the video feed with stunned reverence. Becker looked at him and nodded once.

"What do we do now?" Guttman asked.

Quinton caught a glimpse of movement as a double-ended, bullet-shaped aircar came to a stop between the two ships. Counter-grav emitters kept it hovering one foot or so above the floor. A large hatch opened on the side and light spilled from the opening, bright and welcoming.

"Quinton," Maelyn said, "has there been any other contact?"

"No, but the data connection is still there. I think we're being invited to go somewhere."

The spider-drone's armored body spun toward Quinton. "I'm not staying behind," Harper said.

"No one is staying behind this time," Quinton said. He looked at the holoscreen, and Maelyn nodded in agreement.

Becker stood up and cleared his throat. "Is anyone worried about the Union ships in the star system?"

"I think we're pretty well protected for now," Quinton replied.

"He's right," Oscar said. "Did you see what we had to fly through to make it here?"

"Let's go," Quinton said.

They left the bridge and exited the rear loading ramp of the *Wayfarer*. Maelyn and the others met them outside the aircar. The air was crisp, with a slight chill.

"I'm getting atmospheric readings," Maelyn said. She pulled off her helmet and the others did the same.

Guttman checked his weapon and kept looking around as if he expected to be attacked at any moment. "This is just like that starbase, except there are more ships here. If these star fighters are here, there must be other ships."

"They're not yours," Corvax said.

Guttman frowned. "I don't see anyone here claiming them."

"Let's not divvy anything up just yet," Quinton said and entered the aircar.

The others followed.

"What's the matter with you?" Simon said to Guttman.

"What?"

"You're a real piece of work. You think everything is just there for you to take."

Guttman shrugged. "What do you think *they're* doing here?" He jutted his chin toward Quinton. "And if it's not us, then it'll be someone else. There's no room for being high and mighty."

The spider-drone began tapping one of its legs on the ground, and the drone's red optics swung toward Guttman. "How about showing one iota of respect."

Corvax and Bradshaw looked at him with the artificial eyes of the CDA.

Guttman bit his lower lip for a moment and looked at Quinton. "I apologize," he said and looked away from them.

The aircar's hatch closed, and several chairs rose from the floor near everyone except Harper, Corvax, and Bradshaw. The others sat down.

"They're so comfortable. We need these on the *Nebulon,*" Kieva said.

Maelyn agreed.

The aircar accelerated away from their ships and sped across the cavern, heading straight at a featureless metal wall that popped open an instant before they hit. The aircar then darted into another brightly lit bore.

Quinton glanced at the others. "Reminds me of traveling in some of the moon stations in the core star systems," he said and paused. "What's wrong?"

"There's so much metal," Becker said. "I've never seen this much in one place before."

Guttman blew out a breath. "I'm glad someone finally said it. I'm barely keeping it together here."

"We're heading toward another wall," Simon said.

Once again, a hatch opened at the last minute. There was a brief darkened area and then they emerged into another brightly lit bore, this one no wider than two or three of the aircar in which they rode.

The walls weren't featureless, but speed reduced those features to a blur. They traveled for so long that even Quinton was wondering just how big this place was. It easily dwarfed any space station he'd ever seen. He glanced at Maelyn, and her eyes gleamed with excitement. There was a fresh spurt of acceleration and a sideways surge of inertia as the aircar swept through a curved junction and darted into yet another tunnel.

A status window appeared on Quinton's HUD.

Pre-Check of Personality Matrix Construct Integrity Complete.

Confirm identity is Quinton Aldren.

Acheron Confederacy Navy.

Rank: Commander.

Galactic Personality Matrix Construct.

Authentication Procedure Step Two: Virtual Intelligence Integrity Check.

Are you ready to proceed?

Quinton stared at the question for a few moments. "Radek," he said subvocally. "What do you make of this?"

"It's an additional integrity check for a virtual intelligence. I would have expected this to happen as part of the other check, but since that was designated a pre-check, they might have changed the procedures."

Quinton tried to think of a reason to take one all-inclusive integrity check and divide it into multiple steps, but he came up short.

"These checks are prerequisites for assuming command of an Acheron Confederacy Naval vessel or installation, such as a starbase or space station," Radek said.

This place was much too big to be a ship.

"This tunnel is going on forever," Guttman said.

"I saw a chamber earlier that contained more ships," Simon said. "We're traveling so fast that I hardly got a good look at them. They might have been Condor class."

The aircar scooted down the very center of the tunnel.

"I keep waiting to arrive," Maelyn said.

The others agreed. The PMCs were quiet.

Quinton looked over at Corvax, Bradshaw, and Harper. "Have you gotten anything through the data comlink about integrity checks for your VIs?"

Corvax and Bradshaw exchanged a glance and shook their heads.

"I haven't received a data comlink," Harper said.

"Same here. There's been nothing since I provided my identification on the ship," Corvax said.

Bradshaw nodded. "You're the Galactic, Commander."

"It might be because you're the ranking officer here," Maelyn said.

Quinton considered it. He just needed to find a way to stop the massive broadcast that would reactivate the PMCs scattered across the galaxy. Without those signals, the Sentinels would go back to the deep dark.

"Why would they run a separate integrity check for your VI?" Simon asked.

"That's the thing," Quinton replied. "They're like the psychological evaluations commanding officers go through before assuming command of anything—a ship, a fleet, a starbase. The PMC integrity checks are similar. I've just never had a specific request for Radek before."

"What's wrong with that? Wasn't this part of your training?" Maelyn asked.

"It's usually part of..." Quinton began and stopped. "Never mind. To answer your question, no it wasn't. Radek, or any VI, is integrated into a PMC. They bridge the gap between the human-to-machine interface. If I grant the request, I might be unresponsive for the duration of the check."

Becker frowned, leaned forward, and rubbed the palms of his hands together. "Let me see if I understand this. We're being taken somewhere, and you haven't even finished authenticating to whatever this place is yet?"

Quinton pursed his lips while he considered it for a moment, then nodded. "When you put it like that, it sounds... There's no turning back now."

Becker sighed and shook his head, then turned toward the window to stare at the dark tunnel. The aircar began to slow and the entire cockpit swiveled smoothly until they were facing back the way they'd come. Quinton felt the drag of deceleration, which continued for almost ten minutes, and then the blurred walls beyond the transparent canopy slowed. He could make out the details once more, including the maws of other tunnels. The aircar slowed virtually to a walk, and they swerved gently down an intersecting tunnel that was only a little wider than the vehicle itself. It slid alongside an entrance and stopped. The hatch flicked soundlessly open.

The others looked at Quinton expectantly. "I'll go first," he said with mock enthusiasm, stepping out of the vehicle and looking around. Then he gestured for the others to follow. Once they were all out, the vehicle's hatch closed and it slid silently backwards, vanishing the way it had come.

Guttman cursed as he looked longingly in the direction the vehicle had gone.

The flashing light of a small sphere appeared, hanging in midair. It bobbed a few times to attract their attention and then headed down a side corridor at a comfortable pace.

Quinton tried to open another comlink session, but they were all denied. The only connection available was the one waiting for his response.

"Let's go," Quinton said and followed the sphere.

It guided them down a corridor past numerous closed doors until they came to an expanse of black walls where thin, pale, glowing lines traveled the length of the long corridor. Quinton peered at the lines and saw that they were actually tiny words written in a flowing white script.

Quinton slowed down and looked at the words. "They're names of people," he said and looked at the others. He turned back toward the names, quickly reading. Many had ACN ranks associated with them.

Maelyn went to the other side of the corridor. "Oh my," she said and leaned closer to the wall. "There are other federations listed here—Tilion Empire Marines, Ixander Star Collective, Alari. And Dholeren United Coalition!"

Becker walk over to her. "The DUC was part of this?" he asked and peered at the wall.

Simon joined them, gesturing toward the wall a few moments later. "The list of spacers here were part of the DUC's lost fleets. I recognize the ships' names. They were lost during the Federation Wars."

"Why would they be listed here?" Becker asked.

"There are Jordani ships and spacers listed over here," Guttman said. "The ships have JFS in the names. That has to be them, right?"

"They helped Browning," Quinton said. Silence nearly swallowed the hallowed halls. "These names are honoring soldiers who died in battle. This corridor is a monument to the fallen. Whoever built this place wanted anyone who came down here to understand the sacrifice of so many. Browning had help, and by the looks of it, he had it from…" Quinton's gaze swept the walls. The flowing cursive script went on and on. He hesitated to guess how many people were listed there.

"Most of these federations or unions are gone," Maelyn said.

Quinton's eyebrows pulled together and his gaze became hard. The white, flowing script was tiny, and yet it filled up the walls from floor to ceiling. Each of these names, ranks, ship references, alliances, and places were tied to the people who'd tried to help Elias Browning—Grand Admiral Browning who had allegedly betrayed the Acheron Confederacy and raided countless worlds on some kind of destructive tirade. The survivors of the Federation Wars believed Browning was a monster, but if he was, why would this monument even exist? If Browning had been so evil, why would so many spacers fight alongside him?

Corvax and Bradshaw watched him. Their metallic faces conveyed a grimness forged in battle and sacrifice in a war Quinton had never been part of. He felt like an imposter, intruding upon the halls of the dead. Corvax and Bradshaw had fought in the Federation Wars. He looked at Harper. The spider-drone stood in the center of the corridor with its optics forward, but Quinton knew he could see all around him. Did they recognize any of the names written on the walls? He wanted to know but wouldn't ask. Some information should only be volunteered, and it was a struggle at times when his past caught up with him.

Even now he felt all those memories of a life long gone bubbling to the surface of his thoughts. He knew the others felt it, too. He remembered the agricultural bot he'd been forced to use. His access to his memories had been severely limited because it hadn't been designed to house a PMC. But for all the agricultural bot's flaws, the limited access to his memories had been both a blessing and a curse. In the avatar he used now, he had no such limitations. Quinton had full access to his life from before, and this monument was just another reminder of what he'd lost. He looked at the others, and his gaze lingered on Maelyn for only a moment before moving on. He just needed to stop the signal and figure out how to get all the resources here to the people who could use them. There had to be a CDA here for Harper to use. Once he did all that, he could move on.

Quinton continued, his footsteps echoing through the long corridor, and the others quietly followed him. The corridor eventually curved and then ended abruptly at a hatch that was large enough for a shuttle to fly through. The middle of the hatch bore the ACN black and gold emblem in stunning clarity. The ACN motto was written in elegant cursive script that surrounded the planet, and beneath it was the word *Salvation*.

Their disembodied guide twitched impatiently and drifted closer to the hatch. Quinton followed, and the massive door slid open as he approached. The door had been constructed of a thick metallic alloy that formed an immensely strong barrier. He followed the guide down the silently opening passage. Once they were all through, the door shut behind them, equally silently, and he tried to suppress a feeling of imprisonment.

The interior lighting began to glow brighter, revealing a spherical chamber that felt as open as the cavern they'd been in before. Smooth walls surrounded them in a colossal display of strength. They stood on a platform that had been thrust out from one curving wall. The platform was transparent, dotted with dozens of comfortable couch-like chairs before what could only be control consoles. The consoles were blank, as if they were in standby.

A holoscreen winked into existence at the edge of the platform.

Authentication Procedure Step Two: Virtual Intelligence Integrity Check.

Are you ready to proceed?

Quinton walked toward the holoscreen on a platform so transparent that he seemed to be striding on air as he crossed. His guide flew toward the display.

He turned to see Corvax, Bradshaw, and Harper fanned out behind him, but the others remained near the chairs. Quinton heard the spider-drone's legs begin to tap the floor in a nervous tick. Turning back toward the holoscreen, he sent an affirmative, and then everything went dark.

29

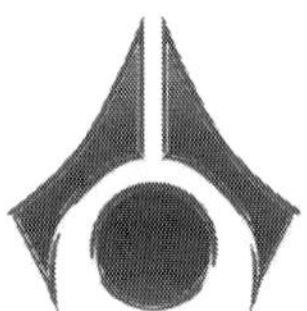

A FLASH of code scrolled so quickly down the holoscreen that Maelyn couldn't read it before it disappeared.

"Dammit all!" Guttman groused, glaring at his wrist computer. "This thing hasn't worked right since we were on that damn outpost."

Maelyn blinked several times. Then her eyes widened, and she stormed toward Guttman. "What did you say?"

Guttman leaned back, frowned a little, and glanced at the others for a moment. "It's nothing. I just need to get this thing fixed, is all."

Maelyn's gaze swooped toward Guttman's wrist computer and then to Quinton. She closed the distance to him, startling both Corvax and Bradshaw.

"Something's not right," Maelyn said.

The two CDAs regarded her and then looked at Quinton. Maelyn moved to stand in front of him. He was completely still. Frozen. Lifeless.

"Quinton!" she shouted.

It was a feeble attempt to get him to respond, and it didn't work.

Her gazed darted to the others, frantically searching for a way to help him. Becker and Simon came towards her with questions emerging from their lips that she couldn't hear. She lifted her wrist computer and tried to open a comlink to Quinton, snarling when it failed. Stalking back and forth in front of him, she shook her head as a tangle of ideas came to her mind and were dismissed, one after the other.

"I can't get a connection," Corvax said.

"Me either," Bradshaw said.

Maelyn flung her arm toward the blank holoscreen. "Well, what about there? Can you connect to that?" Her voice echoed throughout the vast chamber.

Corvax and Bradshaw focused on the holoscreen, but nothing happened.

Maelyn inhaled explosively and stormed in front of them. "You find a way to help him," she said through gritted teeth. "I don't care what you have to do. Do you hear me! Help him now!"

She scowled toward Quinton. The cybernetic avatar that made him look so human now held him prisoner.

"Quinton isn't the only one who's not responding," Simon said.

Maelyn looked in his direction, and he gestured toward Harper. The spider-drone was frozen, just like Quinton, with one of its legs stopped in mid-motion.

A data window flickered on the holoscreen—snippets of something she couldn't quite see.

"Uh, guys," Guttman said in a shaky voice. "This doesn't look right." He held out his arm, showing them his personal holoscreen. It flickered with code just like the holoscreen in front of Quinton.

"What did you do?" Becker asked.

"Nothing," Guttman replied. "I didn't do anything. You think I could do something like this? I don't even know what this thing is doing."

Simon darted over to him. Maelyn looked at Corvax and Bradshaw. "Check that out," she ordered.

The two PMCs did as she told them. Maelyn gritted her teeth and glared at Quinton for a few moments, then joined the others.

SOMETIMES IT WAS the little things that could sneak up and really have a huge impact on your day. One moment Quinton was consenting to having Radek's integrity checked, and the next he was fighting for his life. In the briefest of moments, Radek's security measures went on full alert, but Salvation's computing core must have sensed the danger and quarantined both of them into some kind of virtual holding area. He stood in a virtual reproduction of the chamber his avatar was in with all the others. Harper was with him, but there was something wrong with him.

Radek's security alert referred to the same Sentinel control signal they'd encountered on the Alari Outpost. Quinton tried to connect to Harper's PMC. He'd given all of them the same protections he had in place, so he couldn't figure out how or why Harper was compromised now.

Quinton tried to move, but nothing happened. He was cut off from the cybernetic avatar that housed his PMC, trapped in this virtual environment.

"Harper, can you hear me?"

"Quinton!?" Harper said, sounding confused and disoriented. "Something's wrong. Someone's trying to control me, Quinton. I don't know how to stop it."

Quinton detected another PMC's presence trapped with them. It lurked in the virtual environment but was part of Harper at the same time.

"I'm going to help you, Harper. Listen to me. I'm going to get us out of this."

"Just tell me what to do." Harper was quiet for a few moments. "Commander? No, you already told me the firing solution was wrong. We're not going to attack the Union ships."

"There aren't any ships. What are you talking about?"

Quinton was stuck in the middle of authenticating with Salvation, and it wouldn't allow him to proceed. Something was stopping him.

"The others are plotting to kill me," Harper said. He wasn't even looking at Quinton. "They want to trap the drone by the airlock. Once I'm gone, they think there's nothing you can do about it. Guttman is the worst. I hate his beady eyes. He always thinks I'm trying to get him. He'd never know it if I was. I've sneaked up on him before. I like how afraid he is when I do that."

Quinton tried to open a comlink to Harper, but it was denied. He tried to force his way in.

"It's so hard," Harper said. "I've been trying to keep pushing forward. All those damn diagnostics had the same result. PMC degeneration is inevitable."

Quinton almost found a way to reach Harper, but then it was closed off. He cursed.

"Radek, can you reach Greta?" Quinton asked, hoping that Harper's VI was at least able to communicate with them.

"Yet another in a long line of mistakes, Commander Quinton Aldren."

Quinton scanned out, trying to find the source of the other PMC. Harper whimpered incoherently.

"You can't help him."

"Shut up!" Quinton snarled.

He was able to find the source of the third PMC. It was coming through Harper. The two were linked. It was the only thing that made sense.

"So, you're the Agent of Harding."

"Is that what they call me? Then I guess I am. I suppose *you* might be called an Agent of Browning." He paused, considering. "I don't think you're quite there yet, so there is still hope for you, but this exchange will get tedious if we keep on this way. I'm Admen Desher."

His tone dripped with the pure arrogance of someone with an unshakable certainty of the superiority of their position. Quinton hated it, even if it was partially true.

"You say that like it's supposed to mean something to me. I didn't know Sentinels used PMCs."

"Wrong again," Desher said with wry amusement. "I've reviewed Harper's ESS, particularly his experiences with you. Quite revealing."

"Leave him alone. Get out of his ESS," he snarled.

"That temper is going to get the better of you, but let's not get sidetracked here. I can do what I want with Harper. You've encountered the infiltration protocol before. Yes, I see it now. A Sentinel encounter. Another PMC named Misako. I know that one. Commander Isobe Misako, Intelligence Officer. She was a high-priority target. Sentinels occasionally get the job done, it seems," Desher said scathingly.

Harper's whimper turned into a growl. "Get out of my head!"

"Give it up, Lieutenant Harper. Your PMC was corrupt long before I got here," Desher scorned.

"Don't listen to that asshole, Harper. Let me in, and I can help you fight him."

"Oh yes, do that, Harper. Commander Aldren is going to make everything better."

Quinton tried to force a connection to Harper's PMC but was blocked by Harper.

"That's not going to work," Desher said. "Let's try something else. I think we can be reasonable."

"Go to hell!"

"You're a Galactic PMC—one of Browning's prized Galactics. I thought PMCs like you might have been just a ruse to throw off the Sentinels," Desher said.

Quinton needed to calm down. Flying into a rage wasn't going to help anyone. Desher seemed keen on talking, so maybe he could learn something. "What do you want?"

"The way I see it is that we're stuck here with no end in sight. No one is going to get what they want like this," Desher said.

Quinton would have liked to see what Desher actually looked like, but his voice was coming through Harper. "Get to the damn point then."

Harper looked at Quinton, and Desher's voice came through his lips. "You never wanted this. You're one of the earliest iterations of PMCs meant to fight the Jordanis. I can clear things up for you. The Acheron Confederacy humbled the Jordanis in the most humiliating way possible. The ACN crushed their vast military. Browning was a hero. You would have been, too, if your ESS had gotten to where it was supposed to go. There, that's all done now. Regardless, you can walk away from all of this."

"And leave Salvation to you?"

"I don't want this place. It has no value to me or my mission at all," Desher replied.

"I don't believe you. Haven't you—"

"I had no idea this place was even here. Some kind of automated construction VI with access to too many resources must have built another ACN starbase."

"Then why did you come here? You arrived before we did. How did you find this place?"

"I would have thought that was obvious," Desher said in that same scathing tone that made Quinton want to kick something. "I came here because you triggered the Polaris Operation—part of Browning's pathetic attempts to change the outcome of a war that was decided long ago," Desher said and paused for a moment. "He lost. I'm not going to argue the point with you, but he did. You came here to stop the Polaris Operation. You want to prevent the broadcast of PMC activation signals across the galaxy."

Quinton hated that Desher had access to Harper's ESS. All the chips were stacked in his favor.

"You've got me all figured out," Quinton replied evenly.

"How are you going to stop the broadcast from here? This is just another ACN starbase, albeit a much larger one than the fleet records indicate, but a starbase all the same."

Quinton thought Desher was being a little too insistent on what he professed to know, which made Quinton doubt what he was being told.

"Let's take it a step further. Why would Browning make you a Galactic PMC? Why reactivate you in a galaxy you don't even know and not give you any help at all? The Federation Wars have already been fought and lost. We're in the final cleanup phase of that conflict. You'll never be able to defeat the Prime."

Quinton laughed. "The Prime. That's what you call Miles Harding?"

"The Prime has never been defeated. Everything that has happened is according to his plan."

"His plan, you say," Quinton sneered. "Really? You think he controls everything. Is this place part of his plan, too?"

"Yes," Desher replied without hesitation. "This variable was one of many that could occur. Let's not get hung up on the details. But think about it. The situation is hopeless. You've encountered the Sentinels before. They have hundreds of thousands of warships at their disposal, with more coming online, especially now with all the PMC activity going on. After this broadcast, they'll all be deployed. Also, why would Browning entrust Polaris and Salvation to an ACN Commander who's probably only commanded a small battle group against the Jordani Federation before volunteering for the PMC program. Does any of that sound like a brilliant strategy?"

Quinton let Desher's words penetrate deep into his mind. How many times had he said he just wanted to find a way to become human again? Find another DNA vault and download his PMC into a body that was as close as he was ever going to get to the one he'd been born with. Desher was right. The Federation Wars had been fought and lost. All Quinton wanted to do was put all this behind him and move on with his life, finding a way to coexist until they could combat the Sentinels in a way that wouldn't get them all killed.

"Do you have any idea how many Sentinel fleets must have arrived at this star system by now?" Desher asked. "After the broadcast is sent and all the PMCs scattered across the galaxy start coming here, we'll mop them up in droves. We won't even have to hunt them down, but we'll do that, too, Commander Aldren."

A maelstrom of memories spun up from the depths of his mind—recollections of his life before becoming a PMC, coming back online in a dying world, his time aboard the *Nebulon*, and then more recent memories of commanding the *Wayfarer* with his friends. Becker, Oscar, and Guttman could be wearing on anyone who spent time with them, but so could he. It was messy and it was real. They'd fought together and had even gone their separate ways, but they'd come back together.

Then he remembered obsidian walls along a long corridor and the countless names of the people who had died, people who had sacrificed, people who had made a stand in the face of overwhelming odds. He felt them all as if he were slamming his fists against battle steel, and each recollection brought a piece of knowledge that seemed to snap into place. He knew what Salvation was. He'd figured it out, and judging by Desher's comments, the Agent of Harding hadn't. Desher didn't have the slightest clue, but Quinton did, and the knowledge settled on him like the most hardened battle-steel-armored hull of the most colossal warship ever created.

Quinton focused on accessing the Salvation's systems, but he was still locked out. They wouldn't allow him to assume command with Admen Desher infiltrating Harper's PMC. He tried to think of a way to help Harper and couldn't. He kept remembering Misako leaping out of the Alari Outpost's hangar bay, choosing to sacrifice herself rather than remain controlled by the Sentinels. Now Harper was faced with a similar choice, except his PMC might have deteriorated so much that it was impossible to predict what he was going to do.

"You must know that it is hopeless," Desher said.

Quinton gritted his teeth.

"All that remains now is whether you'll admit it to yourself or not," Desher continued.

"I know exactly what I'm going to do," Quinton replied, hating it.

"I'm waiting."

"You're not even inside this place, and you don't know what it is. You probably followed us through the asteroid field and are using your docking clamps on the outer walls. You're within the dampening field, so somehow you've got a subspace comlink to penetrate all the way here."

"Bravo, Commander. You've got me all figured out," Desher replied.

"Probably not all, but I've got a few things to say to you. First, you almost had me convinced that you knew what Salvation is and what it was meant for. Also, you're so certain that your precious Harding Prime has already won the war. You're wrong."

"Take a look at the galaxy. You're on the losing side."

Quinton laughed. "I wouldn't be so sure about that. I figured out what Browning's plan was, and now I'm going to take this fight to your precious Prime. Wherever he's hiding, I'm going to find him. I bet *you* don't even know where Harding Prime is, do you?"

Desher didn't reply.

"Well, do you? Do you know where he is? Where's he been? If he's already won the war, why hasn't anyone seen him? You don't know."

"Neither do you."

"Maybe Lieutenant Nash Harper can help settle this."

Desher snorted. "You can't save him."

Quinton scowled. "Listen to me. If you somehow survive what's about to happen, make sure you send my regards to your superiors."

"You seem quite sure of yourself. We're in a stalemate. That hasn't changed. None of us wins."

"That's the problem with supreme arrogance. Not only does it make you an asshole, but it blinds to what you should have already realized," Quinton said, and hated what he was about to do. Then he spoke with the command authority of a Galactic PMC. "Lieutenant Nash Harper, Acheron Confederacy Navy, you're hereby relieved of duty. Your service to the Acheron Confederacy is complete. It's time for your PMC to go into standby. Thank you for your service."

Harper let out a soft sigh and disappeared from VR. Quinton heard the beginnings of Desher's venomous scream before it was cut off. At the same time, Salvation's authentication protocols completed Radek's integrity check and began transferring command authority to Quinton.

30

THE SPIDER-DRONE COLLAPSED to the transparent floor. Maelyn spun toward it and the others stepped back.

Corvax stepped toward it and squatted down. "His ESS has gone dormant."

"Dormant? But that means he's…" Maelyn said and hastened to Quinton.

"Harper is dead? Are you sure? How?" Becker asked.

Maelyn stared at Quinton's chest and scanned for the avatar's power core, but the shielding prevented her from seeing it.

Bradshaw came to stand next to her. "His ESS is still working," she said.

Maelyn frowned and bobbed her head a little. Quinton still looked as lifeless as he'd been for the past fifteen minutes. On the far side of the chamber, a tremendous holoscreen flickered to life, and a vast array of data feeds began popping up.

"I don't know what happened to him," Corvax said.

Maelyn looked over at them, and Becker lifted his eyebrows questioningly.

"He's still alive," she said.

Becker let out a huge breath and looked at Corvax. "Can you remote-access Harper's ESS and figure out what happened to him?"

"That won't work," Simon said. "If the core is dead, the ESS is gone, along with all the data on it."

"Maybe Quinton found a way to transfer him to a CDA somewhere," Guttman said.

Maelyn saw Quinton move. He took a few steps forward and rocked on his feet, disoriented, then squeezed his eyes shut and slowly shook his head.

"Just give me a second," Quinton said. His voice sounded slightly modulated, reminding her of when he multitasked within a computer system and stretched his capacity to the limit.

They gathered around him.

"We're here," Maelyn said. "You've been out of it for over fifteen minutes."

Quinton's eyes flashed and tracked back and forth as if he was reading at a fast pace.

"Harper?" Quinton asked. He started to turn but halted.

"His core is depleted. We thought maybe he was transferred out of it into a CDA," Maelyn said.

Quinton pressed his lips together and narrowed his gaze. "No, he was…" He jerked toward Guttman, and the spacer's eyes went wide. "Give it. Your wrist computer is compromised."

Guttman hastily took it off, but Becker intercepted it as Guttman tried to hand it off.

"I'll take that," Becker said. He dropped it to the floor and shot it with his hand-cannon. "No need to take any chances."

Quinton nodded and thanked him.

"What happened to Harper?" Maelyn asked.

"I couldn't help him. His matrix was too corrupt, and when he was infiltrated…" Quinton said and paused. "I'm sorry, the ship is transferring command authority and it's complicated."

"What ship?" Becker asked.

Maelyn lifted her eyebrows.

Quinton smiled, his eyes gleaming, and she felt her own lips lift in response.

"This place is a ship. It's one massive ship. Welcome to the *Salvation*."

Maelyn thought about how long it had taken them to get this far, trying to estimate the size, but she couldn't.

"Did he say 'ship'?" Guttman asked.

Becker nodded.

"Corvax and Bradshaw, I'm sending you a comlink with authentication protocols. I need you integrated ASAP," Quinton said.

"Yes, Commander," Corvax said.

The two CDAs walked away from them and then stood still.

"What's happening?" Maelyn asked.

"The Sentinels are here. There are thousands of them. I'll explain everything."

"Sentinels!" Guttman nearly shrieked. "We've gotta get out of here. This thing must have a heck of a jump drive. Let's skedaddle."

Quinton shook his head. "Not this time," he said with a hungry gleam in his gaze. "This time, we send a very clear message to the Sentinels, with Admiral Browning's compliments."

"What can we do to help?" Maelyn asked.

"Go over to those consoles and we'll get started."

QUINTON WATCHED the others for a moment and then turned toward the massive holoscreen on the far side of the bridge. Even with Radek managing the data feed from the *Salvation*, he still felt as if he was filling up to the breaking point. Knowledge of the *Salvation's* operation and weapons' systems and capabilities, along with live data feeds from their sensors, needed to be throttled or it would overwhelm him. His knowledge expanded with the vast data repositories aboard, and he chased after it because the answers were there—answers about the *Salvation*, Admiral Browning, and the Federation Wars.

"You must pace yourself," Radek warned.

"I know, but there's so much here," Quinton replied.

He couldn't afford to get distracted. Sensor data was still coming in, showing that thousands of Sentinel ships had entered the star system. He searched for the Union Ships that were attempting to flee, but they were within the dampening field. He had to set aside the paralyzing knowledge that he was about to fly a planetoid-class starship that was six thousand kilometers in diameter. He checked the specs multiple times, even though he knew they were accurate. Questions kept mounting, but he had to ignore them. He was going to fly a ship meant to be crewed by half a million people.

The dampening field protecting the *Salvation* was maintained by millions of field generators located throughout the remnant planet clusters, shielding the ship from the rest of the star system. The clusters maintained their formation due to the artificial gravity field powered by an array of the *Salvation's* power cores.

Quinton maintained a comlink with the others but could group them as needed; otherwise, they'd never get anything done. He activated Corvax and Bradshaw. Integrated PMCs could communicate much faster than the spoken word. Once they understood what Quinton wanted, they began to build targeting, and the tactical plot began to update.

Corvax queried Quinton regarding the Union Ships, and he told him to make sure they weren't harmed. Sentinel targeting only.

Bradshaw began to integrate with the *Salvation's* complex engineering components, focusing on the power core infrastructure.

Quinton uploaded multiple versions of his VI assistants into the *Salvation's* systems to scratch the surface of the command shortfall because they didn't have a full crew. He then immediately turned his attention to the tactical plot. Corvax was feeding targeting data in, almost at the same time that the sensor data reported it.

"Time to show ourselves to the galaxy," Quinton said.

He executed an update to the artificial gravity controls and his VI assistants took over. A multitude of the *Salvation's* power cores reported a huge spike in energy draw as the massive artificial gravity field reversed with startlingly accurate precision. The sheer gravitational forces tore apart the remnant planet clusters, expelling them out into the star system. Rocky chunks that had been clustered together suddenly broke apart as the gravitational field reversal pushed them outward at thirty percent of the speed of light. Everything in their path was destroyed. Thousands of Sentinel ships were blindsided by a colossal bombardment that their powerful control VIs had never anticipated. Even with the benefit of increased frame rate to facilitate supercomputing processing power, whole fleets of Sentinel warships were destroyed.

Located in the heart of what had been a cluster of dead remnant planets was the *Salvation*. All the infrastructure that had been used to build the ship had been part of the massive asteroids now pummeling fleets of Sentinel ships. The rearmost ships attempted to evade, but there was nowhere for them to run.

A holographic image of the ship appeared on the main holoscreen. The *Salvation* had triangular halves that swept away from the sphere in the middle.

"Would you look at that?" Guttman said.

"They replicated the emblem of the ACN," Becker said.

Quinton regarded the image with grim determination.

"They're running," Simon said. "The sentinel ships are trying to flee."

Multiple volleys of hyper-missiles burst from missile tubes across the *Salvation's* hull. The hyper-missiles transitioned into hyperspace, delivering antimatter warheads to Sentinel heavy cruisers. Quinton created a firing solution for the Sentinel Dreadnaught class ships, which had the equivalent mass of seven heavy cruisers each. Hundreds more hyper-missiles left their salvos armed with gravitonic warheads. Within moments, Sentinel Dreadnoughts began to drop from the tactical plot as the warheads detonated, creating short-lived black holes that tore the warships apart.

Quinton observed the Sentinels trying to escape, but the *Salvation* discharged its weapons with deadly precision. As he watched the tactical plot, a piece of knowledge sprang to existence. No doubt, Radek thought he needed it. The Sentinels had been the solution to a galaxy overwrought with corrupt PMC-controlled warships. They'd been constructed by pooling the resources of the surviving federations and star unions. They couldn't have known that the wars had been instigated by Miles Harding. Browning had exhausted his resources trying to stop it and couldn't. Admen Desher hadn't lied about that—Browning had been losing the war. He quit the field so they could rebuild, and the *Salvation* had been his solution. Quinton thought about the monument of the fallen that lined the corridor leading to the *Salvation's* main bridge. He and his companions hadn't been alone. They were standing on the shoulders of trillions of people who had died for this. They'd died for a chance to free the galaxy of not only the Sentinels but Miles Harding.

Quinton accessed the communication systems and found the protocols used for Polaris. They were hours away from recalling the PMCs scattered across the galaxy.

Maelyn walked over to him. "Is that all of them?"

Quinton nodded. "Their last known locations."

"What are you going to do?"

"If I let Polaris initiate, many of them are going to die. There are too many Sentinels. We can't get to all of them in time."

"Then don't," Maelyn said. "Stop the signal."

"We need them."

"Yes, but do we need them right now? Like this?"

Quinton considered it for a few moments. She was right. There was a better way than signaling a massive recall. He stopped Polaris and authorized a broadcast to stop the communication drones deployed throughout the galaxy as well. Radek gave him a report. "The signal won't be stopped everywhere in time."

"Then we should go there first."

"Yes, but we can't do everything ourselves. We need to coordinate with others."

Maelyn smiled and turned back to the tactical plot. "Look at them run. I've never heard of Sentinels retreating before."

"It's a tactical retreat, but it's no less satisfying. We should get underway ourselves."

31

Admen Desher flew his ship through the asteroid field. Union ships were also flying through the area, trying to escape the Sentinel fleets he'd gathered there. He regarded the tactical plot, feeling spikes of rage as thousands of Sentinels were destroyed. This wasn't a battle; it was a slaughter. The dampening field had ceased just before the attack, and his ship had happened to be among the Union ships. He guided his ship to stay with them, easily blending in.

The scan data showed him an impossibly deadly creation. He'd been so close to discovering this secret, and to have it snatched away made him want to spit fire. Commander Aldren had beaten him. Galactic PMCs had command authority over their ranks, and it had been able to give Nash Harper a chance to deny the corruption. Admen had lost all control when Harper went offline. Aldren had proven to be a shrewd opponent.

A subspace comlink registered from a Sentinel warship and uploaded a data package with new commands for him to follow, but the warship went offline before Admen could reply. It must have been unable to escape the star system in time. Admen executed a micro-jump that took him away from the chaos. By the time the Union ships noticed, he would be somewhere else. Commander Aldren may have won the battle, but the war was far from over.

"The dampening field is gone, Commander," Pierce said.

Lennix looked at the data on the main holoscreen. The Sentinel fleets were being destroyed. Huge swaths of their numbers had simply disappeared.

Nate Carradine turned toward him. "Analysis of the attack indicates that we're not being targeted."

Lennix had watched in complete and utter shock as clusters of asteroids, scattered by some unseen force, began decimating Sentinel warships. They'd been pursuing his small fleet, and they must have been just as surprised by the attack as he was.

"Commander, we're being hailed," Pierce said.

"By whom?" Lennix asked.

"He wants to speak to you, sir. He knows you're on this ship, specifically."

Lennix sat down and inclined his chin toward the main holoscreen. A video comlink appeared, showing the head and shoulders of someone he hadn't expected to see again. "Aldren," he whispered.

The PMC smiled. If not for the slight glow of the eyes, Lennix would have thought he was human.

"You and I need to talk," Quinton said.

Lennix leaned forward, but his mouth went dry.

"I'm not going to fire on any Union ships."

Lennix looked confused. "Why not?"

"Because you're not the enemy," Quinton said. "At least, you don't have to be. I know what you did with my ID. It's not going to work anymore."

Lennix knew better than to deny it. All their lives were dangling by a very thin thread. "It was the only way to fight the Collective, but when similar attacks began happening elsewhere…" He paused and shook his head. "We tried to stop it. The information broker we used—Admen Desher—he double-crossed us."

Quinton frowned. "Admen Desher was your information broker?"

Lennix nodded. If he kept Quinton talking, maybe there would be enough time to get away.

"I want to know everything about that, but I don't have time right now," Quinton said and leaned closer to the camera. "You owe me, Crowe. The only reason the Sentinels didn't destroy your fleet was because of me. Do we have an understanding?"

Lennix swallowed hard and nodded. "What do you want?"

"I want you to get your fleet out of here. The Sentinels might come back, and it's best you're not here. But I don't want you to throw your ships away trying to take on the Collective."

"I might not have a choice."

"The Collective is the least of our worries. But I need to be clear with you here. If you start raiding Collective targets again, Trenton Draven will be the least of your worries."

"Why do you care about the Collective?"

Quinton shook his head. "I don't. I care about fighting the Sentinels, and you're going to help me do it. So is Draven. There's a lot you don't know, and a briefing is being prepared to explain it all."

Lennix glanced at Nate, who kept his gaze locked on the main holoscreen. He didn't have a choice. He had to do whatever Quinton said, at least for the moment. "All right, we'll cease all hostilities against Collective targets as of right now."

"Good," Quinton replied. "I've cataloged all of your ships here, as well as the reserves that aren't here."

"You don't know where my reserves are," Lennix said.

Quinton regarded him. "Don't make me regret this," he said and shook his head. "You know what? Never mind. I think you're more trouble than you're worth. Goodbye Crowe."

"Wait!" Lennix cried. "Wait. Just tell me what you want."

"First, I want you to leave this star system. Second, you're to continue building up your fleet strength. I'll be in contact with you."

"Why are you doing this?"

"Like I already said, you're not the enemy. You've got a lot to answer for, Crowe, but that can come later. You'll get your chance to balance what you owe me."

Lennix regarded him for a few moments. "All right."

Quinton nodded once. "Good. Now get your people out of here. They have important work to do."

The comlink severed and Lennix looked at Nate.

"We better do as he says," Nate said.

"Give me a broadcast channel to the fleet," Lennix said.

After he was through giving orders to clear the area, he leaned back in his chair.

Nate looked at him. "He could have killed us."

"But he didn't, which means he was telling the truth. He needs us."

"To take on the Sentinels," Nate replied. "He's simply delaying our deaths to a more convenient time."

"That gives us time to prepare. I have no intention of dying."

32

QUINTON STOOD several meters outside the *Salvation's* primary bridge. He'd just added a name to the monument of the fallen, and he looked at the others for a moment before turning back to the obsidian-colored wall that was almost covered with white script. He saluted in the tradition of the Acheron Confederacy Navy. Corvax and Bradshaw followed suit while the others watched in silence.

Among the long list of people who'd died during the Federation Wars was a new name.

"Lieutenant Nash Harper," Quinton said. "Gone but never forgotten."

"Never forgotten," the others echoed.

Quinton looked at the name and wondered how many more would be added to it. After a few moments' contemplation, he returned to the bridge and couldn't help but be impressed by the sight of it all.

"I've heard back from Admiral Brandt. He confirmed that Sentinel activity has decreased everywhere," Maelyn said.

Quinton had expected it.

"Where did they all go?" Becker asked.

"They were probably recalled. Admen Desher must have gotten away and reported to Harding Prime," Quinton said.

"You're really going to do it? You're going to take on the Sentinels?" Becker asked.

Quinton bobbed his head once. "Hopefully not alone. I was expecting the rest of you might help, but I don't have a choice."

"What do you mean you don't have a choice?"

Quinton looked at them. "It's part of taking command of this ship. Do you think Browning was just going to leave it with whoever ended up here first? No, he had a bunch of constraints associated with it."

Becker regarded him for a moment. "So, you couldn't walk away even if you wanted to?"

"I'm not walking away from this. There isn't anyone else."

Becker rubbed the side of his face. "But all those other PMCs. I guess I just thought that maybe there *would* be someone else."

Quinton arched an eyebrow and half his mouth lifted. "Thanks for the vote of confidence. I really appreciate it."

"No, that isn't what I meant."

"Yes, it was."

Becker rolled his eyes. "I just thought maybe there was someone with more experience or someone who knows more about this ship."

"Then I guess it's do-or-die time," Quinton said. "Besides, there are entire training libraries on all the ships' systems, so we can all catch up."

"I guess we'd better get to work then," Maelyn said, smiling at both of them.

Quinton returned her smile. "You should see the orientation program videos. They're something else," he said and gestured toward the main holoscreen.

Two video windows appeared. One of them showed Oscar singing while pretending to fly an aircar that was locked on a maintenance hold.

"Then, there's this one," Quinton said.

A video feed of a small bridge appeared, and Guttman ran into view. He stopped suddenly and stripped off his EVA suit, wobbling on his feet a little.

"Oh, come on!" Guttman said. "You promised you wouldn't do that anymore."

On the holoscreen, Guttman began galloping around while shouting at the top of his lungs. Then he looked as if he were replying to someone. "Servitors are coming? Woohoo!"

Laughter bubbled up out of all of them. Oscar went to stand beside Guttman and the two bowed.

"When did this happen?" Maelyn asked.

"It wasn't all that long ago," Quinton said.

He updated the video feed so they played on a three-second loop. More rounds of laughter bubbled out of all of them.

"As God as my witness, I'm going to find a way to get back at you," Guttman said.

"That's what I keep hearing," Quinton replied.

"He'll have help," Oscar replied.

The two shared a knowing look and Quinton grinned. It felt good. He killed the video.

A few minutes later, Simon called them over to his workstation. Quinton lingered behind and Maelyn strolled over to him.

"They needed that," she said.

"So did I."

Maelyn eyed him. "Is it true? You really don't have a choice?"

Quinton shrugged. "There's always a choice. I just might not like the choices I've got," he said, and Maelyn nodded. "You saw what the *Salvation* is capable of. Would you just hand that off without a way of keeping them in line?"

"When you put it like that, I guess not."

"We've got a lot of work to do," he said, thinking about the endless list of tasks that were still filling up his "To Do" list, and learning more about the ship only added to it. The *Salvation* also carried hundreds of smaller warships in its hangar bays.

"It's a good thing you've got a strong second-in-command."

Quinton frowned. "I do?"

Maelyn smiled sweetly and gave him a teasing look. "Would you rather it was Becker?"

Quinton chuckled and glanced at the others. They were watching Simon's holoscreen with interest, still wrapping their minds around everything that had happened.

"No, he's not ready for this, although neither are you nor I," Quinton said.

Maelyn raised her chin. "I know, but we'll all have to be quick learners."

Quinton considered it for a few moments, then nodded. "I already am, but I'm not sure about you."

Maelyn narrowed her gaze. "I can do whatever you can, except for…" she said and gestured toward him.

"All I'm saying is that there's an extensive interview process so I can be sure your strengths match up with the rest of the team's."

Maelyn's mouth opened a little and then she laughed. "You're… Fine. Let's start right now."

"We can't."

"Why not?"

"Oh, because I need to put together an advisory committee."

"Now I know you're lying. You hate decisions by committee."

Quinton sighed. "Damn, you saw through it. Well, that means you've passed your first test."

"How many tests are there?"

Quinton smiled. "Admiral's Privilege."

ACHERON REDEMPTION

PROLOGUE

A GALACTIC HISTORICAL EXCERPT.

Personality Matrix Construct (PMC) was first developed by Miles Harding of the Acheron Confederacy to upload a person's mind to an Energy Storage System (ESS). With the help of a highly complex set of virtual intelligences, they manage the human consciousness to machine interface. PMCs augmented existing combat technology, vastly increasing their effectiveness, surpassing traditional cyberwarfare suites.

PMC technology was first adopted by the Acheron Confederacy to push back against the tyranny of the Jordani Federation. But the technology couldn't be contained to one federation and spread throughout the galaxy. PMC degradation began to occur with alarming frequency where entire federations lost control of their most powerful warships. Rogue PMCs attacked civilian population centers across the galaxy in an ever-expanding tide of death and destruction, causing the Federation Wars.

Once a highly decorated naval officer in the ACN, Grand Admiral Elias Browning was branded a traitor and war criminal. Browning was believed to be responsible for the corruption of PMCs and the Federation Wars.

To cope with an increasing list of atrocities by PMC controlled fleets, galactic federations devoted their vast resources to the Sentinel initiative to create and repurpose existing fleets. Sentinel warships were operated by highly restricted versions of PMCs, whose only purpose was to hunt down and eliminate all PMCs from the galaxy.

The Federation Wars continued for decades, destroying most federations' core worlds throughout the galaxy. Subsequent skirmishes increased as spacers competed for what little resources were left. All the while, Sentinel fleets roamed the galaxy, hunting for PMCs.

Post Federation War society saw the rise of the salvager unions and mercenary groups. Galactic residents had to adapt to life aboard space stations, colony ships, and planetary habitats on barely hospitable worlds. The central command that controlled the Sentinels had been destroyed during the wars. Attempts were made to disband Sentinel fleets, but all attempts failed, and remnant fleets were no match for Sentinel warships. Spacers soon learned that coexistence with the Sentinels was far less dangerous than resisting them.

Decades after the Federation Wars, Sentinel fleets continue to send scout forces to patrol star systems. The only communication from the Sentinels were to demand the compliance of space stations and starships alike as they searched for PMCs. Something hidden among the vast reaches of the galaxy began broadcasting PMC activation signals, and much to any spacers' surprise was that there were PMCs who answered the call.

The Sentinels increased their patrols, hunting for PMCs and destroying them heedless of whatever stood in their way. On the galactic fringe, one PMC reactivated who managed to avoid the Sentinels. His name is Quinton Aldren, a Galactic class PMC with authority to command other PMCs. Since Quinton's reactivation, startling new discoveries were found about the origin of the Federation Wars. Discoveries that will change the galaxy and expose the true purpose of the Sentinels.

1

"You never talk about your past."

Quinton cast a wry glance toward the young man. "We spent six months aboard the *Salvation*, and you're only bringing this up now, Simon?"

The young spacer smiled and shrugged a little. "I've been busy."

That was an understatement, which Quinton didn't bother to point out.

They weren't currently aboard the cavernous command deck of the *Salvation*. Instead, he'd chosen to begin this mission aboard the ACS *Fortitude*, a heavily modified leviathan class battleship cruiser. The ship had been designed by the Acheron Confederacy to operate with minimal crew, assuming there were specialized Personality Matrix Constructs serving as part of the crew.

"Admiral Aldren," Captain Javier Martinez said, "Nexus Battle Group stands ready." Martinez was new to his rank, like almost all the human crew that served in the fleet of ships that had come from the *Salvation*.

Quinton was standing at the command center that overlooked the entire bridge of the warship. Amber-colored workstations glowed throughout. He had active connections to the computing core, but the data feeds were muted. They weren't in battle or near any star system where the enemy might find them.

"Understood, Captain," Quinton replied.

Quinton found that he missed being aboard the planetoid spaceship. He'd attained the rank of Admiral when he took command of the *Salvation*. He was a Galactic class PMC, but his consciousness predated the Federation Wars. He'd only attained the rank of Commander in the Acheron Confederacy Navy, but his PMC had been lost for nearly a century and everything had changed. The ACN was gone now, like most of the old Federations. Thousands of PMCs had been hunted and killed by the Sentinels—remnant warships left over from the Federation Wars.

Quinton looked at Simon, who simply stared back at him. "Don't make me regret allowing you to tag along."

Simon chuckled. "I'm at your disposal, Admiral."

Simon was an engineer at heart and had become a foremost expert on PMCs. Quinton was glad to have him along as he provided valuable insight into the technical cohesion of the combined human and PMC crewmembers. Quinton suspected that Simon sometimes missed serving with his former captain, Maelyn. He'd been under her command since he was a scrawny spacer, but she was leading her own task force for one of the away teams.

Captain Martinez gave them a sidelong glance that conveyed mild disapproval, and Quinton couldn't blame him. No one particularly enjoyed having a ranking officer supplant command of a ship, and Martinez adhered to the rigid military decorum that was instilled in anyone who'd recently gone through academy training.

Quinton had also brought spacers to observe the bridge crew performing their duties. He couldn't afford to miss any opportunity for his burgeoning fleet to gain much-needed experience. They were all green as far as Quinton was concerned. None of these spacers had served in any military. They'd been trained using rapid training simulations aboard the *Salvation* before being moved to their respective ships. It was the PMCs that were in short supply.

PMCs were comprised of various pre-Federation Wars military members who had volunteered to upload their consciousness into an Energy Storage System. They were all highly disciplined, with years of training, but they came from various timeframes during the Federation Wars. Not all the PMCs who were brought back online were sane. The ones who could cope served on the ships, and the ones who had lost their sanity were put back into permanent standby.

Quinton regarded the bridge officers. He supposed he should be satisfied that they could more or less fly the ships of his fleet without bumping into anything. Specialized implants had assisted in rapid training and response, but they were unproven in battle.

The Nexus Battle Group included one battleship cruiser, along with a few dozen destroyer class vessels and heavy cruisers. Each of the ships had a PMC assigned to them—PMCs that they'd retrieved a few at a time since they were spread throughout the galaxy. PMCs had had to be hidden from the Sentinels, but the time for hiding was over. The Sentinels outnumbered them by more than fifty to one and had more experience in tactical engagement. Until Quinton found the *Salvation*, the Sentinels had warships and armament that made the spacers who survived the Federation Wars seem woefully insignificant. The Sentinels were more than a malfunctioning war machine meant to bring order to the galaxy. They were the end result of the greatest ruse in galactic history, and Quinton was going to stop them.

"Captain Martinez, I have a comlink request from CENTCOM," Ensign Amano said.

"Put it on the main holoscreen," Martinez replied.

An older man appeared. He had hair the color of an old space station that had seen too much service.

Martinez sat up straight in his chair. "Admiral Brandt," he acknowledged and glanced toward Quinton.

Admiral Severin Brandt was the commanding officer of the Dholeren United Coalition (DUC) and was now Quinton's second-in-command. Brandt looked at Quinton. "How's the view from there, Admiral Aldren?"

Quinton smiled. "Best seats in the house."

A data feed became available as an update from the *Salvation* was pushed to the ship.

"As you're no doubt aware, our forces have been deployed across all sectors," Brandt said.

Quinton had put Brandt in charge of coordinating their deployments. Nexus Battle Group would operate as backup to any of the away teams that encountered heavy resistance from local star cluster defenses or if the Sentinels showed up to investigate PMC activation signals.

"Excellent, we'll be ready to respond when things heat up," Quinton replied.

Brandt nodded and leveled his gaze at Quinton. "I still say we should stagger these retrieval missions to more bite-sized pieces."

"I know you do, but if we do that, the Sentinel response times will decrease once they figure out what we're doing. Moving slower will cost us more in the long run," Quinton replied.

By the numbers, he knew he was right, but Brandt was no fool. He'd gone over those same numbers as well. Brandt was concerned about the inexperienced crews that were serving aboard ships armed to the teeth. They could handle smaller skirmishes if they occurred, but anything approaching a highly concerted effort on the Sentinels' part would leave them outmatched.

"We can't afford to wait years to keep training spacers. If we're to have any hope of fighting the Sentinel fleets, we need those PMCs that are waiting out there for reactivation," Quinton said.

Brandt was old enough to have witnessed the Federation Wars and the various uprisings that had occurred since then. Uprisings attempting to destroy the Sentinel fleets had always failed. The price of those previous failures had led the galaxy to abandon the fight, and the spacers of recent generations were conditioned to run when the Sentinels showed up. It was either run or submit to them, hoping they wouldn't be destroyed while the Sentinels hunted for rogue PMCs like Quinton.

"Time is a valuable commodity," Brandt replied.

"If we wait for the Sentinel incursion to begin, it'll make this mission almost impossible," Quinton said and looked around the bridge. "You're right, Severin. We could use more time to prepare. More time to get our feet under us. We'll stumble, but we'll also adapt. This retrieval mission will more than triple our combat capabilities. There are thousands of PMCs on standby waiting to join this fight. We need them."

Brandt regarded him for a moment, and then he nodded. "Very well. But I would rather you stayed aboard the *Salvation*."

"I know you do, but the less the Sentinels know about it, the better off we'll be," Quinton replied.

The *Salvation* had an armament greater than all the ships he currently had deployed, but it was just one ship, and it could only be at one place at a time. They couldn't even deploy the entire fleet because of shortages of trained spacers and a severe lack of PMCs available for tactical engagement.

"Let's begin," Quinton said.

2

LENNIX CROWE DEPARTED the shuttle on the landing pad at Lumina Station, located within a few lightyears of the Cassius Nebula. He strode down the walkway, ignoring the station officials who attempted to gain his attention. Nate Carradine, his second-in-command, intercepted them and paid whatever docking fees were required.

Crowe had plenty of station officials that, for a regular fee, would keep his network of informants apprised of new developments in various sectors. They were particularly adept at reporting new salvage sites, but those hadn't been of interest to him for over six months—not since he'd been recruited by Quinton Aldren. For too long he'd been stuck between an asteroid on a decaying orbit or on the wrong end of a Sentinel attack force and their damn particle-beam weapons. Aldren had spared him and the remnants of the Union fleet, but the price for his life was to join in the fight against the Sentinels. He'd thought he could play along for a while and then break free from Aldren's control, but that was before he'd learned the truth.

A Union squad dressed in plain spacer attire surrounded him. They were seasoned fighting men whose loyalty to him was unquestioned. Lennix only kept the best with him.

Lumina Station was the kind of place you came to and only stayed for a short period of time. It was perfect for arranging a quick meeting place to recruit independent mercenary companies.

Nate rejoined him as he reached the exit doors of the landing pad. "The problem with traveling incognito is that people lapse into bad habits."

Lennix snorted. "I take it you reminded him?"

"Better to breathe another day. I tagged him with a memory stim that'll put him in a brain fog for the next couple of hours."

Lennix nodded and headed toward the small warehouse section of the station, an area that temporarily held storage containers marked for shipment. The dockworkers knew enough to keep their heads down and not pay too much attention to groups that otherwise wanted to be left alone. A few glances at the Union soldiers were enough to divert even the more curious onlookers who aimed to make a quick credit—that and the fact that Lennix engaged a temporary dampening field that scrambled most comms signals. A couple of dockworkers frowned at their wrist computers and then hastened out of the area.

"How many do you think will show?" Lennix asked.

"Enough to make this worthwhile," Nate replied, making a passing motion toward Lennix, and a drone video feed appeared on Lennix's internal HUD.

Multiple groups of armed mercenaries had gathered in one of the empty holding areas. Lennix had paid to keep the area unoccupied just so he could meet with them. Representatives from various mercenary groups eyed each other with suspicion. More than a few of them had faced each other in conflict because they'd been hired by competing interests.

Lennix strode inside, and the dampening field expanded to include the surrounding area.

"I've instituted a comms blackout for the purpose of this meeting," Lennix said.

A few mercenaries began to protest, and Lennix allowed it to go on for a few seconds. It was better to let the blowhards expend their breaths for a minute or two than silence them outright. Among the most vocal was a spacer Lennix recognized.

"Mase Soner, I thought you were interested in earning credits?" Lennix asked and expanded his gaze to include the others. "Isn't that why you're here?"

The merc captain became silent.

"Now for the business at hand," Lennix said.

"Why block our comlinks?" a mercenary named Karl Dupree asked. He wore polished combat armor that was no stranger to battle.

"It's for the protection of all of us. Plus, I don't want anyone else listening in on our conversation. All of you represent merc groups I wish to do business with. You can report to your superiors after the meeting," Lennix said and paused for a moment. "They'll get over it, or they should have shown up themselves."

Several merc captains snickered in response.

"I'm Lennix Crowe, Commander of the Union."

Instant silence settled over the group of merc captains. The Union's reputation had spread far and wide throughout the galaxy. There was a reason Trenton Draven and the Collective had tried to destroy him. The mercs knew it, and Lennix saw no point in trying to hide that fact.

One of the mercs tried to sneakily raise his weapon, but the Union soldier standing next to Lennix was quicker. A crimson plasma blast took out the head of the idiot merc, while those nearby scrambled out of the way.

The rest of the Union soldiers raised their weapons. Several merc captains had drawn their weapons but hadn't fired them.

"Anyone else want to die?" Lennix asked. He'd had his personal shield activated, which gave him enough protection to get away if he really needed to.

"If we start shooting each other, no one gets what they want. Who was that idiot who thought he'd collect on an old bounty?"

Soner glanced at the headless body sprawled on the ground. "That was Godrey."

Lennix glanced at Nate.

"Sancus Company."

Lennix nodded and turned back toward the others. "Anyone else from Sancus here?"

A few moments passed, and then a short, dark-skinned man raised his hand. "Waltin."

Lennix looked at him for a moment. Mercs only respected strength, and Waltin met his gaze. He was seasoned enough not to show weakness. "You can stay, Waltin. When we're done, report back to Stanis what happened to his brother."

Waltin frowned, mildly surprised that Lennix had such intimate knowledge of Sancus Company.

"All right, let's get to it. We're recruiting spacers."

"Who is the Union fighting now?" Soner asked.

"The Sentinels," Lennix replied.

Soner blinked several times. "You can't be serious."

"I'm quite serious."

"I thought you were going to say the Collective, and I would have told you to take your offer and shove it. Now I know you're crazy," Soner replied.

There were more than a few heads bobbing as others agreed with the merc captain.

Lennix had expected that response but was unperturbed by it. "I'm not fighting the Collective anymore. At least for now. There's been increased Sentinel activity throughout the sectors. Another incursion is happening, but this one is going to be worse."

"We can't fight the Sentinels," Soner replied.

Others voiced their agreement. More than a few backed away as if Lennix was holding a grav grenade.

"I'm not asking you to. None of you have weapons capable of doing enough damage to Sentinel ships to make much difference in a battle," Lennix said. Their reactions amused him. They'd just said how they couldn't fight the Sentinels, but at the same time, they were insulted that Lennix pointed out the truth to them. They were outclassed and they knew it. "I *do*, or to be more accurate, the United Federation Alliance does."

"Never heard of them," Soner said.

"You will. Now listen up. I'll go into who the UFA is in a minute. You can't fight the Sentinels in a straight-up battle, but that doesn't mean you can't help us. We need intel of their whereabouts."

Soner's eyes widened. "You want us to spy on the Sentinels?"

Lennix nodded. "For starters. You'll be paid for credible intel, of course, and if you prove yourselves, then let's just say the UFA is willing to provide you with upgraded weaponry that will put you on a more even playing field with Sentinel ships." Lennix regarded them for a few seconds. "Maybe not the big warships, but the smaller frigates and recon ships. How does that sound?"

He watched as they considered his offer. The promise of more powerful weapons was the bread and butter of any merc group. It could provide them with an edge that could easily allow them to dominate engagements with almost anyone. A few mercs glanced at the dead spacer on the floor.

"So, you think you can handle a little recon and maybe a few snatch-and-grab operations as needed?"

He could tell that many of them were intrigued by the offer.

Nate leaned toward him and whispered something. Lennix nodded. "There's also a signing bonus that will be doubled for any intel that we can verify as accurate."

The merc captains regarded each other, except for one. She simply stared at Lennix. He didn't know who she was. "Looks like you've got something to say."

She tipped her head to the side. "This UFA is planning to fight the Sentinels, right? That's where this is heading."

"Who are you?"

"Musso, from Phoenix Company," she replied.

They were a smaller merc group but had proven effective at engaging enemies with superior forces. It was something Lennix could appreciate.

"We don't have a choice. More PMCs are coming online every day. They're coming out of hiding, and they've got a story to tell that will make you question everything you think you know."

"Is that why you're doing this?" Musso asked. Her tone wasn't accusatory. She really was just asking a question, but there were implications within it that Lennix couldn't ignore.

"Yes. No one standing on the sidelines can affect the change that's coming. If you want to know more, then I suggest you join up," Lennix said and gestured toward Nate. "My associate is sending comms protocols for you to follow when reporting in."

"We haven't said whether we'll take your offer," Soner replied.

Lennix smiled. "The terms are fair and the easiest credits you'll earn. Attempting to squeeze me for more will be disastrous for those involved. Either take the offer or don't, but the consequences for wasting my time will be severe."

Soner regarded him for a few moments but remained quiet.

Lennix glanced at Nate.

"It's done."

"Excellent. Gentleman and ladies, this concludes our meeting," Lennix said.

He turned around and walked away. The dampening field was soon disabled, and Lennix had no doubt that the merc captains were reporting his offer. He had no intention of staying on Lumina Station a minute longer than he had to and headed straight back to the shuttle.

Sometime after the shuttle micro-jumped away from Lumina Station and before it entered the landing bay of the Union Cruiser *Savage*, Nate informed him that they were already receiving intelligence reports from the merc groups they'd just left.

"We'll see if any of them pan out," Lennix replied.

Nate twitched one of his eyebrows. "Still reserving judgment, I see."

They left the shuttle and headed toward the bridge.

"I'm practical. We wave a few thousand credits under their noses to encourage cooperation, but that doesn't mean they'll stick around in the long run."

Several spacers moved to the side of the corridor to allow them to pass.

"You're a believer now?"

Lennix gave his friend a sidelong glance. "It's crazy enough to be true."

They entered his ready room near the bridge. Lennix poured himself a drink and passed the bottle to Nate, who poured some of the amber liquid into his glass and swirled it around a little.

"What?" Lennix asked, knowing his friend had something on his mind.

Nate took a hearty swallow and set the glass down. "When you've been around as long as I have, you notice some things. Patterns, if you will, about what people are willing to believe."

Lennix sipped his drink, enjoying the warmth as he swallowed. "A fool's errand then, but we have very little choice. The evidence Aldren has is pretty compelling. Browning was a war hero, after all. I read the reports. He first made a name for himself by defending a third-tier colony world from a Jordani strike group. That's not the kind of person who decides to bring war and chaos to the rest of the galaxy."

"Browning is just one piece of the puzzle. Maybe you're right, but does it really matter? PMCs *did* go insane. Something caused that to happen. The Sentinels were the response to it, and because they're still around, spacers flock to this idea that they've stumbled onto one of the greatest conspiracies in the galaxy. Never underestimate people's proclivity to believe a sensational lie."

Lennix regarded him for a few moments. "Where do you stand on all this then?"

"With you, Lennix. I support the Union, first and foremost."

"It's not that I don't appreciate it, but you sound like you don't believe in the mission."

"You keep me around because I question things like this. Maybe Quinton Aldren is right, and the Harding Prime controls the Sentinels as part of some plan that began well before our time. What concerns me is that we knew our place in the galaxy, and now that will change. I just want to make sure we survive to be on the other side of all this when the missiles stop firing."

"You and me both," Lennix replied.

Nate Carradine had been at his side even before there was a Union. There was very little that could rattle Crowe's cage, but recent events had. He'd be a fool if he didn't consider what Nate was trying to tell him.

A comlink chimed.

"Commander Crowe, I have an alpha priority message for you."

"Send it here," Lennix said.

A holoscreen appeared above his desk, displaying a status window of a waiting secure comlink.

"News travels fast. That's Draven's identification."

"Do you want me to leave?" Nate asked.

Lennix shook his head and acknowledged the comlink.

Draven was lean and, from outward appearances, unassuming. Eyes nearly silver in color but with an artificial ring of green near the irises regarded Crowe.

"I thought it about time you and I had a chat," Draven said.

"Well, you've got me. What do you want to talk about?"

The edges of Draven's thin lips twitched with contempt. "I'll be honest with you—you've been a thorn in my side for much longer than you have any right to be."

"Coming from you, I consider that a compliment."

Lennix knew Draven wanted to kill him and absorb the Union into the Collective, but Aldren and the UFA had put a significant pause on that conflict. Lennix had bled Draven's operations and knew that would never be forgotten. Sooner or later, one of them was going to kill the other. That was just how the galaxy worked.

"I'm sure you do. Our intelligence network has received an influx of data regarding Sentinel operations. I'm assuming this is related to your current mission."

"Assume away," Lennix replied.

Draven looked at him as one would regard a bug that was about to be squashed.

"It is. Final reports are being sent to the UFA," Lennix said.

Draven rolled his eyes. "A new name, but the organizers are much the same."

"Does this mean you won't be joining?"

"I didn't say that. My operations are very much a part of the Alliance," Draven said.

Lennix knew Draven had been given the same offer from Aldren that he'd received. It was hard to set your fleets, even one as powerful as the Collective, against a planetoid spaceship designed to fight a war. Lennix had seen the ship. He'd seen how it had destroyed thousands of Sentinels without taking any damage. Draven hadn't seen the ship and was working from the reports Lennix and representatives from the DUC had provided.

"I'll have my people forward their analysis of the new leads to you as soon as I can."

"Are you part of the current operation?"

Lennix frowned. "What are you talking about?"

"I don't know. That's why I'm asking you."

"I'm not aware of any other mission beyond what I'm already doing," Lennix lied.

"Doesn't it bother you to be kept in the dark?"

"Maybe you just don't like not being in control."

Draven showed his teeth, and there was nothing friendly about it. "I understand now. You've adjusted to being a lapdog, then. Unquestionable loyalty to your master."

Lennix smiled, not rising to the bait. "I have a job to do. If Aldren wanted me involved in some other operation, he would have told me."

Draven chuckled. "Funny thing about informants and spies. They always think they're one step ahead, but they're usually wrong. I expect those intelligence reports ASAP."

Lennix suppressed a cold shudder but didn't blink. "You'll get them."

The comlink was severed, and the holoscreen went blank. Lennix looked at Nate. "What do you think?"

"He's just kicking over a few rocks, trying to get you to give something away."

"We have spies in his organization. Warning them would just draw attention to them."

"And yet there are a few who should be warned that Draven might be on to them," Nate said.

Lennix closed his eyes for a few seconds, pressing his lips together in thought.

"Teagan doesn't go halfway. She'll get in as deep as possible."

Lennix nodded. "I know. She's a lot like her mother."

Nate exhaled through his nose. "She has a lot of you in her as well. If you're looking for my recommendation, I say you should send her a warning."

Teagan Cayne was Crowe's daughter. Her identity had been protected since she was a young girl, but she'd risen through the Union ranks of her own accord. She'd go the extra lightyears it took to achieve her objective. It was plenty to make even him proud but also a little bit afraid that she'd get into a situation she couldn't escape. To make matters worse, while she was undercover in the Collective, she was beyond whatever aid he could give her.

"See to it. Use normal dropbox comms protocols. She'll retrieve it when she checks in, and that will have to be enough," Lennix said.

"I'll do it immediately," Nate said and left.

Lennix poured himself another drink and gulped it down. He didn't trust Draven, and the feeling was mutual, but they had to work together, at least for now.

3

MAELYN HAD SPENT most of her life aboard one ship or another, but none of them had been fresh off the space docks like the ACS *Rubicon*. When the construction platforms built the *Salvation* in secret, they'd also built the fleet of ships that were housed inside it. The *Rubicon* was a fast attack frigate that was half the size of a standard ACN Destroyer. She brought a lifetime of experience in flying multiple classes of ships, but she'd been out of her element when they'd first found the *Salvation*. She was qualified for command up to the frigate class starship and was in the process of certifying for destroyer command.

She felt a lance of pain in her head, and she winced.

Kieva turned toward her. "Are those implants still giving you headaches?"

Kieva was short, blond, and brilliant when it came to all things related to starships.

They were in her ready room off the bridge, and Kieva had been giving her a performance report for the *Rubicon's* sub-light engines.

"Apparently," Maelyn said, rubbing her temples, and the pain lessened until it was almost gone. "I don't even have them fully active. They've been giving me problems since day one."

"Why don't you see the doctor?" Kieva asked.

They didn't have a doctor on the *Rubicon*, just a VI equipped with the medical libraries that had already determined she just needed to keep using her brain implants and the headaches would go away. They were supposed to help bridge the gap between PMCs and everyone else. She hated them. Despite her recent experiences with PMCs, she had a lifetime of bias against their technology. She'd been taught that wearable tech was much safer than brain enhancements.

"I'll follow up with someone when we get back," Maelyn replied.

Kieva arched an eyebrow for a moment. "I bet Simon could have helped with them. I miss him and that adorable little dimple of his that appeared whenever he smiled. I remember when he was gangly and soft spoken. Quiet as a mouse."

Maelyn made a swiping motion with her hand, and the holoscreens went into standby. She stood up.

"He's all grown up now, and he's helping Quinton," she said.

There was a bit of an edge to her voice. She exhaled through her nose. "Sorry."

Kieva smiled in understanding. "It's all right. Our little foster brother is spreading his wings," she said and paused for a second. "I miss the *Nebulon,* too." She glanced toward the door. "I also liked the old PMC we worked with before."

Maelyn snorted. "He's fine."

"Lieutenant Bjorn Kinton is a stickler for regulations, as if he wrote them himself," Kieva said.

"I thought you'd be more sympathetic."

"I am," Kieva said defensively. "I get that they've been in standby for a long time and all that, but a regular old VI has more life in them than what he's shown."

Most of the PMCs they'd retrieved over the months hadn't been aware that they'd been in standby for decades. Admiral Browning had scattered them throughout the galaxy so he could recall them when they'd rebuilt their fleets.

"He has a job to do like the rest of us."

Kieva nodded. "I just get the feeling that he doesn't trust us."

"Why?"

Kieva shrugged and blew out a breath. "I don't know. I feel like it's the same with most of the PMCs they've been able to retrieve. I remember Quinton being out of sorts for a while, but he was in that old agricultural bot, so I could hardly blame him."

Maelyn smiled a little. "He had his moments. You really miss him. Don't you?"

"Not as much as you do," Kieva replied and smiled. "Yeah, I know. Timing. Anyway. We're good to go. Uh, cleared for duty," she said. Her eyes flashed, and she tilted her head toward the door to the bridge.

Maelyn opened the door and they walked onto the bridge. "Thank you, Kieva."

"No problem, Captain Wayborn."

Kieva left the bridge, returning to engineering, while Maelyn walked to the command center where a humanoid consciousness-driven android (CDA) stood. Bjorn Kinton's PMC was housed inside the CDA, which had black and gold accents that mimicked a standard ACN uniform.

"Good morning, Captain," Kinton said.

The CDA's optics glowed a brilliant green, and they seemed to regard her for a few moments.

"Good morning, Lieutenant," Maelyn replied.

She sat in the commander's chair and crossed her legs, powering on her personal holoscreen and scanning the data on screen. Kinton glanced at the screen for a moment before looking away.

"What's the status of our targets?" Maelyn asked.

Kinton updated the main holoscreen with a regional star chart. "According to the data from CENTCOM, these are the star systems where a PMC has been hidden."

Maelyn looked at the data they had on those star systems. PMC retrieval missions were always a challenge because they didn't have specific coordinates that led them to the precise location of the PMC. They were given regions of space where an activation signal was to be used. The signal leveraged communication repeaters throughout the galaxy, which made tracing activation signals difficult, but since they had the general locations of where the PMCs should be, they could move to a location in the vicinity in hopes of reaching them before the Sentinels arrived. They had to wait for an acknowledgment before they could retrieve the PMC. It wasn't a perfect solution, but Maelyn understood why Browning had done it that way.

"Has there been any reported Sentinel activity in the area?" Maelyn asked.

"Negative, Captain," Kinton replied.

The star systems were occupied with various mining and salvage depots. There was a chance that the PMCs had already been discovered and destroyed, or they were in some kind of warehouse facility.

"Lieutenant Flanagan, what's the status of the task force?" Maelyn asked.

"Both the *Delta* and the *Gauntlet* have a green readiness status, Captain. Away teams are ready for deployment," Flanagan replied.

There were three frigates under her command, and each of them had two combat shuttles capable of short-range deployment. Strike teams were aboard the shuttles waiting for the operation to begin. The frigate jump drives were capable of micro-jumps that could bring them inside a star system.

"Comms, begin operation countdown," Maelyn said.

"Aye, Captain. Begin operation countdown synchronized with the rest of the task force," Ensign Geneva Ovano said.

An automated message broadcast throughout the ships of the task force. Spacers reported to their stations, and secure straps extended over Maelyn's shoulders. Kinton sat at the tactical workstation to her right. Maelyn glanced at him and considered saying something. Kinton was a PMC that had been created during the Federation Wars. He never spoke about it. Instead, he focused all his attention on their current mission. As his commanding officer, she had access to the routine PMC integrity checks conducted by Kinton's personal VI, and they were well within normal operating parameters. The VI had endocrine control protocols in place to help manage Kinton's emotional stability. Perhaps Kinton had instructed the VI to keep him even-keeled in order to avoid processing the emotional toll of being brought back online to a galaxy he didn't recognize. Quinton had disabled those protocols as soon as he could. He said it made him feel less than human, but all the PMCs she'd encountered were unique. They were highly disciplined people, and they chose the best way they saw fit to function while they were a PMC. Maelyn didn't know how she would've handled it. Would she have done what Quinton did and disabled the endocrine control protocols that suppressed her emotional response? She liked to think she'd have been brave enough to do that, but not all the retrieved PMCs could handle it. Once those control protocols were disabled, the PMC had to face the significant risk of destabilizing the matrix construct that preserved their consciousness.

There was no recovery from PMC degradation. There had been more than a few casualties, both on the PMC side and the retrieval teams. In response to these risks, Quinton had updated the reactivation signals to include several updates to help prevent deaths. First was a security protocol update that prevented the PMC from being compromised by Sentinel infiltration protocols. The second was an advisory to the VI, warning them to keep the endocrine control protocols engaged until the PMC had been online for a specified amount of time so they could weigh the risk.

Time was another thing that was relative when dealing with PMCs. They could increase their frame rate, which allowed them to speed up their perception of time. Kinton, like other PMCs, could speed up his frame rate, giving him a significant amount of time to analyze and respond to a given situation. Days became hours, hours became seconds, and so on. The limitation came from the processing capabilities of the android and the ship's computing core. The wetware of her brain implants was supposed to give her the same ability but to a much lesser degree. The human brain was a biological computer that relied on chemical and electrical signals to process information. She really needed to make peace with using her implants or she would put herself and her crew at a disadvantage.

The countdown finished, and a PMC activation signal began to broadcast from the *Rubicon's* communication array.

"PMC acknowledgment," Kinton said. "Multiple responses have been received. All are clustered in a specific star system."

"Put it on screen," Maelyn said.

The main holoscreen updated with the identified star system. There was a significant spacer presence there, so they wouldn't be able to jump right to the location of the PMCs. Their rules of engagement were clear. They had to play nice with the local authorities.

"Helm, plot us a course mid system. Comms, request permission from the local space station for a retrieval mission," Maelyn said.

Her orders were confirmed, and the three frigates executed a space jump. She had a limited window from which to negotiate with local authorities, but there was no way she was going to leave the star system without retrieving those PMCs.

4

LIEUTENANT SIENNA HYDEN increased her frame rate as she integrated with the ship's computing systems. Her VI prioritized the data feeds from the ship's sensor array. The activation signal had gotten multiple responses, and Captain Rossing had the away teams deployed for retrieval. Active scans of the star system showed that a strike force of Sentinel ships had just entered the system to investigate the activation signal. She needed to have a tactical assessment ready for when her CO learned of the enemy ships. Her frame rate was increased as high as her CDA could handle, giving her time to review the data.

The Sentinel strike force was comprised of two heavy cruisers and eight destroyers. They'd emerged into the system at almost the exact same time. This wasn't her first encounter with the Sentinels. She'd fought them before, during what spacers referred to as the Federation Wars. They'd chased her strike group relentlessly. Following Admiral Browning's orders, her ESS core was loaded onto a comms drone and jettisoned from the ship. She'd gone into standby, not knowing whether the Sentinels would find her. She never knew what became of the crew of the ship she'd served on. Those records had been lost.

She knew others who'd become PMCs—Garrity, Lambo, Glenn, and others from her cohort had volunteered, hoping to change the outcome of the war. It was the only way to fight Harding Prime and the Sentinel fleet. None of them had been found. She didn't know whether they'd all been killed or if they were like her, stranded in some nameless star system waiting to be retrieved. She'd only been reactivated three weeks prior to this mission, and the other PMCs she knew hadn't been found.

The tactical assessment she'd come up with wasn't good, but it was still possible to retrieve the PMCs coming online. She returned her frame rate to normal.

"Sentinel ships have entered the system. Updating the tactical plot now, Captain," Sienna said.

She watched Captain Anders Rossing as he looked at the main holoscreen. Biometric sensors indicated a spike in Rossing's heart rate.

"Ten enemy ships!" Rossing exclaimed, looking at Sienna.

"We have hyper-capable missiles, Captain. I have a firing solution that should give the away teams enough time to achieve their objective," Sienna replied.

Rossing peered at the main holoscreen and shook his head. "Comms, recall the away team."

"Captain," Sienna said, "there's time for a retrieval. We can still save them."

Rossing hastened back to his station. "Thank you for your tactical assessment, Lieutenant Hyden, but my orders stand."

Sienna increased her frame rate. Why was he so quick to abandon the mission? She'd provided him with a valid response that had a high probability of success.

The comms array had received another PMC acknowledgment. They were coming online.

"Captain, I'm getting an active response from the PMCs in the star system. We cannot abandon them," Sienna said.

"Captain, away teams haven't acknowledged the updated orders," Ensign Goodman said.

Sienna had seized control of the ship's comms systems and blocked the order.

Rossing glared in her direction. "You're way out of line, Lieutenant. I have command authority over this ship and this mission."

"Sir, we can retrieve them. We don't have to run away. They're right there waiting for us!"

"*Reliant*, execute remote override seven, four, zero, niner on my authority. Revoke Lieutenant Hyden's system access immediately," Rossing said.

Sienna was instantly booted from the ship's computer system. She tried to regain access but was unable to breach the hardened security protocols. She turned toward Rossing.

"Captain, please don't do this. They deserve to be rescued. They don't deserve to be abandoned to the enemy."

"I understand your conflict, Lieutenant, but I'm not going to risk the ship and the crew to retrieve three PMCs. The success probability of your firing solution leaves more than a marginal risk of failure. Now, you're relieved of duty," Rossing said and gestured the security detail stationed at the entrance to the bridge.

Sienna watched as the security detail walked toward her, stunners ready to disable the CDA.

She spun toward Rossing. "You're a coward! If it were any of you waiting to be rescued, you'd send in the strike team."

"Get her off the bridge. Store it in a secure container immediately. I knew we couldn't trust those damn integrity checks," Rossing said.

Sienna reached toward the captain, and a blue stunner flash sent her reeling backward. She fell to the floor.

“Comms, get me a comlink to the away team,” Rossing said.

Sienna lay there helplessly as the security detail used a counter grav emitter to raise the CDA off the floor.

“We can’t allow the objective to fall into enemy hands. Cleanup is authorized, and then get back to the ship ASAP,” Rossing said.

Sienna wanted to scream in defiance. She’d been warned by the others. These spacers didn’t trust them and wouldn’t risk anything to help them. Rossing’s last command would destroy the PMCs before they became fully aware to prevent the Sentinels from getting them.

She was removed from the bridge, and the crew regarded her without compassion. Rossing had referred to her as “it.” These spacers didn’t believe a PMC was an actual person. They didn’t view her as being alive. Now she was being tossed aside. She vowed to get revenge. Somehow, she’d make Rossing pay for the murder of the people they’d left behind. She owed them that, even if it cost her everything.

5

QUINTON REVIEWED the latest mission updates from CENTCOM and nearly screamed. He opened a subspace comlink to Brandt's personal workstation, knowing exactly where Brandt was located on the bridge.

Brandt didn't look surprised. "I'm just reviewing the same update."

"Are these accurate? Are there teams out there abandoning PMCs after they've been activated?" Quinton demanded.

The bridge crew on the *Fortitude* became quiet.

Captain Martinez glanced at him but knew better than to say anything.

"That's what the report says," Brandt replied.

"Oh no, I don't think so," Quinton snapped. "These reports don't include the tactical assessments."

There was no way he'd believe that any of his PMC officers would go along with this unless they were faced with an overwhelming attack force.

"I want those reports and I want them investigated. Did you see the report from the *Reliant*? The PMC officer was relieved of duty for failing to comply with the captain's orders when he attempted to abort the mission. I want to know what happened."

Quinton knew he shouldn't be having this conversation on the bridge, but he was so angry that he didn't care. He'd provided safety protocols that would prevent hostile infiltration from Sentinel cyberwarfare suites, and he knew there was a possibility that a commanding officer could also use it if a PMC suffered from severe degradation.

"No more abandoning PMCs. This is what the reserve force is there to support."

Brandt nodded. "I'm already sending out an update. You're about to become very busy."

Quinton glanced at Martinez and raised his chin. "We're ready."

Martinez gave him a firm nod in response.

Quinton turned back toward his personal holoscreen and lowered his voice. "This Captain Rossing is done. Relieved. I'll find someone else to command that ship."

"Quinton," Brandt said evenly, "we're not exactly swimming in capable personnel for these posts."

"I don't care. He can do something else to serve, but he's not fit for frontline duty. I suspect there are going to be more before the mission is done," Quinton replied.

Brandt nodded. "Very well, I'll see to it. We'll get to the bottom of it."

"Abandoning PMCs after activation isn't an option."

"Sometimes sacrifices are required. We can't afford to commit entire ships to death to save a handful of PMCs. That's unreasonable."

"I'm not unreasonable, but I suspect that if the commanding officers know their actions will be brought under scrutiny, they'll be less likely to make rash decisions," Quinton replied.

"I'll make sure they get the message."

Quinton shook his head. "Those PMCs went to sleep because they believed in what they were doing. They deserve better than being left for the Sentinels or being killed as part of a deranged show of mercy. We need those PMCs if we're going to win this war. The sooner this is accepted, the better off we'll all be."

"I hear you loud and clear, Quinton. Now, are you willing to take some feedback from one admiral to another?" Brandt asked.

Quinton nodded.

"Honestly, this doesn't surprise me. Our fleet personnel need time to adjust to a wartime footing. We'll shuffle people around and put them in the right posts so we can achieve our objectives. You have to trust me on that."

Quinton considered this. Brandt was an experienced commander who had more years of experience than Quinton had been alive. He needed to take Brandt's advice seriously, but he was just so furious at the thought of abandoning anyone when it could have been avoided. Too many spacers of this time period were conditioned to run when they needed to stand and fight. The PMCs who were scattered throughout the galaxy understood what it took to fight a war. It was time that everyone else learned those lessons as well.

Quinton sighed. "I understand."

The comlink was severed, and Quinton's reserve forces were deployed. The Sentinels were showing up to the targeted star systems quicker than they'd anticipated. This war may not be what he'd been trained for, but Quinton knew how to fight, and he was going to make the Sentinels pay a terrible price for every PMC they were prevented from retrieving.

He increased his frame rate and did his own tactical assessment of the data provided. Radek prioritized the list of objectives, taking into consideration the time it would take to travel to the star systems. He'd have to divide his reserve forces, but they needed to retain enough combat capabilities to engage Sentinel forces.

Quinton looked at Captain Martinez. "Time to earn those credits."

Martinez nodded. “Good, I’m getting tired of all this sitting around, Admiral.”

Maybe the spacers from this time period weren’t as spineless as he’d thought a few moments ago. Quinton put up his deployment plan on the main holoscreen, and Martinez studied it for a few moments.

“The only feedback I can give you, Admiral, is that we need to account for updated data as we execute these orders,” Martinez said.

“Understood, we can redeploy other teams as they achieve their objectives.”

Martinez frowned in thought. “I’m sorry, Admiral, I hadn’t considered that.”

“It’s all right. You’ll learn. Let’s get to it,” Quinton replied.

6

THE STAR SYSTEM had a simple alpha-numeric designation that Maelyn couldn't be bothered with remembering—a single main-sequence star that had a dozen gas giants orbiting it, along with a few hundred rocky, mineral-rich moons that the gas giants claimed as their own. The automated response from the spaceport showed its location was almost on top of where the PMCs had been detected.

So much for an in-and-out operation. Now she had to negotiate with station officials.

"Comms," Maelyn said, "get me the dockmaster for the spaceport."

Kinton looked toward her. "Dockmaster, Captain? Wouldn't it make more sense to find someone who can give us the authorization we need? We're not going to dock with the spaceport, are we?"

"No, but the dockmaster can give us clearance to enter the area. What do they have for defenses?"

"Mostly mag cannons and other short-range-type defensive measures. They're equipped to deter incoming ships or prevent them from leaving but nothing for a long-range engagement," Kinton replied.

Maelyn had expected as much.

"Captain, I have Jom Thion, dockmaster of the Weyman Spaceport," Ensign Ovano said.

"Send it to my screen," Maelyn said.

A holoscreen activated at her station, and a pale-faced man appeared on screen.

"Captain Wayborn," Jom said, "your ships are unregistered on any of the known repositories."

"They've newly come on active duty. We're responding to a distress call that necessitates our traveling to the coordinates I'm sending to you now."

Jom looked away from the camera. "We've detected no distress beacons of any kind. Perhaps you're experiencing an equipment malfunction."

"There is no malfunction."

Jom looked away again, conferring with someone off-camera. Maelyn looked at the tactical plot on the main holoscreen. The away teams were already on their way and would probably show up on the spaceport's scanners any minute. She staggered her task force so that their own sensor coverage would include the outer system.

"Away team reports mines detected on their trajectory to the target, Captain," Lieutenant Flanagan said.

Maelyn shook her head. The mines would be triggered unless they were granted access by the spaceport.

"Captain Wayborn, we've detected a smaller craft that appears to have come from your ships. You're not authorized to enter this area. Our defensive measures will activate," Jom said.

Maelyn muted the comlink. "Tactical, are you able to disable the mines from here?"

Kinton's glowing green eyes looked away from her. "I'm not sure, Captain. They're scanning for specific transponder frequencies that will grant safe passage. I believe I can retrieve the necessary codes, but I'll need to infiltrate their systems. They might detect the intrusion."

"How long would it take you to get the codes?"

"It depends on the complexity of their system. I'll go as quickly as I can."

Maelyn considered this for a few moments.

"I could hide my presence if we deployed a comms drone," Kinton offered.

Maelyn shook her head. "No, they'll detect that. They're watching us now. Ops, tell the away teams to hold their position."

The dockmaster shook his head, becoming more impatient.

Maelyn unmuted the comlink. "Apologies, I was conferring with my team. I'm going to be honest with you, Jom. We've traced a PMC activation signal to this star system and have had multiple responses. We've come to retrieve them."

Jom blinked rapidly and looked as if he'd swallowed something foul.

"Check your communication logs. The signal would have reached this star system not long ago."

"A PMC activation signal! But that will bring the Sentinels here," Jom said and turned away from the camera.

Maelyn couldn't hear what he said. She spotted someone with lavender-colored skin walking toward the dockmaster, and her shoulders stiffened.

"Dockmaster, grant me clearance to make the retrieval, and we'll take the PMCs away from here. The Sentinels will never be the wiser," Maelyn said.

Jom glanced at the camera. He'd heard her, but he was speaking with a Servitor.

"Time is of the essence, Dockmaster."

Jom stood up, and the artificial beauty of a lavender-skinned Servitor came into view. She had platinum-colored hair that hung past her bare shoulders and a face that looked to have been sculpted. Maelyn had never given Servitors much thought before she'd been betrayed by a spy disguised as one. Servitors were both advisors and companions, professing to heal the galaxy through wisdom and submissiveness. They were healers and well educated. People craved their attention and approval almost to the point of devotion. But Maelyn couldn't look at one now without being suspicious.

The Servitor looked into camera view with wide, expressive eyes. She was the picture of serenity.

"Captain Wayborn, I'm Rowena Mercy, and I'm in the employ of the Weyman Brothers Spaceport."

Servitors tried to assert dominance by adhering to a strict formal engagement. Maelyn had studied their tactics and didn't have time for it.

"Servitor Mercy, where's the dockmaster?" Maelyn replied.

"I'm afraid I'll be taking over these negotiations, as this is a delicate matter."

Maelyn frowned. Servitors were advisors, but they didn't hold posts of authority.

"Grant my shuttles access to the site where the PMCs are and we'll go in peace," Maelyn said.

"I'm afraid I can't allow that. If I did, you'd be putting the entire spaceport in danger from the Sentinels," Rowena replied.

Maelyn leaned forward. "It would be better for you if you just granted us access. Disable the minefield."

The Servitor shook her head and somehow managed to make that look graceful. "Your ships have the designation associated with the Acheron Confederacy. Tell me, do you seek to resurrect their terrible inventions of the galaxy? The very reason the Sentinels exist is in direct opposition to the Acheron Confederacy and their creations."

Maelyn glanced at Kinton and thought she saw the CDA move but couldn't be sure. All the PMCs she'd encountered had unwavering loyalty to the Acheron Confederacy. The PMCs who'd fought in the Federation Wars knew that the galaxy blamed them for the wars.

"You're misinformed."

"I don't see how that's possible. The established history hasn't changed."

Maelyn activated her implants, and the instant headache didn't irritate her because she was already angry. "I'm not here to debate history with you. I'm here to retrieve those PMCs. I would prefer to do it peacefully."

She didn't want to resort to threatening the spaceport into compliance, but she was being backed into a corner.

She opened a comlink to Kinton.

Retrieve the codes. You can hide the infiltration if you use the comms systems of a ship that's already docked. Don't leave any traces of your session aboard the ship's systems or else the Sentinels could target them.

Understood, Captain. Initializing infiltration session.

"Captain," Lieutenant Flanagan said, "several ships have jumped into the star system. They're on the outer rim. Sentinel class ships."

Maelyn sighed explosively and turned back to the video comlink. "Sentinels have just entered the star system."

She heard Jom swear off camera and begin speaking to someone else. Rowena kept her gaze on Maelyn. "You've led them here."

"And I can lead them away from here, but I'll only do that if my shuttles get clearance to enter the area."

She glanced at Kinton, and the CDA gave a slight shake of his head. She didn't want to fire their weapons on the spaceport.

The Servitor looked away from the video feed for a few moments. She nodded and then looked at Maelyn. "Access has been granted. Transmitting clearance codes to your shuttles now."

Finally, she thought.

"Thank you," Maelyn replied and severed the comlink. "Comms, confirm with the away team that they've received the codes."

Ensign Ovano peered at her holoscreen for a few seconds. "Yes, Captain. They're heading to the objective now."

"Tactical—"

"Captain, more Sentinels have entered the system. Updating the tactical plot now," Lieutenant Flanagan said.

A second strike group entered the system from a different origin point, making Maelyn wonder if the Sentinels were coordinating their efforts.

"Captain, we cannot survive a direct engagement with Sentinel forces," Kinton said.

Maelyn studied the tactical plot, and her mind began to race. "We don't need to engage them directly. We need them to chase us. Draw them away from the away teams."

"I have a solution, Captain," Kinton said. "Split our forces. Have two of the away teams micro-jump to the outer system. They'll rendezvous with the other ships before they leave the system."

Maelyn nodded, following Kinton's idea. "Leaving us to pick up the last team and draw whatever Sentinel ships stay behind away from the spaceport. Good idea. Upload the coordinates to the rest of the task force. Comms, alert Captains Fuller and O'Connor of the update. This is time sensitive. They're to execute upon receipt of the updated orders."

"Aye, Captain. Sending updated orders," Ensign Ovano said.

Maelyn turned toward Kinton. The PMC would have increased his frame rate while he ran through a multitude of scenarios. She'd seen Quinton do the same.

The CDA turned toward her. "I'm sorry, Captain. I couldn't extract the clearance codes."

"It's fine. I wasn't sure whether infiltration was one of your specialties," Maelyn replied.

She'd witnessed Quinton bypass enough security systems that she'd assumed this was a skill all PMCs shared, but she'd been wrong.

"Negative, Captain. I'm better with ship-to-ship engagements. I have an idea on how to balance our engagement with the Sentinels."

"Let's have it," she replied.

The tactical plot on the main holoscreen updated as both the ACS *Delta* and the *Gauntlet* executed a micro-jump away from them. She looked at Kinton, but he was watching the main holoscreen.

"There," he said. "Sentinels have altered course in pursuit. They can track hyperspace jumps. They'll follow us as we leave the system. We can use it to lure them into a trap if we coordinate our target destinations to provide cover, effectively blindsiding the Sentinels as they emerge."

Maelyn considered it for a few moments. "They can only guess as to the direction our ships will go, but they won't know the distance. How can we trap them if we don't know where they'll emerge?"

The CDA's head tilted to the side. "We train them. We have our ships execute a series of jumps at the same distance. The Sentinels will assume that there is a limitation with our jump drives and adjust the distance accordingly."

Maelyn nodded. "Bringing them in closer so our trajectories intercept. We'll need to randomize the intercept points to keep them guessing."

"I've already accounted for that in my solution. Do you wish to review it?"

Maelyn wanted to go over it to make sure Kinton hadn't made any mistakes, but their time was limited.

"Your VIs already gave you a probability assessment?" she asked.

"Yes, they're within acceptable error parameters."

"All right, Lieutenant, we'll give this a try. Package up the solution and send it to the other ships," Maelyn said.

"Thank you, Captain," Kinton replied. "Package has been sent via subspace comlink."

Maelyn looked at Ensign Ovano.

"Package has been received, Captain," the comms officer replied.

The tactical plot on the main holoscreen refreshed, showing the two ACN frigates emerge on the outer system. The combat shuttles had already micro-jumped to the coordinates. Those jump drives would be pushed to the limit since they were at the edge of capacity for the small shuttles.

Kinton turned toward Maelyn.

"What is it?" she asked.

"Four Sentinel destroyers are heading toward the spaceport," Kinton said.

Kinton was integrated with the ship's systems and was reviewing the data as it became available. The PMCs coming back online would squawk their locations until the away team retrieved them and blocked the signal.

Maelyn looked at the main holoscreen. The four destroyers had executed a micro-jump toward the spaceport and were increasing their velocity toward the away team.

"Captain, you should recall the away team," Kinton said.

The PMC could run through thousands of scenarios in seconds and must have calculated that the retrieval mission was in danger of failing.

"No," Maelyn said.

"Captain—"

Maelyn gritted her teeth and made a chopping motion with her hand. "Comms, what's the retrieval status?"

"They're making their final approach, Captain," Ensign Ovano replied.

"Captain, there isn't enough time," Kinton said.

Maelyn stood up and went to the tactical workstation where she brought up multiple holoscreens. She initiated a data connection to the mines nearest the away team.

"You're accessing their control system," Kinton said.

Maelyn nodded. "Comms, tell the away team to get a move on it. Enemy ships incoming."

"Are you activating the minefield?" Kinton asked.

"No. That would make them attack the spaceport."

Someone from the spaceport had detected her access and was attempting to block it.

Maelyn looked at Kinton. "Give the techs on the spaceport something else to do."

"My pleasure," Kinton replied.

Maelyn accessed several of the mines' flight control systems and had them fly toward the away team's location. She didn't arm them yet. If the Sentinels were monitoring, they'd know the mines had been activated.

"Captain, Weyman Spaceport is trying to contact us," Ensign Ovano said.

"Don't acknowledge," Maelyn replied.

She watched the icon for the away team's combat shuttle on the main holoscreen. It had an amber color to it, meaning that they hadn't retrieved the PMCs yet. The mines were closing in on the location.

"Captain, perhaps I can be of assistance if you share what you're doing," Kinton said.

"Once the away team retrieves the PMCs, I'm going to initiate a little diversion. Something the Sentinels will be sure to see," Maelyn said.

The icon for the away team became green.

"Captain, successful retrieval of the PMCs," Ensign Ovano said.

"Excellent. Tell them to get out of there because I'm going to blow up that whole area," Maelyn said.

She watched the clock in the upper right corner of her data window. The combat shuttle was quickly moving away. "There, they've jumped," she said.

The mines flew toward the small moon and detonated.

"Antimatter explosion detected, Captain," Kinton said.

"Helm, execute jump. Let's go get our team," Maelyn said.

"Aye, Captain. Execute jump coordinates bravo," Lieutenant Centrich replied.

The *Rubicon* micro-jumped away from the spaceport.

"Comms, thank the Weyman Spaceport for the use of several of their mines. The Sentinels will assume the PMCs were destroyed," Maelyn said.

While they waited for the combat shuttle to dock with the ship, the Sentinels closed in on their location.

She listened to Ovano speak to the spaceport official, after which she closed the connection and turned toward Maelyn. "They're a little upset."

Maelyn smiled. "They'll feel better when the Sentinels follow us out of here."

"Combat shuttle is aboard, Captain," Lieutenant Flanagan said.

"Thank you, Lieutenant," Maelyn replied and watched the tactical plot.

Sentinel destroyers used powerful particle beams as their primary weapons. They weren't in range yet.

"Helm, plot a course away from here. Best speed," Maelyn said.

"Aye, Captain, course programmed into the nav computer," Lieutenant Centrich replied.

Maelyn needed the Sentinels to chase them, and she silently urged them on. Two of the destroyers disappeared from the plot and emerged farther away. They were attempting to cut off her escape.

"Let the chase begin. Execute jump," Maelyn said.

7

QUINTON COULDN'T STOP the Sentinels from discovering the massive PMC retrieval mission he'd dedicated almost all of his resources to achieving. That had never been his plan. He just hoped his forces could retrieve the PMCs before the Sentinels could organize a response. More than half the retrievals had been achieved without incident. The problems came from inhabited star systems. Local authorities slowed the entire mission, denying access to regions where PMCs were located. Some ship captains weren't equipped to deal with this, while others found a way to negotiate for access to the areas they needed to reach. But the delays in mission execution brought the Sentinels into star systems. The Sentinels must have some kind of listening posts designed to detect PMC activation signals. There was no other explanation that made sense. They hadn't found any of these listening posts, and Quinton didn't have the resources to search for them.

"That's the last of them, Admiral," Captain Martinez said.

"How much damage did they do?" Quinton asked.

He was integrated with the ship's computer systems that maintained a subspace comlink to CENTCOM on the *Salvation*. The *Fortitude* was a leviathan class battleship cruiser, one of four in his battle group, along with destroyer and cruiser escorts.

"The Sentinel heavy-cruisers did direct some of their fire at civilian targets in the system before they focused their attention on us," Martinez replied.

Civilian crossfire was something Quinton needed to avoid. They were vulnerable to attack, and his mission wasn't to create a situation where spacers' lives were put in danger.

"We need to draw the Sentinels away from the inhabited systems," Quinton said.

"I might be able to help with that," Radek said.

A glowing, silvery holographic orb materialized nearby. The globe pulsed as Radek spoke.

"What have you got?" Quinton asked. He had hundreds of analyses going on to give them an edge at squeezing every bit of success from the mission.

"Several mission reports have come into CENTCOM where the commanding officer lured Sentinel ships away to designated ambush sites. This allowed some of the smaller groups to whittle away Sentinel numbers, but those ships have limited fire power," Radek said.

"No, the concept is good. I should have thought of it. We need to coordinate with the teams who need support to do our own ambush sites," Quinton replied.

Over the next forty hours they established ambush sites in the dead space between stars. Quinton divided his battle group into multiple task forces and redeployed them as necessary.

Sensors showed Sentinel ships entering a region of space where they expected a small frigate task force to be. Instead, they were met with hyper-capable antimatter missiles that obliterated their forces as soon as they transitioned into n-space.

"Two more Sentinel strike forces have transitioned in, Captain," Lieutenant Weston said.

"Range?" Martinez asked.

"Five hundred thousand kilometers out, sir."

Martinez looked at Quinton.

The newly arriving ships weren't where they expected them to be, which meant that the Sentinels were finally adapting their tactics to stop the ambush.

"We're well beyond their dampening field range. Shall I order our ships to leave?" Captain Martinez asked.

"Wait," Quinton said.

He accessed the comms systems. The Sentinels communicated their standard broadcast as if they were operating from a set of parameters that hadn't been changed. He took control of a single comms array and transmitted a signal to the Sentinel ships.

Authenticate.

Quinton Everett Aldren, Acheron Confederacy Navy.

Unknown Personality Matrix Construct.

ACN Rank?

Quinton considered this for a few moments. He'd tried to initiate contact with Sentinels before.

Admiral.

He sent his PMC identification to the Sentinels. The Sentinels seemed to consider this as if they were reviewing his authentication.

Confirmed.

Threat anomaly confirmed.

Prevention of spread is required.

The Sentinels tried to infiltrate the data comlink session, but Quinton blocked their attempts.

Hostile PMC host detected.

Prevent the spread.

Targets must be destroyed.

Quinton killed the comlink. It was always the same. The Sentinels viewed him as the enemy and would keep attacking until he was either killed or had destroyed their ships. Having no interest in dying, Quinton ordered their withdrawal from the area. They were getting low on ammunition, and he didn't need to engage the Sentinels without the element of surprise. Choosing when to fight was just as important as choosing where.

"Tactical, deploy the decoys," Captain Martinez said.

"Aye, Captain, deploying decoys now," Lieutenant Weston said.

Decoy jump drones flew out of the ship, and their jump drives synchronized with the ships in Quinton's battle group. The ships and the decoys executed their jumps, and the Sentinels would be hard-pressed to figure out which direction they'd need to follow to pursue him. Quinton knew it would be next to impossible.

"Successful jump, Captain," Lieutenant Pitts reported.

"Excellent. Helm, execute the next series of jumps just in case the Sentinels get lucky," Martinez said.

"Aye, Captain," Lieutenant Pitts replied.

Martinez looked at Quinton. "I think our estimates of Sentinel forces need a serious adjustment."

Quinton nodded. "I was thinking the same thing."

He'd underestimated how many ships the Sentinels could devote in their response to the mission. He'd relied on data provided by Brandt's people from the DUC, which used their own intelligence apparatus to make the estimate.

"Admiral, the comms logs indicate that you tried to communicate with the Sentinels?" Martinez asked.

"I did. I'm not compromised," Quinton replied.

"I know that, sir. Your VI reports nominal PMC integrity checks. If you don't mind me asking, sir, why were you trying to contact them?"

"I wanted to see if their response had changed."

"Had it?"

Quinton shook his head. "No."

Martinez nodded once. "I've heard of spacers over the years who tried to initiate contact with the Sentinels. None even got a response, not even through a data comlink. Nothing. It's like they're not equipped to engage in communication with anyone but themselves."

"I don't pretend to understand it. The Sentinels were created to hunt PMCs by Miles Harding. Why wouldn't he equip them to communicate with the remnant federations?"

Quinton's consciousness had been uploaded into a PMC before the Federation Wars. He predated the creation of the Sentinels, which he used to think was a serious liability but had later thought to be an advantage. His lack of knowledge about the Sentinels enabled him to ask questions that others took for granted. Spacers assumed they understood how the Sentinels worked, but they didn't.

"I don't know, sir. I wish I did, but I just don't know. The Sentinels were always there, always a potential encounter, and our response was to be compliant with them," Martinez said.

He was well aware of how spacers had been forced to comply with the Sentinels. "Hope and pray they left you in peace," Quinton said.

Martinez nodded, looking away for a second as if he was ashamed. "It's not like there weren't attempts to resist what the Sentinels did. There were, but the cost was so high, and they were relentless."

"I understand," Quinton replied, even though he didn't. Not really… That wasn't right. He understood the situation, as it were, but still struggled to wrap his mind around a galaxy that was so different from the one he remembered. Spacers reacted differently to him when they learned of his origin. Some treated him as if he were to blame for what had happened over the last century. Others, who were old enough to remember the Federation Wars, sometimes looked ashamed. Martinez wasn't old enough to remember the Federation Wars, but he'd been raised by parents who did. They'd taught their children what had been lost. Quinton tried not to judge the spacers too harshly. The current climate of the galaxy hadn't happened in one day. It'd taken years and decades for the galaxy to descend into its current state. He wished he could just fix everything, make things how he remembered them, but he was starting to believe that those were fools' errands. The galaxy needed to change, but it might not ever go back to what it had been. The question remained as to what the galaxy would become and whether he would survive to see it.

8

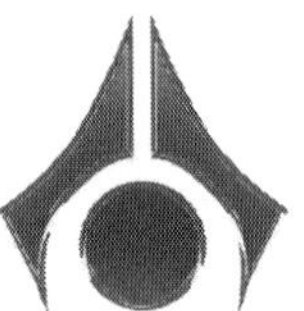

Becker watched as Oscar weaved his way through the crowded, dimly lit bar on some spaceport that he couldn't even remember the name of this time. He'd lost count of how many of these places they'd been to, trying to recruit spacers to join the new United Federation Alliance.

Oscar carried a full mug of dark beer with a frothy top and kept one of his hands in front of it, shielding it from harm. He raised his chin without really looking at Becker and sat on the stool next to him.

"How'd it go?" Becker asked.

Oscar drank from his mug and gave a contented sigh. "You wouldn't think it by the looks of this place, but they have the best dark beer I've ever tasted. I had a few cases sent to the ship."

Becker arched an eyebrow. "How many cases?"

Oscar stared into his beer and mumbled something that Becker couldn't hear as the lively music rose. Hordes of people now had to shout to have a chance at being heard.

Becker leaned forward. "What?"

Guttman joined them. The pudge of his belly shifted from side to side as he part walked and waddled at the same time.

Guttman looked at Oscar and smiled broadly. "Did you tell him?" he asked, tilting his head to Becker.

The song ended, giving them a few seconds of silence.

"I was just about to," Oscar replied.

"We've got five hundred cases of that stuff heading to the ship," Guttman said.

Becker blinked a few times. "Five hundred cases!"

Guttman grinned and nodded.

Becker looked at Oscar. "What were you thinking? I'm not bringing five hundred cases of beer on my ship. I don't care how good it is."

"Technically, it's *our* ship," Oscar replied.

"We're all part owners. That was the dealio," Gutmann said.

Becker shook his head. He knew if he allowed that beer on the ship, he'd have a crew of drunk spacers to contend with. "We don't have room for it."

Oscar shared a look with Guttman. "Yes, we do. I got the aft storage area repaired. The door mechanism had to be replaced. We're all good. Five hundred cases of the good stuff will fit in there, no problem. And the cases are able to interface with most food fabricators on the ship. It's not going to be imitation stuff, so we can sell each case at a premium."

Becker frowned in thought, trying to remember the size of the storage area they were referring to. "So, you're not going to drink it all?"

Oscar shook his head. "No way. Do you know how much each case is capable of creating? It's all compressed. Each case can fill a few thousand of these mugs."

"Three thousand, five hundred to be exact. So, we'll only really need to keep one case for ourselves. The rest we can sell at a profit. It seems that they've had problems getting reliable transport for their products," Guttman said.

Becker's gaze went to the ceiling while he pleaded for patience. "If we were only involved with shipping and receiving, I'd say this was a good deal, but we're not. You guys know it. You know what we're doing out here."

Oscar looked away and took a swig from his mug.

"Becker, come on, man. This is a good deal. Something normal. This is what we *should* be doing," Guttman said.

Somewhere over the last few months, Becker had become the sane one of the group. He had no idea when it'd happened, but it had. They were preparing for war, and there was no hiding from that fact, no matter how many side jobs they did.

Becker sighed and gestured toward Oscar. "Let me taste it. See how good this stuff is."

Oscar smiled and passed the half-full mug toward him.

Becker took the mug and sniffed. Then he took a big sip, holding the dark liquid in his mouth. Tasting the malty sweetness and hoppy bitterness, along with hints of coffee and chocolate, he swallowed and nodded appreciatively.

Oscar gestured for him to return the mug. "Give it back. If you want more, you'll need to go get your own. Come on, give it."

Becker smirked and handed the mug back.

"It's good, right?" Guttman said.

"It is. I don't know how much I could really drink, but I can see why you like it," Becker replied.

He'd learned over the years that there were times to pick his battles, and if he chose to fight this one, he'd probably lose. "All right, but we'd better make a serious profit on this stuff. And I won't have a crew of drunk spacers on the ship. Understood?"

Both men nodded vigorously. Well, Guttman nodded vigorously, and Oscar just raised his mug up a little.

"Okay, what about the real reason we came here?" Becker said.

"Right, the never-ending task of recruitment," Oscar said and proceeded to give him an update.

"Fourteen groups are more than I would've expected from a place like this," Becker replied.

Oscar shrugged. "These are fringe groups. They're desperate enough to take on most work."

"We need more than just informants. Quinton needs people who can be trained," Becker replied.

"There are some of those," Guttman said. "Three groups agreed to send a few hundred spacers to evaluate the training being offered."

"That's right. It's a tough sell. Most of them don't believe the UFA is real," Oscar said.

"They'll learn," Becker said.

A message appeared on his internal HUD. "We've gotta get back to the ship."

Guttman shook his head. "Why so soon?"

Becker scrolled through the message and felt his gut clench for a moment.

"What is it?" Oscar asked.

"Crowe wants to speak to us," Becker replied.

"Us?" Guttman asked.

Becker should have expected that Guttman's first reaction would be to clarify whether Crowe's summons would affect him. He wasn't sure what annoyed him more, the fact that Guttman wanted to know if he was in trouble or the fact that Crowe had asked for Becker specifically.

"Fine," Becker said. "He asked for me, the captain. Come on, let's go. I won't take the comlink here or anywhere near the spaceport."

It was way too easy for someone to intercept the comlink signal near a spaceport.

Oscar drained the rest of his beer, and Guttman sighed.

"Also, I want a lockout code put on our new cargo. And for the case that's going to be available to the crew. I want limits on consumption for daily intake. If they don't like it, they can stay here," Becker said.

Oscar shrugged. "The captain has spoken."

"All hail the captain," Guttman said and gulped the remainder of his beer.

Becker grinned, and they left the bar behind.

They left the spaceport shortly after they returned to the ship. Some of the crew was put out because their shore leave had been cut short. Becker promised to make it up to them, and the beer didn't hurt. When did it ever?

He'd spent his entire life aboard ships, but this was the first one he'd ever owned. There were strings attached—Quinton had made sure of that—but the terms were more than fair. He shared ownership of six ships with Oscar and Guttman. They were transport ships capable of hauling small- to mid-size cargo, but they were quick, and their jump drives had been upgraded from the stock that had been found aboard the *Salvation*.

Their ship was a retrofitted star master class transport ship built over a hundred years ago. The retrofit had been done by the autofactories aboard the

Salvation. They'd more or less rebuilt the ship in its entirety. He walked into his office near the bridge. A few minutes later, Oscar was knocking on the door.

"Guttman is securing the cargo," Oscar said.

Becker nodded. "How'd the crew react?"

Oscar's expression went flat. "It's free beer."

Becker chuckled. It was a small price to pay to increase morale.

A comlink came from the bridge.

"Captain, we've jumped away from the spaceport," Davidge said.

"We won't be staying long. Make sure emergency jump coordinates are ready to go in the nav system," Becker replied.

"Aye, Captain," Davidge replied, and the comlink closed.

Becker activated the wallscreen and stood in front of it. He knew Lennix Crowe was supporting the UFA, but they hadn't spoken.

"Think he still holds a grudge?" Oscar asked.

They'd all left Crowe's Union when a certain PMC had shown up disguised as a beat-up old agricultural bot.

Crowe had a well-earned reputation among spacers. There was a reason the Union had risen amid the salvager groups to be among the most powerful after the Collective. When Becker had left the Union, he'd hoped to get a ship of his own and earn a living in some out-of-the-way fringe location where salvagers didn't often go. Things had changed, but he'd be an idiot not to be cautious when dealing with Lennix Crowe.

Becker sighed. He'd been an enforcer and team leader when he'd been in the Union, but he'd been stuck with too many spacers ahead of him to really rise among the ranks.

"Becker," Oscar said.

Becker shrugged. "I guess we'll find out."

He accessed the comms array and initiated a comlink to his old employer. The subspace comlink was almost instantly acknowledged, and the comms officer routed him through to Crowe.

Crowe's head and shoulders appeared on the wallscreen, and eyes of burnt almond regarded Becker for a few moments. Crowe had a receding hairline, and there were more creases around his eyes and mouth than Becker remembered. He supposed that if the leader of the most powerful salvager operation in the galaxy wanted *him* dead, he'd have a few extra worry lines as well.

"Commander Crowe," Becker said by way of greeting.

Crowe's lips twitched, but his gaze was even. "Captain Becker." His gaze flicked next to him. "Oscar."

Oscar came to stand next to Becker. "Commander," he replied.

"Is Guttman with you?"

Oscar shifted on his feet.

Becker gritted his teeth, feeling annoyed. "What do you want?" he asked. He wasn't going to be browbeaten on his own ship, and the same went for his crew.

The lines around Crowe's eyes deepened. "Well played, Becker. I'm impressed. A pity you didn't show this kind of gumption when you were in the Union."

"I've changed," he said to his old employer.

Crowe regarded him for a few moments and then nodded.

Becker pressed his lips together for a second, then said, "Quinton Aldren turned out to be more than any of us bargained for."

Crowe chuckled and his expression softened in acknowledgment. "You've got that right. I have to admit that perhaps I would have done the same as you did, given the circumstances. However, I didn't contact you to bring up the past. I have a job for you."

Becker frowned. "We're already on a mission."

"This isn't for me. It's for the Alliance."

Becker resisted the urge to scratch the back of his neck. "Okay, what do you need us to do?"

"It's for the recruitment effort. There's a group of mercenaries operating a few hundred lightyears from your location. I'll send you the contact information. They also have cargo that is to be retrieved and delivered to the UFA."

Becker exhaled through his nose. "A cargo run? Why don't you have your own people take care of this?"

A flicker of annoyance shone from Crowe's eyes but was quickly gone. "It's complicated. Will you do this for me? For old time's sake."

Becker saw Oscar look at him in his periphery. "What do I get out of it?"

Crowe blinked and then did something Becker didn't expect. The Union commander laughed. "Becker, I'm impressed with you. You really have changed. All right, I know the rules. No one gets something for nothing."

Becker stared at him without blinking.

"Eventually, this war will be over, and we'll all be able to move on. I don't think we can afford to ignore each other," Crowe said.

"I'm not coming back to the Union," Becker replied.

"No, I wouldn't expect you to, but that doesn't mean we couldn't partner up from time to time."

Becker considered this for a few moments. He didn't want Crowe as his enemy, so dismissing the offer of potential future dealings was something he wasn't willing to do. He regarded Crowe and decided that he wasn't going to leave anything to chance.

"If you're willing to let the past go, then I'm willing to work with you in the future. Starting with this," Becker said.

Crowe looked away from the camera for a few seconds. Becker heard someone speaking off-screen.

"I know," Crowe said to them.

Nate Carradine joined Crowe. "Becker and Oscar, it's good to see you both."

"Hello, Nate," Becker said and then looked at Crowe. "Do we have an understanding?"

Crowe shook his head and showed his teeth. "You're something else."

"You came to me, Crowe, not the other way around. You need us to do something for you, which means that the Union can't be involved." Becker paused for a moment. "Which means this has something to do with the Collective. That's it, isn't it? This has something to do with the Collective."

Crowe gritted his teeth and walked away from the camera.

Nate nodded. "You're right, Becker. This has to do with Draven."

"What is it you're really asking me to do? You're asking me to risk my ship and crew for this, and I need to know why."

Crowe came back on-screen. He clenched a fist and released it. "You know Draven wanted to kill me and destroy the Union. He still does. You've been with the Union long enough to know what that means. You're out, so you can just walk away… Maybe," he said, and leaned forward. "Maybe. Part of the cargo that you're to retrieve is also an intelligence drop."

"What is it?" Becker asked.

"I don't know exactly, but I know it's important."

Becker nodded slowly. "I'll do it. I'll retrieve the cargo, but I want your word that there'll be no revenge from you for what happened in the past. Those are my terms."

He watched as Nate gave Crowe a pointed look. "It's fair, Crowe."

Crowe nodded and didn't look pleased. "All right. A clean slate from here on out."

Becker wasn't sure if he believed him, but he wasn't going to push the matter. "Transmit the data and we'll get this done."

Crowe muttered something and walked away. Nate stayed behind.

"Transmitting the data now," Nate said. "Thanks for doing this, Becker. He's been under a lot of pressure, but I'll make sure he remembers his agreement."

That was as much assurance as he was going to get. "Understood," Becker replied and closed the comlink.

Oscar blew out a long breath. "I'm glad you had to deal with him."

Becker nodded. "You saw him. He's worried about something."

"What do you think it is?"

Becker chewed the inside of his lip for a second, considering. "I don't know. I thought Draven was supporting the Alliance, but that doesn't mean everyone is playing nice."

A chime came from his office door, and Guttman came in.

"What'd I miss?" he asked. "Oh, and the cargo is secure." Guttman glanced at both of them. "Did I miss something?"

"You could say that," Oscar replied. "We just got off a comlink with Crowe."

Guttman swallowed hard. "I'm glad I missed that," he said, quietly.

The conversation with Crowe had left Becker's mouth dry. At least that's what he told himself.

"We'll fill you in, but first, let's go get a drink," Becker said.

9

QUINTON STOOD on the *Fortitude's* bridge. Various sub-windows occupied the outer edge of the main holoscreen with a scrolling list of mission status updates. He found that he needed to divide his time between being fully integrated with the ship's computer systems and being outside of them. He trusted Radek to alert him of new developments that required his attention. His interactions with his personal VI had come a long way since he'd been reactivated.

Simon entered the bridge and walked over to stand next to him. He stifled a yawn.

"How's the withdrawal going?" Simon asked.

"It's going. Updates are still coming in."

Simon nodded and peered at one of the sub-windows. Then he yawned again. "Geez, sorry about that."

"Didn't you sleep any?"

"I did, but I've been on stims for the past few days, and I'm not cleared to take any more. Not all of us can quicken our rest cycles," Simon replied.

"We're the lucky ones."

"How does it feel?" Simon asked.

"What?"

"The rest cycle that you do."

"Oh, that. It's like getting sleep."

"Really," Simon said, unconvinced.

"Yes, really. It's not like they just copy our consciousness into an ESS and let the mind handle the rest."

"I know that. I was just wondering if you felt refreshed. Like when you get enough sleep."

Quinton had gotten used to Simon's inquisitive mind. The young spacer never lacked for questions. He'd been fascinated with PMCs ever since he'd figured out what Quinton was.

"My perception of time is different than yours," Quinton replied.

"Yeah, and you return to normal time because it's your baseline."

"Not just me. It's how PMCs operate. It's part of what keeps us sane."

Simon nodded. "But how does it feel?"

"I'll tell you what. We can look into uploading your consciousness into an ESS and then you can feel it for yourself."

Simon snorted and then looked away. "Maybe one day. I was just curious. When was the last time you got some rest?"

Quinton regarded him for a few seconds. "Just now."

"Are you serious?"

"Yes, I'm serious. It happens that fast. At least for me."

"But that's only a few seconds."

"I needed a break from this line of questioning."

Simon grinned and then looked at the mission status window for the away teams. "Looks like Maelyn—Uh, nothing."

"Her team completed their objective," Quinton replied.

"I know. For a second there, I just thought…" Simon's voice trailed off.

"I kept track of all the teams, Simon."

"No, I know that."

"Where do you think we got the idea of ambushing the Sentinels from?"

"Okay, forget I brought it up," Simon said.

"Forgotten," Quinton replied. "It's been about twelve hours for me since you mentioned it."

Simon grinned. "Now you're just showing off."

Captain Martinez came onto the bridge and walked over to them. "I just came from the CIC. Looks like we're having some issues with the away teams."

"What happened?" Quinton asked.

He could have queried the ship's computing core and found the report, but there were limits to what one mind was capable of, even if that mind was stored in an ESS.

"Some of the retrieval teams are reporting that the PMC update for the activation signal wasn't received, sir," Martinez said.

"How would they be able to locate the PMCs then? I thought the update was part of the activation signal," Simon asked.

"We're still piecing it together," Martinez replied.

"These could be PMCs that were created later during the Federation Wars. They might have had security protocols in place to prevent the updates," Quinton said.

"How are we supposed to know whether those PMCs have been compromised by the Sentinels?" Simon asked.

Quinton considered it for a few moments. "We won't know until they can be tested. We'll need to quarantine them before those teams can return to CENTCOM."

He couldn't allow any of them aboard the *Salvation* until they passed all PMC integrity checks. Not all the away teams had PMCs aboard their ships.

"What are your orders if we find a PMC that's been compromised?" Martinez asked.

Quinton had encountered a PMC that had been infiltrated by the Sentinels. It hadn't ended well. Only a commanding officer could order a PMC into standby, but that could only occur after an authentication session had been established.

"We'll need to establish quarantine sites where they can be properly validated. If the PMC is compromised, then we really don't have a choice. The threat must be neutralized," Quinton said.

Simon's eyes widened.

"Understood, Admiral. I'll work with CENTCOM to route the teams to quarantine locations," Martinez said and left them.

"Is killing them the only option?" Simon asked. Quinton heard the exasperation in his voice.

"We can't afford to bring them back to the *Salvation*. They could report our location back to the Sentinels. They could sabotage our ships. More lives could be lost."

"I understand that, but there must be some kind of alternative. There has to be a way to reverse what the Sentinels do as part of the infiltration attacks," Simon said.

"The risk is too high."

"No, I get it, Quinton. But maybe we can store them somewhere. Give us time to come up with a way to help them."

Quinton inhaled deeply and sighed. "I searched the data repositories on the *Salvation*. Browning had teams working on the exact thing you're suggesting, but they all failed."

"Let me try. I'd rather try and fail than just give up on them. Browning was fighting a war. How much resource could he have devoted to it?" Simon asked.

Quinton regarded his friend. Simon still had a spark of hope that was sometimes rare to see these days. It was a belief that he could impact the galaxy and make things better. Quinton wouldn't be the one to take that away from him, even if he didn't believe his friend would succeed.

"All right, if the PMCs can be safely quarantined and put back into standby, you'll be allowed to study them."

Simon smiled. "Thank you, Quinton. I just don't want to give up on them. People like you have sacrificed so much, and you all deserve our very best efforts."

Quinton stared at this friend. "I should be thanking *you,* not the other way around. I'll tell you what. If the quarantine teams can assure that the PMCs are secured, I'll allow them to be brought to the *Salvation*. You can work on them there, but I need you to do something for me."

"What do you need?"

"I know you'll give it your best, but there comes a time when there's simply nothing that can be done. I don't want anyone to suffer needlessly. Do you understand?"

Simon pursed his lips in thought and then nodded once, looking determined. “I understand. If I can’t help them, then they will be laid to rest with all the respect they deserve.”

Quinton thought of the hall of the fallen on the *Salvation*. It was a record of everyone who had died during the Federation Wars, a reminder to anyone going to the main bridge of the sacrifice that was made by the spacers who’d answered the call to arms and had made the ultimate sacrifice.

“You’re a good man, Simon. Now, help me with the quarantine protocols,” Quinton said.

10

QUINTON HAD BEEN part of large-scale naval operations when the ACN had fought the Jordani Federation. He'd led a battlegroup and been told what his objectives were. Being given orders was much easier than being part of the admiralty who decided what the objective was. Severin Brandt was his second-in-command, and Quinton counted on his experience to help, but they both knew that Quinton had to lead. He was a Galactic PMC in command of the *Salvation*. He looked around the ready room on the *Fortitude*.

"What am I doing here?"

There was no one else in the room with him. No one to answer. No one with the answers. He thought they would find other Galactic PMCs, but they hadn't. Admen Desher, the agent of Harding, had been aware of Galactic PMCs, so why hadn't Quinton been able to find any others? He couldn't be the only one. The war with the Sentinels couldn't reside squarely upon his shoulders. Browning wouldn't have done that. He'd have found a way.

Quinton shook his head and returned his attention to the mission reports. There were groups still coming in, and each time the comms system registered another ship's transponder codes, he found himself looking for a particular one. He reviewed the list, finding the ship he'd been looking for, and sighed.

A comlink chimed on his personal channel, and he acknowledged it, spinning toward the holoscreen as it became active with the video comlink.

Maelyn smiled at him. Her caramel-colored hair was tied back, and she looked tired. Her delicate cheekbones raised as she smiled a greeting.

"Reporting in, Admiral," she said.

Quinton tried to think of a clever response and gave up. "It's good to see you, Commander Wayborn."

"I knew you'd want to hear from me."

"You're right, I did. Although I would have preferred it to have been in person."

She leaned forward and moistened her lips. "Soon. Also, you'll be happy to learn that I'll be testing for..." she said and paused. "Let's just say I'm getting tired of running from the Sentinels."

Quinton chuckled. "Finally going to qualify for a ship with some teeth."

"Yes," she said and winced.

Quinton frowned. "What's wrong?"

"I keep getting headaches from these implants."

"You should check in with a doctor. Do you want to come over here?"

Maelyn shook her head. "No, I'll be fine until we get back. I'll check in with Simon."

Quinton regarded her for a moment. "Simon isn't a doctor."

She leveled a look at him that he'd come to know well. "It's an implant issue."

"Do what you think will help. I read your mission report. You had to negotiate with a Servitor?" Quinton asked.

Maelyn nodded. "The dockmaster put her in charge of negotiations. For a while, I was sure I was going to have to force the issue."

She was dedicated to what they were doing. Quinton wished there were more captains who had even half her tenacity.

"The Sentinels came at you pretty hard. Have you given any more thought to it?" he asked.

Maelyn looked away. "Quinton," she said quietly and paused. "I just don't think it's a good idea."

Quinton stepped toward the holoscreen. "Becoming a PMC is just an option."

"I don't want to become a PMC. I've seen what you have to go through, and the others, and it's just not something I want to do."

"Maelyn, it could save your life. Think of it as a backup just in case."

"I'm not going to die, Quinton."

He stared at her. "I don't understand why you won't even consider it."

Maelyn blinked a few times. "Well, if these implants are any indication, then it'll be painful."

"You're just putting up walls."

"I don't have to explain myself to you. Not for this."

Her rebuke stung more than he cared to admit. "I'm just..." he began and stopped. "It matters to me. I don't..." He clamped his mouth shut. He didn't want to lose her. She was already getting defensive about it, and if he kept pushing, she'd just double down and dig in. "This was where the technology was heading. They were working toward increasing our lifespans beyond what our bodies were capable of, even with prolonging."

Maelyn looked away, considering it for a few seconds. "I'm aware of that. There are moral implications to it. Also, for everything that you're capable of doing, you're also vulnerable."

"What do you mean?"

"If a Sentinel infiltration attack succeeds, you die. You lose all control of yourself."

"I've addressed that. We have protection against that now."

"For now, but what happens when they adapt? I don't want to end up like Harper or any of the others."

He wanted her to reconsider, but he knew she wouldn't. Not now.

"It's not like there are enough leuridium cores available. How would you prioritize who gets a backup?" she asked.

And the walls just kept getting taller.

"I hear you loud and clear. You don't want to do it. No need to come up with all these reasons to make it seem like an impossible task."

"That's not fair."

"It's not. This isn't about being fair. I wouldn't even be here if the contents of my ESS hadn't been transferred into this core," Quinton said, gesturing toward his chest.

Maelyn rubbed the sides of her head. "Look, I'm really tired. Let's just let this go for now. What's our next move?"

"We underestimated the Sentinels' response," Quinton said, relieved to move on. "There have to be even more of them than we thought."

"I wonder if they were kept in standby or something."

"That's what I was thinking as well. Too bad we couldn't find them. It would be easier to take them out while they were in standby."

Maelyn smiled. "I guess we can't have everything."

"Did you have any trouble with Kinton?"

"He's fine," Maelyn said.

Quinton arched an eyebrow. "They can't all be me, you know."

Maelyn smiled. "Yes, he lacks your charming personality."

"People are reluctant to believe the truth about Browning and the Federation Wars, even among our own people," Quinton said.

"It's going to take time."

"We can't afford to sit around and wait for people to work together. There have been reports of COs taking their PMCs into custody. They were quick to abandon the PMCs being activated when the Sentinels showed up."

"I didn't know that."

"There were also reports of PMCs taking command of the ships in order to achieve the objective. If both groups can't learn to work together, then the Sentinels won't have to defeat us. We'll do it for them."

"What does Brandt say?" she asked.

"He says we should rotate those COs out and replace them."

"I think he's right. In the DUC, we wouldn't tolerate any captain who couldn't do the job. I don't see why it would be different here," Maelyn said.

Quinton nodded. "It's just disappointing. I expect resistance about Browning and the Federation Wars, but how long is it going to take for people to get the message?"

"Never underestimate a person's willingness to believe a lie when the truth will cause them pain," Maelyn said.

She was right. To him, the truth was obvious, but the galaxy had been believing a lie for over a hundred years, and it was going to take longer for them to accept the truth.

"We're going to return to the *Salvation*. Do a proper evaluation of the mission. Then we'll be sending out summit invitations," Quinton said.

Maelyn gave him an amused smile. "Brandt is making you meet with government leaders, isn't he?"

Quinton rolled his eyes and nodded. "He says they need to learn to work with me."

Maelyn shrugged. "He's not wrong."

"I know. It's irritating when he has so much good advice."

Maelyn laughed, and Quinton felt his own frustration slip away at the sound of it.

"I'll see you aboard the *Salvation*," Quinton said.

"I'm looking forward to it."

11

BECKER RETURNED the weights to the rack and used a hand towel to wipe the sweat from his face. He never missed a chance to exercise, and the fact that the *Astricus* had a designated workout area made him like the ship even more. Most of the crew made time for it between their duty shifts.

Guttman poked his head through the door.

"Don't be shy. Come on in. The weights don't bite," Becker said.

Guttman shook his head. "I just ate."

"Shocking."

Guttman rolled his eyes. "I just came to tell you that we've entered the Phineas Cluster."

Becker tossed the towel into the nearby dispenser to be washed. "All right, I'll be right there."

He took a quick shower and put on a fresh set of clothes, then went to the bridge. Oscar was peering at a holoscreen, and Becker walked over to him.

"What have you got?" he asked.

"The Crystalline Mines of Taloo. Phineas Cluster."

"Sounds poetic. Has our contact responded yet?"

Oscar nodded. "It just came up. They want us to head to one of the mobile shipping platforms."

Becker frowned. "Not the main depot?"

"No," Oscar replied. "You think something's up?"

"Given the fact that Crowe put us up to this, I wouldn't put it past him to leave certain details out."

"It's a long way to go for a trap."

"Probably not a trap, but I doubt we've been given all the details," Becker said.

Oscar rubbed the dark stubble of his goatee in thought. "Let's have Vikram and the others come with us, then." Becker looked at him. "Just a precaution. No need for us to take all the risk, and it couldn't hurt to have a few people to watch our backs while we're there."

Becker considered it for a few seconds and then nodded. "All right. Take us in."

There were several mobile shipping platforms stationed throughout the star system—large, spinning warehouses that had limited living spaces. No one would stay there for very long, and the lack of recreation simply drove that fact home. Get in and get out. Becker was fine with that.

The *Astricus* was guided to their designated docking area by an automated pilot AI. Several docking arms extended to secure the ship in place.

Becker and the others went to the portside airlock. He looked at Vikram and the others. "You guys are strictly backup. Observe and back up as needed."

Vikram nodded. "You got it, Captain. We'll watch your backs."

The airlock doors opened, and a blast of cold air came in. The air smelled a little sour, which was a sure indication that environmental filters needed attention. Ignoring the smell, Becker walked into the corridor.

Oscar glanced behind them and then looked at Becker. "No Guttman?"

Becker shook his head. "I told him to stay behind. I wanted the ship ready in case we needed to leave sooner than expected."

Oscar chuckled. "Plus, he runs slow."

Becker couldn't argue with that. "If he doesn't drop a few pounds, he won't fit in the ship."

Oscar nodded and then looked pensive. "I don't know what it is. It's really gotten away from him."

"What? What's gotten away from him?"

"It's like he can't get enough of everything. He just keeps eating."

Guttman had always been a big eater—consumer of everything—but now that Oscar mentioned it, he had taken it to a whole new level.

"Maybe he caught something."

"Yeah, gluttony," Oscar said with a shake of his head.

"Guttman has his moments of neediness, but he could have caught a parasite or something like that," Becker replied.

They exited the docking tunnel and made their way to the commons area where they would meet their contact.

"I don't know. Decon would've detected it."

"Not necessarily. Decontamination looks for surface stuff. He could have something inside him."

"Yeah, but his biochip would have detected it. You can't bring it up because he's so sensitive about it."

Becker nodded. "We could just trank him and take him to the doctor."

Oscar laughed. "It just might come to that."

The commons area was a large rotunda with broad windows, giving them a perfect view of the star cluster. Thankfully, the air was much fresher. There were tables and seating areas around them. A table identification flashed in Becker's

HUD, and he walked toward it. Vikram and the others walked away from them but stayed within sight.

Becker strolled to the table and sat down. Oscar sank into the seat next to him. The holographic interface activated, and Becker ordered a malt-flavored nutri-drink with extra protein.

Oscar scanned the menu and put in his own order. A chrome canister rose from the middle of the table and spun toward them. They grabbed their orders and the canister retreated into its compartment.

Oscar sipped his drink and twitched his eyebrows. "Not bad."

Becker set his in front of him and waited. A few minutes passed and he opened a comlink to the ship.

"Guttman here."

"Did any cargo arrive yet?"

"Nope. I've been checking the queue, but nothing has come yet."

Becker frowned. "All right, let me know if something changes."

"Will do," Guttman replied.

Becker checked his comlink to see if he had any messages, but there weren't any. He reached for his nutri-drink and took a sip, holding the malty sweet liquid in his mouth for a few moments before swallowing.

"You're right. It's not bad," Becker said.

A group of spacers walked by, and two of them left the group, heading toward them. They wore dark gray envirosuits, and they still had their helmets on. Becker moved his hand toward the sidearm on his hip.

The two spacers sat down and tapped their helmet controls, and the helmets retracted into their receptacles at the bases of their necks. A man and woman looked at them. The man had steely blue eyes that shone with an intensity that could only come from the extended use of stimulants. He had a patchwork of dark tattoos that covered half his face and neck. He glanced around, doing his own threat assessment.

The woman had dark brown eyes and golden blonde hair tied back into a tight bun. Her cheeks were pink, as if she'd just been running. Her full lips twitched, and she looked at him and Oscar with what might have been a flicker of recognition.

Becker just looked back at them but didn't say anything for a few seconds. A holoscreen had activated as soon as the newcomers sat down. They placed an order, and that same canister returned, bringing their orders.

"So—" Becker began.

"Is your ship the *Astricus*?" the man asked.

Becker stared at the man. "I don't know who you are."

"I'm Victor, and you are?"

"The captain of the *Astricus*. Now, I'm told you have some cargo that needs to be picked up and delivered."

A group of spacers walked by them, and Victor leaned back in his chair. He glanced at the woman.

So she was in charge, Becker thought. He looked at her. "Maybe I should be talking to you?"

The woman smiled, and for some reason, she looked familiar, but Becker couldn't remember who she was. "You must be Becker, which makes you Oscar," she said.

"The one and only," Oscar replied.

Becker smiled a little.

She leaned forward. "You should have been given a set of protocols to be used to complete the transfer."

Becker accessed his wrist computer and made a passing motion toward the woman. "Are you going to tell me who you are, or should I just make up a name for you?"

"You can call me Tia," she said and read the docket he'd given her.

Becker frowned. "You don't look like a Tia."

She laughed. "You look exactly as I remember you."

"Have we met before?"

Tia arched an eyebrow and leaned forward. "When you were with the Union," she said quietly.

She could have been anyone. Crowe's Union employed thousands of spacers. "If you say so. Where is this cargo I'm supposed to retrieve?" he asked.

Tia made a passing motion back to him, and his wrist computer chimed with an encrypted data packet. "The coordinates are in there."

Becker frowned. "Coordinates? I was told the cargo was here."

Tia shook her head. "No, I'm afraid I had to change the location."

Becker narrowed his gaze and then began to rise. "No deal."

Oscar glanced at him and stood.

Victor glared at them, his hand straying toward his sidearm. Then he looked at Tia.

"Good luck," Becker said and walked away from the table.

Oscar leaned toward him. "What are you doing?"

"Something isn't right. We're walking."

"What about Crowe?"

"I don't care," Becker said, and meant it.

He was through getting jerked around by Crowe. He glanced at Vikram and raised his chin toward the exit. Vikram nodded and gestured toward the others.

As they left the rotunda, heading back to the ship, he heard the rapid pace of someone following them.

"Becker, wait!" Tia said.

Becker turned around. Victor scowled at him and had his hand on his weapon.

Becker speared the man with a hardened stare. "You'll confirm that you're as stupid as you look if you draw that weapon."

Victor frowned and sighed explosively.

"Get the hell out of here. Now," Becker said.

Tia turned toward Victor. "Go on. I'll handle this."

Victor shook his head and went back toward the commons area.

Tia turned toward Becker, her expression serious. "Look, I need you to retrieve that cargo."

Spacers walked through the concourse, and Becker gestured toward the window, away from the foot traffic.

"Not until you tell me what it is," Becker replied.

Oscar stood nearby and waited for Tia to speak.

She shook her head. "It's just what the manifest says it is—a shipment of rare materials to enhance the explosive yield of antimatter warheads. It's quite valuable, and I know your associates can use it."

Becker frowned in thought. "How do I know it's not been tampered with?"

"Give me a break. You know there are no guarantees. Whoever you give it to will have to take the necessary precautions. But there's more."

More spacers walked by, and Tia paused until they passed.

Becker narrowed his gaze. "Who are you really?"

She ignored his question. "Hidden in the cargo is a data cache with information about the Collective. Things the Alliance will find useful."

Becker was about to ask another question when a large group of spacers walked by them. Another ship must have arrived. When he turned back toward Tia, she was gone.

Becker looked around, trying to see where she'd gone, but with so many spacers around, it was next to impossible.

"Where'd she go?" Oscar asked.

"I don't know," Becker said, peering through the crowd of spacers.

"Do you want to look for her?"

Becker shook his head. "No, let's get out of here."

Oscar nodded. "What about the cargo?"

They started to walk back to the ship.

"We'll pick it up."

"I didn't think the Union had any spies working out here," Oscar said.

"Did she look familiar to you?" Becker asked.

Oscar sucked in his bottom lip for a second. "She did. Her voice. Something about it."

"Yeah, I think I've heard it before too."

"Well, if she's with the Union, we might have seen her before," Oscar said.

Becker nodded as they turned down the corridor that led to the ship. "I just wish I could remember who she was. I should have gotten a picture."

"Here," Oscar said.

He had a small image on his personal holoscreen.

Becker arched an eyebrow.

"I took pictures of them both. Just in case. What?"

Becker pursed his lips and shrugged. "Nothing. I just never thought you were a voyeur, is all."

Oscar's mouth hung open. "No. No… Eww, no. Stop messing with me."

Becker grinned. "All right, weirdo."

Oscar grinned. "Well, it *has* been a while since we've been to a nice spaceport."

They went back to the ship, and Guttman met them at the airlock. Vikram and the others left them.

"What did she look like?" Guttman asked.

"Here, take a look," Oscar said and gave a sidelong glance at Becker.

Guttman peered at the image for a few seconds and then raised his eyes toward the others, his mouth agape. "Don't you guys know who this is?"

Becker shared a glance with Oscar and shook his head.

"That's, that's, Vonya. Vonya Irani, the Servitor from the *Nebulon*. The one that betrayed us. She gave away the starbase's location to Crowe," Guttman said.

Becker peered at the image. "Are you sure?"

Guttman nodded vigorously. "Oh yeah, I'm sure. I never forget a face. The hair and eyes are different… and the skin, obviously. Here look."

Guttman brought up an image on his personal holoscreen. The image was of a beautiful woman with lavender skin. She wore a formfitting shirt that accentuated her firm breasts, and her dark eyes had violet in them. However, her full lips, the shape of her nose, even the shape of her eyes were the same.

"Oh my God! That's her," Oscar said.

Becker gave Guttman a long look.

Guttman frowned. "What?"

"You saved a picture of her?"

"Of course," he said without a hint of shame. "A beautiful woman like that doesn't come around often."

Becker's thoughts went somewhere between exasperation and a little bit of disgust.

"She was an angel," Guttman said, and then frowned, uncomfortable. "Until she tried to kill us, that is."

"I doubt she meant to lure the Sentinels to that starbase," Oscar said.

Becker rolled his eyes. "Not you, too."

"I'm not wrong."

He wasn't, but Becker didn't want to tell him that.

"Okay," Becker said. "We need to retrieve whatever the hell this cargo is and check it for the data cache before we leave it in a drop location for the Alliance to retrieve."

"Right," Oscar said.

"And we need to warn Quinton and Maelyn about Vonya," Becker said.

His friends frowned.

"Guys, I know she's beautiful, but they need to know about her. Include the two images you miscreants have."

Oscar sighed. "Fine. I'll send an update through normal comms channels."

"Thank you, Oscar."

Oscar shook his head. "You're enjoying this a little too much."

Becker laughed. "It's easy when you give me such rich material to work with. You two are like the gift that keeps on giving."

"I wasn't the one carrying around an image of the Servitor imposter who tried to kill us," Oscar said.

Guttman glared at him for a second. "Hey, come on. A man can dream, right?"

They looked at one another and then laughed.

"It would've never worked between you two," Becker said.

Guttman pressed his lips together. "What do you mean?"

"I remember she spoke with Simon a lot."

"Simon? But he's just a kid," Guttman said and looked at Oscar for support.

"I'm sure it was just friendly chit-chat," Oscar said.

"No, it wasn't," Becker replied quickly, walking toward the bridge.

Oscar put his arm around Guttman's shoulder. "Don't listen to him. What does he know?"

"Simon? Really?"

Becker grinned. Guttman always did wear his heart on his sleeve.

He'd spent over a decade in Crowe's Union and couldn't remember ever meeting Tia. If she was some kind of spy, then that wasn't her name. He'd still send the information to Quinton, and he knew Maelyn would want to know. She'd taken the betrayal personally, as if she should have been able to spot it. One thing was for certain, however. Whoever Tia or Vonya was, she didn't work for the Sentinels.

12

THE FINAL COUNTDOWN clock reached zero, and the *Fortitude* and the rest of the ACN ships jumped the last leg of their journey to reach the *Salvation*. Spacers throughout the battle group gathered near holoscreens, waiting for a glimpse of the planet-sized warship.

Quinton stood on the bridge and waited for the images to appear on the main holoscreen. He'd only been away from the ship for a few weeks, but he was just as excited to see it as the rest of the crew, some of whom would be seeing it for the very first time.

Among the dark space between stars appeared a planetoid ship and the galaxy's last hope of defeating the Sentinels. The battle-steel hull gleamed like a great spherical beacon in the darkness. As they flew toward the ship, Quinton saw fleets of warships orbiting the massive structure. They were like tiny specs of stardust shimmering in the great expanse of the galaxy.

The *Salvation* had triangular halves that swept away from the gigantic sphere in the middle, as if the entire ship was a monument to the ACN. An awe-inspiring silence settled on the crew that served on the bridge of the *Fortitude*, and Quinton imagined that the same silent reverence was occurring on all the other ships that flew with them. The ACN's black and gold emblem could be found on all ships of the fleet. Beneath the emblem were the words of the ACN motto, and Quinton thought of them quietly in his mind.

Perseverance.

Endurance.

Fortitude.

Readiness.

Inevitably, the silent reverie passed and conversations resumed. It was one thing to be told the truth about the Federation Wars and Grand Admiral Browning, but it was quite another to see the product of it on such an unmatched scale. The DUC and many other groups that were part of the newly formed United Federation Alliance professed to be starting a new federation for the future. But the *Salvation* itself was a tribute to the past and the Acheron Confederacy. No one who had seen the ship could deny its heritage.

A challenge request came through the ship's comms system that Quinton had to acknowledge. He transferred his credentials through the data comlink, and his status was confirmed. Since Quinton was the commanding officer of the behemoth-sized warship, the *Fortitude* was given first priority. However, none of the ships had to wait very long to enter. There were hundreds of tunnels spanning multiple kilometers that were more than large enough to accommodate the size of the largest warships. Automated flight control systems engaged from the *Salvation's* massive computing core, and all the ships were guided inside the safety of the *Salvation's* battle-steel hull.

"I'll never get used to that sight, no matter how many times I see it," Simon said.

"Neither will I," Quinton replied.

"They didn't have ships like these," Simon said and paused, looking as if he was about to say something he shouldn't have.

Quinton arched an eyebrow. "Back in my day? Are you saying I'm old?"

Simon grinned.

"No, they didn't. We had warships just like everyone else… *better* than everyone else," Quinton said. He still had the ACN pride in a fleet that wouldn't be squashed anytime soon.

"It still gets me every time I see it. Like, how did they even come up with the plans to make it?" Simon said.

"It's in the archive any time you want to read about it."

"I know. I know," Simon said. "But still. It took decades to build, and by VI-run autofactories, no less."

It was that last part that gave most spacers pause. Building ships wasn't something that was left to the average virtual intelligence. Quinton had invited DUC engineers to review the entire structure, but they hadn't finished yet. After all, the ship was the size of a planet, so it would take some time. However, all systems they'd examined had proven to be better made than they'd ever seen before.

The *Salvation* was designed for long deployments. It had a complex atmospheric system that utilized vast parks and gardens throughout the ship. There were massive lakes that were part of a water purification system. Even though the *Salvation* was a warship capable of delivering untold amounts of destruction, the living areas aboard were nothing short of luxurious. The complex design of the ship left no space wasted, and everything had a purpose, even down to the comfort of the crew. Of all the ships Quinton had ever served on, the *Salvation* was by far and away the best he'd ever experienced. It was as close to a living planet he'd seen in a long time.

Simon looked at him. "You command that whole thing? How does that work?"

"It works with a whole lot of constraints and redundancies."

Simon nodded. "You've mentioned that before. The ship has an intricate system to enforce the rules of engagement."

"You make it sound so simple."

"Simple doesn't mean easy," Simon replied.

"Browning didn't know who was going to find the *Salvation*."

Simon nodded. "He needed a way to keep whoever found it on task," he said and stared at Quinton for a few seconds, considering.

Quinton's expression invited Simon to keep going.

"I'm a little surprised you haven't tried to circumvent those constraints."

During the time Simon had known Quinton, Quinton had had an affinity for bending the rules to achieve an objective, so he couldn't be too surprised by what Simon had said.

"I'd rather pick a fight I had a chance of winning."

"Is that why you haven't used the *Salvation* against the Sentinels yet?"

"The less they know about the ship, the better it will be for us when we do take them on."

Simon nodded. "And now that we've retrieved all these PMCs?"

"It'll help, but we need support from the federation remnants," Quinton said.

Simon pressed his lips together and looked away. Spacers didn't like it when PMCs referred to the current galactic residents as remnants. It reminded them of the loss of a more civilized time in human history. Quinton could sympathize to a point, but he couldn't stop thinking of them as remnants. Spacers survived by salvaging scraps from worlds that had existed before the Federation Wars. Only the very old, and PMCs, were there to remind them of a past that had been much better than what the future had become.

"Simon," Quinton said.

He shook his head in short, jerky movements. "No, you're right. It's what they are."

"They did what they had to do to survive."

Simon sighed and looked around to see if anyone was listening to them. "It's hard. I'm young, so maybe it's easier for me to wrap my mind around the lies. Or maybe it's the other way around. It's easier to manipulate someone like me into believing that everything they've been taught was a lie. That we've been living in a stagnate existence designed by Miles Harding."

"It's not that simple," Quinton replied. "Miles Harding—or a later version of him—is responsible for creating the circumstances that led to the Federation Wars, but we also did it to ourselves."

"He was supposed to be the hero. Someone we were meant to emulate."

"Me, too," Quinton replied.

Simon blinked several times. "I forgot about that. You predate the Federation Wars."

Quinton smiled a little. "Harding's work influenced PMC recruitment. What he was able to do was one of the reasons I volunteered, and learning that he became what he did is sometimes difficult to rationalize. But I reviewed the evidence in the *Salvation's* archives. Sometime along the way, Harding became what he is—this Harding Prime. That's who the enemy is. This is what the spacers need to learn."

"And that's what this summit you're planning is all about," Simon said.

Quinton nodded. "It's what we need to do to build the Alliance. We can't defeat the Sentinels without help."

They left the *Fortitude* as they docked with the resupply depot inside the *Salvation.*

Captain Martinez walked them to a shuttle. "Admiral," he said.

Simon climbed aboard the shuttle and Quinton turned toward Martinez.

"I just wanted to say that having you aboard was educational. I didn't know what to expect, but I appreciate the time you were among us, sir," Martinez said.

"The feeling is mutual, Captain," Quinton replied.

Quinton was silent as the shuttle flew them toward a transit hub. A version of Radek, his VI, had become part of the *Salvation's* computer systems. Radek's integration had occurred when Quinton assumed command of the ship. He spent his time reviewing mission status updates and reports, which he was able to do much quicker now that he was back aboard the *Salvation.*

The shuttle landed and they made their way to the transit hub. Simon stopped walking as he stared at his personal holoscreen.

"What is it?" Quinton asked.

"The quarantined PMCs that we talked about have arrived. They're being transferred to a secure lab," Simon said.

Quinton nodded. "Go. You don't need to be at the briefing. Give me a status update later. And, Simon, be careful."

"I will," Simon promised and walked toward another tram.

Quinton watched him go for a few seconds, appreciating that Simon wanted to find a way to help the PMCs that had been compromised. Most spacers would have assumed they were beyond hope. Quinton was one of them, but he liked that there were spacers like Simon who questioned things and used their impressive intellect to help. His opinion of Simon had done nothing but increase ever since he'd met him.

"Hey there, stranger. Are you lost?"

Quinton smiled as he turned around, recognizing who'd spoken.

Maelyn smiled, her eyes gleaming.

"That would be pretty embarrassing, considering." He took a few seconds to look at her. "You look better."

"I am," she said with a nod. "I got some sleep."

A double-ended, bullet-shaped aircar came to a stop nearby. Counter-grav emitters kept it hovering one foot or so above the floor. A large hatch opened on the side, and they entered. As the hatched closed, the buzz of outside activity disappeared.

Quinton inputted their destination, and the aircar accelerated away, speeding toward a featureless metal wall that popped open an instant before they hit and instead darted into a brightly lit bore.

"It's no wonder you were so tired. You helped twelve other teams with their retrievals. Were you going for some kind of record?"

Maelyn gave a thin laugh that turned into a yawn. "Sorry."

Quinton smiled. "Need me to carry you?"

"That won't be necessary," she replied.

He nodded and then leaned against the side of the aircar. "I appreciate what you did."

"I was just doing my part."

He shook his head and stepped toward her. "No, you weren't. You did more. You always do."

She looked at him with those celestial blue eyes of hers that seemed to reach out and take hold of him. "You would've done the same."

Quinton swallowed. He had, but he also had a much larger attack force than the small frigate group she'd led. She'd done more with less. When Maelyn committed to doing something, she didn't go halfway. They were alike that way, and he thought it was part of the reason they were drawn to each other.

The temperature of the aircar seemed to rise a few degrees.

"There's something we need to talk about," Maelyn said.

Quinton's eyebrows raised. "It's just the two of us in here. Not quite an elevator, but close enough."

She exhaled and smiled with half her mouth. "I could have shot you that second time," she said and tucked a lock of her dark hair behind her ear.

Quinton chuckled. "I know."

There was a fresh spurt of acceleration and a sideways surge of inertia as the aircar swept through a curved junction and darted into yet another tunnel. Maelyn stepped toward him, not quite stumbling, but Quinton steadied her in his arms. Tentatively, slowly, each drew an inch closer, silent, and each still holding the other's steady gaze. Maelyn gently touched his jaw and leaned forward to kiss his cheek. The soft ends of her hair brushed against him. Inhaling the mild scent of her skin, he pressed himself down to her, and she came to meet him, the two of them not so much moving as drifting weightlessly toward the other, attracted by some irresistible force of nature. What had begun so gently took on a life of its own, and they flew to each other, locking open mouths and crossing some line that dared them. They didn't hesitate.

The aircar emerged into a brightly lit cavern and Maelyn pulled away from him, chest heaving. Quinton had never wished to be back in his human body more so than he did right then. She put her hand on the center of his chest—part caress, part barrier.

"Quinton," she said gently, softly, but it still felt like an unexpected splash of cold water on his head.

Quinton closed his eyes for a second, nodding a little. "I know… I know," he said, grudgingly.

The timing was wrong. It was always wrong. He gritted his teeth a little and then tried to cover it up with a small smile.

"We'll have our time," Maelyn said. "I promise."

Quinton swallowed and his chin sank. "I know," he replied, sounding resigned. "It's just," he began, trying not to smile, "you."

Maelyn smiled, and there was something pleasant in the shape of her mouth when she did. "You, too," she admitted.

"At least we're suffering together."

She laughed.

There was a drag of deceleration as the aircar slowed virtually to a walk and they swerved gently down an intersecting tunnel that was only a little wider than the vehicle itself. It slid alongside an entrance and stopped. The hatch flicked soundlessly open.

Outside the aircar, an older man stood in a black and gold uniform. Creases showed at the corners of his eyes and mouth, and his intelligent gaze did a quick assessment that would have no problems guessing what had transpired.

"Hello, Severin," Maelyn said.

They walked out of the aircar.

Quinton raised an eyebrow toward Brandt. "Giving us the personal treatment?"

Brandt chuckled. "Sometimes, this old spacer needs to stretch his legs. I figured we could talk while we walked."

The hatch of the aircar closed, and it silently moved away as they walked down a short corridor that led to one of the *Salvation's* many parks. The warm, fresh air of a veritable forest hovered just a few feet away from the entrance. Benches lined the main path, and the artificial sky above was bright, as if it were the middle of the day. Quinton inhaled the scents of the forest, his artificial detectors interpreting the different smells. He glanced at Maelyn, and she smiled.

"It's almost like being planetside," she said.

Brandt nodded. "All the varieties of parks on the *Salvation* are similar to the colony worlds we found."

"The ones from the starbase?" Quinton asked.

"Yes, the Acheron Confederacy had automated terraforming platforms that made more than a dozen planets livable… more than just livable. They're like the garden worlds that existed before the Federation Wars."

"How has settling them gone?" Quinton asked.

"We've been moving people there quietly ever since we found them, but the secret has become increasingly difficult to keep," Brandt replied.

"We can't afford to let the Sentinels find them," Quinton said.

"Not just the Sentinels," Maelyn replied.

Quinton eyed her for a moment. For years, the DUC had taken in refugees throughout the galaxy. However, the galaxy was a dangerous place. He could only imagine how certain groups like the Collective would leverage the colony worlds. Brandt was right. They needed to move cautiously to preserve and protect those worlds.

"We restrict travel to those planets to reduce the risk of them being discovered. The spacers who are there work to build a home for more spacers to come. They go there knowing that leaving isn't an option," Brandt said.

"They're trapped?" Quinton asked.

"Of course not," Maelyn replied. "If someone really wants to leave, they just need to be kept ignorant of the planet's location."

"But they live there."

"Yes," Brandt said. "But not everyone can navigate the stars, and the spacers that can are required to go through memory modification to remove the relevant information. Don't look at me like that. They volunteer for it. Maybe one day we can change things. I don't like it, but it *is* necessary."

Quinton couldn't fault Brandt's reasoning. How much of what they were doing now was because it was necessary?

Maelyn walked toward a bench. She was hunched, and her hands pressed against the sides of her head. A painful gasp escaped her lips.

Quinton was there instantly.

She looked at him. "Implants," she said.

Quinton gathered her into his arms. "I'm taking you to a doctor."

She winced and then nodded, resting her head on his shoulder as he carried her back to the entrance. Brandt had comlinked ahead, so there were medics waiting to take Maelyn.

Quinton lay her down on the counter-grav stretcher. She looked so small.

"They'll take good care of her," Brandt said.

One of the medics began to push the stretcher away, and Quinton walked with it.

"Quinton," Brandt said.

He clenched his teeth slightly and looked at Maelyn. He wanted to go with her. He knew she'd be all right, but he still wanted to be at her side. They shared a look for a few seconds.

"I'll check on you later," Quinton said.

"Send Simon," Maelyn said.

The medics guided the stretcher away.

Quinton looked at Brandt. "She's been having trouble with her implants."

Brandt nodded. "Ah, that can be painful. They probably just need some fine tuning. Why did she ask for Simon?"

Quinton was a little surprised by the question. Brandt had known Maelyn for a lot longer than he had.

"She trusts him."

Brandt glanced the way the medics had gone. "Ah, she's always been a bit slow to trust."

"Why?"

Brandt regarded him for a second. "Perhaps that's a question you should ask *her*."

Quinton chuckled. "Point taken."

"I've had a chance to review some of the PMCs we were able to recover," Brandt said.

They walked away from the park entrance, instead taking the corridor that led to the meeting rooms they'd be using.

"So have I," Quinton replied.

"There's something I don't understand about them. Most of the PMCs that we've recovered seem to be junior officers. There's the occasional commander, but no one higher in rank," Brandt said.

"Most PMCs are from the Federation Wars. It could be that Browning did this purposefully."

Brandt pursed his lips in thought. "I'd considered that, but I can't find records to support it."

At last, Quinton understood what Brandt was getting at. "I'll check and let you know what I find."

"I appreciate it. I find it curious."

"I'm not sure if it's as big a mystery as you believe it to be. At least when I was recruited, there were age limits to becoming a PMC."

"Age limits, huh?"

Quinton shrugged. "I didn't make the rules. I was hoping we'd find some senior officers too, but until we do, I'm all you've got."

Brandt peered at him in a way only someone with a lifetime of experience could. It made Quinton want to stand up straighter, even though his avatar already had perfect posture.

"I wish I could access Browning's logs. Not just the mission reports, but his personal logs," Brandt said.

This had always been a point of contention. Quinton was the only one able to access Browning's personal logs. He'd tried to find a way to share them, but there were so many security blocks in place that even Radek couldn't find a way through them all.

"I'm sure he had his reasons for putting in those restrictions," Quinton said.

"Maybe, or he was worried about something in them. Something that could affect how we fight the Sentinels."

Quinton had spent a lot of time reviewing Browning's personal logs, and he'd also spent a lot of time learning all he could about the *Salvation*. Even with his frame rate increased to maximum, he still hadn't learned all there was to know.

"I'll make time to keep searching. If I learn something of use, I'll let you know," Quinton said and then added, "Don't have your people try to override the security. Browning didn't do anything without carefully thinking it through. We need to trust his judgment."

Brandt looked at him and sighed. "Yes, sir."

13

Maelyn lay in bed at the medical center.

"Has the pain lessened?" Dr. Corday asked. She peered at her while holding a palm-scanner.

Maelyn nodded. "Yeah, that's better."

"Good. How long have you been experiencing these headaches?" she asked and looked at the holoscreen above the bed.

"About a month. They've been getting worse the more I use them, but the medical VI on the ship advised me to keep using them," Maelyn replied.

Dr. Corday nodded. "Normally that's fine, but in your case, your body was rejecting the implants. The onboard VI should have adjusted for this."

Maelyn frowned. "Are they malfunctioning?"

"That's the interesting part. I'm not sure."

"What do you mean?"

"These implants can stimulate parts of your brain. It's like suddenly having an extra limb. Your brain adapts to the additional input, but like I said earlier, your body was rejecting them."

Maelyn considered it for a few moments. "I can't get them removed. I need them."

"You can still function without them. We could downgrade to the basic implant package."

Maclyn shook her head. "I can't."

Dr. Corday frowned. "You're seeking a command role."

"I'm already in a command role, but we need more. The requirement is the use of the more enhanced implants so I can work better with PMCs."

The door to the room opened and Simon walked in.

"I came as soon as I could," Simon said. He glanced at the holoscreen above her head and then looked at the doctor. "Is this about the implants?"

Maelyn nodded.

Simon walked to the side of the bed. "I think I know what it is."

Dr. Corday's eyes widened. "You do?"

Simon nodded and brought up his personal holoscreen. "This is the configuration of Maelyn's implants. It looks like they were stuck in a learning mode, which can overtax the brain-to-machine interface."

He tapped a few settings and the pressure Maelyn had been feeling went away. She blinked several times and looked up at him.

Dr. Corday tilted her head to the side. "Your stress levels have lowered. Are you feeling better?"

Maelyn blew out a breath and nodded. "Yes, the pain is completely gone."

Dr. Corday sucked in her bottom lip in thought. Then she looked at Simon. "This is the first I've heard of a configuration getting stuck."

"Yeah, the same thing happened to me. Also, it was happening with Captain Martinez on the *Fortitude*. I helped him figure it out. The medical VIs think it's just first-run protocols."

"Okay," she said and looked at Maelyn. "Well, just monitor for it. If you start having pain again, come back here and we'll run some more diagnostics."

Maelyn sat up. "Thank you."

Dr. Corday left the room.

Simon smiled a little. "How you doing?"

Maelyn swung her legs off the bed, her feet dangling, and shook her head. "Better now."

"Yeah, those headaches can be brutal."

She gave him a sidelong look. "You don't say."

Simon offered to help her stand, but she waved him off.

"You know, maybe I should run a few diagnostics on the implants."

"Why?" Maelyn asked.

Simon shrugged. "Just in case. Better to figure out if something is faulty here than out there on a mission."

"You're right about that," Maelyn said.

She stood up and walked to the door. "How long is this going to take?"

"Do you have somewhere you need to be?"

Maelyn nodded, and for a moment she thought about Quinton in the aircar. She felt her face flush and quickly turned away from Simon.

"If you don't need to use your implants, I can just have them run the diagnostic now. It can take a few hours to complete. The data will be uploaded to the ship's computer system," Simon said.

Maelyn looked at him. "Who will have access to it?"

Simon pressed his lips together for a second. "I can restrict access to just you and me."

She nodded. "Do that. I don't want anyone… I just don't want anyone to know, okay?"

"Of course. When it's done, we'll both be notified."

Maelyn smiled. "Thank you, Simon. I really appreciate it."

Simon returned the smile, revealing the adorable little dimple in his cheek. "What are friends for?"

She gave him a playful shove. "You're more than a friend. You're family. We might not be on the *Nebulon*, but we still have each other's backs. Right?"

Simon chuckled. "Of course."

They left the medical center and Simon said he had to return to a lab where he was working on something for Quinton.

She watched him go and then went her own way. She'd intended to head straight to the briefing where Quinton and Brandt were but then decided not to. She needed to clear her head, so she returned to the park and headed inside. She walked along the paths far enough where she could almost fool herself into believing that she stood in a real forest surrounded by tall trees with broad, green leaves. The soil on the ground was soft under her feet. She inhaled deeply and sighed. The tension left her body with each passing breath.

She started thinking about the aircar again. It wasn't the first time they'd had a moment like that. Quinton had a way of reaching her like no one else had. He could be frustrating to deal with sometimes, but over the months, he was getting harder to resist. They'd decided not to complicate things. Instead, they needed to focus on fighting the Sentinels. She wouldn't be a distraction to him. No matter how much he assured her that she wouldn't be, Maelyn knew better. There had been other men in her life, some of whom she'd served with on DUC missions. They all believed they could remain objective, but they'd been wrong. Sometimes the costs of those relationships were too high, and with stakes as high as there were now, she wouldn't take any chances. Her time with Quinton would simply have to wait until after the war was over, even if it meant that they would never be together. What they were trying to accomplish was much too important.

14

QUINTON STRODE down the long corridor leading to the *Salvation's* primary bridge. The black walls were covered in thin, pale, glowing lines that traveled the length of the corridor. Quinton peered at the lines of flowing white script, a monument to honor all those who'd given their lives during the Federation Wars—spacers from multiple militaries representing federations that had been vanquished by the Sentinels long ago. Grand Admiral Elias Browning had united the remnant navies of multiple federations to fight against Harding Prime and the Sentinels, and the corridor was a monument to the fallen.

Quinton always felt an odd sort of stillness when he walked this corridor alone, which he thought had probably been Browning's intention when he'd instructed the autofactories to build the ship. It was a ship Browning had been meant to command, but he never got the chance. Now the responsibility had fallen to Quinton as the only Galactic PMC to answer the *Salvation's* call. The PMC activation signals were to be the rallying cry to unite all those who were left so they could free the galaxy of the Sentinels forever. The survivors of the Federation Wars believed Browning was a monster, largely to blame for the Federation Wars, but why would so many spacers fight alongside him if that were the case?

His footsteps echoed through the long corridor until they ended at a hatch that was large enough for a shuttle to fly through. The middle of the entrance bore the black and gold emblem of the ACN in stunning clarity. The ACN motto was written in an elegant cursive script that surrounded the planet's likeness, and beneath it was the word *Salvation*.

The hatch had been constructed of a thick metallic alloy that formed an immensely strong barrier. However, the door slipped silently to the side, revealing a brightly lit spherical chamber, and Quinton walked toward a transparent platform. Dozens of couch-like chairs were located on either side. Spacers and CDAs occupied the control consoles.

Quinton opened a connection to the *Salvation's* computing core and entered a virtualized interface that transported his perspective into another environment. Galactic leaders throughout several sectors had been invited to a summit that had been organized by Sherilyn Cantos of the Dholeren United Coalition.

He withdrew from the virtual interface and instead routed the specialized comlink to the main holoscreen. A silver orb appeared in front of him as a representation of his own VI.

"Summit communication protocols are for a virtual interface," Radek said.

"I know," Quinton replied.

"I'm unable to connect you to the summit unless these conditions are met," Radek replied.

The communication protocols were in place to protect the summit attendees, but Quinton wanted them all to see the bridge of the *Salvation.* They needed to see it so they could believe that the ship actually existed.

Quinton reviewed the security protocols, looking for a way to supplant them, but they were ironclad—simple and not subject to interpretation.

A few of the spacers working at their consoles looked in his direction, but Quinton ignored them.

He chuckled as an idea sprang to mind. He added a filter to the comlink, which distorted the background behind him. The summit attendees would still be able to see him, but not the rest of the bridge.

"That should work," Quinton said.

"Prerequisite inspection has passed all protocol checks," Radek replied.

"Thank you, Radek. Now get me in there."

Specialized communication platforms had been established throughout the sectors where the galactic leaders were located. Quinton was sure they were trying to locate the source of the comlink sessions in hopes of locating the *Salvation*, but they'd all fail.

An older woman with blonde hair and a mixture of mature and youthful features appeared on the holoscreen.

"Thank you for joining this summit. I am Sherilyn Cantos, senior councilwoman for the Dholeren United Coalition. To protect the identity of all participants, you will not be able to see who else is attending. This is a precautionary measure due to the highly sensitive nature of this meeting." Sherilyn paused for a few seconds. "Now, before you… Ah, the reactions are already coming through."

The meeting session was updated to reveal the number of participants, but their identities were marked as anonymous. Quinton was surprised to see thousands of participants. Before the Federation Wars, there had been hundreds of federations, star unions, empires, and the like, and these were the scattered remnants of the spacers who had survived.

Sherilyn began to speak again. "These are temporary measures that are in place for the beginning of the meeting. As we proceed, you'll have the option of making your identity and affiliation known to the other meeting participants, but sharing your identity isn't a requirement to participate when we come to the discussion portion of this meeting. You are all leaders and representatives of the galactic sectors in this local cluster. We'll be having more of these summits to share new information we believe will have a serious impact on the galaxy. Right now, a data packet is being shared with you that contains recently discovered historical records that challenge the current historical perception of who is ultimately responsible for the Federation Wars. I'll give you a few minutes to review the authenticity of the data I've made available to you."

Quinton had helped prepare the data that had just been shared, copied from the vast archives on the *Salvation*, and he watched the participant count dip as spacers dropped from the meeting. He tried not to think of them in too harsh a light, but if what they saw in the data packet frightened them, wait until he spoke to them.

After about ten minutes had passed, Quinton watched as Sherilyn began to speak again.

"I've given you control over your own meeting session so you can share who you are with the rest of the participants or remain anonymous. It's your choice. Also, by now you've heard of the new United Federation Alliance, of which the DUC is a member. The UFA embraces the revelations found in the data that was provided to you. However, some of this information has been in circulation for months. We have over fifty members who have pledged to join the Alliance, and I'm hopeful that after you review the data and hear what our next speaker is going to say, you'll also consider joining the Alliance."

Sherilyn made Quinton a speaker, and his face was now appearing to thousands of participants.

"I'm Quinton Aldren, a former commander in the Acheron Confederacy Navy. I'm a personality matrix construct, whose consciousness was uploaded into an ESS before the Federation Wars," he said. His appearance changed from humanoid to the standard chrome appearance of a CDA. His eyes had a slight greenish glow to them, and he allowed them to see him this way for a few seconds before changing his appearance back to his preferred configuration. "You've been lied to. All of you. I realize that what I'm about to tell you will be a shock, but you need to listen closely to what I'm about to say. Grand Admiral Elias Browning is not the monster you were led to believe. In fact, everything you think you know about the Federation Wars is false," Quinton said.

Hundreds of participants' comlink sessions took on a yellow border, indicating that they wanted to speak.

"I'm not going to take questions just yet, but I will. First, let's get the obvious stuff out of the way. Yes, PMCs were going insane, which gave rise to the chaos that became the Federation Wars. However, it was Miles Harding—Harding Prime—who was the cause of this. You see, Harding Prime was playing both sides of the war. Admiral Browning and hundreds of thousands of spacers discovered this and tried to stop it. Many of the atrocities attributed to Admiral Browning were large-scale incidences he was trying to prevent. I realize this is difficult for you to believe, and I don't expect anyone to accept what I've said at my word. That's why the data that was recently discovered has been made available to you."

Quinton went on to explain why Browning scattered PMCs throughout the galaxy in hopes that they could be revived to fight against Harding Prime and the Sentinels. During his own presentation, he watched as more and more of the yellow speaker requests disappeared and the number of attendees dropped, but after a few minutes, they rejoined, and he was surprised to see that a vast majority of participants chose not to conceal their identities. Too bad this wasn't the most surprising thing he'd learn at the meeting.

When Quinton was finished speaking, he turned control back to Sherilyn, who then invited attendees to ask their questions.

The session of a speaker became active, and an anonymous image of a man appeared. The man looked to be seated in the shadows and when he spoke, his voice distorted just enough to make it difficult for people to recognize.

"Every so often—decades, in fact—someone comes forward with 'new data' that attempts to explain what really happened in the Federation Wars," the man said.

"I assure you that the data provided is authentic," Sherilyn replied.

"I realize you believe that is true. How often have spacers been told they're being manipulated and lied to? Here we are in another of a long line of people attempting to have us believe that everything we thought we knew was wrong."

"That's because it's the truth," Quinton said.

"Who cares?" the man said. "Who really cares? What does it change? The Federation Wars are over and done with."

"The fact that Sentinels roam the galaxy murdering spacers doesn't bother you? You're fine with that?" Quinton asked.

"They leave us alone if we don't attempt to interfere with them. This system has worked for decades, and we're still here because of it."

Quinton glanced at the others in the meeting. The ones who had shared their identity had given him a view of their faces. Many of them appeared to agree with captain anonymous.

"Anonymity will not protect you from another incursion," Quinton replied.

The man chuckled as the placeholder icon disappeared and a bald man took its place. Although the thousand-odd participants were muted, Quinton couldn't miss their reactions.

"Trenton Draven, leader of the Collective."

Quinton regarded Draven for a few moments. "I'm surprised you support the stance of 'business as usual,' especially given the fact that the Sentinels have impacted your own operations."

Draven smiled, and it didn't reach his eyes. "The Sentinels were lured to star systems. They were there by mistake because they were hunting PMCs."

The Collective was among the most dominant groups in the galaxy. If Quinton could convince him to support the Alliance, then other groups would follow.

"All that stands between you and Sentinel weapons is whether they determine you're a PMC or not. They're no better than machines," Quinton replied.

"There has been peace with them around," Draven replied. "What you're proposing is war. War with the Sentinels."

"That's exactly what I'm proposing."

"Why should we fight another war? Especially for people who have been dead for decades? You say this evidence you've discovered exonerates Elias Browning?"

"I do."

"You don't question it?"

"I'm standing inside a testament to the dedication of what Admiral Browning tried to accomplish. I'm not asking you to do anything because of one man."

Draven nodded. "No, he had followers. That's nothing new. This testament you're referring to. What is it?"

"It's a ship."

"Just a ship?"

Quinton smiled. "It's more than that. It was built to help unite the galaxy and give us the tools we need to destroy the Sentinels."

"A tool to do Elias Browning's bidding."

Quinton felt as if the ground was crumbling beneath his feet. The *Salvation* had been built so they could fight the Sentinels, but Draven was making it sound like his only reason for fighting the Sentinels was because of Browning.

"No," Quinton replied. "Browning knew what was at stake."

"He wanted you to fight another war. Something akin to the Federation Wars. You'd bring that chaos back into spacers' lives? How much is enough?"

"Would you prefer what you have now? Really?" Quinton snarled. "Scavenging an existence by picking away at the skeletons of federations that have gone extinct? Living on overcrowded space stations or colony worlds that can barely sustain life? Scratching away in the hope that maybe someday things will get better? Resenting what was lost during the Federation Wars? That's what you want? Unlike you, I actually remember what the galaxy was like before the Federation Wars. The best of what you have represents the poorest standard of living back then, and you want to cling onto that instead of daring to fight for something better?"

Draven regarded him for a few moments but didn't reply. He seemed oddly satisfied by Quinton's response, and Quinton wondered if he'd said too much.

More people asked questions that were directed at Sherilyn Cantos, and Quinton watched. There was a common theme, and none of it was good.

Quinton accessed his own VI subroutines.

Sapient Combat Simulations Active.

He increased his frame rate, and his perception of time sped up until everyone in the summit became still. He unleashed his VIs. Putting their rapid learning analysis into action, they ran countless simulations on the meeting in its entirety, putting weight on responses and reactions to what people said, attempting to generate a deeper understanding as to the probable outcome. His view of each meeting attendee now appeared with an analysis overlay, giving him inside information into how the attendee was reacting to the meeting based on the recording of the meeting up to the point where he'd sped up his frame rate. A torrent of insight became available to him.

WARNING!

A crimson alert appeared on Quinton's HUD.

Sapient Combat Simulation protocol violation! System aborting.

Quinton frowned.

"Radek, what's happening?"

"You are attempting to use the SCS system to anticipate human reactions and responses. This is expressly forbidden."

The SCS system began to abort.

"No! I need this, Radek. Override the safety protocols."

"Quinton, the safety protocols are there for your protection, and I must advise you not to override them."

"Noted, now override the protocols," Quinton replied.

A series of automated checks appeared, inquiring whether he was sure he wanted to override.

The SCS system remained active, giving him a baseline for the attendees. Then he realized his mistake during his exchange with Draven.

Quinton returned his frame rate to normal and let Sherilyn know that he would like to speak. She granted his request almost immediately.

Quinton looked into the camera, imagining all the attendees on the other side. "I don't want a war. I've tried to communicate with the Sentinels more than a few times when I encountered them. They aren't interested in communicating with me or anyone else. I've seen what the galaxy has become, how you've all survived. This wasn't why we fought the Jordanis. We were freeing the galaxy from an oppressive regime. I see the Sentinels not only as a threat to me and other PMCs, but as a threat to you. If there is a solution out there where the Sentinels could be removed without any spacers losing their lives, I would pursue that. You were taught that the Acheron Confederacy is responsible for the Federation Wars, and perhaps that is partially correct. However, Browning isn't responsible for PMCs going insane. Harding Prime is responsible. His manipulation was the reason the Sentinels were created in the first place, and now they're answerable only to him."

Draven became prominent among the summit attendees, and Sherilyn elevated his privileges so he could speak again.

"What proof do you have of this? What you've just said isn't in the data provided," Draven said.

"I encountered an Agent of Harding. He could control the Sentinels, and he told me about Harding," Quinton said.

"What happened to this agent?"

"He escaped."

Draven seemed to consider this for a few moments. "I think I speak for the majority here in saying that we need time to review this information. You've given us a lot to think about."

Sherilyn began to bring the meeting to a close. "There's something else I'd like to say to all of you. You're the leaders of your people. The information provided to you was given with the intention that it would be shared. We have nothing to hide. Hopefully, this will convince you to support the Alliance."

The summit ended and Quinton felt more dejected than anything else. An extensive analysis from the SCS system found that he'd overestimated the spacers' willingness to accept the truth. He'd thought it would be easier to gain support, especially from Draven. The Sentinels had attacked his assets, but they'd been lured there by Lennix Crowe. There were other locations that had been attacked by the Sentinels that Crowe vehemently denied. Quinton had no way to prove who had sourced those attacks, but they'd used the same methodology. Admen Desher, who gave Crowe a way to fool the Sentinels into attacking different targets, had utilized the same tactics himself. Chances were that Crowe was telling the truth, but that wouldn't matter to anyone else. The attack footprint was the same, and it was impossible for anyone to prove that Admen Desher, the Agent of Harding, had been responsible for those attacks.

Quinton reviewed the meeting in his mind, but it was too fresh for him to think objectively.

A message came from Admiral Brandt.

Not as disastrous as it could have been. The post-meeting review will be in thirty minutes. See you there.

Quinton dismissed the message. Brandt couldn't order him to attend the meeting, but he had a way of compelling him just the same. He found himself thinking about his time on the *Wayfarer,* roaming the galaxy, trying to find Becker and his friends a ship of their own. Those had been simpler times.

15

Quinton walked off the bridge and saw a CDA standing in the corridor, wearing the black and gold accents that most PMC officers from the ACN wore. A PMC comlink became available, and Quinton acknowledged it.

"Admiral Aldren, Commander Ryan Bentlae reporting for duty."

Bentlae was one of the most recent PMCs to be brought back online.

"Welcome aboard the *Salvation*, Commander Bentlae."

Quinton resumed walking away from the bridge and gestured for Bentlae to walk with him.

"Thank you, Admiral. I've been brought up to speed and I'm at your disposal."

Quinton quickly reviewed Bentlae's record and regarded him for a moment. Green artificial eyes stared back at him.

"Federation Wars," Quinton said.

"Before the Blitz Offensive," Bentlae replied, confirming his unasked question.

Browning's personal logs contained entries for the Blitz Offensive. It was the last battle set to destroy Harding Prime. Since the Sentinels were still around, the mission had obviously failed.

"Were you aware of the *Salvation*?" Quinton asked

"Not specifically. Admiral Browning had quite a few ongoing projects."

That was an understatement if Quinton had ever heard one. He laughed, and Bentlae joined him.

"Your PMC identification doesn't indicate that you're a galactic, but you're a commander?"

"That's correct, sir. I didn't qualify as a galactic."

Quinton blinked. "Didn't qualify?"

Bentlae hesitated and then said, "That's correct, sir."

His next question wouldn't inspire confidence in his leadership, but he had to know. "What are the qualifications?"

Bentlae regarded him for a few seconds. "I thought you would know them, sir."

"I'm afraid I don't. I was uploaded before the Federation Wars. Galactic class PMCs came after. I only found out I was a galactic when I authenticated to an old communications node. There have been no others identified among the PMCs we've been able to retrieve," Quinton replied.

Bentlae nodded. "You've probably realized that most PMCs are junior officers, but toward the end of the Federation Wars, things had become desperate. We were preparing to fight the final battle with Harding and the Sentinels, but Browning also needed to prepare for the genuine possibility that he was going to fail. You have command authority over all PMCs, and it's based on certain criteria being met that the elevation of privileges is awarded."

Quinton considered this for a few moments. Before the *Salvation's* computer core granted him access, it had subjected him to a host of integrity checks, including Radek, before it allowed him to take command.

"Are you saying it's because I was activated first?"

"Were you first?"

Quinton looked away for a second. "There were others, but the Sentinels killed them."

"First to survive then."

"There has to be more to it than that," Quinton said.

"There is. Leadership capabilities are among the qualifications. And ingenuity, but also the ability to come up with creative solutions. You must have demonstrated that in your military record," Bentlae said.

Quinton's military record was filled with fighting the Jordani, but he didn't think that set him apart from other PMCs at the time. Perhaps he was thinking about this the wrong way. He assumed he knew all there was to know about his own military record. What if he was wrong? What if his qualification as a galactic was based on things he'd done after he'd been uploaded as a PMC?

Quinton suddenly felt as if an airlock was about to fail, and he was going to be thrust into the abyss.

"Admiral, is everything all right?" Bentlae said.

"Fine," Quinton replied. "I was just thinking. Why don't you join me?"

"I'd be happy to, sir. What are we doing?"

"Figuring out why spacers are reluctant to believe the truth," Quinton replied.

Bentlae remained quiet and followed Quinton.

Bentlae was new, but Quinton couldn't afford to keep a senior officer on the side. PMCs with the rank of commander were few and far between. Bentlae knew what they were up against and would provide valuable insight. That's what Quinton expected of him, and it was what he needed from him—someone to balance out what spacers like Brandt and others knew about the Sentinels. Quinton was hoping to gain insight into how the Sentinels had changed since they were first created. Hopefully, it would lead him to Harding Prime's location.

They walked into the conference room. Brandt and Maelyn were speaking with a civilian PMC named Belinda Hinton. PMCs were created based on specialization, and Hinton's expertise had to do with crew mindset. She was some kind of psychologist, or the future equivalent. Hinton had been recovered just a few months earlier, and she'd helped them improve coping strategies for PMCs.

Two CDAs he recognized looked in his direction and stood up—Walsh Corvax and Chloe Bradshaw. They were former Alari military, a smaller federation that had been allied with the Acheron Confederacy. They were among the first PMCs Quinton had encountered.

The others stopped speaking.

"This is Commander Bentlae. I asked him to join us," Quinton said and sat down across from Maelyn, sharing a furtive glance.

"How are you feeling, Maelyn?" Quinton asked, abandoning any pretext at subtlety.

"Much better. The issue with my implants should be taken care of now," Maelyn responded.

"Good," Brandt said. "Now, you can certify on the more capable warships. We need all the experienced officers we can get."

Maelyn nodded. "Right after this."

Quinton looked at Brandt. "Not a disaster?"

His statement drew a few puzzled frowns from the others.

Brandt nodded. "I expected worse."

"I don't know if that's making me feel any better."

Brandt chuckled. "You want worse? They could *all* have dropped from the meeting, refusing to even consider the things we were telling them."

Quinton sighed and shook his head. "I was hoping for a better outcome than that, especially from Draven. I thought the Collective was open to supporting us."

"I spoke with Sherilyn about that. She thinks he's just feeling us out...You ought to be specific. He *is* working with us."

"He's playing games with us—with me—and I gave him the performance he needed," Quinton replied.

Simon cleared his throat. "I don't understand. What happened?"

"I might have lost my temper a little," Quinton admitted.

Maelyn gave him an "are you serious" look.

"Fine, I did."

Belinda Hinton leaned forward. "Your reaction is understandable."

Quinton blinked. "You're okay with what I said?"

"No, I said it was understandable, but reminding them that their standard of living isn't on the same footing as pre-federation war in such an abrasive manner might cause a setback," Belinda replied.

"We'll need to agree to disagree. Sometimes people need to be pushed. After they get over being reminded of what has been lost, the ones we want on our side will come around."

"Or you could push them to support the Sentinels," Brandt replied.

"We don't want support from spacers who aren't really committed," Maelyn said, and Quinton felt his lips twitch slightly.

"They're already being pushed to accept something they're not prepared to deal with. It's going to take time," Belinda replied.

"They've been down this trajectory before," Brandt said, twisting the cup of water in front of him. "We tried to fight the Sentinels a few times during my lifetime, and each time we were defeated."

"Were you united?" Bentlae asked.

"Not an easy question to answer. There were sizable fleets that pursued the Sentinels. At first, they tried to prevent them from entering occupied star systems. The Sentinels returned with enough ships to make fighting them all but a death sentence. That's the history you're up against, and that's why leaders will be reluctant to support the Alliance."

"Even with the *Salvation*, we couldn't protect everyone," Quinton said.

Bentlae looked at him. "But this ship can take on fleets of ships. Even the Sentinels."

"It can, but they have a lot of ships," Quinton replied.

"We've updated their fleet capabilities based on their response to the retrieval mission," Brandt said.

"I saw the new estimates. Thirty percent more than we previously thought," Quinton said. "Yet, there are no shipyards controlled by the Sentinels, so where did those new ships come from?"

"Excuse me, sir," Bentlae said. "The Sentinels aren't building ships?"

Quinton shook his head. "Analysis of our encounters with them indicate that the Sentinel fleets are comprised of ships built during the Federation Wars."

"That can't be right. Fleets need to be maintained and resupplied," Bentlae said.

"Their armament is designed for a distributed supply interval, meaning that they can travel for a long time without ever resupplying," Quinton said.

Bentlae frowned in thought.

"What is it?" Quinton asked.

"It's just that they had manufacturing capabilities. Maybe the Blitz wasn't as much a failure as we thought," he replied.

"They might have crippled Harding's ability to build new ships," Quinton said and looked at Brandt.

Brandt rubbed his chin in thought. "That would explain a few things."

"Absolutely," Simon said. "It means that there are only so many of them."

"We can cut their numbers down to a size that we can defeat," Bentlae said.

"You're describing a war of attrition—a long, ongoing conflict that takes a toll on all sides. Our numbers will dwindle just like theirs will," Brandt said.

"True," Quinton said. "But is there another way?"

"We still need support from the remnant unions," Maelyn said.

Quinton nodded. "And their leaders are reluctant to commit," he said and frowned. Then he looked at the others. "What we need is a subtle approach."

"You want to be subtle now?" Maelyn asked.

He tilted his head to the side once. "Not to reach the leaders. We need to find a way to pressure the leaders to act, and the best way to do that is to engage everyday, normal spacers."

The others considered this for a few moments.

"How do you suggest we do that?" Brandt asked.

"By utilizing a group that's known throughout the galaxy. We should engage the Servitors," Quinton said.

Maelyn stiffened and her gaze hardened.

Quinton held up his hand. "I know, but I've met another one. A real one, I guess. I'm going to reach out to her and see if she can facilitate a meeting with whoever their leadership is."

"Quinton," Maelyn said, "you think you're the first person who thought they could convince Servitors to help them sway public opinion?"

"I doubt it, but the alternative is to appeal directly to spacers themselves. Maybe we'll need to do both."

"He's right," Brandt said. "It's worth trying."

Maelyn looked down at the table and remained quiet.

"Hang on a second," Simon said. "Won't the leaders who were at the summit resent us appealing directly to their constituents?"

"Not if we go about it the right way," Belinda Hinton said.

Quinton arched an eyebrow toward her, and she continued. "I'm not suggesting we flood the info nets, blasting the information. I'm suggesting we reach out to groups that investigate these kinds of claims. They'll present it to the various sectors in a format that those spacers will understand."

"But we can't control the message then. It'll have their own biases attached to it," Quinton replied.

Maelyn sighed. "You can't control the message, but you can influence its reception by targeting people who are most sympathetic to these ideas."

Quinton regarded her for a few seconds. "Clever. I almost forgot who I was dealing with."

She smiled. "I'm not just another pretty face."

Quinton laughed.

"All right. Let's run this idea through its paces. We need to put a plan together."

Hopefully, the truth about the Federation Wars would spread quickly and pressure the leaders of those areas to act, but it was a fine line they'd be walking. He didn't believe it would be a simple matter of informing spacers of the truth. They would need time to accept it. However, Quinton wasn't sure how much time he could give them, and he doubted the Sentinels, Admen Desher, or Harding Prime would do nothing while this was happening.

16

ADMEN DESHER'S CDA sat in the command chair on the bridge of an SN battlecruiser, the flagship of Scout Force Delta. The CDA was an archaic way to transport his PMC. He'd integrated his consciousness with the ship's vast computing core, which increased his capabilities. The CDA was perfectly still… lifeless. His specialized protocols had negated the micro habits that maintained the illusion that he was human. He was the next step in human evolution, transcending beyond everything he'd been before.

There were other CDA units on the bridge whose ESS cores had been overridden, so they were little more than high-functioning drones. They had a purpose to serve, as he did, but he'd failed to fulfill his purpose. After decades of traveling the galaxy, hunting for rogue PMCs, he'd presided over the biggest failure since the Federation Wars.

A priority subspace comlink registered with the ship's comms system. Admen knew who it was from even before the security protocols had been bypassed, as if they weren't even there. The main holoscreen powered on and the lighting on the bridge dimmed as if there was a massive power draw from the ship's main reactor. The CDA drones throughout the ship all stopped moving at once. He was alone.

Admen withdrew from the ship's systems and back into his CDA. His perception shifted from the vast sensor arrays of not just the ship he was on but of the entire fleet under his command, and he was reduced to the pitiful capabilities of a consciousness-driven android. Inferior optics focused on the main holoscreen where the resolution of a human head made of gleaming chrome regarded him with glowing eyes.

Admen stood up. The CDA's limbs, which hadn't moved in months, effortlessly rose to its feet. He stared at the floor, fearing to gaze upon the Prime.

"I've failed. My mission cannot continue. I wait for your judgment," Admen said.

The sound of a giant inhaling a deep breath could be heard throughout the bridge, and Admen nearly flinched. His protocols prevented such a human display, and yet the Prime exhibited characteristics that made him raise his gaze.

"If I had passed judgment on you already, you would no longer serve. But I'm here because there is cause for celebration," Harding Prime said. His voice sounded deep, as if it were sourced with the power of a massive gravity well from a collapsed star.

Admen lifted his gaze further until he finally stared into the glowing eyes of Harding Prime.

"Thousands of PMCs were activated throughout the galaxy. I deployed the scout forces, but there were already retrieval teams in the star systems. Their forces were minimal. Execution of their retrieval teams was swift. We closed in on the targets, but their ships exhibited capabilities equal to any Sentinel and outperformed our forces. I tracked them across galactic sectors, and our ships were drawn into an ambush. Spacers of this cycle have never used these tactics before. Therefore, I must assume they are from Commander Aldren."

"And after you realized they were luring your ships into a trap?"

"I coordinated our forces so we could overwhelm their traps, but Aldren kept them one step ahead. In spite of all my efforts, we were defeated."

"You were outmaneuvered. However, I've reviewed the mission logs and cannot find any fault with your response to these events. You tried to adapt to a situation that was not anticipated. Not impossible, given the events that occurred nearly six months ago. However, their tactics had changed, and we've learned a great deal about our enemies."

Admen increased his frame rate and allowed his VIs to analyze the data under the new context that Harding Prime had given him. "They revealed their capabilities. There is a limit to their reach."

"Yes. Most of the pieces are on the board, and it's time to move them around. I'm sending you a detailed intelligence briefing that you will review," Harding Prime said.

Admen did as he was ordered. "They're spreading lies about you."

"This was always a war of ideas as much as it was about warships and clever tactics."

"But they're making Elias Browning out to be a hero, and he wasn't."

"This Commander Aldren is part of Browning's plan. They might challenge Sentinel fleets, but not for long. They seek to unite the galaxy against us, but they will fail. It's the war of ideas where our true strength lies. They'll find that our grip on the galaxy is unyielding. I will use them, as I've used them all. Now that Browning's plan has finally been revealed, I am free to act."

Admen Desher considered what Harding Prime had said. "What about their ship? It's as big as a planet, and we don't know what its combat capabilities are."

"It's still just one ship, but I think it will be a fitting destination for me."

Admen's eyes widened. "You want the ship for yourself."

"I need what's on that ship, and you're going to help me draw it out. Aldren believes he can convince the galaxy to join his campaign against me. He'll find that we have allies throughout the galaxy, whether they realize it or not. They are all part of my plan."

"I'm ready to serve," Admen replied. He was eager to begin. He wanted to hunt down the rogue PMCs. "Our infiltration attacks on PMCs have failed. They've found a way to protect against it, and now the enemy has thousands of rogue PMCs on their side."

Harding Prime's eyes flashed. "We've hunted PMCs before. We can do so again, and this time we'll rid the galaxy of them forever."

A data comlink was added and Admen felt a massive download of information enter his system. Harding Prime was equipping him with the tools and intel he needed to fight, and fight he would.

17

"I CAN'T BELIEVE we had to wait a month for this," Quinton said.

Simon shrugged. "You wanted to meet with the leaders of the Servitors. These are their conditions," he said, gesturing toward a holoscreen of the data and high-res images from a stealth recon ship. The image was of a ship that had once been a high-end luxury ship meant for hosting diplomatic delegations.

The ship was considered neutral territory. Active scans didn't detect any weapons, and further analysis of the ship's design didn't reveal any weapons at all.

They stood in a hangar bay on the outer hull of the *Salvation* located a few hundred lightyears from the meeting place. A comlink sub-window to the bridge was on the upper right side of the holoscreen, and Quinton looked at Brandt.

"I don't like it," Brandt said from the main bridge. His eyes darted back and forth as he quickly read the data on his own screen.

"What's not to like? The unsecured location, or the high probability that this could be a trap," Quinton replied.

Brandt looked at him sternly. "That's not funny, Quinton."

"If any of the dozen or so summit meetings we've had for the past month are any indication, we need Servitor support, and we need it now. If this is the only way I can meet with one of their leaders, I'm going to take it."

Most of the summit meetings they'd hosted to gain support to fight the Sentinels had been met with significant hesitation and sometimes outright resistance. There were even promises of retribution for anyone simply considering what Quinton and other Alliance representatives were proposing. He'd thought the near-hysterical response would be a fringe response from outlier groups, but there was evidence of it in the reactions and comments made during the meetings. He could predict the response that they were likely to get after just a few minutes of interaction, which was another problem all by itself.

Quinton looked at Brandt. "I highly doubt that the Servitors are allied with Harding Prime or his Sentinels. You'll be just one space jump away."

Servitors preferred to meet in person, as Quinton had learned when he tracked down Kandria Pavond, a Servitor he'd meet while on a space station before finding the *Salvation*. She'd agreed to arrange this meeting for him.

"We could have invited them aboard the *Salvation*," Brandt replied.

"I did invite them, and their representative refused. This is the only way," Quinton said, and then added, "Besides, I've got Bentlae and fifty soldiers with me. If they're stupid enough to try something, they'll pay for it."

Brandt considered this for a second and then nodded. "I know. It's your call, Quinton. I'm not going to second-guess you. I've made my recommendation known to you. We've been getting new recruits and support has increased, but it's..."

"Not enough." Quinton finished for him. "If this doesn't work, we'll come up with something else."

The comlink window to the bridge disconnected and the sub-window disappeared.

Quinton looked at Simon. "Time to leave."

Simon stood up and they walked across the hangar to the *Wayfarer*. One of the conditions was that no ships with heavy armament were allowed to dock with the luxury ship *Oasis*.

Bentlae followed them, along with a mixed platoon of soldiers comprised of both humans and CDAs. He was allowed to bring a protective detail with him, and he was sure they would do the same. He wondered if their protection would be other Servitors or something else.

Simon glanced at the soldiers and then peered across the hangar. "I thought Maelyn was coming with us."

"She's already aboard," Quinton said.

Simon frowned. "She is? I didn't see her go aboard."

"She's the pilot."

They had a schedule to keep. Both parties had to arrive at the *Oasis* at the same time, or the meeting wouldn't happen. With so many people aboard the *Wayfarer,* it was a good thing they wouldn't be traveling for very long. Quinton and Simon headed to the bridge. Bentlae was setting up a temporary CIC in the mess hall.

Maelyn flew away from the *Salvation* and entered the jump coordinates into the nav computer.

The ship emerged within thirty light-years of the Jade Nebula. They sent a comlink to the *Oasis* and received an immediate reply. They were cleared to approach.

Quinton looked at Maelyn. She sat at the pilot's station and raised her eyebrows when she noticed him looking at her.

Quinton shrugged. "It's nothing."

"You better focus."

"Why? Is it because I'm about to meet a couple of Servitors?"

"Not just any Servitor. It's one of their leaders. She'll be highly intelligent and manipulative."

She had been distrustful of Servitors ever since they'd been betrayed by a spy impersonating one.

Quinton pursed his lips. "You know we could be meeting with a male Servitor."

Maelyn shook her head. "Not a chance. You requested this meeting, and Kandria Pavond set it up. There will be a woman in there."

A short time later they were aboard the *Oasis.* They went through the airlock into the docking tube, then entered the *Oasis* proper. The halls had thick blue carpeting, which Quinton imagined was comfortable to walk on, but those types of stimuli didn't really have an effect on him because of his artificial limbs. Simon commented on the carpets and Maelyn agreed. The walls were pristine—white with gold decorative accents. Maintenance bots ensured the ship's current immaculate state.

A holographic guide led them to the meeting hall. The crew of the ship was cordoned off to an area near the bridge.

They were led to a vast rotunda that gave them a stunning view of the nebula. Holographic golden chandeliers hung high above them, bathing the area in warm light. There were several fountains, and the sounds of carefully coordinated water acrobatics was both spectacular to see and also listen to. The leader of the Servitors was pulling out all the stops for this meeting.

In all of his recent travels throughout the galaxy, he'd rarely seen such a display of splendor. The only other place was aboard the *Salvation,* among its many parks and recreation areas. On the *Salvation*, these luxuries served a purpose that was crucial to maintaining the ship, which was designed for deployments that could last decades or more, but the *Oasis* was a status symbol in a galaxy where spacers struggled to survive.

The human soldiers Quinton had brought with him gazed around, awestruck, but the PMCs remained focused, looking for any sign of danger. Quinton scanned for any type of monitoring devices beyond that of normal life-support functions and didn't find anything.

After they made their way toward the center of the rotunda, a door on the opposite side opened and a similar-sized procession began to emerge. Kandra Pavond lead the procession into the rotunda. She had dark lavender skin and full, soft lips that twitched when she saw him. Her long, silky, black hair seemed to shimmer and sway as she strode toward them with both grace and poise.

Quinton glanced at Maelyn, who gave him an "I told you so" look. He bobbed his head once.

Walking behind Kandra Pavond was a woman with an ageless face that looked to have been chiseled to perfection. She was tall, and her long, slender arms moved with a dancer's grace. Her smoldering gaze seemed to swallow everyone nearby, though maybe it was just Quinton, but he doubted it. A growing silence seemed to take hold of them. It was as if his mind refused to accept what his eyes were seeing. She, too, had dark lavender skin but with long platinum hair that contrasted with her black, form-fitting dress. She was perfectly proportioned, as if she were designed for flawless excellence. Anyone who became a Servitor underwent a transformation if they survived the training, but Quinton couldn't figure out whether they engineered things beyond physical appearance. This woman had a powerful presence that was evident in the way she moved and how her gaze studied her surroundings.

The setting reminded him of the first time he'd seen Maelyn. She was a formidable woman who had appealed to him in such a way that could not be ignored. They'd tried, but sometimes a furtive glance or a comment filled with subtext was made and they were forced to acknowledge the inevitable. Their timing was awful. He wanted to look at Maelyn… and do what? Set her mind at ease? Let her know that these artificially enhanced women held no power over him? No, he wouldn't do that. He didn't need to, and she didn't need his reassurance. Maelyn knew her own worth and knew Quinton wasn't foolish enough to let a pair of artificially perfected faces twist him up into knots. The other men nearby were another matter.

The two Servitors were surrounded by their own protective detail of cybernetically enhanced soldiers. They were cloaked, but they held their weapons with practiced efficiency. They were Yezierians–highly sought-after mercenaries known for their prowess and loyalty to whomever held their contract. They certainly had brain enhancements designed for anything from combat to infiltration. He didn't know what their limits were, and he hoped the CDAs and soldiers he'd brought with him were up to the task should anything go awry.

The Yezierians spread out strategically, locating themselves to be at odds with Quinton's soldiers. There was no open invitation of hostilities, just the calm assessment of well-seasoned combat platoons who served on opposite sides of the conflict. If Quinton were a betting man, he knew who he thought would survive an engagement. He just wasn't sure how high the price would be.

Kandra Pavond smiled. "Hello, Quinton. Quite a difference in locale from when last we met."

He smiled. "Hello, Kandra. Thank you for setting up this meeting."

Kandra gestured toward the Servitor next to her. "I'm proud to introduce to you Yvonne Zariah. She sits on our leadership council."

Quinton wasn't sure whether he should stand up straight, bow his head, or some combination of the two. He did neither. "Thank you for coming all this way, Counselor. If we're exchanging titles, I'm Admiral Quinton Aldren."

"Formerly of the Acheron Confederacy Navy," Counselor Zariah said.

"My reputation precedes me," Quinton said and introduced Maelyn and Simon.

He noticed a passing thought about how Guttman would have loved to be there with them and made a mental note to follow up with Becker and Oscar after the bazillion other things he had to do first.

Counselor Zariah's full lips curved a little. "Rumors abound throughout the galaxy. We were pleased that you finally contacted us."

"Sometimes it's difficult to figure out what's wild speculation and what's truth," Quinton said.

"Kandra has apprised the council of what you wish to discuss, and we've reviewed the data you sent."

"So, we can get right to the point then," Quinton said.

She pursed her lips in thought and then began to walk aside from the others. Quinton glanced at Kandra and then moved to the counselor's side. She gave him a sidelong glance and then looked toward the panoramic view of the Jade Nebula in all its brilliance.

"It's remarkable, isn't it?" she said.

Quinton barely contained an irritated sigh. "I've seen it."

She snorted a little. "Of course, but have you really looked at it? Taken in its majestic beauty as part of a galaxy that is untouched and simply exists?"

They were sparring. Even with the platitudes about how beautiful the nebula was, they were each seeking to influence the conversation in the direction they wanted. Quinton wasn't sure what Counselor Zariah wanted.

Quinton considered his words carefully before responding. "It'll only be this way for a certain amount of time before things change. That's just the way it works."

Counselor Zariah looked at him, her violet eyes considering. She tilted her head to the side, exposing the pleasant lines of a strong jaw and neckline. "And are you that 'change'?"

"Would you prefer that things remain as they are?" Quinton countered.

"Changes introduced over time are less invasive… less violent, and are lasting, but that's not what's in your proposal."

"Spacers have a right to know the truth."

"We're not opposed to the truth. However, we don't view truth as a blunt instrument that creates more chaos than it attempts to solve," she said.

Quinton frowned in thought. "I understand the information we're sharing is difficult for people to accept, but they'll be better for it in the long run."

She arched an eyebrow. "That's just it. You cannot guarantee that. There are too many variables to consider, even for you." She looked at the other PMCs. "Or for them."

She was familiar with how PMCs worked. She knew they excelled at analysis and predictable outcomes.

"Work with me then. If you're so concerned about how the truth will be received, help us deliver the message," Quinton said.

"That's just it. What you're offering brings more chaos into the lives of spacers, not less. The Federation Wars mean something different to us than it does to you. For us, it is the past that we need to move away from, but for you and them," she said, gesturing toward the PMCs, "the experience is more immediate. Your 'truth' might be a huge setback for the stability of spacers everywhere."

"*My* truth?" Quinton said. "I didn't make this up. This is what happened."

"I don't question whether you believe it or not, and I must admit it does put events that have occurred in a different light. However, our options aren't limited to your proposal on how to deal with the problem."

"The Sentinels aren't just a problem. They're a menace. They're the enemy."

"And they're predictable. They only become unpredictable when PMCs are introduced into the mix."

Quinton couldn't allow himself to become defensive, but it wasn't easy. At least this was a discussion, and that was something more than he'd been able to have at any of the summits. "At first, I thought the Sentinels were a malfunctioning war machine left over from the Federation Wars, but they're worse. They're an instrument of control meant to keep the galaxy stagnant in its development."

Counselor Zariah seemed to consider what he said, but he couldn't be sure. Servitors were difficult to read. He engaged his SCS analysis protocols. Multiple VIs began creating various simulations using the data Quinton was able to detect by what he saw. Everything from micro expression, skin temperature, heart rate and more, were scrutinized, but he couldn't be sure whether the counselor's outward expression revealed what she actually believed. Servitors were adept at performing, and to have risen among the Servitor ranks, she must be among the best.

"There is truth to what you're saying, but you also don't acknowledge what the Sentinels have given us," she replied.

"What have they given you?"

"Stability. A chance for spacers to gather together and recover from the utter devastation that came from the Federation Wars."

"Gather together? Scavenging off old spaceships, space stations, dead planets —that's not living or recovering," he said, his voice rising.

Counselor Zariah stared at him. "At least they're not—"

"Killing each other?" he asked.

She blinked at him and frowned in surprise.

"So, the highest standard of living is based on whether spacers are trying to kill each other while competing for the resources that are left."

"You're oversimplifying what I'm saying."

"I don't believe I am."

"We work to spread peace and stability. That's what all Servitors work toward."

"And remain terrorized by the Sentinels, something they can't control or fight against. That's not living. That's dying slowly. That's cramming them into neat little boxes where everyone does exactly as what's expected of them, all so we can avoid another war with the very thing they ought to be resisting. All that's required is one case of mistaken identity or being fooled into attacking a civilian target and the Sentinels kill without mercy and without reason."

"They have reasons. They just don't communicate them to us."

"That's no way to live. That's like living within sight of an auto-defense turret that might open fire at any moment. What's to stop them attacking?"

"Attacking what?" Counselor Zariah asked.

"Anything. Everything. Does it matter?"

She considered this for a few moments, blinking. "Can you protect them? Can you protect everyone from the Sentinels?"

They stared at each other for a few moments, and Quinton became acutely aware of everyone around them. Maelyn, Simon, and the other soldiers listened to them intently. Even the Yezierian mercenaries paid more attention to Quinton and Counselor Zariah than the other soldiers. She was clever. There was no denying that. Counselor Zariah had maneuvered their discussion so he'd have to answer this question, and he had to answer honestly.

"I can't promise that. No one can promise total security like that," Quinton said.

Counselor Zariah smiled a little. "I know, Admiral Aldren. I just wanted to see whether you knew it as well. A lesser leader might have tried to convince me that they could protect us from the Sentinels."

Quinton couldn't help but feel like he'd passed some sort of test, but he wasn't sure what the outcome was. "All right, what does this mean for my proposal? Will you help us convince spacers that they should support the Alliance?"

"I can't do that," she replied.

Great, another door was being shut in his face. Quinton was starting to believe that maybe the spacers had never successfully rebelled against the Sentinels because they were already defeated in their hearts and minds.

He sighed. "That's disappointing. You see, I was under the impression that Servitors endeavored for the benefit of the galaxy."

"We do," she said.

"Then why not help us? With your help, we could get enough support to rid the galaxy of Sentinels forever."

"It's not that simple, Admiral Aldren. There is a price for what you want. The cost in lives to fight your war is much higher than if people endure. Eventually, the Sentinels will fall into disrepair."

Quinton blinked. She didn't completely disagree with what he'd proposed. It just wasn't the right time for it.

"We need time to evaluate how spacers react to what you're telling them. You're going around established government leaders to appeal directly to the people. We will not endorse it, nor will we speak out against it, at least in the immediate future," she said.

"So, you'll wait."

"Yes. Most members of the council believe that civic unrest will spread out of control. That would force our hand."

Quinton regarded her for a second. "And you can't say whether you'll support us or be a voice against us."

She nodded. "I'm glad we know where we both stand on these things. I know you're disappointed, but I think clarity is worth the perception gained from this interaction."

Counselor Zariah turned to leave.

"Wait," Quinton said.

She stopped and looked at him.

"I'd like to make a request for your council to consider. Can you do that for me?"

"I can do that," she replied.

"Not everyone in every sector has reacted to the news about Browning the same way, and it's difficult to determine whether contacting them is doing more harm than good. I want to keep the lines of communication open between us."

"How do you propose we do that?"

"By being open and honest. If the council is leaning toward opposing what we're doing, would you allow us to defend our actions? It might not change anything, but like you said, sometimes a little bit of clarity can go a long way toward lasting peace," Quinton said.

Counselor Zariah pursed her lips in thought, and Quinton didn't think it was for show. She was considering it. "The only thing I can promise is to convey what you've requested. In fact, they'll be able to review the entirety of this exchange." She paused for a moment, looking at him. "You're very different than what I expected, Admiral Aldren."

"I don't know whether that's a compliment or a mere statement of fact."

She smiled a little. "No," she said and walked away from him.

He couldn't think of a snappy reply without making himself appear foolish, so he didn't say anything. There was nothing left for him to do. He signaled to the others, and they headed toward the doors. He needed time to think about what Counselor Zariah had said, and almost as important were the things she didn't say.

18

After they returned to the *Salvation*, they left the Jade Nebula. Quinton made a recording of his meeting with Counselor Zariah available to Brandt and the other Alliance leaders. After weeks of a steady influx of volunteers and provisional support by different galactic groups, civil unrest had spread among spacers across galactic sectors. Some of the allies who'd promised assistance were pressured to withdraw their support, reneging on their promise. This pressure came from spacers in the sectors but also from business arrangements made between various unions.

Trenton Draven, the leader of the Collective, had become more active within the Alliance. He committed more resources and intelligence reports, giving them insight into where Sentinel ships had been spotted. It was something, at least. Quinton wasn't sure what more he could do to convince Draven to commit to the Alliance completely, but perhaps he was expecting too much. Sherilyn Cantos and Severin Brandt believed it was only a matter of time before the Collective joined the Alliance. Quinton hoped that was true.

Quinton was in his quarters aboard the *Salvation*. These "quarters" represented a significant living space that was more like a huge apartment with access to personal gardens. The gardens covered several kilometers in diameter, and he had his own personal lake. His highly acute auditory sensors heard the scampering of Stumpy as the critter from Zeta-Six leaped from treetop to treetop. It had taken Stumpy all of ten seconds to claim the park as his own living space. Radek made sure food was available that Stumpy had to find.

Quinton had an unspoken agreement regarding shared custody of Stumpy with Simon. The young spacer had taken care of Stumpy when they thought Quinton was dead. Stumpy had been extremely wary of Quinton in the beginning, and it wasn't until Quinton spoke that the little fuzzball recognized him. Like a cat, Stumpy had his favorite person, and it wasn't Quinton. It was definitely Simon. Quinton was just a consolation prize.

The door to his quarters chimed and Radek let whoever was out there inside. Quinton wasn't alarmed. No one who didn't have clearance would be allowed through. He did have a meeting with senior staff scheduled, but it wasn't for another half hour. He'd been planning to review more of Grand Admiral Browning's logs, but that would have to wait.

Maelyn lifted her chin in greeting as she walked over to him.

Quinton arched an eyebrow. "You just couldn't wait to see me?"

She chuckled and said, "Something like that."

She joined him at the lake and Quinton updated the atmospheric settings, shifting them from bright daylight to that of a setting star. The artificial skies above became awash with pinks and twilight.

Maelyn looked down. "Don't," she said.

"I thought you'd like it."

She inhaled deeply and sighed, then gave him a knowing look and smiled a little. "I do, but…"

Quinton changed the settings back and the area became as brightly lit as it'd been before. "It's fine. You're early. I guess you wanted to talk to me before the others arrived."

He gestured toward the nearby patio that had a few couches and chairs on it. He sat on one of the chairs and Maelyn took the couch. Rubbing the cushion next to her, she sighed.

"I'm starting to take this ship for granted," Maelyn said.

"It's just a couch."

She looked at him. "This place is breathtaking at the least of times. This is how people are meant to live. We're not meant to stay crammed aboard overcrowded space stations or barely habitable colony worlds."

Quinton's eyebrows twitched. "You'll get no arguments from me," he said and waited for her to continue.

"I've been thinking about your meeting with Counselor Zariah… the Servitors."

She wasn't the only one.

"Okay, what did you come up with?"

"What if she was right?"

"About what?"

"About the unrest that's happening—spacers effectively choosing a side without really understanding why they're in conflict."

Quinton frowned. "It seems pretty straightforward to me."

She gave him a knowing look that was part playful and only slightly annoyed. "Work with me here."

Quinton laughed. "I am." Her gaze hardened. "Okay. I'll be serious. This whole thing was always going to force people to choose a side."

"What if we're wrong to make them choose?"

"You really want to just let things go on as they have been?"

Maelyn shook her head. "No, but people should have the option to sit things out, you know? Not get caught in the crossfire."

"We'll do the best we can, but I'm not sure how it can be avoided."

Maelyn flinched a little and looked away. "What good is freeing the galaxy if we have to burn half of it to do it?"

Quinton stared at her for a few seconds and then also looked away. Maelyn wasn't one to avoid making tough decisions, so he wasn't sure why she was questioning their actions now.

"Maelyn, I don't want to… burn half the galaxy to destroy the Sentinels. Where is this coming from?"

"I know you don't, but what if the Sentinels don't give us another choice?"

"We can't control the Sentinels."

She stared at him. "We have some influence over their actions based on how we conduct ourselves."

Quinton nodded in understanding. "If I could predict how the Sentinels would react to everything we've done and are going to do, I could skip a lot of steps and take the battle directly to them." He paused for a moment. "We'll adapt to the current situation as best we can. I can't promise anything more than that."

"It's such a slippery slope."

Quinton had been on that slope before when fighting the Jordanis before the Federation Wars. "It is. All of us know it. I saw the latest batch of reports. Is that what's bothering you? Do you think we should stop appealing directly to the people and only go through government leaders?"

Maelyn brushed her fingers through her hair and folded her arms. "No. Putting spacers in a position to make up their own minds is the right decision. I just didn't anticipate how much of a divide it was going to cause."

"Neither did I, but you'd know more about that than I would."

She tilted her head to the side and eyed him. "You're part of this galaxy too, Quinton. You're here. You're one of us. There's no going back for you."

Quinton blinked a few times and his eyebrows pushed forward. "I know."

"Do you?"

Twin sapphire eyes regarded him coolly. He nodded.

"Then stop passing judgment on the rest of us. We know things were different in your time. Better. But it's still off-putting."

"I'm not passing... Okay, fine I do judge. I can't help it. I'm not doing it to hurt you or anyone else, even when most spacers regard people like me with fear and vitriol. Things were different in my time. I'd be lying to you if I said I didn't miss those times… my old life. But I know it's gone. Even when we finally defeat the Sentinels, the galaxy won't be the same, and spacers like me will have to find a place in it."

Maelyn just looked at him, and he attempted to read what was in her eyes, trying to guess what she was thinking. She seemed sympathetic without pitying him.

She reached out and touched his hand. "I thought we'd get your body regrown and transfer your consciousness like you wanted."

Quinton did want that, or at least he used to. He wasn't so sure anymore. The cybernetic avatar was several iterations above the standard CDA, and he felt more human in it, but there were differences.

"You do still want that, right?" Maelyn asked.

Quinton stared back at her, feeling that his answer would count for more than he could ever anticipate. If he chose to remain a PMC, would that be it for whatever future was in store for them? It would be so easy to lie right now, but he wouldn't do that to her. She deserved better than a lie.

The door chimed. Radek would start letting the meeting attendees in.

"I don't know," he said and saw her pained expression, but her warm hand stayed on top of his. He swallowed. "Why does it feel like if I choose to remain a PMC, this thing between us is over. I don't want that."

Maelyn pulled her hand away and glanced toward the hall behind them. Quinton heard Brandt speaking to someone else.

Maelyn stood up and turned toward him. "Neither do I," she said.

Brandt walked toward them, followed by Sherilyn Cantos. The director of the DUC's gaze took in the serene sight, and her mouth opened a little, which evaporated into a broad smile.

"Director Cantos, how are you enjoying your first visit to the *Salvation*?" Quinton asked.

Sherilyn inhaled deeply and sighed. "I never expected this. Larger space stations have parks as well, but nothing like this. This is similar to the colony worlds referenced on Starbase Endurance."

"How is the colony relocation effort going?"

"Well. Better than expected, actually," she replied.

Before the Federation Wars, the Acheron Confederacy had a secret automated terraforming project where over a dozen rocky planets without any life on them were transformed into living worlds. The process had taken quite a few decades to achieve. Almost all records of the project had been erased or lost when the Acheron Confederacy was destroyed until Quinton discovered references to a colony world on an ACN starbase that had somehow been overlooked during the Federation Wars. Quinton wondered if Browning had had anything to do with it but hadn't found any record of it. He hadn't searched that hard.

"I see more of the defense platforms for those star systems are getting closer to being completed."

Sherilyn nodded. "We'll feel a lot better about security when they are."

"So will I," said Brandt. "I'm glad we've been able to keep the secret for as long as we have."

The defense platforms could provide enough of a deterrent for most deep space salvagers who happened on those star systems, but they wouldn't be enough against more concerted efforts, and certainly not against the Sentinels.

"References to those systems in star charts show as poor in resources. It's been that way as far back as there *are* references," Maelyn said. "There's no reason for salvagers to explore them when there are much better options. If the Sentinels knew about them, they would have already been there."

They were joined by PMCs Belinda Hinton and Commander Bentlae.

Quinton found that the more people who attended these meetings, the longer they went on, so he tried to limit the participants as much as he could.

Sherilyn looked at him. "We're going to need to expand the scope of these meetings to include more Alliance representatives."

Quinton smiled. "I was just thinking that these summits are much more productive with fewer people."

"The Alliance won't succeed unless supporters believe they have a say," Belinda said. The emerald eyes of her CDA regarded him. "This is beyond standard crew mindset. We're building a new federation, after all."

Maelyn leaned forward. "Those forums have their place, but we can't allow them to bring all forward progress to a halt."

Quinton threw a small nod in Maelyn's direction.

"Would you be surprised if I agreed with you?" Sherilyn replied.

The internal resources Quinton had allocated to SCS analysis tracking this meeting spiked with new possibilities. "A little."

"Quinton," Sherilyn said, "the people who've joined the Alliance need to see you. They need to work with PMCs at least a little bit, so they become more accustomed to it. They're already more open—"

"Minded to working with PMCs," Quinton said, cutting her off. "We don't have PMCs to spare. They're all filling crucial roles here on the *Salvation* and aboard ships of the fleet."

Sherilyn didn't give any indication she was annoyed that he'd cut her off. "Not all PMCs are dedicated to combat and operational roles. There are—"

"PMCs like Belinda and other civilian types are even rarer than the combat PMCs."

This time Sherilyn narrowed her gaze and looked at Brandt.

"Stop it," Maelyn said so quietly that only Quinton heard it.

He looked at her and she gave a slight shake of her head.

"Perhaps it's time for a quick break," Belinda Hinton suggested.

Quinton felt a flash of annoyance. Radek had put up a warning on his internal HUD about the unsanctioned use of the Sapient Combat Simulation system. He'd gotten used to seeing the data analysis windows in his field of vision, but he disabled the SCS system and the data windows disappeared, along with all his insight into the exchange.

"Wait," Quinton said. "The implant-assisted rapid learning is going well. We could try to produce more of those and make them available to members of the Alliance."

Sherilyn considered this for a moment. "They would appreciate it, but it wouldn't instantly remove peoples' biases."

"Bias modification takes time, but it depends on how deeply seated the biases are," Belinda said.

"We've got to start somewhere," Maelyn said.

Quinton nodded and looked at Belinda. "Come up with a plan for expanding PMC interaction with Alliance members, but it cannot interfere with priority mission objectives."

"Understood, Admiral," she replied.

Quinton turned toward Brandt. "We need to locate Sentinel operation bases. We can't fight them if we don't know where they are."

"Agreed," Brandt replied. "We've been chasing down leads that are coming through our informants but haven't found anything yet."

"The priority needs to go up for this. If the informants aren't yielding any usable intel, we need to move beyond that."

"Did you have anyone in mind?" Brandt asked.

The Sentinels had reduced their activity recently, and that made Quinton even more concerned. They were hiding and more likely coordinating for a major offensive. They certainly had enough ships for it.

"It's no secret we're looking for the Sentinels, but while I want to increase our efforts in pursuing them, I don't want to increase their awareness of it," Quinton said.

"Do you think they monitor communications across the sectors?" Sherilyn asked.

"Yes, but I don't know how they do it. I bet it's not everywhere, meaning that they randomize the way they monitor comms, which makes it even more difficult to find."

"Okay, I understand that, but I don't fully understand why you want to pursue this… any more than you did before," she said.

Quinton regarded them all for a few seconds. "It was meeting with Counselor Zariah that got me thinking about it. She asked if we could guarantee the safety of all spacers."

"Yes, and you gave her an honest answer. She was using it to judge your character," Maelyn said.

"The Sentinels must go *somewhere* when they're not roaming the galaxy. They need to refuel and resupply. They must have operation centers, but no one has ever found them. If they did, they were probably hunted down."

Brandt nodded. "They couldn't afford that data to be shared, but I also think they move those operation centers so they never stay anywhere for long."

"That makes it more difficult, but it doesn't change why we need to find them and take them out. If we find those places and destroy them, we can prove to the galaxy that they can be stopped. The Sentinels can be defeated," Quinton said.

"We'd build momentum both on the battlefield and in gaining support," Brandt said.

"Precisely."

Commander Bentlae shifted in his seat, and Quinton knew he did it to remind the others that he was still there. It was a CDA's equivalent of clearing one's throat. "Sentinels operate on the fringes. Spacers restrict their travels to specific regions in their respective sectors. Most of them, anyway. The spacers we need to engage are the ones who also work in the fringes where other spacers are afraid or don't have the resources to go."

Quinton considered this for a few moments and then nodded. "You've got a point. It would certainly narrow our search."

"Yes," Brandt replied. "But those groups are not known for being the most cooperative."

Quinton smiled. "Then we'll just need to figure out how to motivate them. What will it take to get them to work with us?"

"And if they won't?" Brandt asked.

Quinton regarded the DUC admiral. "Then we stop playing nice."

Brandt appeared as if he'd expected that answer, and the meeting ended shortly after that. They left Quinton's quarters. He wanted to check on Simon and the progress he was making with the PMCs he was working on.

"Quinton, a moment, please," Maelyn said.

The others continued down the corridor.

Quinton gestured back toward the door to his rooms. "Do you want to go back inside?"

She shook her head. "No, this won't take long."

"Okay," he replied, and they began to walk at a leisurely pace.

"What are you doing?"

Quinton arched an eyebrow toward her. "You're going to have to give me more than that."

"There's something different about you."

Quinton smiled. "I'd like to think so."

"Stop, I'm serious. You keep cutting people off when they're speaking as if you already know what they're going to say. I've been noticing it a lot lately, and I'm not the only one."

Quinton frowned. Had he been doing that? "I hadn't noticed."

"Well, I have, and like I just said, I'm not the only one."

If he told her he was using the SCS system to analyze all the interactions he'd been having, he didn't think she would approve. In fact, he knew she wouldn't, especially if she found out that it was violating SCS protocols and that he'd been overriding them.

She peered at him. "I know you can increase the speed at which you think, so sometimes interacting the old-fashioned way must be painstakingly slow at times, but you need to stop doing it—cutting people off, thinking you know what they're going to say before they say it. They might surprise you."

Actually, Quinton had reliable data with high probability rates for accurately predicting what they were going to say. It wasn't perfect, but he was getting better.

"Why?"

Maelyn raised her eyebrows. "Why? Because it makes you an insufferable jerk."

Quinton chuckled. "Why don't you tell me what you really think?"

She smiled. "Well, it does. You didn't use to be this way. Did something change? Are your… is everything all right?"

She was going to ask about the integrity checks of his ESS, the psychological profilers that determined whether a PMC was stable or not.

"I'm fine," he said. "I'll try not to cut people off anymore. I promise."

"Good."

"See, I can be reasonable."

Maelyn rolled her eyes, and Quinton laughed.

19

Aris guided the counter-grav platform up to the star class jumper's cargo hold. The doors had several prominent dents and a whole lot of scratches, and he was sure they were wedged shut.

He gritted his teeth and exhaled forcefully through his nose.

"Look at this thing," Augus said from down below, gesturing toward the beat-up ship. "I'm surprised it's still space worthy."

Aris grunted a reply and banged a fist on the door's control panel. It didn't open. Some captains were quite protective of their ships, and others just seemed to give up on them. He doubted that this ship would be in service a year from now.

"That's not going to open it."

Aris looked down at his coworker. "Thanks for that, Augus."

He peered at the scorch marks around the panel. It looked like the captain of this ship used a plasma torch to unlock the cargo hold and then applied patches to reseal it rather than getting it repaired. Aris reached into his toolkit and pulled out a pocket plasma torch. He thumbed the stud on the side, but it didn't respond. He checked the fuel level and saw that it was empty. His eyes went skyward.

"Oh, I forgot to tell you that I had to use your torch yesterday."

Aris shook his head. Augus frequently borrowed his tools and never replaced the power cores. "You don't say. How about throwing up a new fuel cell, will ya?" This was to be his last offload of the day and he was anxious to get home to Riya. Finally, their shifts had aligned so they could be home with their children.

Aris heard shouting from the neighboring platform. An argument had broken out between the dockworkers and the crew of the ship. This was happening more often lately, and Aris didn't care for it at all. He didn't set the purchase price for recovered salvage. He just got to deliver the "good" news.

"Augus. Hey, Augus! Did you hear me? Throw up a fuel cell or we'll never get out of here," Aris said.

Augus stared at the spacers arguing on the nearby platform while he squatted down to reach into the spare fuel-cell pack and rummaged through, pulling one out. More spacers gathered on the main dock, and the level of shouting increased. Aris shouted for him to hurry up. Augus tore his gaze away from the commotion and tossed the glowing fuel cell. Aris caught it and dropped the depleted cell back to his coworker, but the fuel cell bounced off his hand and Augus scrambled to catch it.

Aris shook his head and looked away. He made short work of opening the panel and then accessed the door controls. There was a brown and red lever inside that looked to have been reattached more than a few times. Aris grabbed it and pulled. After a second of resistance, the lever came down. He heard the unlocking mechanism inside, and the exterior cargo hold opened.

Aris peered inside. The hold was jam-packed with material the salvagers had gotten off a derelict spaceship. He studied the cargo with a practiced eye, judging how much the salvagers would be paid for this kind of haul. He doubted it would be much. It never was, and judging by the state of their ship, it never would be. He could tell a lot about a spacer by how they maintained their ship.

"How's it look?" Augus shouted.

Aris looked down. "They've got a full hold."

"Good. I'll be right up," Augus said and gestured toward a member of the ship's crew. The crewman opened a comlink, no doubt alerting the rest of the crew that the offload was about to begin.

"Not that it's worth all that much," Aris muttered to himself.

It took them another hour to empty the cargo hold. Aris had to use the plasma torch to remove some of the larger pieces that the salvagers had shoved inside. The offloading platform was full of various control modules, old sensor arrays, depleted fuels cells that would likely never hold a charge again, and several construction mech suits that hadn't been used in decades. None of it was in working order, but they could be repurposed.

Aris closed the cargo-hold doors and patched the control panel. The counter-grav platform lowered to the floor, and Aris initiated the scans that analyzed the materials found. The captain of the ship watched the scan being performed. He had a rough look to him, as if he was there purely to intimidate the dockworkers. It worked.

Aris kept a stunner in his tool kit that he hoped still had a charge. Several members of the crew watched the scans continue, as if certain they would be given an unfair result. Aris glanced at his partner. Augus was still watching the next platform over. Dock security was trying to sort out the mess. At least backup wouldn't be far if needed. He glanced at the captain and his crew, doubting dock security would arrive in time.

"Problems on the dock?" Captain Jareth asked.

Aris shrugged. "Don't know," he replied, not wanting to bring attention to the low payouts for salvage. "The scan should be done in a few minutes."

Aris walked toward his partner. "How's the rowdy bunch over there?"

Augus glanced at him. "I couldn't really make it out. They weren't fighting about what the salvage they brought was worth. It was something else."

Aris felt a chill on his brow. Tensions between spacers seemed to be increasing. The salvage had already been offloaded and was being hauled away, but there was still arguing going on. Several fights broke out, and security forces were quick to quell them. Riya wanted him to find another job—anything to get off the docks—but without any connections to speak of those jobs didn't pay enough.

His work tablet chimed, and he returned to Captain Jareth. Aris examined the report and then made a passing gesture toward the captain.

Captain Jareth lifted his own tablet and read the report, which contained a detailed list of the materials they'd found. As he read, the lines of his craggy face deepened into a tight frown.

Aris tried to position himself so he could keep an eye on the captain *and* the crew. They seemed to sense their captain's disapproval, and a few glared at Aris, as if the lack of value in their salvage was somehow his fault.

Captain Jareth showed the report to one of them, who quickly skimmed it and nodded.

Captain Jareth looked at Aris. "I guess there's very little point in trying to dispute this."

"You can try. They might give you a few more credits," Aris replied. Several of the crew edged closer to him, and his hand edged closer to the stunner. "You know, I've noticed several ships bringing in some good salvage from Sector 74. Might be worth checking the next time you go out."

Captain Jareth regarded him for a few seconds and the ship's crew waited. "We'll check it out," he said and then looked at the report again. "Aris."

The captain said his name like a dark promise of serious retribution if the tip didn't yield anything useful. Riya was right. He needed to get off the docks. It was getting too dangerous to work them.

"Good luck," Aris replied, keeping his tone light.

Captain Jareth thumbed his tablet, accepting it, and credits were transferred to the ship's account.

Aris backed away and grabbed Augus on his way off the platform.

They crossed to the main dock and Augus shook his head. "I thought he was going to take your head off."

Aris's mouth was already dry, and a shiver went through him. "Same," he said.

Dock security was still trying to quell the fighting on the nearby platform. Several spacers had been taken into custody and were lined up along the walls of the main dock. Other spacers gathered on the dock to watch.

Aris shook his head. "I'm not sticking around for this. You coming?"

Augus stole another glance and then nodded. "Yeah, probably not worth it."

They hastened toward the doors away from the main dock, but the walkways were crowded with spacers and dockworkers alike. Ship traffic had increased recently, bringing with it a surge of spacers staying at the space dock. They brought news with them, and not all of it was well received. Aris normally didn't pay attention to rumors that salvagers brought back from their journeys. Most of it was outright false and meant to mislead other salvagers from finding a good haul.

"Did you hear the latest?" Augus asked as they entered the queue to the commons area.

Aris didn't want to hear about any more rumors. He just wanted to get through the commons area and catch a tram back to deck 92, domicile level. Spacers bunched together as they went through security checkpoints and decontamination.

Augus repeated himself, and Aris shook his head.

"There have been more Sentinel attacks. Remember them happening a few months back? It's started again."

"Says who?"

Several spacers looked over at them, and Aris ignored them.

Augus stared at him for a moment. "You really haven't heard? You don't pay any attention at all?"

Aris frowned and rolled his eyes a little. "No, I'm not obsessed with the newsnets like you are."

"They get it right, sometimes, and those stories are lining up with what I've been hearing other spacers talking about," Augus replied defensively.

"It's probably all coming from the same source."

The line moved forward. Aris hated it. He didn't like crowds, which was why he preferred working on the docks. If he'd gotten done with his work sooner, he could have made it through the checkpoint without waiting in line for an hour.

"That doesn't mean it's not true. You can't ignore this stuff. I've been telling you this for months," Augus said.

A visiting spacer looked at them. He was of average height and wore a tan work suit that would be fine for light duty in a vacuum. "Your friend is right. I've been hearing the same thing at other stations."

Augus smiled and gestured toward Aris. "You see, it's not just here," he said and looked at the spacer, sharing a knowing look.

Aris glanced around and saw that other people were listening and seemed to all share the same knowing look, as if they were all in on some kind of secret.

"Sentinels have always been around. They've been here before, and nothing has happened. It's just the way it is," Aris replied.

"That was before. They attack now," Augus replied.

"Why would they attack?"

Augus shook his head and rolled his eyes. "You've got to be kidding me. It's because of the PMCs. They're being activated everywhere, and it brings the Sentinels, fast."

Aris frowned in thought. Several spacers around them nodded in agreement. The Sentinel attacks had died down almost as quickly as they'd begun. However, he felt his doubts slip away as if he were waking from a nap.

"Watch this," Augus said.

He lifted his tablet and showed Aris several news stories about increased Sentinel activities. Aris watched them, and when they were finished, Augus showed him something else. "This is the latest. It's about some new data cache proving that PMCs are being reactivated to fight the Sentinels."

Aris frowned. "That's nothing new. Sentinels were created to protect us from the PMCs."

Augus smiled, looking as if he knew a secret Aris didn't. "Yeah, but they're also saying that the Sentinels are here to keep us contained. And," he said before Aris could interrupt, "PMCs, the Acheron Confederacy… all that stuff is wrong. Everything we thought we knew about it was wrong."

They edged closer to the checkpoint.

Augus watched him as he considered it.

Aris opened his mouth to speak a few times and then shook his head.

Augus gave him a knowing look. "It's crazy, right?"

The automated checkpoint flashed a green light and Augus walked through it.

Aris kept thinking about what he'd been told, and his mind raced with thoughts that ranged from outright denial to acknowledging that perhaps there was something worth considering.

Aris walked through the checkpoint, and after a quick decom scan, he was allowed into the station proper.

The commons area was even more crowded than the docks. Augus waited for him, smirking.

"So, what do you think about all that stuff?" Aris asked.

"What stuff?"

"Come on, stop jerking me around. I don't have time for this," Aris said. He looked at the corridors across the commons area that lead to the tram system. It was filled with spacers moving through. At this rate, he was never going to get home to Riya.

"Do I think we've been lied to for decades and that the PMCs are our saviors?" Augus asked, and Aris nodded. "No," he said, shaking his head. "No way. If you were smart, you'd believe the same. There's no way the Sentinels are going to hurt us."

Aris was about to reply when the spacer they'd been in line with through the checkpoint came over to them.

"Did I hear you right? You think the Sentinels are here for our protection?" he asked.

Augus sneered. "You're one of those."

The spacer stiffened. "One of what?"

"He didn't mean anything by it," Aris said, but the spacer glared at him.

"Yes, I did," Augus said. "Don't tell me you believe this PMC nonsense. They're a scourge on the galaxy."

"You're wrong!" the spacer shouted and lunged toward Augus.

Aris was shoved to the side, and he knocked into another spacer, starting a chain reaction. The noise level escalated as spacers screamed at one another. Aris spun around. He was knocked to the side as two spacers began fighting right next to him. Several more scuffles erupted all around him. As Aris scrambled to get out of the way, he caught a glimpse of Augus wrestling with another spacer.

A spacer grabbed Aris from behind and pulled him backward. His head slammed into the ground as his vision swam and darkness closed in. He tried to crawl away, but more people stumbled on top of him. He became trapped under a crushing pile of spacers, and the breath was forced from his lungs. Something wet got into his eyes, and he rubbed them and stared at his hands. There was blood on them. Aris tried to crawl forward, but he couldn't move. He couldn't breathe. The last thing he thought of before he couldn't see anything at all was that he just wanted to get home to Riya. He'd promise never to go back to work at the docks ever again, but he never got the chance.

20

QUINTON THOUGHT he'd spend most of his time on the *Salvation's* bridge, but he was wrong. The bridge was probably the second or third location on the ship where he spent his time. On second thought, he'd probably spent most of his time in transit, traveling the ship. Even at the startling speeds that the trams and aircars could move, it still took a bit of time. At least he could get some work done while traveling the planet-sized spaceship.

The *Salvation* was meant to service a crew of over five hundred thousand, which still left plenty of room. At least another hundred thousand could live comfortably on the ship. Most of the *Salvation's* colossal bulk was allotted to hangar bays for the fleet of ships being built and maintained, as well as weapons. The *Salvation* was, first and foremost, a warship capable of delivering huge amounts of destruction. There were also autofactories and processing plants so raw materials could be used to maintain the entire fleet and the ship itself almost indefinitely.

Quinton wondered more than once how long Admiral Browning expected whoever took command of the *Salvation* to war with the Sentinels. In theory, the conflict could go on for many years to come, maybe even decades. He had no interest in fighting a war without end and preferred to believe that he could find a way to defeat the Sentinels quicker than that.

While a passenger on the transit ships, he studied the historical records of all first-hand accounts of the Federation Wars. While doing so, he had Radek execute thousands of analyses to try to identify patterns that could help him defeat Harding Prime and the Sentinels.

The holographic silver orb sprang to life in front of Quinton.

"I have results from my recent analysis of both pre- and post-Federation Wars events, and I've come up with a theory that you'll find interesting," Radek said.

Quinton thought about inviting some of the others into a virtual meeting environment but decided to hold off. He could quickly review the report himself and then decide whether the others should be involved.

"I think the others might be interested in my findings as well," Radek said.

That was a first. Normally, Radek resisted a collaborative approach, especially since Quinton had taken command of the *Salvation*.

"How come?"

"Because some of them might be able to corroborate my findings. They've lived through it. Or they could inform me that my theory is incorrect," Radek replied.

Quinton knew he couldn't fight the Sentinels on his own. He needed the others' feedback, even if the decisions were his to make as to how they would engage the Sentinels.

"All right, Radek. Send out invites."

It wasn't always practical for them to physically meet, especially when several members of his team were on the other side of the ship. When time was of the essence, they needed to meet at a moment's notice.

Quinton entered the virtual meeting environment, which had the appearance of the normal conference rooms found anywhere on the ship. Maelyn and Simon were there. Brandt also joined them, along with Belinda Hinton and Bentlae.

Radek was Quinton's personal VI. All PMCs had personal VIs, but since Quinton had assumed command of the *Salvation*, Radek had achieved a certain level of independence that set him apart from the standard PMC VI.

"What's this about?" Brandt asked.

"I've been studying the records of first-hand accounts of the Federation Wars, and Radek has been running separate analyses, searching for patterns that might help us now. He had some results, and he thought a meeting with people who had actually witnessed these events would be more productive. He assured me it was nothing personal."

The orb glowed a little brighter in Quinton's direction, which was Radek's version of a head nod. "Quinton tasked me with searching for specific events that led to the Federation Wars and how they are linked to the current state of the galaxy. After an exhaustive search, I could not find a single event or action that led to the Federation Wars. My search included the established timeline that, according to DUC records, is the agreed-upon accounting of events."

"We know how the Federation Wars started," Quinton said. "Harding betrayed Browning. Made him appear guilty of war crimes."

"That's only part of it," Radek replied. "You've reviewed battles and strategies that Admiral Browning used to fight Harding and the Sentinels. However, Browning only had suspicions as to why PMCs went insane."

"We've been through this before," Brandt said. "It was the mergence protocol that led PMCs to become unstable."

"This is true, but there's more," Radek replied. "I've studied the Sentinel infiltration protocol, and I believe the earliest instances of this methodology occurred before the Federation Wars began. It was widely believed that PMC instability was attributed to the mergence protocols, and I don't have enough evidence to refute that in my analysis."

"Harding did it," Quinton said. "Before he became Harding Prime, he found a way to manipulate PMCs. Made them unstable. Attack without reason. Browning talks about it in his logs. They tried to stop it."

Brandt looked as if he were searching for something he just couldn't find. "There isn't anything new here. According to the records on this ship, Browning eventually learned that Harding had betrayed them."

"It's more than that," Quinton insisted.

"What do you mean?" Maelyn asked.

"They were friends. Browning and Harding were friends. Harding was the first PMC, and he'd worked with Browning since the beginning. Browning refers to Harding as his friend. There are even multiple instances where he tried to help him."

It had been easier for Quinton to believe that Harding had become corrupt somehow and betrayed Browning and everyone else. That was true to a degree, but the two had been close friends. It still wasn't clear to Quinton why that had all changed.

"In some of the earlier entries, Browning refers to Miles Harding as a younger brother."

"The two were not related," Radek said.

Quinton rolled his eyes a little. "I know that, Radek. They were close friends. Browning tried to take care of Harding."

"What made Harding change?" Maelyn asked.

"Browning wasn't sure. He did say that there were little changes that occurred over time that he hadn't noticed until it was too late," Quinton replied.

"You make it sound like he blamed himself," Brandt said.

"Wouldn't you?"

Brandt considered it for a moment and nodded. "I see your point. That must have been..." His voice trailed off and all of them were quiet for a few moments.

"All right, Radek, tell them the rest," Quinton said.

"Searching for specifics that lead us straight to the Federation Wars is fraught with omissions in the records and non-linear events when thinking of one thing that led to another. The best theory I can come up with that attempts to answer how the Federation Wars affected the entire galaxy can be answered with where the problems began. With Miles Harding. He figured out how to override the safeguards in place that prevented PMCs from making multiple complete copies of themselves. Acheron Confederacy intelligence could never explain how the Jordanis eventually started making their own PMCs. The same can be said for every other star union that had the technology. There is a pattern in the evolution of PMCs in the various star unions. First, there is a demonstration of immediate effectiveness, building trust in the system. Then it eventually spirals out of control, as if it were designed to fail."

Maelyn leaned forward. "Designed to fail. You're saying that Harding copied himself, giving others use of PMCs, but that he wanted it to fail?"

Quinton nodded. "Not only that. It also gave him unfettered access to the space navies of all the key power players across the galaxy. He didn't stop there. Harding eventually expanded to infiltrate smaller star unions as well."

"Admiral, this doesn't make sense," Bentlae said. Quinton gestured for him to continue. "If he gave other federations PMC technology, then how could he copy himself across so many different platforms? All those different federations would have created their own PMCs."

Quinton smiled and looked at Simon. "I bet you could shed some light on that."

Simon frowned. "Me?"

"Yes, you. How would you do it?"

Simon considered this for a few seconds, his face a thoughtful frown. "Slowly. Small pieces designed to emerge as part of the foundation that PMCs all operate from."

"You've lost me on this one, Simon," Brandt said.

"It's the VIs like Radek, or Greta, or the half a dozen others out there. They're all variants of the same base operating system, the same framework. He would only have to include something that would give him access to any PMC he wanted to use later on," Simon said and looked at Quinton. "Am I right?"

Quinton had the advantage of knowing the result of Radek's analysis before his VI shared it with the others. He'd read ahead. "Partially. Mostly, actually. Harding utilized different methods for regaining access that wasn't simply leaving a backdoor everywhere so he could just remote access back into the PMC. He was cleverer than that. He had manipulators that were activated only when certain conditions were met or could be triggered through some specific kind of interaction."

"What kind of conditions?" Brandt asked.

"Could be lots of things, like a certain level of access on ships, or the presence of behavioral traits that would give Harding an edge. He created the technology. He knew how it worked and everything it was capable of," Quinton replied.

"But that would mean we're all vulnerable to it," Bentlae said.

Quinton shook his head. "No, we're not. It's part of the activation signal, but the configuration update purges the questionable protocols, making us more independent. Also, there are the integrity checks that all of us go through to ensure we remain stable. Browning and his team tried to make sure there were enough safeguards in place to reduce the risk of potential compromise."

Bentlae sighed heavily. "I don't know what to think about all this."

"Just wait. It gets worse," Quinton said.

"They didn't think of everything, since PMCs are vulnerable to Sentinel infiltration protocols," Brandt said.

Quinton had found a way to protect against it, but Brandt was right.

"How does it get worse?" Maelyn asked.

"I'd like to know as well," Brandt said. "It's bad enough that Harding caused PMCs to go insane. What could be worse than that?"

"That it was part of Harding's plan," Quinton replied.

The others stared at him.

"Go on, Radek."

"This next part is theory. Harding Prime not only had control of PMCs but was able to influence the entire galaxy by introducing severe psychological trauma on a galactic level," Radek said.

"Think about it," Quinton said. "The first thing anyone ever talks about in relation to the Federation Wars was about how chaotic those times were. Civilizations were falling. Federations that had been around for thousands of years were gone. Entire planets were destroyed. How much galaxy-spanning destruction can people witness before they just want it all to be over?"

Belinda Hinton's eyes drew up in alarm. "You're talking about hysteria on a galactic scale."

Quinton nodded. "That's exactly what I'm talking about."

Brandt shook his head. "But how could he have done it? He wasn't everywhere. He couldn't have had that kind of influence."

"Harding didn't need to be everywhere. He manipulated entire groups against one another. The chaos wasn't just union against union, but spacer against spacer, and the madness was everywhere. Even Browning commented on it. They tried to fight it, but it was like being surrounded on all sides by an all-consuming fire, and there wasn't enough anyone could do to change the outcome."

Brandt's brow furrowed. "He didn't just give up."

Quinton shook his head. "No, he fought."

"But we still don't know what happened to Harding Prime," Brandt replied.

"He's still out there."

"So, Browning did fail."

"I don't think he did," Quinton said. The others gave him doubtful stares, except for Maelyn, who wouldn't rush to an opinion. "At least not entirely. I think Harding Prime is limited somehow. Otherwise, we would've seen more of him, experienced more of his influence. The only thing I can think of is that Browning found some way to trap him," Quinton said.

"How?" Brandt asked.

"I don't know."

Brandt frowned. "Spacers were scared, but I don't know if I'd call it hysteria."

"They were isolated," Maelyn said. "With so many things appearing to happen at once, people felt alone. Too many enemies to fight and spacers looking for a way to survive."

"Yeah, but galaxy-spanning hysteria?" Brandt said.

Belinda Hinton cleared her throat, drawing their attention. "It's rather ingenious, actually. What better way to usher in wide, sweeping changes than during times of great stress and chaos?"

The lines around Brandt's eyes deepened, and he shook his head with a sigh. "The creation of the Sentinels was proposed by the most powerful remnant star unions left. If what you're saying is true, Harding had a hand in all of this."

"The threat of rogue PMCs was very real," Belinda Hinton said. "This wasn't something Harding could fake, which is why there was such a strong reaction to it. Anyone who tried to take a more practical approach would be overwhelmed by the masses, who would most likely be bonded together by a form of fanaticism often observed in extremist groups."

Quinton nodded. "That's right. And it explains a lot, like how there was so much effort put into the detection capabilities of PMCs. This would work against the ones who were stable, like all the PMCs who served Browning."

He looked at the others. Bentlae's gaze took on an intensity, as if he were preparing to explode.

"Unbelievable!" Bentlae growled. "Harding made it impossible to win against him. We never stood a chance."

Quinton watched Bentlae and Hinton. Both were PMCs during the Federation Wars. They'd witnessed all the chaos firsthand and now looked stunned. Quinton stood apart from the other PMCs they'd recovered. He predated the Federation Wars, and he thought this was one of the reasons Browning had made him a Galactic PMC.

Simon shook his head. "But why would he… how could he have… People everywhere were pulled into this, and they didn't have a choice?"

"When hysteria takes hold, it doesn't matter the size of the group. They become radically intolerant of dissonant voices. PMCs like us were the enemy. We became the reason the galaxy was in such a chaotic state. Anyone who tried to be a voice of reason was shut down hard," Belinda Hinton said.

Simon looked at Quinton. "And Admiral Browning didn't know about that?"

Quinton shook his head. "I don't think so."

"He was probably so busy reacting that neither he nor anyone else could figure it out," Maelyn said. She raised her index finger to her lips in thought. "Or maybe they did figure it out but weren't able to change the prevailing narrative."

She looked at Quinton, who said, "I told you it was worse."

"Okay, but this was decades ago. Things are so different now," Simon said.

"Are they?" Quinton asked.

Brandt looked away from them, his brow furrowed in thought.

Simon nodded. "Yes, they have to be. Too much time has passed."

"Yes, but there has been increased resistance to the information we've been making available to everyone," Maelyn said.

Quinton nodded. "It explains why there's so much resistance. Why there's this almost instant denial."

"Yeah, but it's not as bad as what happened during the Federation Wars," Simon replied.

Quinton shared a look with Maelyn.

"Not yet," Brandt said, his voice sounding strained.

"How do we convince spacers that we're telling them the truth?" Simon asked.

Bentlae chuckled bitterly. "No one likes to admit when they've been wrong."

"Yeah, but that doesn't mean we stop trying," Simon said and looked at the others. "Right? We're not going to stop."

Quinton shook his head. "No, we're not going to stop."

Belinda Hinton nodded. "We can't stop, or spacers will never be free."

A few moments of silence filled the virtual meeting room.

"This is a lot to take in and consider," Brandt said. "I know I need time to digest this, and I have a few people I need to contact."

Quinton expected as much, and he didn't even need to access his SCS system to inform him that this was the best outcome he could have hoped for.

"There are resources I also need to engage about this," Belinda Hinton said.

"There are people from the DUC I'd like you to consult with," Brandt said.

"Feel free to consult with whomever you need. This isn't classified. Admittedly, it's outside my expertise. I don't know anything about how to correct a prevailing false narrative. I'm not even sure there's a way, but that's what I want you to work on," Quinton said.

The others dropped out of the meeting, except for Maelyn.

"Thanks for helping me out, and I don't just mean now. I mean throughout this whole thing."

Maelyn smiled a little. "You don't make it easy sometimes."

Quinton grinned. "I know. I'm a handful."

They were both quiet for a few seconds.

"Maelyn, does any of this change how you feel about PMCs?"

She looked away from him for a moment. "Quinton, I don't want to become a PMC, even temporarily."

Quinton swallowed hard, trying not to let her reply sting, but it did.

"And I want your promise that you won't do anything to make it happen," she said.

Quinton blinked a few times. She was afraid he'd find a way to upload her consciousness against her will. He'd thought about it and was even tempted to do it. He looked at her and said, "I wouldn't do that to you. I hope you can believe me."

She regarded him for a few moments and then her gaze softened. "I do believe you."

He'd hoped she'd change her mind about it but didn't think she ever would. And he'd have to accept that because he wasn't going to betray her trust in him.

21

As TEAGAN CREPT along the outer dome of the citadel at Zeta Lyrae, she passed a rooftop sensor, hardly paying it any notice other than a passing glance. Her stealth suit allowed her to blend in even here. She'd expected much better security sensors from such an important facility associated with the Collective, unless the intel Victor had given her was wrong.

She continued her trek, following a path only visible on her internal heads-up display. The security HUD overlay showed data from her suit sensors, as well as the tiny recon drones she'd deployed.

The citadel nearly gleamed with a yellowish-brown metallic alloy that could withstand all but the most devastating of bombardments from a fleet of warships. Trenton Draven, or one of the Collective's subsidiaries, had spent quite a bit of credits for what appeared to be pre-Federation Wars armorplast. She'd also spotted several point-defense platforms armed with rapid-fire frag cannons. They appeared to be well serviced and ready to protect the citadel should the need arise.

After a week of reconnaissance of this part of the station, she felt as if she knew all its outward appearances. The citadel was a type of stronghold that serviced this sector. All the financial records showed that it was part of the Hazelton Group assets. Records showed that Hazelton managed sector security, both for the station and for the star cluster. Nothing in the financial records indicated that there was any type of link between Hazelton Group and the Collective. Lesser operatives would have moved on to another target, assuming they were even capable of infiltrating one of the most powerful unions in the galaxy.

Teagan ran toward a small sensor array and squatted down next to it. Her stealth suit should be enough to fool most of the sensors she'd found, but she suspected they'd been placed specifically to lure unsuspecting operatives into a false sense of security. She surveyed the area, waiting. Years of training in Crowe's Union and a lifetime of missions had taught her never to accept what she saw at face value.

"You were wrong, Father," Teagan said quietly, thinking about her last conversation with him and Nate Carradine.

She focused her attention on her breathing, using controlled breaths to measure the time and observe her surroundings. Her patience paid off. A wedge-shaped reconnaissance drone flew in a wide arc nearby. Several more flew in formation, heading toward her location. Teagan smiled and thrust out a hand. Six small spheres detached themselves from her forearm and flew away with increasing velocity, gaining the attention of the reconnaissance drones. Teagan waited for a seven-count, then stepped lively toward the edge and vaulted over the side. The artificial gravity field was much weaker outside the station, but she still swan-dived downward. She activated the small counter-grav emitters in her suit, which kept her body at a steady distance from the side of the dome as she glided down. She increased the gravitational field in the hand emitters and swerved, so she glided parallel to paths below. She grabbed a handhold and used it to propel herself faster.

Teagan looked below and angled toward the rooftop of a long corridor that connected the citadel to the building next to it. With her head thrust forward, she kicked away from the citadel, moving beyond the artificial gravity field. A short burst from her suit jets propelled her free fall. Her pulse quickened, and she kept her arms pinned to her sides. As she raced toward the rooftop, the artificial gravity emitters on her suit slowed her descent into a controlled swoop. Teagan's lips curved upward and she inhaled, enjoying it probably a little too much. She reached out toward the handles on the rooftop and propelled herself forward, moving toward her target.

A comlink appeared on her HUD and she acknowledged it.

"You're almost there," Victor said. "How's the view, Tia?"

His tone sounded a little strained and less than curious about her progress.

"Stimulating," Teagan replied.

Victor began to reply and stopped. She relished his hesitation, but he hadn't suffered enough yet for her to disable the explosive charge.

"You didn't tell me about drones," Teagan said.

"Give me a break, Tia. I didn't know about them. Otherwise, I would've told you. Do you think I'd take a chance like that?" he asked.

Teagan snorted. "No, I suppose not, especially if you want to keep your head."

He laughed mockingly.

"Don't expect any sympathy from me. You brought this on yourself," she admonished.

Victor didn't respond.

Teagan cleared her throat.

"I brought this on myself. I shouldn't have tried to betray you to that agent."

"There, you see? That wasn't so bad, was it?"

Victor released an explosive breath.

"I'm closing in. Disable the security locks on my signal," Teagan said.

She angled toward a maintenance hatch and passed it. A short distance away was a smaller hatch for repair drones.

"Ready," Teagan said.

Victor transmitted the drone transponder codes and she broadcasted them from her suit. The small hatch was only a meter in diameter. Someone Victor's size would never fit through, but Teagan was slender. The hatch popped open, and she glided through. She slowed down as her stealth suit's VI increased power to her gravity emitters. The tube stretched out ahead of her and she coasted without slowing, not touching any of the walls.

"I'm in," Teagan said.

She couldn't hide from the sensors in the transit tube, but she'd gotten a power signature from the maintenance drones she'd tracked. The VI of her stealth suit mimicked the power output, and her counter-grav emitters were configured to match those of the standard model repair drones used for maintenance.

"Good," Victor said. "Since you're inside now, will you disable the collar?"

"Don't you like your new necklace?"

"Not especially."

"You know the deal. When I get what I need and am safely out of here, then you'll be fine."

Victor was silent.

The tunnel opened to a charging station. Spherical repair drones sat in their charging cradles, waiting for instruction. She spotted a control panel on the far end of the chamber.

"What's the matter, Vic? Afraid I'll treat you like you treated me?"

"Come on, Tia. Enough with this already. You're almost out of range."

Teagan chuckled. Victor thought she'd used the standard transmitter range for the collar, but she'd found a way to increase it.

She closed in on the control panel and said, "Just trust me the way I trusted you."

Victor muttered a curse. If given a chance, Victor would have killed her. The galaxy never pitied the weak. It was one of her earliest lessons. Her temporary partner had rolled the dice and lost.

Teagan used her implants to initiate a comlink session with the control panel. She then ran a trace program that gave her access to the nearest data node and switched her comlink session to it.

"Hey Tia, what do you think about what's been going on?" Victor asked.

She triggered the locking mechanism for the door, and it silently slipped to the side. She walked through and it closed behind her.

"I'm in," she said.

"Did you hear me?"

She rolled her eyes. Victor had hardly said anything when they first started working together, and now she couldn't get him to shut up. She walked down the dimly lit corridor.

"Huh?"

Victor sighed. "The stuff about the Sentinels."

"What are you talking about?"

He covered the microphone. "...such a bitch."

She grinned. "That's the spirit."

"Why do you do this?"

"Because it's fun," she replied.

There was a data core here in the depths of the citadel, and she was going to access it. Most security systems focused on preventing unauthorized entry from the outside. However, they lacked detection capabilities for trusted system sources.

She lifted her hand and a small scanner feed appeared on her HUD, giving her an inside view of the data lines behind the wall. She found the one she wanted and followed it.

"Did it bother you?" she asked.

"You think?" he said. "Sentinels were created by Harding and they're... you saw it right?"

"I did," she said.

The data line angled away from her, and she started walking faster. Teagan sent a small broadcast signal, and a door appeared a few meters from her location. She hastened toward it.

"I'm inside the data node. Just a quick data dump and we're done," Teagan said.

The brightly lit data node was lit up from the small computing core inside. There were rows of octagonal-shaped processing units—definitely not the standard processing units if this were just a station computing core. If she had to guess, this data core was much more important than she'd first realized.

She headed deeper into the room, following the highlighted path on her HUD. The specific processing unit she was going to use flashed on her HUD, and she walked over to it and connected a data-dump device to the side. The data dump began to offload, and she waited.

A minute went by, and she frowned. Glancing at the comlink session she had with Victor, she saw that it was grayed out. The connection had been lost. Pressing her lips together, she tried to initialize a new connection, but it didn't work. She glanced around at the computing core, thinking there was something interfering with her comlink. She checked the security alert system, and it was quiet. If they'd detected her, there would be all kinds of alarms being raised.

She checked the data dump progress and sighed, then decided to lean up against the wall to wait.

Victor's comlink became active.

"Oh good, the collar didn't malfunction," Teagan said.

"Ha, ha," Victor sneered. "I had to switch locations."

Teagan frowned. There was something in Victor's voice that hadn't been there before, something beyond anticipation.

She sighed. "What did you do?"

"What do you mean?" he asked a little too quickly.

Gritting her teeth, she triggered the detonator signal. No confirmation registered, and she heard Victor laughing.

"Wow, that's it. You don't waste any time, do you? Just like that, you were willing to blow my head off. Well, I disabled your damn collar!"

Teagan sprang across the aisle and snatched the data-dump device from the processing unit. It wasn't finished querying the data core or dumping what it found. She initiated a data session to the device and began transferring the information to her suit systems.

She reached into a small compartment on her waist and placed a small disc-shaped charge on the processing unit. She wouldn't be able to cover up her tracks the way she preferred, but it beat the alternative.

Teagan ran toward the far end of the computing core.

"That's it, Tia. Run away. Run. Run. Run. Maybe they won't catch you," Victor said.

A message flashed on her HUD, and she smiled. "Goodbye, Victor."

Victor shouted a half-strangled cry that was cut off when the comlink went dark. Why have only one detonator available when you could have three? There would be nothing left of Victor's body, and the explosive charge would sanitize any kind of DNA evidence.

At least she hadn't slept with him. She took a small amount of pride in not giving in to any of Victor's charms.

She kept scanning security channels, searching for some kind of alarm. Someone had bought Victor off to get him to betray her. Had he told them where she was? She couldn't be sure, and even if Victor could talk, he'd never tell her. The galaxy only respects strength.

Teagan never executed any operation without having a few alternative escape routes just in case. Betrayal was an occupational hazard that occurred entirely too often. At least she'd killed that bastard. Now all she needed to do was escape.

She ran down the maintenance corridors, increasing her distance from the computing core. Teagan selected one of the alternative escape routes and set that as default on her HUD. The path in front of her updated and she followed it. A few minutes later, her security scanner showed several alarms, confirming that Victor really had sold her out. He'd informed security forces of her escape route and they'd tracked her progress. Victor wouldn't have alerted them until after she was already inside, but he'd been unaware of her alternate escape routes, which should give her an edge over the security forces. Time to employ some misdirection of her own.

She uploaded several infiltration protocols onto the station's computer system. They quickly deployed multiple instances that would confuse security personnel who were monitoring her breach of their systems.

It didn't take her long to reach the outside. With the station's security monitoring systems compromised, there was no way they would notice another open hatch.

She vaulted over the walkway and engaged her suit's counter-grav emitters. Her suit's scanners detected security drones patrolling the area, but none of them had noticed her yet.

She initiated a recall of the flight harness she'd deployed a few days ago and received confirmation. A few seconds later, she spotted the harness speeding toward her.

A proximity alarm flashed on her HUD. Several security drones were coming toward her on an intercept course. Teagan blew out a breath. Her stealth suit couldn't protect her against the weapons those drones carried. This was going to be close.

The flight harness swooped underneath her, and she spread her arms out wide. The harness wrapped around her suit, its systems going online with her suit computer. She initiated boosters, disabled her counter-grav emitters, and sped away from the security drones. They couldn't keep up with her. She set the navigation coordinates and the flight control systems took over. Teagan became a passenger in her own suit. It was the only way she'd be able to escape.

The security drones quickly fell off her scanners as she moved out of range. Their onboard systems would likely report the anomaly, but it would take time for station security to organize a response. Teagan didn't intend to waste any time. The security in this station was top-notch, and it wouldn't take them long to regroup.

She reached her ship, and as soon as she was aboard, she initiated a micro-jump away from the station. Ten seconds later, the ship executed a much longer jump, stressing the drive to its limit. It would require a longer recharge time, but that was the price of crossing such vast distances.

Teagan removed the flight harness and put it in its cradle, giving it a companionable slap of appreciation, then initiated the removal of the stealth suit and stepped out of it. She put her equipment in maintenance mode, which would take care of diagnostics and the recharge they'd need when she used them again.

She looked at the data-dump device and considered what to do with it. She was supposed to upload the data into a secure comms drone and send it to the closest drop point so that a Union team could recover it.

"Welcome back, Tia," said Greta. "Secure comms drone is ready."

Teagan peered at the data-dump device with a thoughtful frown.

A circular panel opened next to the nearby workbench. It was Greta's way of prompting her into following Union protocols.

"I'm going to hold onto it, Greta."

"Tia, this isn't protocol. I must insist—"

"Override. Authorization Teagan Cayne."

Using her implants, she transmitted her identification to the ship's computer core.

"Override accepted."

"Good. And retire the Tia persona. I won't need it anymore."

"Understood," Greta replied. "Shall I purge recent identity?"

As a rule, Teagan tried not to reuse a persona more than once, but sometimes it was unavoidable. "Yeah, I won't keep that one."

A holoscreen appeared, showing the current list of aliases Teagan maintained. The Tia alias had been expunged. She peered at the list of aliases and focused on one of them. It was much too dangerous to ever use again, but she couldn't bring herself to erase it. She selected the alias, and a profile picture came to prominence on the holoscreen.

Her blonde hair, brown eyes, and tanned skin were replaced with something much more exotic. She studied the curves of her face from the delicate cheekbones to her full lips.

"My name is Vonya Irani," Teagan said, and the edges of her lips lifted a little.

She'd changed so completely for that alias, from the dark lavender skin color to the silky platinum-colored hair. As she looked at the image, she remembered the smile of a young spacer aboard the *Nebulon*. He had an adorable little dimple that appeared when he smiled, and there was something about him that made her want to stay with him. She thought about Simon sometimes during downtime between missions. She could hear his laugh and the sound of his voice when he spoke. He was so curious about her… about Vonya, she corrected. He was attracted to her, that much was obvious, but during her time aboard the *Nebulon*, she'd found that she enjoyed his company more so than anyone else in a very long time.

Teagan looked away from the holoscreen. When she'd seen Becker and Oscar in the Phineas Cluster, she felt a thrill at the thought that they might recognize her. She'd thought Toros Becker might have, but he hadn't. She knew it was careless of her to tempt fate like that, especially after what she'd done, but she hadn't known her actions would lure the Sentinels to that starbase. She'd been trying to neutralize Quinton's access to the starbase so Union ships could take control of it from the DUC. In that scenario, the lives that would have been lost were only those who'd chosen to fight. Then the Sentinels showed up with a fleet of their own ships. Teagan had done the only thing she could have done. She was already off the starbase when the Sentinels came. Her eyes became tight around the edges and her throat thickened. She'd run away, leaving the crew of the *Nebulon* to their fates aboard the starbase. She thought they'd all died, that Simon had died. The thrill of using her skills in deception had been matched by one of the DUC's finest agents, Maelyn Wayborn, and she'd come out the victor, but it was a hollow victory for her because she'd left behind something much more valuable than a starbase.

Teagan thought about her time aboard the *Nebulon*, living with its crew, and sometimes enjoying the fantasy that she was a Servitor traveling the galaxy.

She grabbed the data-dump device and powered off the holoscreen, heading to the showers. She'd spent almost forty-eight hours in a stealth suit, and the first thing she wanted to do was get clean. She needed to wash the mission off her skin. Hopefully, it would also wash away the nostalgia she was feeling. There wouldn't be a future where she could indulge her foolish fantasy of lounging in Simon's embrace.

The shower started off as hot as she could take, and she washed every inch of herself, but no matter how long she washed, she couldn't dismiss the ghosts from her past. She changed the temperature of the water to cold and stood beneath it, stubbornly refusing to move. She exhaled forcefully and after a minute, she began to shiver. She stayed there as if serving some kind of penance, but what she really wanted was to forget. She should purge Vonya Irani's alias from the computing core. Gritting her teeth, she slapped the controls and the water stopped streaming.

Teagan stepped out of the shower and began to dry herself. Greta had had one of the maintenance drones leave some clothes for her to wear, and she quickly dressed and walked toward the bridge. At the central workstation, she kept shifting in her seat as if she couldn't get comfortable. After a few minutes, she sighed in disgust and stood up.

Teagan activated the main holoscreen and brought up her list of aliases, selecting Vonya Irani's alias. A list of options appeared, and her gaze slid to the option to purge. Teagan swallowed hard and then shook her head. She made a swiping motion with her hand and the windows on the holoscreen disappeared.

A maintenance drone carried in a tray of food for her. She picked something at random and started chewing it, not paying any attention to the taste. The galaxy only respected the strong, but was Quinton right? She'd seen the reports across multiple systems. Her father served the Alliance because, for the moment, Quinton Aldren could protect him from Trenton Draven and the Collective. Teagan knew that much, but what if Quinton had been right? Were they all living in some kind of prison without walls? Even her? She'd always served the Union's interests. One day she'd command the Union, but for now, she was a like a coil in a jump drive. By itself it wasn't very effective, but when it was part of a group, it had the power to fold space and time. What if the machine that was the galactic civilization after the Federation Wars itself was wrong? Could it really have been designed to be as it is now? Teagan frowned at the thought, but it kept coming back to her. She could put it aside for a while, but downtimes between missions were tough. If the galaxy was going to change, she needed to decide what her role was going to be. Otherwise, she'd be stumbling in the dark in a world of someone else's design, and that was something she couldn't tolerate. She was in control of her own destiny.

22

QUINTON WALKED through the corridors of the *Salvation* wearing the black-and-gold-trimmed uniform of the Acheron Confederacy Navy. Conversations hushed for a brief period of time while Quinton walked past them, and spacers stared at him for a second before remembering to salute. Bentlae and Simon walked with him.

"Is it always like this?" Simon asked.

Quinton looked at his friend. "They're just shocked that you left the lab."

Simon chuckled. "*That's* what it is. But seriously, it seems like there are more and more people aboard all the time now."

"There are," Quinton replied.

The Alliance was getting volunteers more frequently, and powerful factions throughout the galaxy were finally taking notice. The United Federation Alliance was becoming something that couldn't be ignored.

Commander Bentlae wore a uniform similar to Quinton's, but Simon wore common spacers garb with a tech specialist insignia on his arm.

"I'm surprised you wanted me to come to the meeting," Simon said.

"Maelyn said you've been all but sleeping in the lab and the change in scenery would do you good," Quinton replied.

Simon had thrown himself into his work. He was trying to find a way to help the PMCs that had been compromised by Sentinel infiltration protocols, and he hadn't been successful. Quinton didn't think it was possible to help those PMCs, and Simon was going to have to accept that.

"What have you been working on?" Bentlae asked.

"Trying to reverse what the infiltration protocols did to the PMCs who are being brought back online."

Bentlae looked at Quinton. "The protocols are irreversible."

"They shouldn't be," Simon replied.

Bentlae ignored him. "All that's being done is lengthening their agony. This needs to stop."

"I haven't been hurting them," Simon said quickly.

Bentlae shook his head. "Don't you think what you're doing has been tried before?"

"Bentlae," Quinton said, "Simon is taking every precaution."

Simon nodded. "I am. I promise you that I am. You can even stop by the lab, and I'll show you."

"Not necessary."

"Simon is trying to help," Quinton said.

"They can't be helped," Bentlae replied.

Quinton looked at Simon. "You've been at it for a while now. What have you got to show for it?"

Simon frowned in thought for a few seconds. "First, I'm not experimenting on any PMCs. Okay? Understand?" Bentlae nodded once. "I've been analyzing how the infiltration protocols affect the base VIs that are used in managing the interface between the PMC and the outside world."

Bentlae shook his head. "I know what you're trying to do. It makes sense until you realize that the effects are impossible to measure and analyze without a consciousness loaded into the ESS."

Simon blinked a few times.

"Is he right?" Quinton asked.

Simon looked away and nodded. "It's as if the infiltration protocols themselves work together like their own VIs. I've never seen anything like it."

"That's because you're treating the problem like it's just a complex computer system that hosts a virtual intelligence, but it's more complex than that," Bentlae said.

Quinton eyed the ACN commander for a few moments. "You seem to know a lot about it."

Bentlae sighed and nodded once. "We tried to help our own, Admiral, but Browning ordered us to stop because we couldn't spend more time and resources on it. Not with everything else that was happening." He looked at Simon. "I appreciate that you're trying to help, but it's a fool's errand, Simon."

The young spacer inhaled and sighed.

"I don't like the thought of giving up any more than you do, Simon, but maybe it's time to step away from this for a while," Quinton said.

Simon's eyebrows pushed forward into a tight frown. "There has to be a way to reverse it. I just need to figure out how. I don't want to abandon them. They deserve better than what they got."

"You're right. They do deserve better."

"I'm all they've got, Quinton. No one else is even willing to try."

Quinton felt an enormous sense of pride in the young man. Sometimes, when people hit a wall, they gave up, but not Simon. He dug in and refused to quit.

"You don't have to give up on this, Simon. We'll store them, and they won't be destroyed. You can come back to it after you've given the problem some space. All right?" Quinton asked.

He could have ordered Simon to stop and have the ESS cores of the compromised PMCs removed from the lab, but he wouldn't do that. He couldn't —not only because it would crush Simon's spirit and foster resentment that wouldn't help anyone, but because of what the young man had said. They were the only ones those PMCs had. In a galaxy filled with the harshness of war, they needed to preserve what hope they could, even if it was in an effort that might never succeed. The difference was in the trying and not giving up.

"Yes, Admiral," Simon said.

They headed to an audience chamber meant for hosting large meetings, something beyond the normal conference rooms. They weren't holding any more summits, but they did have regular meetings with members of the Alliance. Membership was granted to groups who provided support to the Alliance. It required a certain level of commitment, but Quinton wasn't sure how many groups would stay when things got harder for them to ignore.

They walked into a multi-level chamber and were greeted by hundreds of individual holoscreens that showed representatives and their advisors. Quinton strode toward the central platform with Bentlae, while Simon went to one of the observer platforms on the side. Sherilyn Cantos, Severin Brandt, Maelyn, and a dozen more representatives from the DUC were already in the room. Among them were a few representatives who wore the emblem of the Acheron Confederacy. Since the Federation Wars, the DUC had taken in refugees from all the fallen federations. They hadn't turned anyone away, and for nearly a century, galactic society had blamed the Acheron Confederacy for the Federation Wars. Seeing spacers acknowledge the Acheron Confederacy was a symbolic gesture that wasn't lost on anyone at the meeting. Maelyn had told him there were plenty of places where the risk of such a display was life-threatening.

Quinton looked at the holoscreens, searching the delegates who were in attendance for anyone else brave enough to show the Acheron Confederacy's colors or emblems. Among the hundreds of holoscreens, he did see a few dozen out there, and it ignited in him a sense of grim satisfaction. There were spacers out there willing to accept the truth.

Sherilyn looked at Quinton. "Thank you for joining us, Admiral Aldren."

Quinton was about to reply when another holoscreen came on, indicating that an additional group had arrived in the meeting. It took him all of half a second to realize that it was Trenton Draven of the Collective.

Sherilyn looked at the new holoscreen and her eyes widened. Then she smiled. "Director Draven, thank you for joining us."

"I appreciate the invite. Allowing me access here will greatly influence the decision to join your Alliance," Draven replied.

Quinton watched the leader of the Collective, who was one of the most dangerous people in the galaxy. Maelyn had told Quinton that no one knew for sure just how extensive the Collective really was. Quinton recognized the tactic—leave spacers room to speculate and they'll invent something more powerful and capable that will more than likely be further from the truth. However, when he looked at Trenton Draven, there was something in his gaze that made him think he would be a fool to underestimate the man. An old friend in the ACN had once told him to always watch out for the man who had nothing to prove because they were either the most foolish or the most dangerous spacer in the room. Given the unspoken deference shown toward Draven, Quinton knew which of those sentiments applied to the leader of the Collective.

Sherilyn Cantos conducted the meeting for the next few hours, giving delegates a chance to speak and ask questions. Trenton Draven remained quiet for the duration, and Quinton wondered what he was thinking. He was tempted to enable his SCS to come up with a guess but decided not to, something that was much harder to do than he thought it should be. There were protocols embedded into all PMCs to help the human consciousness inside cope with being in an altered state, and it was imperative that the PMC kept their connection to their humanity. This necessitated highly advanced android bodies designed for PMCs, but only Quinton's prototype avatar was best suited to that purpose.

As he listened to the various delegates' participation, he noticed a pattern in their comments and questions. Quinton supposed that even after a century, there were some things that just didn't change. Spacers wanted to be enticed in exchange for their support. Quinton wasn't surprised… Well, he was a little surprised. He'd hoped that after the spacers learned about the real reason for the Sentinels being created, they'd be eager to provide as much support to the Alliance as possible. But all they were really concerned with was how to gain access to even more resources and supplies. Many wanted to come to the *Salvation*, which Quinton had already refused to consider previously, and Sherilyn deftly denied their requests, using her skills as a leader for longer than Quinton had been alive. The last thing Quinton wanted for the *Salvation* was to host senior delegates as some sort of compensation.

A high-priority message appeared on Quinton's HUD, and he acknowledged it.

"Admiral," Commander Boschevets said, "one of our drop points has received a high-priority message from Counselor Yvonne Zariah. It's addressed to you personally. Given who it was, I thought it best to inform you about it immediately."

"Thank you, Commander," Quinton said.

He'd accessed the ship's comms systems as soon as Boschevets said Counselor Zariah's name. A message from the leadership council of the Servitors wasn't something he could ignore, and he doubted she'd send him a message just because. He was charming, but he wasn't *that* charming.

Maelyn looked at him.

Quinton opened a comlink to her. Now that her neural implants were working properly, she didn't have to rely on her wrist computer.

I've just received a message from the Servitors. It's a video-recorded message. I'm going to start it now.

A new window appeared on both their HUDs, and the recording began.

"Admiral Aldren," Counselor Zariah said, "it is with great regret that I must contact you under these circumstances, but we are in need of your help. The Sentinels are targeting our training installations, and we're unable to evacuate them in time. Protection of these installations was arranged by local star system authorities, but they are no match against Sentinel warships. All attempts to communicate with the Sentinels have failed. We've scanned for rogue signals, thinking that perhaps the Sentinels were being lured to those locations, but we haven't been able to find any." She paused and looked directly at the camera, and Quinton felt as if she were staring right into his eyes. He knew what the Servitors were capable of, what kind of response their appearance was meant to attain, but he couldn't put a logical spin on the fear and desperation in her eyes. "Do you remember our conversation about whether you could protect spacers from the Sentinels? Will you help protect us? Their attacks aren't limited to a single star system. They've spread out, and we're not sure how many are being attacked. The council believes that the Sentinel attack is in response to the new Alliance and to the data regarding the Federation Wars that has spread throughout the galactic sectors. We've remained neutral, but we need your help. If the Alliance will help us, then perhaps I can convince the council to change their stance and join. Please help us, Admiral Aldren."

The recorded message ended, and he shared a look with Maelyn. She gave him a slight nod.

"Director Cantos. I'm sorry, but I need the floor. I've just learned of something that cannot wait," Quinton said.

Sherilyn's eyebrows raised and then she nodded. "The floor is yours, Admiral Aldren."

Quinton stood up. He couldn't remember the protocol for speaking at these meetings, but it didn't matter right then. "We've just received an alert that Sentinels are attacking numerous star systems. They seem to be focusing their efforts on Servitor training locations."

"Where did the alert come from?" Brandt asked.

"It came from Counselor Yvonne Zariah through one of the drop points," Quinton replied.

Activity seemed to occur all at once from each holoscreen. Quinton couldn't hear them, but he could guess as to what was being said.

"Counselor Zariah wasn't sure how many star systems were being attacked, but she did ask for help from the Alliance," he said in a firm voice that carried throughout the chamber.

Many of the delegates stopped their sidebars to listen.

Counselor Zariah's message had included a list of the star systems that had been attacked. Quinton took control of the virtual meeting environment and opened a data session to everyone in attendance. Then he uploaded the list.

"Those are the star systems that need our help."

A holoscreen became outlined in yellow, indicating the delegate wanted to speak. It was Trenton Draven, and Quinton cleared his session to speak.

"Thank you, Admiral Aldren. What do you intend to do?" Draven asked.

"I'm going to help as many of those star systems as I can."

"You'll do that on your own authority? Do you speak for the Alliance?"

Quinton's authority extended to the *Salvation* and the fleets of ships associated with it, but even then, there were incredible limitations embedded within the security protocols for the ship. Browning had put in safeguards against whoever took command of the *Salvation* so they could only operate within the confines of engaging the Sentinels. He was limited with most other engagements. Draven was aware of those limitations, and his question indicated as much.

"I do not speak for the Alliance. However, in regard to the Sentinels, I have the ultimate authority to engage them, and I won't stand by and watch them begin another incursion on the galaxy. Some of the star systems listed should be of interest to you. Do you plan to help us, or are you still going to require more time to ponder the situation?"

Quinton could give as much as he could take, and he'd just put the leader of the Collective on the spot in front of a whole lot of groups.

Trenton Draven regarded him for a few moments. The edge of his mouth twitched, but his eyes were steady.

"The Collective stands ready to render assistance, be it for evacuation of star systems in need or to engage the Sentinels. Our fleets are prepared," Draven said.

Quinton had the urge to increase his frame rate just so he could get his thoughts in order. He increased it just a little bit so he could quickly be sure he'd heard the leader of the Collective correctly.

"Thank you for your support," Sherilyn said and paused for a moment, regarding the camera feed and making it appear as if she were appealing to whoever was watching. "Admiral Aldren has stated the objective, but we can't do this alone. All of you have offered provisional support to the Alliance, but more is required."

"Excuse me, Director Cantos," Draven said.

"Yes," Sherilyn replied.

"Surely you don't expect every member of the Alliance to assist in the fighting. If anyone had ships capable of engaging the Sentinels, it would have been done by now."

"No suicide missions for this," Quinton said. "Support can be provided by assisting with evacuations and repairs to space stations and star ports as needed. However, if your ships enter a system where spacers are hopelessly outmatched, we expect you to alert the Alliance immediately and wait for support."

"Director Draven, we'll coordinate our efforts, so we'll need all of you to confirm the status of your own locations. Information is our biggest ally. It will help us prioritize where to deploy our fleets," Sherilyn said.

Draven looked at Quinton. "There is a risk of spreading your forces too thin."

"This may come as a shock to you, but this isn't the first battle I've been in. Every PMC in the Alliance has extensive experience, and I intend to leverage it against the Sentinels," Quinton replied.

Sherilyn kept the virtual meeting going to keep communications open, but that responsibility would eventually be shifted to a DUC ship. Quinton couldn't host all communications across the Alliance and use the *Salvation* to engage the Sentinels at the same time.

Brandt walked over to him. "I assume you want me on the secondary bridge."

"Correct. Contact me when you get there," Quinton said.

Brandt hastened toward one of the exits.

There were dozens of messages waiting for Quinton's attention, but he had withdrawn from the *Salvation's* computing core.

Maelyn walked next to Quinton. "What do you think?"

"About what?" she asked.

"Do you think Zariah was lying?"

Maelyn shook her head. "I don't think so. As much as I don't like the Servitors, they aren't known for lying to people."

Quinton nodded. "I didn't think so either, but you know how it goes."

"I would have spoken up if I thought she was misleading you," Maelyn said and smiled.

"I'm glad you have my back."

"Always," she replied.

They walked out of the meeting room.

"Quinton," Maelyn said, "I've completed my training for—"

"I know. I have a ship for you and a new XO that I think you'll enjoy working with. I think you're kindred spirits. Anyway, you need to head to your ship, unless you'd rather join me on the bridge."

Maelyn smiled a little, but it didn't reach her eyes. "I'll be more useful to you out there."

He'd known she wouldn't take him up on his offer. She needed to be out there just like he needed to remain aboard the *Salvation*. They walked toward the nearest transit location where an empty aircar waited nearby. The hatch opened and Maelyn glanced at it.

Simon walked over and hugged her. "Stay safe, Captain."

She laughed. "You too, spacer. Look out for our admiral here," she said, tilting her head toward Quinton.

Simon chuckled and walked to a nearby aircar, giving them some space.

Multiple aircars came and left as they ferried passengers to different parts of the colossal ship.

Quinton was about to make what he thought would be a witty remark, when Maelyn stepped closer, closing the distance between them. Then she pressed her lips on his. The kiss was fierce and filled with promise, and he loved every second of it. She pulled away, her lips lifting into a small smile that made him ignore everything around him. Older men might think he was being a fool, but he knew a thing or two about missed opportunities, and he wasn't about to let this small one slip away.

They each backed away a few steps, not wanting to be the first to look away. Quinton grinned and so did she. "We're a pair."

She stepped into the waiting aircar, and the translucent hatch closed, speeding her away. She waved as she disappeared into the distance.

Quinton walked toward the aircar where Simon waited.

The young spacer raised an eyebrow, but before he could speak, Quinton said, "A wise man knows when not to say anything at all and to just go with it."

Simon chuckled, and then the aircar whisked them toward their destination.

23

THE PILOTLESS TRANSPORT shuttle flew toward the ACN Challenger Class Destroyer, *Ascendant*. The shuttle was remotely piloted by the *Salvation's* computing core, and Maelyn watched its perfect approach vector through the main holoscreen. She'd worked tirelessly to qualify not only to command a destroyer class warship, but to also lead a battle group. Since she was now able to utilize her implants, she'd used the rapid learning simulations available on the *Salvation*. Without accelerated learning programs, Quinton wouldn't have been able to crew anywhere near as many ships as he had. Guided training simulations had given her a solid foundation, and she had a lifetime of experience aboard various ships. Her aptitude tests revealed that she was best suited to command destroyer class ships or below. Maelyn wasn't the least bit surprised by this, as she'd never wanted to fly behemoth-sized ships, and she never wanted to command the *Salvation*. She was best suited for a smaller, precision strike force, and the *Salvation's* aptitude tests had reinforced that. Her implants with VI assistants helped the rapid learning training simulations become committed to the memory centers of her brain. She'd underestimated just how well those simulations could impart knowledge. Over the weeks, she'd amassed years' worth of experience in ship and fleet tactics. And the training wasn't a download of someone else's experience. Through her implants, the *Salvation's* computing core analyzed her brain and experiences, then adapted the training scenarios that could quickly be integrated. They weren't actual memories being inserted into her brain, but they were the suggestions of them, which allowed the brain to accept or reject those suggestions. Over time, with continued use of her implants, the training VI had been able to better match training simulations with her particular learning style.

As the shuttle flew toward the *Ascendant*, she got to see her ship for the first time. There were thousands of shuttles leaving the *Salvation*, taking passengers to their ships. As captain of the *Ascendant*, she wore the ACN black and gold uniform. Truth be told, Maelyn was in awe of what Admiral Browning had accomplished. She wished she could have seen the core worlds of the Acheron Confederacy before the Federation Wars. They'd been capable of so much, and even though they were gone, they'd left the spacers a way to free themselves from what had been unleashed on the galaxy.

The aircraft landed on the access hatch midships, and a section of the shuttle's floor pulled away, revealing a small airlock. She climbed down the ladder onto her ship.

A female CDA in the same uniform gave her a crisp salute. "Welcome aboard the *Ascendant*, Captain Wayborn. Lieutenant Commander Sienna Hyden, ma'am."

As the PMC mentioned her name, her service record appeared on Maelyn's internal HUD. She quickly read it and frowned. Maelyn returned the salute and began walking toward the bridge.

"I didn't have a chance to review the service records of the crew before I came aboard."

Artificial green eyes regarded her for a moment and then blinked. "Understood, Captain. I can give you a report if you wish."

Maelyn considered it for a moment and then understood Hyden's meaning. She opened a comlink to the PMC. "Go ahead, Lieutenant."

Hyden accepted the comlink and transferred a report that included her evaluation of the crew and the ship during the weeks she'd been aboard. In the span of a few moments, Maelyn was able to absorb the information in the report.

"Thank you for that," Maelyn said.

They walked down the corridor toward the bridge, and Maelyn instead chose to enter her ready room. "A quick word, Lieutenant Commander."

They walked into her office and Maelyn turned toward her XO. The PMC had feminine features based on what Sienna Hyden must have looked like when she'd been human.

"I think there's something we should get out of the way regarding your previous command under Captain Rossing," Maelyn said.

The CDA didn't stiffen, but it was the lack of reaction that made her believe Sienna might have engaged her endocrine control protocols to help govern her emotions.

"What is it you would like to ask me, Captain?"

"Do you have any trepidations serving under another captain? I'd rather know about it now and clear the air before we engage the Sentinels."

"Captain, you have access to my PMC integrity checks and could access that data any time you wish."

Maelyn nodded. "I know that, but I'd rather hear it from you."

"Yes, I do, Captain. My concern is that PMCs like me aren't counted as equal members of the crew despite our rank and service history. These concerns are not just my own, but are shared by many others of my…"

Maelyn gave her an inquisitive look. "Kind?"

"PMC guidance protocols advise against regarding oneself as something different than other human beings."

"That puts us in a difficult position, because you *are* different, as are others like you."

"Yes, Captain."

"You're a member of my crew, and I'll treat you with the same respect I would give anyone else," Maelyn said, regarding her XO for a moment. "I don't expect you to believe me, but I do ask that you give me the opportunity to prove to you that not everyone feels the same way about PMCs."

Lieutenant Commander Hyden blinked a few times. "I appreciate that, Captain."

"You've sacrificed so much—you and every other PMC that we've managed to retrieve—and I want you to know that I will do everything I can to make sure no one forgets and that we honor your service."

She smiled. "Thank you, Captain. That really means a lot to me. I've heard about what you did during your last mission. You wouldn't abandon the PMCs being reactivated, and you helped others achieve their mission objectives. It's an honor to serve under you."

Maelyn smiled a little. "Thank you for that, Lieutenant Commander. Now let's head to the bridge and get this ship ready to depart."

"Lead the way, ma'am."

The ships of the fleet maintained a ready status, and automated resupply drones made sure that they were fully stocked with ammunition and supplies. These ships had been constructed while the *Salvation* was being built, and they were designed to require minimal crew as long as they had PMC support aboard.

Maelyn was leading a battle group of twenty destroyers and fifteen cruisers, and more than half of them had PMCs aboard. She was able to review the ship's systems in as little as fifteen minutes, recalling Brandt's comment that that task would normally have taken a few hours to complete.

She sat at the command station on the bridge and opened a comlink to engineering. A familiar voice answered.

"Engineering," Kieva said. "Oh, sorry, Captain."

Maelyn knew the status of engineering, but she just wanted to speak to her longtime friend and engineer.

"How's my ship?"

"Purring like the great kitties of old, Captain. She's got teeth. I can't imagine another kind of ship that could be more ready to engage the Sentinels."

"Excellent," Maelyn said.

She closed the commlink, and an alert appeared on her workstation HUD. It was from the *Salvation*.

Maelyn accepted the comlink and smiled. "Admiral Aldren."

Quinton smiled. "How do you like your new ship?"

"I can't wait to take her out."

"You won't have to wait long. The orders are coming." He leaned closer to the camera. "You know, I could demote myself and be there in an hour."

Maelyn snorted. He had his charms, and they always seemed to work on her. "I would have enjoyed the company."

Quinton's eyes softened and he looked at her for a few moments longer. She knew that look. He was afraid of losing her. No amount of quips could cover up the fact that they cared about one another. Maybe she was being foolish and should have let him create a backup of her mind.

"Thank you for assigning Lieutenant Commander Hyden to my command."

Quinton nodded. "I had a feeling the two of you would work well together," he said. He shrugged and rolled his eyes a little. "I guess, if I *had* to be replaced..."

She could tell he was dragging this out and she didn't mind. Quinton could multitask like no one she'd ever seen, but time was running out.

"Good luck, Admiral Aldren."

Quinton's face became serious. "Good hunting, Captain Wayborn. Until we meet again."

They shared one last look, and then the comlink closed.

A few minutes later, they received their orders from CENTCOM.

"XO," Maelyn said, "alert the battle group of our immediate departure."

"Yes, Captain. Comms, alert the battle group," Lieutenant Commander Hyden said.

Maelyn looked at her XO. She hoped they had enough time to really get to know one another because she thought they could be good friends one day.

24

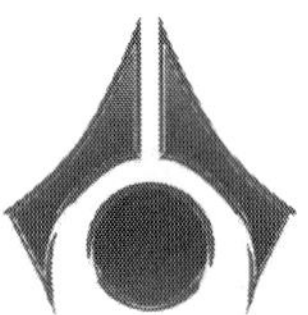

QUINTON STOOD on the central platform in the spherical chamber that was the *Salvation's* main bridge. Dozens of comfortable, couch-like workstations were spaced throughout the cavernous room, which was bursting with activity. Primary and secondary teams occupied the rows of workstations, representing a mix of PMC and human bridge officers.

Quinton was integrated into the *Salvation's* massive computing core, as were the other PMCs on the bridge. However, there were hundreds of PMCs who served aboard the *Salvation's* key systems, along with tens of thousands of human crewmembers. Integration into the *Salvation's* computing core was essential for maximum efficiency of the planetoid spaceship.

Quinton had integrated into many ships' computing cores, and he had instant awareness of data—from scanner arrays to onboard weapons systems, and even deployed hyper-missiles—but the *Salvation's* computing core was more complex than a single warship. There were too many systems, sensors, and sheer amounts of data for any one person to monitor, even with increased frame rates and an ESS that processed information at the speed of light, which was why there was a complex hierarchy of data access that helped filter the data up the chain of command, avoiding bottlenecks in the flow of information. As commanding officer, Quinton could access any of the ship's systems he wanted, but it would be foolish of him to do so. Running a ship was a team effort, and the *Salvation* was no exception, even if the crew signature was comprised of different individuals. Quinton hadn't been idle over these many months while they'd built up their strength. Augmented implants had been provided for the human crew, along with rapid learning simulations that built upon the vast experience of multiple federation space navies. Admiral Browning had ensured that tactics and capabilities of all the known space navies were available in the *Salvation's* vast data repositories. The Acheron Confederacy Navy hadn't been the most capable federation space navy just because of the superiority of its technology, although that was part of it, but the bigger part was the training of ACN personnel, from the lowliest spacer to that of the highest officer.

Quinton was not only able to take advantage of all that, but also of the allies who had supported Browning during the Federation Wars. He'd reviewed Browning's personal logs, but he wasn't finished going through them all. Browning might not have been a PMC himself, but he was the most driven person Quinton had ever studied. He wished he could've met him, wished Browning were here now, because when it came right down to it, Browning was the best person to defeat Harding Prime. Quinton was merely the PMC who had stepped up to fill the shoes of a much greater man than he could ever be. He smiled as he imagined what Browning's response to thoughts like that would have been—probably the proverbial "kick in the ass." Quinton was here, and Browning was gone. It was *his* job to see that the Sentinels and Harding Prime were defeated.

Quinton looked at the massive holotank that displayed a galaxy map showing fleet deployments, as well as reported star systems under Sentinel attack.

A comlink came from Brandt on the secondary bridge.

"UFA civilian delegate transport ships have left. Sherilyn will continue to send us intel as it comes in," Brandt said.

"Good," Quinton replied. "We can't protect all these star systems at once. Where did Harding get so many ships? Are you sure he's not building them?"

"We've been trying to get an accurate count of Sentinel ships for over fifty years, and each time we thought we had a handle on it, there were always more," Brandt replied.

Quinton peered at the holographic galaxy map. He could focus in on individual star systems, and there was even more data on each level, but he couldn't allow himself to get distracted.

"As to your second question, our intelligence assets all maintain that there are no Sentinel shipyards still building ships," Brandt said.

Quinton looked at the comlink sub-window. "No insult to the DUC spy network, but no one knew about the *Salvation* either. Harding could have shipyards hidden somewhere."

"I don't think so, Quinton, and not just because I don't want to believe it. Harding is a genius when it comes to systems and technology, but the engineering of ships was never associated with him. The ACN taught him about weapons systems and ship capabilities, but they didn't teach him how to build a fleet."

"He could have learned or gotten someone to do it for him."

"Well, he did create the original Sentinel fleet. After that, he took control of existing warships and added them to his fleets."

Quinton nodded, conceding the point. "Why would he need to build more ships when he already had so many to begin with." He studied the galaxy map for a few seconds.

"I can't see any pattern as to why these star systems were attacked," Brandt said. He looked at Quinton and frowned. "What is it? You suspect something."

"I do, but it'll be difficult to prove, and in the end, it might not make any difference," Quinton said, scanning the data on the screen. Radek was conducting multiple data analyses and probability scores, suggesting the most likely reason for the targeted systems being attacked. "Maybe it's not a tactical decision based on the resources in those star systems."

Brandt considered that for a few moments and then nodded. "They don't need the resources."

"Right, so this attack is in reaction to something. I think it's because the spacers in these systems were starting to believe the truth. They're being targeted to send a message to other star systems. We have to help them," Quinton said.

Brandt's eyebrows pulled forward. "That would mean that the Sentinels are more capable of monitoring individual star systems than we suspected. God, Quinton, I can't… I don't know what that means."

"It's not as difficult as you might think. Most public data—things like current events—are broadcast on newsnets. It's the perfect way to see which narratives are being pushed and challenged, depending on the sources of the information."

"Is there something you're not telling me?"

"It's not new. The Jordani's did it. I've been on a few counter-intelligence missions to expose insurgents and the like. I don't have to tell *you* that wars are fought in many different ways, even when there isn't an active engagement."

Brandt bobbed his head once. "How do you want to proceed?"

"Since we can't protect all those star systems simultaneously, we'll have to do a sweep—several sweeps launched from different star systems. I want to delay the Sentinel response for as long as possible," Quinton said.

"What about the Collective?"

"What about them?"

"Draven wants our help defending his star systems in return for his support."

Quinton needed to prioritize where his fleets were deployed and do it in such a way as to not appear to be assigning priority according to what a star system's perceived worth was. "Draven has defenses for his core systems… assuming he shares them with us. He'll need to hold on until we can get to those systems, unless he's going to volunteer that kind of data."

Brandt smiled a little. "I see your point. I can coordinate with him. He'll want to know where our ships will be deployed."

Quinton chuckled. "He can wonder all he wants, but he's not cleared to know. If his systems come under serious attack, he needs to let us know so we can help him with his defenses, but that doesn't necessitate him knowing or having any input on our operations. He's stayed on the sideline for so long that I doubt he'll be surprised by our stance."

"I'm glad you said it."

"I did learn a thing or two from you, Brandt."

The comlink was severed and Quinton began issuing orders to his fleets of ships. More than half the effort of battle went toward the preparation and placement of military assets. He wouldn't have his ships going blindly into star systems where the Sentinels were located. They'd have to do some reconnaissance first to assess the situation. After that, the fleets and battlegroup commanders would come up with a response.

Quinton increased the *Salvation's* battle readiness because it would be impossible for him to keep his ship secret any longer. This was likely a big part of the Sentinels' strategy. They wanted him to bring the *Salvation* into this fight, which was exactly what he would do if he had hundreds of thousands of warships at his disposal—lure out his quarry and assess its capabilities so he could formulate a strategy to neutralize the threat. Quinton aimed to keep the Sentinels, Admen Desher, and Harding Prime off-balance as much as he could, and that meant he had to limit the number of Sentinels reporting back to Harding Prime—a task much easier said than done.

25

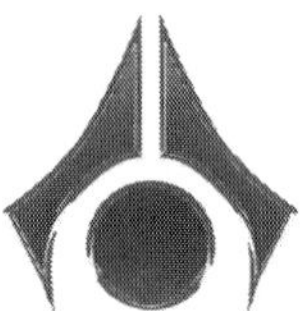

Maelyn peered at the tactical data on the main holoscreen. They'd entered the Epsilon Odysseus Star System, which was home to several large space stations, as well as orbital salvage processing stations. Epsilon Odysseus was known for its high metallicity throughout the system of planets there.

They'd tracked the Sentinels through three different star systems in the sector. They'd been too late to prevent an attack, but the Sentinels hadn't destroyed all the habitats in those systems. They'd done crippling damage to more than half the installations, dividing their attacks between automated processing centers and habitat decks where thousands of spacers lived and worked. She couldn't do anything to offer immediate help to those star systems, other than assuring the survivors that help was on the way. She sent a jump-capable comms drone to bring her report to CENTCOM, apprising them of the situation. She'd given her assessment on the amount of assistance those star systems needed, but they were hardly in the systems long enough to do a proper assessment. Maelyn did the best she could and tried to be as fair as possible.

A fresh set of icons appeared on the tactical plot as a third of her battle group entered the star system on the far side from her own ships. She held another group in reserve, waiting for active scan confirmation of Sentinel ships before they'd respond. If Sentinels weren't detected, they'd jump to the next star system on their list, and the rest of the battle group would catch up.

"Contact," Lieutenant Donavan said. "Sentinel destroyers. Leviathan class. Eight ships detected so far, Captain."

Her tactical officer updated the plot on the main holoscreen. It wouldn't take the Sentinels long to detect Maelyn's battle group.

"Helm, execute a micro-jump. Bring us in there. Tactical, I want a firing solution with tachyon lance ready to go when we get there," Maelyn said.

Tachyon lances fired a large, focused beam of highly energized particles, capable of massive damage, even to the battle-steel hulls of armored warships.

"Yes, Captain, firing solution ready," Lieutenant Donavan said.

"Course ready, Captain," Ensign Goodman said.

"Engage," Maelyn said.

The *Ascendant* and the other ships in her task force micro-jumped, beating the gamma burst from their system jump by over thirty seconds.

Sentinel destroyers were firing their weapons on one of the processing centers in orbit around an inner planet.

"Fire," Maelyn said.

Tachyon lances from six ACN destroyers fired at the unsuspecting Sentinel warships. Highly energized particles raced toward the enemy ships faster than the speed of light.

"Direct hit on five targets," Lieutenant Commander Hyden said. "Hull penetration on three of the targets. Two ships have been disabled."

"Remaining enemy ships have increased their velocity. They're moving on an intercept course, Captain," Lieutenant Donavan said.

The Sentinels seemed to respond to new threats in the same way—quickly and recklessly. Maelyn believed this was because for far too long the Sentinels had gone unopposed.

The tactical plot updated and two of the enemy ships went to amber status, while the rest still showed a readiness status.

"Helm, alter course fifteen degrees. Let's lure them away from the processing centers. Tactical, do we have the angle for another shot?"

"We can hit one of them. It'll take time to line up the remaining two ships here, Captain," Lieutenant Donavan said.

"Focus on the ship we can hit," Maelyn replied. "Ops, have Captains Tolliver and Bala break off and engage the two we can't reach."

"Aye, Captain," Lieutenant Linda Norquist replied.

Maelyn saw the power draw from her ship's main reactor spike as their primary weapon primed. They'd taken the Sentinels by surprise and prevented them from angling the prows of their ships to fire their weapons.

A lance of highly energized particles slammed into the enemy ship's armored hull. The *Ascendant* was perfectly aligned, and the lance penetrated through to the other side, gutting the interior of the ship. The Sentinel destroyer tried to angle away, but that made the damage worse, and the ship blew apart.

"Direct hit, main reactor. There's nothing left of them, Captain," Lieutenant Donavan said, his voice high with excitement.

"Excellent work," Maelyn said.

The tactical plot showed the status of the remaining two disabled ships switch to red. The other ships in her battle group had destroyed them.

"Let's focus. This isn't over yet. There are three more ships in this system, and they know we're coming," Maelyn said.

She looked at Sienna, and the PMC gave a slight shake of her head. "Not yet, Captain."

Maelyn nodded. "Comms, have there been any broadcast comlinks from the Sentinels?"

Lieutenant Tom Ellis peered at the multiple windows on his holoscreen. "Negative, Captain, but our sensors might have missed it."

Maelyn's gaze flicked toward Sienna. "They would have reported in. They should have signaled for backup units once they were under attack."

"That is their standard operating procedure, but we took them by surprise. Perhaps they never got the chance, ma'am."

"Captain," Lieutenant Donavan said, "Bravo Task Force has destroyed the remaining three Sentinel destroyers."

"Understood," Maelyn replied and looked at her comms officer.

Lieutenant Ellis shook his head. "No subspace comlinks have been detected."

Maelyn considered this for a few moments and peered at the main holoscreen. No more enemy ships had been detected, and if the Sentinels hadn't reported the attack, it wasn't likely that more would be coming.

"Comms, send a message to the system governors informing them that the Sentinels have been destroyed," Maelyn said.

"Aye, Captain," Lieutenant Ellis replied.

She checked the status of the ships in her battle group. The enemy had barely fired back. Even though the Sentinels were leviathan class ACN destroyers, their jump drives were limited so they couldn't execute micro jumps. However, that wasn't evident across other Sentinel warships. It was impossible for them to predict, and they couldn't rely on known ship signatures.

Maelyn looked at her XO.

"Luck of the draw, Captain," Sienna said.

Maelyn didn't like it. She'd take the win, but something felt off about this encounter. Even if the Sentinels were surprised, why wouldn't they report the attack? She said as much to Sienna.

"It could be that they knew help wouldn't arrive," Sienna replied.

"Perhaps," Maelyn agreed.

"Captain, we've received a priority update from CENTCOM," Lieutenant Ellis said.

"Send it to my workstation," Maelyn replied.

She quickly read the new orders. "Nav, plot a course to the Arcturus Star System. Ops, send an update to the rest of the battle group once Nav has our course."

Maelyn saw that Sienna had brought up information on the Arcturus Star System.

"What's so special about this star system?" Sienna asked.

"It's highly populated. There are millions of spacers there," Maelyn replied, reading the data on her screen. Lists of salvager groups operating in the star system were among the data, and she recognized some of them. "The Collective has a big operations base there."

"The Collective began from the remnants of the Tillion Empire Military, now one of the most powerful groups in the galaxy," Sienna said.

"No one knows for sure just how big the Collective really is. Trenton Draven has been able to hide that through different corporations and star unions," Maelyn replied.

They came up with an approach to recon the Arcturus Star System and Maelyn's battle group left the Epsilon Odysseus System, despite protests raised by the system governors. She understood their frustration. They'd just been attacked. Lives had been lost, and their only means of protection was leaving them to engage the enemy in another star system. It was unlikely that the Sentinels would return to Epsilon Odysseus, but there was no way Maelyn could guarantee that, which was what the system governors wanted.

She'd redeployed her battle group so they were split down the middle, with Maelyn leading one group and Captain Tolliver leading the second group.

Tolliver would enter the system first and lead the scouting force. Maelyn's task force entered on the opposite side of the star system. As they emerged from the hyperspace jump, scan data from Tolliver's task force began coming in.

Maelyn peered at the data. The tactical plot on the main holoscreen changed to reflect Arcturus's system of planets and features. She tilted her head to the side. The Arcturus Star System was part of a sextuplet system of eclipsing binary star systems. Arcturus was the outermost binary star in the system.

"They haven't detected anything," Maelyn said and shook her head. "Tactical, have any enemy ships been detected by our scanners?"

"Negative, Captain," Lieutenant Donavan said.

The star system had multiple massive space stations that had taken up locations closer to the star where traditional life-giving planets could support life. However, this star system didn't have any planets in the traditional Goldilocks zone. Instead, the interior rocky planets had been destroyed during the Federation Wars, leaving massive fields of asteroids.

They flew toward the space stations. Since their location was surrounded by a significant asteroid field, the Sentinels could be hiding.

"Captain, I'm receiving a comlink from someone near the space station," Lieutenant Ellis said.

Maelyn frowned. "Near?"

"Yes, ma'am. It's hard to pinpoint exactly, but I don't think they're on the actual space station. They're asking to speak to the leader of the battle group, Captain."

"Send the link to my station," Maelyn replied.

A video comlink was established, and a woman with golden blonde hair and large brown eyes appeared. The woman stared at her for a moment, and her eyes widened in recognition. Maelyn frowned and blinked several times, her brain racing to make the connection.

"Captain, thank you for taking this comlink. You and your battlegroup are in imminent danger."

That voice… It sounded so familiar to her, but she couldn't identify it.

The woman's eyebrows pushed into a concerned frown while her eyes darted to the side, checking something off-screen. "Captain Wayborn, are you receiving me?"

Maelyn narrowed her gaze. The intonation and speech pattern of how she pronounced her name sent a jolt through her brain. She knew who this woman was. How many times had she thought about the one operative who'd managed to fool her, almost taking her life and those of her crewmembers aboard the *Nebulon?* She looked at the screen and her expression deadpanned. "Yes, I'm receiving you," she said, sending a text message to her XO.

Find the source of the signal.

"Who are you, and what kind of danger are you talking about?" Maelyn asked.

"I'm Teagan Cayne, Captain. You and the other Alliance ships need to leave here immediately. This is a trap..."

Maelyn leaned toward her holoscreen, peering at the woman. "You!" she snarled. "You! What happened to your blue skin and platinum hair, Vonya?"

The woman stopped speaking for a moment and blinked in surprise, but she quickly recovered. "Please, you need to listen to me. You're right. My name isn't Vonya. It's Teagan Cayne."

"Right, sure you are," Maelyn said, her voice dripping with sarcasm. She looked at her XO. "Do you have a lock on her location yet?"

"You're wasting time—"

"No, I'm not. You have so much to answer for. I let you on my ship and you betrayed us. Left us for dead, and for the Sentinels, no less. Once I get your location, I'm coming for you," Maelyn said. She gritted her teeth and turned away from the video comlink.

"Maelyn, please, I know you have no reason to trust me. My name really is Teagan. Lennix Crowe is my father."

Maelyn grinned bitterly, unable to believe the audacity of this woman. "You're something else. Lennix Crowe doesn't have a daughter. What danger are we in? There are no Sentinels here."

The video comlink wavered as if the signal was being disrupted.

Teagan leaned toward the camera. "Listen to me. You can't trust your allies... betrayal. They're going to betray you—"

Maelyn heard a shriek of frustration before the comlink severed, and she looked at her comms officer.

"I'm sorry, Captain. The signal is gone," Lieutenant Donavan said.

"Tactical, is anything showing on our scans?" Maelyn asked.

"No, Captain, there's nothing here. I couldn't pinpoint her location."

After all this time, Vonya, of all people, was trying to warn her, as if Maelyn would be foolish enough to listen to a spy. Vonya or Teagan—whatever her name was.

Lennix Crowe's daughter?

"Captain, I've analyzed her vocal patterns," Sienna said.

Maelyn swung her gaze toward her XO.

"Aside from masking her location, there was no other signal augmentation detected. She's telling the truth. At least, she believed she was."

Maelyn pressed her lips together and looked at the main holoscreen as if the tactical plot could give her further insight. Why would Vonya warn her? It didn't make any sense. She was a master of disguise. Surely she could fool whatever analysis Sienna was capable of doing. Not all deception was carried out through artificial enhancements.

Maelyn squeezed her eyes shut. She was too angry, and it was clouding her judgment. "Ops, set Condition One. Helm, plot a course into the star system. We'll take our time. There could be a Sentinel attack force hiding among the asteroids."

While her orders were carried out, she wondered who Teagan had meant when she told her that they couldn't trust their allies. Who couldn't they trust? Had she named someone before the signal was disrupted? A calmer and more logical part of her mind was considering the warning as factual, but she couldn't leave the star system without doing a sweep. There was no indication of an attack force that her battle group couldn't handle.

Maelyn looked at Sienna, and the PMC gave her a grim nod.

"Into the inferno we go," Maelyn said quietly.

26

Becker stood in the cargo hold and watched as the dockworkers finished guiding the counter-grav platforms stacked with storage containers. One of the dockworkers walked over to Oscar, holding out a tablet. Oscar quickly read the manifest and checked the list with the containers.

Becker walked toward the ladder and slid down to the main level. "How's it look?"

Oscar thumbed the tablet and returned it to the dockworker. "Looks good. This is the last of it."

They heard Guttman singing as he strode through the cargo bay doors with a spring in his step. He spotted them and gave them a smile from ear to ear.

"He did it," Oscar said.

Guttman grinned as he shuffled toward them, doing a kind of happy dance. "They're all gone. I just sold the last batch. We need to get more of that beer. They kept asking if Borealis Station was going to be one of our regular stops."

"How much did you sell them for?" Becker asked.

Guttman's face became solemn for a second, and then the grin reappeared. "A lot more than what I paid for it. Here, take a look."

Guttman used his wrist computer to send them the data.

"You know, that's not a bad idea," Oscar said with a thoughtful frown.

Becker looked at the bill of sale and smiled. "I've got to hand it to you, Guttman. You made us a hefty profit, but what about the duty fees that go to the station?"

Guttman's face blanched. "Isn't it time to go? Aren't we leaving now?" he asked, hastening to close the cargo doors.

Becker shook his head. "You didn't."

Guttman held his hands out to the side. "What?"

Becker gritted his teeth and exhaled forcefully through his nose.

"Don't get like that. It's not what you think. But we should go sooner rather than later," Guttman said.

Becker walked toward the ship intercom and opened a comlink to the bridge. "Yeah, Hayley, we're all set here. Time to go."

"Understood, Captain. I'll get us underway," Haley replied.

Becker pulled his finger from the intercom and glared at Guttman.

Oscar walked over to them. "I said it's not a bad idea."

Becker glanced at Oscar. "What's not a bad idea?"

"Establishing regular stops for our ships. Something with a schedule that spacers can depend on," Oscar replied.

"That is a good idea," Becker said and then looked at Guttman. "But we can only do that if we remain in good standing with the docking authorities. Now tell me what you did and whether this is going to come back to bite us in the ass."

Guttman's smile drooped a little. "The buyer met me on the docks to take possession of the canisters. He wanted all of them, so I never got to actually pay the duty fees."

"And the dockmaster has no idea we just sold cargo on his dock. They monitor for that, Guttman. What's the matter with you?"

"I know. I wouldn't have done it, but they had already taken care of the monitors in the area."

Becker inhaled deeply and sighed, grabbing his anger and choking the life out of it. "No more. You hear me? Never again. I don't care who it is."

Guttman nodded and then frowned. "What if—"

"No! My God, I don't care what kind of… don't double down on this. Don't you know who owns Teratek Industrial?"

Guttman swallowed and shook his head.

Oscar rolled his eyes. "Guttman, come on," he said, looking around to make sure none of the crew could overhear them. "The Collective."

Guttman's mouth hung open a little. "Oh."

"Yeah, 'oh,'" Becker replied. "You know—"

"No, don't say it. I won't do it again. Promise," Guttman said quickly.

Becker heard the ship's engines engage. At least they were off the docking station. They just needed to put some distance from the station before they could leave the system.

"So back to the other thing," Oscar said and then added, "Shipping."

Becker nodded. "I think the idea has merit. It's not unheard of, though."

"Yeah, but if we can establish shipping routes, we'd bring in regular business."

"As long as it lasts," Guttman said.

Becker shook his head, and the others looked at him. "Aren't you forgetting something? Sentinels? The Alliance? Any of this ringing a bell? It's not like we've been helping them with recruiting for months."

Oscar looked away and frowned.

Guttman sighed heavily, and his shoulders slumped. "Geez, Becker, when did you become such a killjoy?"

Becker snorted. "*I'm* the killjoy? You guys are acting like there isn't a war about to begin at any moment and just want to go on like none of that is going to affect us. That's not being a killjoy; that's being practical. Now, come on. Get your heads on straight."

Guttman winced. "All right, geez. No need to go all high and mighty with us."

"Becker's right," Oscar said, shrugging. "It's still a good idea, though."

Becker nodded. "It is. We can look into it, but right now, we don't even have a place to set up shop. We have three ships doing salvage runs. It's a good start, but if we're going to get into shipping, we might be stepping on a few toes."

"So what? We're not looking to take over anyone's business, but clearly, there's a need for more regular contact between spaceports," Oscar said.

Guttman's lips lifted into a broad smile. "I love this."

Becker shared a glance with Oscar, and the two of them gave Guttman an appraising look.

"Love what?" Oscar asked.

"This!" Guttman replied, gesturing to all three of them. "Working together. Figuring it out. Not dealing with someone breathing down our necks about a damn salvage quota. And no one trying to kill us."

An audible chime sounded from overhead.

"Captain, report to the bridge," Haley said.

There was an alarmed tone in her voice. Becker hastened over to the intercom, giving Guttman a sidelong glance. "What is it?"

"Captain, there are a couple of ships on an intercept course. They look like they've come from Borealis Station."

"I'm on my way," Becker said and speared a look toward Guttman. "No one breathing down our necks, huh?"

Becker palmed the door controls and headed toward the bridge, hurrying through the ship and ignoring the questioning looks from the crew he passed.

"Get to your stations," Oscar said.

Becker walked onto the bridge and Haley stood up from the command center.

On the main holoscreen was a chart of the star system, and there were three ships on an intercept course.

"Corvettes," Becker said.

Haley nodded.

Corvette interceptors were the ships of choice to quickly move through a star system on security patrols. They carried a light weapons payload, and a lesser captain would allow themselves to be delayed until a cruiser showed up. Becker didn't intend to wait that long.

"Have they hailed us?" he asked.

"Negative, Captain," Haley replied. She'd gone to the communications workstation.

Oscar went to the pilot's station, and Guttman approached the operations workstation.

Becker brought up the tactical plot. They were still connected to the Borealis Station Network, which broadcasted ship locations within its vicinity.

"I don't like this," Becker said. His gut instinct was flailing with alarm. "Oscar, let's charge up the jump drive."

"On it," Oscar replied.

Becker watched the ship traffic leaving from the station.

"All this for some duty fees? Seems a bit over the top to me," Guttman said.

Becker scowled in Guttman's direction. "I told you they don't play around."

Guttman grimaced and looked away.

"They're hailing us, Captain," Haley said.

"Oscar?" Becker asked.

Oscar stared at the navigation interface on the holoscreen in front of him. "Got it. Course is in."

"Good. Execute," Becker replied.

"Bye, bye, Borealis. Maybe next time," Oscar said.

Becker waited for the jump drive to engage. It didn't, and Oscar's eyebrows drew up in alarm.

"Captain, they say we're in a dampening field," Haley said.

The tactical plot flashed an update, and several more corvettes appeared on the plot behind the *Astricus*.

"Shit," Becker said. "All right, Haley, send it to my station."

A second later, a video comlink appeared on Becker's holoscreen. The head and shoulders of a dark-skinned woman appeared, and she was smirking at him.

"Captain Becker," she said.

"That's me."

"I'm Captain Terallo."

"Look, Captain. I think there's been a misunderstanding."

The smirk never left Captain Terallo's face. "You tried to run. Only someone with something to hide runs."

"We were cleared to leave by the dockmaster."

Terallo chuckled. "Captain, you're not going anywhere. Check your scanners again."

Becker did. More corvettes appeared, along with two cruiser class ships. He looked at the comlink. "Look, my associate—"

"Spare me the excuses, Captain Becker. You're being detained. Any attempt to run and we'll…" she said with a shrug. "Just don't."

"Why are we being detained?"

"That's above my pay grade, Captain. My job is just to prevent you from leaving."

Becker inhaled deeply and sighed. He couldn't escape, not like this. The *Astricus* had some weapons and a few tricks, but he couldn't engage all those other ships, especially not in the middle of a dampening field.

"Well, I'm not going anywhere."

Captain Terallo smiled. "You're more sensible than the dossier indicates."

"Can you tell me who wants me detained?"

Captain Terallo gave him a pointed look. "You're guests of the Collective. Stay put, Captain. Instructions will be sent to you shortly."

"You don't want us to return to the station?"

Captain Terallo waggled her dark eyebrows once and severed the comlink.

"Just to be clear," Guttman said, "this isn't about the dock fees, right?"

Becker shook his head.

"Oh good," Guttman said, and Becker glared at him. "Well, not good, but you know what I mean. It's not my fault. This is something else."

"Yeah, it's worse," Becker replied.

27

The *Salvation's* main bridge was bursting with activity and Quinton stood in the center of it all. Reports from deployed fleets were pouring in as the bridge crew tried to make sense of the data. Some of the reports about a Sentinel presence were false. Scan data didn't reveal any recent gamma bursts from a ship entering the star system through a hyperspace jump. Other reports were accurate. Sentinels had attacked, and Alliance fleets had arrived in time to engage. Fighting the Sentinels was hardly ever limited to a fleet engagement between two known attack forces. Some Sentinel ships were capable of micro-jumps in system, and others were not. Each engagement taught them something, so Alliance ships could adapt to use better tactics against the Sentinels. The strength of the Sentinel fleets was in their numbers. A small scout force was rarely without backup forces within a few hundred lightyears. This was something Alliance ships had to account for in their tactics. It was difficult to engage the enemy when expecting a superior attack force to enter the system almost on top of the Alliance ships.

Quinton didn't know who was commanding the Sentinels. He didn't want to assume it was Harding Prime because there was no evidence to support it. He kept thinking about Admen Desher, who was a bit of a mystery. Desher was an Agent of Harding, who had traveled the galaxy on a mission to destroy any PMC he found. Desher had command authority to summon Sentinel ships. Could he be organizing these attacks? They were essentially using Sentinel scout forces to lure in an Alliance response, and then the real attack force would arrive. As much as Quinton had studied the data found on the *Salvation* in Browning's logs, he had never interacted with Harding Prime directly. Harding Prime was himself a mystery to Quinton, whereas he'd encountered and outsmarted Admen Desher in the past. However, he had to wonder how many Agents of Harding there were. Bentlae and other PMCs had recounted that there had been many during the

Federation Wars. Agents of Harding had sought to infiltrate Browning's ranks. The Federation Wars had been fought over a long period of time, with all sides seeking to create an advantage. The only way to detect whether a PMC was an Agent of Harding was through established PMC authentication protocols.

In response to Sentinel ambush tactics, Quinton had to ensure he had enough reserve forces to bolster Alliance ships. Trenton Draven had deployed his own fleets of ships to assist in the defense of other star systems. Brandt coordinated with Draven's fleet commanders, and they had been extremely helpful to Alliance ships. They were still sustaining losses, but so were the Sentinels—a lot of them.

"Admiral, we're receiving reports of significant Sentinel presence in the Vopurn Expanse," Lieutenant Xander said.

His tactical officer made that data available to him, and Quinton reviewed it. Significant Sentinel presence didn't begin to describe the tens of thousands of ships that were pouncing on three Alliance fleets only numbering in the thousands.

"Helm, plot us a course to Vopurn Expanse. Get us as close to the Sentinels as possible," Quinton said.

"Aye, Admiral," Lieutenant Stasya Orlova replied.

"Tactical, I want a firing solution ready to execute as soon as our scanners report on Sentinel locations. Priorities are their Dreadnoughts," Quinton said.

The nav system updated with a course to Vopurn Expanse, and the system of jump drives spiked a significant power draw from ten reactor cores. The *Salvation* entered hyperspace for a brief moment and emerged into a cluster of stars.

Scanner arrays began reporting the locations of the Sentinel forces, and the Alliance ships quickly updated them with their own tactical data. The star cluster was really a place where three star systems had collided. Orbiting planets hadn't settled into any sort of stability and wouldn't for a very long time.

The Alliance ships were defending a spaceport and mining stations in the system's interior. One fleet of eight hundred ships protected the interior star system, while the two remaining fleets had divided their forces in an attempt to draw away the Sentinels.

"Comms, inform the fleet commanders that help has arrived," Quinton said.

The *Salvation* had enough weaponry that even a Sentinel attack force that numbered over thirty thousand ships wouldn't require Quinton to use their most powerful weapons.

"Admiral, I have a firing solution. Dreadnought priority targets have been identified," Lieutenant Xander said.

Quinton studied the firing solution and authorized the attack. Scattered across the *Salvation's* massive hull, interior hatches opened for thousands of missile tubes. Multiple volleys of hyper-capable missiles with fusion warheads raced out of the missile tubes and transitioned out of n-space. The missiles emerged within three light-seconds of their targets and detonated their payloads. Soon, the tactical plot was awash with fusion warhead detonations that severely cut down the Sentinel forces.

"That got their attention, Admiral," Lieutenant Walsh Corvax said.

"Good," Quinton replied.

He wanted the Sentinels to come after him. Better that they attack the *Salvation* than wipe out three of his fleets.

"Comms, inform the fleet commanders to withdraw. We'll take it from here," Quinton said.

It took a few minutes for the tactical plot to refresh. The fusion warheads had blinded the sensors, but while their initial detonations were extremely powerful, they also quickly dissipated, which was exactly what he wanted. He had much stronger weapons in his arsenal. With a signal volley, he'd destroyed seven percent of the Sentinel's forces—enough to get their attention but not enough to make them run. He didn't want them to run. In fact, running was the last thing he wanted them to do.

A comlink from Brandt came from the secondary bridge. "They've taken the bait."

The remaining Sentinel forces were changing course to put them on an intercept course with the *Salvation*.

"Nearly all of them are coming. I thought they would have been more tactical with their attack," Brandt said.

"They have their priorities. They want to see what we're capable of and report back. The intel is worth more than the loss of ships," Quinton replied.

"Admiral," Lieutenant Xander said, "I have another firing solution ready for your approval."

A sub-window appeared on Quinton's holoscreen with his tactical officer's firing solution. Xander had adhered to the limitations Quinton had placed on him in terms of what weapons he was authorized to use against the enemy.

"Wait until they're fully committed. Then, let's show them something else," Quinton said and updated the tactical engagement parameters.

Lieutenant Xander looked at him, and there was a hungry gleam in the PMC's eyes.

With the discharge of any type of weapons, situational awareness was essential for minimizing and preventing collateral damage. The *Salvation* was capable of annihilating entire planets, and while there were no habitable planets in this star system, spacers lived with the knowledge of predictable orbital expectations. He didn't need to disrupt those expectations and create a worse situation for the spacers who would live here for years to come. Perhaps it was the ACN officer in him, but Quinton preferred that his attacks only impact his intended targets. He was a perfectionist like that.

Sentinel warships had high-energy weapons capabilities that were effective at both long- and short-range targets. Dreadnoughts were equipped with spinal-mounted heavy weapons that could pierce armor and overwhelm shields when their attacks were coordinated.

Quinton watched the tactical plot on display in the immense holotank. Sentinel destroyers screened their larger counterparts in anticipation of the volley of missiles their tactical computers predicted would be coming. They staggered their formation, expanding equal distances apart and in depth while allowing for many thousands of ships to fire their weapons at the *Salvation*. The fact that they'd adapted so quickly and with such precision wasn't lost on Quinton. He had no choice but to be impressed. Their computing cores must be linked with highly capable VIs that drew from over a century of knowledge gathered while participating in massive fleet engagements.

Heavy plasma cannons from more than six thousand Sentinel Dreadnoughts fired immense, high-energy, oviform emerald bolts, streaking their way toward the *Salvation*. After a short primer period, the cannons fired again and again.

"Power taps have been brought online. Energy fields are stable. Lances are ready, Admiral," Lieutenant Xander said.

Quinton lifted his lip in a snarl. "Fire!"

Colossal lances of cyan beams, flashing tremendously energized particles, surged from over a thousand superconductive lenses distributed across a quadrant of the *Salvation's* upper hemisphere. The beams crossed the expanse, reaching the Sentinels at relativistic speeds, causing massive damage to anything in their paths, be it the bolts of a plasma cannon or the armored hull of Sentinel warships.

The hulls of thousands of Sentinel warships gleamed brightly before the massive beam sloughed through layers of armor, annihilating the vulnerable interior. The enemy ships attempted to evade the powerful beams, but the weapons systems of the *Salvation* were controlled by highly trained and highly effective teams of PMCs, all of them with their Sapient Combat Simulation systems and frame rates at near maximum capacity. PMCs armed with legions of VIs could outperform Sentinel VIs.

"You can run, but you can't hide," Quinton said.

"My God," Brandt muttered.

"Helm, all ahead full. Let's close the gap," Quinton ordered.

"All ahead full, aye, Admiral," Lieutenant Stasya Orlova said.

Twenty percent of the energy drawn from the *Salvation's* power taps diverted to the ship's reactionless drive, and the planetoid ship accelerated at a rate that would impress starship captains of any generation.

Completely integrated into the *Salvation's* computing core, Quinton took in the data from the sensor arrays feeding the ship's tactical computers. Unable to repel or even do much damage to the *Salvation's* hull, the surviving Sentinel warships attempted to flee the system.

They didn't let them, and Sentinel warships were destroyed by the hundreds. The Sentinels equipped with jump drives capable of micro-jumps were pursued by either hyper-capable missiles that were fired from the *Salvation* or a ship from the three Alliance fleets still in the star system.

There was no escape, and the destruction of the Sentinel ambush was absolute.

"My God," Brandt said. "The firepower from this ship is without equal."

Integrating with the ship's system always gave Quinton an odd sense of detachment and expansion of his awareness. He withdrew from the *Salvation's* systems.

Looking at the holoscreen with Brandt's video commlink, Quinton smiled. "We kept it a secret as much as we could, but it's time they knew what they're up against."

Over the next six hours, they resupplied the ships in the star systems. An extensive scan of the wrecked Sentinel warships revealed no power core signals. The *Salvation's* attacks had been so devastating that there wasn't much left inside the hulks they were able to find.

Simon walked to Quinton and stood by his side. "I can't believe how destructive those lances were. The energy requirements are beyond anything I've seen before, but the power taps all remained within stable ranges of operation."

Quinton nodded. "You can learn the specifications of the weapons systems and test fire them, but it's different when they're used in actual combat."

Simon looked at him, lips pursed a little in thought. "I see the shock has already worn off."

"I'm sure you can make an accurate guess as to why that is," Quinton replied.

Simon chuckled. "Yeah, I think I can." He paused for a few seconds. "There have been other ambush sites, but none with an attack force this big."

Quinton nodded. "You're right. It's not a coincidence."

Simon frowned. "I hadn't said that."

"But you were."

Simon shrugged and shook his head a little. "You're right, I was. Anyway, I went over the sensor data and there's no way for us to determine whether any of the Sentinels escaped."

"It's probably safe to assume that at least one of them did, or at least got off a hyper-capable comms drone to report on the tactical data they collected."

"I thought you didn't like to assume. You do realize what the root word of that is, right?"

Quinton smiled with half his mouth. "Sometimes it can't be avoided."

"Admiral," Lieutenant Traver said, "we've received an alpha priority message. It's from Trenton Draven."

Quinton opened his personal holoscreen and gestured for Simon to stay while accessing the message.

"Admiral Aldren, Omicron Prioxis is under attack. The Sentinels are overwhelming our defenses. I've attached the tactical data from our sensors. I… We need the Alliance's help if we're to survive. I know there's been friction between us, and that you view the Collective's reticence—my reticence—to openly help the Alliance as detrimental to the Alliance's objectives. But Omicron Prioxis is one of our core systems, with ships and resources capable of helping you against the Sentinels. I assure you that if you help us defend the system and prevent the Sentinels from obliterating it, I will commit the Collective's extensive resources to the Alliance without delay. You must hurry. All of our lives are depending on the Alliance. On you."

The video message finished and then the tactical data and information about the star system became available.

Simon's mouth hung open a little and then he looked at Quinton. "You just had the leader of the Collective ask for your help. The leader of the whole damn Collective."

He didn't know anything about Omicron Prioxis, but one of the things he'd accepted since taking command of the *Salvation* was that he didn't need to do everything on his own. He sent out an alert to his senior officers and uploaded the data to the *Salvation's* computing core.

His senior officers joined a virtual meeting session.

"Brandt, what do you know about Omicron Prioxis? Is it really part of the Collective? What's so valuable there?" Quinton asked.

Brandt's gaze was away from the camera, looking at the tactical data. "Omicron," he said with a frown. "Yes, that system is known to be part of the Collective. The DUC archives show it tagged as a mining outpost, but the data on that is probably outdated. According to the data Draven included, it's a system rich in rare minerals, as well as materials critical to enhancing the capabilities of weapons yield and jump-drive range. The system has extensive defensive capabilities. It doesn't appear that the Sentinels attacked all at once. They sent a scout force and then called in reinforcements."

Quinton increased his frame rate, and Radek retrieved the data they had about Omicron Prioxis. It was a massive star system that was home to a red dwarf star. There were multiple asteroid belts from planetary collisions when the system was formed. It was home to a dozen ice planets, four Jovian planets, and eight Neptunian planets. The Collective had built multiple space stations and starbases. They had more defenses there than Quinton had seen anywhere else, which could only mean one thing. Draven was telling the truth and this star system was crucial to the Collective.

Quinton updated the data on the star map.

Simon exhaled explosively. "Are those numbers correct?"

"It's what they reported," Quinton replied.

"That's nearly a hundred thousand ships!" Simon said.

"More than enough to overwhelm even the defenses the Collective has deployed in that star system," Brandt said.

Quinton peered at the data. "We have to help them. I don't think we can win this war without help from the Collective."

Quinton studied the tactical data provided by Trenton Draven. The Sentinels had sent a scout force, and when they were met with resistance, they brought in more ships. The conflict had escalated from there as the Sentinels probed different areas of the star system. Each time the Sentinels were beaten back, more of their warships entered. Their behavior matched what Alliance forces had observed. If the Sentinels didn't have enough firepower to achieve their objective, they brought back enough ships until the objective—whatever that may be—was achieved.

Standing on the extended platform of the bridge, Quinton ordered Alliance reserve forces to the high-priority system and redirected other fleets as well. A countdown time appeared on one of his status windows. Alliance fleets would converge on Omicron Prioxis when the timer expired.

Battle assessments from previous encounters with the Sentinels provided statistical probabilities of the chances that the Alliance fleets could defeat the enemy force, and this was going to cost them. He couldn't account for the star systems defenses, and he didn't know how many warships the Collective had defending it. None of the statistical probabilities meant anything without that intel.

The *Salvation* emerged from hyperspace into the Oort of the Omicron Prioxis's outer system. Subspace comms confirmed the arrival of the other Alliance fleets with a vector to their defense priorities.

The star system was home to four space stations, twelve different mining stations, and six starbases. Scans revealed that the starbases were of a modified Jordani Federation design. Quinton remembered that the Jordanis were mostly reliant upon kinetic weaponry for their starbases. There was evidence of that in the scans, but there were also hangar bays, which meant that they had small combat ships to help with the defense. Squadrons of attack craft could evade heavy weapons and wreak havoc on larger ships. Quinton approved of the strategy.

Quinton glanced around the bridge and noticed that the bridge officers watched the tactical plot shown in the massive holotank with wide-eyed amazement—both his human and PMC crew.

"Stay focused," Quinton said, snatching their attention. "Concentration on the objectives. We need to relieve pressure on Collective forces and maximize the impact our fleets can project onto the enemy."

The moment of frozen awe was dissipated, and the bridge officers went back to work.

The Sentinels had divided their considerable forces, attacking multiple targets at once. Essentially, wherever they encountered resistance, they concentrated their efforts. It wasn't the most well-thought-out strategy and was predictive.

Quinton had his fleets jump to the Oort so they could assess the situation and then execute micro-jumps to strategic locations.

"Quinton, once we attack, they'll redirect their forces," Brandt said.

He nodded. "We need to use that, and time is running out. They'll detect us soon enough."

"We need to prioritize civilian targets. That means we should focus our efforts on the space stations first and then work our way out from there."

Quinton had considered that and said so. "Getting in that mess isn't the problem. It's getting back out again. Once we show our teeth, then..." he paused for a moment. "Let's coordinate with Draven on this and leverage his forces in our plan."

Trenton Draven was aboard a battleship carrier that was part of the main battlegroup defending Aurora Station. The leader of the Collective looked a little haggard, with worry lines creasing his forehead.

"I hope you've got a good plan," Draven said.

Quinton and Brandt explained what they intended.

"I should have seen their attack pattern sooner. Their reactionary and escalation methodology is so obvious now that you've pointed it out," Draven said.

"You're doing the best you can," Quinton replied.

"Okay, we can update our tactical response after. Where do you want our forces?"

Quinton smiled. "Sending you a data burst now. Countdown will begin upon receipt."

Draven looked away from the camera for a few seconds. "All right, we've got it."

"Good. Now let's give the Sentinels something their tactical VIs won't expect."

The comlink to Draven shifted to a secondary priority and passed to a comms officer under Brandt's command.

"I know we're both on the same ship, but it feels like we're not," Brandt said.

Quinton chuckled a little. "I know what you mean. Time to kick a hornet's nest."

Brandt smiled. "Another pre-diaspora saying. You're just full of surprises."

"I like to keep you on your toes. You never know what's going to come out of my mouth."

"Let's hope we can keep the Sentinels off-balance. I can't imagine they have more warships in reserve in this sector," Brandt said.

Quinton closed the comlink. He integrated into the *Salvation's* computer systems but allowed enough of his attention to maintain awareness of his avatar's location on the bridge. He engaged the SCS system and began collecting data from a multitude of sources as they were prioritized from Radek, PMCs serving on the *Salvation*, and PMCs that served aboard Alliance ships in the star system. He could never analyze the raw data feeds. The sheer amount of data processing required was way beyond even his cybernetic avatar, but the *Salvation's* computer core processing strength was beyond that of the entire fleet, even if they functioned as a distributed computer system. The *Salvation* was meant for this fight, and Quinton was starting to believe that he was up to the task of defeating the Sentinels and Harding Prime.

Alliance fleet warships micro-jumped out of the Oort of the outer star system, bringing them within firing range of the Sentinels that converged on the four space stations. As soon as Alliance ships emerged, they used the tactical data provided by Collective ships and targeted Sentinel warships.

Trenton Draven provided them with the ships' identifications, which were then broadcast through secure comlink channels. Hyper-capable missiles with fusion warheads raced from Alliance heavy cruisers while Challenger class destroyers used their tachyon lances to devastating effect on their targets. The Sentinels' rear ranks were taken completely by surprise. Sentinels began to engage their engines using emergency boosters to execute evasive maneuvers as if they'd been moving in slow motion and had suddenly sprung to life.

There were tens of thousands of Sentinel warships, from the smallest destroyer class to the behemoth super-Dreadnoughts. Quinton monitored the tactical data as it reached the *Salvation*. The speeds at which the Sentinels were moving in a concerted coordination was sure to stress even the most powerful of the inertia dampeners. If any of those ships had human crew aboard them, they would be dead. A human crew was always the limiting factor when it came to fleet engagements. CDAs could withstand the powerful forces, but Sentinels were in danger of breaking the superstructure of their warships. And still, they realigned their ships to face the new threat.

The *Salvation* emerged from its micro-jump near Aurora Station, home to over forty million spacers and station defensive systems that fired their weapons at the Sentinels. The station commanders must have coordinated their attacks with the Collective fleets, trying to push back the Sentinel warships.

Quinton made sure his comms officers informed them that the planetoid spaceship that had emerged from hyperspace was there to help defend the station.

"Aurora Station acknowledges our fleet presence, Admiral," Lieutenant Traver said.

"Good," Quinton replied. He didn't want to be concerned with friendly fire from their allies.

"Admiral," Lieutenant Xander said, "I have multiple firing solutions ready."

"Let's show them our teeth, Lieutenant," Quinton replied.

Powerful Hercules class missiles began pouring out from tubes across the entirety of the *Salvation's* surface. Quinton expanded their available warhead arsenal beyond the standard fusion warheads to also include gravitic and antimatter warheads. Tens of thousands of hyper-capable missiles raced toward Sentinel warships. PMCs ensured that the deadly missiles could reach their targets despite any interference from cyber warfare defenses used by Sentinel warships. It was a numbers game. The farther a missile penetrated the defensive screens of the Sentinels, the more intel was distributed to the other ships and weapons systems. PMCs using Sapient Combat Simulations further increased the precision accuracy.

With so many detonations happening, it was impossible for the sensor arrays to detect the amount of destruction being dealt to the Sentinels. However, the Sentinels had thousands of ships to spare, and they pushed toward the *Salvation* with relentless determination.

Thousands of super-Dreadnought class Sentinel ships fired their own high-powered tachyon lances. Highly energized particles blazed forth with the fury of thousands of exploding stars, and there was nothing Quinton could do as the *Salvation* took the brunt of the attack.

The *Salvation's* internal sensors began reporting damaged sections as the Sentinels' heavy weapons pierced the battle-steel hull. He checked the tactical plot and frowned.

"Admiral, hyperspace jumps detected. Enemy ships are converging on this location," Lieutenant Walsh Corvax said.

"Admiral, reports are coming in from Alliance ships of more enemy forces entering the star system," Lieutenant Traver said.

Quinton increased his frame rate more than what he already had.

"Where are they coming from?" Quinton asked.

"Admiral, it doesn't make any sense," Walsh replied. "They're micro-jumps, but they're new detections. Maybe the Collective ships missed them, and they were hiding—"

"Waiting for the Alliance to show up," Quinton finished.

A silver orb materialized in Quinton's virtual command center. "Quinton, analysis of Sentinel attacks reveal that they are no longer targeting Collective forces."

Quinton considered this. "We're the bigger threat, so they just reprioritized."

"Negative, they're not targeting any Collective targets at all," Radek replied.

"Radek is right, Admiral," Walsh said. "Collective ships are broadcasting new identifications. Something isn't right with it. It's almost as if—"

"They're using Sentinel communication protocols," Quinton said and gritted his teeth.

He activated a comlink to the secondary bridge. "Brandt, do you still have a tactical comlink session with Collective ships?"

Brandt blinked and checked the status, and his thick eyebrows pushed forward. "Negative, they're registering an L.O.S. Same with the Aurora Station. What the hell is going on?"

Quinton sent a comlink to Draven's ship. It was refused. "No, dammit. This can't be happening."

Damage alarms began filling the onboard operations monitoring systems. Alliance fleets reported an increase in friendly fire occurrences.

"Comms," Quinton said, "alpha priority message to the fleet. Zulu. Zulu. Zulu. The Collective has allied with the Sentinels. They're to execute emergency ACN orders 74JAN."

"They betrayed us. This whole thing was a ruse to bring us here," Brandt said and sagged into his chair for a few moments. Then he sat up. "Could the Sentinels be controlling them somehow?"

Quinton considered it for half a millisecond. "No, there's too much coordination involved. We need to focus on getting our ships away from here."

He wanted to scream, howl, and rage, but he wouldn't allow it.

"Walsh, give me the status of the retreat."

"Alliance ships with functioning jump drives are leaving the system. Ships that have taken damage are engaging the enemy, buying time for the others to escape."

Quinton balled his hands into fists. "Tactical, I want a firing solution on Collective forces. Since they've thrown their lot in with the Sentinels, I want to give them a parting gift."

"Aye, Admiral," Lieutenant Xander said.

A few seconds later he had a firing solution ready.

"Fire!" Quinton said.

Nothing happened.

Lieutenant Xander's eyebrows raised in alarm. The CDA turned toward Quinton. "Weapons systems are not responding."

"What?! Have the Sentinels infiltrated our systems?"

"I've run a diagnostic. It's like the system is denying the firing solution, Admiral. There's a warning on my screen with a violation code," Lieutenant Xander said.

Quinton accessed the tactical workstation's data sessions and saw the violation code. He tried to override the security protocols and was booted out of the tactical computer system.

"Radek, what the hell is happening?"

"Violations of authorized command for fleet engagement. The *Salvation's* computing core will deny access to its systems when these violations occur," Radek replied.

"But they're helping the Sentinels, dammit! They're the enemy!"

"Warning, if you persist in trying to use the *Salvation's* weapons against civilian targets, command authority will be revoked. There will be no further warnings."

Quinton was stumped, and even though his frame rate was increased to the max, he felt like the bottom of his mouth had hit the floor and his thoughts flatlined. Browning had put preventative measures into the *Salvation's* computing core that forbade Quinton from engaging with what it thought were civilian targets. Just because a space station had heavy defenses didn't mean it was a military installation. He was in a no-win situation where he couldn't fight back against the forces that were trying to kill him. Just the Collective, it seemed.

Quinton looked at the tactical plot and saw that the Collective fleets were in full retreat, heading for cover to the space stations throughout the systems. The same thing was reported by Alliance ships.

Trenton Draven hadn't just decided to betray them. He'd planned for it, and he'd coordinated this whole thing to lure him out so the Sentinels could finish him off.

Quinton reduced his frame rate to normal. He couldn't do this alone. He needed his entire crew. The tactical plots showed Alliance ships going from green to red status. They were being destroyed. The crews of those ships were dying.

"We need to rescue our remaining ships. Helm, plot a course through the system that will allow them to dock with us."

"No, Quinton," Brandt said, his voice harsh with a truth that Quinton didn't want to acknowledge.

He could find a way. He had to.

"I'm not leaving them behind!" he snarled.

"It's a fool's errand, Quinton. They want you to do that. Look at the plot. Look at it. Sentinel ships have increased to over two hundred thousand. It's too much, even for the *Salvation*. There's nothing for us here anymore. We have to leave."

Quinton stood rooted in place, unable to move or think. It was as if his brain refused to process anything else. Alliance ships were being destroyed. Their human and PMC crews were dying. They'd followed him, believed him when he told them all that he could fight the Sentinels. He blew air out between his teeth and looked away from the plot for a second, glaring at everything but seeing nothing. How could this have happened? How could he have fallen for this trap? How could the Sentinels—

"We must leave," Brandt said. "Order the retreat. Get us out of here."

Quinton gritted his teeth, longing to crush the truth. Then his emotions seemed to drain away as if the stopper had suddenly been removed. A small status window appeared on his internal HUD.

Endocrine management system has been engaged.

Quinton stared at the message for a long second. Radek must have done it.

"Helm," Quinton said, his voice sounding oddly modulated but strained. "Execute emergency jump."

"Aye, aye, Admiral, executing emergency jump," Lieutenant Stasya Orlova said.

Tens of thousands of ships converged on the *Salvation's* location, flying through a field of wrecked ships, trying to destroy the one thing that could stand against them. Multiple barrages of plasma cannons fired at them. With a planet-sized target, very little precision was required. The Sentinels weren't trying to find some critical system because they didn't know any of them. They fired their powerful weapons in a massive screen, knowing that eventually they'd hit something vital and would then exploit the weakness.

There was a massive spike as the *Salvation's* jump drives primed their capacitors, building up the energy, pulling from the power taps until it reached critical levels, and then the planetoid ship disappeared from n-space.

28

MAELYN FELT a tinge of a headache form at the front of her head, and it had nothing to do with implants. Not anymore. Not since Simon had helped her with them. She'd even gotten used to the occasional diagnostic check-ins that assured her that there was no implant rejection. Her headache came from studying the tactical plot on the main holoscreen.

"There's too much metallicity in the asteroid field, and it's making it difficult to determine whether there's anything but mining ships in the vicinity," Sienna said.

Her PMC executive officer had put her considerable skills at work to try to find anything that would put the space stations or her battle group at risk.

"She lied," Maelyn said.

Sienna looked at her with her head tilted slightly to the side. Artificial eyes that looked mostly human but with a slight greenish glow regarded her. "My analysis of Teagan Cayne's message hasn't changed."

They'd been flying toward the star system's inner planets, but it was taking a long time. They had to be cautious with their approach.

"Captain," Lieutenant Ellis said, "we've received an update from Legacy Station. They've provided deep space sensor readings of Sentinel warships en route to the inner system."

Maelyn looked at Lieutenant Donavan. "Anything on our sensors?" she asked.

"Negative, Captain. They could be beyond our sensor range," her tactical officer replied.

The only way she could confirm whether the Sentinels were there was to send one of her own ships on a scouting mission.

"Comms, send a message to Captain Callahan to take the *Culver* and scout the coordinates where Legacy Station's deep space sensors spotted the Sentinels. They could be trying to sneak up on the system," Maelyn said.

"Aye, Captain," Lieutenant Ellis replied.

Sienna walked to Maelyn's side.

"Captain, we need to know what kind of defenses they have here. If the Sentinels are coming and their ships are equipped with drives capable of making micro-jumps, the situation here can become more complex rather quickly."

Maelyn nodded. "Probably not much more than a local security force, but you're right. We need to know."

She brought up another sub-window on her personal holoscreen.

"Comms, open a comlink to Legacy Station. Tell them I need to know who I can coordinate with to secure the star system," Maelyn said.

Lieutenant Ellis spoke to the station representative for a minute. "Captain, I have Commander Peydafar Singh."

She had the comlink routed to her station, and the display showed an older, thin, olive-skinned man with a large nose and eyes that were entirely too close together.

"Senior Fleet Captain Wayborn?" he asked. His tone was mild, but his mouth drew up in the middle as if he wore a permanent sneer. It was gone in an instant, replaced by a slick smile that didn't reach his eyes.

"Commander Singh, I'd like to know what security measures you have in place." Maelyn asked.

His eyes blinked in rapid succession. He cocked his head to the side and pursed his lips. "In place?"

Maelyn arched an eyebrow, wondering if she'd been given the right contact.

Commander Singh laughed with an awkward cadence, then slapped the palm of his hand down on the armrest next to him. "Is just a joke, Captain. The look on your face was priceless."

Maelyn suppressed a frustrated sigh. "You are the commanding officer of the *Ruma*, correct?"

Commander Singh schooled his features and nodded. "Yes, yes, I am the fleet commander here at Arcturus."

Sienna shifted her feet and looked at Maelyn with her mouth partially open.

Commander Singh smiled in the way of a man who approached entirely too many women looking for a good time, and it didn't matter how many times he was turned down or slapped. This star system was supposed to be home to a major operations center for the Collective. She didn't think they put idiots in charge of anything dangerous, but she was beginning to think she'd need to revise her opinion of that.

"Commander, we've received data from Legacy Station that a deep space scanner array has detected Sentinel warships on their way here. I'm here from the Alliance to help with the defense of this star system," Maelyn said.

Commander Singh nodded, and then one of his officers approached him. Maelyn couldn't get a good look at who it was because their back was to the camera. "That is correct."

Maelyn waited for him to continue, but he just waited, and she gritted her teeth a little.

Singh grinned again, and her patience had reached its limit.

"Is there an executive officer I can speak with?" she asked.

Commander Singh waved the question away. "Now, now, Captain Wayborn. No need for anything like that. I take the security of Arcturus very seriously. You want to know what security measures we have in place. Sending the data to you now."

Maelyn looked over at her comms officer for a beat and decided not to chase the fleeting thought of abandoning Arcturus to the idiot they'd put in charge of their own security.

A list of defenses appeared on the main holoscreen. The data showed that the three space stations had little more than a basic point-defense system that primarily used a flak cannon. She knew that the Collective had a reputation of ruthless business practices, but based on what she read on the main holoscreen, she was beginning to believe that nothing but pure negligence governed this entire star system. How was she going to help defend a system that hadn't even taken the time to bolster its own defenses, ever?

"Is this accurate? You only have six cruiser class ships?" Maelyn asked.

Singh nodded, and the floppy hair seemed to move a beat behind his head shakes. "Oh, we also have corvettes."

Maelyn watched him for a few seconds. "How many?"

Singh shrugged. "About fifty or so. They patrol out to the smaller outposts."

A range of expressions vied for attention on the incompetent commander's face, but his beady eyes were freakishly without any emotion.

"One second, Commander," Maelyn said and muted the comlink.

Singh looked like he hadn't heard her and leaned toward the camera with a hand near his ear. Maelyn was about to unmute the comlink when he smiled and laughed as if they were sharing a joke.

"Take all the time you need, Captain. But we'll need to do something about our defense before the Sentinels arrive," he said.

Maelyn turned away from the video comlink.

Sienna turned toward her. "These people are doomed. They have nothing in terms of defenses, and what little they do have… it's a disgrace. They're going to die because of this. Did you see the bridge where he was sitting? It looks like it hasn't been cleaned in months. I doubt they've done any proper maintenance on that ship."

Maelyn heard a few of her bridge officers chuckle a little.

"As entertaining as Lieutenant Commander Hyden's assessment of the… spacers here is, we still have a job to do," Maelyn said. Her crew turned back to their stations, and Maelyn looked at Sienna. "I happen to agree with you."

"Tactical, can you confirm the number of cruisers here?"

"Yes, Captain, a moment please," Lieutenant Donavan said. He peered at the data on one of his holoscreens. "It's accurate, ma'am. We've only detected six cruisers, like he said. None of the corvettes, though they could be in a hangar on any one of the stations here."

"Understood. Thank you, Lieutenant," she replied.

Maelyn looked at the tactical plot on the main holoscreen. Captain Tolliver had his task force making steady progress through the asteroid field to the inner system where the space stations were located. They were of a similar distance.

A comlink came to Maelyn's personal channel. She frowned and then acknowledged it.

"He's lying to you. Singh is a conman, not to be underestimated," Teagan Cayne said.

Maelyn began to trace the signal. "You, again."

"I'm trying to help you."

"I don't need your help. The Sentinels are on their way here right now."

Teagan gave her an exasperated look. "Who told you that? Singh?"

"No," Maelyn replied and paused. She glanced at the status of the trace. It was scattered through multiple communications arrays throughout the system. Maelyn was impressed.

"You're focusing on the wrong thing. Singh is playing the fool to get you to lower your guard," Teagan said.

"Oh yeah? And what are you trying to do?" she asked.

Sienna came over to her and peered at the holoscreen.

Teagan glanced at the PMC. "Good! You have one of them."

"Excuse me?" Sienna asked frostily.

"Singh only has six cruisers. We've scanned the system," Maelyn said.

Teagan shook her head, and a data file became available on the comlink. "Here. Have her use these protocols. You can listen to their comms chatter. Do you really think Draven would leave something like this guarded by only six cruisers?"

The seed of doubt Teagan had planted took root and grew with abandon. She'd thought there was something off with Commander Singh. She looked at Sienna and sent her the file. "Check these protocols. Quickly."

Sienna stepped away and stood still. The PMC didn't need to use an actual workstation.

Maelyn checked the trace. It was still running. How many communications nodes had Teagan used? "We're checking."

"Good, then maybe you'll finally listen to me."

"Why are you doing this? Why the sudden change of heart?"

Teagan looked away for a moment and then back at Maelyn. "It's because of what you found. You and Quinton, that is."

"Don't tell me you're a believer now."

"Is that so hard to believe? You and I have traveled this galaxy. We've been around other spacers. We know what's been happening and how things are almost the same everywhere. That can't be a coincidence."

"And this led to a change of heart?"

Teagan shook her head. "I didn't know you would be here. I had my own mission."

"That's right. Your father is Lennix Crowe."

Teagan smirked. "Boy, you really don't like to lose. I knew that was Quinton's thing, but you're no different."

Maelyn leaned forward. "Listen to me," she snarled.

"Captain, you need to see this," Sienna said.

Maelyn looked at her XO. "What?" she snapped.

Sienna gestured toward the main holoscreen. "I've scanned for that secure communications protocol. They use a standard check-in and acknowledgment. These are the returns I'm getting."

At first there were ten returns, then that number quickly increased to twenty. In less than a minute, there were several hundred. They were scattered throughout the asteroid field, and her ships were right in the middle of them.

"There. Now you believe me," Teagan said.

Maelyn swallowed and looked at her screen. Teagan had been telling the truth. "I may have been wrong about you."

Teagan shook her head, looking relieved. "No, you're exactly right about me, but I didn't know the Sentinels would come to that starbase."

Maelyn believed her. She'd been so angry with herself that Vonya…Teagan had successfully fooled them all that she'd made her the reason for all those deaths. She never suspected that perhaps Teagan wasn't fully aware of what she'd done. If she really was Lennix Crowe's daughter and agent, sent to capture Quinton, she would have had to use the tools Crowe had given her. If she believed that, then she had to believe that Teagan Cayne was Lennix Crowe's daughter.

"Is Simon with you?" Teagan asked.

Maelyn's mouth opened a little and then she shook her head. "No, he's not here. He's… he's with Quinton."

Teagan looked as if she'd just been given bad news. Did she actually care about Simon?

Teagan recovered quickly and nodded.

Maelyn stopped the trace.

"You have to leave here," Teagan said.

Maelyn glanced at the data on the main holoscreen. "We can't."

"Why not?"

"Because we're caught in the middle of a dampening field. They must have engaged it when we sent one of our ships to confirm their Sentinel detection."

Teagan inhaled and sighed. "What are you going to do?"

"I don't suppose you can help me deactivate the dampening field?"

Teagan shook her head.

Maelyn suspected as much. Dampening fields were tricky to figure out. They could be deployed via specialized drones or sourced from any of the ships hiding in the asteroid field.

"Then there's only one thing I can do."

Teagan looked at her and waited.

"I'm going to fight," she said and regarded Teagan for a moment. "Good luck, and thank you."

Teagan looked at her sadly and then severed the comlink.

Sienna looked at her. “What are your orders, ma’am?”

Maelyn brought up the comlink with Commander Singh. It was muted and he was checking his hair.

She swung her gaze toward her XO. “I want to know what ship that bastard is on, and I want it targeted first.”

29

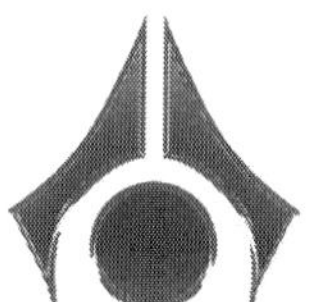

QUINTON MOVED the holoscreen with the long list of damage reports away from him. He had thousands of engineers stationed throughout the ship who would leverage the *Salvation's* considerable repair drones and materials to fix the damage. If a critical system had been hit, he'd know about it and prioritize accordingly. He didn't need to do it all himself.

The virtual meeting room that connected key personnel throughout the ship was still being used.

"How could Draven be working with the Sentinels? How could that have happened?" Simon asked.

"*When* did it happen?" Brandt asked.

Simon nodded. "And how could we have missed it? How'd they even communicate? The Sentinels don't communicate with anyone."

Quinton shook his head. "Yes, they do," he said, and the handful of conversations going on became quiet. "Admen Desher," he said, and his gaze swept across the others, allowing them to catch up to him. "Agent of Harding. He sold his services to Lennix Crowe to lure me out. I guess now we know he escaped when we found this ship. He did this."

"But Draven was coming around. I thought he was committed..." Simon said and paused before he finished his thought.

"The only thing Draven is committed to are the lies he fed us," Quinton said.

"We need to alert the rest of the fleet," Brandt said.

"There could be traitors among us," Simon said. "How are we supposed to determine who has ties to the Collective?"

Quinton watched as they all looked at him. "Brandt is right. We need to warn the other fleets. But I won't tell those ship captains that their crews can't be trusted without sufficient evidence."

Brandt nodded. "It would cause dangerous divides. I'm not sure how to handle it."

"We'll handle it by leveraging our most secure assets. PMCs are deployed throughout the fleets. There aren't enough of us to hold a post on every ship, but capital ships certainly have them aboard in executive officer positions. We alert them and they will alert the commanding officers," Quinton said.

"What about the other ships? The ones that aren't from the *Salvation*. What do we tell them?" Brandt asked.

"We'll need to give them a different set of coordinates… probably multiple sets of coordinates, until we can weed out the people we can't trust," Quinton said.

Simon glanced away, looking as if he couldn't believe what was happening, and for some reason, Quinton felt a pang of guilt deep in his gut.

"We need to focus on getting our people out of this trap. That's the priority. We can do root-cause analysis afterward," Quinton said.

"Admiral," Corvax said, "I have to point out that there could be significant Sentinel presence in other star systems as well. This was a widespread operation that took a lot of coordination. They won't simply stop because we left the system."

Quinton looked at his tactical officer. Corvax's specialization was defensive measures and risk assessment. It was his job to point out the risks involved in doing these things.

"Understood. We'll have to be cautious, but we can't afford to play it safe," Quinton said.

"We should leverage our fleets as part of the retreat. They can check on the fleets that were deployed in nearby star systems. Investigate anomalies. Then they can go to whatever waypoint we tell them to," Brandt said.

"That's good, Brandt. Then we'll prioritize the rest and go down the list. We can't race across the galaxy. We need to be methodical in order to maximize rescuing as many as we can," Quinton said.

Simon's eyebrows peaked and he looked at Quinton in alarm. He was worried about Maelyn. He gave Simon a small nod. Quinton was worried about Maelyn too, but he knew she could take care of herself.

"There's something I don't understand," Brandt said.

Quinton looked at the old DUC admiral. "Can it wait?"

"Actually, no, it can't. We can't make tactical decisions unless we know what restrictions are in place."

Simon frowned and looked at Quinton.

The PMCs at the virtual meeting looked at Quinton, expectation in their meaningful looks. Human crew members like Brandt, Simon, and half a dozen others waited for his response.

"You're talking about the alert. The one about me. The violation," Quinton said.

Brandt stared at him and didn't blink.

Quinton exhaled forcefully. "The *Salvation* has built-in limitations about which targets can be engaged. I'm free to use our weapons against the Sentinels and other military vessels, but I cannot… the ship will not target anything that has a significant civilian presence."

"How does the ship know whether there are civilians there or not? What about if weapons from a space station fire on us?" Simon asked.

"The ship monitors us. It's Radek to a certain extent. It's all part of when I took command."

"It's a failsafe," Brandt said.

Quinton nodded. "It's Browning's way of keeping me in check."

"How did Draven know about it? I thought the Collective warships moved to protect the space stations, but I guess that isn't right. He was using them as shields. But again, how could he have known?" Simon asked.

"He might not have known. It could have been a gamble," Quinton said.

Simon swallowed. "That's a hell of a gamble."

"Admen Desher could have told him. He could have made a guess as well," Quinton said.

"If the Sentinels start using space stations as a way of shielding themselves from our weapons, that's going to hinder our capabilities," Brandt said.

Quinton shrugged. "Not if we don't let it," he replied.

Brandt considered this for a second and nodded in acknowledgment of the point.

"We can discuss our limitations as part of the rules of engagement later on. We have a job to do, and Alliance ships need our help," Quinton said.

He quickly checked the fleet deployment statuses. They were all moving through their lists of star systems that had Sentinel ships attacking the spacers who lived there, but a large percentage of those systems were associated in some way with the Collective. As he looked at which battlegroups were investigating those systems, there was one in particular that leaped out to his attention, and it happened to be the one they were farthest from. Maelyn had good instincts. She wouldn't fall for a trap that easily. Then again, he wouldn't have thought that about himself.

30

FLEET OPERATIONS, no matter how meticulously they were planned, rarely went off without a problem. Quinton had found that working with experienced spacers like Severin Brandt reinforced those lessons from long ago. At least, it felt like a long time ago. How much could a person age in the span of a year?

The human crew had gone through several shift rotations so they could rest, but the PMCs rested differently in their consciousness-driven androids. Increased frame rates sped up the rest they required. Quinton's rest cycle could be measured in seconds, but he hadn't taken any. Anyone—human or PMC—could delay resting, but eventually they wouldn't be able to put if off any longer. However, Quinton could find ways around that requirement. Sometimes a rest cycle could give a person some distance to reconsider a problem, but that same distance from a problem was also a hindrance. He wasn't going to rest until all Alliance fleets were accounted for, and he might not even then.

Quinton wished he could have lost count of how many star systems they'd been to, but that was part of the problem. He couldn't forget. Whether knowing details and facts was part of his personality or part of the abilities instilled in PMCs, he didn't know.

Simon hastened toward him, stopping to examine the tactical plot in the holotank.

Quinton turned toward him. "You're just in time."

They'd found evidence of betrayal among star systems that had a significant Collective presence, and there was little doubt in anyone's mind that Trenton Draven was working with the Sentinels—with Admen Desher. Quinton tried to push those thoughts aside, but they were always there, waiting like an apex predator in the shadows.

Some of the Alliance fleets had escaped the trap. They'd either received the warning ahead of time, or their captains had refused to travel to inner star systems without credible evidence of Sentinel warships. Other commanders were more thorough in how they executed their orders. They'd had to fight their way out of the trap, but what made it worse wasn't that they had to fight the Sentinels. They'd also been flanked by security forces that the Alliance was there to help. As far as betrayals went, Quinton couldn't think of anything worse than being stabbed in the back by the people they were supposed to protect.

According to regs, Quinton was emotionally compromised. Assessing emotional instability was a fine regulation when preserving the functional capacity of a single ship and maybe even a battle group, but for multiple fleets, the regulation was unsuitable. They were all angry, hurt, bitter, and more than a little afraid. Quinton settled for lowering the settings of his endocrine control systems just enough to take the edge off. Radek was monitoring him and could increase them as necessary.

He checked the status of the fleets he'd deployed in teams to conduct system sweeps. They weren't going to any system where there were reports of Sentinel attacks. Quinton wouldn't waste Alliance ships on that anymore. Their first priority was to regroup after they'd accounted for all their ships.

The *Salvation's* crew threw themselves into their work. They were the heart of the Alliance fleet and couldn't afford to spend any more time in shock. Quinton had given them a direction to focus on, and they were doing their jobs so he could do his.

They were about to jump to the Arcturus Star System. This was the last known location of Maelyn's battle group, and there hadn't been any check-ins since. Quinton had pushed the *Salvation's* jump drives to their limits, which was happening across the fleet, but his engineering teams found ways to squeeze every bit of efficiency from their ships.

A countdown timer appeared, and a monotone voice broadcasted the countdown to the entire ship. They were in a combat-readiness status, and no one could be sure of what they would find when they reached the Arcturus Star System.

Quinton reviewed the data about the system. Maelyn wouldn't have simply loitered in the Oort. She would have done a sweep of the interior system, which meant she'd traveled through the dense asteroid field. There was very little doubt that Maelyn's battle group had fallen into the same trap they all had.

Quinton fully integrated into the *Salvation's* systems. He inserted his own VIs into the sensor arrays so he could be among the first to learn what had happened.

The countdown timer reached zero and the *Salvation* left n-space for the duration of a hyperspace jump to the middle of Arcturus Star System. When they reemerged into n-space, active scans immediately began their analysis of the system. No matter how fast Quinton could access the information, it wasn't fast enough. Impatience was the doom of all who needed to know something quickly, and he needed to know.

Please be there, he said to himself.

"No Alliance comlinks detected," Lieutenant Corvax said. A few moments passed. "It's a comms blackout, Admiral. It's affecting the area near one of the space stations."

"Dampening field to block communications and jump-drive navigation systems. Helm, bring us in," Quinton said.

"Scanners are showing ship wreckage in the asteroid field. We can't identify who they are," Lieutenant Donavan said.

"Understood," Quinton replied.

Analyses from the *Salvation's* VI began to populate the tactical plot. Active scans were running through the entire system. They hadn't detected any ships in the outer system of planets. Quinton suspected that since the trap had been sprung there, most of the ships were located in the inner system of planets. But dampening fields, as well as the abundance of asteroids, would interfere with the ship's scanners.

The numbers of wrecks in the system reached into the hundreds, and the *Salvation's* computers attempted to reduce the number of false positives while trying to give the most accurate guess as quickly as possible. After that, it was up to his tactical officers to review the data. Quinton didn't wait for them. He was scanning through the same data.

"Ops, deploy scout drones from sectors 5 to 30," Quinton said.

"Yes, Admiral, deploying scout drone package now," Lieutenant Chloe Bradshaw said.

The *Salvation* flew toward the asteroid field at best speed while hundreds of scout drones approached the area much more rapidly, increasing their scanning capabilities and providing more detail. If and when the scout drones went offline, they'd know where the dampening field began. Once inside the field, Quinton would find the source and take it out.

As the scout drones got closer to their designated coverage areas, they were finally able to glimpse the edges of the dampening field.

"Ops, arm the drones. Enable seeker mode," Quinton said.

"Yes, Admiral, seeker mode enabled," Lieutenant Bradshaw replied.

Scout drones were equipped with low-yield explosives that were enough to cripple the smaller ships that he suspected were maintaining the dampening field. They could also extend the range quite a bit.

Quinton watched as the drones armed themselves and began disappearing from the tactical plot. A bulge began to appear in the dampening field as the drones confirmed Quinton's suspicions. The tactical plot updated as more data came in.

"Helm, all ahead full. Get us in there," Quinton said.

His orders were confirmed, and the *Salvation* accelerated.

Active scans began detecting weapons discharge, as well as ships in the regions closest to one of the space stations. Piercing the dampening field was like the calm before the fiery barrage that was the organized chaos of a battlefield. A casual observer would see only chaos, but Quinton and the crew of the *Salvation* saw the familiar patterns of an ongoing space combat.

Alliance ship communication pings registered with the *Salvation's* comms systems, and they were finally able to gain their first real insight into the situation at the Arcturus Star System. There were no Sentinels in the system, at least none that their scanners had been able to detect. However, they did scan wreckages of a Sentinel battle group comprised mainly of destroyer class vessels.

"Tactical, I'm going to need multiple firing solutions to help the surviving Alliance ships," Quinton said.

"Understood, Admiral," Lieutenant Xander said. After a moment, he continued, "Admiral, there are no active Sentinel contacts. These are Collective forces."

"Target them, Lieutenant. They chose a side, and now they'll live with it. No quarter will be given to the enemy warships," Quinton replied.

Scan data of the space station armament became available. They were mainly armed with mag cannons.

"Firing solution ready, Admiral," Lieutenant Xander said.

"Fire!"

The *Salvation* unleashed its fury onto the Collective forces as hyper-capable missiles burst from hundreds of missiles tubes. They disappeared from n-space and sped toward their targets through hyperspace.

The enemy ships had divided their forces in order to focus their efforts on destroying the battlegroup. Quinton opened subspace comlinks to their missiles, and his awareness was transported onto the battlefield. There was an abundance of interference from weapons discharge between the fusion warheads and the smaller tachyon lance used by the Alliance destroyers, but Quinton didn't care how effective their weapons were. He was here. He'd brought help, and now he had to reach them in time.

Quinton scoured the sensor data and finally found what he was looking for. The ACN *Ascendant*, Maelyn's ship, was besieged by enemy ships. Its flight pattern was that of a dying ship limping off into oblivion. The operational point-defense cannons continued to fire, protecting the ship as much as they could. Rear mag cannons belched a steady burst at the enemy ships nearby, but there was no detection of the destroyer's primary weapon systems. The ship and its crew were battered and barely clinging to life.

Quinton seized control of the *Salvation's* tactical combat systems and overrode the missile control systems. He increased his frame rate and brought an entire quadrant of the *Salvation's* tachyon lances to bear, firing them at the tangle of ships determined to finish off the *Ascendant* and the remnants of the Alliance battlegroup.

Power spiked to critical levels from the *Salvation's* power taps, and a thick green bar of highly energized particles so dense that it was nearly a solid object lashed toward the enemy ships. Hyper-capable missiles emerged into n-space and detonated both fusion and antimatter warheads, unleashing huge amounts of devastation. Collective ships, like an unsuspecting hunter, were torn apart by the colossal forces of the *Salvation's* weapons.

Quinton devoured the data feed as the enemy ship counts plummeted from his attack, but was it enough? He was destroying them so quickly that they had no chance to escape, but he couldn't do anything about the weapons that had already fired. Plasma cannons belched out their fiery payloads in controlled bursts, and with so many enemy ships, they were impossible to count. They slammed into the battered hull of the Alliance ships that should have quit the field long before the *Salvation* arrived.

With his frame rate increased, Quinton was forced to witness events in frustratingly slow motion, but he couldn't lower his frame rate. There had to be something he could do. Enemy ships and their traitorous crews were dying all around him, and he didn't care.

He watched as the *Ascendant* limped away, trying to evade the barrage of high-energy plasma bolts speeding toward it. Then one of the main engines failed, causing the ship to tumble, and Quinton's gut sank with the speed of a gargantuan singularity from which he was helpless to escape. Gritting his teeth, he seized control of a communication's array and opened a subspace comlink to the *Ascendant*. The ACN destroyer's computer system seemed to take an entire millennium to acknowledge his request. When it finally did, he used his command authority to access the *Ascendant's* systems, frantically navigating to where he knew Maelyn would be. She was a senior fleet captain and there was nowhere else she'd be but on the bridge. Just as he was about to finally see the bridge—just as he was about to finally see *her*—the comlink severed. Everything blanked out, and Quinton was once again inside the *Salvation's* computer systems.

There was one final, fragile automated response shared between ships. Then the data feed registered the *Ascendant's* destruction.

Quinton's mind flatlined, refusing to believe the data he was seeing. He searched the scan data, hoping escape pods had been jettisoned. There had been time. The crew could have escaped. Maelyn could have escaped.

There were no escape pods.

There was nothing.

Maelyn and the rest of her crew were dead.

Simon had been in awe of what PMCs could accomplish. They were capable of amazing things that even he, with radically advanced implants, couldn't scratch the surface of. During his many months aboard the *Salvation*, Quinton had always emphasized the limitations PMCs had, and they were the same limitations that everyone had to deal with. While PMCs could compartmentalize their focus to an amazing degree, they couldn't account for all possibilities, even after factoring in their ability to alter their perception of time so they experienced it at different rates than Simon ever could. Once events were set in motion, PMCs could only influence those events.

Simon monitored the tactical plot, and his implants sped up his reaction times, but it was the tiniest fraction of what Quinton was capable of doing. He and the rest of the human crew monitored and reacted to events as they unfolded as best they could, doing their utmost to support the objective. At some point, Quinton had stopped issuing orders and began controlling the *Salvation's* weapons systems directly. The Collective's ships were trying to finish off the remaining Alliance ships.

A fearsome howl erupted from Quinton, startling everyone on the bridge. Even the PMCs, in their consciousness-driven androids, flinched at the sound. The data on the tactical plot flashed, and more Alliance ships' statuses switched to red.

Simon's eyes widened and his jaw went slack. He watched in vain, hoping that the ship statuses would switch back to green, but they didn't. The *Salvation* was closing in on the area, and the sensors had given an accurate detection.

All enemy ships in the area had been destroyed.

Simon blinked several times as he peered at the holoscreens of his workstation, desperately searching for emergency broadcast beacons, but there was too much interference. He would have to wait.

A comlink to his workstation became active without his acknowledging it, and Admiral Brandt looked at him. "Simon, Quinton won't respond. I can still see him active in the computer systems."

Simon glanced to where Quinton stood on the bridge, completely still. Then Simon looked back at the comlink. "Admiral, I… I think he's in shock. Maelyn was on the *Ascendant*. The ship has been destroyed."

Brandt closed his eyes and winced but then inhaled a steadying breath and sighed. "My God," he said and paused for a moment. "Okay, I need you to snap him out of it."

"Snap him out of it? How?" Simon asked.

Brandt's gaze hardened. "Get in front of him. Make him listen to you."

"But, Admiral, he's integrated with the ship's systems. He can just ignore whatever I might try."

"Wrong. Get his attention. I don't care how you have to do it, but we need him. Brandt, out."

The comlink disconnected and Simon sagged in his seat a little.

Maelyn was dead.

He tried to push the thought from his mind, but his brain wouldn't cooperate.

She was his family, an older sister who looked after him and guided him, who'd taken him under her wing.

Stop it! Simon gritted his teeth and then stood up. He raised his left hand to his forehead and pressed his thumb and index fingers to the side of his head.

He looked at Quinton standing on a platform that extended toward the massive holotank. Simon inhaled deeply and held his breath, then walked toward his friend while blowing out the air through his teeth. His stride was short but steady, and he watched Quinton for some sign that he was aware of his surroundings.

Simon called out to Quinton as he closed the distance. A few bridge officers looked at him but didn't say anything.

Simon stopped next to his friend. The slight glow of Quinton's artificial green eyes pulsed in a quick cadence that reminded Simon of a processing core. He stepped in front of Quinton so he was squarely in his field of vision.

"Quinton, Admiral Brandt needs you to respond," Simon said and waited.

Quinton could have been a statue for all the response Simon got, but he wouldn't give up. He tried to open a data comlink to Quinton, but the connection was refused.

"Okay, no data connections, but I need you to respond to me. Give me some indication that you're still there," Simon said.

Long seconds went by, and Quinton didn't respond.

"Radek, can you hear me?" Simon asked, hoping that Quinton's VI would respond.

Nothing.

Brandt contacted him again.

"He won't respond to me either," Simon said. "He's not frozen or anything."

Brandt considered it for a moment. "Hit him."

Simon's eyes widened and stepped back. "Hit him?"

Brandt nodded. "Yes, hit him."

"Admiral, I can't—do you know what he's made of? He'd barely notice it if I hit him."

Brandt shook his head. "I thought you were smart. Hit him in a way that he'll be sure to feel it. Don't you have a palm stunner? Give him a jolt."

Simon swallowed and thought about it, glancing at his hands for a second. "Sir, I don't think this is a good idea. Can't you just take command?"

Brandt glared at him. "Webb! Dammit, I'm giving you an order! Don't stand there and tell me what my job is! Now, I told you to get his attention. If he doesn't respond, then I want you to hit him with your stunner."

Whenever someone addressed him by his surname, it was never anything good. He gave Brandt a slight nod and used his implants to activate the palm stunner. Maelyn had told him how to configure its power output so that it could affect Quinton or any other CDA.

Simon stepped back with his right foot and raised his hand, palm facing toward Quinton's chest. A blue glow came from the palm stunner, and he tightened his muscles and thrust his hand out. A burst of energy came from the stunner, and at the same moment, Quinton grabbed him and swung Simon off his feet.

"What are you doing!" Quinton snarled while holding Simon in the air.

His feet dangled and Quinton glared at him.

"Quinton, it's me."

Quinton lifted him higher and took a powerful step forward.

"I know it's you!"

Simon's breath came in gasps. Would Quinton kill him? He looked as if he were about to throw Simon across the cavernous room. He could do it, too. Simon knew how strong Quinton's avatar was. He'd seen it in action. Simon wouldn't stand a chance.

"The stunner," Simon gasped.

"Doesn't work on me. You've got five seconds to start making sense right now."

"Brandt told me to get your attention. He said you weren't responding to him. We didn't know… he thought you were in shock because of Maelyn…" Simon stopped speaking.

Quinton's gaze softened and his face crumpled. "She's…" he shook his head once. "Her ship was destroyed," he said and lowered Simon to the floor.

Simon had never been so happy for his feet to touch the ground. He looked at his friend and put his hand on Quinton's shoulder. "I know."

"I tried to save them."

"I know you did. Believe me, I was watching, and I couldn't keep up, but…" Simon said and inclined his chin toward the holotank.

"Admiral Aldren," Lieutenant Traver said, "we're receiving multiple comlink requests from the space stations, and there are more ships coming from them. Uh, civilian ships."

"What do they say they want?" Quinton asked and walked toward Traver's workstation.

Simon walked with him, muttering to Brandt to wait. Quinton glanced at him. "It's Admiral Brandt on a comlink. He wants to speak with you."

Quinton gestured and a holoscreen appeared with Brandt's vidcom. "Sorry, Admiral," he said and glanced toward Simon for a second. "Lieutenant Traver was just telling me about multiple comlinks coming from the space stations. Apparently, there are civilian ships leaving those stations."

Brandt considered this for a moment and then nodded. "Go on, Lieutenant."

"Station officials are begging us not to destroy them," Traver said.

"Okay, tell them if they cease all hostilities, we'll do the same," Quinton replied.

"Understood, Admiral."

"What about those ships? Could they be hostiles as well?" Quinton said and looked toward Corvax. "Scan those ships for weapons' payloads. Confirm any detections and issue a warning. If they don't alter course, take them out."

Simon looked at Quinton. "I thought we couldn't fire on civilian ships."

"If they're carrying armed explosives, they're elevated to hostile enemy ships," Quinton replied.

"Admiral," Traver said, "we're receiving multiple requests for refuge."

Simon's mouth hung open for a few seconds. "They're refugees?"

"That's what they say," Traver replied.

Quinton looked away from them and was quiet for a long moment. "Denied."

"Quinton, they need our help," Simon said.

Quinton shook his head. "How can we be sure they really are refugees? We can't. Ask Brandt if you don't believe me."

Simon swung his gaze toward Brandt.

Brandt sighed heavily. "We can't be sure."

"Okay, but that doesn't mean we have to leave them behind. They can't all be part of what happened. Brandt, please," Simon said and looked at Quinton. "*Please*."

Quinton regarded him, but the hardened glint in his eyes didn't fill Simon with confidence.

"I was a refugee. The DUC took me in. Maelyn took me in. She'd never condone leaving spacers behind."

Quinton's glare wasn't as baleful as it had been before, but it still made Simon's mouth dry.

"Do what you want, but it's the truth," Simon said. "Leaving refugees behind is just wrong. There's more than enough room on the ship, and there are enough security measures to prevent anything from happening. All we need to do is coordinate transportation of the refugees to the DUC."

Quinton sighed heavily and a painful expression passed so quickly that Simon wasn't sure he'd seen it. "Fine, we'll take in the refugees."

"Thank you," Simon replied, relieved.

Quinton leaned toward Simon, artificial eyes glaring. He looked as if he were about to yell, but then something changed. Quinton turned and walked away from him.

Simon thought about following him.

"Let it go," Brandt said. "You got him out of it, and now you need to give him some space. I'll deal with him."

Simon felt as if something cold had settled into his gut as he walked back to his workstation and sat down. When he reached toward the holo-interface, he noticed his hands were shaking, and he couldn't get them to stop.

Traver called over to him. "Sending you a comlink. They asked for you personally."

Simon threw him a nod and looked at his holoscreen.

A vidcom became active, and a young woman was staring at him. She had golden blonde hair and large brown eyes that reminded him of warm milk chocolate and caramel. He thought he recognized her, but there was something he couldn't quite place about her.

"Simon," she said, sounding relieved. "I'm so glad you're safe."

Her voice. He'd heard it before, but the face didn't match his memory. "Vonya?" he said quietly.

A hint of a smile lifted her full lips and her eyes softened. "It's Teagan," she said.

Simon swallowed nervously. He didn't know what to think. His emotions were raw, and seeing her just pushed him over the top. He looked around to see if anyone was watching or listening. Then he turned back toward the holoscreen. "Where are you?"

"I'm one of the ships heading to you."

"If you come here, they'll take you into custody," he said.

Teagan nodded a little. "I know."

"Then why are you coming? You have to know what will happen if you do."

Teagan tilted her head to the side a little and smiled. "You were always so nice to me."

Simon clenched his teeth for a second. "Yeah, and you deceived us. You sold us out."

Teagan looked at him, her expression unreadable. "There are things I need to tell you. I need to speak to Quinton."

Simon glanced toward where Quinton stood and shuddered a little. "You don't want to talk to him right now. Believe me. You might not survive the conversation."

Teagan looked away and it reminded him of how Vonya moved. A memory hovered in the back of his mind. They'd been aboard the *Nebulon*, sitting together in the galley. She could have had her pick of anyone on the ship to spend time with and she'd chosen him.

"I know, but I have to. I need to do this. Will you please help me?"

Simon considered it. As much as it surprised him, he was tempted, but she had betrayed them. Like everyone else on the *Nebulon*, he'd been fooled by her "Servitor down on her luck" disguise. He remembered all the time they'd spent together. He'd missed her but had to keep that to himself. Maelyn hated the mere mention of Vonya or the Servitors. And yet, he still wanted to help her. But Simon pushed those thoughts away. He shook his head and glared at the holoscreen.

"No," he said. "I won't help you."

She turned her face away. "I'll find some other way," she said, quietly.

In that moment, Simon didn't think he'd ever seen anyone so lovely look so utterly alone. He severed the comlink before he changed his mind.

31

"How much longer are we going to have to wait?" Guttman asked.

Becker watched as Guttman continued to pace the length of the bridge. Each time he waddled past, it spiked his irritation.

"Are you in a rush or something?" Oscar asked.

Guttman stopped pacing and shrugged. "I just don't like waiting around. First, they tell us we can't leave. Then they make us return to the space dock... another part of the dock anyway. Now they ignore us. For hours!"

"I thought you were feeling better," Oscar said.

Guttman frowned. "Huh?"

"The parasite. It was making you irritable."

"That's an understatement," Becker grumbled.

Guttman turned toward him. "Well, excuse me if my affliction bothered you so much. It's not like I could help it."

Becker rolled his eyes. "You're just a beacon that attracts trouble."

"No," Oscar said, quickly, "a tractor beam for trouble."

Becker snorted. "A black hole for trouble."

Oscar laughed.

"Ha, ha. Very funny. That parasite was no joke."

"We know. You almost ate all our food."

Guttman pressed his lips together and glared. "That's not my fault. Come on, you guys said you weren't going to hold that against me."

Becker shook his head. "Forget I said anything," he said and stood up. He inhaled and blew out a breath. "Guttman's right. This is taking too long."

"Heh! You see. Even Becker finally agrees with me."

"So, what should we do about it?" Oscar asked.

Becker walked toward the main holoscreen. There were external video feeds across multiple windows showing the area around the ship.

"I doubt they forgot about us. If I knew where those corvettes were, I'd consider escaping," Becker said.

"Same," Oscar agreed. "The only one who was ever good at getting around station security was Quinton."

Becker nodded. "He made it look easy."

"Captain," Haley said, "I might be able to help with that."

Becker's eyebrows peaked and he bit his lower lip a little. "All right, what have you got?"

He walked over to Haley's workstation and Guttman came to stand next to him.

"I've been monitoring communications ever since we arrived. Since then, they've been redirecting all outbound ship traffic back to the station."

"Okay, but what does that mean?" Guttman asked.

"It means we weren't detained because someone in the Collective has it out for us," Becker replied.

"So they're not looking for us specifically?" Oscar said.

Becker looked at Haley and smiled.

"That's what I was thinking," Haley said. "I couldn't be sure at first, but as more time passed it became obvious."

Becker folded his arms across his chest and turned toward the main holoscreen. He took a few steps toward it.

"I guess it's good that they're not looking for us, but we still can't leave. It's not like we can access their scanners to find where those interceptors are," Guttman said.

He was right. If they used the *Astricus's* scanner array, it would just bring unwanted attention to their ship.

Oscar snapped his fingers and pointed at Becker. "What about using someone else's scanner—not the station's but one of the other ships nearby."

Becker shook his head. "Nah, they'll detect it and trace the hack attempt. We can't sneak our way out of here by doing that…" He blinked a few times and then turned toward Haley. "Can you access Borealis's comms systems?"

Haley pursed her lips in thought. "Maybe. What do you want me to do?"

Becker gave her a crooked smile. "We just need temporary control. Enough to broadcast a message for a little while."

Guttman tilted his head to the side. "What good is that going to do?"

Oscar chuckled. "I like it. Oh man, that's goooood," he said, drawing out the word.

Becker looked at Guttman. "Alone, we wouldn't get very far. But if we get a bunch of ships to leave all at once, there's no way those corvettes can stop us."

Guttman's eyes widened and then he smiled.

"You gave me the idea," Becker said.

"I did?" Guttman said.

Becker nodded. "You were complaining about being stuck here, and I'm willing to bet that there are a lot of other spacers who are just as anxious to leave."

A small laugh bubbled from Guttman's mouth.

Becker looked at Haley, eyebrows raised.

"Just give me a few minutes, Captain. I'm pretty sure I can get you tempo control," Haley said.

Becker clapped his hands together and returned to his workstation, opening a ship-wide broadcast. "Crew of *Astricus*. We've been sitting on our sorry asses long enough. Get to your stations. We'll be departing in a few minutes." Becker closed the channel, and then he said quietly, "Hopefully."

After a few minutes, Haley made a 'hmm' sound.

"What's the matter?" Becker asked.

Haley looked at him. "Oh, it's nothing, Captain. I just found a few hack protocols in the ship's computer system. They're really good. The strange thing is that the protocols became available after I started putting my own bypass together."

"Oh yeah," Oscar said. "They're from Quinton. He told me he included a few things on the ship when we left."

"Fine with me," Becker said.

Haley peered intently at her personal holoscreen and then smiled. "I'm in, Captain. I have their command interface up."

"Good, just send a broadcast to all docked ships that they're cleared to leave. Set it on a loop and then see if you can lock them out of the system for a while. It doesn't have to be clean. We just need some time to get out of here."

"Understood, Captain," Haley replied.

Less than a minute later, Borealis Station began broadcasting clearance authority for ships to leave.

Becker waited for the broadcast to cycle one more time and then looked at Oscar.

"Other ships are starting to leave," Oscar said.

"That's all we need. Get us out of here," Becker said.

"You don't have to tell me twice," Oscar replied.

The *Astricus* severed the umbilicus to the space dock and Oscar navigated away from the station. Active scans showed that the corvette interceptors were on the far side of the station. They tried to order the ships back to the dock, but with hundreds of ships departing at once, there was little they could do.

Once they reached a minimum safe distance from the station, they executed a hyperspace jump and left Borealis Station behind.

32

Simon stood in the workspace he'd appropriated as his own personal lab. Multiple amber-colored holoscreens surrounded him, showing numerous data windows from the analyses he had running. He'd dimmed the lights. Sometimes he preferred working like this. By limiting the distractions, he felt closer to the data he was working with. It helped him focus, and it also gave his tired eyes a rest from the bright lights.

Simon rubbed his eyes and turned toward one of the holoscreens, crossing his arms and rubbing his chin in thought. The screen showed a complex, multilayered simulation of a PMC in an ESS. There were tiny bursts of sparkly brilliance that was similar to the synapses firing in a human brain. Normally, it was comforting to him to look at, almost hypnotic, but not this morning. He compared it with another data window that showed a partially formed PMC.

"These are new PMCs," Radek said.

"They were recovered from the ships destroyed in the Arcturus Star System," Simon replied, keeping his tone even.

Radek could detect spikes in emotions through his biometric sensors.

"Understood. However, I don't recognize this one."

"That's because the ESS core was damaged. I was trying to see if there was a way I could save them."

"Oh, I see. I'm afraid there's too much data degradation for a proper retrieval. Shall I send a maintenance drone to move it to permanent storage?"

"No!" Simon said quickly and winced. "Um, no, that's fine. I want to… I just don't want to give up on them yet."

Radek was quiet for a few moments. "Simon, I understand the desire to hold onto hope even in the direst of circumstances, but I assure you that this data matrix is not recoverable. I cannot even identify who they were. It's best that they be laid to rest with the utmost respect for their sacrifice."

Simon's eyes tightened and he shook his head. "Not yet," he replied, his voice sounding thick.

A few seconds passed, and Radek said. "Very well. I will leave you alone now."

Simon let out a long exhale. "Thanks, Radek."

He checked that Radek wasn't trying to monitor what he was doing. There had been a few times when the VI had chimed in to offer help. Simon wasn't opposed to help, but he wanted it on his own terms. He'd instructed Radek that he didn't want him monitoring what he was doing without being aware of it. Since then, Radek had respected Simon's wishes.

A chime came from a nearby delivery hatch. Simon walked over and opened the hatch, seeing a small, metallic data core. He reached inside and picked it up.

"Lights," Simon said and lifted the data core to get a better look at it.

The lighting in his lab increased to Simon's predefined preferences. The data core was from a retrieval drone that he'd sent to search through the Alliance ship wreckage. He pressed his lips together as he carried the data core and carefully placed it on a matter-transference pad. A blue ring glowed on the pad, and the small data core rose an inch into the air. Then it disintegrated into tiny pieces, absorbing into the pad itself.

A new data window appeared on his primary holoscreen. The data retrieved was in a holding area. Simon studied it for a few seconds and then engaged the mergence protocol. The newly retrieved data darted toward the data window where the partial PMC was located.

Reconstruction starting. Twelve hours to completion.

A progress bar appeared that showed the time remaining underneath it.

Simon closed the holoscreen and locked his data session. He would have used the *Salvation's* computing core to process the data reconstruction more quickly, but then too many people would start asking questions that he wanted to avoid. He'd do it from here and wait, hoping for a miracle.

A comlink chimed and Simon answered it.

"Admiral Brandt."

"Simon, where are you?"

"I'm in my lab, sir."

Brandt regarded him for a few seconds. "I need you to stay close to Quinton."

Simon nodded. "I know that. I'll head back to the bridge. I'm… I just needed some time to myself."

Brandt nodded in understanding. "It's fine, but it's important that you're there for Quinton. He needs personal connections now more than ever. You're friends."

"We are, but sir, he almost…" Simon didn't finish. When he'd tried to stun Quinton, he thought Quinton was going to kill him.

"Yeah, I get it, but he needs to see familiar faces—people who know him and not just what he is. He's been more detached, and I'm worried about him," Brandt said.

Simon nodded. "It's the endocrine control system helping to reduce the impact of his emotions. That's how Quinton explained it to me. It's something he can control."

"Yeah, and he might need a friend to remind him of that. Look, I know this isn't going to be easy, but it's what has to happen. With Maelyn…gone, you're all I've got, kid."

Simon looked away from the holoscreen and nodded. "I'll return to the bridge at once, sir."

"Thank you, Simon."

The comlink severed and Simon left his lab to head toward the transit station. One thing he could say about the *Salvation:* For as big as the ship was, the designers had made getting around the vast distances easy and quick.

A text message appeared on his internal HUD. He glanced at it and dismissed it. It was another request from Teagan that he go to the refugee camp. She was relentless. He didn't want to see her.

Simon rolled his eyes. He *did* want to see her. Just knowing she was on the ship had been on his mind since that first request after she was aboard.

He walked to the transit station and headed toward the nearest open aircar. After stepping aboard, the door slid shut.

"Destination?" asked a monotone voice.

Simon was about to answer when someone knocked on the window. He turned around and saw Teagan standing there, giving him a pointed look, as if daring him to ignore her.

"Well, are you going to let me in?" she asked.

Simon palmed the door controls and the door slid open. He leaned forward and glanced around. "How did you get here?"

Teagan stepped aboard and the door slid shut. Simon was pretty sure the temperature had gone up inside the aircar, but he couldn't have sworn to it. She was almost as tall as he was, with long slender arms and a small waist. Her high cheekbones and large eyes seemed full of a promise that he couldn't look away from. There was a flirty tilt to her mouth, and Simon felt the breath catch in his throat.

She quirked an eyebrow at him. "You mean without a security escort?" She gave him a demure smile and her eyes gleamed. "I'm a spy, Simon. Getting into and out of places is what I do."

Simon didn't respond. He looked out the window and chuckled. "I think *they* might have something to say about it."

Teagan kept her gaze on him, even when the aircar doors slid back open to reveal two men wearing black uniforms with gold trim along the cuffs and shoulders. They sported the security force insignia on their arms.

Simon flicked his gaze toward her. "Looks like someone noticed that you left."

The two men stood behind Teagan. She glanced at them and winked. "Hello, boys."

One of the men looked at Simon and his rank insignia. "Apologies, Lieutenant. We've been searching for her," he said and looked at Teagan. "Miss, refugees are not allowed beyond the established areas for your use. You'll need to come with us."

Teagan turned back toward Simon. "Help a girl out, Simon. I came all this way to talk to you."

Simon stepped toward her, and she pursed her lips.

"I'd have thought you'd get the message when I didn't respond to you." He inclined his chin toward the two security agents, and they beckoned for Teagan to follow them.

She didn't move, looking amused.

"This isn't funny. They'll force you to go if you don't listen to them," Simon said.

Teagan arched an eyebrow and leaned toward him a little. "Remember when Guttman tried to grab me?"

Simon grinned and gave a slight roll of his eyes. Guttman had gotten a little too handsy with her and she'd put him in his place. She could handle herself.

Simon looked at the two agents. "You guys might want to have those palm stunners ready."

Teagan's mouth hung open and her beautiful eyes widened.

The two security agents grabbed her by her arms and gently pulled her out of the aircar. Teagan looked at Simon imploringly, but he reached toward the door controls, intent on closing them and leaving.

"Wait," Teagan cried. "Simon, I have proof that the Collective isn't the only major power working with the Sentinels."

His hand hovered by the door controls, almost grazing them. Why did she have to look at him like that? He blinked, then lowered his hand and stepped out of the aircar. The two agents glanced from Teagan to Simon.

"Give me the proof. I'll make sure it gets to the people who need to see it," Simon said.

Teagan's lips quirked at the sides. "Not until we've had a chance to talk."

"We're talking right here."

She gave him an exasperated look. "I meant with a little more privacy."

Simon stared at her. She was the embodiment of trouble—beautiful, flirty, appealing to him in every way, even more so than when she'd disguised herself as Vonya the Servitor. He *should* just walk away, tell Quinton about her offer and be done with it. He didn't need the distraction right now.

"Look, if you don't like what I have to say, I promise I'll go back to the refugee area and wait to be transferred to the DUC authorities," Teagan said.

He sighed. "You might go back to the refugees, but I doubt you'll really surrender to the DUC."

She tipped her head to the side, exposing the smooth, tan skin of her neck and jawline. "I might surprise you. Come on, it's just a conversation. The length of time traveling on that aircar there. You can have them follow if you want," she said, tilting her head behind her. "Or have others waiting. I don't care."

Simon sighed. It wasn't that long of a ride, and he could finally get some answers from her.

He looked at the security agents. "I'll take it from here. Log that she's with me."

They let go of Teagan's arms. "Very well, sir."

Simon stepped back onto the aircar, and Teagan followed him. Her hands were clasped in front of her, the very picture of cooperation.

"Destination?" a monotone voice asked.

"Take us to the bridge," Simon replied.

"Acknowledged. Arrival will be in thirty minutes."

The aircar sped away from the platform.

Simon crossed his arms and leaned against the wall. He expected Teagan to look pleased with herself, but instead, she seemed reserved, almost vulnerable. He wondered if it was some kind of act, as if she was playing another part. How many personas had she adopted over the years?

"You have thirty minutes," Simon said. "Now tell me about this proof you have concerning the Collective."

SHE SIGHED and her hands came to her sides. "We should clear the air first."

Simon's eyes flicked skyward for less than a second. "You betrayed me and my friends, then left us for dead. What else is there to say?"

"Is this where you expect me to grovel for your forgiveness?"

Simon frowned, disbelieving what he'd just heard. "Fine, you don't care."

"I didn't say that, but it's the truth, isn't it?"

"If this is your version of an apology, then you suck at it," Simon said.

He was starting to regret letting her come with him.

Teagan shook her head and smiled a little. Then a small giggle escaped her lips.

"You think this is funny?"

"No—Well, a little. Meaning this here," she said, gesturing between them.

"Is this all you wanted then?" he asked and then shook his head and walked toward the opposite end of the aircar.

"Simon," she said, following him. There was a slight pleading tone to her voice that made his stomach flip flop. "Look, I didn't know the Sentinels were going to come to the starbase. By the time they came, I was already gone. There was nothing I could have done."

Simon looked at her. "That's it?"

"What else do you want me to say?"

Simon blinked a few times. "You're unbelievable."

"Me? You are!" she replied in the same exasperated tone that he'd just used.

"I think you have that backward."

Teagan raised her chin and shook her head. "Not from where I'm standing. I had a job to do, and I did it. You expect me to apologize for it, which I won't do."

"You've made that abundantly clear."

"Give me a break, Simon. You and the others were doing the same thing. It's how the galaxy works."

"No, it's not. We were trying to help Quinton."

She locked eyes with him. "With the understanding that he would give you something in return. I was doing the same thing."

"You were working for Crowe's Union. You're Lennix's daughter!"

"Yes, I am. Quinton was extremely valuable, and my father wanted him for the Union. I told him I could get it for him."

"Yeah, and..." He stopped speaking, not quite sure where he was going with that line of thinking. Maelyn used to tell him that was his brain trying to keep him from getting into trouble.

"How many operations did you and Maelyn do together? Weren't you trying to infiltrate the Union when Quinton showed up?"

"Don't you dare say her name," Simon snarled, balling his hands into fists in frustration.

Teagan looked away from him for a few seconds. "I'm sorry she's gone. I warned her about the trap, but by the time she listened to me, they were too deep inside it."

Simon started to speak a few times but couldn't find the words. Teagan's eyebrows raised, her eyes challenging.

"You warned her? Uh, tried to warn her?"

"Yes," Teagan said, and then her expression softened. "I have a recording of the vidcom if you don't believe me."

"I'd like to see it."

"You really don't trust me."

He shrugged. "Can you blame me?"

Teagan blew out a breath.

Simon looked at her perfect lips and the shape of her mouth. "Just send it to me later," he said.

Teagan closed the distance between them and placed her hand on his shoulder. "I'm sorry about, Maelyn. I really am. She was... formidable. And as far as Endurance Starbase goes, if I'd known that what I'd done would cause the Sentinels to attack, I wouldn't have done it. The code I used was supposed to slow Quinton down so my father could take possession of the starbase. The only loss of life would have been if the DUC fleet refused to give it up."

He felt the warmth of her hand through his shirt and tried not to take comfort in it. He searched her eyes, trying to find a hint of deception, but he couldn't see any. "I don't know what to think. How am I supposed to believe you? You're the best liar I've ever met. You fooled all of us."

Teagan shook her head. "Becker suspected something. He and Quinton would have figured it out."

Simon glanced at her hand and then looked up at her face again. "What about me? All that time we spent together on the *Nebulon*. Was that just part of the job? Something to do to pass the time? When you were alone, did you find it amusing that I... I can't be the first guy you've charmed."

Teagan crossed her arms over her stomach and her eyes became sad. "At first, I was just getting to know everyone on the ship. It was part of the job. Get to know your surroundings. Determine who's a threat."

Simon snorted bitterly. "I guess I wasn't much of a threat. That's why you spent so much time with me."

"No," she said, quietly. "You were something I hadn't anticipated. I like you, Simon. Spending time with you on the *Nebulon* was easy… I really miss it. I miss you."

Simon drew in a quick breath. "Really?" he said.

Teagan stepped closer to him. "Yes. I didn't realize how much I'd missed you until after it was over."

Simon licked his lips and swallowed. "I wish I could believe you."

"I wish you could believe me, too," she replied. She stared into his eyes, and he felt himself wanting to give in. He wanted to believe her. "I came here because Maelyn told me you were here."

Simon didn't know what to say. Was she lying? God, he wanted to believe her. He'd missed her, too—more than he'd thought he would. He'd had to keep it a secret for so long that he sometimes thought he'd been wrong about it.

"I could have just sent the data to the ship. I didn't have to come here."

"Then why did you come here? For me?"

"That's a big part of it, Simon. Do you know how hard it was not to come find you?"

She seemed sincere, but she was a professional liar. She knew how to manipulate people. So did Maelyn. He'd seen her do it, but it was for DUC Intelligence. Teagan served Crowe's Union, and they served the DUC. Maybe it really was as simple as that.

"What else then? Why come here at all?"

"The message. The data is being circulated around the galaxy. About the Sentinels, Miles Harding, all of it."

"You believe it?"

"Yes. It explains a lot. I've traveled all over the galaxy. Once I saw that data, the pattern was so obvious. I don't know why I didn't see it before. These attacks. The Sentinels… Harding Prime is trying to reassert the narrative he created."

Simon considered it for a few moments. "None of us saw it either."

Teagan regarded him.

There was something else he wanted to ask her, but he was afraid of what it would mean. He didn't want to be fooled again.

He opened his mouth to speak, but Teagan folded her arms around his neck and drew his mouth to hers. Her lips pressed against his in gentle surges, and Simon wrapped his arms around her waist and pulled her body to his. Their kisses were deep and urgent, her tongue finding the depth and sweetness of his open mouth while he explored hers. All thoughts of whether she was lying to him fled his mind. She moaned softly, and they began to sway, doing a slow dance in some sort of delicious vertigo.

Eventually, they came up for air.

"You have no idea how much I've wanted to do that, and more," Teagan said.

"Me, too." He wanted to kiss her again and almost leaned forward, but a thought suddenly occurred to him. "Is this the real you? Is this what you really look like?"

She smiled. "Would you believe me if I said yes?"

Simon grinned a little and nodded.

She smiled again and her eyes widened in delight. "Good answer."

"I feel like the biggest idiot asking you this, but you really came here for me?"

"Yes. I don't want to lose you, Simon. I liked being Vonya. It's not always like that with disguises. Becoming Vonya was the most challenging disguise I'd ever tried. The Servitors' training and method of speaking were all part of it, but I started to love being her. I got to be with you, and you were so sweet to me. But there was more to it. People confided in her and wanted her advice. It was something I never thought would affect me. Kinda like you, and your boyish charms, and that adorable little dimple that appears on your cheek when you smile."

Simon tried not to smile and failed. If he was dreaming, he didn't want to wake up, ever. He knew that believing her left him vulnerable, but if he didn't, he'd regret it for however long he lived. She was here, telling him that she wanted to be with him. He wasn't going to lie to himself and try to behave as if he didn't want the same thing.

"You're good," Simon said.

Teagan smiled and kissed him again. "You have no idea."

Simon was certain that he didn't. He glanced at the info screen nearby. They only had a few minutes before they reached their destination. Where had the time gone?

Teagan followed his gaze. "Oh, our time is almost up."

"This was just the warm-up. Now you need to convince Quinton to listen to what you have to say," Simon said.

"He'll listen to me."

Simon frowned. "How can you be so sure?"

"Trust me, when he finds out what I learned, he'll be less concerned about me and more concerned about the level of deceit shown by the Alliance's supposed allies."

"Now I can't wait to hear about it," he said and glanced at the time again. Then he smiled and pulled her toward him, eager to kiss her one more time before they had to get out. Teagan giggled and pushed him against the wall. It was the best time he'd ever had in an aircar.

33

FLASHES OF LIGHTNING split the artificial atmosphere of Quinton's quarters on the *Salvation.* Thunder crackled across the sky and rain began to spatter on the ground. Sheets of rain bombarded the lake, and the wind gusted with a fury that barely scratched the surface of Quinton's inner suffering.

The configuration of his vast quarters updated according to his mood. The gale was a fitting selection, and the force of it would have surprised him if he'd taken the time to notice. He stood on the lakeshore just a few meters from the waves—a solitary figure at the apex of a storm. Lightning arced nearby, striking the water and radiating across large swaths of the surface before it dissipated. An analysis of the lightning's power appeared on his internal HUD. He must have overridden the security protocols because it was lethal to anyone without armor. From within his detached state, he wondered what would happen to him if he were struck by lightning. Would it damage his cybernetic avatar? He was protected by it, but there were limits. He'd almost died once while trying to fix the jump drive coils on the *Wayfarer*—a case of either fixing the ship or being captured by the Sentinels. But what would the lightning do to him in this instance? He'd already been struck by a different kind of lightning, and it had thrown him into a havoc that challenged even Radek's logical approach to dispassionate analysis. Quinton must be really bad off if he'd managed to frighten his emotionless VI.

Although Radek didn't need an endocrine control system, Quinton's was enabled at the lowest possible setting, and this storm was the result. What would the storm become if he disabled the system entirely?

If he wanted, he could have increased his frame rate to experience time so quickly that he'd move past the worst of the pain, and this torture would be a distant memory. But what would that cost him? Would he have to wait for years?

If Radek could read his thoughts, he would have put the calculation on his HUD.

It didn't matter. He wasn't going to increase his frame rate. In fact, he thought about slowing it down instead. Because if he was feeling all this pain and loss, it meant she was still near. If he slowed his frame rate, he could remain in this moment when Maelyn had only just died. His life would become the suffering that he felt, but at least he felt close to her.

He hadn't even been there for her at the very end. He should never have allowed her to go on this mission. He shouldn't have let her lead her own battle group. And why wouldn't she let him preserve her consciousness? At least then she would still be alive, and instead of him standing here in a storm, they'd be speaking about how they'd been lucky she'd let him download her. There were engineers working on building more cybernetic avatars like the one Quinton used, which was an advanced upgrade over the CDAs most PMCs used—as close to human as they could be without flesh and blood. Maelyn might have grown to like being in her own avatar if she'd given it a chance.

Why didn't you listen to me?

Quinton accessed the endocrine control system on his internal HUD and stared at it. The option of it taunted him. Why had they developed this capability when PMCs were first designed? Had Miles Harding included it when he created the technology that allowed him to become a PMC? Quinton wasn't sure and didn't care enough to look it up in the *Salvation's* vast array of data repositories.

He continued to stare at the control systems. If he increased it, he wouldn't feel anything at all, but if he turned it off, he'd feel everything all at once. He closed his eyes, but his internal HUD was still there.

Why didn't you listen to me? I tried to tell you, but you just wouldn't listen.

They'd been flirting with the deadliest of creatures without completely understanding the stakes, and the deadly creature had turned out to be their own ignorance—a belief that since they'd beaten the odds so many times, they could take on risks they shouldn't have taken, and this was the price. He was through with hiding behind an artificial emotional suppression system. Quinton gritted his teeth and his upper lip lifted into a snarl. Then he disabled the endocrine control system.

And screamed.

His scream pierced the storm louder than the howling winds and tumultuous thunder. Waves whipped up by the high winds raced toward the beach with renewed fury and crashed into him. They also smashed into several boulders next to him, and the splash burst in all directions. He turned his face toward the boulders and glared. Then he stomped over to them, his footfalls sloshing through the receding waters. He smashed his fists into either side of a boulder, penetrating into the rock, and heaved it up, holding it over his head. Then he spun, building up enough force that it began to slip from his grasp, and he flung it high into the air. He watched the boulder reach the apex of its journey and then sink toward the lake. Growling, Quinton threw another boulder. Then another one. He threw them so fast and with such force that two of them collided in the air, splitting into multiple pieces and pelting the lake.

Quinton stood hunched over, his hands on his knees. The habits of his mind caused his breath to come in gasps, but he could have thrown a thousand boulders and never grown tired. And that was why Maelyn wouldn't allow herself to become like him. He was stuck in a place where he was partly human and partly something else. He'd heard other PMCs say that they were more than humans, that they were the next step in evolution, but Quinton had never even considered it. He was only supposed to be a PMC for a short time while the ACN fought the Jordani Federation. After his service was complete, he was to have been put into a newly grown version of his body. He'd told Maelyn that, but it hadn't changed her answer.

He'd never gotten the chance to say goodbye to her. If only he'd acted sooner, he might have at least been able to say goodbye, and he might even have been able to prevent her ship from being destroyed in the first place. If only… If only he had someone to blame. His mind grabbed onto that thought, suddenly distracted from his pain.

The Arcturus Star System was controlled by the Collective, and that meant Draven was responsible. He could destroy the entire fucking Collective, and he didn't have to use the *Salvation* to do it. He would crush the Collective and every single spacer who was part of it. If they were living on a space station controlled by the Collective, they were the enemy. He could hunt them all like prey. The Collective could be declared the enemy just like…

His thoughts crashed and a barrage of memories flooded his mind. His life before he'd become a PMC seemed so distant that it sometimes felt as if those memories belonged to someone else, but the more recent ones pulled at him like the heaviest of black holes. Maelyn would never want him to do it. She'd rail against any such actions against spacers who were just trying to live their lives. And the more he thought about it, the more he realized that he could never do those things anyway. They were just the dark thoughts of a man who'd lost the woman he loved. His memories were perfectly preserved and would never fade, but there weren't enough of them. They were all he'd ever have, and they'd never be enough.

Quinton stopped the storm. Within a few minutes, the rain ceased, the winds died down, and the clouds dissipated. He heard water dripping from nearby trees. Soon, the cresting waves stopped, becoming smaller. Without the high winds to fuel them, they would eventually return to a flat calm. Artificial sunlight pierced the remaining clouds, and Quinton felt its warmth on his face. He looked toward the patio furniture, at the couch where Maelyn had sat the last time she'd come to see him.

"What good is saving the galaxy if you have to destroy half of it to do so?" Maelyn asked.

The couch became blurry, and Quinton sank to his knees. He wasn't sure how long he stayed like that. He purposefully ignored the clock on his HUD. Sometimes he didn't like being so connected to... everything.

"Quinton?" Simon said.

Quinton turned toward Simon, who stood inside Quinton's quarters at the edge of the patio, and he wasn't alone. A woman stood behind him, but Quinton couldn't really see her.

He stood up.

Simon's eyebrows peaked. "The door was unlocked. You didn't answer any of my comlinks."

Quinton looked at him for a long second and sighed.

"I tried to find you on the bridge," Simon continued.

"I needed some time to myself," Quinton replied.

Simon glanced around the area. Trees had been knocked over, and branches were strewn across the patio, some floating in the lake.

"I better get back to you. You can show yourself out," Quinton said and turned back toward the lake.

"Quinton, we need to talk to you."

"It has to wait." He walked toward the lake but heard Simon following. He squeezed his eyes shut. "This isn't a good time," he said, putting a bit of steel in his voice.

"She meant something to me too, you know," Simon said.

Quinton winced a little. Simon was right. The young spacer had spent a lot more time with Maelyn.

"I tried to find her. I searched. I thought that if we could recover her body, there would be some way to bring her back. She might have been—"

"She wasn't," Simon said, interrupting him.

Quinton gave him a sidelong look, a little irritated at being cut off.

"I looked, too," Simon continued. "I hoped that maybe she'd managed to get on an escape pod, but she must not have been able to."

Quinton regarded him. The young spacer was grieving, but at least he was much better composed than Quinton at the moment. Quinton wanted to tell Simon how he'd tried to reach Maelyn in time but couldn't. But Simon had been there. He knew what Quinton had done. Bringing it up again would just start another cycle of pain, and nothing new would be gleaned or put to rest. Although he didn't think he'd ever be able to put any of this to rest, that didn't mean he had to spin around in circles of grief and anger.

Quinton glanced toward the woman who waited just beyond the doorway to his quarters. He couldn't get a good look at her. "Who's your friend?"

Simon's gaze darted toward her for a second. "It's part of why I came to find you. There are things I just learned about that you need to hear," he said and then gestured toward Quinton's quarters.

The woman walked outside into the sunlight, her golden hair glistening. An analysis appeared on Quinton's HUD and a warning flashed. Quinton stepped in front of Simon faster than the young spacer could react.

"Don't you know who this is?" Quinton asked with a hand extended toward her. She stopped.

"He knows who I am," she said.

Simon came around and put himself between Quinton and the woman again. "I know who she is… who she really is, I mean. Please just listen to me. She's trying to help us."

Quinton glared at the woman who had pretended to be a Servitor. "She's a spy. You can't trust anything she says," he said and moved toward her, pushing Simon back a few steps. "Who do you work for, Vonya?"

She didn't back up or even blink. She regarded him coolly, as if she'd expected this reaction from him.

"Is it the Collective? Do you work for Draven? Did you set this all up?" Quinton fired his questions in rapid succession.

"I don't work for Trenton Draven or the Collective," she said.

Simon tried to stall Quinton from reaching her.

"It's all right, Simon. Let him come," she said.

Simon glared at him—actually glared at him. "Stop!" the young spacer said forcefully.

Quinton sneered at him.

"My name is Teagan Cayne. I'm Lennix Crowe's daughter."

Quinton stopped. His eyes widened and his mouth opened a little. "You're Crowe's daughter?" he said, and the analysis on his HUD updated. He had a record of Crowe's DNA and peered at Teagan. It was a fifty percent match. She was telling the truth. "You *are* his daughter. Why are you here?"

Teagan blinked in surprise, and she glanced at Simon.

"I checked your DNA with your father's. It's a match. Now answer my question."

"I didn't know," she said and shook her head. "It doesn't matter. I tried to warn Maelyn about the Collective's trap."

"She wouldn't believe you."

Teagan shook her head sadly. "Not at first, and by the time she did, it was too late to escape. I did what I could for her and the rest of the battle group."

Quinton's behavioral analysis of Teagan indicated that she showed all the physical signs of expressing genuine regret, but she'd pretended to be a Servitor. If she was one of Lennix Crowe's top operatives, she was a skilled liar.

"There's no way I can determine whether you're telling me the truth," Quinton said.

"She is," Simon said.

Quinton frowned and looked at his friend. The same behavior analysis began to show for him. Quinton blinked and stared at both of them. There were traces of each of their scents on the other, particularly around the mouth. They'd been kissing.

"Simon," Quinton said.

The spacer seemed to be expecting it and nodded. "We were friends aboard the *Nebulon*."

Quinton snarled and stepped toward Teagan. "What did you do to him? Did you use some kind of inhibitor?" He grabbed her shoulders and lifted her from the ground. "Tell me!"

"I didn't do anything," she said in a frustratingly calm voice.

Simon grabbed Quinton's arm and tried to free Teagan. "Let her go."

"So, she batted her eyelashes at you, and you just what? Rolled over for her? She's playing you for a fool," Quinton said.

Simon shook his head. "She's not."

"I'm not," Teagan said. "Quinton, look at me. You can tell whether I'm lying or not."

"Can I? Can I really? You're trained. You can beat whatever detection I'm able to perform," Quinton said.

Simon pulled out his sidearm and pointed it at Quinton. "Put her down, or I swear I'm going to shoot your arm off."

He meant it. The palm stunner Simon had tried to use on the bridge wouldn't work, so he'd gone for the next best option.

Quinton's reaction times were more than capable of disarming his friend, but he wasn't going to do it. He lowered Teagan to the ground and let her go.

Simon exhaled forcefully and put his sidearm away.

Quinton held his hands up in front of his chest. "All right. You've got my attention. I'm not going to pretend I understand, but I'm willing to listen. After that, I make no guarantees," he said and looked at Simon. "And that sidearm isn't going to help you if I think she's trying to hurt you or is in any way responsible for what happened in Arcturus."

Simon inhaled explosively, but Teagan placed a restraining hand on his arm. "Simon, it's fine. He's agreed to listen. It's fine. We shouldn't expect anything more from him at this point."

His friend sighed and nodded—a gesture that appeared to be more to himself than in acknowledgment of anyone else.

Teagan told him how she'd tried to warn Maelyn about the trap that was waiting for the Alliance ships. To prove it, she shared recordings of their conversations. He watched them, committing them to memory. Everything she'd told them seemed to be the truth, but he wasn't ready to trust her yet. He couldn't be sure what her motivations were.

"Lennix never mentioned you," Quinton said.

"He wouldn't. Do you blame him?"

"I don't know."

"He doesn't show any favoritism or leniency because I'm his daughter. Never has. I rose through the ranks by proving myself," Teagan said.

Quinton recognized the surety in her tone, born of accomplishment. Maelyn has—had—the same confidence.

"You didn't come all this way to tell me that you tried to help the Alliance ships," Quinton said.

"No, that was to get you to listen to me. I needed you to believe me at least a little bit."

"So, this was just to whet my appetite. I get it."

Teagan shook her head. "No, it wasn't. I was establishing credibility, but I also know you cared about Maelyn. I'd want to know what happened if I were you."

"Okay, why are you really here then?"

"I'm here to help you."

Quinton arched an eyebrow. "Really?"

Teagan nodded. "Yes, really. I've seen the data you've sent everywhere—the information about the Sentinels."

Quinton glanced at Simon. He nodded.

"And?" Quinton asked.

"I believe you," Teagan said and smiled a little. "It may not seem like much, but I'd like to offer my services."

"What about your father?"

Teagan snorted. "I'm a big girl, Quinton. I can do what I want."

"Okay. Simon didn't bring you here for that, so tell me the rest."

The edges of her lips twitched, and she nodded once. "For the past seven standard months, I've been working on infiltrating the Collective. It was my father's highest priority."

"Why?"

"Because he doesn't trust Trenton Draven," Teagan replied.

"Neither did I, but I had to work with him." Quinton shook his head. "I really thought he was… he fooled me, too, and a lot of other people."

Teagan nodded. "He's very good at manipulating everyone. He knew you needed his resources to fight the Sentinels. Anyway, I've been working my way across various groups, looking for where his core enterprises were and how they all function together. It's really quite extensive."

"What did Lennix want you to find?"

"Draven was trying to absorb the Union into the Collective. He wanted my father out of the way, and my father wanted anything he could leverage against him."

Quinton considered it for a few seconds. "You mean for after the war."

"He never said as much to me, but I think you're right. Draven had protection because of his association with the Alliance, but now… all bets are off, it seems. However, there's more. I have evidence that the Collective has been colluding with various groups within the Alliance."

Quinton gritted his teeth. "Which groups?"

"I have a list. Many are smaller groups that he likely forced to do what he wanted, but there's one I think you'll be more interested in than all the others. I know I wouldn't have expected it."

"Tell me who they are."

Teagan glanced at Simon for a second, and Quinton realized that Simon didn't know who she was talking about either.

"The Servitors. Their lead counselor, Yvonne Zariah."

Quinton felt as if his gut had sunk through the floor. "Counselor Zariah is working with Draven? You have proof of this?"

Teagan nodded gravely. "They've been colluding for months."

"Months!"

Quinton hadn't meant to shout, but he couldn't help it. He'd tried to convince the Servitors to help him when all along they'd already decided to stand against him and the Alliance. They'd deceived him since the beginning. He'd been manipulated. Quinton blinked several times and turned away from the others. Had Kandra Pavond been part of the deception? Were all the Servitors part of it, or was it just their leadership? There wasn't any way for Quinton to figure it out

—not by himself. He turned back toward the others and raised his gaze to Teagan.

She swallowed nervously and looked a little afraid. "I only learned about their alliance just before the attack. Here, look at the data I've retrieved. I didn't know about it until recently. I swear it. Please, you have to believe me."

A data repository became available. Quinton snatched it out of the air, and Radek began running multiple analyses on it.

"I got into one of the Collective's core systems data centers and found the information there," Teagan said.

Quinton reviewed the data and scanned the high-level analysis Radek performed. "I believe you," he said.

Simon visibly relaxed.

"That's all I have, Quinton. I was supposed to bring that data to my father, but I chose to bring it to you instead," Teagan said.

Quinton regarded her for a few moments. "Thank you. I appreciate you taking the risk."

Teagan bit her lower lip for a second. "What happens now?"

"I don't know. I need to share this with my senior officers and the select members of the Alliance," Quinton said and frowned. "We need to figure out who we can trust."

"I can help you," Teagan said.

Quinton looked at Simon.

"I believe her," Simon said. "We need her help."

"How do you think Brandt will react when he learns who she is?"

"I thought you were in charge," Teagan said.

"I am, but this is a group effort."

"Brandt won't be a problem," Teagan replied.

Simon frowned. "How can you be so sure?"

"Because he's not stupid. With allies falling by the wayside, you need all the help you can get," Teagan replied.

"What about your father?" Quinton asked.

"You let me worry about my father."

"Do you think he'll try to cut his losses?" Quinton asked.

He was testing her, and she wouldn't back down.

"I doubt it, Quinton. The Collective wants him dead. You don't want him dead because you need him. He's not stupid either. Also, his intolerance for what the Sentinels actually are means that he can't go back to the way things were."

"What do you mean?" Simon asked.

The doors to Quinton's quarters opened and Becker, Oscar, and Guttman strode in. He really needed to lock those doors. Guttman was his usual loud self, and they heard him before they saw Becker leading the others toward the lake.

Becker looked at Teagan in recognition.

"It's all right. I know who she is. She's with us," Quinton said.

Becker considered it for a second, glancing at Oscar and Guttman. "You're the admiral."

Guttman stared at Teagan for a few seconds.

"I'm sorry. I'm just trying to imagine the way you were before."

Becker grunted and shook his head. "Well, get over it," he said, inclining his chin toward Simon.

Guttman frowned. "What do you mean?"

Oscar looked at Simon and Teagan for a second and then gave Becker a nod. "Would you look at that," Oscar said and smiled at Simon. "Good for you, kid."

Simon smiled a little.

Guttman frowned and then sighed.

Becker looked at Quinton. "You'll have to fill me in, but before we get to that..." he said, gesturing toward Guttman.

"Guttman, come on, man," Oscar said.

"Oh, that's right. I've got it right here," Guttman said.

He opened his bag and handed a stack of cups to Oscar. "Pass those out," he said.

After Oscar gave them each a cup, Guttman filled the cups with a dark liquid. He came to Quinton and offered. After a moment's hesitation, Quinton held out his cup, and Guttman filled it.

Becker held up his cup and the others joined in. He looked at Quinton.

"Go ahead," Quinton said.

"To Maelyn Wayborn. Gone, but never forgotten."

They repeated the toast and drank.

Quinton lowered his cup. "Never forgotten," he said quietly and drank. The liquid tasted bitter and wouldn't affect him the way he wanted, but there was nothing he could do about it. At least he'd gotten to have this moment with his friends, remembering someone who was no longer with them. And not just someone, but a person who had affected all of their lives in a meaningful way.

Becker drank some more and sighed. He looked at Quinton. "Now tell me why she's got a free pass," he said, jutting his chin toward Teagan.

34

THE *SALVATION* and its crew left the Arcturus Star System, transporting millions of refugees who no longer wanted to remain in the Collective's controlled space. Quinton couldn't be sure there weren't Collective operatives among the refugees. It was a safe bet there were, but Sherilyn Cantos had assured him that their protocols would help mitigate the risk.

They salvaged what they could from the warships that couldn't be repaired. Even though they'd blocked communications from the space stations in the star system, Quinton knew their time was limited before Draven and the Sentinels coordinated another attack, and there was nothing to be gained by fighting another battle in the Arcturus Star System.

They executed a series of hyperspace jumps, meeting up with DUC transport ships to offload the refugees in large groups. They couldn't offload them all at once, so multiple waypoints were scheduled in secret to avoid any unwanted attention. Even though the *Salvation* was the size of a rocky planet, it wasn't designed to accommodate millions of people. The *Salvation* was, first and foremost, a ship of war, and most of its systems had been designed with that purpose in mind.

Quinton walked inside a conference room near the bridge. He hadn't been back to his designated quarters in over a week, and he wasn't sure when he'd go back. He really didn't need them and had offered them up as a recreation area to the families aboard the ship. Almost none of them had ever set foot on a planet, much less one with a breathable atmosphere. Most planets post-Federation Wars wouldn't even have been considered before. They were planets with harsh climates that required people to live under crowded domes and wear environmental suits when they left the safety of the domes. There were some terraforming efforts in various star systems, but the process took years, and according to Brandt, they suffered a lot of delays, both intentional and otherwise.

The door to the conference room opened and Becker walked in, heading straight toward Quinton.

"You really want someone like me here?" Becker asked.

Quinton nodded. "I need all the allies I can get."

Becker eyed him for a second. "Thanks, I guess."

Quinton chuckled a little. "I trust you. That goes a long way."

"More allies running for the nearest airlock?"

"You could say that," Quinton replied.

Severin Brandt and several others entered the conference room. The virtual meeting room was also occupied by more Alliance leaders, as well as several senior officers selected by Quinton and Brandt.

Quinton started the meeting.

"The last of the refugees have been transferred to the transport ships," Sherilyn said.

"Good," he replied.

"What do you want to do with the volunteers?"

"They need to be vetted, and I don't want to do that here. Where are you taking them?" Quinton asked.

Sherilyn's holographic image glanced toward Brandt and then she looked at Quinton. "With so many refugees, the only place they can be safe is the colony worlds."

"How did they react to the news?" Becker asked.

"We didn't give them a choice. They don't know where we're taking them. I don't want to chance one of them sending a comlink out to a Collective monitoring station," Sherilyn said.

"Or the Sentinels," Quinton added. The others looked at him. "Somehow, Draven and Counselor Zariah have formed some kind of alliance with the Sentinels," he said. His gaze strayed toward Teagan Cayne, and his wasn't the only one.

"Will you move against the Collective now? Cripple his enterprise?" Lennix Crowe asked.

Quinton looked at the Union commander. "Eventually. The goal of this meeting is to figure out our next move."

"This is our highest priority," Sherilyn said.

Crowe frowned. "There are so few of us here. Have that many groups abandoned the Alliance?"

Sherilyn shook her head. "We've limited these meetings to key personnel, but the decisions will be conveyed to the others at the appropriate time."

Crowe looked at Quinton. "I understand the need for discretion, but how long can we keep this up?"

"As long as we need to," Quinton replied. "That's the way it needs to be for now. It's not bravado, but having both the Collective and the Servitors turn against us was something none of us anticipated." He pressed his lips together for a second. "Well, some of us might have anticipated it, but it couldn't be proven until recently," he said and looked at Teagan.

Crowe's gaze flicked toward his daughter for a moment. The two shared a glance that Quinton couldn't begin to interpret.

"The truth is that there are likely more groups like the refugees who don't support what the Collective has done," Quinton said.

"We can't transport all of them to the colony worlds," Crowe said.

"You're right, Lennix," Sherilyn said. "Their location must be kept secret. That's why anyone who goes there isn't allowed to leave."

"Yes, but are they defended?" Crowe asked.

He didn't know where the colony worlds were located.

"Their defenses are not your concern," Quinton said, and Crowe glared at him a little. "At least not right now."

"Fine," Crowe replied. "How are we going to prevent the Sentinel incursion that's coming? With the number of Sentinel warships being reported, it's going to be like nothing we've ever seen before."

Quinton looked around the conference room. There were a few empty chairs, and more than once, he wished Maelyn was there. He'd underestimated how much he'd relied on her, especially at times like these. She'd helped bridge the gap he felt with the spacers.

"We have plans in place to defend strategic star systems," Brandt said.

Crowe nodded. "But going on the defensive isn't a long-term strategy." His tone was that of someone making a statement that should already be known to the other spacers in the room.

Quinton wondered if this was how Grand Admiral Elias Browning had felt. They'd been surrounded by enemies, and if enough allies believed their situation was hopeless, self-preservation would've taken over.

"It's not," Brandt said. "We need more allies. Then we can shift the balance against the Collective and the Sentinels."

"Why did the Servitors choose to betray us?" Crowe asked.

Quinton turned toward Crowe's hologram. "The Servitors want peace in the galaxy. They're not interested so much in the truth."

"And that's what led them to…" Crowe paused for a second and regarded Quinton. "You were the target. I don't have to tell you what they did."

The edges of Quinton's lips twitched in acknowledgment. "It's okay. We don't have to avoid the topic. Counselor Yvonne Zariah was able to fool me. Both she and Trenton Draven knew how we'd react. They hatched an elaborate trap to lure me to a place where the Sentinel fleets could destroy us."

"They underestimated how powerful your ship is," Crowe said.

"They also exposed its weakness."

Crowe frowned and looked at Brandt.

"The *Salvation* is only one ship. We can only be in one place at a time," Quinton said.

"Yeah, but…" Crowe began and stopped.

"We have to consider that perhaps there are too many Sentinel warships," Quinton said.

Brandt's gaze darted toward him. "What are you saying?"

"We overreached. Tried to do too many things at once and got burned because of it. That's what I'm saying," Quinton said and paused for a few seconds. "I'm saying that maybe we can't unite the galaxy against the Sentinels like we'd hoped."

Everyone in the room and in the virtual conference room stared at him in shock. No one spoke, as if they were all afraid to utter a single word.

Sherilyn cleared her throat. "Admiral Aldren has a point. Avoiding the mere thought of addressing our own flaws isn't going to help us in the long run."

"Are you sure?" Crowe asked scornfully. "Because it sounds to me like we're giving up. What happened to inspire the galaxy to fight the Sentinels? Just as we start to gain momentum, we're going to stop?"

"No one is saying we're stopping," Brandt replied.

"Then what are we saying?" Crowe said and gestured toward Quinton. "And I want to hear it from you."

"I'm not saying we should stop what we're doing, but our strategy has to change. Not only that, but we also need to consider that our reach is limited in comparison to the Sentinels. Wait a second," Quinton said, holding up his hand. "You asked a question and I'm going to answer it. One of the things we lack, that the Alliance lacks, is a single place to call its own. We're fragmented, and if we stay like that we'll never survive."

"You're talking about something more than fortifying a single star system," Brandt said.

Quinton nodded and looked at Sherilyn. "The UFA needs a place to call its own. Sooner rather than later."

Crowe watched them, and then his eyes widened a little.

"We'll establish a federation that will one day challenge the Sentinels," Quinton said.

"It will also make us a target," Sherilyn said. "You think that since we're fragmented we're not strong? Not true—not in the way you might think. It prevents the Sentinels from finding us. You've already said you couldn't defend us against the Sentinels in what you refer to as a straight-up fight."

Quinton nodded. "You're right. I did say that, and I meant it. However, the *Salvation* has the means to build new ships—technology that can be duplicated. We build up our strength."

"But what about the spacers who've… we can't abandon them," Sherilyn said.

"Even Browning accounted for the possibility that this would be a long war that couldn't be decided in a single battle. And there's nothing we can do that doesn't involve significant risk."

The meeting went quiet as the participants considered what had been said.

"I think we need time to process this information. See if we can come up with other solutions," Brandt said.

Quinton didn't think there were any other possibilities. They weren't just fighting the Sentinels. That was too simplistic a view, and that had been reinforced by the reports of what his fleets had encountered across multiple star systems. The Sentinels were a huge proponent of the war, as was Harding Prime, but spacers were as well. The spacers made up the entire galactic society, and the entire post-Federation Wars society that emerged seemed to exist only to reinforce a narrative that kept them subjugated. They were survivors. They'd endured hardships. Quinton could see it in people like Brandt and Sherilyn, but it also gave rise to ruthless leaders like Trenton Draven, and even Lennix Crowe. Quinton glanced at Teagan. It was his conversation with her that had helped him realize this, but more than that, it was Maelyn.

What good is saving the galaxy if you had to destroy half of it to do so?

The meeting ended and people began leaving the conference room. Quinton knew Brandt wanted to speak with him, but he sent a message to Lennix Crowe first. The Union commander was outraged by these developments, and Quinton understood that.

Quinton entered his own private meeting room, and a few seconds later Lennix Crowe appeared.

"I'm going to keep this brief," Quinton said. "I have a job for you, and I think it's something you were probably considering anyway. But you need my help to get it done."

Lennix regarded him for a moment and his gaze narrowed a little. "I know you're not a coward. So, was all this talk about withdrawing and building up our strength just some kind of misdirection?"

Quinton shook his head. "No, that's what we're going to do."

The surety of his tone left little doubt that Quinton had already decided on their new course of action.

"However, as you pointed out, we can't *not* maintain a presence in the galaxy. Also, there's a reckoning that needs to happen. Don't you agree?"

Lennix leaned forward. "I'm listening."

35

THE DOOR to the dimly lit conference room opened and Brandt leaned inside.

"Quinton, what are you doing in here?"

Quinton had several active holoscreens open in front of him. He turned toward Brandt. "At the moment, I'm reviewing the latest intelligence reports. Also, Belinda sent me an update of her observations about fleet cohesion."

Brandt crossed the room to stand next to him, scratching his beard. "Don't you usually do this on the bridge?"

"I needed a change of scenery."

Brandt gave him a sidelong look.

"All right, Radek informed me that the bridge officers were becoming concerned because I never left the bridge."

"You're still near the bridge."

"Nobody is perfect."

Brandt blew out a breath. "I guess not. What was in Belinda's report?"

"She sent it to you, too."

"I know, but I haven't had a chance to read it. I don't have your bandwidth when it comes to reviewing information."

Quinton snorted. It wasn't the first time Brandt had commented about his limitations. It was right up there with getting too old. "There's growing discontent among the PMCs. Several hundred of them are requesting that their bodies be regrown. They want to be human again."

Brandt looked away. "This is ridiculous. Lights," he said, and the lighting increased its luminosity until the room was well lit. "What do you think?"

"I think it's their right to make the request."

Brandt walked over to the refreshment module near the wall and poured himself a glass of water. He turned toward Quinton. "I sense a 'but' coming."

"They all have a term of service to fulfill before they'll be released from their contract."

Brandt sighed and rubbed his beard in thought. "Are we asking too much from them?"

Quinton chuckled bitterly. "The alternative is worse. They're just blowing off some frustration. I get it. I want the same thing sometimes. Only…"

He didn't finish the thought.

Brandt did him the courtesy of not bringing up painful memories. "Sherilyn told me that making the colony worlds the heart of the UFA is gaining traction. But you know what the concerns are."

Quinton nodded. "They want the *Salvation*."

"You got it."

"What do you think I should do?"

"There isn't an easy answer to give you. They want security. They don't want to lose the worlds that the Acheron Confederacy terraformed in secret. I can see that it makes sense for a short duration, but we're not dealing with the real issue here. The Sentinels are still out there, and they'll eventually find the colony worlds. What do we do then? Hope that whatever defenses we've built are enough to hold out against them? That's a hell of a gamble."

Quinton's eyebrows flicked toward the ceiling for less than a second. "It doesn't inspire confidence."

Brandt shook his head. "No, it doesn't. I still say there's more to learn from Browning's entries."

"I've looked."

"Look again."

"If only it were that simple."

"It might be," Brandt replied.

"Reviewing the thoughts of a dead man isn't going to save us. It could take years."

Brandt shrugged. "Then that's what it takes."

"I could lose sight of what we're doing if I'm… not gone, but when I increase my frame rate like that… there's a cost, is all I'm trying to say. Spacers already don't trust me. I don't need to add absentmindedness to their list."

"Well then, you'll have to rely on the rest of us to help you."

"I already do."

Brandt looked at the holoscreens for a few seconds. "You know what made Maelyn such a good operative?"

"She knew how to read people."

"You're right about that. She understood people. You were lucky she found you. I don't know if anyone else could have helped you."

Quinton's thoughts flatlined. "I could use her help now."

"Me, too. Look, think about what I said. There has to be something in Browning's log entries. Something we can use."

Brandt left the room and Quinton dimmed the lights a little. He didn't need lighting at all, but if someone else found him standing alone in the dark, they'd be even more worried that he was losing his mind.

Quinton closed the holoscreens and left the conference room. He needed a change of scenery and walked away from the bridge, moving with a determined stride, although he didn't really have a destination in mind. Brandt had encouraged Quinton to search Browning's logs for answers so many times that it had become something they both acknowledged without a lot of effort. Brandt was relentless when he thought there was more to learn about something.

Quinton had searched Browning's logs on many occasions, looking for anything that had to do with the Sentinels and the *Salvation*. Browning had never seen the *Salvation*. It was one of many efforts he'd overseen before he launched what had been his final assault on Harding Prime. Browning hadn't kept the location a secret. It was one of the first places Quinton had sent a scout force, but there was no trace of anything. Too much time had passed for them to find evidence of a space battle having been fought there. It was yet another in a long line of dead ends.

Quinton soon entered a transit hub and walked toward the nearest empty aircar. Several spacers watched him.

"Destination?" a monotone voice asked.

"Just take me for a ride until I tell you to stop."

"Understood, Admiral Aldren."

The aircar sped out of the transit hub, traveling so fast that the scenery was little more than a flurry of images, but he looked out the window for a while anyway before opening a data connection to the *Salvation's* core computer system and accessing Browning's logs.

A special holoscreen appeared and showed an extensive list of log entries. Some of them were simple text-type logs, and others were video logs. There were also hundreds of thousands of mission reports. He'd asked Radek to analyze them for pertinent information, which never yielded anything. It was as if Browning had designed his log entries to resist VI analysis.

Quinton frowned, considering.

"Okay, Admiral Browning. What would you do?" Quinton asked.

There was a flash from the specialized holoscreen, and then a recorded video log appeared.

Elias Browning was an older man. Gray hair, mixed with flecks of darker hair, was scattered around his short-cropped head. His brow lines were deep, as if chiseled by the decades of pressure, firm in the knowledge that he'd lost a war. Yet, there was still fight left in his eyes. His gaze promised something that made Quinton want to stand up straight. Quinton wished he could have met him, that he could have spoken to him.

Grand Admiral Elias Browning regarded him, or at least the camera in front of him. "I don't know which of you will find the *Salvation*. There were thousands of possibilities. However, I knew the question you asked was inevitable. Given what you're doing, I didn't want your answer to be met with stubborn silence. You asked what I would do. If I knew how to defeat Miles Harding, I would have done it. The truth is that I don't know how to defeat him. He wasn't always the way he is now. He was a good kid in the beginning, and it might surprise you to learn that it was a version of Miles Harding that helped me figure out what the

Prime was doing." Browning paused and shook his head. A sneer was moments from his lips, but the moment passed, and he looked at the camera again. "The only advice I have to offer you is what I tell every commanding officer serving in the fleets. Remember who the real enemy is. The only way the galaxy moves forward is without the Sentinels and Harding Prime. The only way."

The recording stopped and Quinton stared at the empty holoscreen for a few minutes. Recent events had certainly shown him that he couldn't force wide, sweeping change on the galaxy. He wasn't convinced he'd been wrong to try, but Browning was right. They needed to focus all their efforts on the true enemies.

The aircar continued its trek through the *Salvation,* and Quinton thought about Browning's recording. When he mentioned Miles Harding, there'd been pain in his gaze.

He'd been a good kid.

They'd been friends. That's the only explanation for it. Browning and Harding had been friends, but what had gone wrong? Why had Harding betrayed Browning? Browning referred to the "Prime" as if he were a separate person. PMCs that came out of storage had indicated that it was the mergence protocol that caused PMCs to go insane—the mergence protocol that had been modified by Harding—but what if it was the mergence protocol that had created Harding Prime in the first place?

Quinton glanced at the holoscreen and blew out a long breath. Browning had somehow made his log entries difficult to analyze, not wanting a VI to do a detailed analysis and provide only the highlights for whatever Galactic PMC found the *Salvation.* He wanted whoever found it to have to work for the information. Knowledge and insight required time and effort.

"Okay, Admiral Browning. I have another question for you."

36

QUINTON OPENED the door to Simon's lab. A short distance inside, a wall of storage crates blocked his way. He called out Simon's name and heard some shuffling behind the wall.

"Quinton, come in. Watch out for the crates. I've been rearranging things in here," Simon said.

Quinton walked to the end of the wall of crates and came around the other side. "Are you alone?"

A creature screeched from on top of a high shelf, and Stumpy glared at him with animalistic posturing. Then the creature turned away from him and groomed himself. He paused for a second, craning his neck around to peek at Simon and then continued grooming.

"He's still upset with you," Simon said.

Stumpy hadn't appreciated the storm Quinton unleashed in his quarters.

When Quinton had rescued the creature, he'd never intended it to become a lifelong companion. Stumpy was more Simon's pet than Quinton's. "He'll live," he replied, deciding that he'd ignore the little fuzzball with huge ears. He glanced at the storage crates and then back at Simon. "Look, I said you could try to help PMCs that have been infiltrated with Sentinel protocols, but it's time to put this effort to rest."

Quinton looked at an active holoscreen nearby, and Simon hastened in front of it. He held his hands up in front of his chest. "I'm really close, Quinton."

"Not from where I'm standing. This place is a mess. Besides, I'm going to need you on the bridge, and we can't afford any more distractions. I know you did your best, but sometimes it's not enough," Quinton said.

Simon closed the holoscreen and sighed. "You came all the way here to tell me in person?"

"I was in the area. Where's Teagan?" he asked, heading back around the wall of storage crates.

"She just stepped out," Simon said.

Quinton looked at him as they left the lab. "You and she?"

Simon smiled and nodded. Then his eyebrows pushed forward in concern. "We're trying to be discreet."

"Don't," Quinton replied. "You never know how much time you'll have. Don't waste a second."

Simon swallowed and lowered his chin. "I won't."

They walked in silence for a minute.

"So, what are we working on?" Simon asked.

"We're hunting Sentinels."

Simon's eyebrows peaked and his mouth hung open a little. Then he blew out a breath. "Okay."

"I'm glad you understand. Most people would have started asking a lot of questions by now."

Simon grinned.

They walked into the transit hub and Teagan met them there. She looked at Quinton. "You want to hunt Sentinels?"

Quinton glanced at Simon.

The young spacer shrugged one shoulder and tipped his head to the side. "You didn't say it was a secret."

"Yeah," Quinton said, entering an aircar.

Teagan and Simon followed him.

"How are we supposed to do that?" Simon asked.

"I was hoping you guys might have a few ideas about that," Quinton replied.

Simon glanced at Teagan, who considered it for a moment. "I think I can come up with something. Do we just want to take them out, or do you have something else in mind?"

Quinton smiled, appreciating that there were people who just wanted to get the work done. "I'm glad you found your way back."

Teagan blinked in surprise and then smiled. She was a beautiful woman, and Quinton could understand why Simon was smitten with her.

"I won't let it go to my head, Admiral," she replied.

"That's probably a good thing."

Simon cleared his throat. "Who else is going to help with this?"

Quinton considered it for a second. "The usual crew. Maybe a few others. Probably your father for sure."

Teagan snorted. "He's going to hate this."

Quinton grinned. "I know. You should have seen his face with the last thing I gave him to do."

Simon frowned. "What do you have him doing?"

"Uh, uh," Quinton replied, pointing a finger at him. "Admiral's privilege. Don't worry about it."

"Okay, let me get this straight," Simon said. "First, you want us to withdraw and build up our defenses, but you still want to fight the Sentinels?"

"Hunt the Sentinels."

Simon pursed his lips. "Is there a difference?"

"Of course there's a difference. Hunting is much different than fighting. Teagan, I expect you to educate him better, otherwise someone could take advantage of our young spacer here," Quinton replied.

Teagan grinned.

"You're in a better mood," Simon replied.

"A little," Quinton said and paused for a moment. "I got some clarity on some things. But yeah, I don't want to just fight the Sentinels. I want to hunt them down wherever they are."

"Why the sudden change?"

Quinton shrugged. "Not a change, really. We're not meant to waste away on old ships and space stations. We're meant to colonize, explore, and build things. We're meant to thrive. We're not meant to cower, embracing old rivalries or celebrating victimhood."

"But you said we tried to do too much. We can't unite the galaxy."

"We can't. I haven't changed my mind about that."

"Okay," Simon replied, drawing out the word.

"We can't solve the galaxy's problems. I thought we could help with some of that, but that's not what I'm supposed to do. And before you ask, hunting the Sentinels is what I'm supposed to do. Hunting the Sentinels and taking out Harding Prime. It's simple and liberating all at the same time. The rest of the galaxy will need to take care of itself. Spacers can believe whatever they want, and they can do whatever they want, but what they can't do is stop the Sentinels. It's what Browning intended all along."

Simon leaned against the wall and sighed. "You make it sound so simple."

"It is," Quinton replied. "That doesn't mean it's going to be easy."

They stopped at the conference room near the bridge. The room was filled with people, and there was a virtual meeting already set up, with holographic images of the remote attendees. Among them were delegates of the UFA.

Simon looked at Quinton.

"I multitask really well," Quinton said.

Simon and Teagan found a couple of open seats and sat down.

Brandt stood up. "Admiral Aldren, you called this meeting."

"Thanks," Quinton said and turned to address everyone else. "I'm going to get straight to the point. We need to hunt the Sentinels. We've been too reactionary to events, and it's cost us."

Multiple speaker requests became active, and Quinton acknowledged Sherilyn Cantos.

"We've just suffered a huge betrayal that almost led to our utter defeat. More than half of our allies have abandoned us because they believe we can't protect them, and you want to hunt the Sentinels? Am I correct in my understanding?" Sherilyn asked. The leader of the DUC was the senior council representative for the United Federation Alliance, and it was her job to raise the questions that were, no doubt, on everyone's minds.

She watched him expectantly, waiting for his response.

"Losing support from the Collective and the Servitors was a major setback," Quinton said, noticing that many of the delegates were shouting their responses, as if that could overcome the fact that their microphones were muted. "Let me finish. You'll all get to ask your questions. All that I ask is that you hear me out," he said.

One by one the delegates settled down.

"When we found the *Salvation*, I thought it was to become a beacon or a rallying cry for the galactic remnants to support the fight against the Sentinels. I underestimated the extent of how much the Federation Wars had scarred the galaxy. There are limitations to what I can do. Many of you are afraid that the UFA is dying or already dead. That's why former allies have left us. It's not their fault. In the face of what happened, they need to put their survivability ahead of the things we'd like them to believe. Knowing the truth about what happened during the Federation Wars carries a price, and while I might feel it's righteous of me to give that information out to everyone, it doesn't entitle me or the UFA to their support." Quinton paused for a few seconds, allowing what he'd said to be considered by the attendees. "The UFA isn't dead, not as long as we remain. The *Salvation* represents a joint effort of the federations of old, and after Harding and the Sentinels are defeated, I will turn control of the *Salvation* over to the UFA leadership."

Brandt's eyes widened, as did many of the others in the room. Multiple people began speaking at once, both in the physical room and in the virtual room. Quinton had unmuted all the microphones, and there was a startled silence when everyone realized they could now hear each other. More than a few chuckles came from the attendees.

"Admiral Aldren, this is a lot for us to consider," Sherilyn said.

"I know. That's why I'm going to leave you to it. Senior officers will join me on the bridge. Oh, and if anyone has any good ideas for finding the Sentinels, let us know," Quinton replied.

"Wait," Sherilyn said. "You're just going to leave us?"

Quinton nodded. "I thought there would be a lot more to discuss, but I think it would be best if you handled that among yourselves. I have a few ideas of my own for finding the Sentinels, and I can't be tied up here while you decide whether you can support this effort or not."

Sherilyn nodded. "I see. You are committed to this course of action."

Quinton regarded her for a moment. "It's the only action I can take."

Quinton walked toward the door, and senior navy personnel followed, as well as the spacers he'd asked to join him on the bridge. The delegates would no doubt debate the issue for hours on end, but it wouldn't change what Quinton was going to do. It would be easier if he had their help, but he'd found that after months of trying to convince spacers to join them, actions spoke louder than words.

37

QUINTON WALKED TOWARD THE BRIDGE. The massive doors slid open, and he entered. He heard Brandt chuckling behind him.

"That's one way to negotiate for their support," Brandt said.

"What do you think they'll do?" Simon asked.

"They'll talk for a while before they eventually agree to it," Teagan replied.

"How do you know?" Simon asked.

"Because Quinton has what they want. This ship."

Quinton turned toward them. They were a mix of human and PMC crewmembers.

"There wasn't anything left for us to do in that meeting," Quinton said.

"How do you want to begin?" Brandt asked. "Oh, and Sherilyn will be able to deal with them."

"Good. I feel like I just threw her a few armed explosives to juggle."

"She's been doing it for years."

Becker entered the bridge.

Quinton gestured for Becker to join them. "We need to leverage our contacts to locate the Sentinels. Current sightings. The things we've been doing, but I'd like to concentrate on smaller groups if we can."

"Why do you want to focus on smaller groups?" Simon asked.

"Because I want to capture some of them."

"It's never been done," Brandt said.

"There's a reason for that," Becker replied. "They coordinate with a larger attack force, so they always have a backup."

Quinton nodded. "I know. I want to spread their forces thin. Like what they did to us."

"Why do you want to capture one?" Simon asked.

"To be able to find out where they go when they're not scouting star systems.

They have to refuel eventually, and after the most recent campaign, they'll need to replenish their ammunition."

"How are you going to lure them out?" Brandt asked.

"By leveraging one of our greatest assets," Quinton said, looking at the other PMCs.

Brandt stared at him. Then he looked at Walsh and Chloe. Both PMCs shrugged.

Quinton smiled. "I've learned a few things from the person who started all this."

Brandt's eyes widened. "Browning?"

He nodded. "And Harding. They were friends."

"Shut the front airlock!" Simon blurted.

"There's a lot more to it, but when this all started," Quinton said, gesturing toward himself and the other PMCs, "Browning spoke of Miles Harding as… it's like he was his younger brother. The two were close."

"What the hell happened then?" Becker asked. Then he shook his head. "Never mind. We've already been searching for Sentinels. How is this any different? Most spacers aren't going to volunteer any information, and the ones that do are just blowing atmosphere out the airlock."

"I had a feeling you'd bring that up. One thing I can always count on is for spacers to ask what's in it for them. I say we offer a bounty for information about the Sentinels," Quinton said.

Becker frowned and looked at the others. "A bounty. What are you going to pay them with?"

"You tell me. What do spacers want more than anything?" Quinton asked.

He watched them as they all considered the question.

"We're not a complex bunch, Quinton," Becker said. "Clean air to breathe, food, and open space to fly."

Teagan laughed. "Maybe that's all *you* want. Spacers want what we all want. A home. Not a room on a space station. Not to live in a habitat or inside some kind of dome. They want safety. They want solid ground beneath their feet. They want to live on a habitable world, not something where they can scarcely survive. After decades in space, they want a garden world."

"You mean the colony worlds. The planets that the Acheron Confederacy terraformed in secret," Brandt said. He looked at Quinton, his brow furrowed. "You can't do that."

"Why not?" Teagan asked. Brandt glared at her. "Seriously, why can't he? Why do you get to decide who gets to live on one of those worlds and who doesn't?"

"I don't get to decide."

"Then why can't he do it?"

Brandt shook his head and looked at Quinton. "There have been other star systems where garden worlds were discovered. Spacers from all over descended upon it and fought over it until the planet became unlivable. That's what will happen if you do this. We'll lose what little we have left."

"It doesn't have to be that way," Simon said, and Brandt swung his gaze toward him. "It doesn't. We can still control how they reach those worlds. They have defenses in place. We can scrub computer systems on ships so their locations can't be shared."

Brandt exhaled explosively. "These are temporary measures," he said.

"You're right, Brandt," Quinton said. "They are, but so is keeping those worlds a secret."

Brandt's shoulders slumped a little. "What happens if the Sentinels find them?"

"They might be a little busy because of it, but I'm aware of the risk. You know we don't have to share *all* the colony worlds. They're not all in the same star system or even cluster of stars."

Brandt looked away from him. "There has to be a better way—something else we can offer in exchange for information about the Sentinels."

"Quinton is right. It's the one thing that will get spacers to take notice," Becker said.

Quinton looked at him and smiled. "See, it doesn't hurt nearly so much as it used to, but I can do the same."

Becker chuckled.

"You'll never get approval from the UFA to do this," Brandt said.

Quinton expected it. "I know, but I'm going to do it anyway. Hold on," he said before Brandt could interject. "I'm going to bolster the colony worlds' defenses just in case."

Brandt shook his head. He wasn't happy with it, but he wouldn't leave. Brandt knew what was at stake. Quinton was taking a huge risk.

"How do you plan to lure the Sentinels?" Becker asked.

"I think you're going to enjoy this. It's pretty sneaky," Quinton said and began sharing the finer points of the plan he'd come up with.

38

Quinton was true to his word. He ordered several fleets to form a special task force for the purpose of defending the colony worlds. With those fleets came orbital defenses and autofactories that would assist the colony worlds with building their own defenses. The organization and deployment of these resources was given to a commander that Brandt had recommended.

Quinton looked at the galaxy map that was showing on the main holotank, peering at the data that showed fleet deployments. To say that he'd spread his forces impossibly thin was an understatement, but it was the only way to lure the Sentinels out.

Over the past few weeks, he'd deployed specialized stealth drones throughout the known star systems wherever there was a human presence. The stealth drones included VIs with enhanced security protocols designed to bypass security systems.

Simon worked at a nearby workstation. He looked over at Quinton. "I never expected us to have this kind of penetration so quickly."

Quinton nodded. To augment the stealth drones' capabilities, they would be under the direction of a PMC that was within subspace communication range.

"Increasing power to our comms systems," Lieutenant Traver said.

"Acknowledged," Quinton replied.

The countdown for this mission had begun weeks ago. News had spread to UFA allies and independent groups alike that there was a bounty being offered for any information leading the UFA to Sentinel ships. Since then, the communications network the DUC had deployed throughout the galaxy had been nearly overwhelmed with spacers volunteering information. Teagan had been right. The promise of life on a garden world was too good to pass up despite efforts by the Collective and the Servitors to discourage belief in what they termed false claims.

A text message appeared on his HUD from Radek.

I thought you'd be interested in viewing this message personally.

Quinton opened the attached message, and a video log became available. He accessed it and Kandra Pavond's lavender face appeared. Her dark hair was pinned up and she wore a common spacer's garb, but she somehow managed to make even that look amazing.

"Quinton, this is the first chance I've had where I could risk contacting you. The Servitor Council used to be the voice for us, but now we're fractured. I wanted you to know that not all of us went along with Counselor Zariah and the rest of the council's plans to ally with the Collective and, in turn, the Sentinels. I understand that trust is in short supply where Servitors are concerned, but I wanted you to know that you do have allies. I don't know what will happen or where we go from here, but I do know that the changes you've wrought among us were a long time coming, and perhaps long overdue. Farewell."

Kandra stared at the camera for a few moments longer, looking as if she wanted to say something else, and then stopped the recording.

"Do you believe her?" Simon asked.

Quinton frowned and looked at him.

"You shared access to your data feeds with me."

He had.

"I do. She didn't ask for anything. She just wanted me to know that not all the Servitors had gone along with what their leadership decided. I can tell by the look on your face that you don't believe her. She could be lying, but if she is, there's nothing to be gained by sending the message. She knew we wouldn't trust her, and I don't, but I do believe her. I hope she finds her way through all this."

Simon regarded him for a moment. "I'm just surprised you feel that way."

"None of this is black and white, Simon. There are divisions everywhere, even within the UFA, but I want to believe there are people out there doing what they can for their future."

Simon's eyebrows drew together in concern. "This isn't the first time you've spoken like that—like you don't think you'll be around after all this is over."

Quinton smoothed his features. "I don't know."

"Okay, how about this? If you had access to Maelyn's consciousness, would you create a PMC from it?" Simon asked.

Quinton stared at his friend. "What have you done?"

Simon held up his hands. "Nothing! Really, I haven't done anything. It's just hypothetical."

Quinton's gaze sank to the floor. He'd felt a spike of hope ignite inside him and then dissipate just as quickly. He'd tried to find Maelyn's body just for that purpose, but it was gone, and he wasn't sure he'd have gone through with it if he *had* found it. "She didn't want me to."

Simon nodded. "Yeah," he replied quietly and then turned back toward his holoscreen.

Quinton watched the countdown dwindle to zero. "All right, Admen Desher, answer the call."

Across galactic sectors, communication arrays began broadcasting a PMC broadcast signal that contained Admen Desher's identification. He'd thought Admen Desher was simply a more capable Sentinel, but he was something else. He served Harding Prime, and over time Quinton began to suspect that Desher was some kind of PMC that Harding had convinced to join him.

Quinton had tried to interact with the Sentinels, but every time he tried, they refused all communications beyond the initial contact. Lennix Crowe had provided him with all the comms he'd had with Admen Desher. He'd pieced these together with his own encounters and come up with a partial identification that would draw the Agent of Harding's attention, and with him, the Sentinels.

The response wasn't immediate, but it did build over time. Active broadcasts from thousands of drones and hijacked comms stations popped up on the galaxy map above the holotank, and reports began to come in about Sentinel scout ships investigating the broadcasts. Alliance ships engaged those scout forces, attempting to capture a Sentinel warship. It wasn't enough that they disabled the engines of the Sentinel warships; they also had to remove the capability for the ships to initiate a self-destruct.

Quinton had Radek conducting his own analysis separate from the tactical data feeds.

Simon looked at Quinton. The young spacer had noticed the spike in processing resources devoted to the *Salvation's* communications systems.

As the PMCs aboard Alliance ships gained access to the computer systems aboard Sentinel warships, they ran their own analysis on them, searching for communication protocols and navigation entries. Both comms and navigation would lead him where he needed to go. The Sentinels must receive their orders from somewhere, and Quinton was willing to bet that it would lead him to Harding Prime.

"They're adapting their tactics to respond to the Alliance fleet presence, Admiral," Lieutenant Corvax said.

"Understood. The race is on," Quinton replied.

Data extracted from Sentinel ships were copied and transmitted through secure communications channels that were eventually retrieved by the *Salvation*. Quinton had every conceivable security protocol in place to prevent Sentinel attack codes that could impact the *Salvation's* computer systems.

Quinton knew the Sentinels would eventually figure out that they were being lured in with the broadcasts. However, it was unlikely that they'd cease investigating.

Quinton activated another communication package and sent it out over subspace comms. Several new broadcasts began to appear on the galaxy map. He'd enabled the new communication monitoring protocols based on what had been extracted from the Sentinels they'd managed to capture. There hadn't been nearly as many as Quinton would have liked before gambling on such a tactic, but they were in a race, and it was one he had to win.

Alliance ships scattered across the galaxy moved among the different star systems. They were attempting to capture more Sentinels, but fewer and fewer reports were coming in of successful captures. The Sentinels had begun putting bigger scout forces together that were large enough to make the successful capture of their warships almost impossible.

Quinton sent out a recall notice, which began to make its way through the massive communications network that had come online.

A new broadcast appeared on the galaxy map, and Quinton focused his attention on it.

"Helm, plot a course to these coordinates," Quinton said and forwarded a new set of coordinates to his helmsman. "Comms, send out those coordinates to Alliance fleets within a ten-thousand-lightyear range. They're to converge on that location."

Quinton waited a few seconds. "Helm, where are we with that course?"

"Course laid in, Admiral. Ready to engage."

"Make it so," Quinton replied.

The *Salvation's* power taps were engaged, and the additional power was directed toward the planetoid's array of jump drives. The ship left n-space for a few moments and then emerged near an uninhabited star cluster—uninhabited but for the thousands of Sentinel warships that began appearing on the tactical plot.

"Holy shit, you were right," Simon said. "He answered."

Quinton threw him a nod. He'd goaded Admen Desher into responding. Now it was up to the *Salvation* to capture him before he escaped.

"Helm, go emergency. Take us to the origin of the broadcast!" Quinton shouted.

"Aye, Admiral," Lieutenant Orlova replied.

"Tactical, I need your team to punch a great big hole through those warships and get me to the alpha target," Quinton said.

The *Salvation* was capable of a multistage attack that enabled it to engage anywhere, from across vast distances to right on the enemy's doorstep. Space fleets had to be designed for this, and they usually fell short, with federations preferring more of a specialized attack style rather than comprehensive attack capabilities. Browning had designed the *Salvation* to accommodate all attack scenarios, and Quinton was going to use every one of them before he was done.

Hundreds of hyperspace-capable missiles with fusion and antimatter warheads launched from the *Salvation's* missile tubes and disappeared from n-space, crossing the vast distance to where the Sentinel armada waited.

Alliance fleets began to appear, entering the area from different vectors.

The *Salvation* sped toward the enemy ships even as thousands more Sentinel ships entered the system. The star cluster wasn't inhabited by anyone, which was a serious misstep on Admen Desher's part. They pinpointed Desher's broadcast from a Sentinel capital ship so large that it had two massive spinal-mounted plasma lances. The Sentinel capital ship was surrounded by Sentinel warships, but the Alliance's powerful missiles controlled by hundreds of PMCs had the highest rate of hitting their mark, and the enemy was paying the price.

The *Salvation's* powerful tachyon lance of highly energized particles burst from across the ship's many launchers. Without the risk of civilian casualties,

Quinton was free to unleash the full armament against the Sentinels, and enemy ships were destroyed by the thousands.

Quinton watched as they closed the distance. Throughout the battle, he'd been analyzing the Sentinel capital ship's capabilities. The closer the *Salvation* got, the more unlikely it was that Admen Desher would escape.

A swarm of attack drones flew from small hangar bays and executed a micro-jump, controlled by Quinton's VI. They breached the capital ship's point defense systems and swarmed the hull. Powerful cutting lasers penetrated the layers of armored hull, and Quinton urged them onward. They pierced the hull and penetrated the interior of the ship. Quinton signaled the other drones in the area of the breach, and they converged on the location.

Once inside the ship, Quinton would have access to their computer systems. The attack drones carried subspace transceivers and opened a link directly to an isolated comms system aboard the *Salvation*.

Quinton fully integrated into the isolated comms system and linked with the Sentinel capital ship's computer system.

Sapient Combat Simulation systems were initiated, and he unleashed millions of copies of his VI henchman into the enemy ship. Sentinel computer systems were built with hardening security in mind, but the threat they were designed to mitigate was from that of a single PMC—not a PMC that had a computing core the size of a moon. Quinton overwhelmed the internal defense protocols, but he couldn't control the entire ship. As various systems became compromised, the others went offline, and its combat capability plummeted. Quinton seized control of the ship's communication systems and found an old, early-series CDA sitting on the bridge.

The CDA's dimly lit scarlet eyes were the only indication that there was a consciousness still inside. A bitter laugh sounded throughout the bridge.

"I underestimated you, Quinton."

"You're not the only one."

"What do you want? You've won. The ship is disabled, and the last data feeds I saw from the sensor array indicated that your forces were winning."

Quinton chuckled. "I'm sure it's only temporary. In fact, I know there are thousands of warships on the way."

Desher's CDA sat up in the chair. Its movements were slow, as if it hadn't been used in quite some time. The fact that it was an earlier series of CDA that Quinton was actually familiar with indicated that Admen Desher predated the Federation Wars.

"I had no idea how old you were. I guess we have that in common," Quinton said.

Quinton put an image of himself on the main holoscreen. He wore the black and gold of the Acheron Confederacy Navy.

"ACN," Desher said bitterly.

"The same as the faded colors on that CDA. What happened? At first, I thought you were just another Sentinel, but you're different. Harding must have needed someone more capable."

"God, you're so arrogant. I can see it on your face. You think that since you defeated me, you can defeat Harding Prime. You're a fool."

"So, you'll have no problem sharing his location with me then," Quinton replied.

Desher laughed, and it had a lifeless bitterness to it. "That would be a negative, Commander Aldren," he said, addressing Quinton by his old ACN rank.

While Quinton spoke with Desher, he scoured the ship's computer systems, searching for mission data.

"Updated incursion parameters," Quinton said. "You convinced the Collective to help you, and this is what you're going to do?"

"They'll outlive their usefulness."

Several alerts appeared on Quinton's HUD—specialized targeting information for priority targets. They were DUC-controlled systems. All of them.

Desher lifted his gaze toward the holoscreen. "If you hurry, you might make it in time, but then again, it could already be too late."

The aged CDA sank back into the command chair and its scarlet gaze faded. Desher was gone.

Quinton uploaded the data he'd found to the *Salvation*. If Harding Prime knew the location of the DUC core systems, then he either knew of the colony worlds or he intended to find them by destroying the core systems.

Lennix Crowe hated being kept in the dark, but his orders from Admiral Aldren were clear. The Union Cruiser *Savage* led a battlegroup of old Jordani warships that had had their weapons and computer systems refitted with upgraded components. At least that would put them on equal footing if they engaged the Sentinels.

He strode onto the bridge and walked toward the command station.

Nate stood up. "The shuttles are on their final approach to the main hangar bay, Commander."

"Who are they?"

"They didn't say anything after they provided all the necessary clearance codes provided to us by CENTCOM. They said they'll debrief you when they come aboard," Nate said.

Lennix watched the video feed showing a pair of combat shuttles flying into the *Savage's* main hangar.

"Let's go greet our new guests. Lieutenant Engstrom, you have the con," Lennix said.

Nate followed him off the bridge and they made their way to the hangar.

The elevator reached deck seventeen and Lennix walked onto the deck. He'd ordered four armed squads to meet them in the hangar just in case he didn't agree with Aldren's new orders. Lennix had never been much of a follower, and this was the first time he'd been kept in the dark like this.

Nate glanced at him. "I was just as surprised as you were that Teagan found her way to the *Salvation.*"

Crowe's eyes flicked upward for less than a second. "We'll sort that out later."

Nate nodded. "Of course."

The two combat shuttles were sleek and dark, with copper accents that made Lennix want to keep them for himself. They must have come from the *Salvation.*

Loading ramps lowered from beneath the belly, and six chrome-colored CDAs walked down the ramp of one of the shuttles. Six more came from the other shuttle.

Aldren had sent him twelve PMCs! His mind raced with possibilities.

The CDAs changed their accent colors to ACN black and gold, and the leader walked toward them.

"Commander Crowe, I'm Chief Travis Woolridge. I'm here with the rest of Admiral Aldren's mission orders."

The other CDAs began offloading large storage containers.

Chief Woolridge glanced toward the squads of armed spacers, and Lennix suspected it was more for his benefit than for the PMC's awareness.

"Welcome aboard, Chief. Do you need help offloading the cargo?" Lennix asked.

Woolridge shook his chrome-colored head. "Negative, my guys can handle it. The weight doesn't affect us much. Is there someplace we can talk? We're on a timetable here and we need to get moving yesterday."

Lennix glanced at the storage containers being offloaded onto his deck and then back at Woolridge. "Very well. Follow me, Chief."

39

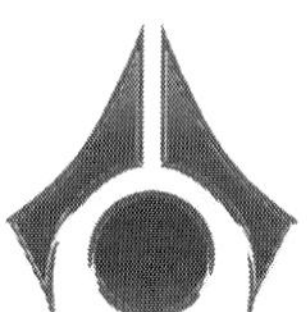

Quinton ordered the Alliance fleets to disengage and withdraw from the remaining Sentinels. Alliance ships were starting to show signs of wear and tear, along with decreased combat capabilities, which included the *Salvation*. During the battle, Sentinels began focusing their attacks on the *Salvation's* weapons systems, and a number of them needed to be repaired. It was a tried-and-true tactic when combating a fleet with superior firepower—keep hitting their weakest point until eventually striking a killing blow. The *Salvation* was the most powerful ship Quinton had ever seen, but even it had limits. Maybe if Browning had somehow found a way to build ten *Salvations,* he could engage the Sentinels differently.

Quinton reviewed the damage reports and, more importantly, the casualty reports. Entire ships and crews were unaccounted for, and there was no end in sight. Alliance ships were running low on missiles and other ammunition, and there wasn't much time to resupply them.

"They're targeting the DUC, Brandt," Quinton said.

Brandt stared back at him through the vid-comlink. "They want the colony worlds. The DUC core systems change from time to time. They're mostly space stations and old colony ships that have been retrofitted for long-term living. There are still a significant number of spacers living on them, but we've been offloading those stations for over a year."

"Doesn't matter. Harding Prime isn't going to stop with the space stations. This next incursion is going to be brutal—worse than before—and no one is going to be spared," Quinton said.

"No one… you mean he's going to—"

"I meant that no one is going to escape this unscathed. He's not going to kill every spacer he comes across, but he *is* going to focus on non-compliant star systems. After all the work we did telling the spacers the actual cause of the Federation Wars, there are divisions everywhere."

Brandt frowned in consideration for a couple of seconds. "We stopped Admen Desher, and the Sentinels just keep coming. Harding Prime is still one step ahead of us."

"No, we're catching up to him. Harding Prime can't work through Desher anymore."

"Did Desher give you Harding Prime's location?"

"No, and their navigation systems are regularly purged, so only a few hundred entries of recent destinations can be found in them. They're still being reviewed."

"I thought you said we were catching up to them. It doesn't sound like that. It sounds like we're going back to square one."

Quinton smiled. "I have a few ideas about that. You didn't see their reaction to the false broadcasts ostensibly giving away the *Salvation's* location."

Brandt's jaw slackened, and then he blew out a breath.

"I underestimated how much they want this ship. I think I can get him to give away his location. With his lead agent gone, Harding Prime has to be monitoring the Sentinels and whatever intelligence net he's got deployed. They're too well informed otherwise."

"But the DUC and the colony worlds. We can't leave them unprotected," Brandt said.

"We'll try to lure them away, but once I've located him..." Quinton's voice trailed off and Brandt nodded in understanding.

"That's why you offloaded so many autofactories and the tech platforms."

Quinton regarded the old spacer. "I don't think we're going to be able to deliver on the promise I made, Brandt. I'm sorry."

Brandt sighed heavily. "I'm sorry, too."

LENNIX CROWE HAD BEEN AROUND dangerous people almost his entire life. He was one of them, but watching what the PMC commandos could do had impressed even him.

The *Savage* loitered way out in the Oort of a Collective-controlled star system —one of their core systems. Chief Woolridge used their stealth combat shuttles to intercept incoming freighters and attach a payload to the outer hulls that no docking authority would give a passing glance. Then, they went on their way without the freighters even knowing they'd been there. PMCs could easily manipulate a ship's computer systems so they wouldn't be discovered.

Lennix had watched Woolridge and his squad of PMCs do the same thing on smaller salvage ships as well, and he studied the video feed from the away team. The PMCs moved as if they were showing off just how much better they were at this than anyone who was part of the Union could ever hope to be. Lennix had offered to send out some of his own people to help, but Woolridge declined, saying it would be less efficient.

Lennix rolled his eyes. *Less efficient?* Most of his spacers earned their livelihoods salvaging from wreckages in places that were extremely dangerous. *Less efficient, pfft.* Woolridge and his team had only been brought out of standby a few months ago. However, watching the video feed convinced him that Woolridge's confidence in his team's capabilities was well placed.

"Remarkable," Nate said.

"Maybe I could convince them to join us," Lennix replied.

"Doubtful, but at least the targeting is good."

Lennix nodded. His daughter had infiltrated the Collective and, over the months, had built up an accurate accounting of their operations—in particular, their senior leadership.

"If this works, we don't have to worry about Trenton Draven anymore," Nate said.

Lennix's lips lifted a little. "We'll have our pick of whatever is left."

"Do you think that's why Aldren gave us this mission?"

"I doubt he was doing us any favors. He just knew this was something we'd go at full tilt."

Nate nodded. "He turned out to be much more than I expected. It's hard to believe he was just an ACN commander."

"He doesn't talk about his past much. That's what I've been told anyway, but Severin Brandt wouldn't follow Quinton's lead if he weren't confident in his abilities. But you're right, he's not at all what we thought he was, especially when he was inside that old garden robot."

Lennix watched the PMCs deliver another payload. Launching their weapons at core Collective star systems wasn't feasible, so Aldren had come up with an impressive alternative. He was using the space traffic heading into the star system to deliver his payloads. From there, they would seek their targets. If it worked, Lennix would have delivered a crippling blow to the Collective. But he had a plan of his own. He wanted Draven to know who had beaten him.

40

QUINTON STOOD in his office near the bridge. He had very little time left. They'd pushed out an update to the comms beacons they had deployed throughout the galaxy, which also included monitoring stations that they'd commandeered and still had control over. Even with the use of subspace, it took time for comms to span the millions of lightyears across the inhabited sectors of the galaxy.

The door to his office opened and Brandt stormed inside.

"What do you think you're doing?" he asked, glaring at Quinton.

"I've ordered all non-essential personnel to leave the ship," Quinton replied.

"Why are you ordering *me* away? Last I checked, I was your second-in-command. What are you doing?"

Quinton disabled the active holoscreens around him, and the almost silent buzz and flashes of refreshing data feeds ceased. It was just Quinton and Brandt.

"I need you to help defend the colony worlds."

Brandt let out a frustrated neighing sound. "Bullshit! You want me out of the way. Without another XO, there's no one to challenge your orders."

Quinton let the silence stretch for a minute. "There's something I have to do, and it could mean losing this ship. If that happens, you're the only other person familiar enough with it to defend against it."

Brandt frowned. "Lose the ship. Defend against it. What are you saying?"

Quinton walked around his desk until he stood in front of the old spacer. "Desher told me that Harding wants this ship, and not only wants. He needs it."

"For what?"

"Browning's last mission might have been partially successful. Harding has been limited. I think he might be trapped."

Brandt considered this for a few seconds. "If he's trapped, then we can wait him out."

Quinton shook his head. "Come on, you know we can't. A defensive strategy isn't going to get it done. Harding still commands the Sentinels." Brandt looked away, and for a moment, the old spacer showed his many long years. "Your people need you. The Alliance needs you."

Brandt lifted his gaze. "The Alliance needs you too, Quinton. You're playing a lot of this close to the chest. Don't think for a second that I haven't noticed."

Quinton gave him a weak smile. "So, are you going to follow orders, or am I going to have to convince you?"

The old spacer stood up straight with a proud gleam in his eyes and saluted Quinton in the tradition of the Acheron Confederacy Navy. Quinton returned the salute, then stuck out his hand. "It's been an honor, Admiral Brandt."

Brandt shook it. "I know it bothered you how people regarded the Acheron Confederacy, but no one will forget now that we've set the record straight. I'll make sure this continues. Good luck, Admiral Aldren."

The old spacer turned on his heels and walked out of the office.

Quinton waited for a beat and then followed him, walking down the long corridor toward the main bridge. Darkened walls with flowing white script gleamed in the dim light. The names and ranks of all the spacers who'd given their lives in the Federation Wars adorned these walls, and Quinton felt the weight of them all as if they were watching him.

Outside the bridge, Becker, Guttman, Oscar, Simon, and Teagan waited for him. Guttman gestured toward the others when they saw Quinton.

Quinton slowed down and looked at them. He could almost imagine Maelyn and Kieva standing with them. They'd all been there since the beginning when they'd been aboard the *Nebulon*.

All of them regarded Quinton as he walked toward them.

Becker glanced at the others. "We're not leaving."

Quinton smiled a little. "Was it something I said?"

Becker shook his head, not giving in to Quinton's attempt at humor. "No, it was something you did. We're with you, Quinton."

Quinton looked at the others and stopped at Guttman.

Guttman shifted his feet, swaying a little. "Yeah, yeah." He leaned toward Quinton. "I know where the nearest escape pods are, just in case."

Oscar rolled his eyes and gave Quinton a knowing look.

Quinton looked at Simon.

"We're not finished yet."

Quinton glanced at Teagan. She smiled a little, but there was something in her stance that conveyed she was protecting Simon. He thought Maelyn would approve. She'd loved Simon like a brother.

He knew he couldn't convince them to leave, and if he was being honest with himself, he didn't want them to. "All right, then," Quinton said, "let's finish this."

The massive doors to the bridge opened, and they walked inside.

41

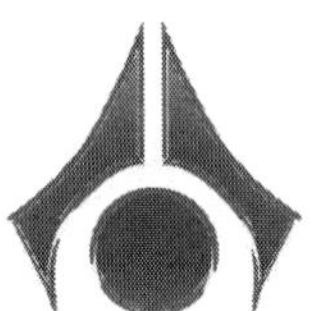

Quinton received confirmation that Brandt had reached the battleship-carrier *Avalon*. He glanced around the *Salvation's* bridge. The workstations were divided between chrome-colored CDAs and their human counterparts. The planetoid spaceship required a crew of half a million, but with the help of PMCs, he'd been able to drastically reduce that number. With the exception of Brandt, because he was part of Quinton's contingency plans, he wasn't going to force anyone to leave. He couldn't fight the Sentinels on his own, but he promised himself to do what he could for his crew should the need arise.

Quinton walked to the edge of the extended platform that put him closest to the holotank. Turning around, he opened a holo-interface and selected the option of a ship-wide broadcast, also adding the rest of the fleet. At the same time, he sent the command to broadcast the *Salvation's* location in deep space.

"Alliance Fleet, this is Admiral Aldren. Across the galaxy, the enemy is outside our airlock. By now, you've heard that there are fleets of Sentinels on their way to the DUC core systems, and from there, they will move on to the colony worlds. Our forces have been divided so that our homes will have a fighting chance. This will buy us time to find Harding Prime and destroy the Sentinels at their core. The plan is simple—either we fight or we die. This ship was built in the tradition of the Acheron Confederacy Navy, but what I see is the culmination of many star unions. We are their descendants, and it falls to us to finish this fight. Stay focused. Stay vigilant. *Salvation* actual, out."

Quinton closed the broadcast comlink. The warships that were part of Brandt's battle group disappeared from the *Salvation's* sensors as they left n-space.

The *Salvation's* broadcast had contained a general PMC-activation signal with Miles Harding's identification. The broadcast was repeated throughout every beacon, monitoring station, and ship comms that they had throughout the galaxy. He was giving Harding Prime an open invitation to come to the *Salvation*.

Multiple Sentinel contacts began to appear on the galaxy map. Broadcast comms usually didn't require an acknowledgment, but Simon had found a way to force it. Those comlink acknowledgments ran through a filter so their monitoring systems wouldn't be inundated with returns from ships they didn't care about. They were only interested in the Sentinels. It wasn't a perfect system; there was no such thing, but the comms filter managed to reduce most of the noise that came from the detections.

Sentinel response was quick. No sooner were the unintended acknowledgments received than additional reports of Sentinel fleets entering hyperspace began to appear. They were taking the bait, but Quinton couldn't be sure they were fully committed until more of them were detected.

A secondary tactical plot showed Sentinel detections a mere lightyear away from the *Salvation.* They'd deployed sensor platforms scattered along best-guess approach vectors. The Sentinels would send several scout forces to validate the broadcast, and then more of their fleets would arrive.

The tactical plot updated, showing more Sentinel fleets being detected.

"Tactical, we need to filter the Sentinel fleet detections to highlight large attack forces and those from previously unknown origin points. We're searching for outliers," Quinton said.

"Understood, Admiral," Lieutenant Xander said.

Quinton was partially integrated into *Salvation's* computing core and saw Xander begin to build a data filter with the new specifications.

"I have something," Simon said.

"Go ahead," Quinton replied.

The galaxy map updated, and a sector became highlighted. "Tracing the jump points and knowing the range of the drives used by Sentinel warships, it appears that many are coming from this nebula."

Quinton peered at the data, receiving a confirmation from Lieutenant Xander.

"Helm, plot a course for the nebula to be executed on my orders."

"Aye, Admiral, uploading course into the nav systems," Lieutenant Orlova replied.

Quinton checked the nav systems, looking for any data they had on that region of space. The galaxy was an immense place, and as much as the federations of old had explored and colonized, they hadn't been everywhere. There were still galactic regions that were unexplored.

"Multiple Sentinel fleets detected," Lieutenant Corvax said.

Quinton checked that the remaining Alliance fleets had the coordinates, and once that was confirmed, he ordered the jump.

The *Salvation's* jump drives became active, and the planetoid ship left n-space along with thousands of Alliance ships. Jump drives folded space, and the only limiting factor was the capability of the jump drive itself. The *Salvation* had an array of powerful jump drives, and with power taps pulling energy from outside of n-space, the range the ship could cross was greater than all the ships in the Alliance fleet. They usually had to hold back in order for the rest of the fleet to keep up with them, but not this time. They were in a race against time.

The *Salvation* emerged into n-space.

"Ops, begin active scans," Quinton said.

His orders were confirmed. The *Salvation's* powerful sensor arrays began sweeping the area, searching for the Sentinels and Harding Prime.

Browning's logs contained locations of where he thought Harding Prime was. Quinton had checked those locations with the current star charts and even sent a few scouting missions. Nothing was ever found. However, none of the scouting missions had come to this location. The nebula was only referenced by an alphanumeric because it hadn't been explored.

"Gravitational anomaly detected, Admiral," Lieutenant Xander said.

A sub-window appeared, and Quinton peered at the data. The analysis suggested a cluster of singularities had converged in a single location.

"Doesn't look like they've been there long," Simon said.

Guttman looked at him and frowned. "How can you tell?"

"The effects of a singularity can be traced across billions of years, and the ripple effect of the gravity waves from this cluster is less than a hundred years. So, either they're very new, as in they just formed by collapsing stars, or they're artificial," Simon replied.

"He's right," Quinton said. "Helm, take us in. Comms, update the fleet with the coordinates of the anomaly."

"Aye, Admiral, sending secure comlinks to the fleet," Lieutenant Traver replied.

They executed a micro-jump, which closed the distance to the cluster of singularities.

"It's difficult to get a reading, but there seems to be a structure that could be a ship. However, these aren't traditional singularities. The scan data show that it's a region stuck amid folded space just beyond n-space," Lieutenant Xander said.

"Browning's trap," Quinton said, quietly. His mind raced with possibilities of how the trap could work. If they'd used power-taps to pull energy into the trap, then it was feasible that Harding had been trapped since the Federation Wars. Admen Desher had been in contact with Harding Prime, so either the trap had partially worked, or Harding had been slowly breaking free of it.

"Tactical, be ready for enemy forces to converge on the area."

Klaxon alarms blared as the sensor arrays detected thousands of Sentinel warships entering the area.

Quinton increased his frame rate and completely integrated with the *Salvation's* computer system. He sent his orders to the team leaders and then took control of select communications systems throughout the ship.

"THEY KEEP COMING," Becker said and tore his gaze from the main holotank.

"Why is it so quiet?" Guttman asked, looking around the bridge. The PMCs had all gone silent.

"Quinton has integrated with the ship's computer system," Simon said. "He's just given the tactical officers orders to engage the enemy ships."

Becker's eyes widened. "The ship is moving toward whatever the hell that thing is."

Simon looked at the holoscreens in front of him where he had multiple sub-windows open.

"What is it? Is that where Harding Prime is?" Guttman asked.

Simon scanned the data, also using his implants to help him process the information. "I think so. It's some kind of trap."

"Why the hell aren't we firing all our weapons on it right now?" Becker asked.

"The target is off-limits," Lieutenant Xander said. His voice sounded slightly modulated.

Simon couldn't imagine how many things the PMCs on the bridge had going at once.

Becker shook his head. "That doesn't make any sense. Simon, what do you think?"

Simon glanced at Teagan, and she gave him a small nod. He turned back toward Becker. "We have to trust Quinton."

Becker barked out a frustrated breath. "The enemy is right there! We could fire the lances and the missiles and everything else we've got, and take out whatever's in there."

"That assumes our weapons can reach it."

"I know. That's the problem."

Simon blew out a breath. "Look, that whole area is distorted as if it's stuck in the middle of an array of jump coils, but I think it's holding him there."

"What does that do?" Guttman asked.

"It keeps him from going anywhere, and it also prevents him from entering n-space, but that doesn't account for—"

An alert appeared on their holoscreens, warning of a system compromise. Main communications had stopped responding.

Guttman cursed and looked at Becker.

Simon reviewed the damage reports. "Quinton isolated certain comms arrays. I need to bring them online."

"Before the rest of the fleet arrives," Becker said.

"Tell us what you need us to do," Teagan said.

Quinton had had Simon review the *Salvation's* communications systems looking for ways to harden them against tampering. Had he suspected what was going to happen?

"All right, let's get started."

QUINTON SEIZED control of the *Salvation's* communications system, and the automated monitoring processes determined that his control of the system indicated compromise by a hostile entity, which was exactly what Quinton wanted.

He had multiple system sessions open and was monitoring for the arrival of the Alliance fleet.

A comlink came from within the anomaly, offering a PMC exchange. Quinton blocked it and instead made an open channel that didn't require that they authenticate. At the same time, he initiated a small data comlink to every PMC serving aboard the *Salvation* and set an automated comms session that would initiate a similar comlink to PMCs serving aboard Alliance ships. The data window showed hundreds of connections, with more coming online. He moved the data window aside.

The open channel was a virtual meeting room, and he detected another presence in it with him.

Quinton enabled a virtual image of himself standing in a holographic replica of the *Salvation's* computing core. A massive golden sphere spun and pulsed as the *Salvation's* colossal computing core processed untold amounts of data.

"Impressive."

The voice was deep with the promise of power and seemed to come from all around him.

Quinton had a sinking feeling that he was in way over his head.

A figure materialized in front of him, easily twice Quinton's size. Humanoid in appearance, the chrome gleamed from no discernible source of light.

"You should see the real one," Quinton said.

The figure lowered its glowing eyes toward Quinton, who fought an urge to back up and close the virtual meeting room, but he could do neither. With an open session such as this, both parties could control it. In a sense, it was similar to neutral territory, but Quinton had his doubts about that, which tended to happen when the creator of PMC technology stood in front of him.

"Harding Prime. It looks like you've been stuck here for a long time."

One of Quinton's many flaws was that he became more sarcastic when he was intimidated. He'd been working on it, but sometimes he lapsed into old habits. No one was perfect.

"You refused to authenticate as per standard procedure," Harding Prime said.

Quinton nodded. "Of course. I didn't want to become like the Sentinels."

Harding Prime looked amused.

"I realize you've got this whole 'I'm bigger and smarter' thing going on, but I thought we could talk."

Harding Prime didn't quite move forward so much as appeared within arm's reach of Quinton's virtual avatar. "Insect!" he growled, seizing the avatar.

Quinton tried to get away and couldn't. His eyes widened in surprise. Harding Prime had not only seized his avatar, but he'd taken control of the data session Quinton was using.

Harding Prime smiled, and even that gleamed with a pure white light. "You can't control the session. Everything you can do was created by me. I'll put this in terms you can understand: One could say I wrote the training manual."

A deep, sadistic chuckle seemed to bubble out of everywhere.

"Okay. Okay," Quinton said quickly. He couldn't move his arms. "Admen Desher spoke so highly of you. I guess I just expected more."

"He served his purpose. He brought you to me."

"I think you've got that backward. You see, I used him to find *you,* and that brought *you* to *me.*"

Harding Prime arched an eyebrow. "Did you now?"

Quinton cursed inwardly. This wasn't going according to plan. In fact, the entire plan was falling apart. Then the virtual meeting disintegrated around them, and Quinton felt as if he were being forced back into the *Salvation's* computer systems, except he wasn't alone. He was bringing a little something extra, and as he tried to stop it, he realized how futile his attempts at blocking Harding Prime really were.

This didn't mean that Quinton was going to give up. Harding Prime may have a toehold, but the *Salvation* was Quinton's, and no one was going to start tearing up his place.

"He was your friend. Browning was your friend. How could you betray him? He tried to help you," Quinton said.

They were still contained within the comms systems that Quinton had isolated on the *Salvation.*

Harding Prime regarded him, as if considering whether Quinton was worthy of a response. He seemed to surround Quinton, and Quinton wasn't sure how he'd done it.

"I've been trapped for almost a century, and you think that playing to my sympathies is going to stop the inevitable?"

Harding Prime raced through the *Salvation's* systems, going straight toward the computing core.

"Speaking of the trap, is that why you need this ship? Is it because it's the only computing core available large enough to accommodate your…ego?"

"My plans are beyond your comprehension."

Quinton moved his avatar in front of Harding Prime. "A century alone with no one to talk to, and you really can't be bothered. I've tried talking to the Sentinels, but they're not much for communicating either. I bet that wore down your patience after a while."

Harding Prime tried to move around him, and Quinton materialized in his path again. Harding Prime created copies of himself and Quinton did the same.

"I'm a quick learner," Quinton said.

Harding Prime snarled and began to chase him. He used a strike protocol to unravel Quinton's avatars, which he returned in kind. Harding Prime was the culmination of thousands of iterations of the original Miles Harding, which meant he was extremely intelligent. There was no way Quinton could compete with that, so he had to play to his own strengths, and what he really needed was time.

SIMON and the others helped the PMCs on the bridge however they could, but something else was happening to the ship—something beyond the battle being fought.

"Simon, I think it's getting near time," Teagan said.

Guttman nodded. "I'm glad someone finally said it. It's usually me."

"Where are we going to go?" Becker asked. "The Sentinels aren't trying to destroy the ship. They're disabling the weapons systems."

The *Salvation's* combat capability was sinking fast.

"Not yet. We can't go yet," Simon said. Quinton would have signaled for them to evacuate or have someone else do it.

He turned toward Corvax. The PMC was unresponsive, so Quinton tried to open a comlink to him.

Corvax acknowledged. "We're all connected." His voice was even more monotone than before.

Simon frowned. "What do you mean? Who's all connected?"

"PMCs everywhere. Quinton has connected us all."

"Why?"

Corvax didn't reply right away.

A barrage of damage reports appeared in the main holotank.

"We serve the galactic… abandon ship…"

Corvax's voice kept going in and out, as if there was interference from something.

"You heard him! Abandon ship," Guttman shrieked and flung his hand toward the door. "We have to get out of here."

Simon spun around, his breath coming in gasps. There had to be more he could do. Why wouldn't Quinton fire the *Salvation's* weapons at the anomaly? Something could get through and destroy the structure within.

He ran to his workstation and brought up the tactical interface. He tried to target the anomaly, but his firing solution kept getting rejected.

"Simon, we have to go," Becker said.

"Go if you want. I'm not leaving," Simon snarled in reply.

Becker opened a ship-wide broadcast. "Abandon ship. All hands abandon ship. Head to the nearest escape pods or egress ships. Abandon ship."

Simon ignored him and kept trying to find a way around the security lockout that prevented him from targeting the anomaly where Harding Prime was trapped. Something must have gone wrong, and Quinton was unable to do it. He tried to open a comlink to Quinton, but it didn't connect. It was as if Quinton wasn't there anymore. He glanced at Quinton's avatar and could see the leuridium core glowing from inside his chest.

Simon slammed his fists on the console. "Damn it!"

Teagan was at his side and placed her hands on his shoulders. "Simon, it's time to go."

Simon gritted his teeth, and his throat became thick. This couldn't be it. This wasn't how it was supposed to go.

She rubbed his shoulder. "It's all right," she said quietly and repeated herself.

"What if he needs our help? We can't leave. *I* can't leave. I promised her I would help him."

Teagan squatted down so she was eye level with him. "She would understand, Simon. Maelyn would understand. You have to trust Quinton. Look at them all. They're part of something that we can't participate in. It's time for us to go."

Simon glanced toward the door. Becker, Oscar, and Guttman were waiting.

Teagan said his name and squeezed his hand. He felt his shoulders slump. She was right. There wasn't anything he could do here. He trusted Quinton.

Simon stood up, and they left the bridge behind.

"It's about time," Guttman said and looked at Simon. "Come on, kid, we need you. The escape pods aren't far."

"We're not going on an escape pod," Becker said.

Guttman's mouth hung open. "What do you mean we're not?"

"Just what I said. I'm not about to leave my ship behind."

Simon opened a data session and began copying things to the *Nebulon*. He then tasked maintenance drones from his lab to move several storage containers to the ship.

"He's right," Simon said. "We can make it to our ships if we hurry."

42

Quinton continued to block Harding Prime, delaying him from accessing the *Salvation's* core. It was the same fight being fought on infinite fronts, and the only thing it achieved was stalling Harding Prime from reaching his objective. The strength of a PMC came from its ability to think and process information. Intelligence mattered, but so did the agility of the mind. As intelligent as Harding Prime had become, he'd lost the malleability of his mind, his ability to think beyond an objective, no matter how complex the analysis. Quinton had started walking the same path as Miles Harding and hadn't even realized it. He'd used Sapient Combat Simulations in his interactions with people throughout the galaxy, believing it would give him an advantage in negotiations and planning. SCS had given him those things, but the price was the very thing that sets humans apart from machines. Browning must have suspected as much, which was why the PMC activation signals contained a configuration update that limited the application of the SCS and the mergence protocol.

Quinton was pushed to his limits as he struggled to keep up with Harding Prime's relentless attacks. Being trapped for nearly a century had given the Prime ample time to learn patience and focus. With severe limitations to affecting the galaxy himself, he'd been able to manipulate events and people everywhere. But now that his freedom was close at hand, he fought with a fervor that Quinton couldn't hope to match. Whatever humanity had been part of Harding Prime was gone, but he wasn't merely an intelligent machine. He was stuck somewhere between, and his psychological wounds still afflicted him, but Quinton suspected that Harding wasn't even aware of them anymore.

Quinton slowly and purposefully stopped fighting. Harding Prime surged all his efforts, and Quinton made his final stand before the *Salvation's* computing core system.

Harding Prime paused, and a virtual chrome-colored CDA sprang to existence. Quinton created his own avatar and regarded him.

"Why did you stop?" Harding Prime asked. "You think you're so clever. Do you honestly believe that I didn't anticipate you guiding me here?"

"I can't stop you."

"It's about time you realized that."

"And I can't stop the Sentinels and the incursion you have planned."

Harding Prime narrowed his gaze suspiciously. His gaze lifted toward the golden core and then, after a few moments, lowered back toward Quinton.

"You surrender."

It wasn't a question.

Quinton gritted his teeth as Harding Prime pushed toward the barrier that was between him and full access to the *Salvation*.

"Lower this immediately. You've surrendered. I'll bring you in line with all the rest of the PMCs that Grand Admiral Browning secreted away throughout the galaxy. I can't believe you were his agent. You! A mere ACN commander thought he could defeat me. You alone—"

"Uh, I never said I surrendered," Quinton said and lowered the barrier that separated the comms systems he'd segmented from the rest of the *Salvation's* systems.

Quinton strode toward Harding Prime. "I'm a Galactic PMC of the Acheron Confederacy Navy. And I'm not alone!"

With thousands of PMCs connected to the *Salvation's* computing core, Quinton engaged the mergence protocol for all of them. As a Galactic PMC, he could command them, but he didn't have to. All of them were from a time when they'd witnessed the galaxy they knew descend into chaos and ruin. He'd never have to command them to do this. They volunteered. They knew the price that would be paid if they failed.

Quinton merged his consciousness with all of them and initiated a PMC authentication session with Harding Prime. Harding Prime's virtual avatar ran towards the *Salvation's* computing core, leaping into the air as he tried to escape the inevitable framework he'd created. Harding Prime had corrupted the mergence protocol in order to create the Sentinels. They were all lesser versions of Harding Prime. Quinton's new mergence protocol contained thousands of individual PMCs, of which Harding Prime was but a single voice with no standing save one. Quinton was the Galactic PMC, and within him was the ability to command other PMCs. Harding Prime tried to resist being merged with the *Salvation's* core, but it was too late for him. He had never built any safeguards to prevent it.

Quinton felt as if his mind had expanded to oblivion. It was almost too much for him to even comprehend. Browning hadn't selected him because he was the most brilliant ACN officer to ever become a PMC. Browning had picked him because even though he could comprehend the big picture, it didn't inhibit his ability to focus on the important things—things that people with superior intelligence tended to overlook. Single experiences, memories, and the like, grounded him, just like the woman he'd loved and his companions who'd helped get him here.

Quinton took the Sentinel command protocols from Harding Prime and used the *Salvation's* remaining communication arrays to broadcast new orders for the Sentinels. They were the kind of orders that couldn't be disobeyed or questioned.

SIMON ENTERED the hangar bay and ran toward the *Nebulon*. Teagan ran with him, along with a dozen or so spacers they'd encountered along the way. Becker and the others headed to their own ship in a neighboring hangar bay.

Simon sent his authentication toward the ship's computer system, and they ran up the loading ramp.

"We need to finish the pre-flight checks," Simon said to Teagan as they ran to the bridge. It had been months since he'd been aboard the *Nebulon*, but he'd spent years on this ship and knew it better than any other.

He went to the commander's station and checked the ship's systems. Teagan sat at the workstation next to his.

"Pre-flight status is green," Teagan said.

"Same here," Simon replied and began to engage the *Nebulon's* flight control systems.

Teagan cleared her throat. "You can command, or you can fly, but I wouldn't recommend doing both. Why don't you let me fly us out of here?"

Simon frowned. "Are you familiar…" he stopped speaking. "All right, take it," he said, relinquishing control.

The *Nebulon's* engines engaged, and they flew out of the hangar bay.

"No automated guidance systems anymore. Looks like I'll have to fly us out of here the old-fashioned way," Teagan said.

"I can take over if you need me to."

She blew out a short breath. "Please. You wouldn't believe some of the buckets I've had to fly. Remind me to tell you—"

"Watch out!"

A proximity alarm sounded as another ship nearly collided with them. Teagan avoided the ship and glanced at Simon.

"Don't you trust me, Simon?"

Simon winced. "Yeah, I do, but it's my new ship, and I don't want you scratching the hull."

They both grinned.

They entered a large bore that would get them to the exit. Teagan increased their speed and Simon entered the jump coordinates that would take them away from there.

As soon as they were clear of the bore, Simon engaged the *Nebulon's* jump drive and they micro-jumped away from the *Salvation*.

LENNIX CROWE INITIATED a comlink to the space station.

"Who is this?" Trenton Draven answered irritably.

"I thought you and I should talk," Lennix replied and then enabled his camera so Draven could see him.

Draven leaned toward his screen and narrowed his gaze. "You! And you didn't even attempt to hide your location." He looked off-screen, and after a few moments, he frowned in confusion.

"I don't know what happened to the Sentinel warships that were loitering here in the Oort. If they detected us, they didn't seem to care," Lennix said.

Draven sneered toward the camera and cursed. "Crowe, I'm going to take your entire operation without absorbing it into the Collective. I'm simply going to destroy it just to spite you. You chose the wrong side."

Lennix laughed. "That's funny because I was about to say the same thing about you. Check your scanners. Look at where those Sentinels have flown to."

Draven rolled his eyes and looked away. He yelled at someone off-screen.

"It looks to me like they're on an intercept course with the star. Now correct me—"

"Shut up!" Draven snarled.

Lennix smiled and continued. "Correct me if I'm wrong, but I don't think even the armored hulls of those ships can withstand exposure to the interior of a star… Uh, no they can't. They disappeared off our scanners. I guess it's too late for them." Lennix leaned toward the camera and glared at Draven. "And it's too late for you. Goodbye, Draven. You don't need to worry about the Collective anymore. I'll take it from here."

Draven was in the middle of shouting orders to someone when the comlink severed.

Lennix looked at Nate.

"The package has been delivered, Commander."

Lennix leaned back in his chair with a huge smile on his face. He looked at Chief Woolridge. "Do you mind sticking around until we can secure a few things on that station?"

"Of course. That is, until I receive updated orders from the Alliance."

"After we get things sorted out here, I'll initiate a check-in with CENTCOM."

QUINTON FELT himself slipping away a little bit at a time. The *Salvation's* engines put them on an intercept course with Browning's trap. He'd inputted a destination into the *Salvation's* navigation computer, but it didn't matter where they were going because they'd never reach it. When multiple jump-drive fields crossed over, the result was always destruction.

Harding Prime still struggled against Quinton's control as if he refused to accept that he'd been defeated. Quinton wished the cost wasn't as high as it was going to be, but he had no choice. His orders had been sent out and were now being propagated throughout both the Alliance network and millions of communication stations the Sentinels used to coordinate their fleets. Across the galaxy, Sentinels were ceasing all hostilities and would fly into the nearest main-sequence star, ridding the galaxy of their presence once and for all. The only compromised ship remaining to be destroyed was the *Salvation*.

Quinton couldn't purge Harding Prime's corruption. The computing core had absorbed thousands of PMCs. The price for controlling Harding Prime was to also absorb the corrupt protocols that compromised PMCs, which led to the destabilization of the consciousness inside. Having no wish to experience insanity firsthand, Quinton did the only thing he could.

It was a good death.

43

SIMON INHALED the freshest air he'd ever breathed in his life. It was warm and carried the earthy and floral scents of blossoms, sweet clover, and damp wood. He looked around the well-manicured garden that seemed to just keep going, with earthy paths throughout. A steady procession of shuttles flew toward the designated landing zones near UFA headquarters. The sprawling building had open-air decks on multiple levels like some grand staircase. He could still see the support columns of the unfinished parts of the building that was still under construction.

The soon-to-be officially named colony world was the temporary headquarters of the United Federation Alliance. Nearby was a replica of the monument to the fallen that had been the corridor leading to the *Salvation's* main bridge. The expanse of black walls appeared even more impressive in the direct sunlight. Names and ranks of spacers, worlds, and everything else the survivors of the Federation Wars could think of had a place on this monument. But they couldn't include everyone. In the months after the *Salvation* had been destroyed, the survivors worked tirelessly to build a haven for all spacers. The Acheron Confederacy had given them over a dozen terraformed worlds and the technology that could repeat the process across the galaxy. One day, spacers wouldn't salvage supplies from the skeletons left over from the Federation Wars. They could build a new world. It also helped that Severin Brandt commanded the most powerful fleet in the galaxy, remnants from the *Salvation*.

The Dholeren United Coalition had been dissolved, along with many other groups, to formally become the UFA. The old federations and star unions would have a place in the UFA's archives, and Simon hoped that the generations to come wouldn't waste the opportunity that had been given to them by the sacrifice of so many.

Simon inhaled and sighed. He couldn't recall spending so much time without wearing some type of envirosuit, but he remembered Quinton telling him that wearing plain clothes used to be considered normal. He smiled and thought he could get used to it.

"Hey there, spacer," Teagan called to him.

He turned toward her. She wore a silver gown that left her strong white shoulders bare. She smiled and rested her hand on her hip. He could *definitely* get used to not wearing envirosuits all the time.

"You sure you want to do this?" Simon asked.

She strode toward him, and the swing of her hips made his mouth open a little. There was a pleased tilt to her mouth as she watched him, and she arched a tawny eyebrow.

Stumpy ran along a thick tree branch and howled.

"I think he likes your dress," Simon said.

"He can howl all he wants, but I'm still not picking him up." Teagan glanced at the creature. Stumpy leapt toward a neighboring branch away from them. "I doubt he'll come back to the ship."

Simon shrugged. "At least he's got a home now." He paused for a few seconds, and she turned toward him. "Your father," Simon began.

"He can wait. Besides, he's got enough to deal with. It'll take him years to consolidate what remains of the Collective. It'll fracture when what's left of senior leadership makes a power grab."

"Yeah, but he wants you to be part of it."

She took his arm and they started walking. "I know, but like I said, he can wait."

"It's not everyone who'd defer the opportunity of starting a union or new federation."

She stopped walking and leaned toward him, speaking softly. "How many times do I have to tell you that I'm not interested in taking over the union or whatever my father creates. That's his." She eyed him. "I've got what I want, and if I find something else I want, I'll get that as well."

Simon frowned playfully. "I'm not sure how to react to that."

Her eyebrows twitched. "If you think you're getting away from me again, you've got another thing coming."

An alert chimed and he opened his personal holoscreen. He smiled and looked at Teagan. "It's working! The new data storage is working."

Teagan smiled. "See, with the profit you'll make off this, I won't need my father's union. We can start one of our own."

"That's not what this is for."

"Simon, there's a business part to how the galaxy works."

"I understand that, but—"

"That doesn't mean we take advantage of anyone, but no one should expect something for nothing."

He considered it for a few seconds and nodded.

The Sentinels had all been destroyed. A few hundred PMCs had survived because they'd been serving aboard other Alliance ships that helped defend the core systems from the Sentinels. They continued to serve on Alliance ships, but some had elected to have new bodies grown and their consciousness transferred into them. However, many of the surviving PMCs wanted to stay just as they were but with a cybernetic avatar similar to the one Quinton had used. Alliance engineers had been able to reproduce the avatars and were in the process of moving PMCs into their new bodies. They could be so lifelike that Simon suspected most would remain in those avatars for a very long time.

"I heard from Becker that he's going into business with your father," Simon said.

"My father is first and foremost a businessman."

"They're supposed to be partners, but do you think it'll really work out?"

Teagan shrugged. "Only time will tell." She paused for a moment, considering. "This new data storage."

"Yeah, it's something else. I'm able to store data out of n-space so data storage limitations become a thing of the past. There's no degradation in accessing the data or transferring it or anything like that."

"How'd you come up with it?"

"I was thinking about the ESS and leuridium cores. They were used for PMCs because of their reliability and stable energy state. And the trap Browning created made me question whether it was possible to remove that limitation as well."

Teagan frowned. "So, you think you can store a PMC core with this new data storage… medium, and the avatar would just maintain a connection to it?"

Simon nodded. "You see, even if the avatar gets destroyed, the PMC isn't dead. They're preserved until a new connection can be established."

"How long have you been working on this?"

"In pieces, for a while. I was trying to help the PMCs that had been exposed to the Sentinel infiltration protocols, but I couldn't figure out a way to separate the corruption from everything else."

Teagan glanced at the monument of the fallen for a long moment. "It's too bad this new data storage wasn't available before the *Salvation* was destroyed. We might have been able to save the PMCs on there, as well as the Alliance fleets in the vicinity."

Simon swallowed and turned away from her.

Teagan's eyebrows peaked. "Simon?" He looked at her and she pursed her lips in thought. "You did something."

He smiled with half his mouth. "I do a lot of things."

"No, this is something big… something more," she said, and her eyes widened.

"I couldn't save them all, but we didn't lose as many PMCs as we thought."

Teagan blinked several times. "How did you… What did you…"

"I had a little help," Simon said with a grin. "All right, Radek, I think we can let Teagan in on our little secret."

44

SHE BECAME aware in such a way that it was similar to waking up, but without the restful feeling of having had a good night's sleep. It was like an awareness came to the forefront of her mind, and she didn't know how it happened. She simply was there, and anything that had come before simply wasn't.

System diagnostic running.

The amber-colored words appeared amid the darkness of her thoughts. She inhaled and felt her chest rise, and air came in through her nostrils. She tried to open her eyes and couldn't, so she focused her attention on the dispassionate words that were within her field of vision.

Where was she?

She had the vague notion that her implants were going through some kind of self-check, but it was taking much too long to complete.

Veris initiation complete.

System startup complete.

PMC startup protocols have been initialized.

She felt a flash of annoyance race through her mind.

Initialization of VI interface is complete. Designation Greta.

Autonomous mode is waiting for confirmation of PMC integrity check.

"Hello, I am Greta, your personal virtual intelligence. Please stand by for first-time operation systems check. As integrity checks run through their diagnostic protocols, you will experience a variety of sensations akin to the tingling of your extremities when you had a physical form. These sensations are normal and will not hurt you in any way."

Physical form? she thought. What happened to her body? She felt a tingling sensation on the tips of her fingers and toes that traveled throughout her body. She lay on something cold. She tried to open her eyes again but couldn't.

"Ocular systems will be brought on momentarily. One moment, please."

She felt her face scrunch into a slow-forming frown, and then her eyes opened.

"Excellent. PMC interface with the ESS core is optimal. The disorientation you're experiencing should be almost gone," Greta said.

She worked the muscles in her mouth and swallowed. "Where am I?" she asked.

Directly in front of her face was the reflective surface of a nearly transparent ceraphome shield that distorted her view of the room she was in.

"I've been given updated protocols to follow once you've been activated. Can you confirm your identity?" Greta asked.

The walls in her mind seemed to disappear, and her awareness stretched to embrace the memories that had been locked away. A few things became immediately apparent. Her sense of time was off. What had felt like minutes to bring her back online had only been a few seconds. A frame-rate indicator appeared on her internal HUD. It flashed before fading from view as her thoughts focused on something else.

A silvery reflective orb hung in the air near her face, and she knew it was Greta. The VI waited for her response with all the patience of something that could wait forever and be entirely content in doing so.

"Maelyn Wayborn," she replied.

"Excellent," Greta said.

The orb flashed and disappeared. The ceraphome shield became translucent, and she was staring at the dimly lit azure glow of the ceiling above her. The medical capsule she lay on lifted her up so she could see the rest of the room. It was circular, with smooth white walls bathed in bluish light. On the other side was another capsule, and she could just make out the outline of someone inside.

Maelyn tried to move her arms, but a message appeared on her HUD.

Autonomous mode not authorized.

Before Maelyn could voice a question to Greta, a holoscreen became active a short distance from her. Simon's head and shoulders appeared, and a recorded video message began to play.

Simon gave her a guilty smile. "Hello, Maelyn," he said and paused for a moment. He looked away from her for a few seconds, as if he was summoning the courage to deliver news that she wasn't going to like. "Yeah, so I managed to upload your consciousness into an ESS core. I know you must be furious with me for doing it, and if not, it'll come." He lifted his hands in a pacifying gesture. "Please, just hear me out before you do anything rash. Will you do that for me?"

Maelyn glared at Simon, and then her gaze slid down toward the other capsule. She couldn't see who was inside, but she had a really good idea who it was.

"Quinton," she scowled.

"Ah, you see, I thought you might have thought this was something Quinton had done," Simon said. He must have made his video recording interactive, based on her response. He was way too clever for his own good.

"Go on," Maelyn replied.

"Quinton had nothing to do with this. In fact, he didn't even know I was working on it. Honestly, he would have forbidden it if he'd known. He respected your wishes, Maelyn. Please believe me," he said and shifted in his seat, sighing.

"You died in the battle. Your entire battle group was decimated by Admen Desher's fleet. It was a trap, and you sacrificed yourself."

Maelyn looked away from Simon, biting her lip, and her chin trembled.

She'd died?

A few seconds passed and she cleared her throat. "I can't remember any of this."

Simon nodded. "You won't remember it. Your PMC was pieced together from all the brain scans I did to get your implants to work right."

"My implants," she said and considered that for a few moments. "You were trying to figure out a way to upload my consciousness without me knowing. That's it, isn't it?"

"I did, and I'm not sorry I did it, Maelyn."

Maelyn gritted her teeth, and she tried to raise her arms. "Damn it, Simon! Remove this block right now."

Simon's gaze softened and he leaned toward the camera. "Look, I know you hate this, but hear me out. Please? Can you just do that?"

She grimaced. "What choice do I have? I can't even move."

"I know you, and I know being a PMC isn't what you wanted," Simon said in a soothing tone. "I also know you'll never listen to me if I have to force you to do it, so that's why I'm going to give you the option to end it right here and now."

Maelyn still couldn't move, but she suddenly had access to a control interface for her ESS. She could terminate her existence and be done with it.

"There. Now you have all the power. You can simply cease to exist, and everything ends for you," Simon said.

Maelyn seized access to the control interface, intent on doing just that.

"But before you do that, I want you to know that your decision will not only affect you. It'll terminate Quinton as well."

Maelyn froze. She'd been moments from doing it—ending this quasi existence. Being a PMC was something she'd never wanted. She looked at the capsule across from her. The ceraphome shield became translucent, and she saw Quinton inside. His eyes were closed, appearing as if he were asleep.

PMC Quinton Aldren—Standby, appeared on her HUD. She tugged her gaze toward Simon. "You bastard."

Simon smiled and the adorable dimple on his cheek appeared, showing hints of that boyish charm she'd grown to love in the man she considered family. She loved him like a brother, and she still felt that love inside her amid the anger that had become a tight ball inside her chest.

It felt so real.

She looked down at her arms. They appeared to be of flesh and blood, but she knew they weren't. She was in the prototype CDA that Quinton had. Her "skin" was made from advanced composites that comprised her musculature. She had a full-sensory interface. She could see, smell, and feel. The air smelt a bit stale, as if the environmental systems hadn't been used in a long time. The filters probably needed to be changed.

Autonomous mode activated.

The restraints that kept her in place retracted, and she stood. She wanted to see her face, and a window appeared in her HUD. Her long dark hair came past her shoulders, and celestial blue eyes stared back at her. She blinked and felt her lips lift in response. It felt so real that she might have been fooled into thinking she was in her own body. There were some differences, but the sensory inputs were all online. She tilted her head to the side and touched her chin, sliding her fingertips down her neck. It felt like her skin. Her skin! She stood there naked as the day she was born, and despite the cool temperature, she didn't feel cold. She just had the awareness that the air was cool, but *she* wasn't.

Maelyn turned toward Simon. The VI that controlled the video recording of him waited for her. "All right, Simon. Say what you've got to say."

Simon smiled. "Oh, thank God, Maelyn. I really wasn't sure what you were going to do," he said and shook his head. "Never mind that."

Simon spoke at length about what had happened after she died—how Quinton had fought Admen Desher and the Sentinels, and how he'd united all the PMCs against Harding Prime and used the mergence protocol to defeat him. The cost was that Quinton and the crew of the *Salvation* had died. Simon had come up with a way to retrieve the data cores of most of the PMCs, and they were working to grow new bodies for them. The retrieval process wasn't as reliable as they'd hoped, and they failed as much as they succeeded. Simon didn't know why, but he wasn't going to give up on it.

"Why am I here?" Maelyn asked. "Why didn't you try to regrow my body like the others?"

"It wasn't going to work for you," Simon replied. "You weren't a PMC first. The brain scans we had of you were never in an ESS and hadn't undergone all the integrity checks necessary." He paused for a moment, looking troubled. "Honestly, I didn't want to see you die in front of me. I couldn't go through it. It was hard enough to go through the first time. The only way I'm going to know this worked is if you contact me. No one knows I've done this."

"Quinton didn't know?"

"No, he didn't. I had to convince Radek to take a snapshot of Quinton's ESS without his knowing it. So, if he does wake up, I'll need you to explain things to him," Simon said. He looked away for a few moments, nodding toward someone off-screen and then looking back at Maelyn. "I think he knew he was going to die, and he was all right with it. He'd achieved his purpose. He'd stopped the Sentinels. The rest is up to us. But that wasn't good enough for me. Quinton deserved better than that, and so do you, Maelyn. You both deserved better. While I might not ever know what happened with this, I like knowing that there's a chance the two of you are out there living the lives you deserve among the stars. You could say I'm playing God, and maybe I am." He shrugged. "Some might argue that none of this is real, that you're not really Maelyn anymore, and maybe to a certain extent, that's true. But I don't care what anyone else thinks. I wanted both you and Quinton to have this chance, and now you've got it. The rest is up to you."

Simon smiled a little. Then he reached up and the video flickered off.

Maelyn shook her head. "Oh Simon," she whispered.

She'd died, and yet she was here on a ship somewhere in the galaxy. She looked at Quinton. They'd both died, and yet they were here. Quinton didn't like to talk about his past. She'd thought it was too painful for him, and she supposed that was part of the reason. She also thought it was his way of moving forward. The implication of developing PMC technology was the merging of humans and machines. They could live well beyond the capabilities that even prolonging provided. Was this what she wanted? And how many people who thought they wanted to live forever actually had the option? The mere thought was daunting, and she retreated from it. It was too much to think about.

Maelyn looked at Quinton and a smile lifted her countenance. She didn't have to be alone—not anymore and not ever again. But the ESS control interface was still active. She could end it here and now, and she would simply fade to oblivion. This ship would never be found as it drifted amid the great expanse between stars.

She walked toward the capsule where Quinton slept, and the arguments in her brain melted away as she looked at him. Memories flooded her thoughts, from Quinton trapped in the agricultural bot to when they'd found each other on that Alari Starbase. He had a way of making her smile. They'd lifted each other up, and she had been closer to him than anyone else.

Maelyn closed the ESS control interface. She wasn't going to end her life, not now. She lifted her hand toward the capsule and sent the PMC activation signal. A few seconds later, the capsule opened, and Quinton looked at her. He blinked, confused.

She felt her heart begin to race and dismissed the thoughts that told her she resided in an artificial body meant to mimic life. These were emotional responses. She was alive.

The restraints holding Quinton's body in place retracted.

"Maelyn," he said. "How? Where are we?"

"We're in a ship. I think it's the *Wayfarer,*" she said.

Quinton stepped toward her. "You're here? You're really here?" He paused for a moment. "I knew he was working on something, but he hid it from me. I should have guessed."

Maelyn smiled, and her vision blurred for a moment as tears welled up. "He found a way."

Quinton stepped closer to her and looked at her for a long moment. "Feel real enough for you?"

Maelyn nodded and laughed. "Yes," she said.

Quinton pulled her into his arms, and they held each other.

"Where should we go first?" Maelyn asked.

Quinton smiled. "Anywhere you want." Then he looked at her questioningly. "Couple's privilege?"

Maelyn shook her head a little. "I think we can dispense with the privileges—captain's, admiral's, or otherwise."

"Partners then."

She leaned toward him, pursing her lips. "I was thinking of something a little more intimate."

They'd waited long enough.

THE END

AUTHOR NOTE

Thank you for reading *Federation Chronicles.* I hope you enjoyed it. The characters were fun for me to write and I hope you liked getting to know them. Please consider leaving a review for the book. Reviews help my books get discovered by other readers. Also, consider telling a friend about the book or share it on social media. Word of mouth is crucial in helping authors write books that readers want to read.

Again, thank you so much for reading one of my books. I'm so grateful that I get to share these stories with you.

If you're new to my work, here is a little bit about myself. I worked in IT Security for 20 years, and in 2013 I decided I wanted to change careers. I picked up the bones of an old book I'd started writing a long time ago and finished it. Readers liked the story I'd written, so I kept on writing more. For about four years, I wrote in the early morning hours before my workday began. After releasing my 10th book in 2017, I learned that I was going to be laid off from my job. My employer gave me six months notice, which, while not ideal, wasn't as bad as it could have been. I had to decide whether I was ready for my hobby of writing books to be my new career. I'm a family man and responsibilities that need to be fulfilled. After quite a bit of soul-searching and data crunching, I decided to take the leap and see if I really could take my hobby of writing books and make it my career.

I had six months.

I wrote the first two books in the First Colony series, and on my last day at my old job, I started writing the third book in the series. I said a few prayers and released the first book in the First Colony series. That book and the other books in the series skyrocketed to the top of the charts and stayed there for over a year. I was awestruck, and although it's been a few years since that happened, I still am. I plan to be around for a long time writing books, and I hope that you find some fun escapism in the stories that I write.

Thanks again for reading one of my books. If you wouldn't mind, please consider leaving a review for this book. Reviews really do help, even it's just a few words to say that you really liked this book.

https://kenlozito.com/my-books/

I do have a Facebook group called **Ken Lozito's SF readers**. Answer two easy questions and you're in. If you're on Facebook and you'd like to stop by, please search for it on Facebook.

Not everyone is on Facebook. I get it, but I also have a blog if you'd like to stop by there. My blog is more of a monthly check-in as to the status of what I'm working on. Please stop by and say hello, I'd love to hear from you.

Visit www.kenlozito.com

Thank you for reading!

If you're looking for something else to read consider the following series I've written.

First Colony - A story about humanity's first interstellar colony.

Ascension - A story about humanity's first alien contact.

Visit KenLozito.com to learn more.

ABOUT THE AUTHOR

I've written multiple science fiction and fantasy series. Books have been my way to escape everyday life since I was a teenager to my current ripe old(?) age. What started out as a love of stories has turned into a full-blown passion for writing them.

Overall, I'm just a fan of really good stories regardless of genre. I love the heroic tales, redemption stories, the last stand, or just a good old fashion adventure. Those are the types of stories I like to write. Stories with rich and interesting characters and then I put them into dangerous and sometimes morally gray situations.

My ultimate intent for writing stories is to provide fun escapism for readers. I write stories that I would like to read, and I hope you enjoy them as well.

If you have questions or comments about any of my works I would love to hear from you, even if it's only to drop by to say hello at KenLozito.com

Thanks again for reading ***Federation Chronicles***

Don't be shy about emails, I love getting them, and try to respond to everyone.

ALSO BY KEN LOZITO

Federation Chronicles

Acheron Inheritance

Acheron Salvation

Acheron Redemption

Acheron Rising (Prequel Novella)

First Colony Series

genesis

nemesis

legacy

Sanctuary

Discovery

Emergence

Vigilance

Fracture

Harbinger

Insurgent

Invasion

Impulse

Infinity

expedition earth

Ascension Series

Star Shroud

Star Divide

Star Alliance

Infinity's Edge

Rising Force

Ascension

Safanarion Order Series

Road to Shandara

Echoes of a Gloried Past

Amidst the Rising Shadows

Heir of Shandara

If you would like to be notified when my next book is released visit kenlozito.com

Made in the USA
Columbia, SC
22 August 2023